D0434973

The
Reluctant
Suitor

The Reluctant Suitor

KATHLEEN E. WOODIWISS

wm

WILLIAM MORROW
An Imprint of HarperCollins*Publishers*

HarperCollins books may be purchased for educational, business, or sales promotional use. For information please write: Special Markets Department, HarperCollins Publishers Inc., 10 East 53rd Street, New York, NY 10022.

FIRST EDITION

Designed by Bernard Klein

Printed on acid-free paper

Library of Congress Cataloging-in-Publication Data
Woodiwiss, Kathleen E.
The reluctant suitor / Kathleen E. Woodiwiss.—1st ed.
p. cm.
ISBN 0-06-018570-8
I. Napoleonic Wars, 1800–1815—Veterans—Fiction. I. Title.
IS3573.O625 R4 2003
813'.54—dc21   2002041087

03 04 05 06 07 WBC/QW 10 9 8 7 6 5 4 3 2 1

*To my very good friend
Laurie McBain.
If we thought any more alike,
we'd be identical twins.*

The Reluctant Suitor

One

✳

Wiltshire countryside, England
Northeast of Bath and Bradford on Avon
September 5, 1815

Lady Adriana Sutton whirled through the gracefully arched portico of Randwulf Manor, spilling effervescent laughter over her shoulder as she deftly avoided the reaching hand of an eager young swain. In copying her lead, he had jumped down from his mount and raced after her in his zeal to catch her before she could dash up the stone steps and escape into the Jacobean mansion of her family's closest neighbors and friends. At her approach, the massive door was drawn open and, with quiet dignity, a tall, thin, elderly butler stepped aside to await her entrance.

"Oh, Harrison, you're positively a dear," Adriana warbled cheerily as she flitted through the spacious vestibule. Safely ensconcing herself in the hall beyond the steward, she spun about and struck a playfully triumphant pose for the benefit of her pursuer who came to a teetering halt at the threshold, causing her to lift a brow in curious wonder. As zealously as Roger Elston had dogged her heels in his nearly year-long quest to claim her for his very own, even intruding when not invited, it seemed as if his dread of the late Lord Sedgwick Wyndham, the sixth Marquess of Randwulf, had actually intensified rather than abated in the months following the nobleman's death.

If there had been occasions when Lord Sedgwick had grown exasperated by the apprentice's impromptu visits, it certainly hadn't been the elder's fault, for Roger had seemed unusually tenacious in his endeavor to win her hand, as if that had been even remotely possible. His gall had reached amazing limits. Whenever formal invitations had been extended to select groups or close friends were enjoying private dinners with the Wyndhams or her own family, as long as she had been a participant, her single-minded admirer would present himself on some pretext or another, if only to speak with her for a moment or two. It made her rue the day she had ever yielded to his first unannounced visit to her own home at Wakefield Manor. Even after his audacious proposal of marriage, which her father had answered forthrightly by explaining that she was already committed, Roger had continued to chase her hither and yon.

As much as she had foreseen the need to issue a stern directive that would have permanently banished the apprentice from her presence, Adriana had not yet subdued the qualms that plagued her. At times, Roger seemed like such a lonely individual, clearly evincing his troubled youth. Whenever she came nigh to severing their association, she found herself inundated with reminders of all the helpless creatures that her lifelong companion, Samantha Wyndham, and she had once nurtured as children. To exhibit less compassion to a human being in desperate need of a little kindness had seemed inequitable in comparison.

"I do believe that dastardly fellow is afraid of you, Harrison," Adriana teasingly surmised, lifting her riding crop to indicate her boyishly handsome admirer. "His reluctance to confront such a man as yourself has plainly led to my advantage. If you hadn't opened the door when you did, Mr. Elston would've likely caught me and made me rue the fact that Ulysses and I left him and that paltry nag plodding along behind us again."

Although Roger had not been invited on their planned outing today, he had nevertheless shown up at Wakefield Manor just as her friends had arrived on horseback to join up with her and a recent female acquaintance. What else could she have done other than politely offer the man a mount? In spite of his awareness that she was obliged to another by a formal agreement her parents had signed years ago, Roger's perseverance seemed indefatigable, causing her to wonder if the man actually thought he could, by his own resolve, put to naught such a contract and win her hand.

In a guise of perplexity, Adriana gathered elegantly arched brows as she laid a slender finger aside her chin. "Still, as much as I've tried to rein in Ulysses, I fear he can't abide the sight of another steed racing ahead of him. He refuses to walk beside any of the geldings from our stables, as Mr. Elston can well attest by his efforts to keep up today. Indeed, I wouldn't be at all surprised if the gray considers it a personal affront to be associated with them. You know yourself, Harrison, that Lord Sedgwick used to complain fairly often about the stallion's indomitable spirit."

The steward's ephemeral grin hinted of a humor more often masked by a dignified mien. "Aye, my lady, that he did, but always with a twinkle of pride in his eye because of your ability to handle such a headstrong stallion. His lordship took enormous delight in boasting of your accomplishments to any who'd lend an ear. Why, he was just as proud of you as his own darling daughter."

Having been in the Wyndhams' employ for several decades, Harrison had a fine recollection of the Suttons' arrival at Randwulf Manor in a quest to show off their third and newest daughter. Slightly more than a score of years later, the lady now held claim to the affection of nearly everyone living on the premises. As for her riding skill, Harrison had heard enough praise from his late lordship to be conversant of the fact that the girl rode well enough to ruffle the pride of equestrians who considered their own talents unmatched. In view of her present companion's lack of experience in that area less than a year ago, it wasn't at all surprising that he continued to lose without fail. If anything, his defeats had strengthened his determination to succeed, to the degree that he usually fared better now than other participants in their spontaneous races. At least this time he had been nigh upon the girl's heels when she had darted through the doorway. But then, considering the long climb from the hitching posts to the manor, her pursuer's leaping strides had allowed him more of an advantage in the final moments of their contest.

"To be sure, my lady, no other steed has the heart to match the heroic efforts of the gray... *or* those of its spirited rider. Nevertheless, Mr. Elston does seem determined to catch you. Perhaps he will someday."

Long years of service had established Alfred Harrison as head steward of Randwulf Manor, in all aspects a rightly deserved position dutifully carried out with loyal dedication. In the presence of such a respected pillar of the household staff, Roger Elston did indeed feel uncomfortable barging into the manor. As much as he craved to have the lady for his own, he couldn't dismiss the fact that he was taking much upon himself by fraternizing with affluent aristocrats who had grown up with lofty titles and well-respected names. His impertinence had already tweaked the ire of a veritable legion of titled lords vying for the maiden's hand, but months ago he had decided the prize was clearly worth any altercation he'd be forced to surmount. Had not his own sire inherited a sizable woolen mill on the outskirts of Bradford on Avon and bade him to learn its management and the woolen trade, he would never have left the London orphanage wherein he had lived since he was nine and, for the last ten of his eight and ten years' residency there, served as a tutor. Truly, considering his less than humble circumstances, it was a miracle he was even allowed in their presence. If not for the Wyndhams' deep, long-abiding affection for Lady Adriana and their reluctance to embarrass her by questioning the one who trailed in her footsteps, a man of his low estate would have been turned away at the door.

Sweeping off his hat, Roger drew himself up in stilted decorum and sought to claim the steward's attention, if only to remind the man he was awaiting an invitation to enter, but he froze in sudden prickling apprehension as his ears caught the low, muffled growls of the pair of aging wolfhounds that freely roamed the palatial manse and the grounds around it. Months ago, he had learned that when Leo and Aris were afoot, he was not always safe, whether in the house or the grounds around it. Indeed, the two seemed ever-eager to sink their sharp fangs into him. Even if the manners of the family members had always been above reproach, the same could not be said for their two pets.

Elaborately ornamented stonework clearly evidenced the artistry of talented masons of bygone eras in the fluted and festooned archways that on two levels and four sides set apart the enormous great hall located at the heart of the manor from the elegantly vaulted passageways that surrounded it. Two of these corridors began at the vestibule, which was itself spacious enough to accommodate a throng of people. From the entrance, the hallways on both the north and south sides almost traversed the entire length of the manor. The expansive great hall, which they buttressed, was typical of those built in ancient castles, where trestle tables, replete with thronelike chairs, provided dining reminiscent of the Middle Ages. The southernmost corridor offered access to the drawing room, at the door of which the lady and the butler had paused to talk. Just beyond that massive chamber, stone archways similar to those encompassing the great room defined the boundaries of the gallery. The library with its handsomely paneled door was immediately adjacent to it. At the end of the passage was a pair of deeply etched crystal doors that led to the enormous, glass-paned conservatory presently glowing with the reflected radiance of the afternoon sun.

The rumbling growls could have come from any of these areas on the south end of the manse, yet the open stone archways bordering the gallery made it completely accessible to the hounds. It was also a room where the pair could often be found basking in the warm maze of fragmented sunlight.

Cautiously Roger craned his neck as he tried to see into the gallery, though from where he stood it was impossible to view the interior of the room. But then, even had he been standing directly in front, the stained-glass windows lining the exterior wall would have made it difficult for him to ferret out the wolfhounds. Framed within elegantly arched stone casings similar to those on the opposite side of the room, the vividly hued windows presented an impressive collection of artistic memorials. Among ancestors honored for their valiant contributions to the Wyndhams' legacy were battle-garbed knights immortalized for their separate acts of courage, several ladies for their righteous causes, and a gentlemanly scholar holding an olive branch. Yet, in seasons stretching from the advent of winter until the coming of summer, the sun cast its rays upon the leaded panes from mid-afternoon nigh to the approach of dusk, causing strangely distorted configurations of multicolored shafts of radiance to flood into the room, doing much to confuse the eye and muddle the senses of the beholder. It was nearly three in the afternoon now, and already there was a riotous blaze of vibrantly hued streaks stretching as far away as the great hall.

Roger blamed his sudden dizziness on the variegated brilliance imbuing the corridor rather than his own swiftly palpitating heart, but he had cause to reflect upon a possible error in his reasoning when he found himself meeting evilly glinting eyes amid the dazzling array of sunlit colors. Beneath those piercing orbs, sharp, white fangs were bared in fixed snarls. The threat was obvious . . . and immensely terrifying; any moment now the huge beasts might decide to rush upon him and close their steely jaws on his legs or arms, if not his throat. They only awaited some menacing gesture to incite them to attack. For that reason, Roger dared not twitch a brow.

Incredible as it began to seem as the moments flew past, the animals remained rigidly poised for battle where they stood, as if some magical potion had transformed them into two granite effigies, which to Roger's regret he could not trust to remain stationary beyond a second's passage of time. In spite of their frozen posture, their hackles now formed distinct ridges along their backs, conveying their unwavering distrust of him or anyone else they loosely regarded as an outsider . . . except that in this case they had taken up what had every appearance of being a protective stance on either side of a tall, uniformed officer who was standing in the passageway near the far end of the gallery. The fact that he was leaning heavily on a cane indicated that he was just another wounded participant from their war with France, perhaps even from the more recent battle of Waterloo or the subsequent skirmishes still raging in that foe's country. From what could be roughly ascertained, the fellow had been halted by the lady's arrival in the manor, for his slowly exacting perusal seemed riveted entirely upon her.

No reasonable explanation could be found for the wolfhounds' acceptance of this newcomer, at least none to which Roger was privy. Stalwart loyalty of the sort he was now witnessing was normally reserved for the immediate family, as had frequently been demonstrated by the dogs' fierce devotion to the late lord. Roger had oft suspected and yet had never found viable proof to privately convict the marquess of abetting the hostility of his pets in order to deter the many suitors seeking Lady Adriana's attention. Prior to Lord Sedgwick's illness and death, the hopefuls had been wont to descend in droves on the neighboring country estates of Randwulf and Wakefield in their eagerness to be anywhere within close proximity to Adriana Sutton. Not only was the lady breathtakingly beautiful, but perhaps of more interest to some than to others was the fact that, upon her marriage, her groom would become the recipient of a dowry generous enough to greatly elevate his status from pauper to fortunate gentleman.

The hounds had belonged to the nobleman, after all, and if Lord Sedgwick had been of such a mind, he could've easily encouraged their aggression. Although outwardly he had seemed pleasantly amused by the gallants who had found themselves genuinely besotted with the lady, he had once decreed his own son should marry the lady, which in Roger's mind had seemed reason enough for the elder to use crafty subterfuge in allowing the dogs to frighten off lovesick swains.

It was still a mystery to Roger why the hounds tolerated the servants, though some came and went, unless their uniforms somehow set them apart from visitors and strangers in the dogs' minds. Having nurtured as many aspirations as the rest of Lady Adriana's admirers, Roger had followed her to Randwulf Manor on more than a score occasions, and had concluded that Leo and Aris bestowed upon her alone the same affection they extended to family members. Bearing that in mind and considering the dogs' intolerance for outsiders, Roger was more than a little curious as to what connection this officer had to those living in the manor.

Unable to bring to mind any definite memory of such a man from previous visits to the mansion, Roger was put to task to figure out precisely who this newcomer was. If merely an acquaintance or a distant relative of the family, then why would the dogs accept him so readily? As perplexing as that question was, Roger couldn't shake the impression that he had seen the officer somewhere before or at least someone who bore a close resemblance to him. Such a face was unforgettable. It had all the characteristics he had come to envy: strong, noble features and a handsomeness significantly more manly than his own fine, good looks, which in recent years he had begun to suspect would remain annoyingly boyish far into the future. Although he had recently passed his twenty and seventh birthday, he was continually vexed by people who mistook him for a stripling lad.

If the officer was indeed a guest in the house, Roger had to mentally revile the air of authority the man conveyed, which no doubt stemmed from a haughty attitude or perhaps even his military rank. He certainly couldn't have commanded respect merely by his length of years. At the most, he looked no more than thirty and five.

The stranger's imposing presence seemed highly inappropriate in the late marquess's home. Having elevated a dark brow to a lofty height in some exasperation with the elderly butler, who at the moment seemed oblivious to everything but his own animated conversation with the lady, the officer gave every indication that he was expecting an introduction to the maid, as if he had some indubitable right to receive one. Perhaps, like his predecessors, he had become enthralled by her uncommon beauty, a premise that ofttimes had sorely nettled Roger's mood when he found himself in the midst of her audience of aristocratic suitors.

Who the devil was this chap anyway?

That question was swept from conscious thought as Roger was jostled aside by the late lord's only daughter. After falling well behind during their afternoon race, Samantha Galia Wyndham Burke had only just now arrived at her family's country estate. Much in the manner of her closest friend, she seemed playfully intent upon eluding the man who had given chase, in this case her sandy-haired husband of nearly two years. In tossing a quick glance over her shoulder, she found him closing the distance between them at a rapid pace.

Perceval Burke's height and long, leaping strides definitely gave him an advantage in his pursuit. Amid squeals of laughing protest, he gathered his wife in the crook of an arm and, with a devious chuckle, swept her around to face him. "Now I have you, my lovely."

Dragging off her bonnet, Samantha peered up at her handsome husband through long, silky lashes as the corners of her soft lips curved coyly. "Should I believe I am in danger, sir?"

Sandy brows arched diabolically above gleaming blue eyes. "The worst kind, I fear."

In sweetly contrived contrition, Samantha lowered her gaze as her gloved fingers toyed with the buttons of his suede waistcoat. Even so, her lips seemed inclined to twitch as she strove to restrain her merriment. "I suppose I must pay penance."

"Aye," her husband murmured huskily, squeezing her arm. "I shall see to it without delay upon our arrival home."

The entrance of the third couple was considerably more dignified than the previous two. For some time now, Major Lord Stuart Burke had been hindered by a particularly painful wound, which he had received in the left buttock during the Battle of Waterloo. Yet his courtliness remained above reproach. Having drawn within his accommodating arm the daintily gloved hand of Miss Felicity Fairchild, a young, immensely fetching new-comer to the small nearby town of Bradford on Avon, Stuart escorted her into the great hall with all the gallantry of an officer and a gentleman, while she, with small, mincing steps and demure little smiles, glided along beside him.

Greatly encouraged by the arrival of the couples, Roger followed in their wake and sought to fortify his entrance further still by the example Perceval had set. Daring much, he dashed toward Adriana with every hope of catching her unaware, for if there was one thing at which he excelled, it was his speed and maneuverability. Having had to fend for himself and his mother amid the squalor of London streets prior to her death and his internment in an orphanage, he had learned the necessity of being swift at a very early age. It had either been that or have the stolen food stripped from his grasp by officials, an incident that had usually ended in a magistrate determining the fate of the thief.

The briskly advancing repetition of metal striking marble immediately claimed Adriana Sutton's attention. Recognizing it as a sound that normally accompanied Roger's every footfall, she glanced around in some surprise. It was as she had feared: The rascal was coming toward her with all possible speed.

In spite of the destructive and painful havoc the metallic wedges had wreaked upon her slippers and feet in the past, Adriana was far more dedicated to the idea of keeping the apprentice at bay. An unwed maid, she would allow no man the same familiarity Perceval had recently evidenced with his wife. She had *yet* to find *any* man *that* engaging. However disappointed she had been earlier to find herself once again in the company of Roger Elston, she could not bring herself to discomfit him by demanding a halt to his antics in the presence of her highborn friends. Her mother had never been one to abide rudeness of any sort, even when it was bestowed upon one who frequently forced his company on others.

Challenged to defeat the purposes of her indomitable suitor, Adriana spun away from Harrison with a well-feigned, lighthearted laugh, managing by a narrow margin to avoid Roger's outstretched hand. Dedicated to the idea of staying out of the apprentice's reach (as much as he would have had it otherwise), she continued her whirling dervish past the first several archways of the gallery, vaguely aware of Leo and Aris scurrying out of her way. Immediately on the heels of their flight, a wooden object rattled to the floor and then skittered across the marble somewhere ahead of her, making her wonder what the animals had inadvertently sent flying. She was just thankful she hadn't heard an accompaniment of shattering glass. The metallic clacking, which had been nigh upon her heels, ceased abruptly as the hounds leapt from the gallery, where they had briefly sought refuge, into the hallway behind her, forestalling the apprentice's advance. As for what the animals had actually overturned, Adriana's curiosity went unappeased, for in the very next instant she came to a mind-jarring halt against an obstacle firmly rooted in her path, giving her cause to wonder if a tree had suddenly sprouted to soaring heights in the passageway. Taking into account her dazed senses, the notion seemed justifiable as she reeled away haphazardly.

The threat of falling seemed imminent as her booted toe struck the decorative molding at the bottom of an Italianate ornamented archway. Or was it a wickedly twining root over which she stumbled?

In the next instant, a long limb stretched forth from the seemingly oaken structure and clamped about her waist in an unyielding vise. Before her wits had time to clear, she was swept full length against a solid structure, which seemed far more human than any tree could have come close to duplicating. Once upon a time, she had plowed into her family's portly cook in her haste to escape to the stables. The experience had been much like landing upon a pillow, a memory that now convinced her that whatever the nature of the one who currently imprisoned her, one fact was certain: The form was *definitely* not of feminine origin!

Lady Adriana Elynn Sutton had grown up in her family's ancestral home no more than a hundred furlongs away, the youngest of three female offspring and, from her earliest years, a companion and close confidant of Samantha Wyndham. Although in many respects she had always been her father's darling, she had nevertheless caused her mother and sisters untold hours of despair. Not only was she dissimilar in appearance from the three, being tall, ebon-eyed, and dark-haired like her handsome sire, but in a variety of other ways too numerous to mention.

Her mother, Christina, was the quintessence of a lady who had tried to sculpt her three daughters in the very same mold. To some degree she had been successful. The elder two, Jaclyn and Melora, had heeded their parents' counsel and, when it met their mood, could convey a genteel demeanor that observers found both pleasing and attractive, to the extent that Jaclyn was now married, living near London, and the mother of two children. Melora, the second born, was not long from being wed. Adriana, on the other hand, had given every indication that she had been cast from an entirely different mold. Her siblings had even suggested that she was more like her paternal aunt than the family could bear.

Except for a contract of courtship and betrothal that had left her uncertain as to her future, Adriana considered herself as yet uncommitted and wasn't at all eager for that circumstance to change. She was reluctant to assume lofty airs for the benefit of high-ranking guests and, in her mother's opinion, had even seemed rebellious at times when, instead of donning her finest gowns, she'd appear before their visitors in riding attire, offer gracious excuses with enchanting smiles, and then flit out the door in a dizzying flash before any had the inclination to object.

Unquestionably her equestrian abilities ranked among the best in the area, especially when she rode the proud Andalusian stallion her father had had imported from Spain especially for her. But to achieve such skill as an accomplished rider, she had dedicated herself relentlessly to hours of training, something her fainthearted siblings had been disinclined to do soon after discovering they were not always safely ensconced in a sidesaddle. A tumble or two had made them keenly aware of that fact and abruptly turned their interests toward more ladylike activities.

Her mother had fretted untold hours over the tomboyish ways of her youngest offspring, who had proven far more adventuresome than her siblings, not only while racing Ulysses across the rolling fields or sending him flying over steep hurdles, but in her avid fascination with archery and firearms. Under her sire's doting tutelage, she had acquired a keen eye for both and, from a goodly distance away, especially with the Ferguson rifle he had bestowed on her, could take down a stag or some other game to relieve the monotony of the fare served at the family table or to deliver dressed-out portions to people in need, most often to a couple who had taken in a dozen or more orphans. It was the opinions of her tutors that her doting sire had found most satisfying, however. According to those worthy scholars, Adriana Sutton had an intellect keen enough to be envied by many a learned gentleman.

In spite of such lauding praises from her instructors, her *lack* of certain accomplishments had earned sharp disapproval from her dainty, green-eyed, flaxen-haired sisters, a condemnation greatly strengthened by the fact that she was totally lacking any skill with a needle. She was especially loath to sing or play the harpsichord, at which both Jaclyn and Melora excelled. She was also fairly selective in extending her friendship to those of her own gender, for she couldn't endure twittering little gossips who were forever whispering snide comments in others' ears about this or that young lady who just happened to be more appealing than the little talemongers. It seemed deplorable to her sisters that she had far more gentlemen friends than feminine companions. "Why, what would people think?" they complained. Yet, inexplicably (definitely to those who frowned on her flawed, ofttimes unladylike behavior), Adriana Sutton had been much favored by the late Marquess of Randwulf, his family, and their loyal servants, many of whom had watched her grow from a painfully thin chit to an intriguingly beautiful young lady.

Now, here she was, caught in an unyielding vise that, by rights, should have made her hackles rise. At the moment, however, she was experiencing some difficulty in discerning reality from illusion. Under the circumstances, Adriana thought she had had every right to entertain the whimsical notion that a tree had taken root in the hall, for the towering form against which she had been swept left her inundated with impressions of a steely oak. The smoothly draped black skirt of her modish riding habit and its short, double-breasted Spencer jacket of forest-green velvet, fashionably set off by a creamy-hued jabot, seemed insufficient protection against the stalwart frame, for she had cause to wince within the unyielding embrace of the one who clasped her so tightly.

In a sudden, peevish attempt to push herself away and regain her dignity, she was relieved to find the man's arms falling away. Upon reclaiming her freedom, she sought to retreat farther still from the fellow. Alas, her effort to escape fell far short of her expectation, for in backing away, she stepped on a stick or some other long, wooden object, which promptly slid forward beneath her booted foot, throwing her completely off balance. Her arms flayed wildly about in a frantic attempt to catch herself as the man reached for her. In desperation she clutched the first thing that came within proximity to her hand, the waist of the finely tailored red coat. Even then, her feet seemed to twist beneath her. The sole of her boot slipped, making her lose what little equipoise she had gained. Her frantic gyrations to recover her aplomb ended abruptly when her right thigh slammed into the manly loins. Her victim seemed to choke from her haphazard assault, but that was hardly the end of her disgrace. Her skirts rode nigh up to her knee as her left leg slid down the outer side of a hard, muscular limb, seemingly with the same intent as a skinning tool. It was difficult to determine who winced more from her outlandish feats, the officer or herself. Adriana only knew the inside of her leg felt as if it had been scraped raw after skimming down the man's smoothly tailored white wool breeches. If any wrinkle had existed in his trousers, she had no doubt she would've been the first to discover it.

Diligently she sought to regain her modesty as well as her dignity as she strove to unmount the iron-thewed thigh, but, as much as she tried, she couldn't ignore the fact that her softer parts felt sorely abused. Considering her discomfort, she had reason to doubt that she'd be able to grit out a smile, much less laugh at her own clumsiness. She could only wonder in agonized reflection what havoc she had reaped upon the man.

"I'm sorry . . . ," she began, blushing hotly as she endeavored to hide her burgeoning chagrin and distress. She feared her pantaloons had cut creases where previously there had been none. "I didn't mean—"

"Never mind," the officer strangled out. The tendons in his cheeks fairly snapped as he struggled for control. His arm came around her waist once again, and he lifted her easily, shifting her weight off his thigh before settling her feet safely to the floor between his own shiny black boots.

Still struggling to surmount his manly discomfort, the officer closed his eyes and bent his head forward to await its ebbing, allowing Adriana to catch a vague scent of his cologne. Mingled with an underlying essence of soap and an equally indistinct trace of the fine, costly wool of his uniform, the pleasantly aromatic bouquet drifted upward into her nostrils, and twined tantalizingly through her senses. Adriana had never in her life experienced the like of such strangely provocative stirrings. Indeed, the manly fragrance seemed far more intoxicating than a glass of port on a warm evening. As difficult as it proved to be, she sought to lend her attention to what she was actually seeing rather than the warmly titillating ambience through which she had just drifted.

Another painful grimace evidenced the man's continuing discomfort, tightening chiseled features and compressing well-formed lips as he endured the torment in silence. Stoic-faced, gentlemanly decorum didn't seem at all conducive to abating his pain, however, for with a softly muttered apology he reached down between them beneath the protective shroud of her skirts.

Adriana made the mistake of glancing down before it dawned on her just what he was doing, gingerly readjusting the torpid fullness defined by his narrow-fitting breeches. Just as quickly, a breathless gasp was snatched from her throat, and her eyes went chasing off. She suffered through an endless moment of excruciating embarrassment as she tried diligently to banish from mind what she had just seen and to keep her thoughts firmly fixed on logical matters, such as the reason for this officer's presence at Randwulf Manor. Yet it was impossible to ignore the heat creeping into her cheeks. It certainly didn't help that she felt much like a ship adrift in some strange sea halfway around the world.

Purposefully, Adriana focused her gaze within an area no higher than closely cropped, dark brown hair and no lower than broad shoulders adorned with gold epaulettes affixed to the blazing red fabric of his military blouse. It seemed the only way she could keep her thoughts well in line with what was proper for an untried maid, but she never in her life imagined the alluring quintessence of masculinity could be embodied so completely in just one man.

In the midst of a handsome arrangement of chiseled features, darkly translucent gray eyes were now thankfully devoid of pain, at least enough to communicate some evidence of humor above a waywardly charming grin. Still, white teeth, as perfect as any she had seen in many a year, seemed far too bright to allow for sober reflection. Neatly clipped side-burns accentuated crisply chiseled bones beneath sun-bronzed cheeks. Poorly suppressed amusement momentarily compressed manly grooves that formed deep channels on either side of his mouth. Any woman would've stared in admiration at the intriguing results that perhaps had evolved through the years from simple dimples. Yet those indentations troubled Adriana, for they seemed to pluck at fibers long entrenched in her memory, as if strumming some tantalizingly evasive tune she had heard ages ago but now had difficulty bringing clearly to mind. If some faint recollection of those devilish creases actually did exist, then surely it was no recent memory and in all probability had been relegated to the dark, fathomless depths of her brain, where she could imagine such thoughts and remembrances of forgotten years were now moldering from disuse.

"Considering the discomfort we have shared in this past moment," the officer murmured in a warmly hushed tone meant for her ears alone, "I think I should at least know the name of such a captivating companion before another calamity befalls us . . . Miss . . . ?"

The warmly mellow tones of her captor's voice were imbued with a rich quality that seemed to vibrate through her womanly being. To Adriana's amazement, the sound evoked a strangely pleasurable disturbance in areas far too private for an untried virgin even to consider, much less invite. As evocative as the sensations were, she didn't know quite what to make of them. They seemed almost . . . wanton. But then, the image that had recently been scored into her brain had undoubtedly heightened her sensitivity to wayward imaginings. If not for the man's sterling good looks, she'd still be struggling to drag her musings away from his loins.

"S-Sutton," she stammered, and could have groaned in chagrin at the clumsiness of her tongue. Her present failure to articulate clearly could in no wise have been due to any painful bashfulness suffered in the presence of men, for hardly a month passed without some new request for her hand

being addressed to her or her father. If anything, those pleas had become
rather hackneyed, solidifying her disinterest while she awaited some news
of the one to whom she had been promised.

Prior to this day in history, she had considered the darkly handsome
Riordan Kendrick, Marquess of Harcourt, without equal among those
who had petitioned her father. Riordan had definitely seemed the most
charming, and although his persistence hadn't equaled Roger's, she definitely counted that a point in his favor. Indeed, his manners were suave
and polished. Yet, she couldn't recall a time wherein she had been so completely awed by Riordan's shining black eyes as she was now by the thickly
lashed, luminous gray depths presently sparkling with amusement above
her own. She hadn't seen eyes like that since . . .

"Sutton?" A well-defined eyebrow jutted sharply upward in what could
only have been astonishment. A sort of incredulous awe seemed to spread
over the officer's features as he looked her up and down. Still, he seemed
hampered by lingering doubt as he thoughtfully canted his head and
peered at her more closely. As much as he searched her face, it was as if he
just couldn't believe what he had heard or, for that matter, was actually
seeing. "Not . . . Lady . . . Adriana Sutton?" At her cautious nod, his grin
deepened by nearly the same astonishing degree his arm tightened, crushing her soft bosom against the unyielding hardness of his broad chest.
"My goodness, Adriana, you've become thoroughly enchanting in your
maturity. Never in a thousand years would I have dreamt that one day
you'd be so utterly ravishing."

At this questionable familiarity and praise, Adriana suffered through
another scorching blush. Whoever this stranger was, he had somehow
gained knowledge of her name. But that hardly put to flight *her own* confusion *or* her discomfort. Considering the intensity of his embrace, she
feared her ribs would crack beneath the strain. She suffered little doubt
that her breasts would be tender for days to come merely from his
painfully constricting clinch. She just wondered how the fellow would
react if she adjusted *them* beneath his very nose.

Perhaps the officer had passed too long a time in the company of fighting men and had forgotten that a gentleman didn't clasp a lady as tenaciously as he seemed wont to do, but Adriana had every intention of
instructing him in the error of his ways. Though she had earlier shunned
the idea of chiding the apprentice in front of witnesses, this man didn't

seem the least bit hindered by a retiring nature, certainly not after he had made use of her blanketing skirts. On the contrary, she wondered if she had ever met a bolder man.

"Please, sir! Kindly release me and allow me to breathe! I can promise you that you're not confronting the enemy here in this place!"

A soft, amused chuckle issued forth from the officer, but it wasn't until her toes actually touched the floor that Adriana realized he had swept her, with uncommon ease, off her feet. It wasn't his physical prowess that astounded her as much as the fact that he was so tall. The top of her head barely reached his shoulder. Her own father and Riordan Kendrick were tall men, yet there had only been one other she had known who could have equaled this officer's height, and that had been the late Sedgwick Wyndham.

"Dearest Adriana, please forgive me," the man murmured, making no attempt to curtail his grin. Casually he glanced aside and accepted with a murmur of thanks the fine, black, silver-handled walking stick the elderly steward handed back to him. Then his eyes gleamed once again into hers. "I certainly didn't mean to distress you by my failure to heed gentlemanly manners, but I'm afraid I forgot myself in my eagerness to renew our acquaintance. When I saw you talking with Harrison, I was hoping for an introduction, but I never imagined for an instant that I already knew you."

Dearest Adriana! Renew our acquaintance! Already knew you! Was the man making overtures?

Of a sudden, Adriana found the officer's brazenness too much to bear. Cheeks aflame, she spun away, snapping her skirts about with enough force to whip them across the tops of his highly polished black boots as well as his costly walking cane, the end of which he had braced on the floor. She could only believe *that* instrument had created their difficulty in the first place. It would probably prove just as valuable as a chastening rod should she decide to take offense at the man's audacity and lay it over his fine head.

Only when she had halted the length of one archway away did Adriana dare face the officer again. She did so quite saucily, flipping her skirt about once more before freeing it and lifting her chin in an attitude of haughty displeasure.

The officer's lips widened leisurely into a rakish grin as his gaze ranged over her. Though she had been leered at any number of times while strolling along the streets of Bath with her paternal aunt or with her sister in London, this was an entirely different matter. Those warmly glowing gray orbs gave her cause to wonder if his expression would have changed even remotely had she been standing before him entirely naked. Indeed, she could almost swear from the way he was looking at her that he had designs upon her person and was already portioning off the areas where he would begin his manly seducement.

The gall of him! she thought in rising ire and readied her tongue to flay the hide off this one who had proven himself no gentleman.

"Sir, I must protest!"

A second or two passed before it dawned on Adriana that the words had not issued forth from her lips, but from Roger Elston's, of all people. Taken aback, she glanced around to find him stalking toward them with lean features contorted by rage. The way his hands were clenched into white-knuckled fists, he seemed ready to confront the man, with fisticuffs if need be.

The wolfhounds had plopped themselves down on the floor near the stranger's feet, but when they became aware of Roger's advancing presence, they leapt to their feet with a fierce barking that sundered the confused blend of curious questions that had been evoked from the other occupants of the hall. Glinting eyes and evilly bared fangs left little doubt that the dogs would attack if Roger advanced but one step closer. The threat was enough to bring him to a stumbling halt.

Roger had never noticed any trace of frailty in the physical prowess of either canine during his previous visits to Randwulf Manor, though both Aris and Leo were at an age of ten and eight years. Regretfully, he detected none now. The prime condition of both animals had made him grateful for those far too rare occasions when, for some reason or another, they had been left behind during the equestrian outings of family members and their many friends. More times than he cared to recall, however, the inseparable pair had been encouraged to race alongside their mounts. In most cases, they had dashed far ahead to scout out the brush or hilly terrain in their eagerness to sink their fangs into larger animals or else gobble up the smaller ones, depending on what they discovered.

Roger had found himself facing a similar threat the first time he had followed Adriana to Randwulf Manor. The hounds had rushed upon him, barking so ferociously that she had been forced to intervene lest they rend his flesh. On later occasions, he had seen her calm the animals with softly scolding tones, doing much to solidify the premise that the huge beasts adored her as much as any member of the Wyndham family. Her proximity usually bolstered his confidence, but at the moment the lady was staring agog at the pair, as if unable to believe they'd leap to the fore in defense of a perfect stranger. Except he wasn't a stranger.

Months ago, Roger had been brought brutally to the full realization of his paltry lineage. Such an occurrence had taken place soon after he had arrived in his quest to be with Adriana. He had not been the only one who had come for such a purpose. Nearly a dozen other gallants had been just as bold. Later, the lot of them had gathered in the Wyndhams' drawing room, where, during the course of their tête-à-tête with Samantha, her family, and other acquaintances, Roger had become increasingly mindful of the vast array of portraits adorning the walls. An impressive collection of faces evidenced the very handsome and distinguished line from whence the Wyndhams had descended. In an attempt to appease not only a curiosity about nobles in general, but specifically those related by blood to his host, Roger had carefully studied each likeness. One painting in particular, a full-length oil of Sedgwick Wyndham himself, standing majestically beside the very same fireplace over which the portrait now hung, had taken precedence over all the rest, lending largely to Roger's burgeoning disquiet. The portrait, painted less than two decades ago, had not only affirmed the striking good looks of his lordship at an age of about forty or so, but also the youthful fitness of the pair of wolfhounds.

No one after meeting the marquess could have lightly dismissed the ability of the artist, for the latter had painted his subject with incredible accuracy, to the extent that even now, many years later, people were still held captive by the darkly lucent gray eyes that seemed to sparkle back at them from the canvas. The refined visage, captured for generations to come, was so strikingly handsome that an ordinary man could easily feel insignificant in comparison.

Still, whatever feelings were normally stirred within the breasts of those gazing upon the portrait seemed as naught when compared to the emotions that had occasionally been elicited in the actual presence of his lordship. It was as if those darkly translucent orbs had had the ability to see the innermost secrets of a man's heart and, more disturbingly, to turn one's focus inward. Roger had likened such an experience to peering into the intricate mechanisms of one's own character. Thereafter, he had hated Lord Randwulf for what he had been able to discern about himself, not the least of which was the bleakness of his own aspirations. Adriana ranked among the nobility, an earl's daughter, no less. She was at ease and content within the realm of the landed gentry, and yet Roger, aware of the fate looming over him if he failed to win her, had dismissed the restrictions of his common birth in his strengthening desire to have her for himself.

Now, here he was again, no longer confronting the handsomely aging marquess, but one who bore a striking resemblance to the elder. A rapidly intensifying gloom grew apace with his heightening perception of just who this visitor was. As fervently as Roger yearned to deny the likelihood, the similarity between father and son was too great. The heir of the late lord had finally, at long last, returned home, perhaps to claim his marquessate and, with it, no doubt, the hand of Adriana Sutton. What man in his right mind could long reject a woman of such exquisite beauty . . . or a dowry large enough to stagger a pauper's wits?

Beneath the piercing challenge of the officer's sharply inquisitive stare, above which a dark brow had been arched condescendingly, Roger yearned to vent several insulting epithets, if for no other reason than to convey his own mounting frustration at the injustice of one who was already wealthy being able to claim the rich dowry that would come to him through marriage to the Lady Adriana. Yet, with the wolfhounds braced to attack, Roger could not find the courage to do anything more than retreat behind a huge, potted plant occupying the nearest archway bordering the great hall.

Adriana could find no plausible explanation for what she had just witnessed. Indeed, she had to wonder what madness had taken hold of the animals. They absolutely abhorred outsiders. Even with frequent visitors, they were disinclined to make friends, as had oft been evidenced by their refusal to accept Roger as anything less than an enemy. Yet, for some unfathomable reason, they seemed motivated to defend this uniformed officer, whom she could only believe was some distant kin of the family. If a stranger, she had no idea what mission he was on.

It was Samantha who put the mystery to flight when she seemed to awaken from a daze and, with an ecstatic shriek, ran toward the officer. "Colton! Dear brother, is it really you?"

Before the man had a chance to reply, Samantha reached her own conclusions and threw herself into his arms, nearly choking him in her enthusiasm. This time he managed to retain possession of his cane as he embraced his sister in return. A full moment passed before Samantha relaxed her stranglehold and, with a jubilant laugh, leaned back against a steely arm. Equally oblivious to the angry resentment with which Roger Elston was presently trying to cope and the emotional upheaval that had nearly buckled the knees of Adriana Sutton, who all but gaped at the officer, Samantha could only revel in her own spiraling joy, hardly able to believe that her brother had finally, at long last, come home.

Reaching up, Samantha clasped his sturdy arms and sought without success to shake them. Undeterred, she declared gaily, "Oh, Colton, I hardly recognized you. Why, you must have grown taller by half a head in the years you've been gone! I never once imagined that you'd be as tall as Papa. You look so . . . so . . . *mature*, or should I say more truthfully, so very handsome and distinguished?"

Adriana closed her mouth, realizing her jaw had plummeted to a depth that equaled her shock. Though it was difficult to do anything more than gawk at the new Marquess of Randwulf, a man to whom she had been pledged ere her seventh birthday, she searched the manly features for some hint of the youth she had once known. Years ago, their respective parents had made every effort to convince the lad of the judiciousness of the contract his father had proposed, but at the age of ten and six, James Colton Wyndham had been no less than adamant in his refusal to consider their future courtship and betrothal and had departed, never to be seen again until this very day. Adriana would have felt vindicated if in his maturity he had been as hideous as a warthog. Instead, she was struck with a sense of awe at the changes that had occurred since he had taken leave of Randwulf Manor. As a lad, Colton had proven time and again that he had had a mind and a will of his own, and after so many years, Adriana had begun to think, as his sister had, that he would never return. Now, at an age of thirty and two years, he was no longer a youth, but a man in every sense of the word.

It was a simple fact that Colton Wyndham was far more magnificent in his maturity than he had ever been in his youth. Indubitably he was now taller, stronger, heavier, and incredibly more handsome and virile. With noble features, crisply wrought cheekbones handsomely defined by bronzed skin and striking indentations, a lean, straight nose, and darkly lashed gray eyes as translucent as a moonlit pool in a heavy glade, he now possessed the refined, aristocratic good looks that could make any maiden pine for want of him. No wonder she had fancied herself in love with him at so youthful an age. He had been her prince, her champion in gleaming armor. Now he was home, ready to assume the marquessate. Though she suspected he had yet to be informed of the conditions his father had laid out for them, she wondered if, in keeping with what he saw fit, he would comply with the requirements of the contract or renounce them altogether, just as he had done years ago. The uncertainty created a strange, uneasy feeling in the pit of her stomach, and she had to wonder what would cause her greater turmoil: the implementation of the nuptial agreement or its expected negation.

Brotherly affection was evident as Colton leaned on his cane and, with his free hand, chucked his sibling gently beneath the chin. "Dear sister, by this time you've probably heard that Bonaparte has been vanquished once again. Perhaps the good captain of the ship has even dropped anchor and put his illustrious passenger ashore at Saint Helena. If we are indeed fortunate, the emperor will never again escape to stir up the ugly worm of war. 'Tis a hungry maggot whose ravaging fangs feed upon the lives of men with little regard for the legions of widows and mothers it leaves grieving in its wake."

Samantha traced trembling fingers over a handsome groove in her brother's cheek. "I had thought you'd return sooner, Colton. Papa kept asking for you on his deathbed, but he finally lost all hope of seeing you. He died with your name on his lips."

Colton clasped his sister's hand within his and pressed a gentle kiss upon her thin knuckles. "Please forgive me, Samantha. My regrets in that area are immense. When you first sent word of Father's illness, I was unable to leave because of our conflict with Napoleon's forces. Later, when news of Father's death came, I was hampered by a leg wound the surgeons deemed so serious that they warned me they'd have to hack it off nigh my hip if the infection worsened. If not for my good fortune in having seen a sergeant heal his own festered wound by unspeakable methods—maggots, no less, and a repulsive mixture of moss and clay—I wouldn't be here today a whole man...if at all. Even so, it took some time before I was able to walk with any proficiency. Then, to obtain my release from service, I was required to go hither and yon. Officials seemed indisposed to issue the papers granting my release, since by that time it was evident that I would keep my leg. They kept assuring me that I was being considered for brigadier general, that I could have any assignment I wanted. They were especially reluctant to let me go, considering that some of our troops are still engaged with the enemy in certain areas of France. I had to tell them more than once that I was ready to come home."

Samantha and Adriana's minds had snagged on his debilitating injury and the bizarre cure, and, for a moment, couldn't seem to move beyond that. Much of what he had stated afterward had been lost to them. The remedy that had brought about the cure seemed so grotesque they were both seized by convulsive shudders.

Samantha could do nothing more than clasp a trembling hand over her mouth as she waited for her queasiness to pass. At long last, her eyes fell to her brother's cane and when finally she lifted her gaze to meet his again, she spoke haltingly in a voice fraught with concern. "And . . . there is . . . no lingering malady?"

Colton's own tone was muted as he lowered his head near his sister's. "Only a slight hindrance that requires the aid of a cane in walking, but, with any luck, exercise, and enough time to perfect a proper healing, my dependence upon it will likely cease. With each passing day, my leg is growing stronger. I'm confident my limping gait *will* wane, precisely to what degree remains to be seen."

Squeezing her eyes shut against encroaching tears, Samantha leaned into her brother and felt his arm slip about her shoulders. Tearfully she mewled, "I can only thank a merciful God for your safe return, Colton. Our prayers have truly been answered."

His hand moved in a slow, circular motion between her shoulder blades. "I have every confidence that I'm here, hale and hearty, because you and our dear mother proved faithful in offering entreaties on my behalf," he rasped near her ear. "I must thank you from the bottom of my heart for your petitions, for there were indeed many close calls in this latest campaign against Napoleon's forces."

Adriana was reminded of her own fervent supplications whispered in the night-borne shadows of her bedchamber. She had lain awake many a night, unable to endure the thought of Colton lying dead, wounded, or perhaps even abandoned on a battlefield somewhere. He was the only male offspring of parents she had loved almost as much as her own. Once he had even been the hero of her girlish fantasies, more than enough reason for her to offer countless prayers for his safety.

Samantha couldn't ignore the inquiry burning within her heart. Leaning back against her brother's supporting arm, she searched his features with an intensity that encompassed the full sphere of her concerns. "Does your presence here at Randwulf Manor mean that you intend to assume the responsibilities of the marquessate?"

Colton met her dewy-eyed gaze unwaveringly. "As the one upon whom the title rightly falls, dear sister, I'd be remiss in my duties to the family if I allowed it to be bestowed upon our cousin, Latham."

Struggling against a confused blend of thankful tears and jubilant laughter, Samantha relented to both, vividly evidencing her overwhelming relief and joy. Latham's latest visit had set her at odds with their cousin. He had arrived on the pretext of attending her father's funeral, but had entered the manor with the air of a pompous lordling, single-mindedly intent on inspecting his newly acquired domain and the furnishings therein housed. Indeed, he had barely paid proper respect to the dead before insisting that Harrison take him on a tour of the mansion and then had grown annoyed when the steward, out of his fierce loyalty to the family, had asked his mistress if she'd permit the man to look about. Considering the galling height of Latham's arrogance, Samantha had almost expected him to demand an immediate accounting of the family treasures. In spite of her own enforced restraint throughout most of his visit, near its conclusion she had answered him rather caustically when he had asked where her mother would live in the coming months. Quite aloofly she had informed him that Lady Philana would remain at Randwulf Manor as *mother* of the heir.

"Latham will be disappointed," she murmured with a radiant smile. Although her elation was entirely due to Colton's willingness to accept the marquessate, which had been a heartfelt desire of their father, she was grateful that she wouldn't have to choke on the bitter bile of resentment while making an apology to their cousin. "I'm sure Latham thought you were dead when you failed to return from Waterloo. If not for assurances offered by men in your command, Mama and I would've certainly lost heart. Yet it seemed you were gone so long after most of the officers had returned home that we had begun to fear you were opposed to giving up your commission and taking on the responsibilities the title demanded. But now you're home, and all is well. In fact, if I had known you'd be here, I would've insisted that we ride over after collecting Adriana and our guests and have you join our outing."

Chuckling softly, Colton shook his head, denying the possibility. "I'm afraid after traveling so far by coach I was immensely relieved just to have it behind me. Then, too, my leg would've prevented me. It still pains me when I ride or when I'm physically confined, as I was on the trip here. Unless I'm able to walk out the stiffness that comes upon me, the discomfort doesn't relent. As it happened, Mother and I were able to spend some time talking together. I left her resting upstairs a few moments ago and thought I'd just ramble about the old place, get reacquainted with the older servants, and have a look around the grounds with Leo and Aris. I had barely begun my tour when Harrison opened the door to let in your guests."

Samantha's lips curved mischievously as her eyes swept him from the top of his head to a finely booted toe. "You left here hardly more than a lad and have returned here a man. . . ."

"To find you a woman," Colton countered with a chuckle. "You were a wee chit of eight when I left. Now look at you, a real beauty you are." Retreating with the aid of his cane, his granite gray eyes sparkled with delight as they swept over her. "Mother sent a lengthy letter describing your wedding a couple of years ago, and I must confess at the time it caused me a great deal of shock. I'm still having trouble believing what I'm actually seeing . . . my little sister all grown up and married."

"I suppose you were still imagining me as that scrawny little girl who followed in your wake, but whether you realize it or not, brother mine, I'm twenty and four now, which, of course, makes you positively ancient." Beneath his contrived glower, she danced away, merriment rippling in musical waves behind her. Upon facing him again, she clasped a hand behind her ear, as if straining to hear. "Forsooth, I do believe I hear your bones creaking from old age."

Her brother burst into hearty laughter. "If they are, dear sister, I can truthfully attest 'twas entirely due to the rigors of war, not old age." Much like a rooster strutting before a hen, he limped about in a circle, smoothing a lean hand down the side of his blouse. Whether intentional or not, he drew the ladies' attention to the sleekness of his waist. "If you haven't yet noticed, I'm exceptionally well preserved."

Although in full agreement with his claims, Samantha rolled her eyes, as if to convey her skepticism. "No one would ever believe that merely looking at you."

Thrusting up a hand to halt her criticism, Colton struck a commanding pose, yet he made no attempt to curb the amusement shining in his eyes. "Enough of this nonsense, minx! I've been waiting hours to meet everyone."

The statement was barely out of his mouth when, to his sibling's surprise, he pivoted about on his good leg and approached the tall, dark-haired beauty he had had the pleasure of encountering moments earlier. It had been some time since he had felt the intriguing softness of a womanly bosom pressed against his chest. As for the lady's long, sleek limbs, he was led to think that he had never caressed any that had evoked his imagination as much as those he had recently felt sliding against his own. The lingering impression of those trim thighs entangled with his own had done much to awaken a manly craving that had gone unappeased for some months. Although it was fairly safe to say Gyles Sutton's daughter was an innocent and likely ignorant of her affect on him, he could believe she had branded her very image upon his mind and body.

Years ago, he had resented his father's prediction that one day he would come to savor the company of Lady Adriana. Little had he guessed after his lengthy absence that at their very first meeting he'd be taken aback by the uncommon pulchritude of the very one he had adamantly rejected. Search as he might, he could find no lingering evidence of that thin little thing with huge, dark eyes who, along with his sister, had once tagged behind his heels whenever her parents had visited.

For a young girl whose looks had once been so uninspiring, Adriana Sutton was now no less than a rare gem. The enticingly slender nose, the elegant cheekbones, and the delicate structure of her winsome face in its entirety were admirable enough to bestir the heart of many of his gender, but it was her large, silkily lashed dark eyes, slanting ever-so-slightly upward beneath gracefully sweeping brows, that revived images of the young, gangly sprite she had once been. Still, after so long a time, those memories seemed as fleeting and whimsical as the wind rustling through the trees.

As a young girl, Adriana had always been thin and tall. Even now, she was nearly half a head taller than his sister. Although slender still, she had more curves than he would've ever supposed possible for one he had once likened to a twig. Perhaps his lengthy abstinence had much to do with the fact that he was still keenly aware of the lingering impressions her soft bosom and slender limbs had left upon his frame.

A few curling wisps had escaped from underneath her rakishly slanted top hat and the heavy chignon at her nape, leading his gaze to delectable little areas a man might be tempted to stroke with his tongue. The long, ivory column of her throat, visible between her jabot and dark hair, might well prove a delicate sweetmeat that his parted lips and nibbling teeth could leisurely savor. So, too, her dainty, pearl-adorned ears. The tantalizing fragrance that had wafted from these areas as well as the smooth temple even now, in recall, seemed to twine like silken vapors through his very being. A natural rosy hue had imbued her cheeks even before she had become aware of his presence, yet the places where her skin had been fair and smooth as creamy silk, he now detected a deeper color, giving him cause to wonder if his close inspection had stirred forth a blush from the lady.

As much as his heart rallied in admiration at what he saw before him, conversely his self-esteem suffered from the smarting darts of his erroneous judgment of the past, for it was a simple fact that Adriana Sutton was a strikingly beautiful young woman. Indeed, rarely, if ever, had he seen such perfection. For the first time since his ten-and-six-year absence from home, the full weight of his refusal to accept the betrothal his father had proposed struck his pride a blow that equaled a broadside across the prow of a ship, leaving his heart listing with a sense of regret to the leeward. Had it not been for his limited foresight and his own headstrong obstinacy, by now he'd have already laid claim to the lady.

"I beg your pardon for not recognizing you at the onset, Adriana," he murmured warmly. "Your appearance has changed by such an astonishing degree that I'm left in awe. I suppose I was still thinking of you as a little girl, but that is definitely no longer the case." His eyes twinkled above a lopsided grin. "Father always said you'd be a beauty one day, but I never imagined you'd become a goddess."

The vague smile that touched her lips was the best Adriana could manage with any semblance of calm. It didn't help that moments earlier she had been forced to construct a cool reserve from the ashes of a resentment she had struggled to maintain throughout the uncertainty of war. Even after feeling as if this man had ripped out her heart so many years ago, it was all she could do to carry on with her stilted aloofness. She was so very, very relieved he was home and safe from the hazards of war that she wanted to throw herself in joyful delight into his arms, much as his sister had done. Still, what loomed before them filled her with a consuming dread that he would revile the agreement that had been drawn up in his absence and, in rebellious resentment, leave Randwulf Manor once more, never to be seen again.

"You're very kind, my lord, but there is no need to apologize," she replied, struggling with a tremulous smile. "Your lack of recognition is quite understandable. I was, after all, a mere child of six when you left. I can only guess at the many changes that have occurred in your life since your departure, yet, from all outward indications, you have endured the years very well in spite of the many battles you've fought."

"I'm definitely older and a bit more scarred," Colton admitted, casually indicating the tiny nicks that added subtle character to his handsome face, "but in my lengthy absence from home, I've learned to appreciate the people I left behind more than I once did. I've often thought of the anguish I caused by my departure and have lamented it time and again, but, of course, like wine foolishly spilled, there was no real remedy for the mistakes I made. Once I set my heels to the flanks of my horse, I dared not glance back at the havoc I left behind me; I could only look forward with the hope that someday I would be forgiven for the pain I caused."

Considering what had yet to be revealed, Adriana could only wonder if he'd still have regrets when a similar announcement was made to him. Years ago, his reaction to the proposed edict had left such an ominous impression in her mind that she knew with a certainty that she wanted to be far away when the second pronouncement was issued. "I share in the immense relief of your family, my lord, and do take comfort in the fact that you're back home where you belong. Samantha has been fretting night and day since your father's death, and I had no idea what more I could say to rally her hopes."

"You used to call me Colton years ago," he reminded her, moving forward a step. "Is it so hard for you to do so now?"

As he encroached into an area that she would've quickly deemed intrusive had it been some other man, Adriana realized that his proximity stirred feelings she had previously considered benumbed. Long ago, when she had been no more than a child, this man had shattered the image she had formed of him in her mind. In every way, he had been an heroic knight to her. To forestall such a trauma from ever happening again, she had to keep herself on an even keel, her sights firmly fixed upon the horizon, for there was no guarantee that the sails that had once been filled by her girlish desires and aspirations would be less susceptible to the freshening breezes of his charm. She couldn't allow him to fill those vulnerable canvas shrouds with any degree of hopeful expectation ever again, at least not until she was reasonably confident that he'd prove himself more compassionate now than he had then. Only when she had been reassured of his benevolence toward her would she yield him her companionship . . . and perhaps, in time, her heart.

"Please forgive the faults of my youth, my lord," she replied, daring to meet his gaze as she retreated a step. "That was a very long time ago when I was naught but a child. I can only hope that among the basics my mother has tried to teach me in your absence, I've learn to show proper respect for lords of your noble standing."

Slanting his head at a curious angle, Colton considered her at length and had to wonder why she refused to be so informal with him after he had invited her to. "I must assume by your answer that you're averse to the familiarity."

"If not with the show of etiquette my mother would demand of me were she here, my lord, what would you suggest?"

His eyebrow quirked with some amusement. "Come now, Adriana, our parents have not only lived near each other for nigh on to thirty or more years, but they have been intimate friends since well before I came into the world. My goodness, I even remember the day you were born and the fuss I made carrying in the flowers Mother had picked from her conservatory when she took Samantha and me over for a peek at the newborn. You were the tiniest, reddest, most outraged little creature I had ever seen in my life. Can you not agree that the close camaraderie of our families allows us some privileges above the usual stilted decorum of strangers?"

Adriana was convinced that he had plied many light-of-loves with similar persuasive reasoning. As handsome as he was, she could imagine that he had grown quite adept at swaying besotted young maids from the path their parents had urged them to follow. He did seem to have a way about him, and she could not fault any woman for falling under his spell, for she found to her amazement that her heart was not so distantly detached as she might've imagined it to be. Even his deep, mellow voice seemed like a warm caress stroking over her senses.

Shaking off the effects of his winning smile, Adriana took herself mentally in hand and reminded herself of what she'd likely suffer once the truth came out, at the very least the pain of his rejection. Better to remain aloof and save some minute portion of her pride against that coming day, she reasoned. "I'm afraid, my lord, that your lengthy absence has made us that very thing. Strangers we have become, and I fear there's no remedy to be found in the space of a few moments or even a matter of hours."

The tantalizing channels in his cheeks deepened as he offered her a smile that seemed every bit as persuasive as it once had been. "Will you not relent, Adriana?"

Staring into those darkly translucent eyes that had ensnared her own, Adriana felt as if she were being swept back in time to her childhood. As a young girl, she had absolutely adored Colton Wyndham. He had been the brother she had never had, a hero second only to her father, a knight more worthy than any of whom she had either read or heard. Then had come the fateful day she had learned he wanted no part of her. The question that remained was whether he'd react any differently today once he realized that nothing had changed during his absence.

Colton argued his case unrelentingly. "If you insist upon rejecting my plea, Adriana, then I'm left wondering if I must restrict myself to the stiltedness of addressing you in like manner. Considering the close ties of our families, does it not seem ridiculous that we should be held to such rigid reserve?"

"Far be it for me to presume upon your forbearance, my lord. Whether or not you adhere to a strict code of gentlemanly conduct is entirely limited to your discretion."

"Ouch!" Colton feigned a grimace and clasped a lean, brown hand to his scarlet blouse as if denoting the place where she had wounded him. "I must confess that my conduct has not always been displayed in proper form, Adriana. Still, as much as I once deserved to be socially cut from your presence, I thought I had managed to learn a few manners over the years."

"I wouldn't know anything about that, my lord. You've been gone half your lifetime and most of mine."

"Aye, that I have," he admitted, "and though I had expected changes in my absence, I never once thought I'd have to be so confoundedly reserved with the youngest daughter of my family's closest friends."

"Your marquessate gives you leave to do as you please, my lord."

Colton sighed in vexation and, leaning on his cane, folded his free arm behind his back as he gazed down into the face of the delectable beauty. "My dear Adriana, you look like something a lonely man far from home would dream about in the wee hours of the morning. Had I been able to store such a memory in my heart years ago, it would have surely given me hope in times of need. Your words flow so silkily from your lovely lips and, at the onset, seem as pleasing as the delicate scent of roses that clings to you, but alas, their sharp thorns prick my unwary hide, leaving me to wonder at this deep chasm I now find betwixt us. Can you not forgive the callousness of my youth? I would hope that I am a different man today than the boy I once was."

Her hesitant smile was brief enough to seem terse. "If I appear rude, my lord, I suppose one could say I've learned from my betters."

Colton winced again, feeling as if she had just sunk her fangs into him. "Aye, I was rather rude to you back then," he admitted in a hushed tone, "and for that, I must make amends. I never intended to hurt you, Adriana. You were an innocent, and I brought shame upon myself by wounding you as I did." He studied her at length, saying nothing more until he became aware of a blush invading her cheeks. With a charmingly wayward grin, he stepped forward, once again invading the forbidden boundaries she had mentally erected around herself. Leaning his head near until his cheek almost brushed the brim of her top hat, he murmured above her ear, "But let me assure you, my dear, you have no betters. You have become a rare jewel, the very finest I've ever seen. The sight of you definitely makes me wish I hadn't acted so foolishly and left home in such a fretful temper."

Adriana's head snapped up, and for a moment she searched those dancing gray eyes for what they would reveal. Thoroughly confused, she accused breathlessly, "You jest with me, my lord."

Colton laughed softly, pleased that he had put to flight her aloofness. "Perchance I do, Adriana." A long interval passed before he leaned forward again, barely breathing above her ear, "Then again, perchance not."

Though Adriana stumbled back a step in sudden confusion and made a desperate attempt to respond in an intelligent vein as she opened and closed her mouth several times, she realized the futility of her effort, for he had disconcerted her to the point that she could manage no adequate rejoinder.

Colton reached out and, gently laying a hand alongside her cheek, placed a lean thumb across her softly enticing lips, stilling her attempts. "Have pity upon me, Adriana, I can bear no more holes in my hide right now. My wound has yet to heal."

Turning from her without further adieu, he moved away, leaving the lady clasping a trembling hand to her burning cheek, that same cheek that his palm had caressed in a strangely provocative way before he had drawn back. In spite of the wayward racing of her blood, Adriana became certain of one thing. Colton Wyndham had not changed one whit since his departure, for even now, with nothing more than a word or a warm touch of his hand, he seemed able to scatter her wits in a thousand different directions. He had done it countless times by teasing her when she was a child, and then, more devastatingly before his departure, by his angry refusal to entertain their future marriage. As much as Adriana would have denied her susceptibility moments earlier, she realized that he had disconcerted her once again, only this time by creating peculiar little bubbles of delight she couldn't seem to hold in check.

Two

❋

"Samantha, my dear sister, do you intend to do the honors, or must I introduce myself to your husband?" Colton demanded with a chuckle. "Delay no longer. Acquaint me with this new member of the family."

"Gladly!" Samantha replied with buoyant eagerness. Accepting her commission, she fell in beside her brother and considered his proficiency with the cane as they progressed across the great hall. "'Twould seem you've become quite handy with that stick."

Colton lifted his wide shoulders, casually dismissing his skill as anything worthy of praise. "'Twas either that or trip over the blasted thing, and I wasn't willing to endure *that* disgrace again . . . *or* the pain associated with a fall. I was enormously put out by the experience the first time it happened and became firmly dedicated to the idea that it shouldn't happen again. So far, it hasn't."

Tucking her arm within the crook of his, Samantha stroked a hand over the scarlet fabric of his sleeve and was wont to admire the muscular firmness she felt beneath it. Heretofore she had thought her predilection in the area of men's physiques slanted only one way, unequivocally toward the tall leanness of her own husband, which in truth bordered on thinness. But her brother's physique definitely caused her to rethink her stance on the matter, for her former preference now seemed unfairly biased.

Although Colton's tall, broad-shouldered form was sleek enough to complement *any* garment, it was also hard and muscular, attesting to his immense physical prowess.

"Was this the first injury you ever suffered?"

A soft chortle wafted from Colton's lips and seemed as pleasing to Samantha's ears as a burbling brook. The childhood memories of her brother, which she had stored in her heart as something immensely precious, had abounded with recollections of his warm, melodious laughter. Until this very moment, she hadn't realized just how great a void that its absence had actually left in her everyday existence.

"Indeed, no, my dear, but it *was* the only one that ever became tainted. 'Twas a very chilling experience indeed to come to the realization that I'd either lose my leg or die from gangrene poisoning, the initial evidence of which set me back upon my heels. It was my first *real* experience with fear. On the battlefields where I fought, there was always the chance I'd never leave them alive. The square formation, which Wellington often used, held solid in most cases, even against cavalry, but the outcome could never be predicted. Thus, I fought with every measure of skill and wit at my command to preserve my life as well as my company of men. I was too busy to think much about that cold, menacing dread called death, but it came upon me with devastating precision when I realized there was very little that could be done to stop the spread of tainted flesh other than chopping off a limb. In many cases, the amputation of a limb often speeded that event. My goading fear spurred me to try the good sergeant's remedy in spite of how loathsome and foul it seemed. You see, maggots eat only putrid, not healthy flesh—"

"Oh, please! I'm feeling sick! Say no more!" Samantha pleaded tremblingly as she clasped a handkerchief over her mouth. A distressing coldness swept through her as she was brought once again to the realization of her brother's narrow escape. "However the cure came about, I'm immensely relieved it was effectual."

The dark, manly brows flicked upward in agreement. "So am I, of that I can heartily attest."

Samantha preferred not to dwell on what might've been had he not found the means to control the spread of the infection. Purposefully she changed the subject, for her own sake, as well as his. "Tell me, Colton, do you recall the Earl of Raeford?"

"Of course. Father and he were good friends, were they not?" At her nod, he continued, "Mother sent a letter describing your wedding soon after it took place. I assumed at the time that your groom was the younger of Lord Raeford's two sons. As I recall, I was several years older than the elder brother, but I'm afraid I missed the opportunity to become better acquainted with either of them while I was still at home since my own friends were usually here, demanding my attention when I wasn't at my studies."

Sweeping a hand toward the far end of the hall, his sister indicated the tall, sandy-haired man who, with the young woman upon his arm, had been the last to enter the manor. Presently, the couple were engaged in a muted exchange liberally punctuated with confident grins and coy, flirtatious smiles. "Stuart . . . or Major Lord Stuart Burke, as he is known in more formal circles, or even Viscount, if you prefer, is an honored guest of our riding party today. For that distinction, Stuart was given a choice of the area in which we rode. 'Twould seem the rolling countryside is his preference. Adriana knows it as well as her own reflection, but I fear I've never been as adventuresome on a horse as she . . . or you, for that matter. Going up a hill while sitting in a sidesaddle is bad enough, but coming down leaves me wondering if I'll arrive at the bottom with or without the horse." She smiled as her brother responded to her wit with amused chuckles, and then veered astray of the main topic long enough to interject, "It always puzzled me why, with your vast equestrian skill, you refrained from joining the cavalry, Colton, but, of course, that is now neither here nor there. You certainly proved your worth many times over in the infantry." She patted his arm affectionately before returning to the original subject. "Actually, today's ride was Stuart's first since surgeons pronounced him fit to carry on with normal activities. It also happens to be his birthday, which we'll be observing here at dinner this evening. Now that you're home, 'twill surely be a threefold celebration."

" 'Twould seem I couldn't have chosen a better time to return. Your planned events will allow me to get reacquainted with everyone, but, as yet, the only person I've been able to recognize since my arrival is Mother. She's still as elegant as she once was. On the converse side of that, Adriana was definitely the most befuddling. Even after she told me who she was, I had difficulty believing it was true."

Samantha giggled. " 'Tis a wonder she didn't send you reeling for daring to take hold of her. Adriana can be quite standoffish when it comes to men trying to handle her. In the past she has come close to blackening the eye of many an overeager swain before Father banished them from her sight. I've seen them leaving here with their tails tucked between their legs. Once they regained their footing, however, their hackles rose, and they ceased to be gentlemen, blaming her when it was really their fault for being so free with their hands."

Colton rubbed the back of his forefinger across his mouth as he sought to subdue the grin that seemed wont to manifest itself. Had he known the identity of the beauty to begin with, he'd have likely been more cautious. Considering what she had managed to do to him, he'd have definitely had cause to reflect upon the possibility that she had been trying to exact revenge for past offenses. "Well, if you're at all curious, she left me wondering if I'd ever be the same man again."

Samantha peered up at him in growing bemusement, but Colton didn't care to explain his witticism. The fact that his privates still felt as if they had been caught in a clothes-press right along with his trousers made him wonder if it would be safe to approach the lady again without donning a full suit of armor.

Leaving his sibling still puzzling over his statement, he approached the sandy-haired man who had entered hard on his sister's heels and whose presence had recently been discovered by the wolfhounds. It was evident that this was one young man the animals enjoyed having around, for he was now squatting on his heels beside them, stroking their long coats.

Colton grinned and stretched forth his hand as he neared. "I think after two years it's about time I welcome my only brother-in-law into the family. What say you, Perceval?"

The low, throaty, canine moans of appreciation ceased abruptly when the younger man jumped energetically to his feet. Readily accepting the proffered hand, Perceval chortled at the unexpected exuberance exhibited by the other and responded with equal fervor as he pumped his brother-in-law's hand. "Thank you, my lord. It's good to have you home."

"None of that *my lord* stuff, do you hear?" Colton protested, his chuckles doing much to soften his gruff reprimand. "We're brothers now. Call me Colton."

"An honor I gladly accept," Perceval replied jovially. "And if you'd reciprocate in kind, I'd be especially pleased if you'd called me Percy. All my friends do."

"Henceforth I shall consider myself among them," the new marquess avowed with a slanted grin. "Percy it is then."

Joining them, Samantha settled her hands on her narrow waist, as if sorely put out with both men. "Well, it's obvious you two don't need *me* to make the introductions."

Colton grinned at her girlish antics. "Mother filled me in on the details of your nuptials in her letters and did much to refresh my memory during our visit this afternoon." Arching a brow, he looked down his handsome nose at his younger sibling, simulating a lofty manner. "'Twould seem, m'dear, that our mother is thoroughly delighted with your marriage, but she's beginning to wonder if she'll *ever* have a grandchild."

Witnessing the swift descent of his wife's jaw, Percy threw back his head and roared in hearty amusement. "'Twould seem, m'dear, your brother comes right to the point."

Samantha tossed her head saucily in the air. "M'dear, m'dear, m'dear. If I were at all a suspicious sort, I'd say the two of you have already been tippling Papa's port or else his favorite brandy in the drawing room."

"We'll get to that after dinner, m'dear. I've come to enjoy a glass of the latter myself before retiring in the evening," Colton assured her with a brotherly pat upon her shoulder.

Percy turned to him in a more serious vein. "You can't imagine how relieved we all are to have you finally back, Colton. Samantha insisted I keep her abreast of the battles in which you were engaged almost as soon as the couriers arrived at the palace with the outcome. It certainly helped that we had a town house nearby, so I could get a message to her posthaste and she could then expedite the news to your mother. The awareness that you were constantly in the midst of conflicts wherein so many lives were being lost on both sides filled us all with enormous dread. Your name was on everyone's lips, especially your father's while he was yet alive. Although you may not be entirely aware of it, your parents were very proud of you and your accomplishments."

Percy tossed a grin toward his older brother, causing that one to arch a brow warily. "I'm afraid you put poor Stuart to shame with your many exploits and daring-dos."

Evidencing nothing more than a minor hitch in his gait, the elder brother approached as a lopsided grin slowly made its way across his lips. "One day, Percy, you may experience for yourself the hazards of being on a battlefield while cannonballs are being lobbed all around you," he warned, doing his best to present a sober demeanor as he made much of chiding his younger brother. "For too long now you've been allowed to serve as a wet-nosed whelp of an emissary to the Prince Regent, but let me assure you, much more will be required of you should Napoleon return yet again."

"God forbid," Colton muttered, as if in a muted prayer.

Percy exaggerated shock at his sibling's repartee. "What's this? My own brother belittling my valiant attempts to keep his majesty apprised of our troops' activities? Wet-nosed whelp, bah!" Rising to every degree of his slender, lofty height, he looked the elder Burke up and down as if highly offended. "You have no idea how difficult the riggers of diplomacy can be, else you'd refrain from such malicious slander."

Samantha patted her husband's arm cajolingly. "Don't vex your poor brother, dear. He has suffered considerably after that leaden ball shredded a tree and sent huge splinters flying into his flesh. I wouldn't doubt the roar of cannons makes him quake in terror after the endless torment he suffered at the hands of surgeons who took their time prying all those pieces out. 'Twill be a miracle if Stuart doesn't box your ears for claiming *anyone* can put him to shame."

Her brother-in-law gave her a bow, abbreviated rather harshly by a sharp reminder of his past wound, which at unpredictable times caused painful twitches. "Thank you, dear Samantha. 'Tis immensely gratifying to realize my brother married above himself when he took you to wife. Obviously you have the intelligence he has been lacking all these many years." He ignored Percy's spluttering protests and dryly digressed into difficulties associated with his injury. "Though the wound has mended to a goodly degree, I doubt my pride ever will. Blasted luck, what with so many thinking the worst, and my own brother chortling like a village idiot over the precise location of my injury. Though I've tried time and again to explain how I came to be wounded from the rear and have repeatedly given my pledge that I was charging to the fore rather than retreating, my companions . . . *and* brother . . . still hoot in disbelief. Callous oafs, that's what they are. 'Tis sure they're no friends of mine."

When the mirth finally subsided, Stuart faced his host in all sincerity. "I'm especially honored by this opportunity to renew our acquaintance, my lord. Wellington sang your praises so often during our latest campaign, we entertained no doubt that you did a great service for our country, not only at Waterloo, but on other battlefields you've traversed throughout your illustrious career. From all reports, your regiment proved itself as valiant in battle as any in the British army."

"I was fortunate to command men of exemplary courage," Colton assured the major. "Whatever tribute has been bestowed on me, I owe the greater part of it to them, for 'twas their valor that helped us win the day over the enemy."

"They did indeed prove a shining example of a well-disciplined force," Stuart agreed, "but I also heard in the ceremony wherein your men were being honored that they vowed to the very last man that whenever there was ground to be gained and they had to charge into the ranks of the enemy, you led the way into the thickest of frays and inspired them to accomplish daring feats of their own. They were dreadfully disappointed that you were not there to receive your medals, but I can understand how your injuries might've prevented your appearance. May I say, my lord, that few officers have received such glowing accolades from their men as yours bestowed on you that day."

Uncomfortable with such praise, Colton murmured his appreciation but otherwise remained mute until the lengthy silence made him glance about for some other avenue upon which to turn the subject. He noticed that the young man who had voiced some outrage at his familiarity with Adriana had taken himself to the far end of the hall. It was just as well, for the hothead seemed well out of harm's way there, at least from the wolfhounds. His host would be another matter entirely if the lad didn't mind his manners, which he seemed incapable of doing. In spite of the distance between them, Colton could feel the heat of the glare that smoldered in those pale green eyes. It hinted strongly of an unreasonable jealousy that revolved around Adriana, but then again, Colton mentally smiled as he mused, not so unreasonable when a lady was as exceptional as she obviously was.

Colton was convinced this individual was none other than the one his mother had spoken of earlier that afternoon, Roger Elston, the apprentice who, against all odds, was striving desperately to win Adriana's hand in marriage. In his opinion, the man was definitely reaching beyond his limits.

In presenting an ignoring back to the man, Colton found himself facing the young, fair-haired woman who had approached. "Your pardon, miss, I hope we haven't been boring you with all this recent talk of war."

"Oh, no, my lord!" Felicity Fairchild protested, fairly breathless with excitement. It certainly wasn't an everyday occurrence that a bookkeeper's daughter was able to converse with a high-ranking lord of the realm, but here she was just the same. "On the contrary! 'Tis thrilling to hear stories of great courage."

Realizing she had neglected her duties as hostess, Samantha hastened to make amends. "Please forgive my oversight, Miss Fairchild. I'm afraid I became a bit addled after recognizing my brother. Even now, I can hardly believe he's actually home, after all these many years. With his permission, I'd like to introduce him to you."

A brief moment was spent performing such a task, at the end of which Felicity sank into a graceful curtsey before the new marquess. "'Tis an honor to meet a man of your renown, my lord."

"The honor is entirely mine, Miss Fairchild," Colton responded, managing a crisp bow in spite of the rigidity still vexing him after his lengthy carriage ride. His first experience with enforced immobility had, of course, come after his wounding. He had lain far too long on a cot awaiting the surgeons' decision before realizing he'd have to save his limb himself or else say good-bye to it, for every one of them had seemed intent upon hacking it off and being done with it. That was about the time he discovered that idleness could be far more vexing than rigorous activity. Throughout his military career, the latter had become part of his way of life. Even now, interminable periods of imposed inactivity seemed to shorten his temper and, because of his wound, stiffen his muscles.

"Miss Fairchild happens to be Samuel Gladstone's granddaughter," Samantha explained. "Do you perchance recall the elder, Colton?"

"Of course, he's the miller who owns Stanover House. Our family used to visit there at least every Christmas Eve. I can still remember the enormous feasts his servants laid out for his close acquaintances and the people living in the area."

"For some months now, the miller has been feeling poorly, so Mistress Jane . . ." Pausing, Samantha tilted her head aslant as she peered up at her sibling questioningly. "You *do* remember his daughter, Jane, do you not?"

"As a matter of fact I do, but it has been quite some time since I've seen or spoken to her. She moved to London well before I left home."

"Mr. Fairchild worked at a London counting house until Mistress Jane availed upon him to leave their service and move to Bradford, a change that now allows her to watch over her father. God forbid that Mr. Gladstone should expire, but the mill would become theirs under such circumstances."

Responding in polite deference, Colton bestowed his attention upon the fetching blonde. "I'm sorry to hear that your grandfather has been feeling poorly, Miss Fairchild. During my absence from home, my mother and sister kept me abreast of his many deeds of benevolence. Without question, Mr. Gladstone is a most admirable man."

"I must confess we weren't able to visit Grandpa but on rare occasions while we were living in London," Felicity responded prettily, "but since our move to Bradford, I've come to realize he has fortified himself with many loyal friends over the years. I'm amazed at the number of aristocrats who come to visit him. 'Twas precisely how I came to meet your sister . . . and Lady Adriana."

Samantha slipped an arm through her brother's. "Mr. Gladstone seems to have taken on new life since his daughter and her family have moved in with him. No doubt, his spirits have been greatly buoyed by Mr. Fairchild's decision to manage his mill. God willing, with the elder's mind now at ease, we shall be seeing a vast improvement in his health in the weeks to come."

Felicity lifted a sweetly appealing smile to Colton. "Grandpa would be thrilled to hear stories of your experiences in the war, my lord. Not a day goes by that he doesn't receive a friend, an employee, or some distant relative into his bedchamber for a chat, a tipple, or a game of cards. He'd enjoy it immensely if you were to visit him."

"I'm sure he has been much encouraged by the company of so many," Colton surmised pleasantly. "I shall make a point of calling upon him once I've become settled."

"He's not the only one who has reaped benefits from visitors," Felicity declared, flicking her long, dark eyelashes to good advantage as she cast glances toward the other two ladies. "The kindness your sister and Lady Adriana extended toward me when they invited me on this outing today left me fairly amazed by the graciousness of both. In London, I was never able to meet individuals of similar noble standing. Yet the two made me feel as if I had truly been welcomed into the area. Were I as wise as the sages of old, I might've recognized them as two angels on missions of mercy."

Colton laughed in hearty amusement as a memory from his youth came winging back. "Miss Fairchild, I should warn you that you were *not* the first creature these *angels* have taken under their wings," he observed drolly. "Lady Adriana and my sister have been companions since well before the younger could talk, and I can verify from firsthand knowledge that both women have long championed hospitality as a valiant cause to be nurtured. However, they have not always limited their benevolence to humans. Although I shall likely be chided for making comparisons between past and present, I distinctly recall that, at a fairly early age, the two were wont to bring home injured animals or their young, and as dedicated as they were in that mission of mercy, I can only believe they continued in that endeavor long after I left. While I was still at home, they made every effort to nurse whatever creature they had found back to good health, but if one happened to expire, they'd sob their hearts out till none could bear their lamentation a moment longer. In truth, Miss Felicity, you're only one of a strange collection these *angels* have brought home over the years."

"Colton, for shame," Samantha scolded, her smile doing much to negate her rebuke. "Miss Felicity will surely be taken aback by your comparison."

Facing the fair-haired woman, he clasped a lean hand to his scarlet blouse as if to offer a pledge. "Truly, Miss Fairchild, I meant no disrespect. Actually, there's no real comparison between you and the furry or feathered creatures my sister and her most valued friend were inclined to bring home. I'm certain in your case both ladies were delighted to be able for a change to extend the benefits of their hospitality to one of their own species."

He glanced toward Adriana, who was standing a short distance away, listening to their conversation as she rested a slender hand on the massive staircase's heavily carved Jacobean newel. Though he offered her a warm smile, she met his gaze with a gravity that brought back memories he had tried so often to suppress, that of a thin little girl with enormous eyes whose heart he had once broken. How could he have known so long ago that Harrison had let her in with her parents and had asked them to wait outside the drawing room from whence moments later he had launched strenuous objections to his father's plans to sign a betrothal agreement committing them to each other?

He held out an arm invitingly, desiring to have her near. "Come join us, Adriana. Standing there like that, you remind me of that little girl I once knew who always hung back with a yearning look in her eyes whenever Samantha would come to me, pleading for a favor. It always seemed as if that little girl, with her huge dark eyes, really wanted to join us, but wasn't quite sure if she should. Please do. I can promise you, I've truly enjoyed seeing you again."

A tentative smile tugged at the soft lips as he beckoned her forward, and when she finally complied, albeit hesitantly, he laid an arm about her shoulders. "My sister hugged me and welcomed me back, Adriana. Might I dare hope that you're delighted enough with my return to do the same?"

"Welcome home, my lord," she murmured, offering him a tentative smile as she drew a step closer.

"Come, give us a hug," he urged warmly, as if she were only a child of six again. "And a kiss." Her apparent reluctance caused him to crinkle a brow above a warmly glowing, yet somewhat dubious stare. "You're not afraid of me, now are you? Where is that little girl whose pluck won my father's admiration?"

Considering that every eye in the hall was upon her, Adriana mentally took a deep breath to barricade herself against the nervous jitters. How could they understand that in all her life this was the only man who, as a youth, had wounded her so deeply that she hadn't yet forgotten it? She had often wondered if that singular experience had been the reason she didn't allow suitors to get too close even now.

Tentatively she slipped an arm about his shoulders as he bent near to accommodate her height. Even so, she felt her heart hammering in her chest and found that very strange indeed, considering that she had come to believe that no man frightened her. She was rather surprised to hear the chortling laughter of the other nobles as her lips brushed his warmly bronzed cheek.

"There now, that's better," Colton murmured near her ear before he drew away. When Adriana looked up, she found her gaze ensnared by the glittering sheen of the gray eyes. A pleased smile curved his handsome lips, deepening the furrows in his cheeks. His voice was husky and muted as it invaded her senses. "Now I truly feel welcomed home."

"So that's how you wrangle a kiss from the pretty ones," Stuart observed drolly from several paces away. Grinning, he eagerly beckoned to Adriana. "Leave that wily rascal, my girl, and come here to me. Although I may not have known you as well as his lordship before his departure, I've certainly become better acquainted with you since. Am I not more deserving of your affection? Am I not more pleasing to look upon?"

Chuckling at the other's playful cajoling, Colton laid a hand lightly on the sleeve covering Adriana's forearm, as if to forestall the possibility of her falling into the man's trap. "Stay near, my dear," he advised roguishly. "You need my stalwart protection, for the major is obviously a rake, of whom tender young maids such as yourself should be wary."

At the major's scoffing hoot, Colton slipped his own arm about the lady's shoulders and faced his challenger with a grin that seemed waggishly proud of his triumph over the other. Colton was amazed to feel his senses awakening to the delicate scent of roses that clung to the lady. Dipping his head near the brim of her top hat again, he breathed in the intoxicating bouquet.

"Your fragrance reminds me of Mother's rose garden from years back," he murmured warmly. "Do you suppose there are any blooms in it this time of year? I'd be pleased if you'd show it to me ere the day is over."

If the warmth in her cheeks didn't cause her enough chagrin, Adriana could feel the heat rising to her ears. To her regret, her tormentor noticed and seemed somewhat amazed as he brushed a fingertip along the dainty fold curving over the top of an ear, just beneath the brim of her hat. "I do believe you're blushing, Adriana."

Although Colton would've acted no differently had he thought of the young man who had chased her into the house, it soon became apparent his presumptuousness in handling the lady with casual ease snapped that one's restraint. With eyes blazing, the fellow crossed the hall with long, outraged strides.

The brisk, intrusive approach of metallic-clad heels claimed Colton's immediate attention, bringing him sharply about to face the man with an eyebrow arched at a challenging angle. Just as quickly the hounds launched into fierce barking, setting themselves before their master and the girl at his side.

Being accosted by a stranger in one's own home was enough to tweak anyone's temper, but Colton considered the apprentice's actions immensely galling, especially since he seemed desirous of separating him from a woman whom he had known even before she had been a toddler running underfoot.

Well able to defend himself without the wolfhounds' protection, Colton thought it was time that Roger Elston became cognizant of that fact. The man was obviously being less than rational in his passion to protect . . . or, more accurately, to place a barrier around the lady in his desire to keep other males from sniffing her scent, which in this case was very pleasant and not anything approaching what dogs would be interested in following. As for the human breed, well, that was an entirely different matter indeed. He hadn't indulged in a woman's sweet fragrance in many a month, and this one seemed especially evocative. Even now, the memory of her sleek, delectably curved form pressed close against his own did much to awaken his manly imagination.

Pivoting about-face on his good leg, Colton leaned heavily upon his cane as he progressed rapidly toward the north end of the manor whereupon he snatched open a door leading from the morning room to the outside terrace. At his whistle, the hounds dashed through without pause and bounded off toward the distant woods. On closing the portal, Colton limped back to face his would-be rival from very close range.

"Did you have a matter you wished to discuss with me, Mr. Elston?" he asked crisply.

Roger was startled by the fact that the man knew his name and could only believe that others in the family, namely the marchioness, had spoken of him earlier, in what context he likely would never know. Though he opened his mouth to retort to the other's challenge, he came abruptly to the realization that he now held claim to the keenly attentive ear and eye of everyone in the room. The men definitely seemed to be peering down their noses at him as they awaited his reaction, but then, they'd probably say it was only his imagination.

Grinding his teeth in vexation, Roger swung his head about, much like a bull in close confinement, and finally mauled a surly reply. "Not really."

"Good!" Colton shot back. "Then, if you'd kindly give me some space, I shall finish my discussion with Lady Adriana."

Colton perused his adversary with a blatant disinterest that did much to rankle the younger man. Beneath an unruly mass of light brown curls that fell over a smooth brow was a face that seemed unusually youthful. Indeed, Colton almost expected to see a bit of fuzz on the pale cheeks, but that idea was quickly dispelled when he noticed a recent nick just below a bushy sideburn.

Roger could feel the vivid heat creeping up to the roots of his hair as he found himself the recipient of the other's inspection. Smoldering with inner rage, he maintained a stony silence, prompting his host to elevate a challenging brow.

Nothing to do but ignore the man, Roger thought furiously and turned rather stiltedly to face the dark-haired beauty. As much as he longed to, he dared not touch her for fear his boldness would be openly reviled and he'd be humbled before his lordship. His proximity went against all protocol. To silently imply any right to a lady of the peerage, especially in front of another nobleman, was at the very height of lunacy.

Throughout his lifetime, Roger had found numerous reasons to lament his paltry upbringing, but never so much as now when he saw the very real threat of losing Adriana to a man who had everything, including entitlement to the lady. Although the regal beauty had known only a life of privilege, she had seemed little affected by her noble status. Even so, she had given him absolutely no reason to hope that her feelings for him would eventually deepen into something more satisfying in spite of the fact that he had indicated as much to his father, who had then seen some advantage in investing a tidy sum in gentlemanly attire for him. The clothing that had once sufficed for a tutor had seemed paltry indeed among landed gentry and had proven a painful embarrassment to him on more than one occasion. Yet even now Roger feared such extravagance would come to naught and he'd rue the day he ever deceived his parent, for no matter how diligently he sought to bestir some deeper affection within the heart of the tall, slender, stirringly beautiful brunette, she seemed content to keep him at arm's length, offering him nothing more than a congenial graciousness, and *that* strictly on her terms.

He stretched forth a thin hand in invitation, exercising caution lest he touch her and she pull away. "Should we not be going now, my lady?"

Colton shifted his gaze to Adriana to determine her response to the apprentice's impertinence to urge her to leave. He hardly expected his scrutiny to be challenged, and yet, beneath his close attention, she lifted her delicately refined chin with stately aloofness, as if daring him to question her association with a commoner.

Colton felt his hackles rise, a reaction almost as unsettling as the surgeons telling him he'd likely lose his leg. Never before had he considered himself disdainful of common men. Almost half his lifetime, he had trudged in their footsteps through rain-soaked muck, raced ahead of them amid the thunderous din of exploding cannons, fought hand to hand beside them against the fury of the enemy, and many times had fallen asleep within a handbreadth of the very ones who had called him "milord Colonel." He didn't know precisely what there was about Roger Elston that nettled his mood and temper. Having only this hour met the fellow, he was incapable of laying a finger to the exact cause. It could hardly have been spawned by his own jealousy. Considering his lengthy absence, the girl was merely an acquaintance from his past, definitely exquisite beyond a mortal man's comprehension, but one who over the years had become estranged to him. Whatever the cause of his vexation, he accepted it as fact that he disliked the apprentice intensely.

The lady's unspoken challenge did much to rally Roger's hopes. It was rare indeed that she had encouraged him, and he felt a surge of boldness in his desire to establish her as his own fiancée, yet when he actually tried to take her hand, he felt an icy shiver of rejection as she retreated a step and then, as if blind, looked through him rather than at him. The lady definitely had a way of conveying her annoyance, and he could only construe by her frosty detachment that she hadn't appreciated his attempt to demonstrate some right to her. Nor apparently had she deemed herself answerable to the marquess for her conduct or her association with a miller's apprentice.

Eager to solidify her lifelong companion as a member of the Wyndham family any way she could, Samantha seized upon the tenuous situation to make her brother aware that Adriana was not only desired by scores of aristocrats but also by ordinary men who struggled against the futility of their aspirations. As much as her friend would've dismissed such a suggestion, Samantha had long perceived that Roger was desperate to have her any way he could.

"I fear once again I've failed to introduce you to another one of our guests, Colton. Mr. Roger Elston, to be precise." She took a moment to take care of that formality, and then went on to explain, "Mr. Elston has been acquainted with Adriana for almost a year now. He accompanies us fairly frequently on our rides about the countryside. Under Adriana's tutorship, he has become an accomplished equestrian, which definitely leaves me feeling ill-suited for a saddle. Fairly soon now, Mr. Elston will be finishing his apprenticeship and will then be assuming the management of his father's woolen mill, the one that once belonged to Mr. Winter."

"Mr. Winter?" Colton repeated, unable to recall the name. His irritation with the apprentice still nettled him, and although the muscles in his face felt as rigid as unseasoned leather, he struggled to convey an aplomb that was at best hard won. He flicked his brows upward in an abbreviated shrug.

"I'm sorry, I have no recollection of a Mr. Winter from my boyhood days here."

"Thomas Winter. Years ago, he owned that large mill just beyond the outskirts of Bradford. You probably passed it often, but had no reason to notice it in your youth. Mr. Winter never had any offspring, and after being widowed, he kept to himself until, about four or five years ago, he wed a very pleasant woman from London. Upon his death some months later, his widow inherited everything. She, in turn, married Edmund Elston, Roger's father. Poor thing, she took ill not long after that and died. That's when Mr. Elston became sole proprietor and summoned Roger to Bradford to learn the trade."

In spite of the brewing abhorrence he had felt toward the man earlier, Colton stretched forth a hand in an offer of goodwill, primarily for the benefit of Adriana and the other guests. "Welcome to Randwulf Manor, Mr. Elston."

Having nurtured a festering resentment for this particular nobleman well before their introduction, Roger was as unwilling to accept the proffered hand as the man had been reluctant to extend it, but in so doing, he suffered a measurable shock as the long fingers closed about his own hand. They were leaner, stronger, and far more callused than he would have ever supposed of a nobleman. No doubt the wielding of a sword required a firm grip even from a pampered aristocrat.

"Waterloo was an enormous victory for Wellington," Roger stated stiltedly, eager to convey his knowledge of that event. "Any officer would've deemed it a privilege to serve under his leadership."

"Aye, Mr. Elston," Colton agreed, just as rigidly. "But let us not forget the contributions of General von Blücher. Without him, 'tis doubtful the English would've fared as well. Together the two men, with their armies, proved a force Napoleon could not long withstand."

"In spite of what you say, had Wellington been solely in charge, I'm willing to wager the French would've been no match for our forces," Roger boasted.

Colton cocked a querying brow, wondering if the apprentice was deliberately trying to antagonize him . . . again. Still, he was curious to know how the fellow had arrived at his conclusions. "Excuse me, sir, but were you there to witness our confrontations?"

Roger chose to avoid the marquess's pointed stare and flicked his fingers across his sleeve, as if to dislodge a tiny fleck from the cloth. "If not for a recurring and ofttimes debilitating malady I've suffered since my youth, I would've willingly volunteered my services. Indeed, I would've enjoyed killing a few of those frogs."

Colton's face clouded as he thought of the terrible waste of men's lives that had taken place, not only at Waterloo, but on other battlefields he had traversed. "'Twas a bloody campaign for everyone," he stated ruefully. "To my regret, I lost many friends during the course of our struggles against Napoleon. Considering the legions of French killed at Waterloo, I can only sympathize with the untold numbers of parents, wives, and children left grieving and destitute. 'Tis unfortunate indeed that wars must be fought because of the ambition of one man."

Adriana studied the handsome face of the one to whom she had been promised years ago and saw a sadness in the dark gray eyes that had not been there in his youth, making her wonder if his goals had changed much since that memorable day of his departure. It seemed as if a century had passed since she had overheard his vehement protests. Had the agreement met with his approval, they would have been wed soon after her seventeenth birthday, but the idea of that proposal had set him at odds with his father, so much so that he had left home. She really had no wish to be around when he learned that Lord Sedgwick had carried through with his plans and signed documents committing his son to a term of courtship prior to a formal betrothal actually being initiated. If her ears had burned red hot from Colton's first diatribe, then surely, this time, they'd be singed black from his explosive anger.

"The English were bound to win," Roger declared loftily, touching a pinch of snuff to his nose, an affectation he had recently acquired in his efforts to emulate wellborn dandies. Yet, as much as he had thought the practice widespread, he was just beginning to suspect that none of the men presently occupying the great room cared for the habit, for he usually educed an amused smile or two whenever he went through the process of using it. Struggling hard to maintain a dignified mien in spite of an encroaching urge to sneeze, he snapped the small, enameled box shut and forcefully pressed a handkerchief to his left nostril where the sensation was more pronounced. Gaining some relief, he sniffed and, with watery, reddened eyes, offered a succinct smile to the other man. "As they say, my lord, right shall always prevail."

"I'd like nothing better than to know for certain that that premise would always be the case, Mr. Elston, but I'm afraid it isn't," Colton rejoined soberly. "As for the English, I cannot declare with any degree of truth that we're always right."

Roger was taken aback. He had never traveled beyond the shores of England, and had been led to believe that all foreign powers were not only inferior but contemptible in comparison. "I say, my lord, that's rather unpatriotic of you to doubt our country's integrity. After all, we're the greatest nation in the world."

Smiling rather sadly, Colton offered some insight into observations he had made during his career as an officer. "Far too many Englishmen trusted in the logic that right would prevail, but they were buried where they and their men fell. I know, because a number of them were close acquaintances of mine, and I helped bury them."

Roger cocked a quizzical brow at the man. For nigh on to a year now, he had repeatedly been subjected to tales of Colton Wyndham's daring exploits on the battlefield. Although envious of such fame, he had admired the nobleman, yet some months ago genuine hatred for the man had taken deep root when he had learned that the beautiful Adriana had been selected by the late Lord Sedgwick to become the wife of the very one who stood before him now. The inevitability of their meeting had solidified Roger's aversion well before he had ever laid eyes on the one who would claim the marquessate. After hearing the man voice such feeble inanities, he felt justified for having come to despise him. Colonel Lord Colton may have been considered a hero by the standards of many, but Roger had formed his own opinions as to what made one a champion among men, and it was his belief that his lordship fell far short of that sterling crusader who rode his charger into the thickest of frays and, sparing no quarter, wet his sword time and again with the blood of the enemy.

Curling his lip sardonically, Roger dared to present an inquiry in tones not altogether respectful. "And what fine logic did you take into battle, my lord?"

Unable to ignore what had every element of being a disparaging challenge, Colton made a point of elevating his brow to a skeptical level. Considering the fact the apprentice was more than half a head shorter and probably lighter by as much as two or three stone, he decided the fellow was as impetuous as he was impudent. Or perhaps the little pip had foolishly concluded he was an invalid merely because he required the assistance of a cane.

"Simply put, Mr. Elston, it was either kill or be killed. I trained my men to be ruthless in the midst of our many confrontations with the enemy. It was the only way they were going to stay alive. I, myself, fought with desperation, not only to preserve my life, and the lives of my men, but to defeat the foes of my country. By some strange miracle, I survived, as did most of my regiment, but after considering the bloody aftermath and the staggering number of soldiers lying dead upon the battlefields we trod, my men and I were simply grateful to have fallen under God's mercy."

"Come, you two," Samantha chided, sensing Colton's growing animosity toward their guest. Perhaps she had misjudged the depth of Roger's resolve to have Adriana for his own, for he seemed unable to hide his frustration with the situation in which he found himself. Slipping an arm through her brother's, she gave it an affectionate squeeze in an attempt to soothe his vexation. "This talk of war and killing will soon bring the brumes of gloom down upon us if you do not soon desist."

Though still struggling to curb his annoyance, Colton managed a wane smile of reassurance for his sister. "I'm afraid the war has left its mark on me, my dear. If ever I had a talent for being an entertaining conversationalist, I fear that is no longer the case. I have lived, breathed, and talked of war for so many years that my dialogue has been sharply limited to my experiences. If anything, I've become something of a bore."

"Doubtful," Samantha countered with a fond chuckle. She had never known her brother to be anything but fascinating. But then, she had to admit she was naturally biased in his favor.

Having witnessed for himself the fire that could light the gray eyes of his host, Roger retreated a discreet distance behind Adriana, having no wish to provoke her by yet another display of jealousy. As persistently as he had tried to establish some claim upon her, he had come to realize underneath that outer layer of softly refined femininity, the lady had a temper that could set him back upon his heels. To rile her again would be complete folly, for she'd likely exile him henceforth from her presence.

Felicity was thankful when manly tempers began to cool, since the easement of tensions allowed her to reclaim the attention of the marquess. She did so, demonstrating a congeniality she hoped would be in marked contrast to Lady Adriana's rejection of his request for casual addresses, which the man seemed prone to ignore anyway. "My lord, I would deem it a privilege if you'd dispense with the formality and merely call me Felicity."

Adriana couldn't resist a surreptitious glance toward the pair. The blonde's invitation brought back her own rejection of Colton's plea to use her given name and had been so winsomely requested that she couldn't imagine *any* man refusing, much less one who, until recently, had been sequestered in the lonely, far-flung camps of the soldiers.

"Miss Felicity," Colton responded, salting his response with proper formality and a fair measure of his usual persuasive charm as he bestowed a winning smile upon the fair-haired beauty. "However sweet your given name, Miss Felicity, 'twould seem that Fairchild is far more appropriate, considering how winsome you are to look upon."

"Oh, you're too kind, my lord." Although other young women might have been tempted to gush with pleasure, Felicity smiled demurely as she cast her darkly lashed eyes downward to good advantage. Endless hours of practice in front of a silvered glass had helped her to perfect a variety of facial expressions. With diligent dedication she had cultivated her manners and nurtured her looks, all with the hope of attracting a titled lord who'd take her to wife, an idea instilled within her by her sire in spite of her mother's efforts to keep her offspring's feet firmly on the ground instead of the lofty clouds wherein she was wont to dally in endless daydreams.

Still, *Miss* Felicity was not *quite* the appellation she had desired from his lordship. Something a little more intimate would've been her preference since he seemed to use Adriana's name with casual ease. Just the same, she smiled at the inroads she had thus far made. Of course, she would *now* be required to extend a similar invitation to the two women or chance evoking suppositions that she was throwing herself at the nobleman.

Turning a smile upon Samantha, she spoke with well-contrived humility. "I'm overwhelmed by the kindness you and Lady Sutton have bestowed upon me, Lady Burke. Nothing I can offer could come close to comparing. Just be confident that I'm grateful for your gracious benevolence toward me and would be pleased if you'd both consider using my given name as well."

Cognizant of the earlier exchange between her brother and Adriana, Samantha deemed it prudent to answer for her friend as well as for herself. "Lady Adriana and I would be delighted to forego the formality, Miss Felicity. Please, kindly do the same."

"Thank you, Lady Samantha." Felicity dipped into a curtsey, mentally congratulating herself. Having grown up entirely in London, she was even more of a stranger to the area and its habitants than Roger Elston, but the warmly sincere geniality of Lady Adriana and Lady Samantha had worked to her advantage when, barely a week ago, the pair had accompanied their mothers on a visit to the bedside of her ailing grandfather, bringing with them a delectable broth, scrumptious pastries, and medicinal herbs purportedly of rare quality. The gifts had been their tribute to Samuel Gladstone, who, over the years, had become not only a wealthy miller but a well-respected patriarch among the citizenry of Bradford on Avon. Proving themselves gracious and warmly congenial young women, Samantha and Adriana had talked glowingly about the area and the people living in it and then had lent sympathetic attention to her diffident complaints about feeling lonely and very much a stranger. That was when the pair had insisted she accompany them on their equestrian outing. If not for her ploy, Felicity knew her chances of visiting Randwulf Manor or, more farfetched, being invited to join aristocrats at their leisure would have been nil. Who among her cynical peers in London would've ever believed she'd be associating with landed gentry so soon after moving to a quaint little town the likes of Bradford on Avon, or, for that matter, conversing with a marquess whose refined good looks could put to shame many of his gender? Here, indeed, was a man who, by his own aristocracy, could open for her a variety of doors into the world of the nobility.

Percy glanced at his brother, wondering how he was reacting to the winsome blonde's obvious fascination with their host. A stranger to Felicity before they had ridden over to the Suttons' to collect the younger two women (and, not surprisingly, the apprentice), Stuart had made his annoyance known soon after learning of the invitation the ladies had extended to the miller's granddaughter. He had definitely balked at the idea that he'd be required to serve as escort to a total stranger for the entire day when he had actually been looking forward to spending some time with Adriana. Although Stuart had grudgingly acquiesced, he had promised dire repercussions on his sibling if the lady didn't live up to his expectations. As it turned out, after meeting Felicity, he had given himself over with enthusiasm to his commission. In a private moment, he had even expressed gratitude for being allowed the pleasure of meeting such a divine creature.

At the moment, however, Stuart didn't seem to mind that Felicity was plying Colton with coy looks and subtle smiles, since his own attention had strayed to the lady he had hoped to escort through their outing. Any man would have considered Adriana a desirable young woman, and from all indications, Stuart had also become one of her admirers.

The swiftly evolving situation gave Percy cause to mentally scratch his head. He knew Samantha would be shocked once he told her, perhaps even a bit worried by the turnabout, for there was only one man his wife considered suitable for her best friend . . . none other than her own brother.

Colton Wyndham had also given himself over to pondering matters. He was a man who had experienced the rigors of war much too often of late. If he set aside his suspicions as to Felicity's ambitions, then there was much to admire, for she had an overflowing coffer of physical assets: pale gold hair, liquid blue eyes, and a mouth that at first seemed a bit too full and soft, yet on further consideration proved quite appealing. Wispy curls framed her youthful face to good advantage beneath a wide-brimmed bonnet fetchingly tied with a wide ribbon as blue as her eyes. The coy glances she cast his way were provocative, assuring him that were he of such a mind, she'd be willing to accept his attentions, to what degree he could not determine. Yet he was rather amazed to find himself comparing the pulchritude of one young lady to that of another, the latter being the raven-haired perfection he had rejected long ago and been surreptitiously admiring since her entrance into Randwulf Manor.

"Please allow me to express my condolences over the loss of your sire, my lord," Felicity murmured, managing an appropriately sympathetic expression as she strove to divert his attention from the earl's daughter. As far as she was concerned, Lady Adriana had already received far too much of his consideration. But then, in view of the lofty title, wealth, and fine looks of her host, Felicity didn't doubt that she'd have cast any woman with tolerable good looks a rival. This was precisely the kind of opportunity her father had predicted would come to pass if she kept her dignity and didn't yield her innocence to some lowborn rogue. "I know you were deeply saddened by news of your father's death. Yet, for the sake of your fine family and all your friends, I'm heartened by the knowledge that you'll be assuming the duties of the marquessate."

"'Tis truly good to be home again. I've been away much too long," Colton admitted, glancing about the interior that for so long had seemed like nothing more than a pleasant memory from his youth. When his hired livery had left the stand of trees buttressing the lane in front of Randwulf

Manor earlier in the day and he had caught sight of the Jacobean structure, his heart had swelled with exhilarating joy at the realization he was
finally home after spending half his lifetime in other parts of England
and the world. The manor had seemed like a pale-stoned jewel amid the
verdant lushness of a gently rolling countryside liberally adorned with
evergreens and deciduous trees. The mansion was a three-storied edifice
adorned with countless, closely spaced mullioned windows, four symmet-
rical bays, and a flat roof edged with lacy stone fretwork. It had been built
on a small rise, which bore neatly trimmed hedges and colorful floral beds.
Familiar gargoyles, lions, and urns, made of similar stone as the parapets
upon which they sat, had greeted him as he made his halting ascent toward
the gracefully arched portico, behind which the massive front door had
loomed. Although absent for ten and six years, he had been amazed by the
fact that everything was just as he had remembered it.

Colton glanced aside, noticing that Roger had removed himself from
their present company. *Good riddance*, he thought, but then had to wonder
just where the apprentice had taken himself, since he was nowhere in sight.
It was too much to hope that the lad had left. Wherever he was, one could
almost lay odds that he was sulking and devising a plan to claim Adriana
for himself.

Relenting to a chuckle, Colton confessed, "I'm afraid I would never
have known my own sister had she not recognized me. When I left, she
was no more than a child, Lady Adriana a couple years younger. Now I
understand from Mother that the eldest of the Suttons' offspring has
children of her own and the second-born will soon be getting married.
Considering the length of time I've been away, I'm surprised that Lady
Adriana is still unattached."

In spite of the fact that she had been staring at him intently, Colton
realized Adriana had likely missed his comments, for she seemed to
awaken to the realization that he was smiling at her. Beneath his lingering
stare, a blush crept upward into her cheeks, but she quickly averted her
gaze. Even so, he found himself astounded once again by the transforma-
tion that had taken place in his absence. How could a young chit, whom
he had once likened to a scrawny little scarecrow, have grown up to be
such an exquisite, *indeed* nigh flawless, example of pulchritude?

Sensing her stilted aloofness, he managed a wry grin as he cast a brief
glance toward the other occupants of the room. "I'm afraid Lady Adriana

has never quite forgiven me for being that obstinately brash, headstrong young whelp who, against his father's wishes, left home to seek his own way in life."

Though his comment readily drew amused giggles from Felicity and, more reluctantly, a subdued chuckle or two from the other men, Colton hadn't meant to be humorous. He had merely been trying to express his regret for hurting an innocent little girl so many years ago. The betrothal idea hadn't been her fault, but when he had stalked out of the drawing room after angrily refusing to consider an agreement involving a betrothal to a thin, lackluster sprig and had found himself facing the wide-eyed stares of the girl and her parents, his cruel words had come back to haunt him. Though the elder two Suttons had been taken aback by his outrage, it had been Adriana's stricken look that had haunted him throughout the years, for she had seemed completely devastated by his adamant refusal to consider their future union. Well before that event, he had become cognizant of the fact that she idolized him as much as his own sister. She had never had a brother, and perhaps for that reason she had mentally set him upon a pedestal as her champion, for there had been more than a few instances wherein he had rushed to the girls' defense after they had gotten into trouble trying to save some injured younglings and found themselves facing a formidable stag or some other furious parent instead. A deep regret for his cruel comments had swept over him after seeing the crushed look on her thin face; he hadn't meant to wound her so severely. In deepening chagrin, he had stammered through a difficult apology, and then had hurriedly taken his leave, unable to bear her obvious misery.

Stepping beside her friend in the protective manner of an older sister, Samantha decided her brother needed to be enlightened for his own good before he became the recipient of the news that awaited him. Perhaps with such a warning, he'd think twice this time before rejecting his options out of hand. "'Tis highly unlikely that Adriana has given much thought to you over the years, Colton. She hasn't had time with all the handsome suitors vying for her attention." Ignoring the insistent prodding of her elbow, which no doubt was intended to warn her to veer away from the subject, Samantha pressed on puposefully to give her brother something to think about. She was almost sorry Roger wasn't in the room; for the apprentice needed to be reminded that he was only one small fish in the stream and, even if he had the nerve to intimidate his aristocratic rivals pell-mell, he'd soon find himself gobbled up for a morsel, for there was always a larger grayling swimming somewhere in the same waters. "Her admirers flock to the Suttons' stoop with all the eagerness of smitten swains, each vying for the honor of being the one Adriana will eventually choose, but, as yet, their pleas have been for naught." This time Samantha became the recipient of a menacing glower, but she casually shrugged away her friend's intimidation, deeming herself totally innocent of any wrongdoing. "Well, it's the truth, and you know it."

In spite of the indignant little snort that came from Adriana, which seemed to suggest the contrary, Colton realized his sister had done her best to put him in his place. Even to him, his smile seemed lame. "I can see why bachelors are anxious to win the lady for themselves. She's truly a beauty, the finest I've ever seen."

Felicity took exception to his declaration. When her own hair glistened like pale gold in the sun and her eyes took their color from the very skies, why would a man of great renown and evidently extensive experience prefer the dark-eyed, dark-haired looks of a peevish young woman?

Adriana didn't necessarily appreciate the fact that she was being discussed as if she were some unusual artifact a continent away. She faced Colton, managing a trace of a smile. "I'm afraid your sister has been inclined to exaggerate over the number of callers vying for my attention, my lord. You'll learn after a time that Samantha can go on a bit long over nothing in particular whenever she wants to make a point."

Percy's muted chortle affirmed in Adriana's mind that he had already discovered that truth about his wife. In immediate response, Samantha settled her arms akimbo and gave them both an exasperated look, evoking more chuckles, this time from the pair.

Allowing Percy the privilege of dealing with his wife's challenging questions, Adriana returned to the business at hand and served swift death to the notion that she hadn't heard Colton's earlier comments. "You made some reference to my sisters a few moments ago, my lord, and I'd like to take this opportunity to verify that Jaclyn is living in London now and has two children, a boy and a girl. Melora's wedding is swiftly approaching, at the end of this month, in fact, and although invitations have ceased to be necessary between our two families, I shall see that you receive one. Melora would certainly be disappointed if she didn't get to see you before she and Sir Harold leave on their honeymoon. They'll be making their home at his estate in Cornwall and won't be returning to Wakefield until the latter part of October, at which time my parents will be giving a ball to celebrate the advent of the hunting season. I'm sure you recall how our fathers always enjoyed getting together with close acquaintances after the adjournment of Parliament to plan their hunts and talk of old times. Naturally their wives and daughters will be attending as well, and of course there'll be lots of food and dancing, perhaps even a witty game or two for those who enjoy such things. It probably has been some time since you've indulged in similar diversions."

Colton grinned down at her. "I've been away so long I'm afraid you'll have to introduce me to your parents."

A smile curved Adriana's lips as she elevated a brow. "You *have* been gone a long time, my lord. *I* certainly didn't know you."

"For a moment there, I thought you were merely going to slap me for past offenses," he quipped, his lips twitching with ill-suppressed humor. "In the future, I shall be more wary of the way you take your revenge."

The intense heat infusing her cheeks made Adriana immediately thankful the miller's granddaughter stepped forward to reclaim the marquess's attention. One could almost imagine the blonde had become infatuated with the man . . . or perhaps his title.

Curious about his availability, Felicity Fairchild did indeed desire a moment of his time to appease her curiosity. "Will we have the honor of meeting your marchioness fairly soon, my lord?"

Colton would've been convinced of the woman's diffidence if not for the nervous little smile tugging at the corners of her mouth. It was as delightful as some witty tale, assuring him that he had awakened the lady's interest. "Except for my own mother, Miss Felicity, no other lady presently claims that distinction in the family."

Struggling valiantly to curb her elation, Felicity managed a demure response. "I must have been mistaken about such matches being made in one's youth."

Unnerved not so much by the woman's speculation but by the threat of the truth slipping out, Adriana held her breath for fear that it would. Though the woman's conjecture was an accurate assessment of the state of affairs, in this case Colton Wyndham was the last to know just what had taken place in his absence.

Samantha noticed that her friend was looking unusually apprehensive, no doubt with good cause. She, too, remembered how vehemently her brother had protested their father's attempts to arrange his life and could only wonder if he'd react any differently to the news awaiting him now that their sire was dead. If he hadn't yet realized their father had wanted the best for him, then she surely had. Adriana was the sister she had never had, and she was reluctant to lose her to some other man's family.

Three

✺

"Tʜᴇʀᴇ you are," Samantha said with a gently welcoming smile after catching sight of her mother descending the stairs. A month earlier, Philana Wyndham had passed fifty and three years, and though her tawny hair had become frosted with white over the passage of time, she could have easily passed for a woman ten years her junior. Still slender and very striking, she bore herself with an elegance that seemed ageless. In spite of the fact that at the moment her vivid blue eyes bore a telltale wetness, they were her greatest asset.

A wealth of inexplicable emotions swept over Colton as he watched his mother approach, forcing him to swallow against a gathering thickness in his throat. In his eagerness to find his parent soon after his arrival, he had limped through the front door without pausing to herald his entrance by way of the heavy wrought-iron door-clapper. His abrupt, disquieting invasion into the vestibule had caused Harrison's jaw to plummet forthwith, but after the steward had settled his widened eyes upon the intruder, his qualms had instantly vanished. The resemblance between sire and son had been too close for a loyal servant to mistake. The aging man had fought a difficult battle with encroaching tears as he spoke of his late master's death and then had wept unabashedly when Colton laid a comforting arm about his shoulders and mourned his father's loss with him.

Upon leaving the butler, Colton had hastened up the stairs as quickly as his hindered gait had allowed. When his mother had responded to the knock upon the door of her chambers with a muted bidding to enter, her knees had nearly buckled beneath her when he had limped into her sitting room. Sobbing with overwhelming joy, she had rushed into his opening arms and then been nearly squeezed breathless by his long, encompassing embrace. Later, her tears had turned to grieving sorrow as she reminisced on the relatively short illness that had taken the husband she had so thoroughly adored. Sedgwick had always been so hale and hearty, she had murmured as twin rivulets streamed down her cheeks. Earlier in the day, he had even been out riding with Perceval and Samantha and seemed quite jovial, in spite of the gall of that young upstart, Roger Elston, to come to the manor in search of Adriana, who, along with her parents, had been invited to dinner. Although it had been evident to nearly everyone that the girl had been mortified by the apprentice's unexpected arrival, Sedgwick had hidden his annoyance with the younger man and bade another place be set at the table rather than allow Adriana to fret for fear she had caused the difficulty. Before retiring later that night, Sedgwick had had his customary brandy in the drawing room, but hardly an hour later, Philana had awakened to find him writhing beside her in a cold sweat as wrenching pains tore at his stomach. His condition had gradually worsened during the next two months until finally he succumbed to the unknown malady.

Colton wished he could erase the lingering sadness still shadowing his mother's eyes, but he knew she would continue mourning the loss of her husband until the day she died. His parents had been deeply devoted to each other, loving and cherishing one another as if each gave the other the very breath of life. With similar dedication to their offspring, they had carefully brought them up, teaching them honor and dignity and giving them a zest for the wonders to be found in every facet of their lives. During the years Colton had been away, he had often been too busy to think of home and family. In the quiet times, however, he had found himself yearning to see his parents, but he had learned from past experiences that looking back had a way of binding his heart in chains of remorse. The past was behind him, he had oft reminded himself. It couldn't be rewritten. He had chosen the path he had trod. He had made a life for himself far beyond his sire's control. He was his own man, had been for more than a decade, and except for having hurt the ones he had left behind, he felt no regrets for his accomplishments.

Philana paused as the steward came toward her. After years of loyal service, there was no need for him to ask her bidding. Philana supplied it readily in a hushed tone. "We'll have our tea in the drawing room, Harrison."

"Yes, my lady. As to dinner tonight, Cook would like to know if everyone now present will be staying."

"Yes, I believe they will, Harrison."

Adriana moved near to correct that premise. "Your pardon, my lady, but I don't think that will actually be the case." Dipping into a respectful curtsey as the older woman faced her, she explained, "Mr. Fairchild kindly bade us to have Miss Felicity back at Wakefield in time for him to fetch her home before the approach of evening. Stuart will be escorting us there, and then the two of us will be returning here before tonight's celebration. As for Roger, he will not be attending." She heard the apprentice's sharp intake of breath and turned slightly to look at him pointedly as he entered from the drawing room where he had obviously taken himself for some moments. Considering his earlier attempt to accost their host, she deemed her announcement justified. Besides, her patience with him had been tested far too much for one day. Facing her hostess again, she offered the conjecture, "Our brief absence will allow your family some privacy to revel in the fact that Lord Colton is home again and ready to assume the marquessate."

Adriana tried to blank her mind to the presence of the one who had once again awakened a tumult within her, but when Colton stepped near, she knew it was futile to ignore him. Lifting her gaze to meet those darkly translucent gray eyes, she was amazed by the strange fluttering of her heart as his smile brought into play those deep channels in his cheeks. Somehow she managed a semblance of calm in spite of the chaotic drumming in the area where that organ was housed.

"I'm pleased and thankful to know that you're back, my lord." She couldn't believe how breathless she had become, as if he had snatched the very air from her lungs. "Now your mother and sister won't have to worry or wonder if you're safe."

Colton gathered the slender hands within his, giving Adriana no chance to retreat. He had noticed shortly after his sister had recognized him that the lighthearted ambience the brunette beauty had displayed upon her initial entrance into the manor had vanished. He couldn't much blame her for sobering in his presence, considering the last time they were together he had been in the midst of an angry revolt. In spite of her reserve, he felt challenged to bridge the chasm between them. After all, he couldn't allow a close neighbor to continue to think ill of him, could he?

Then, too, there was the fact that he was a man who appreciated the friendship of a very beautiful and equally intelligent woman. The first asset she had achieved with stunning perfection during his absence; the latter was the primary reason his father had once been so adamant that she'd eventually become his wife. Intellect had always been a very important issue throughout the Wyndhams' ancestry, and thus Sedgwick had settled his mind on one who'd do much to fulfill those requirements.

"Please extend my regards to your parents and tell them that I shall enjoy seeing them, fairly soon, in fact, if it would serve their pleasure. I will send a missive over to Wakefield Manor to inquire into the suitability of such a visit and shall hope an appropriate time may be found." His eyes delved into hers, seeking he knew not what. "And if you'd permit me a few moments of your time while I'm there, Adriana, I'd be grateful. We have much to reminisce over."

His voice was a husky murmur, incredibly warm, melting her, Adriana feared, from the inside out. She couldn't believe what he was able to do to her emotions, *and* with very little effort. By rights, she should've been turning her nose up at his request. As for that, she wished in good manner she could deny it, for she realized he had a way of affecting her that made her leery of future encounters. Yet she could find no viable way of escape without lending the impression that she hadn't yet forgiven him. That was far from the truth. In spite of his angry departure from home, in her heart she had always held an image of him as her betrothed; after all, it was what their parents had always wanted and had taken measures to bring into fruition.

His eyes never wavered from hers as he lifted the back of her hand to his lips. *Stop him!* her mind screamed. *He's using you for a plaything!*

"Your visits will always be welcomed," she murmured as she diligently tried to slip her fingers from his grasp, but, as persistent as always, he would not relent. "As much as our parents were wont to call upon each other while we were growing up, one could almost say that Wakefield is merely an extension of your home."

Colton searched the delicate features, yearning to see some evidence of a soft smile. "I liked it far better, Adriana, when you used to call me Colton. Have you forgotten how you'd get so angry at me and kick my shins for teasing you and my sister, and then chant after me when I'd finally relent and start walking back toward the house, 'Colton's aboltin' down the hill; scared o' his shadow, an' me, too, I hear'?"

Adriana rolled her eyes, wishing he'd do her a favor and just forget all those excruciating memories, but she seriously doubted he would, since he seemed to enjoy teasing her about the past. His tenacious grin seemed to bear that out. "Your memory serves you better than mine, my lord. I had clearly forgotten all about that. But you must consider I was but a child then, and of course that was well before you acquired a marquessate. You've been gone so long that calling you by your given name would be akin to casually addressing a stranger. If I were to be so bold, my mother would surely take me to task."

"Then I shall have to speak with your mother and convince her that the familiarity has my complete blessing. Until then, Adriana, would you kindly consider my request?"

Adriana felt as if he had just backed her into a corner from whence she could find no escape. His perseverance was beyond belief. Barely had she begun to think she had won the battle of wills when she was again faced with the prospect of having to relent merely to erase the notion that she was harboring a grudge against him. "I will consider doing so . . ."—she waited until his grin widened to convey his triumph, and then added puckishly—"in good time, my lord."

Colton rolled his eyes skyward, realizing there was still a bit of the minx in the lady, but he couldn't help but chortle in amusement. When he lowered his gaze again, those gray orbs warmly glinted into hers, and as his lips slanted into a grin, he did his best to pay her back full measure with a madrigal.

> *My love in her attire doth show her wit,*
> *It doth so well become her;*
> *For every season she hath dressings fit,*
> *For Winter, Spring, and Summer.*
> *No beauty she doth miss*
> *When all her robes are on:*
> *But Beauty's self she is*
> *When all her robes are gone.*

Adriana's mouth descended forthwith, and much as in the days of her youth when she had become annoyed with him, she hauled back an arm, intending to give him a good wallop, but amid his uproarious laughter, her sanity made a timely return, forestalling the exacting of her revenge.

"You're a devil, Colton Wyndham!" she cried, and then clapped a hand over her mouth as she realized he had gotten exactly what he had been after. Shaking her head at his antics, she lowered her arm and relented enough to give him a grin as memories of the fun that Samantha and she had once had with him came flooding back upon her.

Colton didn't leave off his teasing, but made much of savoring her name. "Adriana Elynn Sutton. Beautiful, to be sure."

She eyed him suspiciously, much like a chick scurrying to find cover from a circling hawk, curious to know what he was up to now. "'Tis a simple one, nothing more."

"It has the flavor of sweetmeat upon my tongue. I wonder if you would taste as sweet."

Adriana wished she could fan her burning cheeks without evidencing the fact that he had been successful in unsettling her. "No, my lord, I fear I'm rather tart and sour. At least, that's what my sisters aver when they're angry with me."

"I assume that's when they've tried to manipulate you into doing what they want, and, in return, you've snubbed them with your fine, dainty nose in the air."

That was close enough to the truth to give Adriana goose bumps. "Perhaps."

Colton leaned near to tease. "So, Adriana, who will be there to challenge you once Melora leaves the nest?"

Her delicately boned chin raised a notch as a smile flitted across her lips, and she met his gaze with a brow pointedly raised in a challenging mode. "I assumed that was the reason you came home, my lord. As I remember, you were quite fond of doing that very thing ere you went away. You seem quite adept at it still."

Throwing back his head, Colton laughed again in hearty amusement. "Aye," he admitted. "I definitely have recollections of having teased you unmercifully a time or two."

"More like a few hundred or more," she countered, yielding him a brief glimpse of a grin.

Becoming aware of his mother's close attention, Colton shifted his gaze to her and found a troubled look in the blue eyes as well as a perplexed smile gently curving her lips. He had no way of discerning what thoughts were being formed behind that gentle mask of concern, but he rather suspected that it was not for him she fretted, but for Adriana. And why not? Considering the strict upbringing of young, wellborn ladies, he could only assume the girl was an innocent, ignorant of the wiles of men. Such an idea didn't displease him. During his years as an officer, he had experienced enough of the wayward life to know that he didn't care to marry a woman who was easy game for rutting bachelors. If duty demanded he beget a lineage worthy of the marquessate, he didn't want to suffer any doubts as to their sire.

"I shall be here when you return, Adriana," Colton confided in a warm murmur as he smiled down at her again. Once more he lifted her thin fingers to his lips and bestowed a lingering kiss upon them, yet he had cause to wonder at the slight tremor he detected. About then was when he noticed a blush infusing her cheeks. In some surprise, he asked, "Do I upset you, Adriana?"

His breath was like a soft, warm breeze caressing her brow, and though Adriana would have hurriedly retreated, the advance of metal-clad soles coming upon them very quickly brought her around in surprise, just in time to see Roger lunging toward Colton with a fist drawn back with mean intent. A startled cry escaped her, and just as quickly the walking stick went skittering across the floor again as the marquess caught Roger's extended arm and drove his own hard, clenched fist into the apprentice's belly. Roger doubled over instantly with a loud groan that was promptly silenced by a second blow, this time against his lean jaw. The force of the slanted, upward thrust sent Roger flying backward until he came to earth again some distance away. There, in total oblivion with nary a moan escaping him, he lay with arms and legs splayed upon the marble floor.

Harrison had quickly emerged from the back, having heard a muted scream. He didn't need anyone to tell him what had happened; he had foreseen the likelihood of the confrontation between the pair after witnessing the apprentice's initial advance upon his lordship. Hurrying to fetch the marquess's cane, he picked it up and held it as Colton flexed his hand.

"Shall I have a groom from the stables return Mr. Elston to his home, my lord?" Harrison asked in a barely audible tone. Feeling no sympathy for the unconscious man, he peered down at him as he offered the conjecture, "Mr. Elston will likely be out for a while. He can sleep more comfortably in his own bed."

Colton finally accepted the walking stick from the steward. "Take care of it as you see fit, Harrison. If the decision were left to me, I'd kick the lad out and let him come around when the dew falls on his face."

Harrison allowed a twitch of a humorous smile to show. "'Twould be his just due, my lord, but with the ladies leaving and Lady Adriana returning here for dinner . . ."

Colton clasped the smaller man's shoulder and squeezed it fondly as he grinned. "You're right, of course, Harrison. We can't fret the ladies nor should we have a blight on this evening's festivities."

Adriana stepped forward with a scarlet hue infusing her cheeks. "I'm sorry this happened. 'Twas clearly not your fault. Roger can be quite volatile at times when there's no cause."

"He's anxious to preserve you for himself, but I assume that will never come to fruition. . . ." Colton lifted a brow questioningly as he dared to delve into those dark, shining orbs. "At least, I hope not."

Adriana did not dare imagine that he was probing for an answer because he was interested in her. Perhaps he was only hoping to see Roger's purposes defeated. Lowering her gaze, she hurriedly retreated.

"It's getting late," she stated breathlessly.

Feeling the presence of another nearby, Colton glanced around and was surprised to find Felicity standing close beside them. Her lips curved winsomely as she extended her hand, obviously expecting the same degree of attention as he had bestowed upon Adriana. Gallantly he complied, causing the young woman to catch her breath in excitement.

"It has been absolutely divine meeting you, my lord," she said with bubbling enthusiasm.

"The pleasure has been all mine, Miss Felicity," he murmured with a cordial smile. "Good day to you."

Bracing much of his weight upon his cane, he stepped back a respectful distance. Only then did he turn and shake the hand of the man who had followed her. "I'm pleased that we could finally renew our acquaintance after all these years, Major."

"We're all greatly relieved that you're home, my lord," Stuart assured him, smiling amiably.

"Forego the formalities. My invitation to you is the same as I gave your brother. My name is Colton. You have my permission to use it as a friend."

"I shall do so on a regular basis if you will also respond with similar familiarity," Stuart replied and was pleased when he received an affirmative response. Retreating toward the entrance, the major waved a hand of farewell to the family as he grinningly announced, "Lady Adriana and I shall see the lot of you later."

The threesome took their leave, but after servants carried Roger out, several moments passed before Colton turned to find his mother watching him curiously. He presented an arm. "Harrison informed me earlier there's a nice, cheery fire in the drawing room that will take the chill from our bones. I was on my way there when our guests arrived. Will you join me, Mother?"

Philana slipped a slender hand within the crook of his arm. "Of course, dear."

"Ready for tea, anyone?" Colton asked, lifting a questioning grin to his sister and her husband.

"I am," Percy eagerly declared and, taking his wife's hand, gently squeezed it. "Shall we, my love?"

"By all means," Samantha agreed cheerily.

Upon entering the drawing room, Colton seated his parent at the tea table just as a servant arrived with the silver service. In good manner, he stood back as Percy assisted Samantha into a chair and took a place beside her. Only then did Colton settle himself rather stiffly into his own seat, managing to hide a wince of pain as his muscles twitched uncomfortably in his thigh. Having been admitted back into the house by Harrison, the two wolfhounds found the family and plopped themselves down on the rug near their master's chair.

"Look at that," Philana bade in amazement, indicating the animals. "Leonardo and Aristotle still remember you, Colton, after all this time."

Shaking his head as he laughed, he readily denied the possibility. "They have merely accepted me as a replacement for Father."

His mother smilingly disputed his claim as she stirred a spot of cream through her tea. "Nay, my son, I think 'tis something more. You've no idea, of course, how deeply the hounds mourned your departure; 'twas as if they had lost their dearest friend. Only when your father was here within the house did their doldrums ease. After his death, Samantha and I tried everything we could to relieve their misery, but we proved poor replacements indeed. Loyal as Aristotle and Leonardo have been to the family throughout the years, they have never been as partial to Samantha or to me as they were to you and your father. Remember, they *were* your dogs before they became Sedgwick's."

Leaning down, Colton generously ruffled the coats of each in turn, evoking low, deep-throated moans of pleasure. "You brutish pair, do you actually remember me?"

As if in answer, Leo, the largest of the two males, lifted his head and rubbed it against Colton's arm, drawing a chuckle from the man for his display of affection and gaining several more fond strokes along his back. Aris refused to be ignored. Sitting up on his haunches, he placed a massive paw upon Colton's arm, winning for himself the same loving attention his rival had reaped.

Lilting laughter floated from Philana's lips. "And you say they've forgotten you. My dearest son, I think you labor under a misconception."

"I've been gone for sixteen years," he pointed out with a skeptical chuckle. "It seems beyond a dog's capability to remember a person who has been absent for that length of time."

"And yet, 'tis obvious they have," Philana maintained, indicating the animals and the attention he was presently receiving from them. "If they hadn't known you, they'd have likely gone after you with teeth bared. I doubt anyone has ever told you that we had to keep the pair leashed after you left home for fear they'd run off in search of you. Until then, you were the only one who had walked or romped with them outside. But then, I was of a mind to join them in that quest. The afternoon of your departure, I stood at the window for what seemed an eternity after you had ridden out of sight. I was so in hopes you'd turn back. What is more, your father was there beside me, watching just as anxiously as I for any sign of yielding. But you never once looked back. At times, it seems as if I can still hear the pensive sigh your father heaved when he finally realized his hopes were in vain and turned away from the window. It was the first time I had ever seen him so completely dismayed, as if his heart had been seriously wounded."

In thoughtful silence, Colton sipped his tea as he stared at his father's portrait above the massive fireplace. No one knew how desperately he had missed his family, especially his father, but as much as their separation had beleaguered him, it was far too late to make amends.

Philana eyed her son contemplatively, wondering where his thoughts had strayed. She ventured a possibility. "Miss Fairchild is quite lovely, is she not?"

Colton nodded in distraction and then, with a curious frown, turned back to face his parent. "Who is this Roger Elston fellow, anyway?"

Philana lifted her slender shoulders in a casual shrug as she exchanged a glance with her daughter. "A wealthy miller's son who for some time now has been following Adriana about, hoping against all odds to win her hand."

Samantha took her cue and, settling a slender hand upon her husband's arm, squeezed it. "What do you want to bet that I can beat you at a game of chess?"

Percy grinned back at her. "I'll yield you that decision if I can choose what your penalty will be when you lose."

Arching a brow above sparkling gray orbs, she challenged, "Penalty, noble sir? Or mayhap you mean reward since I will likely win."

His own eyes glowed into hers as the wavering movement of his hand indicated some flexibility as to the actual outcome. "We'll see what comes of the game, my dear. Should I win, I may be persuaded to have pity on you. Will you not consider doing the same?"

The corners of her lips curved upward enticingly. "I suppose I could be persuaded to be lenient."

As the couple crossed to the gaming table at the far end of the room, Philana leaned back in her chair and considered her handsome son. When he had swept into her chambers earlier that afternoon, she had been struck with a treasured memory of his father's equally enthusiastic return home after spending a week in London a mere two months following their marriage. Never had she imagined her son would come to look so much like his sire. The fact that he did eased to some degree the anguish of her loss. "As you saw for yourself, Roger is quite possessive of Adriana."

Colton snorted in irritation as he exercised his hand again. He could tell by the way it was aching that he had hit the apprentice with all his might. Just as he had once rallied every fiber of energy in his determination to stay alive on the many battlefields upon which he had fought throughout his career, so he had reacted to Roger's attack in the very same way. It was just second nature for one constantly in danger to respond with all the physical forces at his command. "The lad made that obvious. But tell me, Mother, how does Lord Gyles feel about the apprentice's obsessive pursuit of Adriana?"

"Although he has never said anything derogatory about the young man in our presence, I imagine Gyles feels precisely the same way your father did. Sedgwick was absolutely convinced that Roger is an opportunist. As beautiful as Adriana is, the fact that she'll also make some man very rich when she marries has encouraged those of meager circumstance to test their luck, which has likely led Roger to do the same. Gyles has certainly been generous with his daughters in establishing properties and enormous funds for their dowries, but both Jaclyn's husband and Melora's fiancé were already wealthy in their own rights before petitioning Gyles for their hands. I don't mean to infer that there aren't those of wealth and prestige seeking to gain Adriana as their wife. The Marquess of Harcourt has the looks and wealth to have any lady of his choosing; it's understandable that he has set his sights upon the loveliest in the area. Occasionally he has joined other besotted swains when they've ventured here to be with her, but he has always behaved in a gentlemanly fashion." Philana flicked her delicately arched brows upward briefly to lend emphasis to her words as she added, "That's more than I can say for Roger, as you have so recently evidenced."

"The only Lord Harcourt I can remember was ancient even before my departure. As I recall he had a son living in London."

"You may know the man better by the name of Riordan Kendrick."

"Colonel Kendrick who gained fame as a hero in our confrontations with Napoleon?" Colton asked in amazement.

"The very same."

"He is kin to Lord Harcourt?"

"Riordan Kendrick was Lord Harcourt's grandson before the elder passed on. Riordan is about your age . . . or somewhere thereabouts," Philana explained. "His father, Redding Kendrick, assumed the duchy when the old man died, but he rarely comes to this area except to whisk in and out on brief visits with his son. On the other hand, Riordan seems to enjoy the family's country estate and has acquired it from his father who really has shown no interest in being this far away from London. But then, perhaps Riordan chooses to remain in the area because of Adriana."

Colton paused to take a sip of tea before offering the conjecture, "Obviously there has been no match made between this Riordan Kendrick and Adriana. Otherwise Roger wouldn't seem so hopeful of winning the girl."

"From what Samantha and I have ascertained from those who know the man, Riordan is definitely interested in changing those circumstances."

Colton traced the tip of his finger over the teacup's delicate handle. "And Adriana? How does she feel about the man?"

"Oh, I believe she likes him very much. Of all the young men who come around, he has been the only one she will sit and converse with for hours on end. The man has a good head on his shoulders. Your father said as much. Of course, there are always others here vying for her time, trying to thwart Riordan's attempts to win her. It's a wonder some of those gallants didn't show up here today, but then, many of them have been reluctant to intrude upon us after your father died. Frankly, prior to Sedgwick's passing, I wouldn't have put it past a number of them to have had spies watching Wakefield Manor to see in which direction Adriana would ride after leaving home, because it wasn't long after she appeared that they'd begin arriving on some pretext or another."

"Considering the rarity of the prize, Roger has certainly set his sights high, too high in my opinion." Frowning thoughtfully, Colton posed a question to his mother. "Can Adriana not see the apprentice for what he is?"

"Adriana isn't necessarily thinking of marriage when she allows the apprentice to join her and her companions. She has merely been reluctant to send him on his way because she believes he has suffered terrible hardships throughout his life. You know how she and Samantha always were as children, taking in stray animals and coddling them until they were healed and able to fend for themselves." Philana lifted her slender shoulders, finding no need to explain their compassion to one who had seen it for himself. "In the face of Adriana's gentle empathy, Roger has just presumed too much."

"I thought she'd be married by now. One look at her leaves me wondering why she isn't."

"She will eventually," Philana replied after a lengthy space and lifted her gaze to peer at her son over the rim of the teacup. Pensively, she sipped the brew again and, after a long silence, settled the cup back upon its saucer. "Your father certainly didn't care for Roger. As much as he tried to treat the young man with kindly deference, Sedgwick couldn't ignore the underlying tension between them. For one thing, Roger didn't appear to like the way Adriana doted upon your father or, for that matter, the converse. Call it jealousy, if you will. It seemed that way to me whenever I'd catch Roger watching the pair of them together. I suppose on the reverse side of that, Sedgwick considered Roger an interloper. You know yourself that your father always held the girl in high esteem, far above her sisters. She never made any pretense of being prim or skittish, and I think Sedgwick admired that about her, among other things. In fact, when Adriana left him behind in a horserace to the manor, he boasted about it for days on end. No one had ever beaten him before, not even Gyles. But then, your father admired her mind just as much as her courage. Even with all those qualities, she *is* still quite beautiful, is she not?"

A slow grin crept across Colton's lips as he leaned back in his chair. "I'm totally astounded by the changes that have occurred in the girl since I left home. Never for an instant would I have guessed this afternoon that the lady who bolted into the foyer was Adriana Sutton. Without question, she has become a rare beauty."

"Quite so," Philana agreed, managing to curb a pleased smile. "Of course, your father never wavered in the belief that she would come into her own one day, but there were other, more important reasons he had for securing her as your future wife."

"I know Father had my best interests at heart," Colton reluctantly admitted. "But, at the time, I just couldn't accept at face value what he was proposing. For a young man to be betrothed to a mere chit leaves much to chance, and I wasn't willing to let fate fall where it would. I had to be certain that I wouldn't come to regret the betrothal...."

"Are you saying you would now be more amenable to such a contract?"

A casual shrug prefaced his reply. "I think it would greatly behoove me to get to know Adriana better ere I make any serious considerations along those lines. In one respect, she is right. We *are* strangers."

"Even though she was the only choice your father ever made for you?" Philana gently prodded.

"I prefer making my own selections when it comes to a wife, Mother. I haven't changed at all in that respect."

"Then you're still opposed to the idea of taking her for your bride?"

"For the present moment, yes, but that doesn't mean I won't come to desire her as my wife in time. Unquestionably, she is difficult to ignore."

Philana considered her son closely. "I can imagine that Roger Elston would go to great lengths to have the girl for his wife."

Colton flicked his brows upward and, with a half-angry snort, lent emphasis to the derision detectable in his tone. "A blind man could see the fellow was keen on having her ... *as if* he has any rights at all where she is concerned. At every turn of the hand, he seemed eager to challenge me for even daring to talk with her until he went too far, and I have no idea why."

Taking in a deep breath, Philana braced herself for the moment ahead and then, after a brief uncertainty, plunged headlong into the quagmire of the situation. "Perhaps that is because Roger is aware the two of you have been promised to each other."

The hand Colton had lifted to his brow slowly lowered as he stared at his parent in astonishment. "What are you telling me, Mother?"

Percy and Samantha turned in surprise at the harshness of Colton's tone and looked from mother to son before exchanging a worried glance with each other. Sensing his wife's rapidly mounting concern, Percy reached across the table and squeezed her thin fingers, silently reassuring her that all would work out well.

Philana folded her own slender hands in her lap, trying to subdue their telltale trembling as she searched for the appropriate words to explain what had been done. The last thing she wanted was to drive him away from the family again. "Your father was convinced that, given enough time, you'd change your mind about Adriana and come to see her as a potential asset to the Wyndhams . . . the way he always saw her . . . even at the very beginning . . . and continued to see her for the rest of his life. Sometime after you left, he and the Suttons signed the nuptial agreement, pledging her to you."

Try though he might, Colton couldn't subdue the sneer in his tone. "Leaving home didn't profit me in the least, did it, Mother? I'm still committed."

"Not altogether," Philana replied, her voice losing its strength under the strain and at the possibility of opening old wounds with what she was about to reveal. "If you abhor the agreement so much, you can free yourself from it. Your father went to great lengths to make allowances for such a provision in the contract. They were there at the very beginning, but you refused to listen. You have only to pay earnest court to the girl for ninety days, and if, after that length of time, you still wish to avoid marriage with her, you can nullify the agreement. It's as simple as that."

Colton stared at his parent, reading the tension in her face. Only now did he realize how much she had aged during his absence. Although still very lovely in a priceless, elegant way, she had allowed the burdens of her family and her concern for him to etch her face with tiny lines. His breath eased outward in a long sigh. "Ninety days, you say?"

"Ninety days of earnest courtship." Philana stressed the point. "That is the stipulation your father required in exchange for your freedom."

Thoughtfully Colton sipped his tea. It was the standard practice that if he refused to consider the terms of the contract, even the three-month tenure, then he'd be forced by his own recognizance to compensate the Suttons for his offense, but he wasn't worried about that. Even without the largesse of the marquessate, he had managed to save enough in his career as an officer to accomplish that feat. Still, by so doing, he'd be closing off future access to Adriana as her suitor, and that was precisely where his manly instincts rebelled. He'd be wiser by far to test the susceptibility of his own heart in a compatible relationship ere he severed his association with the lady completely. It was a simple fact that she was far too beautiful for any man to turn his back on, much less one who had grown tired of the tawdry women who had frequented the encampments of the soldiers, or the others he had visited off and on.

"I suppose if I can endure the stress of endless skirmishes for sixteen years of my life, I can suffer through three months of courtship with an utterly beautiful young woman." He allowed a meager smile to convey his scant attempt at humor. "But after my lengthy experience as a bachelor, I'm afraid I'll have to relearn the art of chivalry. There wasn't much need for it in our encampments."

Philana lowered her gaze to hide the suspicions that flared within her mind. At times, her husband had voiced his concerns about the kind of life their son was mayhap leading when he wasn't battling the enemy. Each camp had its share of harlots and loose women, he had fretted, and after so long a time, and no matter how much a father might wish otherwise, a man far from home would have difficulty remaining indifferent to temptations constantly at hand. Carousing with strumpets was hardly the way of life one expected of an exemplary existence, but, as parents, they had been unable to hope for anything better.

Colton cocked a querying brow at his mother. "Does Adriana know about this agreement?"

"Yes, of course."

All too clearly he remembered the coolness in the girl's tone at odd and sundry times. "I take it that she's none too thrilled by the arrangement."

"Adriana will fulfill her part of the bargain to please her parents."

"You mean that she'd actually agree to marry me just to satisfy them?"

"The girl will do the honorable thing. . . ."

"Though she may thoroughly loathe me?"

"She doesn't loathe you. . . ."

"Pray tell, why not?" he demanded, and then couldn't help but scoff. "Don't tell me she has forgotten the vehement protests I made the day I left. If I discerned anything in her manner today, then I'm willing to wager that Adriana is still bristling over the incident."

"I'm afraid she was very much hurt," Philana admitted. "After all, you were the one she and Samantha looked up to when they were both young. Had you been a god, they could not have adored you more. You must know that, considering the way they followed at your heels. Naturally, Adriana was wounded by your fierce rejection and could only believe you hated her. She blamed herself for your departure and suffered some chagrin until Sedgwick talked to her and explained that some young men like to make their own decisions in life and that your rebellion was mainly due to what he had tried to enforce. In most cases, time has a way of healing old wounds. After all, Adriana was only a child. Many things are forgotten along the path from youth to womanhood."

"While in Africa I learned that elephants do not forget. Though it's true that Adriana was very young at the time of my infraction, I don't think she has forgotten either. I definitely caught glimpses of a coolness in her manner toward me today."

"You'll soon learn that Adriana is far more congenial toward friends than suitors. Sometimes I think the girl is just as averse to marriage as you are, but I believe that will change once she becomes convinced you are serious."

"Dearest Mother, though you may well desire a marriage between us as much as Father once did, you must understand that it may not come to fruition. I'll not bind myself to a woman simply because she's the primary choice of my parents. There has to be something more between us—"

"Before we were married, your father and I were allowed no other choice but to accept the dictates of our parents," Philana interrupted. "And still, not too long into our union, we came to realize that we loved one another deeply. I cannot believe you and Adriana aren't meant for each other. Whatever your father saw in the girl initially, he became even more convinced of it after she grew into womanhood. He remained firmly committed to the idea that she'd be an excellent choice for you. Considering how much your father loved you, do you honestly think that he would've wanted you to be miserable married to a woman you'd eventually come to abhor?"

"Adriana was no more than a child when Father arranged our betrothal!" Colton protested. "How in heaven's name could he have imagined that she'd become anything but a gawky little twig?"

"She has good blood and comes from a handsome family," Philana insisted. "Her appearance was bound to improve . . . as you can see that it has!"

"Father made his decision six and ten years ago, when she looked like a castoff collection of odd parts! Not even an accomplished seer could've foreseen the uncommon beauty she has today!"

"Nevertheless, as you can see for yourself, your father's predictions have proven accurate," his mother stubbornly asserted.

"Thus far," Colton acknowledged tersely. "But that doesn't mean that Adriana and I will come to love each other."

"Only time will establish what your feelings for one another will be."

He threw up a hand in frustration. "As you say, Mother, time will bear that out, but unless I am reasonably convinced that we can share some love or affection for one another, I shan't be asking for Adriana's hand in marriage. I refuse to go through life regretting the fact that I accepted someone else's choice rather than my own."

"Have you . . . a choice in mind then?" his mother asked haltingly, fearful of what he would say.

A heavy sigh slipped from his lips. "Thus far, I have found no woman to appease me or satisfy the demands of my heart."

"And what are they?"

Colton shrugged, not knowing the answer to that himself. "Perhaps that is merely to fill the abyss I yet feel in my personal life."

Lifting her teacup to her lips, Philana held a steady grip on its delicate handle in an effort to hide the telltale trembling of her fingers. She felt a strong compulsion to suggest that Adriana would likely be the only one who could satisfy that void, but she knew her son would not appreciate such a trite statement, though it could very well prove to be true.

After a long, thoughtful moment, Philana resettled her porcelain cup upon its saucer and announced quietly, "I shall leave you to decide when we should approach the Suttons about this matter, but know this, my son: Adriana's appearance had little sway over your father's judgment. He assumed it would improve, perhaps not to the degree that it has, but more than anything else, it was her character and intellect that he admired. The manner in which she and her siblings were brought up promised commendable behavior and principles, but in Adriana's case those qualities have become jewels in her crown."

Feeling as if a trap were closing in around him, Colton glowered across the room until he realized he was staring once again at the portrait above the fireplace. In a way, it was like looking at a reflection of himself; the resemblance was so very, very close, not only outwardly, but inwardly as well. His father had always had a mind of his own. Only Philana, with her soft, gentle ways, had been able to sway him one way or another. Colton had to wonder if Adriana would be as capable of softening *his* heart. As yet, no woman had ever succeeded.

Other thoughts intruded, prodding him with spurs that made him mentally wince. How would he feel if he were to have a son as rebellious as he had proven to be? Would the day ever come when he would yield to arguments put forth by an offspring? Or would he hold firm to his own convictions and resolve, just as his father had before him?

An inward honesty prevented Colton from offering dry, empty platitudes in defense of himself. Having been an officer nearly half his life, he knew he wouldn't enjoy the prospect of being faced with revolt, even if it duplicated his own refusal to comply with his father's wishes.

Four

⁂

Now that Colton Wyndham was home and lord of the manor, he was deserving of chambers worthy of a marquess. Yet servants were still unpacking his possessions, freshening the linens on his bed and generally dusting and airing the several rooms that comprised his new, second-story apartments on the southernmost side of the house. When Colton expressed to Harrison a desire to find a quiet place to take a nap, the steward suggested that he retire to the room he had once occupied in his youth until the new accommodations were ready.

Colton didn't mind; he was too near exhaustion to care much where he slept. Just as long as he had enough privacy to doff his clothes and stretch out upon something approaching a serviceable mattress, he'd be content. After all the narrow canvas cots he had slept on during his military career, his old bed with its down-filled mattress would seem like a luxury. Thus, he stripped away his uniform and, in complete exhaustion, sprawled upon the bed that Harrison had had the foresight to send servants to turn down.

Having gotten little rest during the lengthy carriage ride from whence he had bade farewell to his troops, he felt both mentally and physically drained. But then, perhaps that wasn't entirely due to his journey. The news of his pending betrothal to Adriana had set him back upon his heels. Once again, he found himself reliving those moments preceding his break with his father and his departure from home.

Thoroughly incensed that his sire would seek to arrange his life by committing him to a mere slip of a girl ten years his junior, he had stormed out of the house in rebellious resentment. Even at the age of six and ten, he had been acquainted with far more comely maidens to whom in years to come he'd have dutifully promised to give his protection and perhaps even his heart had his father considered any one of them suitable as a future spouse for his son; but almost from the time of her birth, the late Sedgwick Wyndham had been especially partial to the youngest daughter of his closest friend and neighbor. Never mind that the girl had seemed destined to remain not only a spindly little reed but a plain, awkward gamine with enormous, ebon eyes and a thin face. How could *anyone* have expected anything more? That was the way she had always looked, and in contrast to her two older sisters, who were petite, fair-haired, and exceptionally pretty, as well as closer to his own age, Adriana had seemed like nothing more than a dark, nondescript shadow in an otherwise extraordinarily handsome family. Notwithstanding, his father had set his aspirations resolutely upon six-year-old Adriana, recognizably the most studious of the three siblings, and deemed her a prudent match for his only male offspring. In that decision, Sedgwick had remained firmly dedicated, even declaring he would have no other for his son.

Colton had balked, to the point that he had left home the very day of his angry confrontation with his parent. He had entered military academy, at which time he had gained the support of his maternal uncle, Lord Alistair Dermot, who had confessed with a mischievous gleam in his eye that over the passage of some years he had been secretly yearning to find a righteous cause to go against the dictates of his brother-in-law, whom many of his peers had considered keenly intuitive in evaluating the worth of a person. Just once, Uncle Alistair had said, he wanted to prove Sedgwick Wyndham capable of committing errors in judgment, but no matter how much he may have longed for that event to come to fruition, Alistair had failed to gain the evidence he had sought. Now it seemed the contrary was true.

During the course of the next two years, Colton had learned the art of war and, in 1801, had gone to Egypt as a young officer, second lieutenant

grade, where he had seen service under Lieutenant General Sir Aber-
combe. From there, he had distinguished himself time and again in many
bloody conflicts against the enemy, daringly leading his men into the
thickest of frays or, when the enemy swarmed upon them, either standing
firm in a solid square of armed men facing four sides or else advancing or
retreating as a block, an infantry formation upon which commanders of
the British Empire even now often relied. During the next fourteen years in
which Uncle Alistair and letters from family members had been his only
contact with home, a series of promotions had elevated him to the status of
colonel in command of a sizable regiment under Lord Wellington. Though
Waterloo had recently evinced the deterioration of Napoleon's ambitions,
Colton had let it be known that he intended to carry on with his military
career. Wellington had been delighted and assured him that if his wounds
healed properly he would make general ere the year was out. Then had
come news of his father's death, and Colton had had a change of heart.
After finally getting on his feet again, he had discharged himself from the
surgeon's care and begged leave of Wellington and the English army. Casting his sights toward home, he had sworn an oath to himself that he
would do his duty by his family and to his newly acquired marquessate. In
spite of their past disagreements, he had felt an enormous pride in his
father's accomplishments. Even to think of the title being bestowed upon
another had gone against everything he had held dear, and he had become
increasingly resolved to keep the marquessate firmly within his grasp.

In his years as an officer, he had never given serious consideration to the
girl he had once rejected except to lament the fact that he had hurt her
deeply by his adamant refusal. He had certainly never imagined that one
day she would reach the extraordinary degree of exquisiteness she had
attained during his absence. Had someone swung a wood plank across the
back of his knees and swept his legs out from under him the moment she
announced her name, he couldn't have been more surprised.

Still, her unrivaled beauty would mean little to him if the two of them
proved incompatible, which had seemed the way of it shortly after Samantha had recognized him. The girl's stilted aloofness had evidenced something closely approaching resentment. Then, too, considering the number
of years he had held staunchly to his decision not to yield to his father's
dictates, he couldn't envision himself accepting a betrothal merely to pay
tribute to the elder's memory. Something more promising would have to

manifest itself ere he'd relent and turn his thoughts in line with what his sire had decreed for him.

A PAIR of hours later, Samantha left Percy chatting with her mother and went upstairs to seek out her brother. At her light knock, she heard his muffled, halting footfalls and the thump of his cane approaching the door. When the portal was drawn open, she found him garbed in older military attire that had softened over the years and clung more readily to his tall frame, evincing his broad shoulders and the sleekness of his hips.

"I hope I'm not disturbing you," she ventured apprehensively. Of a sudden, he seemed like a stranger, and she felt a surge of regret for having come. "Were you still resting?"

"No, actually, I was considering taking the dogs out for a short walk. My leg could use the exercise. It tightens up on me when I sit for long spells, as was the case during my journey here." Leaning heavily upon the cane, he backed away from the entrance and, with a welcoming grin, pulled the door wide. "Come in."

"Are you sure?" she inquired in a tiny voice, closely reminiscent of the way she had sounded as a child.

Old memories of happier times came winging back to Colton, drawing a chuckle from him. "Indeed, please do. You don't know how often I reminisced on your visits to my room after I left here. Whether you came to beg for help in repairing a broken toy or to be read a story, you made me feel cherished as a brother. After so long a time, I feel honored that you still have a desire to seek me out."

Moving inward with more enthusiasm, Samantha glanced about the chamber, finding it basically unchanged from the last time she had entered it years ago. As a child, she had idolized her brother and suffered through a painful loneliness after he had gone away. As much as she had tried earlier that afternoon to subdue the anxieties aroused by his conversation with their mother, she had found herself beset by a niggling apprehension that he'd revolt against the arrangements that had been made during his absence and once again take his leave. After being his own man for half his lifetime, he had grown accustomed to doing just as he pleased. It was understandable that he might resent intrusion into that area now.

Her smile wavered between uncertainty of the future and gratification that he had at last come home. "You can't imagine how much I've missed you, Colton. During the first several years after your departure, there were times when I felt so lost and forlorn that I just wanted to sit down and have a good cry. After Papa's passing, I found it doubly hard to stay here in the manse, especially without Percy. Every room seemed to echo with Papa's deep voice and laughter. If you're not aware of it, Colton, you not only look like him, but your voice has the same mellow tones that his had."

"Uncle Alistair complained about that on a fairly frequent basis," he acknowledged with a soft chuckle. "I suspect I startled him more than he cared to admit whenever I'd come up behind him unawares and say something. Once, he even called me Sedgwick before he realized his error."

The silkily lashed, dark gray eyes sparkled with amusement. "Dear Uncle Alistair, what a darling he is."

Never having thought of his uncle in that precise way before, Colton offered her a skeptical grin. "Well, he certainly helped me out when I was in dire need, but I always assumed that was only because he wanted to thwart Father any way he could."

Samantha's soft smile hinted otherwise. "Uncle Alistair seemed to enjoy giving the impression that he and Papa were ever at odds. Some of their views were dissimilar, granted, and neither was hesitant about speaking his mind. At times, when they argued, one could even believe they were the fiercest of enemies, yet if anyone spoke against the other in either's presence, woe to the fellow, for his ears would soon be ringing. I must admit Uncle Alistair had me completely duped until I saw tears welling up in his eyes at Papa's funeral. That was when he acknowledged he had never known a more honorable nor a more intelligent man than our father. He even avouched that he had never been more pleased about a wedding than the day his sister married Sedgwick."

Totally astounded by her claims, Colton could only stare at her as he tried to mentally assimilate what she was telling him. Initially, Alistair had led him to believe that his aim was merely to show up Sedgwick as being opinionated and self-willed. Now Colton was hearing something totally contrary to that premise. Feeling a bit dumbstruck at this new perspective of their uncle, Colton could only shake his head in wonder. "I suppose I'll have to reform my thinking and consider that Uncle Alistair's grumbling complaints about Father were merely for my benefit. Should I also negate the idea that he was actually looking for a way to recompense Father for his flaws when he offered to support me?"

A smile traced across Samantha's lips as her translucent gray eyes sparkled back at him. "The likelihood has merit. He probably didn't want you to feel beholden to him."

The manly brows flicked upward in amazement. "I should've known something was afoot the night I went to pay my debt to him and he told me that he had just bought a small estate near Bradford on Avon so he'd be able to visit his sister whenever he wished. The very thought of their proximity left me wondering how he was going to cope with Father's presence since our parents were together so much."

"After Uncle Alistair moved into his estate, he seemed to enjoy testing Papa's knowledge about this and that during his many visits here. I thought for a time he was merely trying to tweak Papa's temper, but at the funeral he confessed that whenever he wanted to know how some mechanism worked or some such thing, he'd just ask the one most likely to have that knowledge . . . our father." Having started weeping, she tried to laugh it off as she drew a dainty handkerchief from her cuff and hurriedly dabbed at the tears trickling from her eyes. "Foolish me, getting so emotional."

"I must give Uncle Alistair credit for his cunning. He certainly had me fooled," Colton admitted, a pensive grin slanting across his face.

Seeking another subject that would stem the emotional watery flow, Samantha turned her attention to her surroundings. Not since she had moved from her bedchamber just off the bathing room across the hall had she been in this area of the manse. Upon maturing, she had taken larger chambers in the north section, near the suite of rooms their parents had resided in for the whole of their married life and where her mother had chosen to remain after Sedgwick's passing. Samantha suffered no doubt that the happiest years she had ever spent in the manse were those wherein she had been ensconced across the hall within close proximity to her brother.

"Nothing at Randwulf Manor has really changed since you left, Colton, especially in this part of the house. Of course, your new chambers are far more impressive, but I have always thought these bedrooms cozier."

Samantha ran slender fingers fondly over the top of the desk where her brother had once studied languages, arithmetic, and science, among a host of other subjects that his private tutor had considered needful for a maturing young man, if only to help one face without shirking the difficult challenges of the world. According to the gentlemanly scholar, Colton had demonstrated himself of superior intellect in his studies in spite of the fact that he had also evidenced a tenaciously stubborn streak, which Malcolm Grimm had declared had often tested his patience. According to the man, that tendency had provoked lengthy debates between them, which had proven beneficial to them both. The scholar had also considered Colton unique among his peers in that he had carefully researched his facts before settling his mind firmly upon a matter. In a vast majority of the cases, which the two had passionately discussed, Mr. Grimm had been quick to acknowledge that the youth had established himself correct in his hypotheses.

Samantha smiled at her brother over her shoulder. "When I saw you standing in the hall outside the gallery this afternoon, I first thought you were a stranger. Then it finally dawned on me that you had the looks of someone I had known very well. Of course, your features aren't the only things you've inherited from Papa."

Perhaps it was his own intuitive instinct that led Colton to think she was referring to his willful independence. "I can imagine I've been just as stubborn about the betrothal as Father was. It certainly didn't help that we were at opposite ends of the spectrum."

Samantha chewed a lip worriedly as she strolled across the darkly hued oriental rug cushioning the floor. Upon reaching the fireplace mantel, she traced a finger reflectively over the elaborate scroll that finished its marble edge as she broached the main reason for her visit. "I tried to ignore your conversation with Mama this afternoon, but it was impossible. You must be aware that it's a subject that deeply concerns me."

"The agreement that Father arranged between Adriana and me, you mean." Colton rubbed his neck where tension had formed a kink soon after he had been told of the contract to which his father had committed him. It was not that he was against seeing Adriana again, or even courting her. In truth, he yearned for feminine companionship, the sort that lent no shame to a man, and she *was*, after all, far more exquisite than even the rare few he had deemed exceptionally beautiful during his lifetime. Still, he was a man who had considered his independence of great import; he wasn't necessarily anxious to give up that autonomy immediately upon his return home. He had no wish to hurt Adriana *or* his parent, but it would probably come to that should he decide not to marry the girl, for he wasn't at all sure a demure young lady with Adriana's strict upbringing wouldn't bore him nigh to his grave.

During his absence from home, he had deemed it prudent to shun lengthy entanglements and had avoided innocents with doting, ambitious fathers, many of whom had been his superior officers. He had had no lofty reputation to uphold and, for the most part, had casually sought the company of vivacious, exciting women. Then there had been the widows of close friends, who had come to him in the dark of night, at odds with themselves as they sought to assuage their sorrow and loneliness with one who had shared in the loss of their loved one and yet could be trusted to understand and hold his tongue.

Apart from his temporary light-o'-loves, he had become involved with an actress in London, which, taking into account his infrequent and limited visits to the city, had been a fairly casual affair in spite of the fact that it had been going on for perhaps five years now. Still, he had never considered his involvement with the beauteous Pandora Mayes of any consequence. He had merely deemed it safe to be with her in view of her inability to have children and the fact that he had never heard her name bandied about among the officers and bachelors. Yet, even while pampering her with lavish gifts, he had been fairly forthright and warned her that one day their affair would have to end. The less Pandora had known about his aristocracy, he had decided, the fewer inquiries she'd be inclined to make and the less likelihood she'd be able to embarrass him later on. It hadn't been until an article extolling his valor had appeared in the *London Gazette* that the actress had learned of his father's marquessate, but, even then, he had casually brushed off her questions by explaining that he had left home much at odds with his family. He had never declared that as an aristocrat he was bound by the requirements of his birth to marry a lady from among his peers, but in that area, he had made a private commitment to himself that when the time came to marry, he'd do the honorable thing and faithfully adhere to the union lest he embarrass his heirs by begetting nameless contenders for the marquessate.

Though the Wyndhams and the Suttons had been close friends and neighbors for what seemed an eternity, Adriana was almost a complete stranger to him. Still, he had to admit that he was as intrigued as any man could possibly be. Beyond being incredibly beautiful, she had a body that seemed far more tempting than any he had ever held. Softly rounded in all the right places, yet slender and long of limb, she had whet his imagination to such a degree that he found himself wondering if he'd find her just as enticing waking up naked beside him in the mornings.

Samantha turned to face her brother, beset by her own deepening apprehension. "The contract concerning you and Adriana is exactly what I mean."

Colton made no further effort to curb a mounting desire to jeer. "Apparently I'm the last one to know how well Father planned my life."

"He did nothing more for you than he did for me."

Fairly amazed by her statement, Colton could only stare at his sibling. The couple seemed so taken with each other that he found it hard to believe that a betrothal had been arranged for them. "You mean that your marriage was someone else's idea?"

Samantha inclined her head with a well-defined nod. "Aye, 'twas, and though you may have difficulty believing that it's possible, we love each other deeply."

"When did this come about? On your wedding night?"

Samantha's eyes flared with indignation at the mocking derision in her brother's tone. He had made it clear from his youth that he didn't believe in arranged marriages or betrothals and was highly cynical of their outcome. Now he was letting his skepticism spew over like a boiling cauldron. "Our love for each other began to sprout during our courtship. Since then, it has firmly taken root. Truly, we find it difficult to imagine how our love could have come about if Papa hadn't planted the idea and initiated our betrothal."

"Am I supposed to believe that kind of devotion could happen between Adriana and me?"

Samantha was frustrated by his obvious scorn. "You must know by now that Adriana and I are as close as sisters."

"I'm aware of that, Samantha, but as much as you may cherish her, I tell you now that that fact will in no wise influence my decision. By the terms Father laid out for me, I find myself committed to three months of courtship with Adriana. I will honor that agreement, but as far as the rest, I shall offer no empty platitudes or promises." He shrugged his shoulders with a casual air of indifference. "Simply put, Samantha, what will be will be."

Clasping a fist to her breast, she looked at him beseechingly. "Colton, I beg you . . . *please, please* don't hurt Adriana. As much as you may resent the arrangements Papa made for you, none of it has ever been her fault."

A pensive sigh escaped his lips. "I know that, Samantha, and I *will* make *every* effort to consider the merits of our future together. I shall also try to conduct myself in a manner Father would've deemed appropriate, but until I'm completely convinced that Adriana and I can come to love each other, I won't make any promises that I may later come to regret. Neither will I exchange nuptials with her to please family members. You must accept the fact that though I've agreed to court her, there still remains a very strong possibility that nothing will come of it. In view of the fact that the contract was drawn up without my knowledge by our parents, warning Adriana to be on her guard seems the only way to forestall the likelihood of her being seriously wounded by my rejection."

Samantha realized her pleas had profited nothing. Having gained no commitments from her brother, she and her friend were no better off now than they had been earlier. The arduous task of waiting would now begin, and only time would reveal whether Sedgwick Wyndham had been right all along when he had offered the comment that Adriana and his son were so well matched they could've been joined at the hip.

Thoughtfully, Samantha tilted her head aslant as she considered her handsome kin. "There is one thing I would have you explain, Colton, if you'd care to enlighten me. My question has nothing to do with Adriana, so you needn't be on your guard. I've just been curious about something, that's all."

His lips traced upward. "I'll try my best."

"Earlier this year, Mama and I were told by several acquaintances that they had met you in London. We were certain after being away for so many years you'd come home during that brief span of peace since we were there in London ourselves, but, of course, you never did. It has been our deepest regret that you didn't get to see Papa while he was still alive and in good health. Couldn't you have seen fit to visit us while we were all there?"

Colton was reluctant to upset his sister any more than she had been. Had it not been for the fact that on the day of his departure, his sire had forbidden him to darken the door of the family homes until he could yield himself to the idea of discussing plans for his betrothal to Adriana or, as it had come to be, the elder had been laid to rest in a grave, he would have visited much sooner. "I'm sorry, Samantha, I went to London on official business for Lord Wellington and, while there, I had to stay within an area wherein I could be located easily by couriers. I wasn't there long before other commanders and I were sent to join Wellington in Vienna to discuss Napoleon's return to France. I had my orders; I had to obey them."

"Papa kept asking for you on his deathbed," she said in a small voice, futilely struggling to suppress the tears that still seemed inclined to come whenever she remembered their father's muted pleas to see his only son.

The unrelenting remorse Colton had suffered over his father's death had lain like an arduous weight upon his chest since news of that event had reached him. As much as he wished he had the ability to reverse time and events and substitute those sorrowful moments with happier, affectionate moments, he could not. He was merely a man, after all.

Noticing the wetness glistening in the eyes that were so very much like his own and their father's before them, he limped toward his sister and, slipping his arms about her, breathed a humble supplication against her hair. "Dearest Samantha, please forgive me. We were confronting the enemy when your first missive of Father's illness came, and I was bound by duty to remain with my regiment. Then, later, after his death, I was prevented by my wound from making a departure. It was some time before I could even leave my cot."

Realizing her own dialogue had turned morbid, Samantha became immediately repentant. "I must ask your forgiveness in return, Colton. You can't imagine how truly relieved and grateful we all are to have you finally home and to know for a certainty that you're alive and well." Amid a profusion of tears, she slipped her arms about him. "Mama and I have been so dreadfully worried about you. Though Papa dared not speak of his fears while the fighting was so intense, he, too, was deeply concerned for your welfare." Striving diligently to pull herself together, she took a deep breath, seeking to subdue the emotions that even now threatened to undermine her efforts to speak. Forcing a smile, she stood back with eyes still brimming with moisture. "In spite of your differences, he loved you very, very much."

His sister's words wrung Colton's heart, and it took a concerted effort for him to move beyond his regret. He had loved his father deeply, but he had abhorred the tradition that allowed parents to select spouses for their offspring. But then, he wondered if he'd have felt any different had he been the parent.

ADRIANA raced up the wide staircase of Randwulf Manor in an anxious quest to get bathed and dressed before dinner was announced. She hadn't imagined that Stuart and she would be returning so late, yet when Mr. Fairchild had arrived at Wakefield Manor to fetch Felicity, he had proven quite verbose in his praise of his daughter and the beneficial changes he had purportedly been making at his grandfather's mill. No one, least of all her mother, had wanted to appear rude and urge him on his way until Stuart, seeing their time dwindling rapidly away, had hurriedly explained their need for haste before begging leave of the Fairchilds. Whisking Adriana out the door, he had promptly handed her into her parents' waiting landau and then had urged Joseph to use all possible speed to get them to the neighboring mansion. He had quickly ascended into the conveyance just as the whip cracked above the horses' heads and then, as the team shot forward, had fallen into the seat beside her, readily evoking their merriment.

Dinner at both manors was always served punctually every evening, which meant by the time they arrived Adriana had little more than an hour to bathe, dress, and reasonably coif her hair before joining the Wyndhams downstairs in the great hall in time to drink a toast to Stuart's birthday. She just hoped there would be enough hot water simmering in the kettles above the fire in the bathing chamber to allow her to prepare a bath for herself fairly quickly. It would prove especially beneficial if Helga, the family's upstairs maid, could lend assistance helping her dress. From previous experience, Adriana knew the woman could speed her on her way.

Years ago, the bedchamber into which Adriana fairly sprinted had graciously been designated as her own. After sweeping her undergarments and gown onto the bed and dropping her slippers beside the chaise, she rushed into the bathing compartment, which nowadays was rarely used unless the house was overflowing with guests. As a child, Samantha had wanted her ensconced nearby whenever she came to spend the night, and had claimed for Adriana the bedchamber on the opposite side of the narrow bathing compartment from her own room. It was rare nowadays that Samantha took advantage of the chambers she had been given as an adult much less those from her youth unless Percy was perchance required to travel alone as royal emissary for the Prince Regent.

As much as Colton had once disliked having to cross the hall to use the bathing room and had squabbled countless times with his younger sibling over her tendency to monopolize the facility and leave it a total disaster after her lengthy baths, that would no longer be the case. Henceforth, as lord and master of the house, he'd be residing in his own spacious, recently renovated chambers replete with his own private bathing room. Considering the limited luxuries even an officer garnered in the military, such comforts would seem rather grandiose until he got reacquainted with the better things in life.

Considering her tardiness in returning from Wakefield, Adriana had to glumly face the realization that her toilette would be greatly shortened in contrast to what she normally enjoyed. Although she may have acquired a few manly skills from her father throughout her lifetime, she definitely relished occasions to luxuriate in certain feminine pleasures, such as soaking in perfumed baths. As closely as Colton had seemed inclined to approach her earlier that afternoon, she definitely wanted to rid herself of any scent closely resembling a horse. Besides, her black crape gown ornamented with black velvet Vandykes silhouetted upon white satin around the décolletage and the bottom of the hem was new and quite lovely. Before donning her lace and satin chemise and the stylish gown, she yearned to indulge in a warm fragrant bath.

Flames crackled and danced around the belly of a large kettle hanging in the bathing chamber's small fireplace, lending a cheery warmth to the narrow room, which in the winter months proved especially needful. Yet when Adriana flicked slender fingers through the liquid simmering in the cauldron, she groaned in despair, for it was hardly more than lukewarm. The best bath it promised to yield would be a shallow, tepid puddle in the bottom of a huge tub. Although several large pitchers stood beside the washstand, full to the brim, they were there merely to refill the kettle or to blend with the boiling water once it had been poured into the tub.

Heaving a dejected sigh, Adriana glumly crossed to the huge, copper tub where an empty pitcher had been left. What she saw there caused her to catch her breath in sudden elation, for a fairly deep bath had already been prepared for her.

"Oh, Helga, you're such a dear," she crooned in appreciation, and made a mental note to thank the servant profusely for her foresight. The maid could only have run ahead when she had seen her coming, for steam was still drifting over the surface of the water. On an ornate linen rack near the end of the tub, a large linen towel and a bathing cloth hung, evidencing the thoughtfulness of the older woman.

The elongated copper bathing vessel, replete with tall sides and a rounded back, had always been comfortable. In her youth, Adriana had also used it for a hiding place during games of hide-and-seek. Several times she had lain flat and fully clothed on the bottom while Samantha searched high and low for her. The elevated sides had allowed her to remain undetected. Even now, as a grown woman, she had to use the small step kept conveniently near when either entering or exiting the vast confines of the copper vat.

The water was sufficiently hot for a soothing soak, a treat Adriana greatly anticipated. Hastily stripping off her boots, riding habit, stockings, and undergarments, she left them in a disorganized heap on the floor and stepped to the tub. From a vial of rose oil, she drizzled several droplets over the surface of the steaming liquid and then flicked her fingers back and forth to swirl the scent evenly throughout. A sigh of pure delight escaped her lips as she settled into the fragrant water. The bath was actually deeper and hotter than Helga normally prepared, but it was a change Adriana appreciated. It was now comparable to that which her own maid, Maud, prepared for her at Wakefield Manor.

Thoughtfully, Adriana drizzled the contents of a saturated sponge over the pale, rounded hills of her bosom as she leaned back against the curved end of the tub. The warmth of the water proved immensely relaxing, and after the shock of Colton's return, the confrontation that had ensued between him and Roger, and her tardy return to Randwulf Manor, she felt much in need of a few moments of quiet repose. Perhaps it would even rejuvenate her spirits, which in the last few hours had been suffering mightily from her growing anxieties over the contract and its possible effect on Colton.

Dismissing that fear from her mind took determination, but Adriana folded a wet cloth, laid it over her eyes to block out the glow of the oil lamps hanging overhead, and slid down into the tub until the liquid lapped at her chin. She deliberately turned her mind to the fictional story she had been reading the night before. It had been immensely slow-paced and had soon issued her into the arms of Morpheus.

The tale proved equally effective in recall, for the next thing she became mindful of was a low clearing of a throat interrupting her dreams. Reluctantly rousing herself, she mumbled sleepily, "Thank you for preparing a bath for me, Helga. It has been no less than heavenly."

Instead of the cordial reply she expected from the plump maid, a deep, throaty "*Ha-hmm*" intruded, causing Adriana to gasp in sudden alarm and snatch off her makeshift blindfold. For barely an instant, she gawked at the tall, near-naked man looming over the tub before her dark eyes descended and promptly widened in horror. He wore nothing more than a towel around his narrow hips and that linen was bulging ominously in front. In the passing of a heartbeat, Adriana scrambled to sit upright and, upon achieving that position, clasped her arms tightly around her legs as she sought to hide her nudity from the new Marquess of Randwulf.

Having leisurely observed the beauty to his heart's content while she slept, Colton made no effort to curb an amused, all too confident grin. "I hope I'm not intruding, my lady."

His casual statement ignited Adriana's temper. Angrily she railed at him, "Why are you here and not in the master's chambers?"

He gave a succinct bow, which seemed at the very least absurd, considering the brevity of his attire. "Your pardon, Adriana, but I was told a bath awaited me here." His tone was warm and mellow, somewhat unnerving to the one who had just screeched at him. "Indeed, had I known we'd be sharing one together, I'd have returned posthaste rather than spend so much time walking the dogs."

"We're not sharing anything!" she cried, hauling back the sodden washcloth and letting it fly. Never would she have imagined it would fall short of its mark (his grinning face) and plop across the ominous, towel-covered shelf protruding from the area of his genitals. It caught and hung half-mast where it landed until Colton made a point of plucking it up by a thumb and forefinger. Shaking his head in chiding reproof, he displayed the deepening grooves in his cheeks as he draped the sopping cloth over the rim of the tub.

"*Tsk, tsk!* Such a temper you have, my dear! 'Twould seem it hasn't changed much at all since I left home. And here I was ready to accept your invitation."

"You conceited buffoon!" she shrieked. "Do you actually think I was waiting for you?"

Her show of outrage bestirred his hearty laughter. Thoroughly incensed, Adriana glowered at him until his amusement dwindled to nothing more than a slanted grin. Meeting her furious glare with glowing eyes, he lifted bare shoulders, which, in contrast to his taut, lean waist, seemed even wider and far more firmly muscled than even his short-cropped military blouse had revealed.

"You can't really fault a wounded officer recently returned from the wars for hoping that such would be the case, now can you, my dear? You're the most enticing female I've seen in . . . well, perhaps my whole life."

"I doubt your mother has it in her to run a bawdy house, my lord, nor would I be one of the attractions even if that were the situation," she stated caustically.

Colton had to wonder if the lady's indignation was merely a ploy. Long ago, he had become inured to the schemes of lonely wives and harlots who had followed their camps. The latter had used coyly diverse methods in order to entice him into taking them into his cot, and he had to admit that at times he had seriously been tempted by their invitations, but the idea of falling victim to a malady that would perhaps taint him for the rest of his life had been a very sobering restraint. In Adriana's case, however, he couldn't believe the Suttons had been anything but protective of their offspring. Yet as much as he yearned to taste and relish firsthand her creamy form, he had to consider at what cost he'd be doing so and what she'd require of him. *Almost* betrothed was definitely not the same as actually *being* betrothed, and being lured into marriage by such a delectable form fully visible to his hungry eyes was an inducement he *hoped* he'd be able to resist, though, truly, at the moment, he desired to throw caution to the four winds and dally to his heart's content with the lady, for he had serious cause to doubt that he had *ever* seen the like of such perfection before. Her beauty certainly made his past conquests seem paltry in comparison.

When he had first entered the bathing chamber, he hadn't noticed her over the rim of the tub; but after doffing his clothes, he had stepped to the huge copper vat and, upon espying within its confines a nymph as ravishing in her naked glory as any man was capable of imagining, he had experienced a most titillating shock. If after their collision in the gallery he had suffered even the smallest scrap of doubt as to the desirability of the lady's form, then it had definitely been sundered by the flawlessness to which he had become privy. For a moment, he had savored the delectable details of her womanly curves—admiring her intriguingly round, delicately hued breasts; her smoothly taut belly; and the long, sleek limbs that were far more admirable than any he had ever seen—fully aware of his body responding to the stirring sights. He had almost been reluctant to wake her. If not for the threat of a manservant coming to see if there was anything he needed, he'd have gladly relished the sights until the rising of the sun.

"Have you no sympathy for what I've suffered?"

"None at all," Adriana declared flatly. "But since you seem to belabor your hardships overmuch, no doubt to evoke sympathy where there is none, I'll relent and leave the bathing chamber entirely to you!" She glanced around for the towel and, upon finding it missing, realized it was the very one that provided him with what little modesty he was presently enjoying.

"Turn your head, you jackanapes, or, better yet, close your eyes before they pop out your head! You've left me nothing to cover myself."

Colton chuckled softly. If the lady knew how long he had ogled her during her nap, she'd realize it was far too late for her to try to salvage her modesty. "That's a bit like closing the fence after the horses have escaped, isn't it, my dear? I assure you, 'twould not wipe from my mind the loveliness I've savored for the last several moments."

In spite of his unrelenting stare, Adriana braced her hands upon the rim of the tub as she emitted a frustrated snarl. Pushing herself upward, she set her rounded bosom momentarily a-bounce, evoking a low strangled groan from Colton as the sights tweaked his goading desires to an even higher level. Knowing the pain that would come swiftly to assault him if he didn't find release for his pent-up desires, he could almost wish he had not viewed such a delectable form, for he feared hereinafter he'd be tormented and hard-pressed to forget what he had seen.

Wondering what malady had suddenly beset the man, Adriana cast an oblique glance at him, only to find his warmly glowing eyes devouring her nakedness as if he were strongly tempted to do more than just stare. Angrily she held up a hand to ward him off. "Stand back, you blackguard, and give me room to depart," she commanded. "And while you're doing so, try not to stumble over your drooling tongue. I don't have enough hands to cover myself and climb over the rim of this blasted tub at the same time. Trying to preserve my modesty would likely cause me to break my neck."

"Would you like assistance?" Colton offered solicitously, stretching forth a hand in hopeful anticipation. At the moment, he thought he'd even be willing to take his chances bedding the lady; it was a fact he'd never be able to find such satisfactory appeasement for his throbbing desires elsewhere. Indeed, he seriously doubted he had ever known the extent of such blissful torment or experienced the degree of rutting heat he was now battling. If not for the fact that he had long been coached in the ethics of a gentleman, he'd have left this vision of Venus little opportunity to deny him. "I'm more than willing to verify with more credible evidence that what I'm seeing is actually mortal and not some wondrous vision I've conjured from yearnings long starved. Only by touching you will I be able to ascertain that you're real and not some figment of my imagi—"

"A slap in the face would supply that evidence just as well," Adriana shot back in rapid fire. "Try anything, Colton Wyndham, and that's just what you'll be getting."

A heavy sigh did much to express his disappointment. Such sights to which he was now conversant as she stepped over the rim of the tub came nigh to dissolving the strength from his limbs. As far as other areas of his body, it had the opposite effect. Never before had he viewed such long, sleek limbs wondrously crowned by a dainty nest of womanly perfection or the like of such temptingly round, creamy hued orbs. His palms all but itched to feel the silkiness of that luscious fullness within his grasp.

Facing what promised to be a lack of appeasement, Colton knew he'd soon be suffering the torment of the damned when the curse of his lengthy abstinence began to tear at his vitals. He'd rather not have to endure that discomfort . . . if the lady would only relent.

Stretching forth a hand as he offered her a cajoling smile, he appealed to her with all the charm he was capable of putting into play. He had not come this far through life without becoming aware that the vast majority of women he had known had been intrigued . . . and captivated . . . by the grooves that deepened in his cheeks with every smile from his lips. "Will you not relent, Adriana?"

Sharply elevating a brow, Adriana considered the lean hand a brief moment before lifting a challenging gaze to meet his. As they lit upon that handsomely chiseled visage, her eyes were immediately drawn into the snare, and for a moment she found herself susceptible to the appeal of that wondrous smile. Still, the memory of his angry departure years ago was not far from mind and served as a very effectual deterrent against a disastrous thaw. She met his warmly alluring eyes with a cool stare as she warned him crisply, "You lay a hand upon me, Colton Wyndham, and I'll scream until your mother comes running. That much I promise you."

"In that case, my dear, I shall comply with your wishes," he avouched with an unwavering grin, acquiescing with an impromptu bow as he retreated from the tub. "I wouldn't want to shock my mother unduly by our mutual state of undress, especially yours, which you flaunt with such grace and style."

"Flaunt!" she railed in outrage, thoroughly incensed by his audacity to lay the blame on her. "You lecher, you know you gave me little choice in the matter. Whether fortuitously or deliberately, you intruded into my bath while I slept. If by chance, then you should've been enough of a gentleman to leave ere I ever awoke."

"What? And ignore what I truly believed was an invitation?" he asked with an incredulous grin. He chuckled softly as he served quick death to that notion. "My dear, as utterly tempting as you are, you couldn't expect that of a saint, much less a man who has eyes in his head and has become your ardent slave."

"Just how many women have you addled with fabricated protestations of that sort, milord?" Adriana asked snidely. "If *any* believed you, then they must have been a simple lot."

Colton refrained from boasting of his previous success with similar platitudes. The fact that this particular lady was disinclined to accept his cajolery made her rather unique among the women he had known. Even if this beauty was the one his father had chosen for him, he was nevertheless intrigued by her aloofness. It was a simple fact that an easily won prize wasn't treasured by its recipient half as much as one that had been obtained by great toil and difficulty. Her disinterest in his propositions did much to challenge him. It certainly heightened his interest, if indeed it could be intensified any more than it was already.

The casual lifting of his broad shoulders was only briefly considered by Adriana before his limping retreat drew her dark eyes downward again to the bulging towel. Only then did she notice the purplish, puckered scar slanting downward toward the inside of his right thigh, but it was only a fleeting glance, for it was impossible to ignore the protuberance beneath the linen. On rare occasions from the windows, she had seen Ulysses servicing the mares in the fields stretching out beyond her bedchamber, a fact that would have seriously shocked her mother had she known. The bold lance seemed a necessary prelude to the joining of two beings of different genders. Even concealed beneath the towel, it posed a threat that unnerved her . . . and yet, at the same time, awakened a strange pleasurable excitement at the core of her being. This was the closest she had ever come to viewing a naked man. Once she wed, her maidenly curiosity would be appeased, yet she couldn't deny there had already been moments when she had wondered what she'd see on her wedding night.

Becoming cognizant of the fact that Colton was grinning like some hopeful lecher beneath her fleeting glances, she groaned in embarrassment and clasped her arms over her nakedness as she faced away. "Have you no shame, sir?"

"Why? Because I make no pretense about my vulnerability as a man or that I desire a woman as beautiful and perfect as ever I've seen?"

"Just tell me one thing," she demanded, tossing another glare over her shoulder. "How long were you standing there ogling me before you decided to awaken me?"

It took an Herculean effort for Colton to drag his gaze away from her long, shapely legs and fetching derriere in order to meet the lady's gaze. "Long enough to know I won't ever forget what I've seen here this evening, if that's what you're wondering. As for ogling you, it was impossible not to. I doubt I've ever met a lady more ravishing devoid of clothing than she is properly garbed. The sight of Venus sleeping in my bath awoke a slumbering dragon that I fear will not be placated till satisfaction is found with such a comely maid. I'd certainly feel sufficiently welcomed home from the wars if you were to relent and take pity on me, Adriana."

"*Please*, forgive me for *ever* thinking you were a gentleman," she derided. "You've done much to prove yourself a full-fledged lothario. In addition to your impertinence to ogle me and suggest that I might be amenable to pacifying the *dragon*, you've had the effrontery to take the only towel, which is further proof that you should've stayed under your father's roof a bit longer and learned a few more manners before running off to become your own man."

"Your pardon, Adriana, but I thought you'd be offended by the sight of my male nudity and sought to protect your virginal senses from such a view. Please accept my humble apology for not thinking of your basic needs first." Giving her a brief, impromptu bow, he straightened and whisked the makeshift skirt from his hips. Holding the towel out to her, he offered it to her with a wayward grin. "At least now it's warm."

A shocked gasp was snatched from Adriana's throat as she gaped in shock at his bold blade of passion. Then, with a mortified groan, she turned abruptly about, her face flaming.

Stepping close behind her, Colton leaned over a sublimely naked shoulder. Her dainty pink nipples proved so enticing that it became a test nearly beyond his ability to resist to keep himself from stroking his fingers across them in awe. Smiling, he heckled in a husky whisper, "After all the fuss you made, my dear, would you have me believe you don't want the towel now?"

"Will you *please* just leave me alone!" she begged in exasperation and tried to toss back an angry glare, only to find his face too close to allow her to do anything more than stare into those warmly glowing orbs. They ensnared her own before his gaze dropped to her lips. She felt his hand settle lightly upon her ribs, and for a wild, crazy moment, she thought he intended to kiss her, for his head lowered ever so slowly as his lips parted. Foreseeing the imminent threat, she stepped free of his hand and gathered her dignity, at least what little remained of it. "If you don't mind, my lord, I'd like to get dressed *before* we're late for dinner."

"Colton," he insisted, as a grin curved his handsome lips. "You must call me Colton. 'Tis the price I demand for letting you go."

"What will you do if I scream?" she challenged, lifting her slender nose higher in the air.

He grinned back at her. "Admire the wondrous sights until everyone comes running."

Adriana rolled her eyes at the thought of the humiliation she'd suffer from such an occurrence. A heavy sigh exaggerated her capitulation. "If you insist . . . Colton."

Chuckling softly, he retreated, once again admiring her very shapely backside as he did so. "Well, actually, however much I'd rather keep you prisoner, I can see the necessity of letting you escape. I'm still in need of a bath, and since you appropriated mine, and there's no time for servants to prepare another, I'll have to make use of what you've left."

He was greatly disappointed when she made use of the towel, yet when she faced him, tucking a corner into the deep valley between her breasts, he readily decided that Pandora Mayes had never looked remotely as alluring draped in a towel as this young beauty.

"Do you perhaps need assistance in readying yourself for dinner, my dear? Helga has kitchen duties since one of the scullery maids fell ill tonight. I rather suspect it was due to tippling so much of Father's brandy, since Harrison said that he found what was left of the crystal decanter shattered on the drawing room floor, but that's neither here nor there. The simple truth is that Helga won't be able to assist you. Can I be of service in her stead? I'm quite adept at fastening tiny hooks and buttons. Although the temptation would be enormous, I'd even promise not to look any more than I have already."

An angry snarl issued forth from Adriana's gnashing teeth as she struck out at him with the backside of her arm. The blow hardly fazed him as it came in contact with the taut muscles across his midsection, but the pain she encountered caused her to cry out in sharp surprise. Her sudden anguish drew more chuckles from the naked man. Mortified and enraged, she clasped her throbbing forearm against her midriff and stalked past him into the adjoining room.

Immediately upon passing the door, she turned abruptly to make sure he wasn't following her and found him sauntering leisurely in the opposite direction toward the tub. At its edge, he bent, testing the warmth of the water and, in so doing, bringing into view other manly parts. As much as she was wont to gape in virginal innocence, her eyes were drawn to a small, purplish birthmark shaped like a flying gull that marred the otherwise unblemished skin of his right buttock.

After dumping a pail of hot water into the tub, Colton turned to face her again in all his naked glory. That damnable grin, which seemed naturally inclined to curve across his handsome lips, had not diminished in the least. "What? You haven't gone yet?" he inquired, his eyes casually flitting the entire length of her towel-covered form. "I thought you were in a hurry to leave my sight."

Had she not been so fearful of waking the dead, Adriana would've screamed at him in fury and called him every foul name in her limited repertoire of insulting appellations. Glowering at him with dark eyes fairly snapping with fire, she caught the edge of the door and sent it flying forward with all her might. Alas, the force of her outrage caused the solid plank to rebound before the latch could catch. As it swung back, she shoved the door forward again with another raging snarl. This time she was able to savor some small bit of satisfaction as the latch clicked firmly into place.

DREADING her encounter with Colton Wyndham after their meeting in the bathing chamber, Adriana dallied upstairs as long as she dared, but the appointed moment approached, leaving her no other choice but to make her descent. By the time she arrived, Colton had already joined his family and their guests in the drawing room, and though he remained standing with his white-garbed backside to the warmth radiating from the fireplace and seemed content to quaff the dark red wine in his goblet, his eyes above the crystal rim were vividly alive with manly admiration as they swept upward from her black silk slippers, leisurely perused the tempting roundness visible above her bodice, and then moved higher still to the upswept coiffure elegantly adorned with a black plume. Feeling as if he had just stripped her down to bare skin, Adriana turned aside and sought some other area of the room where hopefully she'd be able to escape those shining orbs. Alas, they seemed to feed upon her every movement, following wherever she led.

Samantha had occasion to pass close in front of her brother, but, in doing so, was brought up short. Peering at him rather strangely, she leaned near, sniffed, and then wrinkled her nose in disdain. "What in the world are you wearing, Colton?"

Somewhat confused, he hefted his cane in one hand, and with his glass clasped in the other, spread his arms wide as he looked down at his uniform. "What does it look like I'm wearing? 'Tis the best I have until I fetch my tailor from London."

Samantha giggled. "Why, Colton, I never would've expected you, of all people, to indulge in a ladies' scent. If my nose hasn't deceived me, I'd be inclined to say the scent is closely reminiscent of the one that Adriana is fond of wearing. In fact, I think the pair of you have used the same perfume tonight."

All eyes turned upon the brunette who, with unswerving dedication, drained her goblet before placing it on a serving tray of a passing servant and accepting in its stead a fresh glass. Uncomfortable beneath the curious attention that had descended on her, Adriana carefully avoided meeting anyone's gaze as she awaited Colton's answer. Although she feared the shame that would descend on her if he proved callous, she had too much backbone to turn tail and run.

"Merely a mistake, my dear Samantha," Colton murmured with a soft chuckle, "one that I had no time to rectify if I wanted to be down here for dinner at the appointed hour. Once I realized my bath had been permeated with the scent, it was too late to bid servants to bring up enough buckets of hot water to suffice for another one. Alas, I had spent too much time outside walking the dogs and was much in need of a bath to consider foregoing it. Frankly, I hadn't realized anyone else had been using the bathing chamber near my old room or that some lady had been there fairly recently."

Laughter rippled effervescently from his sister's lips. "'Tis a wonder you didn't come across something far more shocking than a vial of bath oil. For some time now, Adriana has been using those rooms if she has been riding and needs to bathe and change here for dinner. I'm sure it's her fragrance you're wearing this evening, but I must admit, I prefer to smell it on her, not you."

"I'm in full agreement," Colton avowed, casting a slanted grin toward the younger woman. "Although divinely alluring on the lady, it seems a bit sweet for my personal taste."

"I'm relieved to hear you say that," his sibling responded with a teasing smile as she flicked a glance down his tall form. "You had me worried there for a moment. Truly, the scent left me wondering what the war had done to you."

Noticing that Stuart had approached and was now standing at his sister's elbow, Colton stretched forth his hand to the man. "I'd like to join those who've already extended hearty wishes for your health and good fortune on this event, Stuart. May you enjoy not only this one, but many more birthdays in the years to come."

The viscount responded with a wide grin and a hearty shake of the other's proffered hand. "I didn't have a chance to converse with you very long this afternoon, so before too much time has elapsed, I'd like to take this opportunity to invite you to join me and a small company of my friends on a hunt, that is, if you're up to venturing out. We'd be delighted to have you come with us."

Colton exaggerated a wince before shaking his head. "I must confess I still have some difficulty riding, as you may well understand, but I shall consider your invitation with considerably more enthusiasm once my leg is completely healed."

"I had the same problem not too many days past," Stuart confided as his own feigned grimace turned easily into a grin. "I've become rather loath to lie upon my stomach. For too long now, it seemed it was either that way or no way at all."

The men laughed together over the hindrances they had been forced to surmount, those in the past and some that still lingered. As their amusement ebbed, Colton extended an invitation of his own to the viscount. "Now that you're more or less in the family, Stuart, you must visit Randwulf Manor more often. I'd enjoy hearing stories of the military campaigns in which you were involved."

The viscount eagerly accepted the invitation. "I'd be delighted to share them with you and would be grateful if you'd reciprocate in kind. May I also say at this time that I'm pleased to know that you'll be assuming the marquessate. Latham has his good points, but I'm afraid they're far outweighed by his shortcomings. As for your sister and mother, they tried to appear gay and hopeful these past few weeks, yet it was evident to all concerned they were worried about you and afraid you wouldn't come home."

"I shall make every effort not to trouble my family in the future," Colton avowed. "God willing, I'm home to stay."

"That calls for a toast," Percy interjected as he laid an arm about his wife's waist and, with his free hand, lifted a goblet high. "To the seventh Marquess of Randwulf. May he have good fortune and long life!"

"Hear! Hear!" Stuart cried, raising his glass aloft and saluting Colton in like manner.

Silently Adriana joined the toast by elevating her own goblet and was surprised when the darkly translucent eyes touched on her above a warm smile. For a moment, their eyes merged as her own delved into the depths of those glowing gray orbs. She could only wonder what was going through the mind of the handsome man, but when his gaze descended in a slow, sensual caress of her bosom and crape-clad form, she decided it would probably not be to her liking.

Averting his attention lest he arouse to a greater intensity the hunger still gnawing at his being, Colton murmured thanks to all and then, a short time later, shook hands with Stuart as the latter excused himself. Following their parting, Samantha, Philana, and Percy briefly joined Colton to convey their own good wishes upon him. From the women, he received affectionate kisses and, from the younger man, a pat upon the back. Still, he was wont to glance fairly often across the room at the beauty who, with pinkened cheeks, sought to ignore his lingering perusals.

Stuart approached Adriana, bearing two glasses of wine and, with a smile, offered her one as a replacement for the empty goblet she had just set aside. "You're looking extremely beautiful tonight, my lady, but from the way you were glancing around, I'd be inclined to say you were in need of another libation."

"Yes," she agreed with a valiant smile. "It has been a fairly eventful day."

"One to savor for years to come," the marquess volunteered as he limped near. The fact that Stuart had been perusing Adriana with more than casual interest for the better part of their sojourn in the drawing room had not escaped Colton's notice. With slow deliberation he bestowed his own attention upon the brunette, remembering only too well how her wet, beautiful body had gleamed enticingly beneath the warm glow of the lamps. "I understand from Mother that we are all but promised, Adriana."

Stuart's mouth flew open in surprise, and he stumbled back a step. "Your pardon, my lord. I didn't know."

"Actually, I wasn't aware of it myself until earlier this afternoon," Colton admitted, not entirely sure why he slammed the door in Stuart's face the very moment he noticed the major warming up to the idea of wooing the girl. When he still found the idea of a betrothal irksome, how could he come close to explaining the annoyance that had surged within him when he had seen the man approaching her? When had he ever felt even remotely possessive of a woman? That emotion had always seemed foreign to him . . . at least, until this present moment in time.

"You needn't fret that you've offended Lord Colton," Adriana informed the viscount kindly before lifting a brusque smile to the marquess. Her eyes conveyed an unmistakable coolness as they searched those luminous gray depths. "You see, the truth is that Lord Colton has a choice in the matter prior to the actual initiation of any betrothal. A three-month tenure of courtship will see the way of it, yet, from past experience, 'twould seem unlikely his lordship will be interested in solidifying the agreement since it was the very reason for his lengthy absence from home."

"Even so, my lady," Stuart replied in a muted tone. "I'm honor-bound to give him time to consider his windfall before pressing my own suit. All I can say is that I envy the man for the exceptional opportunity he has been granted."

Smiling at the major, Adriana dipped her head in acknowledgment of his compliment. "Thank you, Stuart. I shall remember your kind words."

As the viscount retreated, Adriana peered up at Colton with cool disdain. "Can you tell me why you found it necessary to tell Stuart that we're promised when you know yourself that you have no real interest in courting me? Does it give you delight to chase away my suitors because of some claim that is at best nebulous? Have I done anything to warrant your spite?"

"Nothing that I'm aware of, my dear," Colton replied pleasantly and offered her a confident grin. "But I saw no reason for Stuart to get his hopes up when there'll be a span of three months ere we decide the matter. I shall allow myself at least that much time before determining whether there is hope for us, *if* my father's predictions have some merit after all, or *if* I should negate the whole thing as ludicrous. Until then, my dear, I intend to be as protective of my right to claim you as I want to be. After all, the agreement allows me that privilege, does it not?"

"What could you possibly find of interest in a castoff collection of odd parts?"

Having had those very same words imbedded in his memory by his own remorse, Colton pressed a lean hand to his blouse. "Forgive me for that slur, Adriana. At the time, 'twas said in rage and directed toward my father rather than at you. I didn't know when I issued that cutting remark that you were sitting outside the room. I would never have knowingly hurt you. In any case, it's far from the truth. Indeed, merely looking at you affirms my belief there is indeed a Divine Creator, for you are far too exquisite to have come into existence by mere chance."

Her cheeks warmed at his praise, and feeling suddenly at odds with herself, she sipped her wine again, looking everywhere but at him. "Perhaps we should forget the past," she suggested. "I find it rather troubling to remember the ire you once felt toward your father because of me. Though you may find this difficult to understand, I loved him, too."

"Adriana?" Colton searched the dark orbs that finally lifted to meet his. "Have I your forgiveness?"

Although she hoped a meager smile would suffice for an answer, in the prolonged silence that followed she was certain his eyes searched hers to the very depth of her being. Unable to bear his inspection any longer, she inclined her head in a brief, consenting nod. "Yes, of course, my lord. You've actually had it for some time now. 'Twas impossible to feel any resentment toward you when I was constantly aware of the danger you were in. You were the brother I never had, and I would've grieved nearly as much as your family had you been killed."

His handsome lips curved in an angled grin as he stepped nearer. "After seeing you this afternoon all decked out in a riding habit and then, later, wearing nothing at all, I'm immensely relieved you're *not* my sister. 'Twould be ill met if I were to lust after a sibling the way I've been hungering after you since our meeting in the bathing chamber. I will be hard-pressed to forget the details of the flawlessness I saw before me then. Your breasts are fairer by far than any I've ever seen, and as for the rest of your beautiful body, I can only believe you are without equal."

Adriana cleared her throat in embarrassment and took another lengthy sip from her goblet. A brief moment later, another long sampling drained the contents of the glass, and when Harrison passed, bearing a tray upon which fresh glasses of wine resided, she availed upon him to exchange the empty goblet for a fresh one. As the servant moved on, several more swallows seemed to give her enough courage to ask the marquess, "Have you become a fair judge of naked women since you left home, my lord?"

Colton's lips twitched in amusement as he braced forward on his cane. "Of those I've seen, my dear, you are far and away the most exquisite."

"Well, thank you for that," she said dryly, briefly flinging him a glance.

"As for what your experiences have been, I would assume from your shocked expression in the bathing chamber that I was your first."

"I would hardly boast about such encounters were you wrong, sir," Adriana retorted, feeling fairly faint. Once more inundated with detailed images of his male nudity, she quaffed the wine again, feeling much in need of its lulling effect.

Noticing how the crystal goblet shook in her slender hand, Colton searched the lady's eyes for barely an instant before the dark orbs went chasing off in another direction. Smiling, he leaned forward to speak over her ear. "The sight of my nakedness didn't frighten you, did it?"

"No, of course not," she denied in a frantic rush, staggering back in an effort to put some distance between them. Her retreat was necessary to cool her burning cheeks and to ease to some small degree the unruly pace of her heart. "Why should you think it did?"

Colton curbed a grin. "Because you're trembling, Adriana, and probably thinking the worst. Believe me, after the rending of your virginity, you will be amazed at the pleasure to be found in the arms of your husband. Should my father's desires come to fruition, I can promise you such delight as you've never before imagined." He watched her take another nervous sip and bent over her ear again. "If I'm allowed to be plain spoken on another topic, Adriana, I'd say you're becoming increasingly inebriated. Truly, you needn't be distressed by what you've seen. Making love can be just as enjoyable for a woman as for a man."

As he straightened, she leaned briefly toward him and delivered her own rejoinder in an angry whisper. "Well, any *lady* would be upset if she were involved in this conversation. 'Tis hardly the topic to soothe one's senses."

"I'll allow the subject itself wouldn't soothe you, but the joining of our bodies in the rites of love would do wonders for relaxing you. I'd certainly be willing to give you a fair sampling of what goes on when two people enjoy such intimacy." His broad shoulders lifted in a casual shrug. "Actually, more than a fair sampling, if you'd be of such a mind."

"Will you *please* stop?" she hissed and lifted her eyes to his face in time to see the gray orbs dip into her décolletage. "And stop ogling me. We're not married *yet*, and considering your previous disdain for that idea, 'tis doubtful we *ever* will be."

Colton chuckled softly. "Who knows what will come from our association? I may just decide to forget my aversion to arranged marriages and take you to wife just to show you what delights can be had between a married couple."

Adriana chuckled chidingly. "Oh, what subtle ploys you practice, my lord. You think to soften my heart and get me into your bed by your liberal use of the word *marriage*, but I'm not as gullible as you may think. You'll have to speak the vows with me ere you see me naked again."

His eyes danced as he probed the dark, shining orbs. "And would you, fairest maid, willingly speak the vows with me?"

Considering his question, she feigned a museful attitude. "My parents would certainly be pleased if I were to do such a thing. After all, it was what both yours and mine agreed to, to the extent that they willingly signed the contract. But since I cannot imagine you'll come to want me as your wife, I don't expect such a wedding will *ever* take place."

He grinned down at her. "I suppose if I were to get you with child, I'd have to marry you and save your reputation."

Fairly faint at such an idea, Adriana gulped the last of her wine before passing him the empty goblet. "Would you mind fetching me another? This conversation is too much to bear sober."

The corners of his lips twitched in amusement. "Frankly, Adriana, I think you've had enough, so much so that I'm afraid to leave you. A breath of fresh air would likely do you far more good." He set aside her goblet and reached to take her arm. "Come, I'll escort you out."

"No, thank you," she hurriedly replied, managing to avoid his touch.

She could well imagine his eagerness to *unite* with her in a private place without benefit of wedding vows. "I'll be all right. I just need to sit for a moment. . . . Perhaps I'll just go across the hall into the great room and wait there until dinner is announced."

"I won't leave you," Colton declared, slipping a hand beneath the bend of her arm and turning her toward the door. As he led her toward it, Harrison entered and announced with stately dignity that dinner was to be served.

"Too late," Colton murmured and grinned askance at Adriana. "I'll escort you to your chair instead."

"Why bother with me when you could just as well assist your mother?" she protested, trying to free herself.

"Considering that I've shocked you nigh out of your wits, I feel responsible for your present condition," he replied, a grin flitting across his lips as he drew her against his side. Though she tried to push herself away, he leaned down and breathed above her ear, "Besides, it pleases Mother to see us together, so if you wish her to enjoy the evening, you should consider limiting your protestations and allowing me to attend you for a few rare moments. You'll be rid of me soon enough."

Adriana thought that would be the case as he escorted her into the great room, but she was mistaken. The customary place of honor for the Marquess of Randwulf had always been at the head of the table. It had been that way during the late Sedgwick's reign as lord of the manor; it seemed destined to remain so under the new marquess's authority. Adriana hardly expected Colton to escort her to a place immediately upon the right of the lord's chair, but that was indeed where he led her. Stuart was directed to sit next to her, and Samantha and Percy settled across from them. As the sole marchioness of the household, Philana took her customary chair at the end of the trestle table.

In spite of the fact that the meal was outstanding and the company even more so, Adriana didn't feel much like participating either in the consumption of food or the conversation. The fact that she graciously declined more wine was certainly conducive to the clearing of her head and senses. Still, she felt in dire need of its numbing effects, considering that, throughout the meal, she found herself the recipient of Colton's careful perusal. Her gown gave her little protection from those hungering eyes, and at times the warm glow she saw in them made her feel as naked as she had been in the bathing chamber. She was not at all surprised when she realized her nerves were taut enough to be plucked.

It proved an especially fine feast. Cook had outdone herself in that area in spite of the fact that the new scullery maid, who had secretly imbibed the late lord's brandy, had to be dismissed and then, because she had been so befuddled by the amount she had imbibed, had to be carted home. The groom and his son, who had been assigned that task, had been required to carry the woman into her cottage. The pair later returned with glum tales of her three young offspring, all less than six years of age, looking as if they were in dire straits, being bone-thin, hollow-eyed, filthy, and raggedly clothed. This news was solemnly absorbed by Harrison who would dutifully report it to his lordship at a later time.

In the drawing room that evening, the presentation of several gifts to commemorate Stuart's birthday were made amid bantering comments and cheery wishes. Many of the presents brought hearty laughter, while others drew smiles of pleasure from the man. Percy had had a blacksmith make a heavy metal shield for his brother's backside, which, the younger sibling claimed, could be conveniently strapped on should the elder ever go to war again. Adriana had sewn Stuart a heavily quilted velvet throw to place atop his saddle. Although that, too, drew humorous comment, it would likely prove serviceable in the colder months, especially for one whose hind parts would still be tender from his wound. As for Samantha's gift, she had cross-stitched a pair of stiff flags for her brother-in-law, one with an arrow that indicated a way to the rear, the other to the front.

The evening's celebration finally drew to a close, and once again Colton lent gentlemanly assistance to Adriana by helping her on with her cloak. Had she been given a choice, she would have preferred Harrison's help rather than the marquess's, for the younger man seemed wont to linger overlong at the task as he stood behind her and smoothed the velvet over her shoulders. Not knowing exactly where his gaze was directed, she glanced downward and immediately blushed as she faced him with a brow raised at a challenging angle. He offered no apology for allowing his gaze to delve into her décolletage, but smiled as if his ogling was something to be expected as he snuggled the hood up close around her face.

"The sights are much too enticing for any man to ignore, Adriana, much less one who has seen you in the altogether. If you must know, I enjoy looking at you."

"As if that wasn't obvious in the bathing chamber," she retorted.

"*Shhh,*" he shushed with a grin. "Someone will hear you and think we shared a bath and have good reason to smell the same."

Adriana rolled her eyes, wondering why she even tried to get the last quip in when this man had spent at least the first ten and six years of his life perfecting his teasing banter. There was no accounting for the time he had spent in that endeavor during the latter half.

Philana approached them with a smile. "Adriana, my dear, please inform your parents that I shall be accompanying my son when he visits Wakefield."

Adriana searched the woman's gently smiling face, wondering if she had actually detected a note of resolve in the marchioness's tone. Colton had merely stated earlier in the day that he'd inquire into the appropriateness of such a visit, whereas Lady Philana had simply presumed they'd be going. But then, Adriana couldn't remember a time when the elder hadn't been welcomed with enthusiasm at Wakefield Manor. Indeed, all of the Suttons considered Philana among the finest of women.

"Of course, my lady. Papa should be returning from London late tonight, but upon my arrival home, I shall inform Mama straightaway. We shall send a missive over with dates and times. If none is convenient, select one that will be. I'm sure we'll be able to accommodate you and Lord Colton."

"Thank you, child."

Philana stood back, allowing her son to escort Adriana through the front door and beyond the portico where her family's landau awaited her. Philana couldn't believe how well the evening had gone, for her son had actually seemed quite taken with the girl. The two certainly made a handsome couple, and she was especially pleased that Adriana was tall enough to complement rather than detract from Colton's height. Most women, including Melora and Jaclyn, would've been dwarfed by him, yet she could imagine that when her son entered a room, everyone turned to watch him, much as they had done when his father had made an appearance, not only because of his extraordinary good looks, but also for his lofty presence. Perhaps, after all this time, there was still strong evidence of that Viking lord from ages ago running in the Wyndhams' blood.

Five

EDMUND Elston sat back in his chair as he stared agog at his rumple-haired son who shuffled like an ancient dotard into the dining room. His shoulders were sharply hunched, and he held an arm clasped across his middle as if desperately trying to hold in his entrails. He made his way to the food-laden sideboard, poured himself a cup of tea, and gingerly took a sip. Immediately he winced, lowered the receptacle, and carefully touched the lopsided protrusion jutting from his swollen mouth, drawing Edmund's notice to the left side of his son's face. It was puffed well past his bruised jaw.

Cocking a curious brow at his offspring, Edmund dared to offer a conjecture. "From what I'm seein', boy, I'd say the cove wha' did 'at ta yu sent yu flyin' 'pon yur arse right quick-like. Oo'd yu get inta a row wit', anyway?"

"No one you'd know," Roger mumbled darkly, glowering at his parent from heavily hooded eyes. " 'Twas merely a dispute over a bit of rare property. As for the victor, no one has been able to claim the piece as yet, so its ownership remains in question."

It certainly didn't help Roger's mood to see a contemptuous smirk turning his father's lips. He didn't need to ask why. His untutored sire had come to believe only a bloke who could swig down several tankards of ale or glasses of gin without losing his ability to throw a dozen or so good punches at some ornery cuss was really worth his weight. As for his solitary offspring, Edmund Elston had always considered him less than competent in manly vices.

"Yu'll have ta let 'at there eye heal afores yu go visitin' 'er liedyship 'gain, or she'll be wonderin' if'n yu're man enuff ta do what needs ta be done ta 'er."

"You needn't worry about that," Roger jeered caustically. "The question that *should be* asked is whether the lady will be able to keep *me* content. I'm not nearly as naive *or* inexperienced as you seem to imagine, Father. In fact, the truth would probably surprise you more than you can even imagine."

"Maybe, but the proof o' the puddin' is in the eatin', boy, an' 'ard as I been lookin', I ain't seen 'Er 'Ighness followin' yu 'ome ta 'ave dessert."

"'Tis doubtful a wellborn lady ever would, either—certainly not when her parents might consider her a means to greater wealth and power."

"So's, when yu gonna be seein' 'er 'gain?" Edmund pressed impatiently. "If yu wants me advice, I'd say yu needs ta stop yur shilly-shallying an' gets yurself 'itched ta 'er afore she gets an itch in her pantaloons ta 'ave some other bloke pleasurin' 'er."

By dint of will, Roger refrained from glowering at his sire. "It isn't as easy as you make it out to be, Father."

A loud snort erupted from the elder. "'Ere's ways ta brings 'ese matters ta a 'ead, lad. If'n yu can'ts get coupled ta 'er no other way, then, be damned, force yurself 'pon the bitch. She'll be enjoyin' it soon enuff wit'out yu worryin' 'bout how yu done it ta 'er the first time. Time's awasting, boy, an' if'n yu don't do somethin' ta make the bitch yur own fairly soon, some other gent'll be settin' her back upon her arse an' climbin' on top."

Rage nettled Roger's temper. "Should ever a suitor be so foolish, Father, I have no doubt that Lord Sutton would take him out and, at the very least, castrate him for raping his daughter."

"'Tain't like she's 'is only chick," Edmund observed as he stuffed a scone into his mouth. Throwing up a hand in derision, he talked through his food, spitting out generous particles as he did so. "Why, the bloke's got 'isself two other chits, more'n any man would e'er need ta baits 'isself a fine one. Betcha 'e wouldn't mind yu makin' 'im a wee li'l babe in 'er belly."

An abortive laugh escaped Roger as he settled into a chair at the far end of the table. At times, he wondered if he wouldn't have been better off keeping his position at the orphanage rather than becoming a simple lackey to someone as demanding and uncouth as his sire. The man cared only for himself and seemed especially bent upon wheedling riches and opportunities from unsuspecting dupes. Yet when he had needed someone far more astute than himself to run his mill, he had appealed to his only evidence of progeny and had expected Roger to make haste in leaving everything he had ever known. That was probably the only way the mill could have survived. Although merely an apprentice, Roger was already seeing evidence that the workers, when crucial decisions had to be made, came to him for instructions rather than seeking out his sire. "You don't understand how Lord Standish dotes upon his youngest daughter. I'll warrant she's the light of his life."

"Well, yu 'as ta do somethin'!" Edmund insisted, becoming irate. Fixing a narrowed squint upon his son, the elder shook a stubby finger at him threateningly. "If'n yu don't hurries yurself 'long, yu'll be courtin' Martha Grimbald ere long, 'at much I promise ye, boy. I wants some returns on me investments o' the clothes I bought for ye, an' from what I beens seein' 'ese past months, yu ain't movin' fast enuff ta suit me."

A heavy sigh escaped Roger's lips. Being constantly threatened into a forced marriage with the very rich miller's unappetizing daughter had made him far bolder in his pursuit of Adriana than he would've ever been otherwise. While in the orphanage, aristocrats had seemed as inaccessible as the clouds in the sky, but his father had definitely motivated him in that area by taking him to dinner at the Grimbalds' soon after his move to Bradford on Avon. "I pressed the Lady Adriana for an invitation to the Suttons' Autumn Ball in October. If I haven't obtained a favorable response to my proposal of marriage from the girl by then, I shall take matters into my own hands." He dared not look at his father as he added, "If need be, I'll find her alone . . . and force myself upon her."

"Now 'at's what I've been waitin' ta 'ear. You're a lad aftah me own 'eart."

Roger's hackles rose on end. "May I remind you, sir, that I'm twenty and seven now, no longer a lad."

Edmund blandly dismissed that fact with a wave of his hand. "You're still untried, I'll warrant, else yu'da've done it ta 'er afore now."

"Although *I'll warrant* you haven't known many, Father, Lady Adriana happens to be just that, a lady, not some filthy slut to be taken whenever a man is in a mood, which you seem enormously fond of doing. Frankly, it's rather disgusting to come home and find you laid out stark naked in the parlor with some prurient doxy you've found in an alehouse. You could at least find one who isn't so revolting to look upon to service your needs. That last one nigh turned my stomach."

Edmund snickered as if enjoying some private joke. "Well, she 'ad 'er 'eart in the right place. She pounded me real good, she did."

Roger's lips twisted with rampant revulsion. "If you ask me, the two of you looked like swine wallowing in a pigsty."

"Yu 'ush 'at kind o' talk, yu 'ear! What I do wit' me friends 'as nothin' ta do wit' what yu're supposed ta be doin' wit' M'liedy High and Haughty, an', right now, 'at don't seem too much! Wouldn't 'urt yu none ta wallow a bit wit' 'er."

Roger lifted his shoulders, and then instantly regretted his actions as he was rudely reminded of the place where he had collided rather abruptly with the floor. "You seem to think I can take her ladyship willy-nilly, yet we've never been alone. We're always in the company of others. Never once has she allowed me to draw her away to a private area."

"Then yu'd best find some way ta get the bitch ta yurself, lad, or yu'll be facin' Martha Grimbald, eyeball ta eyeball, in a marriage bed."

Sometime after Edmund had made his departure, Roger still sat in his chair, staring at nothing in particular. In his mind's eye, all he could envision were darkly translucent gray eyes consuming the young woman he had come to admire. Barely had he managed to subdue his aversion to the marquess, then all too quickly he had felt his vitals churning anew. Even now, he struggled against a fermenting vexation as he recalled the way the colonel had carefully scrutinized the raven-haired beauty. Indeed, the man had made no pretense about doing so, as if he had had some special right.

Roger's shoulders slumped beneath the weight of his overwhelming defeat. He probably knew better than anyone that Lord Colton was the only one with that distinct honor. Yet it had taken every degree of restraint he had been capable of putting into play to stand quietly by and watch the man's smoldering gaze glide over the beauty. His own eyes had feasted so often on the perfection of the young woman that he was sure the lady's face had been forever forged upon his memory: the lovely winged brows; the shining ebon eyes fringed with long, silken lashes; the slender, ever-so-winsome nose; and the soft, gently curving mouth. How many times had he yearned to press his own upon those enticing lips? And yet, he had been forbidden to do so, not only by the girl, but by the dictates of her lofty peerage. Gnawing at his very being even now was the vexing reality that she was intended for the likes of a marquess, not a penniless commoner. How could one of his low estate hope to win the esteem of the aristocrats living in the area? They had formed a close-knit circle that not only encompassed the Suttons and Wyndhams, their intimate friends and relatives, but many other nobles affluent enough to own vast country estates to which, upon the adjournment of Parliament, they and their families retreated from their London mansions. They had multiple homes to flee to at different seasons of the year; he didn't even own the bed in which he slept.

His extended stay in the orphanage had not prepared him for the challenges he'd been confronting since meeting the youngest daughter of Gyles Sutton, the Earl of Standish. It had seemed the way of it that if one came to live within the walls of the orphanage at an early age, more often than not one would remain until laid in his grave. Some had considered their existence there a curse they would never be able to shake. Had he allowed that ominous prediction to remain unchallenged, Roger knew he would never have been allowed a glimpse into a world unlike any he had ever known, one that had long been solidified by great affluence and grandly imposing estates nestled in the rolling countryside northeast of Bath. Nor would he have ever become acquainted with the most beautiful woman he had ever seen.

Recognizing himself as an outsider in more ways than one, he had hoped to divert the lady's attention away from her aristocratic friends, many of whom she had known all her life and with whom she shared a relaxed familiarity. After all, he had been considered unusually handsome by many of the women he had met. Now that the younger Lord Randwulf had come home, however, his optimism for accomplishing that feat had plunged to its lowest ebb, all because of what Lord Sedgwick had brought into play with his plans for his son long years ago.

The resentment Roger now felt toward the male offspring of that family was like a hissing, spewing demon roiling within him; he could almost taste the bitter futility of his own aspirations and his ever-growing abhorrence of men like Colton Wyndham. But then, he was just as resentful of the other one desirous of having the girl, a duke's son, no less. Riordan Kendrick! The two men had everything—looks, wealth, charm, and noble names, not to mention that both had been heroes in the latest confrontation against France—whereas he could claim to his credit not even a fair sampling of those same assets. When he didn't even own the clothes on his back, what did he have to offer a lady well acquainted with affluence? Nothing but a mere pittance.

Not so long ago he had sat alone in the Suttons' library, anxiously awaiting Lord Standish's response to what had admittedly been a most presumptuous proposal of marriage. When, after a lengthy space of time, the elder had ended his discussion with his wife and daughter and joined him, Roger had suffered the greatest surprise and, in similar degrees, the most devastating disappointment. In a subdued and kindly tone, the elder had explained there was already in existence a contract between the Lady Adriana and Colonel Lord James Colton Wyndham. Furthermore, Lord Standish had added (possibly to remove any suspicion that he had merely fabricated this story to use as an excuse) that the papers dealing with the particular details of that arrangement had been signed by himself and Lord Sedgwick no less than ten years ago.

Aware of his own audacity in requesting Adriana's hand in marriage, Roger had nevertheless been appreciative of Lord Standish's honorable comportment. When he had then asked the elder what would nullify such an agreement, his lordship had given him little reason to hope that circumstances would change. The contract could only be voided by the death of the seventh Lord Randwulf or his ultimate refusal to accept the terms as stated. Considering the beauty of the maid, Roger had deemed the latter highly unlikely.

Frustrated as he had been with the man's answer, Roger could hardly overlook the fact that, besides himself, there were a fairly sizable number of aristocrats yearning to have the girl. In view of the existing contract, Colton Wyndham, or Lord Randwulf as he would now be addressed in more formal circles, seemed the greatest obstacle to the vast majority of them. Close upon his heels was the other marquess, Riordan Kendrick, or better known to many as Lord Harcourt. He had also shown himself unrelenting in his desire to have the beauty. Only if Adriana were to reject those two or, more far-fetched, be snubbed by them in return, would less prestigious noblemen have a chance, which, in view of their sizable number, left the odds of a simple apprentice winning her somewhat laughable.

Until the afternoon Roger had asked for Adriana's hand, he had only heard rumors of Riordan Kendrick. Then he had seen the fellow firsthand. After concluding his talk with Lord Standish, he had stalked away from Wakefield Manor with his head down, his heart sore, his lips mouthing rancorous words against the memory of the man who had proposed the contract in the first place. To his astonishment, his heel had caught on a paving stone, and in the next instant, he had found himself hurtling forward with arms and legs flaying wildly about as he strove frantically to regain his balance. The awareness of a darkly clothed form, stepping quickly aside, had entered into his consciousness barely an instant or two before he had plowed headlong into the roses and the bordering shrubbery growing alongside the walk.

That event had seemed to portend the collapse of the world around him. Feeling an overwhelming misery because of his hopeless situation, Roger had yearned just to lie there amid the thorns until the end came. Regrettably, the shadow had coalesced into a tall, handsome, nattily garbed gentleman who had proven solicitous enough to help him to his feet. Whatever meager aspirations he had still been nurturing at that point were completely sundered when he had recognized his good Samaritan as being none other than Lord Harcourt. The experience could've been likened to facing his final defeat. If Colton Wyndham were foolishly to reject his enormous advantage, then Roger could entertain no doubt that Riordan Kendrick would step boldly forward to claim the privileged spot the other had vacated. Both men were too good-looking to be considered anything other than rivals of whom a paltry, penniless suitor had to be enormously wary.

In stumbling away, Roger had hidden himself behind the nearest bush where, out of sheer wretchedness, he had heaved up the contents of his stomach. For the rest of the day, he had wallowed in misery and depression upon his narrow cot, unable to think of himself in any other vein than a man bereft of all hope in the near and distant future.

He had first met Lady Adriana in the latter part of the previous year after she and her maid, Maud, had ventured into his father's mill to purchase a piece of woolen cloth as a gift for another servant. Having been instantly smitten by the lady's regal beauty, Roger had eagerly engaged her in conversation and, on subsequent visits she had made to Bradford, had taken every opportunity to speak with her. He had even scraped up enough coins to purchase a small book of sonnets and, during one of her outings, had hurried out to press it into her hand. Willing to do anything to claim even a fragment of her attention, he had spoken of prior difficulties in his life after overhearing townspeople praising the compassion of the winsome maid. She had indeed proven sympathetic, and although he had realized his efforts to see her went against all propriety, he had started delivering gifts to her home and following her much like a homeless puppy. Perhaps his efforts had been similar to the wearing down of a wall, for she hadn't sent him away when he had boldly attached himself to her entourage of friends and smitten suitors. Still, she had laid out rules by which he had had to adhere; to break them would have seen him banished from her presence. They were merely friends, she had insisted; nothing more could come of it. She had rigorously demonstrated that fact by maintaining a respectful distance between them; she hadn't even allowed him to kiss her hand, much less that winsomely curved mouth he yearned to caress with his own. To have done so would have brought an end to their camaraderie, and he had not been willing to chance such a deed for fear of losing her altogether. A fine dusting of crumbs of her time was better by far than none at all.

The real test for any man, Roger had concluded during that time, was fairly simple. All he had to do was win the lady's heart, for, by winning it, he would then gain her father's approval ... perhaps. Foolish logic indeed, for he had soon learned that a goodly number of pompous lords, after striving to evoke her affection, had toppled from their self-erected plinth with scarcely an excuse or a warning from the young lady herself. Those swains had not been chivalrous enough to maintain their silence. In sharp contrast to the glowing tributes the townspeople were wont to heap upon the girl, jeering comments as to the hardness of the lady's heart had been liberally bandied about by the rejected, causing Roger to wonder if Adriana was really as cold and haughty as those arrogant fellows had claimed, or if her reserve had merely become an impenetrable cage she had locked around her heart while she awaited the return of her intended.

Still, his desire to have her as his wife had strengthened progressively, but more crucial than the assuagement of his pining heart was the matter of her generous dowry and her father's wealth, which no roué in dire financial straits could lightly ignore. As a boy, he had been forced into a life of hardship imposed upon him after his father had callously cast him aside right along with his mother, leaving the two of them struggling to put food in their mouths in the slums of London while the elder had courted numerous ladies and caroused with doxies.

When a wildly careening livery had run down his mother, Roger had found himself not only grieving but entirely deprived of anyone who cared a whit. Other than escorting him to an orphanage and laying out instructions for him to be rigorously schooled, Edmund Elston had given no further heed to his offspring. Although it seemed unlikely that it would've troubled his sire, Roger had suffered harsh treatment and frequent whippings from those in charge. After all, there had been no one to whom they had had to answer for the stripes they had laid across his back or the vindictive discipline that had exacted from him. Eventually he had reached maturity in the orphanage, assumed the role of tutor, and had come to understand how certain children could nettle one's temper even while innocent of the charges laid against them.

It was during his adult years he had learned that his sire had found a rich miller's widow to wed. Soon after her death, Edmund had summoned him to Bradford on Avon. No apologies for what he had been forced to suffer were ever offered. The elder Elston had enormous plans for his son; Roger would marry the young daughter of another miller whose holdings purportedly would stagger the wits of the most greedy, among whom he had come to suspect his father was primary. Being the only issue of her sire, Martha Grimbald stood to inherit a sizable fortune upon his death, and once she married, then, as often was the case, that same wealth would fall under the control of her husband.

Initially Roger had been tempted by the idea of such affluence, but after making the acquaintance of the most undesirable Miss Grimbald, he had decided marrying her would be too great a sacrifice for him to endure beyond the measure of an hour. He certainly couldn't imagine himself actually being able to make love to such a thin, hawk-faced spinster . . . even in the dark. After all, he had acquired an eye for beauty, even if he couldn't always afford it. Nevertheless he had done well enough for himself in that area, for his handsome face had led some lovelies to treat him merely for the pleasure of his company.

In placating his outraged sire over his refusal to marry Miss Grimbald, he had woven a hopeful story about his courtship of the beauteous Lady Adriana Sutton, fabricating more than any man had a right to. The idea of an aristocrat in the family had served to mollify his ambitious father, and Roger had been given time to woo the girl.

It certainly didn't help his situation now that the very handsome and distinguished Colonel Lord Colton Wyndham, the seventh Marquess of Randwulf, had finally come home. The stories about the couple would soon be making their way around Bradford on Avon. What he'd actually tell his sire once the elder confronted him about that matter was something he hadn't quite figured out yet, but he could see that day rapidly approaching. If, in the meantime, Lord Colton could do him a favor and fall over that fine cane of his and break his bloody neck, then perhaps he'd be able to survive without being forced into exchanging marriage vows with Martha Grimbald. It was a very sad occasion indeed when a son was compelled to wed a totally unappetizing woman merely to satisfy a debt his father had extended to him in buying him the clothes of a gentleman.

Six

❀

A BRILLIANT shard of sunlight pierced the drapery-shadowed darkness of the spacious, second-story bedchamber of Wakefield Manor. Much like a dazzling, puckish sprite, it streaked across a lengthy expanse of oriental carpet before climbing a low chest that resided against a heavily carved footboard. Upon reaching the sleeping face of the young woman who lay sprawled amid a twisted tangle of sheets and downy comforters on the huge tester, the brightness seemed mischievously bent upon wrenching its victim from an exhausted slumber, which sadly enough had come well after hours of fitful tossing and turning.

Opening one eye, Adriana glared in vexation toward the cause of the provoking light, in this case a tiny gap that servants the previous night had inadvertently left in the heavily tasseled green velvet draperies they had drawn closed over the spacious oriel. The latter amounted to a wide expanse of diamond-paned windows, which consumed nearly the entire east wall of her bedchamber. No matter how diligently the servants tried to ensure the snug closure of the velvet hangings, the early morning rays, on a fairly frequent basis, would find their way in through the tiniest breach.

At times like these, Adriana knew exactly why her sisters had left her, the youngest offspring, the largest and grandest bedchamber in the manse, with the exception of the suite of rooms belonging to their parents. Both Melora and Jaclyn enjoyed sleeping until a late hour, whereas, in sharp contrast, she normally rose soon after the dawning of the sun, or even earlier when she had plans to join their father on a hunt. Unfortunately, this morning she was thoroughly exhausted and suffering an horrendous headache, the likes of which she had never known before. The intensity of it caused her to regret the fact that she had consumed so much wine. Aside from her fatigue and discomfort, she was also feeling a little queasy and more than a little rebellious. Indeed, if Colton Wyndham had been anywhere within striking distance, she'd have boxed his fine, aristocratic nose just for the sheer pleasure of it.

As relentlessly as she had tried to thrust that gray-eyed, handsome devil from her mind prior to succumbing to her lassitude, regretfully he was still very much in residence in the full light of morning. The hardest part had been trying to banish to the nether ends of her memory the sight of him standing gloriously naked in the bathing chamber. No one could have been more surprised by his return to Randwulf Manor than she. After his failure to come home for his father's funeral, she, like his sister, had assumed that he had wanted nothing to do with the marquessate. Then, out of the blue, he appeared, turning her world topsy-turvy. After waiting an eternity for the rogue to show his handsome face, it seemed she might at least have been better prepared, but in that endeavor she realized she had failed most miserably.

Looming in her future now were three endless months of uncertainty during which she'd be forced to bide her time until the rascal made up his mind whether he wanted to accept or reject his father's decree. Duty and honor would serve as a forceful constraint to bind her to a promise her own sire had made years ago. As much as she loved and respected her father, she couldn't bring herself to appreciate the tenuous position he had helped create for her. He just hadn't realized what it would entail.

Adriana buried her throbbing head beneath a pillow, knowing only too well that her future would hang in the balance during that grueling, interminable interval of time. Her father was a man of high morals and principles, and, as such, would do everything within his power to honor the terms of the betrothal contract, though he, too, had grown impatient for the son of Sedgwick Wyndham to return. Yet, if she chose to avoid the anguish she'd likely suffer while waiting for the outcome of the ordeal, she had no doubt her sire would stand behind her decision, though it could well mean going against a pact that he and Sedgwick had carefully considered at great length years ago. Still, if he did, she could think of no assuagement that would absolve him of the shame that would probably torment him in years to come.

Once again, Adriana found herself at the vexing crux of her problem, how to avoid Colton Wyndham's courtship without causing her father anguish. Being romanced and then rebuffed by the marquess might well prove her undoing. Why, oh, why did he have to return at all? Hadn't their fathers realized at the time of their agreement there existed a possibility that her heart would be just as susceptible to Colton today as it had been ages ago? She didn't think she could bear another wounding the like of which she had suffered after his earlier rejection. What could she possibly do to save herself now that he looked like some godly being sent to Earth for the express purpose of stealing the hearts of maidens in every corner of the world? Sheath her own in a bulwark of stone? Not likely!

As much as Adriana yearned to find a way out of her predicament and banish Colton from her mind, both proved impossible feats. When some moments later she stumbled downstairs, he was still wedged securely within a cavernous niche. Thus, with languishing heart and pounding head, she entered the dining room to find her parents already seated at the table.

"Where have you been, child?" Lady Christina asked cheerily. In view of the different habits of her offspring, she had no need to verify the identity of her youngest. "We've delayed breakfast until Cook is nigh cranky."

When no answer came, the older woman glanced up toward her daughter and immediately gasped in shock. Even at an early hour of the morning, Adriana was normally bright and vivacious, truly a pleasure to be around. It was equally rare the girl came downstairs less than neatly groomed for the morning meal. Nevertheless, here she was, still in her dressing gown, her long black hair tumbling in riotous disarray about her shoulders, and faint, translucent shadows evident beneath her silkily lashed dark eyes. The sight was so unexpected that Christina could do little more than gape in slack-jawed astonishment at her youngest offspring.

Growing sharply curious about what had caused this peculiar reaction from his wife, Gyles Sutton twisted promptly about in his chair to find his daughter, still very much in a state of dishabille, weaving an unsteady path toward the table. Stealing the very words from his awestruck wife, he blurted, "Good heavens, child! Have you fallen ill?"

The jerky, irresolute movement of the dark head was somewhere between a nod and a shake as Adriana halted beside her customary place at the table. Beneath the combined stares of her astounded parents, she passed a shaking hand over her face and managed to croak, "Nay, Father, I'm not ill."

Gyles indicated her disheveled appearance as if to draw attention to the fact that she was not already dressed and definitely far from her sprightly self. What he saw convinced him that something was indeed seriously wrong. "If you're not ill, girl, then what the devil has taken hold of you?"

Adriana opened her mouth to reply, only to emit another hoarse croak, motivating her to clasp slender fingers to her lips in surprise. She tried to swallow against the large lump that seemed wedged there, but, in her failure, was forced to respond with a quick, negative shake of her head. In abject misery, she lowered herself as awkwardly as an ancient crone into her chair.

"Well, I know very well that *something* is the matter!" Gyles insisted. Though generally at a complete loss when discerning the moods of the elder two, he knew his youngest only too well. Concern affected his voice. It seemed to rumble upward from somewhere deep in his chest as he cajoled, "Now tell me, child, what is bothering you?"

"Dear..." Christina sweetly plied with a tentative smile, drawing her husband's curious regard. "You didn't return from London until late last night, and I was reluctant to tell you...."

"Tell me what?" Immediately suspicious, he braced a forearm along the table's edge and peered at her intently. More than thirty years of marriage and three daughters had taught him a few things about women...especially his wife. She was never sweeter than when she had bad news to relate. Recognizing the soft plea in her eyes, he became increasingly anxious. "What the hell-fired blazes is going on here?"

"Calm yourself, dear...please," Christina urged and nervously rearranged the linen napkin on her lap.

"Perhaps I will, madam, if you will *kindly* tell me what you have to say," he bargained gruffly, revealing his heightening apprehension. "Now, what is it? I implore you to tell me before I'm seized with a fit of apoplexy!"

Christina glanced toward their butler who had approached and was presently moving around the table, setting their plates before them. Charles was incredibly loyal, but she was loath to discuss family matters in front of servants.

"Madam, I'm waiting," Gyles reminded her.

Christina smiled gingerly, seeing no help for her predicament. "Only that Colton Wyndham has finally returned home."

Gyles's face took on a shade that closely resembled dark magenta. *"The devil, you say!"*

His bellow was loud enough to draw starts from both Adriana and his wife. Charles, however, seemed oblivious to his employer's show of temper. With an uncompromising air of dignity, he fetched the water pitcher from a side table.

Adriana clasped her hands over her ears as her father's thunderous tones seemed to reverberate within her sore brain. Lifting her slender bare feet off the floor onto the seat of her chair, she curled into a small, discomfited knot, and fought against a strengthening urge to cry.

Lady Christina's fingers trembled as Charles returned a glass of water to her hand. Ever the dignified lady, she sat rigidly in her chair as she urged her husband in a gently admonishing tone, "Don't shout, dear. The servants will think you're angry with us."

"Humph!" Gyles peered askance at the butler, who seemed the very paradigm of tranquillity. "Charles should know by now that I lose my temper on occasion, rare though it be."

"Yes, my lord," the butler agreed, revealing no more than a trace of a smile in spite of his amusement. With the possible exception of his lordship himself, everyone in the house was keenly cognizant of the topics that could ignite the man's outrage. More than not, they had to do with matters concerning his youngest daughter and her many suitors. She certainly had a way about her that seemed to bring waves of admirers to their stoop, which, of course, did much to spark her father's protective instincts.

The housekeeper entered the dining room and crossed it with a rapid patter of footfalls. Having been in the Suttons' employ well before their first daughter was born, Henrietta Reeves did not show the slightest hesitation as she progressed toward the end of the table where his lordship sat. Halting beside his chair, she presented a silver dish bearing a rumpled letter sealed with a rather large, incongruous blotch of red wax. "Mr. Elston stopped by earlier this morning, my lord," she explained in muted tones.

"He asked me to give you this as soon as Lady Adriana came downstairs. He said the missive was most urgent."

"Thank you, Henrietta," Gyles replied in a tone only slightly less gruff. He broke the seal as the servants withdrew and, unfolding the crumpled letter, began to read. After a moment, one dark brow arched sharply upward, deepening lines across his forehead that normally were barely noticeable.

The Earl of Standish hadn't needed a thunderbolt to strike him before he had become suspicious of Roger Elston's attempts to play upon his daughter's sympathies. It had been his concern from the beginning that the apprentice was seeking some secure foothold in her life. He had deplored the man's methods. Having been carefully instructed himself in the manners of a gentleman by his own sire, Gyles had long been of the belief that propriety demanded a fellow, no matter his circumstance in life, remain mum about his difficulties except to those who were required to know. Among the citizens of Bradford on Avon, Adriana was notoriously compassionate toward people in need. Thus, when Roger had disclosed to her many of the arduous travails he had suffered in his youth and the years thereafter, Gyles had taken umbrage at his effrontery. It hadn't helped a father's mounting qualms to realize she had perhaps shown a more kindly tolerance of the apprentice than she had ever exhibited toward aristocrats who, while seeking parental permission to woo her, had been more inclined to abide by lofty codes of behavior. If not for his agreement with his old friend, Gyles would have lent serious consideration to the requests he had received for her hand from several noblemen he had deemed above reproach, the most promising being Riordan Kendrick. Approving of such a courtship would have given him good reason to forbid Roger's visits, which to his great annoyance had often come about unannounced and without prior knowledge of Adriana.

Perhaps he was merely reacting to something many would claim as nothing more than a father's overprotective instincts, but Gyles just couldn't shake the suspicion that Roger's main purpose for attaching himself to Adriana was to marry into wealth, just as his unprincipled sire had done before him, or perhaps even to reap the benefits to be gained through the demise of a spouse, by which method, according to rumors, Edmund Elston had profited either by natural or deliberate means.

"What is it, dear?" Christina inquired, unable to ignore her husband's deepening scowl.

Lowering the missive, Gyles lent his consideration to his handsome wife. "Perhaps, my dear, this dispatch has been delivered to our stoop this very morning because Roger has recently become mindful of Colton's return. In any case, he respectfully petitions us to reconsider with all possible speed his proposal of marriage to our daughter...."

Adriana's head snapped up, and she stared at her father as if he were the one who had taken leave of his senses instead of Roger Elston. "What will you tell him?"

"What would you have me tell him, my dear? The truth? That there's little chance that you will accept such an offer?"

She blushed beneath her father's probing stare and considered her tightly entwined fingers. "I thought the last time Roger asked that it would be sufficient impediment if he knew of my betrothal to Colton. I didn't wish to wound him unduly, Father, neither did I want to encourage him, only to soften the blow to his pride. He'd have likely taken exception to any mention of the differences in our lineage. I'm afraid, however, that he has shown himself rather foolhardy now that Colton has returned. For his own good, he must be told that I cannot possibly accept his offer of marriage."

Gyles probed the dark, luminous eyes that lifted to his. The girl's chagrin was all too apparent. "What has happened to finally convince you of this need for honesty, my child?"

Adriana brushed at the tears welling forth, far more angry at herself than she had ever imagined she had been with her father for asking her to let him be completely candid with the apprentice. "I'm afraid Roger acted unseemly toward Colton yesterday while we were at Randwulf Manor."

"Unseemly?" Gyles repeated, elevating a brow as he considered her tears. "How so?"

Adriana tried to swallow the lump in her throat and made a valiant attempt to present a calm demeanor. "No matter how far-fetched it may seem now in retrospect, it became evident at the onset of their meeting that Roger bore a grudge against Colton. If not for the intervention of Leo and Aris, he would've likely set upon the marquess with fisticuffs right off . . . or, at least, so tried. When he finally launched an attack, it was quickly dealt with by Colton. Even hampered by a leg injury, Colton sent him flying across the room, leaving the stable hands the task of carting Roger home. Frankly, I don't understand why Roger took such a chance. Colton has a physique very much like his father's. At the very least, he's half a head taller than Roger and not only heavier, but solidly made." The colonel's nakedness had proven that fact only too well. Never before had she imagined that the flesh over a man's ribs could be so tautly rippled. "Only a fool or a very brave man would've made such an attempt, and yet Roger sought three times to keep Colton away from me. The last one he was socked across the room."

"He dared be so forward?" her mother whispered in horror. Receiving a disconcerted nod from her daughter, Christina turned to peruse her husband's frowning countenance in spite of the fact that he had always been far better at reading her mind than she had his. "Gyles, dear, Adriana is right. Someone must tell the lad it's useless for him to hope that we'll consider his proposal of marriage. It just cannot be . . . certainly not with the betrothal contract to be honored . . . nor without it even. I know Adriana has been unwilling to destroy the young man's hopes because of the past travails he has suffered, first estranged from his father and then orphaned as he was by his mother's death at so young an age. As much as we can sympathize with him for what he has had to endure, 'twould certainly seem from what Adriana has said that he has taken too much upon himself by demonstrating some claim to her, especially when he knows she's obligated to accept Colton's courtship. What must his lordship be thinking now that he has been set upon by the apprentice?"

"You're right, of course, my dear," Gyles agreed. "The lad must be told. I shall make every effort to explain to him the necessity of our daughter marrying a man from the peerage. . . ."

Adriana shook her head passionately. "Nay, Father, I pray you not be so direct with Roger. I fear he'll take offense."

"He does seem to make much ado about his poor lot in life," Gyles replied, trying not to scowl. Had Roger been less inclined to play upon his daughter's sympathies, Gyles thought perhaps he may have been able to like the fellow better. It was a devious way for any man to claim attention from a lady, especially one sensitive to the hardships of others. "Nevertheless, Roger must be told that you have certain obligations and that you cannot possibly see him anymore."

Adriana wrung her hands. This situation was of her own making; she should never have allowed Roger to visit her at her home. It was obvious now he had mistaken her compassion for something more. "Perhaps I should be the one to tell him. After all, it was my fault that he came here in the first place."

"You were only being kind, dear," her mother avouched. "You didn't realize he'd become desirous of having you for himself."

"*Humph!* 'Tis that stubborn whelp, Colton Wyndham, I'd like to horse-whip!" Gyles muttered sourly. "If not for his defiance, I wouldn't have been forced to contend with all the ambitious, young cocks who think they're doing me an enormous favor by plying for my daughter's hand . . . as if she were some aging spinster facing a life of solitude! No doubt, young Wyndham would be astounded at the number of eligible lords I've had to discourage in my attempt to honor our contract with his father. If not for Sedgwick's uncompromising belief that you'd be of great benefit to his son and he'd be just as good for you, Adriana, I'd have begged him to abandon his plans for Colton long ago. Recently I had come to believe the matter was behind us and that the young whelp would never return. But now, it all begins anew."

"No longer a young whelp, my dear," Christina corrected her husband gently. "He's a man now, more than thirty."

Gyles leaned back in his chair, his jaw slowly sagging in surprise. "Thirty, you say?"

"To be precise, Father, thirty and two," Adriana stated.

"I was married and had a daughter on the way by the time I was his age," Gyles declared, as if aghast at the idea that a man could ignore his duties as prime heir for so long a period of time. "By now, Wyndham should be ready to settle down and start a family."

Adriana clasped her arms about her knees and once again knitted her shaking fingers together. Her voice quavered almost as much. "Obviously he had been told about the contract sometime yesterday afternoon, because he was cognizant of it last night. He just mentioned the period of courtship, not the betrothal that might follow. Perhaps he wasn't willing to consider anything more than that in light of his reluctance to return home. In any case, he asked me to give you his regards and to inform you that he'll be sending a missive over to inquire into a suitable time for his visit."

Christina noticed that a brighter pink had swept into her daughter's pale cheeks, a sure sign the girl was upset. Curiously she asked, "Has he changed much, dear?"

Adriana tried desperately not to think of how handsome her would-be fiancé had become during his absence from home or the beauty of his long, muscular torso, which she couldn't help but admire in retrospect. Except for places where there had been a moderate furring of dark hair across his chest, and the thin line that traced down his taut belly to the darker mass, his naked body had gleamed with the luster of warm bronze in the flickering glow of the lantern light. "More than you can imagine, Mother."

Christina's hand began to tremble, so much so that she was forced to lay aside her fork. Making every effort to hide her mounting apprehension, she clenched her hands in her lap. "Has he been noticeably scarred by the war?"

"Noticeably scarred?" Adriana repeated distantly. Though she gazed out the diamond-paned windows toward the rolling hills beyond the manse, she saw nothing but an image of the man to whom she had been promised. Lost in a tangle of thoughts, she barely moved her shoulders in a responsive shrug. "At Waterloo, he was severely wounded and, because of that reason, was prevented from making a timely return."

"Oh, dear, I hope the wound wasn't too dreadful," her mother replied worriedly, imagining the worst. "Can you bear to look upon him?"

"I must admit it wasn't easy to remain composed." Even now, Adriana had difficulty maintaining her aplomb when she recalled the jolt of excitement that had shot through her when she had been caught up against his steely form. Gooseflesh and weak knees were definitely a rare experience for her; she hadn't known such exquisite sensations could be evoked merely by the pressure of a man's body against her own . . . or the *memory* of *that* moment . . . *or* the one in the bathing chamber, which in recall seemed far more thrilling. She certainly had to reform her opinion on the subject of stimuli if being in a man's embrace and seeing him naked could affect her in such diversely tempestuous degrees. After hearing Colton's heated rejection of her so many years ago, she had remained distantly detached from would-be suitors to protect herself against the possibility of ever being wounded again, but the shock of her recent encounter with Colton had awakened sensations far different from anything she had ever experienced before.

Fighting against visions of a hideously scarred man, Christina pressed a napkin against lips, which now trembled with her ever-mounting concerns. "As difficult a task as that?"

"*Hmmm—*," Adriana answered with a slow nod, trying not to think back upon that moment in the gallery when Colton had grinned down at her as he held her clasped against his long body. Had she been able to read his thoughts, she probably would have had cause to slap his face. The prurient glow in his eyes had seemed to warrant such a reaction from her. In the bathing chamber, the pleasure he had obviously derived from ogling her naked form had been confirmed in a most embarrassing way, yet he had seemed totally unabashed by that fact or that she had all but gawked at him. It was rather humiliating to realize in retrospect that the very one who had once rejected her years ago was also the one who had awakened her womanly desires.

"Oh, dear," her mother murmured apprehensively. A disfigured face was certainly no honorable excuse for terminating a contract of marriage, especially when such wounds had been gained in valiant service to one's country. Still, imagining her beautiful young daughter entrapped in the arms of a hideous monster made her stomach convulse. From there, her concerns swiftly mounted by torturous degrees.

ADRIANA struggled up from the depths of sleep and reluctantly lifted her head off the pillow, allowing her to bestow an ominous squint upon her bedchamber door from whence came an insistent rapping. Her father had left the house shortly after breakfast, and she had dragged herself back to her bedchamber to try to get some more sleep with the hope that, if she did, she would feel better. Her mother was too polite to do anything more than gently tap more than three or four times upon the portal, which seemed to leave none other than her sister, Melora, as the determined culprit.

"Enter if you dare," Adriana called out irritably. "Or better yet, just go away. I really don't want to see anyone right now."

As she might have expected from her sibling, the door swung wide. Adriana was just in the mood to set her testy sister back upon her heels for daring to disturb her, but, much to her surprise, it was not Melora who hastened in, but Samantha, wearing a cape and bonnet.

"What? You lazy thing, are you still slumbering at this hour of the morning?" Samantha asked in amazement. She had grown up with this particular individual and been occasionally annoyed by and even envious of Adriana's ability to present a cheery disposition even at the crack of dawn. For once, Samantha could revel in the chance to return a sampling of all the reproaches she had received from the energetic young woman. "Shame on you. Here you are, lying abed amid your silken sheets while others are suffering in misery. Now get up and get dressed. We have some business to attend in Bradford."

Adriana moaned as she buried her face beneath a pillow. "I don't feel at all well this morning," she mumbled miserably from underneath its feathery confines. "Whatever you're up to, you'll have to take care of it without me. My head is aching too much for me to even contemplate leaving my bed, much less my home."

"Nevertheless, you're coming," Samantha insisted, sweeping the bedcovers off her friend as that one tried her best to burrow beneath them. "The scullery maid who was let go from Wyndham Manor last night has three young children who, according to the groom that carried her into her cottage, looked to be very much in a bad way. He said all three were terribly thin and garbed in filthy rags. As much as you may want to lie abed till a late hour, lazybones, we must go see what we can do to help those children."

"Who will *help me* if I become ill?" Adriana demanded petulantly.

"You shouldn't have drunk so much wine last night," Samantha chided. "You know it always makes you sick the next day. Besides, a little fresh air will be more beneficial to you than lying abed all day. Now get up. I refuse to allow you to hide out in your bedchamber like a spineless little coward simply because my brother has returned."

Adriana groaned in rebellion and flopped over on her back. Squinting at the ceiling above her head, she couldn't even begin to imagine the agony she'd suffer trying to get out of bed. "What in the world did I ever do to deserve a friend as heartless as you?"

"Well, if you want me to start naming the reasons, we'll be here for some time, which we don't have," the other woman rejoined sprightly and went to the armoire to search through the gowns it contained. "Now get washed and please hurry yourself along while you're doing it. I don't have all morning to stay here and listen to you whine like a pampered youngling. You're going with me, and that's all there is to it, so you might as well accept that as a fact, because it will do you little good to resist."

"Sometimes I think I hate you," Adriana moaned dejectedly.

"I know, but most of the time you adore the very ground I walk on."

"Humph!"

Less than an hour later, the Burkes' driver nudged the pair of lead horses of the four-in-hand close behind the boot of another conveyance parked in front of a small, shabby hut. In growing curiosity, Samantha craned her neck to peer out at the dapperly garbed driver who stood alongside. At his friendly wave, she frowned in bemusement, recognizing her family's driver, Bentley.

"What on earth is Colton doing here?"

A gasp issued forth from Adriana's throat as she sat upright, her headache forgotten. As she peered out, Bentley waved again. Her response was rather weakly conveyed with fluttering fingers before she collapsed back into her seat again. After their encounter in the bathing chamber, the last person she wanted to meet was the marquess. "Why don't you go inside and ask him while I sit here and wait for you," Adriana hurriedly suggested. "If Colton is already seeing to the needs of the children, then you certainly don't need me with you."

"Nonsense, you're not getting off that easily," Samantha informed her. "You're coming in with me even if I have to drag you."

"I'm sick . . .," Adriana complained, pressing a trembling hand to her brow. Just the idea of having to face his lordship made her stomach roll queasily; no telling what it would do if he gave her one of those confident, manly grins that seemed to have the ability to strip away whatever pride she once had.

"Not as sick as you're going to be if I have to send Colton out here to carry you in," the older woman warned.

A forlorn sigh was greatly exaggerated as Adriana bemoaned her plight. "You're bereft of pity."

"Why? Because I won't let you wallow in the maudlin mire you've created for yourself? I once thought you had fortitude, at least more than you've been evidencing since my brother returned, but obviously I was mistaken about that. You certainly don't appear to have much backbone now. No, nary a thin thread."

Adriana raised her dainty chin as she took umbrage at her friend's claim. "The way I feel right now has absolutely nothing to do with your brother."

"Good, then it isn't going to bother you any if we go in and see what he's about."

Adriana lifted her upper lip in a mutinous sneer as her friend alighted. "If you treat Percy the way you do me, all I can say is that it's a downright miracle he hasn't disappeared over the border to Scotland."

"He can't! If you haven't noticed lately, there's a ball and chain attached to his ankle," Samantha flung back as she sashayed up the rough stone walk.

Mumbling sourly to herself, Adriana made a reluctant descent with the driver's help and followed her companion inside the cramped, dank, sparsely furnished cottage.

As the two women stepped through the open door of the hut, Colton turned solemnly from the cot upon which lay an ominously draped form. He managed a meager smile for his sister before his eyes moved beyond her to the slender woman who had followed. Though Adriana felt his gaze sweep her from head to foot, his inspection seemed more like a strongly ingrained propensity of the human male than anything deliberate, for his expression remained noticeably somber. Behind him, the hearth was dark, dank, and cold. Across the room stood three young children, ranging in age from two to five. Huddled together in a far corner, they stared in wide-eyed trepidation at the strangers who had entered their home. Seeing their filthy state and the thinness of their faces and bodies, Adriana forgot her own misery as her heart went out to them.

"I'm glad you're both here," Colton acknowledged in a muted tone.

Samantha dragged her gaze away from the morbid shape shrouded by a badly frayed quilt and lifted a silent inquiry to her brother. He nodded, affirming her suspicions that the mother of the children was dead.

"Obviously she died shortly after she was brought here," he explained in a muted tone. "She was stiff and cold when I arrived. I can't imagine how she could've consumed so much brandy, but she obviously did, at least enough to kill her."

Once again, his eyes shifted to Adriana. In spite of the gloomy circumstances of the moment, he seemed once again naturally disposed to look her over from pert bonnet to small, neatly slippered feet.

"I haven't been able to approach the children," he explained quietly. "They're terrified of me."

Adriana hurried to the waifs and, in spite of their mewling fear, doffed her cape and wrapped it around the youngest, a tiny girl with straggly, unkempt blond hair and a dirt-encrusted face. Lifting the child within her arms, she held out a hand to the second oldest.

"Come, children," she bade in a motherly tone, "we're going to take you to a nice, warm, wonderful home where there's a very kindly couple who love children."

The eldest boy shook his head. "Can't. Gotta stay here an' look aftah me sister an' brother. That's what me mum tol' me I should do no matter what."

"You can still watch over them at the Abernathys'," Adriana reasoned, "but there you'll be warm, fed, and clothed. Do you happen to know the Abernathys?"

Once again, the boy responded with a negative movement of his head. "Me mum didn't want us leavin' the house whilst she was gone. Said some strangers'd take us ta the work houses."

"Well, let me tell you a little bit about the Abernathys, and then they will cease to be strangers. They're an older couple who live in the country, not too far from here, in fact. They've never been able to have children of their own, and yet, because of their desire to have a large family, they've been taking in orphans and raising them as their own for some years now. They've also adopted animals in much the same manner. Do you like animals?" At the eldest boy's chary shrug, Adriana began to chant off various kinds that she had seen at the couple's home as she playfully tossed her head from side to side. "They have cats and dogs and chickens and geese and goats and sheep and horses and cows...." She paused to drag in an exaggerated breath, and then questioned, "Have you ever milked a cow?"

The eldest shook his dirt-mired head. "Nope. We ain't hardly seen a cow, 'less someone led her past our cottage. We been livin' here since our pa was killed in the war. Me mum ne'er wanted us ta go out."

"You poor darlings, have you never been outside to play or to see the trees or the sun?"

"Only from the windows."

Adriana was totally amazed that a mother could do such a thing to her children. "It's wonderful to be outside when the sun is shining and there are butterflies flitting about, to see the animals, and to breathe in the fresh air. Outdoors is not a bad place at all. Although there are some evil people of whom children must be wary, the Abernathys are very kind, tender-hearted folk who can be trusted. They love to teach little ones all about animals and also how to read, write, and cipher. Can you do any of that?"

Again she received a negative reply from the eldest boy.

"Well, Mr. Abernathy just happens to be a very fine tutor, and he loves children as much as his wife does. Besides that, he's very clever at whittling animals out of wood. Would you like to have a wooden animal of your own?"

This time she smiled as she gained an affirmative response. "Then I can almost promise you ere the evening comes nigh that each of you will have one. But before we can reach the place where the Abernathys live, we must all go for a ride in one of those nice, shiny carriages outdoors. Would you like that?"

The three orphans looked at each other warily.

"Don't know," the eldest boy mumbled. "Ain't ne'er ridden in one afore."

Adriana laughed and cuddled the tiny girl in her arms. "Then you're about to have your first ride in a conveyance fit for a prince. My friends and I will take you to the Abernathys' and introduce you to all the orphans the couple have taken under their wing. You can question them about their home just to see if they're pleased and happy to be living with the family. If they're not, then you needn't stay. We'll find another kindly soul who'll care for you, but I bet the children living under their roof are as delighted to be there as you will be in time. In fact, I don't think I can recommend a nicer place for children to be."

"Me ma's dead, ain't she?" the boy blurted.

Adriana slowly nodded. "I regret to say she is. That's why we've come . . . to help you. But first, I should know your names." She grew thoughtful for a moment as she considered the dirty face of the child she held in her arms, then she peered questioningly at the eldest and ventured a wild guess. "Something tells me that your name is Thomas. . . ."

"Joshua . . . Joshua Jennings," he announced and threw a thumb to indicate the ragamuffin at his side. "Me brother here is Jeremiah. An' me sister's Sarah."

"Well, it sounds as if the three of you were named after characters in the Bible. That's truly an honor. Did your mother name you perhaps?"

"Nah, me pa did. She weren't fond o' readin', but whilst me pa were alive, he used ta read ta us from the good book. He e'en started teachin' me ta read, but, afore he finished, he went off ta fight in the war an' got shot dead."

"I'm truly sorry, children." Adriana looked at each sympathetically, and then asked, "Have you ever heard the story of Joshua and the battle of Jericho, how the men were instructed to march around the city six days and on the seventh to march seven times around it and then to blow the ram's horns . . . ? To everyone's amazement, the walls fell down."

A slow, negative shake of the grimy head provided a mute reply. "Don't recall. Ain't heard no more stories since me pa went off ta war," the lad mumbled and held up four fingers, black as soot. "I weren't but maybe this many when he left. After that, me ma ne'er wanted ta tell us stories. She traded the good book off for a bottle o' gin, an' a few vittles. When she'd work, she'd come home wit' mo' o' the same. She'd stay in bed a few days, sippin' gin, an' then go out an' find mo' work ta buy some more."

"Well, I happen to know that Mrs. Abernathy is very fond of the Bible, and she'd be happy to read it to you. It has some very exciting stories about men and women with names like your own." Indicating the marquess with a nod of her head, she announced, "This nice gentleman here is Lord Randwulf. He will make all the necessary arrangements so you can stay with the Abernathys until you're old enough to go off to learn professions worthy of respect. Now, if you'll let him and Lady Burke help you into one of the shiny black carriages outside, I shall follow close behind with your sister."

Colton was dumbstruck by the young beauty's ability to charm the three, who upon his initial entry into the cottage, had fled with frightened screams into a corner where they had crouched together in absolute terror. Until his eyes had finally adjusted to the gloom, all he had been able to see in the dark, drab, soot-shrouded interior were their huge eyes, wide with a kind of feral fear, staring at him from thin, grimy faces. No matter how he had tried to convince them that he meant them no harm, they had cowered away and then, whenever he'd try to approach, would start screaming, as if they had expected to be soundly thrashed or taken off to some evil place, as their mother had warned. Yet when Adriana had entered, the situation had been entirely different. It was obvious she had a natural way of talking to children that easily calmed their trepidations and won their trust. He had no doubt that one day she would make a wonderful mother . . . possibly for offspring she would bear him.

Once outside, Colton lifted the children in his sister's carriage and then, after handing Samantha in, turned to Adriana, delaying her a moment as he took her fingers within his. "I'm indebted to you," he said in a muted tone. " 'Twould seem I'm not very gifted with children, at least not these poor, frightened waifs. I was at a complete loss until you came. Thank you for your kindness and help."

Adriana couldn't help but smile. His voice, soft, warm, and soothing, had seemed to stroke along her senses. "Poor cherubs, 'tis evident they've been lacking compassion and care for some time, but the Abernathys will change that for the better. They're very wonderful people. I have no doubt these children will come to love them in time, as have others who were fortunate enough to have been found by the couple. Mrs. Abernathy swears they've truly been blessed with a large family now. Still, with so many to feed and clothe, they must work hard to provide for the ones they've taken in. If you're of such a mind, my lord, perhaps you could spare something to help them in that endeavor. 'Twill be greatly appreciated by all concerned. If not, I'm sure my father would be willing to give more. . . .'"

"No need to bother him, Adriana. I'll gladly take care of the matter myself. Indeed, I came here this morning for that precise purpose, to see to the welfare of the children after the groom told Harrison the three were in desperate need, but when I entered and discovered their mother had died, I really didn't know how to go about finding a suitable home for them without hiring some woman to take care of them. It sounds like the Abernathys are the type of loving, caring people these children need. Thank you for coming to my rescue . . . and for comforting the children. If not for you, I'd probably still be in there, trying to win their trust."

"They'll likely want to know in years to come where their real mother is buried," Adriana murmured, pleased that he was willing to subsidize the Abernathys for taking care of the children.

"I'll see that she's buried in a marked grave and that proper words are spoken as her body is laid to rest. I'll make arrangements today and then inform the Abernathys of the time so they can bring the children. In fact, if you're of such a mind, the three would likely be pleased to see you there, for you seem to have won their trust. Would you consider accompanying me to the woman's funeral on the morrow?"

"Of course, my lord." She lifted a smile to him, realizing she was feeling far better than she had all morning. Indeed, after seeing evidence of his empathy toward complete strangers, her spirits had been buoyed by a rekindling hope. The day now seemed far brighter and much more beautiful. "Just let me know what time and I'll be ready."

"I'll send someone over to Wakefield with that information just as soon as I know when the arrangements will be. There's no need for us to go separately. I shall come around to fetch you in the landau about a half hour before the service. Would that meet with your approval?"

"Will Samantha be going?" Adriana asked, hoping to have someone else with them.

"I shall ask her later about going. As for now, we'd better get the children to the Abernathys' so they can be fed, bathed, and clothed."

"Thank you for the consideration you've extended to these children, my lord," she replied with heartfelt gratitude. "'Tis obvious they haven't had much of a life since their father left, but they'll have a much better one in the future."

"'Tis I who should be beholden to you, Adriana. Never once while you and Samantha were tending all those stray animals you were wont to bring home did I lend consideration to the possibility there'd come a day when I'd be overwhelmed with relief to see that gentle, nurturing instinct in action once again. It was definitely helpful in calming the fears of home-less waifs in need of loving care. May I never again laugh at you—or Samantha—about your role as a good Samaritan."

The corners of Adriana's mouth turned upward tantalizingly. "I shall remind you of your words if you ever broach the subject again. As was your wont when you were younger, you seem to enjoy teasing us, no mat-ter the circumstances."

A slow grin curved his handsome lips as his eyes glowed into hers. "Oh, I needn't resort to pestering *you* about your admirable qualities when I *now* have far more intriguing memories to rag you about." Briefly his gaze descended to caress her breasts. "I shan't by any degree forget those reveal-ing moments."

Feeling the heat of a blush flooding into her cheeks, Adriana turned away abruptly and felt his hand sliding beneath her elbow as he lent her assistance into the carriage. Though she was of a mind to snub him, it was the gentle tightening of his grip upon her arm that swept away all thoughts of retribution. If she hadn't lost her wits entirely, then she'd be inclined to think his touch could have been an affectionate squeeze.

So! I hear Colton Wyndham has finally returned to claim his rightful title as Lord Randwulf," Melora announced, plopping herself down beside her youngest sister as they waited for their mother to serve tea. The petite blonde wiggled her hips as if trying to get comfortable on the huge ottoman, motivating Adriana to roll her eyes at her sister's antics. With all the other chairs, settees, and ottomans in the drawing room, it seemed unnecessary for Melora to crowd her off the cushion in order to acquire more room for herself.

"Are you comfortable now?" Adriana inquired, barely able to restrain her sarcasm.

"Yes, thank you," Melora replied pertly, bobbing her head once as if happily reaffirming her answer.

"You wished to talk with me privately?" This time an acute ear would have detected the copious dash of derision flavoring Adriana's tone.

"Yes, as a matter of fact, I do. All these years I've been most curious about something. Perhaps you'd care to enlighten me since Lord Sedgwick doted upon you so much."

A delicately sweeping brow jutted upward suspiciously. "Yes?"

"I've often wondered if Lord Sedgwick ever regretted the contract he initiated between Colton and you and which one actually came to rue his agreement more, his lordship or his son. Had he been able to foresee Colton's willingness to leave home rather than face the rest of his life with you, Lord Sedgwick probably would have chosen Jaclyn or me rather than staking his aspirations entirely upon the idea of Colton marrying you. No one has ever explained just why he seemed to favor you as a choice for his heir. But, of course, that is now neither here nor there. The past has been etched in stone. What can yet be adjusted is still in the future. So, tell me, what do you think of your betrothed now that you've seen him again?"

Bristling at Melora's taunting theories and inquiries, Adriana declared emphatically, "Colton is *not* my betrothed, and he may never be, so stop calling him that. You know the contract as well as I do. He has three months of courtship in which to decide if he'd be amenable to a betrothal before actually committing himself to it, so until then, if you'd kindly refrain from addressing him as such, I'd be ever so grateful for your forbearance, bereft of understanding and diplomacy as it obviously is." Not willing to mention her meeting with Colton that morning, she lifted her shoulders in a noncommittal shrug. "Who can rightly judge the manner of a man in a few hours' time? Colton seems nice enough, but then, we are little more than strangers."

"Is he handsome?"

Adriana was reluctant to give Melora any information that might return somewhat distorted. "He strongly favors his father."

"Oh, then he must be *very* handsome. Didn't you think so?"

"I always thought Lord Sedgwick was a very distinguished-looking man, so I suppose, in that same respect, I must admit that Colton is just as worthy to gaze upon."

"Do you think he's all that anxious to proceed with the courtship after being away so many years? After his rebellious refusal to consider the proposed nuptials so long ago, he'd probably now prefer to negate the whole thing."

Keenly aware of her sister's penchant for tweaking her nose whenever she could and prying into her feelings until every fragment of knowledge had been thoroughly divested of any confidentiality, Adriana bolted from the overstuffed cushion in a bit of a snit and hastened across the room to receive a cup of tea from her mother.

"Thank you, Mama," she murmured, grateful her parent had such a calming influence on her. Leisurely she savored a sip before accepting a plate of scones her mother had spread with a thin layer of clotted cream and strawberry preserves.

Joining her sister, Melora made a point of sizing her up. "You know, Adriana, you really should wear fuller gowns to disguise the fact that you're so tall and thin. And may I also suggest that a little rouge on your cheeks would be beneficial. You look like death warmed over. But then, I'm sure the trauma you've been experiencing since Colton's return has something to do with that. As much as I can sympathize with your mounting fears that he'll reject you as harshly as he did years ago, you really shouldn't allow your emotions to become so obvious. 'Tis the English way to keep your feelings well confined, though obviously you've never learned the art of appearing serene. Everything is written on your face for all the world to see. Why, I can almost read what you're thinking when I look into your eyes."

Adriana bestowed a loving smile upon her mother, trying her best to ignore her sibling, who at times could be as vexing as a hangnail. "The tea is delightful as usual, Mama. You always know just the right combination of cream and sugar to make it so flavorful."

"Thank you, my dear," Christina said, reaching out and squeezing her youngest daughter's hand fondly. "You have such a wonderful knack for making me feel special even when the services I do for my family are so simple."

Imposing herself between them, Melora placed a doting kiss upon the older woman's cheek. "That's because you *are* special, Mama."

"Save some of that affection for me," Gyles bade with a chortle as he strode into the drawing room.

Whirling with a gay laugh, Melora seemed to float across the room toward him in her haste to claim his attention. Bracing her hands upon his wide shoulders as he leaned down to her, she rose on tiptoes and brushed a kiss upon his cheek. Only Sedgwick Wyndham had ever seemed taller than her father, whose own towering height dwarfed her. Even her fiancé, who was shorter and of stockier build, seemed to loom over her at times. "Papa, you know you will always have my heart in your hands."

"Oh, none of that pretty cajolery now," he rumbled through his laughter, squeezing her shoulder fondly. "I know very well your heart has been stolen away by that young buck you're about to marry. I have no doubt when you leave here you'll be taking a piece of mine with you."

Smiling in satisfaction, Melora tossed an imperious glance toward Adriana. She was forever mindful of the amount of attention bestowed on her by her parents, other kinfolk, and friends in comparison to what her sisters received, especially since their father, because of common interests in hunting, riding, archery, and other pastimes, seemed to spend far more time with his youngest than he did his two older offspring. Melora never felt more gratified and victorious than when he bestowed lavish praise or testaments of love upon her in the presence of the other two. Yet she felt a sharp sense of disappointment when she realized that Adriana was oblivious to what was going on behind her. Her sister was staring almost wistfully through the diamond-paned windows overlooking the front lawns and the narrow lane that wended its way past their house toward the Wyndhams'.

Unwilling to let this ambiguous affront go unrequited, Melora offered the conjecture, "I suppose Adriana's wedding can't be too far off now that Colton is back, Papa, unless of course she does something foolish, like allowing that scamp, Roger, to pop in unannounced as he seems inclined to do. I doubt that Colton is going to have enough patience for that, not after the countless battles he has been engaged in since the onset of his military career. From all reports, he was quite a warrior, dashing into danger ahead of his men. No wonder he was seriously wounded."

A sudden clatter of dishes on the tea table caused Gyles's brows to gather in solicitous concern as he peered across the room toward his wife. "Is all well with you, my dear?"

Christina nodded stoically, fearful of making any comment lest she betray her concerns. Since the early morning meal, both Roger Elston and Colton Wyndham had been preying heavily upon her mind, but it was her fear of the latter's scarred appearance that had created her greatest anxiety. As much as Melora had sought information about the man, she hadn't been able to bring herself to talk of his disfigurement, only that he had been seriously wounded. Bravely she offered a smile to her husband. "Would you care for a cup of tea, Gyles?"

"Only if I can sit beside you and our daughters and drink in the warmth of your combined company."

Looping an arm possessively through his, Melora led him to the settee where he took a seat beside their mother. Melora claimed the only available spot next to him and then lifted a smug smile to her sister as that one turned from the window and approached. In an imperious manner, Melora indicated a chair across from them. "You'll have to sit there, Addy. I know how you hate sharing Papa's attention, yet 'tis only fair that you do, considering how soon I'll be getting married and leaving here."

Bestowing a glare upon her sister, Adriana settled into the proffered chair. Though she casually rejected Melora's accusations of possessiveness as nothing more than something brewed from her sibling's imagination, she was annoyed by the other's tendency to shorten her name. "Don't call me that, Melora. You know I dislike that moniker."

Melora dismissed her exasperated directive with a cavalier shrug of her shoulders. "Well, it suits you."

The dark eyes narrowed ominously. "It does not!"

"Does, too!"

"Girls! Girls! Behave yourselves!" Christina urged. "You know it isn't becoming for ladies to bicker. The both of you sound like a pair of old scolds."

Melora offered a pretty pout for the benefit of their mother. "Just because I call Adriana a pet name now and then, she gets all riled and out of sorts. She's so prickly."

Gyles cast a sidelong glance toward his fair-haired daughter in time to catch the superior smirk she tossed toward her younger sister. He also noticed how quickly her expression changed to a look of doe-eyed innocence when he made a point of clearing his throat to draw her attention.

"Is something wrong, Papa?" Melora asked, making every effort to smile sweetly. At the moment, a grimace might have been easier for her to manage.

Lifting his gaze reflectively to the ceiling, Gyles seemed to ponder the decorative molding with close attention. "Ladies shouldn't make haughty faces either. One never knows when paralysis could strike."

"Haughty faces?" Melora repeated in a guise of angelic innocence. "Who . . . ?" She turned to her sibling with widened eyes, as if she were the one at fault. "Adriana, what did you do?"

"Melora." Gyles lowered his head and stared directly into the blue eyes that lifted in sweet confusion to meet his. Beneath his pointed stare, he noticed a red hue flooding into his daughter's cheeks. "You know very well, my dear, that you dislike people calling you Melly. I'm inclined to think that neither Melly nor Addy is as lovely or befitting as the names your mother and I chose for you both. You'd perhaps benefit from the rewards of a more gracious behavior, Melora, if you wouldn't deliberately go out of your way to antagonize your sister as much as you do, especially when you know Adriana detests that particular appellation."

"Are you saying . . . I'm not very gracious, Papa?" the petite beauty questioned hesitantly.

"I'm sure Sir Harold thinks you are. Otherwise he wouldn't have asked you to marry him. Still, there are times when you can be more than a little nettlesome to your younger sister." As much as he had bitten his tongue to keep from challenging his second daughter in what had obviously become a sensitive area, he could no longer refrain from asking. "Did we coddle you so much before Adriana was born that you couldn't bear to give up what may've become a coveted niche in the family? Should I think you're resentful of her because she's now the youngest?"

"Oh, Papa, how could you even imagine such a thing!"

"I do that on occasion when you seem the most spiteful, but please forgive me if I'm mistaken. I'm only trying to find some rationale for your occasional shrewishness. In any case, we'll hear no more of it. From now on, you'll refrain from calling your sister by anything other than what your mother and I do."

Somewhat chagrined that she had been reprimanded in front of one who, in her eyes, would always be a contender for her parents' affection, Melora turned an outrageously smug smile upon Adriana, unable to resist using an address both their parents were inclined to use fairly often with each of them. "*Dear child*, how you do get into a snit over nothing!"

"Melora," Christina said in a softly muted tone, instantly claiming that one's attention. Becoming the recipient of her daughter's somewhat horrified, questioning stare, the older woman shook her head infinitesimally.

It was a silent communication between parent and daughter, nothing more, nothing less, and yet Melora seemed to shrivel in mortification, for nothing seemed more shaming to her than realizing she had displeased her mother.

Melora blinked away a start of tears as she rose and went to Adriana's chair. Leaning down, she wrapped her arms around her younger sister's shoulders. "I'm sorry," she murmured. "I was being peevish. Will you forgive me?"

"Of course." Lifting a smile, Adriana reached for her sibling's hand and gently squeezed it. "As you well know, I get that way at times, too, and must be chided."

The two women laughed, and the tensions were eased enormously as their parents joined them.

Seven

❋

"Samantha's not in the carriage with him," Melora announced, with a full measure of astonishment evident in her tone as she peered out the front window overlooking the drive and glimpsed no one but the colonel in the halting conveyance. "What are you going to do? You can't go with Colton without a chaperone."

"Really, Melora, must you always see a scandal burgeoning from every circumstance that isn't up to your exalted standard?" Adriana needled, responding with a generous helping of sarcasm as she neared the drawing room door. "Though I seriously doubt Colton is even remotely interested in ravishing me, Bentley will be nigh at hand should it become necessary for me to scream."

"But Bentley is on top of the landau," her sister protested.

"As it should be. After all, Melora, he *is* their coachman."

The simple logic of her younger sibling frustrated the petite woman. "Yes, and you'll be inside all alone with Colton."

"Well, it happens to be daylight outside, and his lordship would be extremely foolish to force himself upon me when the door of his coach bears his family's crest. Why, if he were to do such a thing, who knows what other people could see from their own carriages or wagons. Besides, we're taking the three Jennings children to their mother's funeral. I think he can be trusted to behave in a gentlemanly fashion long enough to deliver me to the Abernathys', pick up the children, and then convey the four of us to the church and graveyard. Besides, I just can't imagine his lordship doing anything foolishly untoward, at least what you seem to fear. If he assaults me, then Papa shall definitely instruct him on how to answer the minister as the marriage vows are being spoken." She became a little irate that her sister could consider the son of Sedgwick Wyndham capable of such a deed. "Really, Melora, you think the worst of everyone except Sir Harold, and Colton is every bit the gentleman your fiancé is, perhaps even more so. After all, Philana *is* Colton's mother, and we all know what a gracious lady she is."

"That doesn't mean that Colton didn't learn a way of life contrary to his upbringing while he was away. I've heard some shocking rumors about camp followers who service the soldier's . . . ah . . . needs. You can't make me believe Colton, as old as he is and as long as he has been away from home, hasn't bedded down with some of them."

"You shouldn't besmirch a man's reputation on hearsay, Melora," Adriana chided. "Were he a saint, you'd likely be wont to call him tiresome and unimaginative. I suggest that you give the man the benefit of a doubt until he proves himself a cad." She didn't dare indicate to her sister that she already had serious cause to wonder about the man's propensities after their confrontation in the bathing chamber. Were she to be so foolish, Melora would run straightaway to their parents, claiming that Colton had exposed himself in front of her. She could just imagine her father's hair standing on end as he blustered and irately deplored such shamelessness. It would definitely mean the end of the agreement between their families.

Pausing in the vestibule, Adriana allowed Charles to settle her cloak about her shoulders. She briefly thanked the servant and then fluttered her fingers in a casual gesture of farewell to her sister. "I'll see you later . . . *if* I'm not waylaid."

Smiling in puckish delight as she fairly flitted out the door, Adriana was pleased her timing allowed her to halt Colton in his progress to the front door. His uniform was just as neat and tidy as it had been earlier, making her wonder how many he actually owned to allow him to look so dapper all the time.

"No need to come inside, my lord. I'm ready to leave if you are. Melora's the only one home anyway, and I'd rather not have her curiosity appeased just yet. Sisterly love, and all that, you know."

"Something like you and Samantha?" he asked curiously as he handed her into the landau. From what he could remember of the three Sutton siblings, Adriana and his sister had seemed much more compatible.

His companion skirted around his conjecture. "Perhaps not quite the same. Samantha and I get on famously most of the time."

She said no more, leaving Colton to wonder what had been said between the two. But then, were he to draw conclusions from his boyhood visits to Wakefield, the older sisters had always seemed a bit snooty toward the youngest, as if they just couldn't be bothered by someone so young, thin, or gawky. It would've been more like the Melora of old to find some fault with her younger kin.

In a few short moments, Colton was wont to think that Adriana came nigh to being angelic for the gentle, motherly care she exhibited toward the Jennings children as she bundled them up against the chilled breezes and slowly led the younger two to his carriage. He walked behind them with the older boy, watching her as she pointed out, named, and explained about the different animals the Abernathys kept in fenced areas alongside the walk. He was rather surprised to find himself inundated with strangely evocative impressions of what it would be like to be the lady's husband and the father of her children. It certainly wasn't an unpleasant feeling. Indeed, it was rather gratifying to know the lady suited him to the extent that he *could* imagine her as his wife and mother of his offspring.

The Abernathys had gathered the other orphaned children into their large, many-seated, homemade conveyance, which had been built on a sturdy wagon base. After waving to the younger couple, they led the way to the small church, outside of which the funeral service was to be held, leaving Colton and Adriana to bring the deceased woman's children. According to Mrs. Abernathy, the three hadn't stopped talking about their ride in the fine carriage since their arrival. The change in the youngsters was remarkable. They were now neat and clean, garbed in new clothing, for which Colton had provided funds, and generally seemed content and definitely less fearful. The smaller two sat on either side of Adriana, and eagerly asked her questions. The eldest had chosen a place beside Colton and seemed no less inquisitive as he leaned back against the armrest and sized up the elder.

"Did yu fight in the war like me pa?"

"I was in the military probably longer than your father. Until recently I had made a career of it."

Joshua peered at him with new interest. "Where yu ever wounded?"

"Yes, in the leg."

"Did yu come close ta dyin'?"

Colton inclined his head briefly as he offered the boy a slanted grin. "Close enough to make me apprehensive."

"Apprehensive?" the boy repeated, perplexed. "What cha mean?"

"Fearful."

Joshua seemed clearly taken aback. "Ya mean yu was sceered?"

"Oh, yes. It's quite natural for one to feel frightened of losing one's life . . . or limb."

"Ya ne'er were in danger afore then?"

"Yes, on the battlefield, but I had no time while I was fighting to think about dying. I was too busy trying to stay alive."

"Folks said me pa were a hero," Joshua stated matter-of-factly. "I heerd 'is friends tell me mum 'at aftah 'ey brought 'er news 'e'd been killed. O' course, 'at didn't make no ne'er mind ta me mum. She was jes' skeered o' what she'd be havin' ta do aftah losin' what li'l 'e'd been able ta send 'ome."

Colton laid a comforting hand upon the boy's shoulder. "From what I've heard about your father, I'm inclined to think he was a very admirable man, of whom a son can be extremely proud. I'm sure his memory will be beneficial to you in the future. Perhaps you can be a hero in your own way."

"Ya mean ta go off ta the war an' be killed jes' like 'im?"

Colton exchanged a smile with Adriana before returning his gaze to the boy and shaking his head. "No, Joshua, you don't need to die to be a hero. You can be just as great a hero if you live. Heroes are people who are honorable and do good for their fellow man and their country without taking their own comfort into consideration. You can begin by watching over your brother and sister, teaching them right from wrong, protecting them from people who'd try to hurt them, and helping them with their everyday existence, perhaps lending assistance in bathing or dressing them, putting on their shoes, combing their hair. Being the eldest, you need to cherish and teach them, as your father cherished and taught you."

Adriana quietly listened as she combed her fingers idly through the girl's pale strands. She could find no fault in Colton's words. For the most part, they gave her hope and encouragement that the man's heart was warmly sensitive toward the needs of the children. She could even imagine that he'd make a good father someday, but of course, whether that would also be for her own offspring remained to be seen.

"Lord Randwulf was a hero in the war, too," she volunteered as she bestowed a smile upon Joshua. "He fought to help save this country from the French forces who'd have likely made an attempt to conquer us had they not been defeated."

"I wanna be a hero," Jeremiah chimed in with a grin as he nestled close to Adriana. He jabbed a forefinger toward Colton. "Jes' like 'im. Then I could have a wagon jes' like this one."

"Wagon, eh?" Colton chuckled.

"I wanna be a hero, too," Sarah declared timidly, and then chortled as Adriana tickled her chin. Hiding her face against the side of the woman's breast, the girl peered at the man with one eye and then pointed upward. "Like pretty liedy."

"She is indeed a heroine," Colton agreed as his eyes delved into the dark, silken-lashed depths. "Not only to numerous animals in the wild, but to three orphans in need of nurturing." Speaking to her directly, he added, "You have a very motherly way about you, my dear."

His endearment brought a flush of color to Adriana's cheeks and, in an effort to hide it, she lent her attention to the girl as she lifted her upon her lap. She busied herself rearranging the child's golden ringlets and then, when she had finished, leaned back to smile into the youngster's blue eyes. "You are so very pretty, Sarah. I have no doubt your father would have been proud of you, just as he was of Joshua and Jeremiah."

"'At's what me pa al'ays tol' us, 'at 'e were proud o' us," Joshua stated, and immediately had to brush a tear from his eye. "I wish maybe he wouldna've been a hero so he could be 'ere wit' us today."

Resting a hand upon the boy's arm, Colton squeezed it in silent empathy for what the youngster was feeling. Of a sudden, the child burst into sobs and threw himself upon the elder's scarlet-clad chest. Adriana watched the pair, enthralled by the tender compassion Colton evidenced, for he slipped a comforting arm around the youngster and made no effort to protect his coat as he let the child weep upon it in overwhelming sorrow.

Not many people attended the service. It seemed the dead woman had not been well liked or respected by her neighbors and acquaintances. As much as those who came conveyed their admiration for the father, they quietly defamed the woman for being a selfish, lazy sot who had done nothing for her children except to starve and keep them prisoners in a cold, dark shanty. Many who came expressed their astonishment at the changes that had occurred in the youngsters in so short a time. To all who were curious, Colton and Adriana praised the Abernathys for their dedication in not only caring for the Jennings children, but for all the other orphans they had taken in throughout the years. It was evident to all that the older children who'd been with the Abernathys longer were highly affectionate and respectful toward their adoptive parents, calling them Mama and Papa and answering Yes, sir, or No, ma'am.

When the Jennings children were finally returned to the Abernathys, the couple invited Colton and Adriana to stay for supper. Colton would've refused, seeing as how the couple seemed in dire straits, but Adriana quietly confided that food was something her father always made sure the family never lacked. For Colton's further consideration, she added that Mrs. Abernathy was an exceptional cook and it was an enormous treat to eat anything prepared by the woman.

The evening was passed in jovial pleasure, as Adriana and Colton sat together on a bench, flanked on either side by the Jennings children. The older children of the family were full of stories and eager to share them with their guests, stirring forth hearty laughter from the men and children and more subdued mirth from the ladies. Little Sarah giggled right along with the rest, although not entirely understanding the humorous tales, but she did everything the beautiful lady did and watched her with adoring eyes, warmly savoring her fond caresses and the gentle chucking of her tiny chin.

When finally the Wyndham carriage turned homeward along the moonlit road, Adriana felt inclined to express her gratitude to Colton for what he had done and seemed willing to do in the future for the children. "They'll benefit from your help, my lord, and be better people for it."

"I've done little," he claimed, rubbing a thumb reflectively over the silver handle of his cane. "You and the Abernathys are the ones deserving all the praise, not I."

"I give that to the couple wholeheartedly, yet you've been generous when other nobles would likely have refused."

"If I've been charitable, Adriana, you are the one who has instructed me. Between your efforts and Samantha's, I may yet prove magnanimous one day."

Her soft, winsome mouth curved upward at the corners. "Perhaps you were merely awaiting an opportunity to demonstrate your benevolence, my lord."

"I've normally overlooked those chances most of my life, Adriana.

You've taught me more about charity in these last couple of days than I suppose I've ever given heed to before." Leaning forward over the handle of his cane, he ensnared her gaze through the warm glow cast from the exterior coach lanterns and carefully probed those dark, lustrous orbs as a slow smile curved his lips. "You've awakened emotions within me that I was sure I was incapable of feeling until we became reacquainted: some of which I'm greatly appreciative; others I'm still struggling to restrain."

Growing suspicious, Adriana peered at him charily. "And those you're trying to curb?"

Colton leaned back in his seat and grinned. "Oh, I shan't tuck that bit of knowledge into your pretty cap just yet, fair maid. I must plumb the depth of that matter more fully ere I give that power over into your hands."

"You tease me," she accused with sudden certainty. "I've done nothing, and yet you would have me believe I've either influenced you in some mysterious way or else committed some crime against you. You're teasing me just as you used to do, and to that I say humbug."

A soft chuckle escaped his lips. "I see you're not easily taken in, my dear, but can you not understand what a man like myself experiences in the presence of such a beautiful woman?"

Adriana decided it was probably an appropriate time to worry about the remaining distance to Wakefield. Peering out into the darkness beyond the coach, she had some difficulty finding her voice until she cleared her throat and made another attempt. "Would you happen to know where we are precisely?"

"No need to fear, Adriana. As much as I'd enjoy making love to you right now, I shan't force you to appease my manly bent. However, I hope in time that you'll prove more receptive to my attentions. I can be enormously persuasive when there is a rare and beautiful prize that I'm desperate to have for my own."

Adriana could feel her cheeks warming as she met those smiling gray eyes. Presently, they were softly illumined by the carriage lanterns, and the warmth shining in those translucent depths was unmistakable; so, too, his confidence. "You seem terribly sure of yourself, my lord."

"Oh, I can imagine a woman of your uniqueness must grow bored with the various propositions presented her, and you may indeed wonder what makes my invitation different from those who may've invited you to share yourself with them. On the surface, nothing; but in bed, well, there's the telling of it. I've come to realize over the years that there's an art to every-thing." His broad shoulders lifted in a casual shrug. "For instance, on the battlefields I traversed throughout my career as an officer, I became more familiar with the skills of war. There is also an art to the intimacy a man and woman can share together. It doesn't have to involve going to bed together; yet, if that were to happen, be confident, Adriana, I would be gentle with you and seek your pleasure before having mine. I'd cherish you as something rare and precious, for truly you are that. I've come to realize after perusing you in my bath that I won't be content until I make you mine. You're like a potent wine that has gone to my head. I've never desired another woman as much as I've come to desire you just since I've been home. You must know that by now."

Not entirely sure what he was telling her, Adriana felt led to probe the matter more thoroughly, just in case she had misunderstood what he wanted from her. Surely he wouldn't dare proposition her when they were facing an agreement signed by both their parents. "Should I believe you're amenable to our betrothal?"

His eyes lowered to the elegant handle of his cane again as he traced the elaborate scroll etched in the silver with a neatly manicured thumbnail. "I didn't say that, Adriana."

Her brow arched at a skeptical angle. "But you *are* soliciting me for my favors, are you not?"

"I don't think I said it quite like that," Colton hedged, sensing her ris-ing ire.

Adriana placed shaking fingers against her brow as she closed her eyes. For a moment, she mulled over what she had heard and tried to make some sense of it all. "Just what did you say then? Perhaps I've miscon-strued what you're proposing."

"I do not intend to take you against your will, my dear, but I would very much enjoy being intimate with you."

The audacity of the man! He was far bolder than she would've ever imag-ined. "Do you actually think I'd consent to lie with you without benefit of marriage vows?" she demanded. *The nerve of him!* "Am I daft? I remember too clearly how soon Jaclyn got with child after her marriage. If I were to be so foolish to concede to such an arrangement, *which I'm not*, I'd be invit-ing certain disaster."

Colton chuckled at her protestations. She seemed far more worried about getting with child than being seduced outside of marriage. "I'd do everything I could to prevent that from happening, Adriana," he cajoled. "I could pleasure you as you've never been pleasured before."

The dark eyes narrowed as she fixed a malevolent glare upon the man through the lantern-lit gloom. "Melora warned me that it wasn't safe to be alone with you in a coach, and foolishly I waved away her efforts to caution me. Next time, you can be certain I'll be more attentive to her admonitions, for they have proven to be most perceptive."

Colton felt a pang of disappointment when he realized Bentley was slowing the landau to round the curve into the Suttons' drive. "'Twould seem the chance to discuss this matter more thoroughly has escaped us, at least for this evening," he murmured with a grin. His eyes came near to consuming her as the soft radiance of the lanterns touched upon her fine, delicate features and luminous dark eyes. He heaved a sigh that conveyed his disappointment. "I suppose I must endure the futility of wanting you for yet another night. Little did I imagine when I found you in my bath that I'd be so completely vexed by my desire to have you."

When Bentley drew the conveyance to a halt before her family's Tudor estate, Adriana didn't wait for gentlemanly assistance. She threw the door open, kicked out the step, and alighted with as much haste as one whose tail had just been torched. Thus deserted, Colton descended the same steps with considerably more dignity and followed as swiftly as his hindered gait would allow.

In her eagerness to confront the pair after espying the coach lanterns emerging from the tree-shrouded lane, Melora had caught up her skirts and raced ahead of Charles. Fairly breathless from her flight, she snatched open the portal and ran out in time to meet her sister just as that one came stalking toward the portal.

"I thought you would never return," Melora declared, sizing up her younger sister. She'd have certainly taken the initiative to suggest to her mother that something was *not quite right* if Adriana's apparel had looked the least bit out of place. "I hope nothing serious happened that detained the two of you this long."

"We had dinner with the Abernathys, Melora," her younger sister announced flatly. "We came here straightaway after it was concluded, and if you're wondering if I've been ravished, the answer is *no*, and will continue to be *no* as long as I have breath left in my body."

Melora's jaw plummeted forthwith at her sister's announcement, and Colton coughed behind a hand as he made an earnest effort not to laugh at the petite woman's gaping astonishment. It came to him in that moment that he had never in all his life met such a woman as Adriana Sutton. 'Twould seem that he would have to be far more subtle about his intentions in the future if he meant to be intimate with the lady outside the boundaries of marriage.

Colton swept off his shako as the petite woman faced him. "Good evening, Melo—"

"Come inside, Melora," Adriana interrupted tersely. Pausing at the door, she gave the man a frosty look. "Lord Colton can't stay. He's returning home immediately."

Thus dismissed, Colton had no choice but to acquiesce. "Alas, 'tis true. I cannot stay."

"Good night, my lord!" Adriana stated rather forcefully as Melora pattered after her. In the next instant, he had cause to flinch as the door slammed behind the two women.

As he neared the landau, he noticed the sheepish glance Bentley cast his way before the man quickly lent his attention to the four-in-hand. Even so, the elder's eyes were inclined to wander surreptitiously over his shoulder on a fairly frequent basis.

"Do you have something you wish to speak with me about, Bentley?" Colton asked, fixing a suspicious squint upon the driver.

"Well, ah . . . no, milord . . . I mean to say . . . Well, Liedy Adriana . . . ah . . . well, she does seem a mite independent . . . at times, that she does."

"Yes, and what is that supposed to mean?"

Wary of offending the nobleman, the coachman shot another quick, nervous glance back at him. "I've seen her ladyship . . . ah . . . get miffed afore when a bloke tried gettin' . . . too . . . ah . . . personal."

"Familiar with the lady, you mean?" Colton prodded, peering up at the badly flustered man.

"Ah . . . well . . . ah . . . maybe so, milord." Bentley cleared his throat with some difficulty, as if he had just gotten a huge frog lodged in it. "I overheard what the liedy said on 'er way ta the door, milord. She . . . ah . . . said . . . ah . . . nearly the same thing the night she blackened the fella's eye wit' her purse. She's wont ta swing it 'bout wit' a wee bit o' force when she gets a mite riled, milord, an' I can promise yu she knows how ta use it. Yur sister can affirm what I say. She were 'ere ta witness it. She an' Mr. Percy."

Hefting his cane, Colton closely considered the handle in the moonlight. "And your suggestion would be . . . ?"

Once again, the driver cleared his throat uncomfortably. "I wouldn't think o' suggestin' anythin' ta yu, milord."

"Come now, Bentley, you were here before I left home. If you have a bit of wisdom to share in regards to the lady, you have my permission to voice it. Whether I take it or not remains to be seen."

"In 'at case, milord, I'll be sharin' what little I'd be knowin'. Mayhap 'twould save yu from settin' yurself at odds wit' the lovely liedy. 'Tis fairly easy for a man what's been in the wars to lose sight o' the difference betwixt the ones in the camps an' those at home, but if'n yu were ta remember 'at the Liedy Adriana is more'n a cut or two above 'em women who follow the soldiers, milord, then yu maybe wouldn't be upsettin' 'er so much."

Colton mulled over the man's advice for a long, thoughtful moment. Then he glanced back at the front portal through which the lady had stalked in a fair bit of a tizzy. Perhaps he *had* become too inured to women propositioning him and had lost sight of the fact that there were still some who preserved their purity for their husbands to savor. As much as he would've enjoyed making love to the lady, he had to admire her for her stance. At least, if he did marry her, he wouldn't have to wonder who had enjoyed her before him.

With a sudden laugh, Colton tossed up his cane and caught the shaft in midair. Touching its handle to the brim of his shako, he saluted the man for his wisdom. "Thank you, Bentley. I shall do everything within my power to remember your prudent counsel. The lady is indeed just that, and 'twould behoove me to tread lightly while I'm with her, or she'll likely blacken my eye with her little purse."

Bentley's whole frame seemed to shake as he chortled in amusement. "Aye, milord, an' the Liedy Adriana is just the one what'll do it ta ya, too."

C OLTON nodded mutely as his tailor, George Gaines, asked him a question, but the small, wiry man could tell that his lordship was distracted by his own thoughts and not in a mood to discuss the details of frock coats, waistcoats, and trousers. Though a number of hours had passed since they had departed the nobleman's London residence, a fine Palladian mansion located near Hyde Park on Park Lane, the retired colonel had hardly muttered a word. For the most part, he had stared out the window at the changing countryside, deep in thought, his brows gathered in a frown, his lips compressed, the corners downturned. Only those lucid gray eyes had moved to take in the passing terrain as they traveled westward. Dusk would soon be approaching, and yet the younger man gave no indication that he even noticed the dwindling light.

Colton took note all right, but he was troubled by other matters. It hadn't helped his surly mood one whit to realize that for the past several days, even while taking care of affairs dealing with his marquessate, he had been constantly inundated with thoughts of the brunette beauty he would soon be courting. As much as he had tried to banish her from his mind, he just hadn't been able to, and it had been of no benefit to imagine he could find release with another woman. The very idea of that had set him awry with himself, and he hadn't even wasted his time on what had promised to be a fruitless pursuit. The simple fact was that after viewing the unadorned perfection of the Lady Adriana, no other woman appealed to him. Trying to placate himself with another would've been similar to try-ing to down a pauper's meal when a rich feast had been laid out before him. In spite of his strenuous objections to his father's proposals in the past, it was as if he were some untried youth again, following merrily along the path his sire had chosen for him years ago.

The narrow lane they were presently traversing serviced both the neigh-boring mansions of Wakefield and Randwulf. When the landau passed the thick stand of trees that buttressed the road and broke into the clearing that allowed a sweeping view of the area around Wakefield Manor, he lifted his gaze with a strangely persuasive hope that he might see Adriana. The gray-stoned many-gabled, steeply-pitched-roofed Tudor mansion sat upon the brow of a hill amid tall evergreens, the height of which almost rivaled the lofty chimneys that seemed to pierce the gathering clouds looming overhead. He had visited the warm, spacious, comfortable man-sion many times in his youth, and he had every confidence that the family living there was just as gracious and hospitable as they had been years ago. A man could do no better than to make such people kin by marriage.

The slowing of the landau evoked Colton's curiosity, and he peered out the windows in an effort to discover the reason for Bentley drawing rein upon the four-in-hand. That's when he saw in the field on the far side of the conveyance the two mounted riders racing their horses toward a low stone wall. The lady, riding sidesaddle atop her mottled gray Andalusian stallion, was in the lead and apparently reveling in that fact. Glancing ahead, Colton saw the height of the barrier looming before the pair, and with a muttered curse that drew the tailor's shocked attention, leaned forward in his seat for a better view. In something akin to paralyzed horror, he watched as the two neared the obstacle, but the closer they came, the more his eyes became riveted on the mottled stallion, which bore the elegantly garbed lady. As he held his breath, the steed soared upward, tucking his forelegs beneath him, and seemingly with buoyant ease, sailed over in a high, graceful arc that easily cleared the hurdle. Feeling an overwhelming relief, Colton hardly noticed the man's shiny black steed gliding with equal grace over the same obstacle.

"Reckless wench!" Colton muttered in a sour temper. "Doesn't she care a whit that she could get her fine neck broken one of these days with antics like that!"

By now, Mr. Gaines was eyeing him rather warily. "A friend of yours, my lord?"

"A neighbor with an uncommon passion for horses," Colton muttered irascibly and, hefting his cane, rapped the elegantly curved handle against the roof of the carriage. As the landau began to slow, he faced his companion. "Your pardon, Mr. Gaines. I'll be alighting here for a few moments, but I'll have Bentley take you on to Randwulf Manor with your men." Turning slightly, he cast a glance out the rear window and found the tailor's conveyance just leaving the wooded copse. "Harrison will see to your needs and will show you to an area of the manor where you and your assistants can work undisturbed for the next week."

When the landau came to a halt, Colton made his descent and gave Bentley his instructions, concluding with the directive, "You may return here for me after you've helped Mr. Gaines and his assistants with their baggage."

Colton made no attempt to understand the sudden surge of irritation that swept through him as he watched the mounted equestrians approaching along the road at a walk, no doubt to cool their steeds. Smiling cheerily as the conveyance passed, Adriana waved a gloved hand at Bentley, as did the handsome gentleman who reined his sleek black steed beside the gray stallion.

This was no Roger Elston, Colton determined, wondering at the nettling sense of displeasure he was presently feeling. The man sat a horse as if he had been born to it, and from his white-toothed grin, which seemed to stretch well across his handsomely bronzed face, one could believe the gentleman was enjoying himself immensely. And why not, Colton mentally derided. Even if the two were now in front of the lady's family estate, the man had her all to himself.

Colton faced Adriana and the man at her side as they approached him. "Good evening," he bade, tipping his hat to the lady. She was looking very elegant indeed in black riding attire with a white silk jabot at her throat and a black silk hat perched jauntily upon her dark head. Solitary pearls adorned the lobes of her dainty ears beneath light curling strands that had no doubt escaped during one of her airborne flights. Colton just couldn't imagine their recent hurdle had been the only one the pair had taken in their ride about the countryside. "I thought I'd stop and see your stallion for myself since everyone in my family has been lauding his praises." His eyes flicked over the steed as Adriana stroked the finely arched neck, and he had to agree. Ulysses was an uncommonly fine animal. "He really *is* a beauty."

Adriana fought a battle with herself as she strove to forget the colonel's bold solicitation of her favors not too many nights ago. Had he told her outright that he wanted no part of the contract their parents had signed, she wouldn't have been any less offended. Since he only wanted her on *his* terms, the fact that he desired her had done little to assuage her annoyance.

Smiling stiltedly, Adriana swept a gloved hand about to indicate her tall, dark-haired, dark-eyed, handsome companion, introducing him as he swung down from his steed. "This is my good friend, Riordan Kendrick, the Marquess of Harcourt. Riordan, may I introduce you to Colton Wyndham, the Marquess of Randwulf."

"I've been hoping to have this pleasure for some time now," the man avouched as he approached Colton with a smile and a hand outstretched in greeting. "What soldier hasn't heard of your bravery under fire? May I welcome you home from Waterloo, my lord, and all the other places you've traversed during your illustrious career."

The nettling irritation that had vexed Colton so quickly at first sight of the man rapidly dissipated as they shook hands. "Thank you, Lord Harcourt, and may I return the salute. I've heard many tales of your bravery on the fields of battle."

Riordan chortled and held up a hand in protest. "I'm afraid you've put me to shame in that area, so, please, say no more, my lord."

Each man, upon realizing that Adriana had lifted her knee from around the leg support of her saddle, stepped forward in his eagerness to be the one to help her down. Much to Colton's chagrin, he was quickly outdone by Harcourt's swift agility, and why not, Colton thought rather gloomily, the man wasn't hindered in the least by past wounds.

The way the nobleman looked at the lady when he set her to her feet was enough to tweak the ire of the observer who, until this moment, had considered himself undecided in his intentions toward the beauty. It was only because the man was unscathed from the wars, Colton mused, mentally offering the excuse as he tried to explain away the annoyance he found himself presently battling; it certainly wasn't jealousy. It couldn't be! Never in his life could he remember being envious of another!

That was before he had come home and found himself committed to a contract he had had no part in making, a voice seemed to whisper inside his head. That was before he had discovered that a lady could thwart his sleep. That was before he had realized just how much a man, who was every bit an equal of his, and who, upon the demise of his father, would have an even loftier title, yearned to have her for himself. That was before he had seen in another's face and in that one's dark eyes a love that burned warm and true.

Leading Ulysses behind her, Adriana approached Colton. "Lord Harcourt and I were just waiting for our friends to catch up. Once Sir Guy Dalton and Lady Berenice Carvell arrive, we'll be joining my family for dinner. Would you care to come in and share the evening meal with us?"

"Thank you kindly for your offer, but Bentley should be returning for me shortly," Colton explained, definitely feeling out of kilter with the young beauty. Though she smiled at him graciously, her eyes maintained their coolness. "I brought my tailor and his assistants from London, and knowing Mr. Gaines as I do, I'm sure he's anxious to get started." He was relieved to see his landau returning, for he was feeling at odds with the situation, and Bentley's timeliness would allow him to make good his escape. Though he dismissed the idea that his manly envy had been goaded by the sight of Adriana with another suitor, he realized he was definitely feeling something resembling jealousy.

"Then I shall bid you a good night," Adriana said and, turning about, accepted the proffered arm of her tall, broad-shouldered escort. Had he previously been puffed up by his own experience with women and their desire to please him, Colton suffered something akin to a brutal awakening as he watched the pair strolling off with their steeds in tow, for the lady never once glanced back as she smiled up at her handsome escort.

Bentley's questioning look was the last thing Colton wanted to confront when the carriage halted beside him. "Don't say anything," he urged sourly. "I'm not in the mood to tolerate any of your wisdom tonight."

Bentley glanced worriedly toward the couple. "Do you think Lady Adriana is taken with his lordship?"

"How the hell should I know! All I can say is that she's not taken with me!"

"Maybe she'll think better on it tomorrow," the driver tentatively suggested.

Colton snorted likely an angry bull. "Or more likely when hell freezes over."

Eight

＊

"FELICITY, where are you?" Jane Fairchild called from over the second-story balustrade. "Will you *please* come upstairs and help me turn your grandfather so I can tend his bedsores?"

Ensconced in the downstairs parlor with a leather-bound volume of Jane Austen's *Pride and Prejudice,* Felicity Fairchild wrinkled her nose in sharp repugnance as she turned another page. The *last* thing she wanted to do today, or, for that matter, *any* day, was assist in such a revolting task, especially when it entailed being a nursemaid to a dawdling old fool! Jane Fairchild may well have had that mission in mind for herself when she begged her husband to resign his position at the counting house where he had worked for more than a score of years, but such chores were hardly what her daughter had resolved to do.

Thus far, the only redemptive advantage for moving to a backward town like Bradford on Avon had been her introduction to Lord Randwulf. Her father had been greatly buoyed by the news of their meeting and had eagerly repeated his prediction that she'd marry an aristocrat one day and have wealth in abundant measure. Her mother had long deemed such talk beyond reasonable expectation, considering their own less than noble status, but it was exactly the reason Jarvis Fairchild had acquiesced to his wife's plea to make the move to the Wiltshire town, for it was in this very area he expected his daughter to capture the interest of a certain aristocrat. While on an errand for his previous employer in London some months back, he had overheard two men of consequence expressing some hope that an unattached nobleman would soon be acquiring a marquessate near the miller's town and, along with it, enough wealth to dispense with the notes of indebtedness each of them held. In view of the fact that his daughter turned the heads of nearly every gentleman she passed, Jarvis had foreseen great opportunity to be found in the area.

Slamming the open book down on a nearby table, Felicity muttered peevishly about her mother's penchant to interrupt her reading. With such an irksome chore looming ahead of her, she could no longer concentrate. Vexed and restless now, she catapulted herself from the chair and stalked to the parlor door from whence she stuck her tongue out toward the upper level.

Of course, by then, Felicity deemed herself safe, since her mother had returned to the elderly miller's bedchamber. Jane smiled at her parent and fondly patted his arm.

"Don't bother yurself 'bout me, Jane," Samuel Gladstone gently rumbled from his bed. "Yu've done enough as 'tis. See ta yur family."

"You *are* family, Papa, and it gives me the greatest pleasure to care for you with the same loving tenderness you once bestowed upon Mama when she was gravely ill. Never have I seen a man more dedicated to his wife than you were to Mama."

Samuel forced a grin in spite of the gathering thickness in his throat. "Ah, there was a woman who could touch a man's heart. At times, dearest Jane, I see a glimpse of her in you."

His daughter heaved a forlorn sigh. "I don't seem to have quite the same knack for touching hearts as she did, Papa."

"Oh, yu've got it all right," he reassured her. "The problem yu're facin' lies wit' the sluggishness o' the hearts yu're tryin' ta awake. Mayhap in time they'll respond ta yur winsome ways. Meantime, girl, take courage. Yur deeds are honorable an' true. They'll stand as a testament ta yur character long aftah yu leave this world, jes' like yur mother's deeds have done throughout these many years since her passing."

Having received no further directive from upstairs, Felicity tossed her head with a flippant air as she strode to the front windows overlooking the cobblestone lane that made a meandering descent through the town after curving past the uppermost hill whereon sat the three-story Cotswold manse. In the distance, she could see the ruins of a medieval church with its lofty steeple and, farther on, the bridge that traversed the River Avon and upon which sat a medieval chapel, ofttimes used as a prison or a blind house. Longingly her gaze flitted along the cobbled streets of the area where the shops were located in search of a gallant gentleman who, if she were indeed fortunate, would present himself at her grandfather's stoop and salvage what was left of her day.

Hurrying footsteps, approaching from down the hall, promptly set to flight such wishful yearnings, giving Felicity immediate cause to reflect upon the folly of her defiance. She tried to brace herself for the ordeal of facing her mother, who had a way of recompensing disobedience and feeble excuses in a most effective fashion. In the short time they had been living at Stanover House, Felicity had come to realize her mother had gotten many of her ideas on integrity, hard work, and loyalty from her sire and had long ago dedicated herself to instructing her daughter in the manner in which she had been brought up. In most cases, however, Jane's attempts were repeatedly put to naught by Jarvis Fairchild, who considered himself far more astute and knowledgeable about everything in general. Many times he undermined his wife's valiant efforts by openly deploring them, even in their daughter's presence. Now that he was working nearby, he was inclined to return fairly often to the house, sometimes to search through Gladstone's ledgers or to question the elder at length about older workers, who, unbeknownst to his father-in-law, he had begun to lay off. Felicity suffered no uncertainty that she'd be saved forthwith from any chore her mother required of her if her father were to enter in the next moment or two, but as much as she yearned for that event, such timeliness seemed far-fetched, even to a dreamer.

The scurrying footfalls advanced down the hall, prompting Felicity to creep hastily toward the door with the hope that she could fool her mother into thinking she had actually been about to respond to her summons. The rushing patter of feet drew near the parlor door and then, much to Felicity's amazement, continued on toward the kitchen. Almost laughing aloud in relief, she realized her fears had been for naught. It had only been Lucy, her grandfather's housemaid, hastening to fulfill some new directive Jane had given her.

Smiling smugly, Felicity returned to the window through which she had been contemplating the world. If she delayed long enough, perhaps her mother would even give up on her coming upstairs. After all, caring for the miller was his daughter's responsibility, no one else's.

Leaning near a windowpane, Felicity searched eagerly for a familiar face. Having had her head filled with fantasies of grandeur by her father for most of her life and, more recently, a wee taste of the social life aristocrats often enjoyed, she entertained lofty aspirations of rich gowns, grand balls, and regal courtships. She yearned to be out amongst the bustling shoppers, but she could think of no viable excuse that would be effective in inducing her mother to let her go out, especially now after her assistance had been requested.

Reflecting upon the aristocrats she had recently met, Felicity braced her chin on a slender knuckle and considered the odds of claiming any one of them for her own. Major Lord Stuart Burke was indeed handsome and entertaining, and if she could attract no other, he'd certainly suffice. Still, if given a choice, she'd prefer the very handsome Lord Randwulf. He was not a mere man in her opinion; he was the very essence of the perfect being, and even if debtors were nigh on his heels, she could only guess that the wealth associated with his marquessate would soon absolve him of all those minor inconveniences.

Her eyes wandered dreamily down the lane, and then she straightened with an excited gasp, recognizing the very one she had been daydreaming about . . . Lord Randwulf! At the moment, he was making his way along the thoroughfare with the aid of his elegant walking stick.

Felicity's heart quickened with excitement, and she dashed into the hall, calling toward the kitchen, "Lucy, I need your assistance upstairs in my room immediately! Immediately, I say!"

The servant sputtered incoherently as she stumbled to the doorway. Felicity didn't bother glancing back as she raced toward the stairs. Although she chanced attracting her mother's attention by going to her room, she had little choice. She just *couldn't* let Lord Randwulf see her attired in anything less than her finest.

She was nigh breathless by the time she reached the third level, but she dared not pause. Upon entering her spacious bedchamber, she flung open the doors of the stately armoire residing near the window and began sorting through her gowns in a frantic quest to find her newest day dress. In spite of her mother's vigorous protestations that they could not afford such extravagance, a seamstress and a milliner had been engaged shortly after Jarvis Fairchild had assumed his new position at the mill. A fashionable mauve creation, with bands of creamy silk lutestring edged with mauve cording ornamenting the skirt, small capped sleeves, and full-length sleeves, was the costliest gown she had ever owned and, without a doubt, the most fetching. A matching bonnet made the ensemble even more attractive.

Drawing forth the garment, Felicity lovingly scanned its length. As irresistible as it was, she had worn it more in a short span of time than she had first deemed wise, but the compliments that had been evoked had made it difficult to resist. She suffered no uncertainty that she'd be able to claim the nobleman's attention garbed in such an exquisite gown.

A tiny stain on the bodice caught her eye, wrenching a gasp of dismay from her. Though Felicity had known such mishaps were bound to happen, especially with repeated wearing, she was nevertheless incensed that the spot had not been taken care of by a servant before now. In growing vexation, she whirled as the door swung open.

Clearly winded from her frantic haste to reach the uppermost level, the housemaid bolted into the room and clasped a trembling hand to her bosom as she paused to catch her breath. Her gaze met the seething glower of her young mistress, and in sudden consternation she tottered backward several steps, querying fearfully, "Is anythin' wrong, miss?"

"I'll tell you exactly what's wrong, Lucy!" Advancing until they stood nearly toe-to-toe, Felicity shook the garment in front of the servant's face. "I've told you repeatedly that you are to make certain my clothes are clean and fit for me to wear *before* you put them away in my armoire. You must know that this is my very best gown, and yet you put it away soiled. What is your excuse for your oversight?"

Lucy chewed her bottom lip worriedly. She had been working for the elderly miller for only a few years, yet he had seemed pleased with her efforts. Her confidence, however, had begun eroding shortly after Felicity and her father had started harping at her, making her feel as useless as a toad. "I'm dreadfully sorry, miss. I didn't notice the stain, what wit' it bein' such a tiny little thing, an' all."

"If *I* can see it, then *others* can see it as well!" In a raging temper, Felicity whipped the garment viciously across the servant's face, sending that one stumbling backward with sharply stinging eyes. "Do what you can to clean the spot and make the gown presentable for me to wear. Immediately, do you hear?"

"Yes, miss." Hurriedly gathering the garment within her arms, Lucy blinked repeatedly to clear her now blurred vision as she tried to ignore the painful burning of her cheeks and eyes. Trembling, she set her cap aright and asked in some confusion, "Are yu going out, miss? Mayhap yu didn't hear yur ma. She were askin' for yur help—"

"I can't be bothered with trivial tasks now," Felicity snapped testily, "not when there's a matter of far greater urgency requiring my attention. Now clean the spot off my gown and be quick about it. Do you understand? I need you to help me dress."

"But Mistress Jane wanted me ta hurry back wit' the ointment...."

Felicity leaned toward the maid until the tips of their noses were nearly touching. At such close range, the maid's eyes resembled large, round disks of palest gray. "You will help me get ready, Lucy, or I will beat you until you whimper, do you understand?"

A frantic nod came in quick response. "Aye, miss."

The gown was just being lowered over Felicity's head some moments later when Jane Fairchild pushed open the door. What was all too apparent made the older woman heave an exasperated sigh. "And just where do you think you're going decked out in that finery, young lady?"

Groaning inwardly, Felicity strove to find the opening of her bodice through the skirt's enveloping shroud. She knew from long experience she had to be far more cordial in her mother's presence than she had thus far been with the maid. If not, she'd be denied permission to leave the house, and then she'd spend the rest of the day doing chores. "Oh, Mama, truly, 'tis a matter of gravest urgency."

Jane folded her arms across her midsection and scoffed in disbelief. "And what, pray, has become so pressing since I asked for your assistance?"

Felicity heard the skepticism in her parent's voice and was leery of telling her the truth. No doubt her mother would chide her again for chasing an empty dream.

Dragging the gown down into place, she silently glared at Lucy who had stepped away to await the outcome of the discussion. Hurriedly the girl stumbled forward again and, with shaking fingers, began fastening the garment. Satisfied with Lucy's frenzied efforts to please her, Felicity faced her parent and smiled tentatively.

"You remember Lady Samantha and Lady Adriana, don't you, Mama?" At the older woman's chary nod, she hastened to explain. "Well, shortly after our ride last week, they introduced me to an individual I just noticed in town. I've been thinking it would be nice to make a gift for each of the ladies to show our appreciation for their kindness to Grandfather . . . and also, for inviting me on their ride. If you'd allow me to speak with this individual, I'm sure I'd have a better idea what the two ladies would enjoy in the way of handmade gifts."

A thin brow arched dubiously. "And does this acquaintance happen to be a man, by any chance?"

"We'll be in plain view of the house, Mama," Felicity assured her nervously and decided that it would better serve her purpose to reveal the lordly status of the man. "'Tis Lady Samantha's brother, the Marquess of Randwulf, Mama. . . . He'd certainly be able to advise me, for he knows both women well. I also wanted to thank him for his hospitality since one of the houses we visited was his."

"Don't let your dreams get entangled with him, child," Jane warned with motherly concern. "He must marry a lady from among his peers."

Irritated with her mother's predictable statement, Felicity dared to protest. "For heaven's sakes, Mama, I only want to ask his advice about the gifts and thank him for his kindness."

Jane nodded slowly, taking in her daughter's appearance. "And there you are, looking as radiant as a rainbow in the sky." She waved a hand in a submissive gesture, having felt inclined herself to repay the ladies in some way for the costly herbs they had brought her father, as well as for their kindness to her daughter. "Very well, Felicity. I approve of your desire to show our gratitude toward the ladies, but, mind you, don't be long. Your grandfather wants you to read to him for a while this afternoon."

Felicity groaned petulantly. "Not from the Bible again."

"For shame," Jane scolded. "It gives him comfort while he's ailing, and as far as I'm concerned, you need a good dose of its wisdom. You're far more concerned with your appearance than you should be."

"'Tis boring reading that stuff!"

"Perhaps to you, but not to him," her mother averred.

Felicity sighed, as if relenting, but dared no other comment. It was a fact that Jane Fairchild loved and respected her father; it was more than Felicity could say for herself when it came to the elder.

Some moments later, Felicity hurriedly snuggled into the costly cape her father had purchased for her as she made her way rather briskly down the steep thoroughfare toward the place where she had last seen the marquess. Hopefully, Lord Colton would merely conclude she had come out for a bit of fresh air and exercise rather than for the purpose of chasing him down like a hound on the scent of an animal.

Smiling as if she had nothing more important to do with her time than enjoy the pleasant weather, Felicity nodded graciously to passersby who responded in kind or politely tipped their hats in greeting. At last, out of the corner of her eye, she espied the one for whom she had been feverishly searching just stepping from a silversmith's shop. He was using his walking stick with surprising proficiency as he descended to the boardwalk. Indeed, in a few weeks he'd likely be using it as a swagger stick.

Felicity could only guess the cost of his new gentlemanly attire and was sure such an expenditure would stagger the wits of a dedicated dandy. She had never seen the like of such handsome lapels or smoothly folded collar. Every seam and stitch evidenced tailoring only noblemen could afford. With such expensive tastes, she could well imagine why his creditors had been so eager for him to assume the marquessate.

Oblivious to his admirer, Colton Wyndham turned crisply on his good leg and progressed toward the far end of the thoroughfare. His destination, Felicity determined, was a fine black landau harnessed to a smartly matched four-in-hand that sported bobbed tails and stiff, brush plumes atop their heads parked alongside the lane in a narrow niche beyond the bridge, a place that posed no hindrance to other carriages and wagons moving to and fro along the narrow, cobblestone lane.

Though such haste was hardly conducive to the impression Felicity wanted to convey, she soon realized if she didn't hurry herself right along, she'd lose more than merely an opportunity to converse with the marquess. Her future aspirations might well depend on this very man. In spite of leg muscles that must have still been weak from his injury, the man moved with an agility that threatened to extend the distance between them in short order. As much as Felicity strove to breech the gap, with every step she lost more ground.

It came to Felicity of a sudden that if she didn't stoop to using some rather unladylike tactics, she'd likely see her hopes dashed by his lordship's departure. To have cajoled her way out of the house alone had been a rare event indeed; she just couldn't contemplate failure now when the prize she craved seemed to dangle like a delectable sweetmeat just beyond her grasp. In desperation, she laid a slender hand alongside her mouth and called out, "Oh, Lord Randwulf!"

Her immediate success made her heart soar, for the man turned promptly about to scan the street behind him. Espying her rushing toward him, he smiled and reversed his direction. As they came together, he touched the brim of his silk hat politely in gentlemanly salutation as he offered her a dazzling grin.

"Miss Felicity, we meet again."

"Yes," she gasped, clasping a hand to her heaving bosom. She was so thoroughly winded she could manage no further statement.

"Out for a stroll?"

An imperceptible nod and a demure smile had to suffice as Felicity struggled to regain her composure. Even so, she doubted she had ever heard a more pleasing voice in all her life. The smoothly melodious tones sent little shivers racing through her whole being.

Gallantly Colton rescued the lady from her breathless dilemma as he turned in the direction of her grandfather's residence and began to progress up the street, closely adhering to the code of behavior that frowned upon two members of the opposite gender halting on a thoroughfare merely to converse with each other. Although he considered it a silly rule himself, as a gentleman he could hardly dismiss the voracious eagerness of gossips to devour a lady's reputation for minor offenses. "You have no idea, Miss Felicity, how relieved I am to be able to identify at least one face among the residents of Bradford. I fear its inhabitants have become strangers to me during my absence. The older ones seem familiar enough in spite of the ten and six years I've been away. Even so, it takes me a while before I can recall their names. As for the younger ones, I'm afraid I'm totally at a loss." He glanced around at the quaint little shops lining the cobbled street. "Still, except for a grand new house or cottage here and there, the town is much as it was when I left."

Felicity peered about her, finding it difficult to rally the same degree of enthusiasm he was exhibiting. She couldn't imagine living for the whole of one's life confined in such an unimpressive town. "My grandfather must be the oldest living resident hereabouts." She flicked a smiling glance aside at his lordship, well aware that her dark lashes emphasized the blue of her eyes from that particular angle. "He says he remembers the events that took place when you were born. According to him, your father was so proud over the birth of his son that he invited not only his relatives and a whole host of acquaintances from London, but everyone from the surrounding area to your christening. Grandpa said it was quite a mixture of aristocrats and common folk, yet they were all on their very best behavior out of respect for your father. As for myself, I know only a few people hereabouts. If not for the kindness of your sister and Lady Adriana, I wouldn't know anyone at all. To be sure, both ladies proved far more gracious than anyone I ever met in London."

"A great metropolis, London. You must miss it immensely after living there all your life."

"I admit that at times I find myself recalling the sights, the sounds . . ."

"The smells?" he finished with a teasing grin.

She blushed, understanding only too well to what he was referring. At times, the odors wafting from the streets were strong enough to stifle a person. "London does have a few disadvantages."

"A few," he agreed amiably, "but not enough to discourage people from living there. I can understand that you may be lonely for it. If you've never acquired a taste for country life, London would definitely seem far more exciting."

"Lady Samantha said your family has a house there."

"Aye, we do, but as a rule, my parents have always preferred the country, especially during the off-season. My father was particularly fond of hunting, as are many of his old acquaintances and friends. I'm sure he and Lord Sutton contributed largely to Adriana's enjoyment of the sport."

"You mean Lady Adriana enjoys shooting animals? After being so dedicated to nursing them back to good health when she was young?" Felicity shook her head, making much of her bemusement. "I don't understand how she could have become so insensitive about taking the lives of helpless creatures. I would never be able to do such a thing myself. My goodness, I couldn't even kill a pesky mouse."

Colton was amazed to feel his hackles rising at Felicity's trivial disparagement of the woman he'd soon be courting. Obviously she was trying to portray herself as far more compassionate, yet when he recalled the brunette's gentle empathy with the three Jennings children, he felt strongly motivated to defend her against the blonde's wily subterfuge. "My sister has informed me that there's a stipulation to which Adriana closely adheres when she hunts. Any game she kills is either served at her family's table or given to others in need. So far this year, she has donated stores of food and game to help provide sustenance for several needy families through the coming winter, including a couple who has taken into their humble home over a dozen orphans. It seems far more mature and exceedingly more honorable of her ladyship to feed people who are starving or in want rather than ignore their plight while she nurses back to health injured strays that could very well be gobbled down by other animals soon after their release."

Felicity realized her error as she detected a note of ire in the man's voice and hurried to dismiss the notion that she was faulting the other woman. "Oh, please be assured, my lord, I never meant to suggest that Lady Adriana is heartless. . . ."

"A more benevolent young woman I have yet to meet," Colton rejoined with a terse smile. "Of that, I am confident." Recognizing his own growing irritation and impatience to be about his affairs, he lifted a hand to the brim of his top hat, intending to bid the fair-haired beauty an adieu, but in casting a brief glance behind him toward his waiting carriage, he espied two well-garbed ladies emerging from a dressmaker's shop.

The taller of the two was unmistakable; she had been dwelling on his mind almost constantly since he had found her soaking in his bath. Now, persistently in the night-borne shadows of his bedchamber, that singular memory haunted him like some willful, recurring apparition licensed to torment his sleep. From that moment in the bathing room, he had been wont to suspect that his mind had been seared forevermore with an image of her delectable form. As much as he yearned to free himself from the hauntingly persuasive song that lured his thoughts relentlessly toward the dark-eyed temptress, he feared nothing short of taking her into his bed and introducing her to the delights to be found between a man and a woman would assuage his long-starved passions. Still, after realizing that Riordan Kendrick wanted her so badly, he seriously doubted his desires would come to fruition without wedding vows being spoken between them. Whether he desired his freedom more than the lady was a decision he'd have to make very, very soon, or else see his infatuation with the beauty brought to a frustrating end by Lord Gyles's acceptance of Riordan's petition of marriage.

He could only presume the diminutive slip of femininity who hurried along beside Adriana was her sister, Melora. He hadn't gotten that close a look at the petite blonde when he had delivered Adriana back to her father's stoop. In truth, he had been too intent upon watching the irate brunette to pay close attention to anyone else. At present, the two were absorbed in their own vivacious chatter and seemed totally unaware that he was even within the area as they came up the cobbled street.

Excusing himself momentarily from Felicity, he approached the pair until he was nigh upon them, whereupon he stepped into their path. The two came to a startled halt, their mouths flying open in astonishment. Melora emitted something that sounded like a fearful whine as her gaze swept quickly upward. After passing the broad shoulders, she was forced to crane her neck far back to see beyond that point. About that time was when she decided she had seen enough to convince her that they were confronting a living, breathing Goliath. With a muffled groan, she whirled promptly about and launched herself in the opposite direction, leaving her younger sister the task of dealing with this huge monster.

Immediately, Adriana reached out to catch Melora's arm and valiantly dragged her fainthearted sibling back to her side as she squelched that one's mewling alarm with a muted, but firm, "Shush!"

Forcing a smile even as she struggled to subdue a blush stirred forth by memories of the man's intrusion into her bath and his more recent nerve to invite her into his bed, Adriana lifted her gaze to meet the translucent eyes now gleaming back at her. She certainly hoped it wouldn't take forever for her to forget his slow, exacting perusal in the bathing chamber, his shocking, manly display there, or his bold solicitation in his carriage, but the way things were going, she could foresee herself being plagued by recurring reenactments of those moments until she was nigh eighty . . . if she lived that long.

She feigned a cheeriness she didn't necessarily feel, for as yet the man had not responded to her parents' note suggesting several possible times for his visit to Wakefield Manor, which seemed to indicate his disinterest in complying with the terms of the contract. "Why, Lord Randwulf, we meet again."

"Good morning, ladies," Colton greeted, sweeping off his top hat with flamboyant gallantry.

Adriana almost expected his teeth to sparkle with the same devilish twinkle she now saw shining in those gray eyes. Though unspoken, the message conveyed by those shining orbs awakened within her a strange excitement that could be felt all the way down to her nipples. It gave her little ease to realize the man probably knew better than her own mother what she looked like entirely naked.

Clandestinely admiring everything her eyes touched, she briefly scanned his long, muscular frame. From his frock coat to the narrow, pin-striped trousers, his garments were so meticulously tailored she had serious cause to wonder if she had ever seen the Prince Regent as well garbed. But then, when a man had been gifted with a tall, broad-shouldered, lean-waisted, narrow-hipped form the like of Colton Wyndham's, clothes were merely an adjunct to his exceptional appearance. It was probably just as well for the ladies at court that His Highness's face and physique fell far short of such manly magnificence.

Felicity hurriedly joined them, not wishing to lose her tenuous grasp on the marquess, for she hadn't forgotten the attention he had liberally bestowed on the brunette during their visit to Randwulf Manor. "Why, Lady Adriana, how pleasant it is to see you again. His lordship and I were just strolling along, enjoying this fine day, when we happened to notice you."

Whatever elation had briefly surged within Adriana's heart when she had recognized Colton mattered not a wit to her after realizing he had been escorting Felicity about town. Indeed, such momentary delight might as well have been dust from a thousand years past.

"Good day, Miss Felicity," Adriana greeted, hoping her words didn't seem as stiff as her smile. Sweeping an elegantly gloved hand about to indicate her sibling, she strove hard to convey a suitable graciousness. "I don't believe you've yet been given an opportunity to meet my sister. Please allow me the pleasure of introducing you."

Felicity cheerily complied, delighted to include another name in her repertoire of aristocrats. Even so, she found it difficult to ignore the stark difference between the pair. "My goodness, I'd never have known the two of you were even related, much less sisters. You're as different as night and day."

Although Adriana laughed, it sounded false even in her own ears. There were definitely times when she felt like the black sheep of the family. "Don't tell me. Let me guess. I'm night . . . and my sister is day."

"Oh, I hope my comment didn't offend you, my lady," Felicity replied, trying desperately to make amends. "I certainly never meant to imply that either of you suffered any lack of beauty. On the contrary, you are both quite lovely."

Colton had trouble curtailing a grin as he witnessed this innocuous confrontation, but when he found himself the recipient of an icy glance from the winsome brunette, he grew a bit perplexed until it suddenly dawned on him what she might be thinking now that the blonde had joined them. Felicity's statement *had* seemed to suggest they had been out and about together.

"Never fear, Miss Felicity," Adriana assured the woman, managing a rather crisp, albeit pleasant smile. "That remark has been made so often in reference to our dissimilarity that my sisters and I have come to expect it. The simple fact is that my two siblings resemble my mother, and I, my father."

Stepping forward, Colton took her sister's dainty hand within his. "May I say, Lady Melora, that you're just as winsome as you were prior to my departure some years back."

"And you're just as gracious as your father before you, Lord Colton," Melora laughingly replied, craning her neck far back in order to meet his gaze. "But please, forego the formality. Our families have been friends far too long for us to adhere to such rigidity. I give you leave to call me by nothing more than my given name."

"Thank you, Melora, and please do the same." At her consenting nod, he cast a devilish grin toward Adriana, who directed her gaze in the opposite direction, deliberately snubbing him.

In an equally affable tone, Colton continued addressing the elder of the two. "I had the good fortune of meeting your intended, Major Sir Harold Manchester, during our encampment near Waterloo. He said at the time that you were reluctant to marry him for fear of being made a widow. Though merely a bachelor myself, I can understand how, when close bonds are formed in betrothals and marriages, they can reap enormous grief when the death of a loved one severs them. Although one hopes to find the same abiding affection that your parents and, until recently, my own enjoyed throughout their marital unions, I fear 'tis not always the case. You and Sir Harold are to be envied for having discovered such sweet accord before your wedding."

"We do feel immeasurably blessed," the petite blonde murmured, amazed that a worldly bachelor could understand the reasoning behind their decision to delay the wedding.

Melora cast a sidelong glance at her sister, clearly conveying the fact that she considered herself the victor in an earlier argument in which they had become embroiled. Being the recipient of that lofty look, Adriana yearned to chide her kin for being so gullible, yet with Colton and Felicity there to witness her testy response, she didn't dare. Melora had snidely accused her of feigning a bland disinterest in his lordship merely to veil the shame she'd likely suffer if he refused to ask for her hand at the end of their courtship. Obviously, after hearing the man voice insights into rationale she deemed private, Melora was willing to reject claims that he was insensitive to matters that women held dear.

Dismissing Melora with all the dignity she could muster, Adriana directed her consideration to Colton's altered appearance. "I see you've dispensed with your military trappings since last we met and have acquired more dapper attire, my lord. Your tailor must relish the opportunity to clothe not only a hero of the war but a man who does immense credit to everything he wears. Garbed in such stylish apparel, you'll soon be the envy of every roué from Bath to London. Indeed, I wouldn't doubt that you'd put Beau Brummell to task to equal such finery."

Colton didn't know just how to accept the lady's statement. He had seen far too many overdressed roués to have any desire to emulate them. As for Beau Brummell, the man had fallen out of favor with the nobility and, as it had recently been rumored, was heavily in debt and not nearly as stylish as he had once been. "I revere your words since they come from a lady who is herself exceptionally well garbed. You alone have seen me at my worst and must therefore appreciate what fine clothes can do for a man." His eyes glowed insinuatingly above a bold grin, pointedly reminding her that she had seen him without a stitch. "As for my London tailor, Mr. Gaines, he became well acquainted with my clothing needs early on in my career as an officer. His talent has endured throughout the years, and when I brought him from London, he and his assistants immediately set about to furnish me with a whole new wardrobe. Considering how many uniforms Mr. Gaines has made for me over the years, he was overjoyed at the opportunity to finally outfit me with all the paraphernalia of a gentleman. I'm afraid, however, that I've worn a uniform so long that I feel rather ostentatious in civilian attire. Nevertheless, 'twill be something I'll have to get used to. In a way, it's like having to learn to dress myself all over again. As much as I've practiced, I fear the cravat is beyond my present capability."

In spite of her limited encounters with naked men, Adriana was wont to think by the seemingly insatiable tendency of her thoughts to dwell on details of the marquess's muscular torso that his reference to "his worst" was hardly that. In fact, she couldn't imagine anything about him that could be considered even remotely flawed . . . except, of course, his brazenness. As for his complaints about the cravat, she failed to find any defect there either. "Well, honestly, my lord, if you didn't do the honors, then I must lend praise to either Mr. Gaines or Harrison's abilities, for your cravat seems deftly executed."

"Your kindness is exceeded only by your grace and beauty, Lady Adriana," he answered, inclining his head in a shallow bow.

However unintentional or minor his slight toward the other two ladies may have been, Felicity took umbrage at the fact that he had praised neither her clothing nor her looks. In sharp contrast, he seemed eager to voice his admiration of Lady Adriana. Indeed, the lighthearted tête-à-tête the pair exchanged seemed to monopolize the couple's attention.

Felicity cut her eyes toward the brunette, curious to know why the man seemed so taken with her. Hadn't her own father told her that she was far more beautiful than any woman he had ever seen? If that was true, then why wasn't she the principal recipient of Lord Colton's admiration?

Considering the costly garments Lady Adriana wore, Felicity was put to confusion. The black lambskin cape, the deeply hued burgundy taffeta gown with its iridescent sheen, and the black-plumed, saucy bonnet of the same burgundy hue were altogether exquisite, but wasn't her own gown just as appealing? Of course, one had to consider that it wasn't her ladyship's looks or attire that really interested the marquess as much as her family's wealth. With the Suttons' affluence, the lady could afford to array herself in finespun gold . . . as well as to buy herself a nobleman whose tailors kept him heavily in debt.

Felicity sidled nearer the marquess, hoping to remind him of her presence. Even then, her attempt to claim his attention from the other came to naught, for he gave every indication that he had dismissed everyone else from mind as he questioned her ladyship about several young children only the two of them seemed to know anything about, concluding with an inquiry, "Have you looked in on them since their mother's funeral?"

"Yesterday afternoon, as a matter of fact," Adriana replied, for once allowing a genuine smile to curve her lips. "Mrs. Abernathy said she heard them giggling and cavorting outside for the first time since we took them there. Poor little cherubs, they were just skin and bones and, as you well know, in serious need of a bath—" Halting abruptly, Adriana almost cringed as she awaited Colton's reaction to her slip. She wanted to bite off her tongue right then and there for its tendency to clatter on foolishly without the aid of her wits. Why in the world did she have to mention the word *bath*?

The gray eyes glimmered tantalizingly. "'Tis hard to imagine anyone foregoing the pleasure of a bath, my lady, but I suppose the Jennings children were never able to enjoy even a satisfying meal, much less a lengthy soak in a tub."

Adriana tried her best to grit out a smile in spite of the glowing blush on her cheeks. Her *lengthy soak* had allowed him an advantage no other man had ever had over her. Whatever modesty she had carefully preserved until that day in time now did her little good in his presence. He knew exactly what she looked like bereft of all the costly clothes she had come to enjoy wearing. Were she eventually to marry another man, she had no doubt that this man's intrusion into her bath would haunt her throughout her marital union.

Colton glanced askance at Felicity, unable to ignore the fact that she was encroaching unusually close. Her deflated pout gave him cause to wonder if he had been *too* obvious in his eagerness to converse with Adriana. However guilty he had been of limiting his consideration entirely to one woman in the presence of others, Colton tried to ease the hurt feelings he had obviously elicited.

Sweeping his gaze about to encompass the three, he declared magnanimously, "I must say, ladies, you make it dreadfully difficult for a man who has long been bound to the battlefield to decide which of you fair maidens would win the prize for beauty or the most winsomely attired lady in the area. I do indeed feel honored to find myself in your collective company."

"You're very kind, my lord," Felicity replied, conveying her best impression of a genteel lady. The temptation to slip her hand through the bend of his arm was nearly beyond her ability to resist.

"You are most generous with your praise, my lord," Melora added, smiling.

"Be careful," Adriana warned, giving him a sidelong perusal and a brief glimpse of a tight smile. "Your pretty words will likely have us all smitten with you."

His eyes sparkled as they delved once again into the depths of those dark pools. "Then I would count myself fortunate indeed to have such comely maids under my spell."

Felicity gasped suddenly as she wobbled from side to side. In the next instant, she caught Colton's arm and held on with all her might, as if fearful of falling through a crack in the cobblestones. The idea for her ploy had come to her when she happened to recall the incident wherein the brunette had whirled through the elegant corridor of Randwulf Manor into the arms of the marquess. Whether that particular event had been planned or a chance occurrence, only her ladyship could rightly say. As for her own ruse, it certainly gave her the chance that she had been seeking. "My goodness," she gasped, slipping a hand through Colton's arm and drawing it close to her soft bosom. "I would have fallen if not for you, my lord."

Proving unstinting in his willingness to accept the lady's ploy for the accident she claimed it to be, Colton consolingly patted the gloved hand that clasped his sleeve. "I'm pleased to have been of service, Miss Felicity. It isn't everyday a gentleman is gifted with the pleasure of having such a winsome lady upon his arm, however fortuitously it came about."

Felicity beamed with delight, pleased that she had managed to fool the man. "Oh, my lord, you truly are kind."

Adriana subdued an urge to emulate her father's habit of snorting in derision whenever he had reason to doubt circumstances to be what they seemed. If she were to do such a thing, she'd likely scandalize her sister, who'd then break all records racing home to tell their parents of her unladylike manners.

Colton met Adriana's cool stare briefly before her fine nose elevated and her gaze went chasing off. From all indications it seemed the lady was none too pleased with him, which did much to heighten his curiosity. Was she miffed merely because he had lent assistance to another woman?

Reluctantly Adriana turned a smile upon her rival. Although she was fairly certain the two were together for some special purpose, she was most curious to know just what that was. "You're looking so radiant this morning, Miss Felicity, I'm led to wonder if my sister and I are keeping you and his lordship from an important event. Considering the exquisiteness of both your appearances, I can only imagine that you two must be going to Bath, or perhaps to Bristol."

Felicity was suddenly aflutter over the idea. "Oh, yes. Wouldn't a trip to Bath be nice!" She glanced at Colton, hoping to receive an invitation similar to that which her ladyship had mentioned, but she was soon to be disappointed, for the gentleman remained discreetly mute. She sighed and, in a wistful tone, assured them, "I would really like to go there . . . someday."

Colton could not have relished Adriana's probing inquiries any more. Had she asked outright if he had plans to whisk the blonde off in his carriage, her irritation over that idea could not have been displayed more vividly. At least now he understood why she had seemed so annoyed. She obviously thought he was paying court to the lady.

Adriana cast a glance toward Colton and once again found herself the recipient of his warmly challenging gaze. The fact that he had not yet seen fit to disengage himself from the blonde's grasp seemed reason enough for her to snub him. Thus she turned her face aside and endeavored to ignore his unswerving regard.

Nevertheless Colton directed his inquiries to the two siblings. "Will Lady Jaclyn be coming to the wedding? 'Twould please me immensely to see her again after all these years and, of course, to be introduced to her family."

Melora peered up at him with a smile. "Yes, of course. In fact, her whole family will be arriving a day or two before the wedding, so you'll be able to get acquainted with them prior to the nuptials, if you so choose."

Coolly distant, Adriana deigned to meet those glowing gray orbs that seemed eager to meet hers. "I'm sure Jaclyn will be delighted to see you again, my lord."

Having noticed the strange quirk that had briefly elevated her brow when he had spoken of the harmonious compatibility that Melora and her betrothed enjoyed, Colton wondered if she deemed him incapable of experiencing a similar attachment to a woman. Feeling directly challenged, he probed, "And you, Lady Adriana, are you not hoping to mirror your sister's good fortune in finding a fiancé whom you can cherish and who will treasure you in return?"

"That seems to be the wish of every maiden, my lord," Adriana replied woodenly, thoroughly convinced that he was seeking some way to escape what his father had once decreed for him. His delay in answering her parents' missive seemed to bear that out. "As for myself, I suffer no grand illusions about the one who was chosen for me. He seems an independent sort, unwilling to bind himself to nuptials. I shan't be surprised if he departs for worlds unknown rather than comply."

The lady's answer was certainly affective in snuffing the heated lust he had recently been battling, Colton realized, but then, perhaps that would prove beneficial if it meant he could enjoy a good night's sleep for a change, instead of remembering how beautiful the lady had looked in his bath. Even so, he couldn't resist an equally nettling rejoinder. "I've heard that you have many smitten swains following at your heels, my lady. I would think you'd find it difficult to choose among them. Of course, there will always be Mr. Elston, should the others lose all hope of winning you for themselves. He seems adamant enough to stay the course through thick and thin."

The dark eyes flared with indignation. "Mr. Elston is merely an acquaintance, my lord, nothing more," Adriana stated frostily, her temper sorely pricked. "As for the suitor my father chose for me, I must bide my time till the true nature of such a match can be determined. I owe that much to my parents and the memory of the elderly gentleman who extended as much affection to me as he did his own daughter, yet I really don't foresee anything of measurable significance materializing from that relationship."

Colton raised a brow to a lofty level, rather amazed that she put no store in the honor she had been bequeathed by being his sire's only choice for a daughter-in-law. "I take it, then, that you have no interest in this . . . ah . . . relationship?"

"A friendship can hardly be nurtured between two individuals unless they spend some time together, my lord. Thus far, that has not occurred. Even if his lordship and I were to become better acquainted, I cannot hold out any hope that the agreement will bring about the desired end that our parents once hoped it would. We are at the very least strangers, and I cannot foresee that fact changing significantly either in the near or distant future."

Colton managed a laconic smile. It would certainly serve the lady her just due if he turned a deaf ear to the pleas of his parent. "Perhaps with a little patience, my lady, you will come to see the way of it. As will he."

Wondering what he meant, Adriana searched the depths of those dark gray eyes once again for what they would reveal, but the glowing warmth was no longer there. With a clipped smile and a murmured excuse, his lordship begged leave of them all and, pivoting about, limped toward his waiting carriage. In watching his departure, Felicity released a dejected sigh and then, after a moment, made her excuses to the two women before departing in the opposite direction.

Melora pinched her sister's arm, breaking the thoughtful trance into which Adriana had descended as she stared after Colton Wyndham.

"Keep your hands to yourself, Melora!" the younger sibling snapped, turning upon her indignantly. "You hurt me just now!"

"Considering the stone you have for a heart, I was wondering if you'd even notice," Melora retorted. "How could you have answered Colton like that? You might as well have slapped him in the face."

Adriana tossed her head, dismissing her sister's jibe. "If mine is of mere stone, then surely his must be made of hardest granite."

The petite sister elevated a challenging brow. "Two of a kind, in other words?"

Adriana leveled an ominous glower upon her older sister, annoyed because she had made such a comparison. Yet, when she turned aside, a gloomy sigh escaped her, for she had to wonder what in the world Sedgwick Wyndham had thought he had been doing when he had created this hellish torment for her. Would she ever be free of it? Would she ever be able to live a normal life with a husband who loved and cherished her above all other women? Or would she be constantly reminded that she had never been the choice of her husband and that, if he yielded at all, he would do so only to avoid wounding his mother?

SWEEPING off his top hat, Colton stepped into the parlor of Samuel Gladstone's three-story Cotswold house. It had been several days since he had met Felicity Fairchild in town, but he had not forgotten his former promise to look in on her grandfather. That was the reason for his visit this day, to renew his acquaintance with the elder after his lengthy absence.

With the aid of his walking stick, Colton limped along behind Samantha as Jane Fairchild led the way upstairs to her father's bedchamber. At the elder's door, his sister paused to talk with Jane and motioned for him to precede her.

Soon after crossing the threshold, Colton noticed books upon layers of books stacked in nearly every available nook and cranny of the spacious room. A tall, elongated, glass-enclosed wooden case residing against the inside wall was completely full of weighty tomes. On a trestle table near the foot of the man's enormous bed were other volumes of comparable size intermingled with a number of others that were both smaller and larger.

Garbed in clean nightshirt and nightcap, Samuel Gladstone was sitting up in his bed with covers draped across his lower torso and a makeshift desk lying across his lap. Several goose-down pillows had been stuffed behind his back, providing a wealth of cushioning against the lofty Elizabethan headboard.

Colton paused, reluctant to disturb the elderly miller who seemed engrossed in perusing the contents of a ledger. Thus far, the man had failed to notice his entrance. Looking back to Jane for guidance, Colton received encouragement as she urged him on with a smile and shooed him inward with fluttering fingers. He stepped closer to the bed. "Good afternoon, Mr. Gladstone."

Lifting his gaze, Samuel readjusted wire-rimmed spectacles upon his nose as he squinted curiously at his visitor. It was not altogether rare that such a well-garbed gentleman came to see him. Lord Harcourt visited him quite often, in fact, bringing with him others who often left him chortling in glee, but the looks of this one was closely reminiscent of another he had once known and respected for a goodly number of years prior to that one's more recent death. Although equally as handsome and tall, this one who progressed toward his bedside with the aid of a fine walking stick was younger by perhaps thirty years.

Samuel Gladstone slowly waggled a finger at his guest as a smile stretched across his aging lips. "I recognize yur face."

Colton grinned and peered at the elder rather dubiously. It had been more than six and ten years since he had last seen the miller, and in that time they had both aged considerably. Indeed, the elder's hair was now totally white and much more sparse than it had once been. "Are you certain?"

Samuel seemed pleased that he could reply with an affirmative nod. "Though I'll warrant me legs aren't as strong as they used ta be, me noggin's still workin' fairly well. Aye, yu're the late Lord Randwulf's son. Yu've the same looks."

Colton chuckled. "So everyone around here keeps telling me. I can't seem to fool anyone, and yet I've found myself incapable of recognizing any of the townspeople."

"Sit down, sit down," the miller urged, motioning toward a nearby chair. "Yur sister kept me up ta date 'bout places yu were at an' the many conflicts yu fought durin' different times o' yur military career. Most o' the people hereabouts have been mightily impressed wit' yur heroism. Mainly the stories come from others livin' outside our area, men what were in yur command an' others what fought alongside yur regiment." Samuel chortled suddenly in amusement. "O' course, me gran'child can't seem ta talk 'bout anyone else. She told me yu'd been wounded, an' needed a cane ta get about wit'."

Settling into the proffered seat, Colton rested the walking stick across his thighs. "Actually, I'm making a little progress. I've been taking long walks in an effort to strengthen my leg and have even set myself a goal. The Suttons are giving a ball some weeks from now, and if I intend to dance with any of the fetching ladies I've seen in the area, I'll definitely *have* to reduce my dependency upon the cane. Otherwise, I'll be sitting like a peg bored into a stump, glumly watching all the other bachelors doing what I won't be able to do. That notion appeals to me about as much as getting another wound in my other leg."

The elderly miller leaned his head back upon his pillows and gave himself over to a moment of hearty mirth. When finally his guffawing ceased, he urged with a twinkle in his eye, "Now don't go breakin' yur other leg in yur haste ta get yur lame one workin' again. If'n yu find a pretty filly, jes' plead yur infirmity whilst yu lead her ta a dark corner."

Colton readily responded to the man's humor with laughter of his own. "You're a devious man, Mr. Gladstone, but I will be sure to remember your advice if I can't get this leg working the way I want it to."

In gentlemanly manner, Colton rose to his feet as Jane followed his sister into the room, but the woman readily motioned him back into his chair.

"No need to trouble yourself, my lord. Please resume your seat while I go make us some tea."

"Why don't yu sit an' visit wit' us for a spell, Jane," her father urged. "Yu scurry 'round here seein' ta me needs, but yu take little time for yurself. I know how much yu enjoy it whene'er Lady Samantha or Lady Adriana come ta visit, so rest yurself an' enjoy her ladyship's visit. Mayhap Felicity would consider makin' the tea today."

Jane didn't dare glance at her father for fear of what he would see in her face. He was, after all, a very perceptive man. "Felicity isn't feeling well today, Papa. She has been in her room all afternoon."

Samuel Gladstone raised a bushy eyebrow, skeptical of Felicity's claims of infirmity, which he had noticed were now coming with increasing frequency. For his daughter's sake, he refrained from making comment. Jane had a good head on her shoulders, of that he was certain, and although she was more patient than he had ever been, he couldn't fault her for that, for he had not always been wise.

He had come to realize that living in the same house with her family had allowed him insights into characteristics and temperaments to which he wouldn't have been otherwise privy. It hadn't taken him long to come to the awareness that he could hardly abide Felicity's presence in his room. Rather than contend with the harsh, mutinous glares and laborious sighs the girl was wont to unleash upon him after being asked to do him favors, he had decided he'd do his own reading and other tasks, at least as much as he was able. Still, after having only servants doing his bidding since his beloved wife passed on, he had come to appreciate being pampered and coddled by his own sweet, darling daughter.

Jane paused at the door before leaving. "Do you wish me to take the ledgers back to the mill now, Papa? Jarvis will be coming home fairly soon."

"Aye, 'tis much as you said. According ta the ledgers, Creighton and some o' me best workers are still gettin' paid. We'll talk 'bout gettin' the lot o' 'em in 'ere ta tell me what they think be goin' on. I fear henceforth yu may be doin' more'n tendin' ta me needs, but I couldn't think o' anyone I taught any better. Yur accountin' would rival me own."

It wasn't long after tea had been served that Colton and Samantha said their farewells. As soon as Bentley saw them departing Stanover House, he brought the landau directly up the thoroughfare. About that same time, Felicity decided to lay aside her novel and meander across the hall into the front bedroom, the windows of which afforded a panoramic view of the town.

She had barely reached the leaded panes when she caught sight of her mother standing near the lane in front of the house as she waited for Lord Randwulf to hand his sister into his landau. A startled gasp was wrenched from Felicity, not only because she realized the two had come for a visit, but, more disturbing, because they were about to take their leave. In frantic haste, she caught up her skirts and dashed toward the stairs. Her feet were a mere blur of motion as she made a rapid descent from the third story. All the while she sought to smooth her hair and neaten her gown. By the time she arrived at the front portal, she was nearly breathless, but she dared not pause, knowing she had little time to halt the Wyndhams' departure. Snatching open the door, she nearly catapulted herself from the Cotswold house. Alas, the driver had already set the fancy steeds in motion.

Racing down the stone walk, Felicity waved frenetically in an attempt to catch the driver's eye, but even as fast as her slippered feet flew upon the curving path, her efforts proved to no avail. When she reached the end of the walk, the landau was moving smartly down the lane.

Felicity clasped a hand over her racing heart as she wheezed air into her depleted lungs. Still huffing, but now in more ways than one, she whirled upon her parent, thoroughly incensed that she hadn't been informed of the marquess's visit. "Why didn't you tell me Lord Colton was here?"

In spite of her daughter's indignation, Jane lifted her shoulders in a casual shrug. "You told me you were sick and didn't feel like being disturbed under any circumstances. I took you at your word."

"But you should've known I'd want to see his lordship!" Felicity railed back and flung out a hand to indicate the conveyance now descending the hill at a brisk pace. "Don't you care that Lord Colton may never come back because of what you've done?"

Jane seemed to turn a deaf ear to her daughter's arguments as she watched the landau's departure. "I assumed you were feeling too poorly to entertain visitors. If that was not the case, then you should've applied yourself to some of the tasks that needed to be done, and then you wouldn't have missed Lord Randwulf's visit."

"You did that on purpose, didn't you? To punish me merely because I wasn't doing your drudgery! Just wait until Papa hears about this! He won't believe how utterly stupid and petty you've been not to let me know his lordship had come to see me—"

"If I were you, young lady, I'd be careful what you say to me," her mother warned, still staring off into the distance. "You may yet find yourself scrubbing floors before the Suttons' ball rolls around. And if you prove too belligerent, you'll find yourself staying home that night in spite of Lady Samantha's invitation."

Totally incensed at her mother's threats, Felicity leaned forward and fairly railed in her ear, "You can't make me stay at home, not when Papa expects me to go! Now tell me, what feeble excuse did you give his lordship when he asked to see me?"

Highly offended by her daughter's demands, Jane came around with eyes flaring and swept a hand smartly across her cheek, wrenching a startled gasp from Felicity. In a voice that had grown threateningly cold, Jane advised her offspring, "Don't ever shout at me like that again or you will wish you hadn't."

Clasping a hand to her burning cheek, Felicity gaped back at her mother as if thoroughly convinced the woman had taken leave of her senses. Although she had received swats upon her buttocks whenever she had misbehaved as a child, her mother had never once struck her across the face. "I'm going to tell Papa on you!" she shrieked and burst into tears. "He'll make you regret your foolishness in not allowing Lord Colton to see me—"

"His lordship didn't come here to see you," Jane corrected sharply. "He came here to visit your grandfather, and if you really want to know, he never once mentioned you. Should you wish me to explain that fact to your father, I shall do so. Perhaps it's time he realizes Lord Randwulf has no intention of marrying below his peerage."

"Papa believes differently!"

A frustrated sigh escaped her mother's lips. "As beautiful as you are, I can understand why your father has great hopes for your future, but his efforts to push you toward that end may never come to fruition, Felicity, at least not in the way he'd like. If you throw yourself at titled gentlemen, hoping to gain a place as their wife, you may well come to regret it. You could easily be sullied and then tossed aside, leaving you with very little hope of attracting a respectable husband. Rumors have a way of ruining lives. No man wants spoiled goods."

"Lord Randwulf would never do that!"

"Although I would expect that Lord Randwulf is like most men in that he's just as susceptible to a woman's charms and invitations as the next man, I'm not referring to him or anyone in particular. The poorest scoundrel can pose as much of a hazard to a young, innocent girl as any rich, handsome lord if he knows the right words to entangle a gullible maid's mind. You're too naive to realize the risks you could encounter if you throw yourself at them. Although titled lords are deemed gentlemen by society's standards, I fear more often than not they're inclined to turn their backs on women who've born them bastards and, to avoid disgrace, claim it was some other man's chit. If you yield to any of them, then you'll likely reap untold sorrow. . . ."

"You're just jealous, that's all," Felicity accused acidly. "You can't bear the thought that I'm still young and beautiful and whatever looks you once had are gone because of hard work and toil. No wonder Papa loves me and not you!"

Jane staggered back a step, shocked by her daughter's accusation. "Well, I guess I really hadn't thought too much about his love for me. Perhaps I've been too trusting myself, but I suppose I shall have to lend consideration to that possibility. In any case, it changes nothing. You will make every effort to improve your disposition and learn proper respect for your elders or I shall be forced to take matters into my own hands."

"What do you mean by that?" the younger woman asked curtly.

"If any of Lord Wellington's foes had asked him to define his plans before he had set them in motion, I'm sure he would've declined, and so shall I, for 'tis apparent that you and I are seriously at odds. My main concern as your parent is teaching you proper respect, not only for me, but for others as well. From now on, you won't be lounging in your room when there are chores to be done. Nor will you threaten mayhem upon Lucy or any of the other servants in order to get them to complete your tasks. And if you think your father is going to negate what I say, I wouldn't depend too much on that premise if I were you. He'll be too worried about correcting his own actions to concern himself about your many complaints."

Felicity peered at her mother closely, trying to discern her meaning. "What are you saying?"

"That really doesn't concern you, Felicity. 'Tis a matter strictly between your father, grandfather, and myself. Just be aware that henceforth you will either complete my directives or you will have to answer to me . . . and to me alone."

It seemed Roger's good fortune that, on the very same morning he had been wondering how he could resume his courtship of Adriana, he espied Lord Randwulf's coach making a departure from the Gladstones' residence. That fact allowed him an opportunity to ride over to Wakefield Manor to report what he had seen to Adriana and to offer several considerations, which had been obvious to everyone from the very beginning, that Felicity was thoroughly taken with the marquess and that, quite possibly, Randwulf was also interested in her.

Nine

❋

CHRISTINA mentally braced herself for the ordeal of meeting their guests as their butler decorously announced that Lord Randwulf and his mother were awaiting the Suttons' presence in the drawing room. "Thank you, Charles. Please inform my husband of their arrival."

"Yes, my lady."

Several moments later, Christina rapped her thin knuckles on the door of her youngest daughter's bedchamber. "The Wyndhams are here, dear. Are you ready?"

Adriana sighed pensively. As much as she had loved and admired Sedgwick Wyndham from her earliest years, his son set her whole world out of kilter. Merely the memory of his angry explosion years ago left her feeling as skittish as a cat facing a pack of hunting dogs. Yet, when she thought of that moment when she had awakened to find him standing beside the tub in the bathing chamber, her senses quickened with the awareness that he could be hers if only he'd relent and agree to their betrothal. Still, after Roger had informed her that he had seen the man's carriage outside Stanover House, she could only conclude that Colton had been visiting Felicity. Of late, the two had been together far more than what could be ascertained as merely chance meetings.

Perhaps Melora had been right all along, Adriana mused morosely. She didn't want to face the shame of Colton's rejection. What woman would willingly invite such disgrace? It would be doubly hard, knowing that after seeing her entirely bereft of clothing, he still preferred Felicity. That would be an insult she wouldn't likely get over too easily.

Had there not been looming over her head the very real threat that she'd cause her parents shame, Adriana knew she wouldn't have even thought twice about the matter before making good her escape. She'd have slipped out to the stables and raced off on the back of Ulysses to some far-off place she knew not where. It certainly wouldn't have been the first time she had absconded when presented with the prospect of entertaining a visitor she'd been averse to see. Melora would promptly deem her a coward, but if Colton Wyndham's vehement outburst years ago had been able to raise the hair off the back of her neck, then she entertained little doubt that, after disciplining his troops during his lengthy career as an officer, he had acquired the skill to flay the hide off his victims with nothing more than his keenly edged tongue.

Still, whatever she would experience or suffer while confronting the nobleman, she knew there'd be no escaping her own pledge, which she had given at the actual signing of the contract. *An honest man's word is as good as his bond,* her father had often quoted while schooling his daughters in exemplary behavior. Gyles Sutton would expect nothing less from her.

"I'll be down directly, Mama," Adriana answered dejectedly from her dressing table. "Maud is still arranging my hair."

"Please tell her to hurry, dear. 'Tis impolite to keep our guests waiting beyond the appointed time."

"Yes, Mama, I know," Adriana mumbled, none too happily.

Maud chuckled in amusement, sensing her young mistress's glum mood. "Now, pretty mum, meetin' Lor' Randwulf won't be nearly as bad as yu're makin' it out ta be. Cook said she seen 'im the other day in Bradford after some young miss pointed 'im out ta the shopkeeper where she'd gone ta buy spices. She said she nearly dropped her jaw when she turned 'bout ta look. 'Is lor'ship cuts a right fine figger all decked out in fancy clothes, she claims. A real man, tall an' wit' some meat on 'is ribs, not like 'at Mr. Elston, who come prancin' hisself up 'ere yesterday like 'e owned the place. Me way o' reckonin' it, Mr. Elston's a might lank an' bony. Why, 'e don't e'en look like a man, at least not the way 'is lor'ship does."

Adriana heaved a laborious sigh. "Everything you say is true, Maud. Lord Randwulf does cut quite a dashing figure. . . ."

"Then why be yu frettin', m'liedy? Ain't yu pleased 'at such a man'll be wantin' ta court ye?"

"I'm not at all sure that Lord Randwulf wants to court me, Maud. That was his father's idea, not his."

"O' course, 'e wants ta court yu," the portly maid insisted. "Why, yu're the loveliest maid this side o' 'eaven, an' if'n 'e don't thinks so, then 'e's likely a might touched in the 'ead. Why, look at all the lords an' gents what's lost 'eir 'earts ta yu already, mum. Ain't 'at proof o' yur appeal?"

"Not all men are the same, Maud, and Lord Randwulf does seem to enjoy his bachelor status...." Adriana broke off, knowing the servant would never understand the true depths of her fears. What bothered her most was her own fascination with the man. If she was attracted to him to the degree she was now, what would her feelings toward him be once he concluded his courtship? It would not be so much her pride that would suffer should he reject their betrothal as it would be her heart. Dismally she shook her head as a pensive sigh escaped her lips. "Who knows what Lord Randwulf wants?"

Maud chortled. "Doan yu go frettin' yurself none 'bout what 'e may be likin', mum. If'n 'e ain't done so already, 'e's bound ta lose 'is 'eart ta yu afore too long."

Time would indeed reveal Colton's true nature and susceptibility, Adriana mused dejectedly. As for the expected outcome, she was not nearly as hopeful as Maud that it would be to her advantage.

Heaving a sigh, Adriana left her bedchamber, dreading the ordeal of facing Lord Randwulf ... and losing another large portion of *her* heart to the man.

LADY Christina had descended the stairs with an uncompromising confidence that her daughter would soon follow, but upon laying a dainty hand upon the Jacobean knob of the drawing room door, her thoughts immediately became mired in the difficult task before her. At the moment, she had no idea which would prove more arduous: appearing unaffected by Lord Colton's scarred face and form ... or giving her youngest daughter to him in marriage.

Slowly inhaling a deep breath in an effort to quell her anxieties, Christina tried to brace herself for the ordeal ahead of her, but it seemed to loom over her spirit like some darkly menacing shadow. Valiantly she pushed open the portal and entered the room. Immediately she became aware that Lord Randwulf had taken up a stance in front of the diamond-paned windows overlooking the lush grounds and undulating drive. For that fact she was immensely relieved, for the distance between himself and his mother would allow her to welcome the latter before she'd be forced to confront his scarred appearance. The testing of her fortitude would come soon enough once she exchanged amenities with Philana. As for greeting the marquess, it would be an incredible feat indeed if she managed to conceal her repugnance well enough to appear serenely cordial. The only way she'd ever be able to get through those arduous moments would be to keep reminding herself that Colton was her best friend's son and that his wounds had been reaped in valiant service to his country.

Pasting a cheery smile upon her face, Christina crossed the room to the settee where Philana had settled. She gathered the woman's slender hands within her own as she murmured graciously, "This day has been long in coming, dear friend." It didn't help that the words seemed to stick like pitch in her throat. "Your son, home at last. How relieved you must be that he has returned to claim the marquessate."

"Not only relieved, but thoroughly pleased by his desire to assume his father's duties," Philana replied with a radiant smile. "But more importantly, Christina, we have come to speak with you and Gyles about the contract of courtship and betrothal. I do hope Adriana can join us. She is so very much a part of this discussion that I cannot imagine making any decision of which she is not entirely agreeable or privy."

"Maud was just finishing her hair when I left from upstairs. I'm sure she'll be along any moment now, and Gyles...." The door opened behind her, and, recognizing the approaching footsteps before they were softened by the oriental rug, she had no need to turn and look. "Why, he's here now."

"Welcome! Welcome!" Feigning a joyful enthusiasm to the best of his ability, Gyles joined the women. Sweeping Philana's hand to his lips, he kissed it briefly before declaring, "You're looking as lovely as ever, my dear."

A cheery laugh escaped Philana as she waved off his compliment with an elegant hand. "Save that for more gullible fillies, Gyles. I'm old and wrinkled and you know it."

Giving her a one-sided grin, Gyles clasped a hand over his heart as if to pledge his troth. "I see no wrinkles before me, and whatever your age, my dear, your grace and beauty will always remain evident."

Pleased by his reply, Philana dipped her tawny head in appreciation. "You're a true friend, Gyles, even if you have a tendency to lie more than a little."

Chuckling in amusement, Gyles stepped back, delaying the moment wherein he would have to face the younger man. Like Christina, he could not bring himself to do so just yet, though he was keenly aware that Colton had turned from the expanse of windows and was in the process of limping across the room toward them. The muffled thump of the man's cane on the rug seemed to herald defeat, which Gyles feared would come upon them much too suddenly. His wife had tearfully expressed her aversion to the idea of completing the agreement that would bind their youngest offspring to a disfigured man, no matter how many honors that one had received fighting the enemy. Gyles had empathized with her over her fears and, to a great extent, now shared them. Adriana had always been his cherished darling, and he was loath to see her miserably married to a man whose looks would send children fleeing in fright.

Philana swept a slender hand to indicate her approaching son. "Here is Colton safe and sound in spite of a horrible leg wound."

Gyles placed a comforting hand upon his wife's back to steady her and hopefully bolster her nerve as together they turned to face the marquess. Being small and petite, Christina had to lean her head back in order to meet the gaze of the tall man. When Gyles felt a sharp shudder go through her slender form, he tried to prepare himself for what would likely follow. If she fainted, he'd just make excuses that she hadn't been feeling herself for the last several days, which would certainly be no lie since he had never seen her so overwrought, as the result of the approaching ordeal. Better that, Gyles determined, than conveying her aversion to their friend's son.

Silently vowing he'd have more control, Gyles reinforced his resolve by refusing even to blink an eye should he be repulsed by the man's disfigurement. With lofty dignity, he directed his attention upon his guest.

That was precisely when his jaw plummeted.

"Lord Gyles," Colton greeted in deep, melodious tones, offering a smile to each in turn. "Lady Christina."

"My goodness," Christina whispered breathlessly as a deep, vibrant hue infused her cheeks. Heretofore she had considered both her son-in-law, Sir Thornton Godric, and Melora's fiancé, Sir Harold Manchester, unusually handsome men, but she had to admit that Colton Wyndham, with his lean, noble features, stunning good looks, and tall, broad-shouldered frame, easily put to shame the other two. She shook her head in confusion, wondering how in the world she had ever arrived at the flawed notion that the man was hideous to look upon. "You've changed so much, Lord Colton, that I'm afraid Gyles and I are both taken aback."

Colton smiled pleasantly. "Quite understandable, my lady, considering I was hardly more than a lad the last time we saw each other. Ten and six years can make an immense difference in one's appearance."

Gushing with joyful relief, Christina swept a hand toward the settee where his mother had become ensconced. "Please, do sit down, and tell us about the places you've been since last we saw you."

Before Colton could comply, the door swung open once again, drawing his attention to the portal as Adriana entered. In spite of his fairly exacting perusal of her while she slept in the bathtub, he was ever amazed by the true depth of her beauty. If ever he had discounted the possibility that a woman's features and overall appearance could be flawless, then he was swiftly coming to the conclusion that Adriana Sutton would set the standard by which all other women would have to be judged, at least in his mind. If her looks weren't at the very least perfect, they came as nigh to being so as he was able to bear. Her long, thick hair had been smoothed back from her face and caught in a heavy, swirled topknot at the crown of her elegantly shaped head. Several feathery curls had escaped at her temples, in front of her ears and the back of her neck, lending a charming softness to the hairstyle. In contrast to her dark tresses, her creamy skin seemed fairer by far than other ladies'. A faint rosy blush adorned her cheeks and the soft, winsomely curved lips. As for her large, silkily lashed dark eyes, their appeal was so strong that he had to mentally shake himself free of their spell.

Her garments were in the height of fashion, and her tall, slender form complemented them divinely. Swirled braided silk trimmed the high-standing collar, the epaulette-draped half-sleeves, and the waist of her short, cropped jacket, lending something of a military flare to an emerald green creation of soft, woolen crape. A stock of ivory silk, intricately embroidered with silk threads of the same hue, was wound about her slender throat and then folded under and over itself to form a smooth layer, nattily filling in the stiffly erect collar of her Spencer jacket. Generous sleeves of the same embroidered creamy silk flowed with undulating grace from under the half-mushroom-shaped extensions capping her shoulders.

Wide, closely fitting bands of the same fabric subdued the fullness over her wrists and were themselves finished with scalloped ruffles that fell over her slender hands.

Colton was surprised to find himself making mental comparisons between the dainty accoutrements adorning Adriana's ears and the jewelry Pandora Mayes had always been partial to wearing. The former amounted to nothing more than solitary pearls set in delicately swirling nests of gold filigree, whereas the actress had preferred to emphasize her own raven-haired beauty by wearing dangling, oversized baubles. No similarity existed between the jewelry; so too the women. To compare them would have been the same as likening a delicate rose to a cabbage. Pandora Mayes was a voluptuous temptress, knowing well what she was about when she lured lovers into her bed. The actress would have been offended had anyone called her a strumpet, for she had zealously maintained that she extended her favors only to men she admired and with whom she enjoyed lengthy relationships, yet the costly gifts of money and jewels she received from her admirers and lovers put her in a class similar to those who hawked their wares on the wharves and streets of London. Adriana, on the other hand, was exactly the kind of genteel lady he had purposed to marry someday. After Bentley had dared to remind him of the uncompromising principles of the lady, he could only agree that Adriana was indeed a rare find among women.

Colton curbed a smile as he realized the lady had grown chilled while making her descent from upstairs, for the woolen crape swathing her breasts was now slightly puckered over her nipples. Though he had viewed far more of her in the bathing chamber than any proper gentleman had a right to, those taut little peaks brought back memories of the way they had looked unadorned. In the warmth of the water they had been incredibly soft and pink, crowning beautiful, ivory breasts round enough to arouse any man's lusting admiration.

It came to him that no matter the style or beauty of the garments the lady wore, he was far more mindful of the delectable form they clothed. It was definitely the best *he* had ever viewed. A young goddess in her prime, the Lady Adriana promised to bring to a marriage exceptionally sweet provender upon which a man could feast his gaze and expend his appetites. Should he yield his pride and himself to his father's dictates and welcome that which had been intended as a gift rather than a constraining lifetime sentence, he could savor everything about her, from her dainty earlobes to her thin toes. Still, he couldn't quite forget he was being coerced into accepting an arrangement he had spent the last ten and six years avoiding.

"Please forgive my tardiness," Adriana murmured to the occupants of the room, diligently avoiding Colton's gaze after managing to avert her own. His unswerving stare was no less tenacious now than it had been before he had propositioned her in his lantern-lit carriage. Considering the perusals to which she had been subjected in years past, she deemed his inspection far bolder. At least other men had had the decency to size her up with discretion, but Colton made no attempt to hide his penchant for caressing every minute detail *and* at very close range. Indeed, beneath his slowly assessing scrutiny, she felt as if she were literally being devoured. Since his eyes fed upon her every curve, it seemed far-fetched to believe that he'd leave her some meager shred of clothing in his mind.

Stepping behind a Tudor chair, Colton tucked the walking stick beneath his arm and clasped both sides of the tall, ornately scrolled back as he moved it every so slightly toward her. "Come sit down, Adriana."

In the presence of their parents, Adriana saw no other option open to her. No matter how she yearned to flee back to her bedchamber, she could hardly decline his offer without causing some dismay among the elders. She perched rather rigidly upon its edge, fearful of coming in contract with those lean, hard, beautiful hands.

As expected, her efforts failed to keep Colton at bay. The tip of his walking stick returned to the costly rug cushioning the floor as he moved around to her side. Leaning close over her shoulder, he breathed in the scent of her hair and lowered his head further still until his warm breath brushed her cheek. Adriana nearly closed her eyes at the unexpected pleasure his nearness elicited. Indeed, it seemed as if her efforts to remain detached from the man were being seriously undermined by the yearning she felt within the depths of her body. It not only threatened to destroy her cool reticence, but to send her fleeing to the stables.

"Relax, Adriana," he breathed warmly. "I'm not going to eat you . . . at least not yet."

Of a sudden, Adriana found herself trying to collect the fragments of her aplomb from the four winds to which he had just scattered them. His persuasive voice seemed to bombard her very being. She had never known her name could sound so warmly evocative when spoken by a man, or that she could feel as if she were melting inside when those soft, mellow tones stroked across her senses.

A memory of his rage from years past proved sufficient in cooling her mind and in strengthening her resolve to remain aloof from this man. Even more effective was the suspicion that he had been plying his persuasive charms upon Felicity, who had likely accepted them eagerly and without restraint. Considering his indecent proposal after Mrs. Jennings's funeral, Adriana could only wonder if he had used a similar invitation with the miller's granddaughter.

Adriana eyed him obliquely as he pulled another chair alongside hers, bringing the pieces so close that the wooden arms of each were nestled snugly together. She couldn't resist a bit of sarcasm as she offered, "I can move over if you need more room, my lord."

Her barb was not lost upon Colton. Laughing softly in response, he leaned toward her again. "The settee is occupied, my fairest Adriana. Otherwise, I'd have directed you there and taken a place beside you."

"Whatever for?" She feigned bewilderment. "Surely you have no interest in closely assessing the choice your father made for you years ago when you stood at the threshold of manhood. Truly, my lord, I thought we were here to discuss your plans for dissolving the agreement." She elevated a brow challengingly. "Was I mistaken?"

Colton managed a contrived grimace, as if sorely pricked to the core. "Though my eyes detect no evidence of a shrew, my dear, there are times when you definitely make me think I've been deceived. Forsooth, maid, you can draw blood with the injuries you inflict."

Adriana scoffed, winning a chiding frown from her mother and another amused chuckle from Colton. She couldn't fully explain why she should feel so many confused emotions whenever she was with the man. On occasion, she was sure that a porcelain figurine or a heavy pot would serve her untold delight if she were to crown him with either. Then, just as often, she was forced to do battle with those disturbing little bubbles of delight he elicited within her. When she was thoroughly convinced that he was merely going through the formality of considering their courtship for his mother's sake, and that at an appropriate time he intended to deal a death blow to it, she had to wonder why she should be so susceptible to him.

"No doubt, my lord, your conclusions have been drawn from your vast experience," she rejoined coolly. "To become an authority on termagants, one must meet them on a fairly frequent basis. No doubt you've had many such experiences during your absence, perhaps even a few since your return." Lifting her gaze to his, she waited for her taunt to strike home, but he only smiled ambiguously. Reading nothing from his expression that lent evidence of her barb's success, she prodded with a more pointed stick, "Or do you cast the blame upon my poor tongue merely to ease your own conscience as you diligently strive to withdraw yourself from the contract?"

For the very first time since her beloved Sedgwick initially proposed a betrothal between their son and Adriana Sutton, Philana felt a spark of hope that a marriage would actually take place between the pair. Colton was too good-looking to be ignored... or rejected by the fairer gender. Most young ladies would be tempted to fawn over such a handsome man and, no doubt, offer their bodies as a token of their infatuation. She found it enormously refreshing to see how adroitly Adriana put her son in his place. Coolly rejecting his advances would likely set the handsome scamp back upon his heels, and deservedly so. He was too confident of his persuasive charm with women and probably wouldn't know how to handle a rebuff.

Missing the real import of his daughter's jibe, Gyles pressed, "Is that true, your lordship? Do you wish to withdraw from the agreement?"

Slowly straightening, Colton smiled as he lent his consideration to the elder. "On the contrary, Lord Gyles, I wish to proceed with the courtship with all possible haste. Since being informed of my father's contract with you, I've read with great care the document you both signed. According to the provisions set forth, I have three months of earnest courtship in which to decide my fate... unless, of course, the lady is otherwise inclined."

Cocking a magnificent brow inquiringly, he peered down his noble nose at Adriana, awaiting an answer. When she maintained a cool reticence, he again settled in the chair beside her and bent toward her with a grin. "What say you, my dear? Do you have any objections as to the date upon which such a testing of our emotions should commence? If you have none, then may I suggest that we start today?"

The sooner to be through with me, Adriana mused derisively, feeling her hackles rise. Although strongly tempted to reject Lord Sedgwick's edict rather than leave herself open to the many antics of his handsome son, she couldn't actually bring herself to the point of doing so. As much as her pride would've benefited from releasing Colton Wyndham from the obligations to which he had long been averse, she knew that she'd have to yield him that distinct privilege, for she couldn't bear the thought of hurting Philana or shaming her own parents by being the one to negate their hopes and wishes for the future. "If you wouldn't mind a short delay overmuch, my lord, I'd prefer to mark the beginning of our courtship with the date upon which the Autumn Ball takes place, the twenty-first of October."

"So long a wait? Why, that's fully a month away!" Colton was taken aback by the idea of such an extended interval. His primary reasons for agreeing to the courtship was simply to prove to his mother that love could not be forced by a mandate drawn up by one's parents. Once that reality had been established, he'd be freed from his commitments. At least, then, if he wanted to marry Adriana, it would be entirely his own decision, not because he felt compelled by his father's dictates. In his opinion, the protracted wait before the initiation of their courtship made the arrangements even more arduous.

Bracing a finger alongside his cheek and his chin upon his thumb, Colton assumed a contemplative pose as he considered Adriana at some length. He was a man who had made his own choices for most of his life, but after viewing this lady in his bath, he had never known so many sleepless nights. As much as he yearned to appease his manly appetites with her, how could he, like some lapdog, blandly accept his father's will over his own? Somehow he'd have to get through the courtship without yielding his heart, his mind, and, more difficult to be sure, his body to the temptations that would be ever at hand. Only then would he remain his own man. Once he managed to accomplish that feat, then he could turn his mind to more serious considerations . . . courting the lady without having to hide his own desire to solidify their union. "The twenty-first, you say?"

"Or whenever you wish, my lord, as long as the Autumn Ball has begun," Adriana answered aloofly.

Colton was curious to know where the girl stood with the miller's son. "And what of Roger Elston? Will you allow the apprentice to visit you until then?"

Adriana felt her cheeks growing hotter by the moment beneath his close perusal. How dare he question *her* after he had taken it upon himself to visit Felicity. "Prior to your return, my lord, I had given Mr. Elston leave to attend the ball. For the sake of propriety, I must inform him of the need to halt his visits, but 'twould seem somehow less rude if I were to tell him at the conclusion of the ball."

Colton teased a curling strand that seemed wont to nestle against her cheek. Such a delicate little ear, he thought, and wondered how she'd react if ever he'd run his tongue into the tempting crevices and fragile ridges that formed the outer configuration. Devilment shone in the gray eyes as he laid a finger aside the lady's chin and turned her face toward his. Probing those dark orbs, he questioned softly, "Would you object overmuch, my dear, if I were to lend my attentions elsewhere that evening? It seems only fair . . . since you will be otherwise engaged."

Adriana presented her profile to him again and aloofly elevated her brows in a quick, upward shrug. She didn't need to be told the name of the woman he had in mind. "I shall not be otherwise engaged, my lord. I merely gave Roger permission to attend the ball if he so desired, but please do whatever pleases you. I have no claim upon you."

"Oh, but you do, Adriana." Capturing the lustrous curl that teased her cheek, he rubbed it between his fingers and admired its natural tendency to curl softly about his digit. The silken strands were as fragrant as the lady's body, and he could feel his senses reacting as surely as if he had quaffed a strong potion. "We're bound by a contract as surely as if we were already betrothed. That alone gives you entitlement to say yea or nay when it concerns my conduct with other women. And if we're affianced, doesn't that mean we're as good as married?"

"That's hardly the way of it in this case!" In some irritation, Adriana flung up a hand as if brushing a pesky insect away from her cheek and in so doing managing to break his grasp on the coiling strand. "We're *not* married, my lord, and even if we *were* truly betrothed, I'd give you permission to lend your attention to whomsoever you please . . . just as long as you'd agreed to leave me alone in the process. . . . Now stop that!" she snapped in fiery indignation and slapped the back of his hand as he reached out again to entrap the curl. "Leave my hair alone!"

"Adriana!" her mother gasped, taken aback by her daughter's display of temper. "For shame, child! Slapping his lordship, what will he think?"

"*Tsk, tsk!*" Colton chided through a widening grin as he leaned toward the enticing beauty. "I think you have little regard for me, Adriana."

"That may well be true, my lord," she retorted hotly. "After all, you're no more than a stranger to me. . . ."

"Adriana!" Christina was shocked by her daughter's bluntness.

"You're presenting a definite challenge to me, Adriana," Colton accused, amusement gleaming in his gray eyes. "I've never before known a woman who seems so loath to accept my attentions." If anything, he had become inured to the fairer gender fawning over him. It was fairly refreshing to be on the opposite end of the spectrum from whence he normally found himself. To chase after a young, beautiful lady who seemed totally devoid of any interest in him? Most intriguing . . . and *challenging!*

Adriana's tone was snide as she yielded to a strengthening urge to reproach him. "I'm sure you've left many a heartbroken maiden in your wake, my lord, but I shall try not to offer adulations that have no doubt become hackneyed to you through numerous repetitions."

It came as something of a shock to Colton to realize that he was enjoying this feisty tête-à-tête perhaps as much as he had ever relished the final capitulation of a beautiful, well-versed enchantress. The women he had known had all been experienced in the game of love, and he had never once doubted his appeal. That was certainly more than he could say for himself in this instance. Still, a little more kindling seemed in order to thoroughly test the true depth of the girl's tenacity.

"What if I were to tell you instead, dearest Adriana, how lovely you are? Little did I imagine when you were a child that you'd become so exquisite. Your beauty takes my breath away."

"Breathe deeply, my lord," Adriana urged loftily, looking neither right nor left as he recaptured her hand. "I'm sure it will come back."

At her daughter's sarcasm, Christina opened her mouth to intervene, but curbed the motherly instinct when Philana reached across the space separating them and gently squeezed her hand, mutely urging her to remain silent.

Colton lifted to his lips the slender fingers of his perspective fiancée, letting his warm, moist mouth linger on her knuckles in a slow, sensual caress.

Adriana became aware of a strange quivering in the pit of her body and realized her breath was being snatched inward each time his lips came in contact with her skin. The rush of feelings he stirred within her was similar to those he had awakened when they had collided in the hall at Randwulf Manor; yet as titillating as they had proven to be, it now seemed only a meager sampling of what she was now experiencing. To be sure, the sensations he elicited were too persuasive for a young lady to bear in front of her parents and still remain poised!

Reclaiming her hand with a vengeance, Adriana shot to her feet and fled to the door. There she faced her guests with flushed cheeks, managing to erect from her shattered composure some semblance of dignity. Feeble as it was, she offered a truthful explanation. "I promised Melora that I'd help her with a few of the wedding arrangements ere the day was well spent." As her eyes swept to their elderly guest, she sank into a respectful curtsey. "Lady Philana, if you will please excuse me . . ."

"Of course, child," the marchioness replied with a gracious smile, holding her son responsible for the girl's flight. She cast a chiding glance toward him. The fact that he seemed amused by it all made her heave a mental sigh. He reminded her too much of his younger years; he was still an unabashed tease.

The dark, silky lashed orbs chilled to some degree as Adriana finally settled her gaze upon the marquess. Her smile was crisp, perhaps even a bit terse. "Good day, Lord Randwulf."

Even Colton flinched as the door slammed behind her, and for a moment, parents and suitor stared at the portal in differing degrees of surprise. Then, almost in unison, Gyles and Christina turned their attention upon the younger man, wondering how he'd react to their daughter's spirited departure.

Bursting into laughter at the girl's fiery display of indignation, Colton thrust a thumb over a shoulder as he indicated the door. Obviously Adriana was no more taken with the terms of the contract than he had been. "I swear that girl has a temper the equal of which I've never seen in one so well bred."

Christina managed a hesitant smile. "I hope my daughter hasn't offended you, my lord,"

Philana began to chortle in amusement. "I don't know about my son, but, personally, I thought she was wonderful . . . as usual. Another moment more and she would have boxed Colton's ears . . . and justifiably so."

Christina didn't know what to say to make amends. She looked almost pleadingly toward the marquess. "At times, my youngest daughter grows a bit annoyed with certain members of the male gender. She doesn't like being pestered, but I never thought for an instant she'd behave so unseemly in your presence, Lord Colton. I shall certainly take her to task for her manners—"

"You'll do nothing of the sort," Philana interrupted with conviction. "My son deserved everything he received for deliberately annoying her. Perhaps next time he'll know better. If not, then he can get used to his fingers being slapped like some naughty little boy's. I can assure you, it wouldn't be the first time. I used to do it on a fairly frequent basis when he was younger. He seemed to take endless delight teasing the girls whenever Adriana came over to play with Samantha."

Gyles rubbed a hand across his mouth several times, trying to banish the unquenchable grin that seemed impervious to his efforts to curb it. Failing in that endeavor, he clapped both hands to his knees and rose to his feet. "I suffer no doubt that my youngest offspring would have given those frogs at Waterloo a proper thrashing. She riles fairly easily at times. She seems to find it especially offensive to be handled in any fashion by eager young suitors."

Adriana paced the confines of her bedchamber in agitation, angry with herself for having allowed Colton Wyndham to affect her in so many widely diverse ways. Never before had she experienced sensations the like of which he had elicited. Nor had she ever felt so much irritation, not only with him, but with herself for allowing his mischievous ruse to get the better of her. His intentions seemed clear enough. Forced by the mandate that his father had set forth, he intended to humiliate her any way he could, if for no other reason than to vent his frustration over the situation in which he found himself. Coming home after years of mutinous refusal to concede to his sire's dictates, only to find himself caught in the same unyielding snare, had likely been a terrible jolt to him, especially if his thoughts had been focused entirely on the marquessate. In view of the depths and heights his resentment had reached years ago, he might well imagine he had cause to hate her, especially if he viewed the situation only from his perspective. He probably wouldn't even realize she had become a victim, too, chained by her dedication to her parents.

A light knock sounded on her chamber door, and at her call for admittance, Melora's maid scurried in and bobbed a sprightly curtsey. "Excuse me, m'liedy, but yur sister be wonderin' what's been keepin' yu since yu came upstairs."

"I'll be there straightaway, Becky."

The door closed behind the servant, and in the silence that followed, Adriana heaved a long, pensive sigh, wondering if she'd ever be able to endure three months of courtship with Colton Wyndham. It was not that she didn't desire it. Indeed, he was the man she had been waiting for all her lifetime. Nevertheless, he seemed capable of creating within her strange emotions that could well prove her downfall, possibly even her capitulation to his invitation. In spite of her outward display of annoyance, she treasured secret memories of him that, at times, left her yearning for the warmth of his arms around her and his lips plying hers with lingering kisses. Just thinking of that long, muscular, naked body against her own stirred a strange, unquenchable excitement that left her whole being burning with desire. Her nipples craved some special attention of which she was totally ignorant, and there bloomed within the depths of her woman's body a hunger that seemed destined to remain unappeased until she yielded herself to him and him alone.

By dint of will, Adriana won a battle with her composure and finally made her way to Melora's room, where she found her sister in a flustered snit. In trying to work out the seating arrangements for the breakfast that would follow the wedding, she had become mired in confusion.

"There you are at last!" Melora cried petulantly. "I was beginning to think I'd have to make all the preparations myself. I've been nigh to the end of my wits while there you and Mama were, taking your own sweet time visiting with the Wyndhams, as if the matter of your courtship couldn't wait for a few more weeks! I say, Adriana, considering all the years Colton has been away, it certainly wouldn't have hurt matters any if you *had* delayed his visit until *after* the wedding. You should've known how frantic I'd be with the nuptials swiftly approaching. Only ten days left!" Pausing, she peered at her sibling, but saw no evidence of sympathy for herself. Glumly, she vented a ponderous sigh. "I suppose the courtship will begin immediately."

Adriana tried to ignore Melora's tiresome tone. "No, as a matter of fact, I've asked that it be delayed at least until the Autumn Ball."

"Thank goodness!" the older sister exclaimed, exaggerating her relief. "Now you can help me as you promised to do. You can start by compiling a list of the guests who'll be coming and where they should be seated for the wedding breakfast. Cook is already busy with preparations, and, of course, the servants have started cleaning every nook and cranny. We can't allow ourselves to be embarrassed by a bit of dust here or a smudged window there. . . ."

Dismissing as unimportant much of what Melora was chattering on about, Adriana sat down at her sister's tall secretary and began organizing the collection of names. She was sure Cook, the assistant cooks, and the rest of the household servants would do their very best to make the wedding breakfast a memorable occasion for her sister. As for herself, she just hoped she could keep her thoughts well away from the area of Colton Wyndham, for she was just beginning to fear that, where he was concerned, her heart wasn't nearly as safe as she had hoped it would be.

Ten

THE weather on the last day of September was fairly heady with the intoxicating smell of autumn wafting on the gentle breezes. With the sun's radiance in evidence, it had proven to be an especially fine morning for a wedding. During the ceremony, the chapel had been filled nigh to overflowing with guests, but as family members and friends collected outside to await the appearance of the bride and groom, they were wont to meander about and exchange pleasantries with relatives and acquaintances. Adriana found herself surrounded by a fairly sizable group of young men eagerly vying for her attention. Among them were members of the best families in England, including Lord Harcourt who had managed to gain an advantageous spot immediately upon her left. Stuart Burke stood on her right and seemed delighted that Colton had deigned to keep company with Perceval rather than the lady. The younger man couldn't help but hope that something had drastically changed in the relationship between the couple that would allow him an occasion to press his own suit.

Adriana was immensely thankful that Roger hadn't taken it upon himself to come to the wedding. Although that would have been at the very height of audacity even for him, since he hadn't been invited, he had not been above making unexpected appearances when it met his mood. If he had been upset after she had collided with Colton at Randwulf Manor, then he'd certainly have been riled at the attention she was presently receiving. Her admirers stood in a wide circle round about her and did indeed prove themselves a jovial group copiously inclined to rag each other about their limited chances with the lady.

"My lords, your pardon," the young knight, Guy Dalton, begged with a broad grin, claiming the consideration of both Riordan Kendrick and Stuart Burke. "I've heard it said that the man who stands nearest to Lady Adriana is usually the first to fall from her favor. If I were either one of you, I'd allow someone else to stand there in your stead."

Stuart hooted at the younger man's ploy. "You, I suppose?"

Lord Harcourt lifted a well-defined brow as his mouth curved in a lazy, self-assured grin. "If it's all the same to you, Sir Guy, I'll take my chances here at the lady's side. But, please, continue salivating in hopeful expectation of that event. One of us may yet change his mind . . . in my case when the netherworld freezes over."

An exaggerated sigh of lament came from Sir Guy. "Well, as a friend I've done my best to advise you both. Go ahead and ignore my warning. Little do I care if the lady tosses you both aside for one perchance as wise and handsome as myself."

Not the least bit remorseful, Riordan chuckled at the other's attempt. "You're a friend indeed, Sir Guy, but I suspect there is that tendency in any man to search out opportunities to benefit himself, even if it means usurping a better man's advantage."

"Please, please," Adriana begged through her laughter. "Desist with this bickering or I shall have to send the lot of you out of my sight."

She swept her gaze around to encompass the entire circle of admirers in her threat, but, upon coming to a breach in their ranks, was shocked to meet through that narrow space the unwavering stare of Colton Wyndham, who stood a short distance away with a hand braced against the stout trunk of a tree.

Garbed in dapper attire that would've come close to putting the bridegroom to shame, the Marquess of Randwulf was the very quintessence of a wealthy aristocrat. Percy had joined him underneath the spreading canopy of limbs and newly reddening leaves, but was chattering incessantly on, glancing hither and yon at this guest or that, completely oblivious to the fact that his companion's gaze was focused entirely upon her. Beneath the brim of an elegant, gray silk top hat, the shadowed gray eyes seemed to glow with a radiance of their own as they fed upon her every word, gesture, or smile.

The intensity of her observer's stare held Adriana's gaze firmly ensnared until his eyes lowered in a leisurely feast that consumed nearly every hollow and curve she possessed. Of a sudden, her robin's-egg-blue woolen frock seemed meager defense indeed from those burning, ravaging eyes that seemed to set her very nipples aflame. At no time before, while fully clothed, had she felt so completely naked beneath a man's stare. The fact that he knew exactly what she looked like underneath her garments only seemed to solidify the evocative sensations. She had never experienced the like of such delicious heat pulsating within her secret parts or felt the exact degree of warmth infusing her cheeks, her throat, her brow, her very being. If it were possible for a maid to be ravished from a distance, then Adriana was sure she had just been stripped, fondled, and deflowered all within the mind of the man who stared at her so intently.

Good heavens! The words, though unspoken, seemed to blare with deafening volume through her mind.

Shaken to the core of her being by the desire smoldering in those dark gray eyes, she turned aside to beg leave of Stuart Burke and then faced Riordan Kendrick, making some incoherent excuse about feeling a bit chilled *(as if that could've been even remotely possible)* and wanting to go to her father's carriage. Gallantly the handsome marquess presented his arm and tossed a victorious smirk over his shoulder at the other gentlemen who voiced protests copiously punctuated with jocular threats upon her escort. After handing her into the conveyance, it was Riordan's wont to stand at the open door of the landau and chat with her, which, of course, encouraged the other gentlemen to flock around. Adriana hardly expected Colton to move to another vantage point, but that's exactly what he did, strolling to the front of the church where he could view her without restriction through the throng. There was nowhere else she could go to escape his vigil, and until the bride and groom came out, it remained as constant as the sun in the sky.

The wedding breakfast was an achievement worthy of praise, or so Melora reiterated before being assisted by her groom into a chair at the head table. Adriana, however, had cause to wonder who had switched the place cards in the seating of family and guests, for she soon found herself shoulder to shoulder with Colton Wyndham. It didn't help her composure one whit to realize he splintered her poise as efficiently as he had earlier that morning. A wan smile was the best she could manage beneath the confident grin he bestowed on her.

"Your pardon, my lord, but I do believe that place is reserved for my aunt," she informed him, willing to send him anywhere in the world rather than submit herself to his close scrutiny.

"On the contrary, Adriana, I think you're the one mistaken." Reaching across the table, Colton flicked the card from its silver holder and handed it to her. "I should be able to recognize my own name after all this time." Challenging her with gleaming eyes, he questioned, "Were you not expecting me?"

"Well, no, I wasn't," she admitted, wanting to pin the blame for his proximity on Melora. It would be just like her sister to do such a thing, especially after Adriana had made certain that Colton would be seated with his uncle and mother.

The Marquess of Randwulf pulled his chair closer to the table, obviously intent upon staying where he was. "I suppose after being surrounded by a legion of men you must find it boring to have to limit your consideration to merely one, but I shall try not to belabor that fact overmuch, however slighted I felt at the time for not being permitted to join them."

Her chin sagged in astonishment at his outrageous charge. "I never said you had to keep your distance from me."

The shining gray orbs challenged her above a lazy smile. "Oh? Perhaps I misunderstood. You did say our courtship was to begin *after* the Autumn Ball, did you not? Was I not to keep my distance until then?"

She sighed heavily, convinced that he was not much changed from that puckish rascal who many times as a youth had teased her unmercifully until she had been tempted to scream, and scream she had, *then*. However, it would hardly be suitable for her to do so at her sister's wedding. "I was merely talking about the courtship itself, my lord. After granting Roger's request to be allowed to attend the ball, it seemed impolite to retract my permission."

"Have you often been of a mind to yield the lad such favors?"

Considering that Roger would've likely taken it upon himself to intrude into the affair, she had thought it would be less vexing to her family and to herself if she just granted him permission to come. She couldn't count how many times since arriving at that decision that she had wanted to kick herself, especially since Colton's return. Roger wouldn't take her intended suitor's presence in stride.

"You have quite a following of admirers," Colton remonstrated as his eyes skimmed over the bachelors who had been among her audience earlier that morning. They were now eyeing him enviously and with keen attention. Smiling, he nodded a greeting to Stuart and then noted that the man wasn't nearly as cheery as he had seemed outside the church. "Are you sure you haven't extended any of your aficionados comparable invitations?"

"*Nooo*," Adriana moaned impatiently. "You're making much ado about nothing."

He cocked a brow dubiously. "Well, I wouldn't necessarily say a score and three men are naught to worry about, especially when every one of them seemed to be drooling in his eagerness to have you. A lone man has to be careful against such odds."

"There didn't seem to be that many," Adriana stated, wondering if he had exaggerated.

"What? You didn't bother to count them for yourself?" Colton laughed. He had to admire her for that; most women would have considered such a number a testament of their appeal and be wont to boast of it. "I can vouch for my ability to count, Adriana. There were indeed that many."

She tossed her head, miffed that he would do such a thing. "Well, you needn't concern yourself about any of them, my lord. I intend to fulfill my part of the agreement whether you do or not."

"Oh, I intend to, Adriana," he averred warmly. "After all, 'tis my father's wish that I consider you as my future wife."

"Why? You really don't have any interest in adhering to the contract beyond the length of the courtship, do you?" She laughed sharply. "I'd really be surprised if you did."

"Let me just say that I shall enjoy the opportunity to mull over that matter at my leisure while courting you. I have that right, do I not?"

"Yes, you do," Adriana reluctantly acknowledged, certain he would do so only because it suited him. Beyond the moment wherein he'd lose patience with it all, there would be no guarantee.

She glanced around, wondering what had happened to her kin and finally espied Aunt Tilly sitting beside Alistair Dermot. At the moment, the woman was involved in an animated conversation with the man, but it wasn't long before Tilly glanced around, as if sensing her niece's stare. Lifting a small name card from the holder in front of her, Tilly shrugged rather impishly as she smiled at Adriana and began to fan herself with it.

Adriana understood all too clearly then. Her aunt had been the culprit who had revised the seating arrangement in at least one small area. Reluctant though she was to apologize, Adriana leaned toward Colton. "I fear I jumped too quickly to my own conclusions, my lord. For that I must apologize. I believe I now know the one who exchanged the name cards." She swept a slender hand gracefully about to bring his consideration to bear upon the older woman. "'Twould seem Aunt Tilly has discovered your uncle. He *is* a very handsome man, and of course, she *is* a widow."

Colton glanced around to find the older woman smiling at them rather guiltily. He winked at her and grinned, winning a vivacious laugh. Her light-hearted mirth drew Alistair's notice, and as the man presented an inquiry, Tilly indicated the younger couple. The elder exchanged smiling nods with his nephew and then bestowed his curious attention upon the beauty sitting at Colton's side. He grinned broadly and lifted his wineglass in salute to his kin, silently commending him on his good taste in women.

"Your uncle seems fairly pleased with himself," Adriana commented, missing the whole gist of the exchange. "Of course, he has much to be proud of, considering you became a national hero after he deemed you worthy of his support."

"I believe he was applauding your beauty, my dear," Colton corrected. "He obviously has cause to think you're my intended."

Adriana was clearly astonished. "Oh, but your mother . . . She wouldn't say anything about the agreement, would she?"

"Perhaps the culprit isn't so much my mother as my sister." Noticing an airy ringlet dangling against Adriana's nape, he stretched forth a hand and rubbed the coiling strand admiringly between his thumb and forefinger. "She's convinced that someday you'll become my wife."

Adriana realized her insides were melting again, as they always did when he touched her in some manner. Sloe eyes lifted from underneath a fringe of jet lashes to meet the softly shining gray orbs, and for what seemed an eternity in the heartbeat of a moment, their gazes gently melded before his own descended to caress her lips yearningly. The unexpected craving to snuggle her cheek within the palm of his hand seemed very strange indeed to Adriana, yet it was no more odd than sensing his lordship was battling a desire to kiss her. Softly she breathed, "I shall have to talk with your sister about her wagging tongue."

Iᴛ seemed nothing short of a century since Adriana had sat beside Colton at the wedding breakfast, when in reality it had only been three weeks. The Autumn Ball was in progress, yet she had delayed joining the guests. Instead, feeling as restless as a caged cat, she prowled through the upper halls of her family's Tudor mansion. It certainly didn't elevate her mood knowing that sometime within the next several hours she'd have to tell Roger that he would have to halt his visits to the manor and to stop following her about hither and yon. Aware of how diligently the apprentice had sought to win approval as well as permission to marry her, she dreaded being the bearer of such news. She just hoped he wouldn't create a scene.

Had she given serious thought to the consequences of yielding to his first unannounced visit to Wakefield Manor months ago, she'd have turned him away right then and there, refusing his gifts of flowers and a second book of sonnets. Yet she had been reluctant to be so harsh, for it had been painfully obvious at the time that the young man was lonely and feeling out of kilter with the small populace of Bradford on Avon. But then, she'd have probably done him an enormous favor by doing so, for he would've then been forced to make friends among the citizens of that small town. And she would've certainly saved herself the anguish she was now suffering, for his first visit had led to another . . . and then another . . . and soon he was popping in unannounced on a regular basis, not only at Wakefield Manor, but at Randwulf, too.

She wished now that she would've allowed her father to tell Roger that he could no longer call upon her. Her parent, in his own efficient way, would've dealt with the matter and suffered no qualms while doing so, but she had been of the belief that if the news came from her, the apprentice could deal with it better. Now, here she was, coping with an incongruous feeling that she'd be kicking a poor, stray dog that had been starving all his life for a few crumbs of kindness and affection. Yet, as arduous as the task promised to be, she saw no help for it. She was committed by contract to another, and as much as Roger was aware of that fact, he seemed reluctant to leave her alone.

Adriana straightened her spine and rolled her shoulders to ease the prickling that in the last hour had intensified in her nape. No matter how difficult the deed looming ahead of her, there was no escaping it. Procrastinating wouldn't help; it would still be confronting her until she spoke her peace. Perhaps her tensions would even ease some slight degree once she put the task behind her. She could only hope so, for she felt terribly beleaguered now.

Lightly skimming a slender hand over the darkly ornate balustrade, Adriana made her descent of the stairs as her eyes followed the undulating rhythm of her bejeweled gown that flowed in shimmering, glistening waves about her long legs. Nothing of what she saw penetrated her thoughts, for her mind moved like a disembodied wraith through everything but the quandaries she faced. Would this present anguish she was suffering be remembered beyond the onset of Colton Wyndham's courtship? Or would the self-willed man give her cause to regret she had ever gone to such onerous lengths for him?

Once again, her mind ranged through the evocative memories left over from the wedding day of her sister. Outside the church the translucent gray eyes had all but consumed her. Then, later that morning, when she had been sitting beside Colton at the breakfast feast, she had felt like dissolving beneath the warmth of his gaze.

It certainly didn't help her composure now to feel a resurgence of the various sensations that had swept over her that day. Though sorely lacking experience in the realm of desire, instinct assured her the wanton yearnings gnawing at the pit of her being were nothing less than cravings that Colton Wyndham had elicited with his slow, lustful perusal. The fact that those feelings were just as potent today completely frustrated her efforts to thrust him from her mind.

Oh, why is he the one I yearn for? her mind railed in anguish.

Shaken by the onslaught of unquenchable desires, Adriana sought to devote her thoughts entirely to how she should go about dismissing Roger from her life. That quandary was as effective as being doused with a bucket of icy water. It chilled her to the bone.

Upon facing the arched, doubled doors leading into the ballroom, Adriana took a deep breath to fortify herself for the challenge ahead as she moved toward the opening, but she was immediately halted by a guest emerging in some haste. Indeed, his alacrity gave her cause to wonder if his coattails were ablaze. The anxious glance he cast over his shoulder made her wonder who or what followed close behind. If his costly garments perhaps denoted the source of his concern, then she'd be inclined to think his tailors were scurrying after him in an attempt to collect his fee. It was certainly not to the benefit of the wastrel that similarly disparaging musings often came to her the very instant she recognized Lord Latham Harrell.

Although Latham's looks were nothing beyond tolerable, his tall, lean form did lend credit to his fashionable attire, but that hardly endeared the pompous man to those who really knew him. Still, the high-minded arrogance he once exhibited at Sedgwick's funeral had apparently flagged, and she could understand why, considering Colton had dashed the man's hopes by coming home and making his intentions clear to all. No longer optimistic about gaining wealth and the marquessate, Latham now seemed as nervous as a rabbit with a fox on its trail.

Upon espying her, the man seemed to forget his reasons for hurrying. Collecting his composure, he swept an arm before him in a gallant bow. "My dear Lady Adriana, you are the very one I've been hoping to see. Indeed, it has been my ongoing desire ever since I saw you at your sister's wedding several weeks ago."

"Really?" Adriana was curious to know what the man could possibly want of her, but the answer came readily enough to her mind. Her dowry! Now that he had no expectations of gaining the marquessate, he would no doubt be required to marry for wealth to support his extravagance.

Latham all but leered at her as he whisked a pale knuckle beneath the curled ends of his thin mustache. An unusual warmth ignited his hazel eyes as they ranged the length of her, causing her to wonder if he imagined her without undergarments under the numerous layers of gossamer silk that had gone into the making of her gown. Had that truly been the case, only a diviner of the thoroughly hidden would have been able to discern evidence of her pale body beneath the uppermost shift of diaphanous silk, for tiny, dangling crystals thoroughly encrusted it. The shimmering adornments, of the same midnight turquoise hue as the fragile cloth upon which they were attached, served as a dazzling armor of defense, yet in a most delicate way.

Latham's gaze reversed itself and seemed inclined to pause overlong on the enticing fullness above her décolletage. From there, it seemed to take a colossal effort for him to drag his gaze higher still. Finally, he glanced aside, as if to reclaim his composure, and loudly cleared his throat before bestowing an ingratiating smile upon her. "I was beginning to fear I'd never find you without your consort of suitors, Lady Adriana. I finally despaired of getting close to you at your sister's wedding, for they surrounded you like an impenetrable rampart. Every eligible bachelor from London to Bath must have been there, except, of course, my cousin. Don't know what *he* was looking at, but after spending so many years in the military, Colton probably got too comfortable with camp-followers to know what *real* beauty is. You know how those officers are wont to dally here and there in their leisure. . . ."

"No, actually I'm afraid I don't," Adriana replied, gritting out a smile. It nettled her sorely that he should seek to besmirch his cousin's character when his own reputation was far from exemplary. Though he seemed entirely in good health, he had begged some dreadful fainting malady to avoid offering his services in defense of his country and then, barely a month after Lord Sedgwick had passed on, had borrowed funds against his anticipated marquessate in order to placate an outraged father whose previously innocent daughter he had gotten with child.

Latham seemed momentarily befuddled by her lack of imagination. "Well, never mind, my dear. My observations wouldn't be fit for sweet, innocent ears like yours." His eyes passed over her again, and as if encouraged by her failure to retreat, he took a step toward her. The huskiness of his voice seemed to convey a warming desire. "I say, Lady Adriana, you are truly the most ravishing creature I've ever seen, and you do yourself such good service by dressing to the occasion. Your gown at the wedding was especially charming, but, my dear, let me say you've clearly outdone yourself this evening. Never in all my life have I seen a more stunning gown *or* a maid more ravishingly beautiful."

"You flatter me, Lord Latham," she accused, boldly using his first name as he had hers. After all, as Colton's cousin, he had visited Randwulf Manor fairly frequently as a lad when she had merely been a toddler clinging to her father's trousers. The man was older than Colton by a trio of years, but as much as he made the pretense, Latham lacked the handsomely refined good looks and polished manners that his younger cousin possessed in abundance.

"You do have quite a following of admirers, my dear, so many I found my head spinning like a whipping top when I saw them gathered around you that day outside the church. Why, even that duke's son . . . what's his name . . . was among them."

Adriana retreated as he advanced another step, preferring to yield him the floor rather than to risk contact. "I believe you're referring to his lordship, Riordan Kendrick, the Marquess of Harcourt."

"Quite a handsome fellow, Lord Riordan. Immensely wealthy, from what I understand, and of course, being the only son, he shall inherit the duchy one day, once his father expires, that is. Has he been courting you long?"

Suspicious of Latham's reasons for addressing his attention to *any* matter, Adriana was somewhat hesitant about answering, yet could not fathom what harm stating the truth would do. "Lord Harcourt hasn't really been courting me. He has merely been visiting Wakefield Manor."

Latham chuckled and dabbed a lace handkerchief to a corner of his mouth, giving Adriana cause to wonder if he were drooling. "Well, my dear girl, it doesn't take much imagination for a body to figure out *why* he would, what with such sublime perfection housed here. I'm somewhat surprised he hasn't obtained a nuptial agreement from Lord Standish. He *has* tried, has he not?"

Adriana hoped her face didn't appear as rigid as it felt. "Of late, my father has been extremely busy addressing other matters. Taking into account that I'm the last of his daughters, he'll probably want to relax for a while before lending his attention to my future. I wouldn't be at all surprised if he doesn't get around to pondering those matters for several months." *At least until Colton Wyndham makes up his mind!*

"Of course! Of course!" Latham chortled. "Delightful news for tardy suitors, eh what?" He raised an eyebrow meaningfully and leaned forward in a confidential manner. His warm, husky whisper clearly conveyed his rising aspirations. "Such news, my dear lady, gives me occasion to hope that I'm not too late in presenting my petition."

Adriana came near to rolling her eyes in disbelief, but she subdued the urge as Latham glanced first to his left and then to his right, as if searching the area for listening ears. She could only wonder what secret he was about to reveal.

Bestowing his attention upon her once again, he smiled cajolingly. "My lady, I do implore you to save a dance for me later on. I'd ask for one now, but barely a moment ago, I was forced to make my excuses to that Carvell fellow, Lord Mansford, who asked me quite boldly to dance with his daughter, a portly young miss who's obviously in a dither to find a husband. Rather than be caught in a lie, I thought to hide out for the duration of the tune. 'Twill be a wonder indeed if Lady Berenice finds a husband. She's pretty enough, to be sure, but I fear her bulk would simply overpower me." His eyes swept over Adriana and began to glow warmly with avid admiration. "I do so enjoy much daintier forms, which, without a doubt, yours takes precedence."

Had Latham been a man to admire, Adriana would've encouraged him to seriously consider Berenice Carvell, in her opinion a very sweet young woman. Unfortunately, her sire seized upon every opportunity to find her a husband and, by so doing, not only embarrassed his daughter, but forced the bachelors he cornered into awkward positions.

Considering the rumors of indebtedness in which Latham had become mired, Adriana couldn't resist taunting him. "Lady Berenice does indeed have a pretty face, my lord, and although a bit bulky as you say, I'm inclined to disagree with you about her chances of being wed, so much so that I'm willing to predict that she'll be married to a fine, upstanding young gentleman ere long."

Arching a brow with rampant skepticism, Latham peered down his long nose at her as he smirked with amused condescension. "Are you gullible enough to believe in miracles, my lady?"

Adriana's hackles rose at his patronizing question, but she managed a musical laugh. "Well, considering Lady Berenice's dowry would choke the wits of a sultan, I'm sure such miracles are well within the realm of possibility. A man may indeed marry Berenice for her dowry, but in time he'll come to discover that he has gained for himself a jewel far more valuable than her father's wealth. Of that I'm confident."

Latham's brows jutted sharply upward in amazement. "I never dreamt her sire was so affluent."

Adriana could almost envision the greedy workings of the man's mind as she cut her eyes askance at him. "Oh, indeed, and considering his eagerness to see her wed, I suffer little doubt that Lord Mansford will prove extremely generous to her bridegroom."

Latham wandered off in something of a daze, leaving Adriana pondering the odds of seeing him dancing with Berenice ere the evening was out. She'd definitely have to warn her friend to be on her guard against the fortune seeker.

Heaving a forlorn sigh as she addressed herself once again to her own predicament, Adriana slipped into the ballroom and took refuge within the shadows shrouding the entrance as she glanced around. Across the room, Jaclyn and her husband, Sir Thornton Godric, stood chatting with her parents, Philana, and Aunt Tilly. Melora and Harold still seemed totally entranced with each other as they waltzed together. Just beyond them, Perceval swept Samantha around the dance floor in wide, graceful rotations. Though married two years, the couple seemed as smitten with each other as the recently wedded pair. There was no question that Samantha greatly esteemed the choice her sire had made for her. To some degree their love for one another rallied Adriana's prospects for herself. She just hoped Sedgwick Wyndham had been equally insightful matching her to his son.

With curiosity, Adriana scanned the faces of the dancing couples in search of the man who, of late, had become the focal point of her musings. If anyone had told her several months ago that she'd be fantasizing about Colton Wyndham at this juncture in her life, she'd have called him daft. But time had a way of putting one's considerations to naught. Her infatuation with the man had deepened by significant degrees since his return. She could only wonder when he'd actually make his entrance. No doubt his appearance would be favorable. The man's penchant for dapper attire left her wondering what exceptional formal apparel he'd be wearing this evening; but then, on his tall, broad-shouldered form, rags would seem like a king's raiment.

Adriana nearly choked in surprise as she finally espied the tall, handsomely garbed Marquess of Randwulf. It was not so much the sight of him that took her aback, but the fact that he was waltzing Felicity Fairchild around the ballroom.

Cheeks burning with humiliation, Adriana pressed back against a French door, hoping the two hadn't seen her. Her moment of obscurity allowed her to watch the retired colonel at some length. From all appearances, he had made remarkable progress in recovering a graceful stride. She could only imagine the grueling extent of his determination to exercise his limb in his quest to overcome his lingering lameness. She remembered the way his wound had looked the night of his return. The sight of it had caused her to consider the pain he had suffered, which had likely been intensified by its tainted condition. It came to her with a fair bit of surprise that at Melora's wedding three weeks earlier he had been without his cane, and yet he had still been hampered by a limp. Now, however, his smooth strides seemed to bear out the successful degree of progress he had made, for his movements seemed as fluid as rippling water flowing over a submerged stone.

Adriana started suddenly when a distant cousin, calling to her from the dance floor, shattered her anonymity.

"Adriana, why aren't you dancing?"

She groaned within herself, wanting to crawl into the nearest cubby. Out of the corner of her eye, she saw Colton glance about, evidently in search of her. When he espied her, he swept Felicity around the ballroom in wide circles, bringing them within close proximity of where she stood.

The blackguard! How could he? Adriana fumed peevishly, still irked that he had all but wheedled a concession from her that had allowed him freedom to direct his manly consideration elsewhere during the ball. His choice of ladies *just happened to be* Felicity Fairchild, a woman who, since her introduction to the man, had been lauding his praises with bubbling enthusiasm to any and all who would listen.

The almost glowing radiance of the fair-haired beauty gowned in a pale, yellow satin caused Adriana to wonder somewhat morosely how he would rate the miller's granddaughter in contrast to one whose eyes and hair were as dark as ebon. A sharp reminder of the insults he had once heaped upon the thin little girl who had adored him seemed to affirm the probability that she wouldn't measure up very well at all.

"She definitely wants him," Adriana muttered petulantly as she considered the blonde's smiling delight.

"Who?" a voice intruded from nearby.

Surprised at having been caught thinking aloud, Adriana turned promptly about to find Roger standing behind her. Although words seemed momentarily lodged in her throat, they came free as she lashed out at him in vexation. "My goodness, Roger, you nearly startled me to death!"

He chuckled, laying the cause of her annoyance to his own tardiness. Heartened by what seemed an eagerness to see him, he readily apologized. "I'm sorry, my lady, but it seemed as if you were caught in a world of your own making. I really had no idea that I would alarm you." He glanced around as several couples danced past, none of whom was even closely reminiscent of the pair Adriana had been eyeing. "Were you referring to anyone in particular?"

"A distant acquaintance, that is all." *Growing more distant by the hour!* Adriana mentally jeered as she caught a glimpse of the very winsome Miss Felicity fluttering long lashes at her tall, handsome partner.

Well, there was no help for it, Adriana decided. As much as she had intended to inform Roger at the conclusion of the ball that she could no longer permit him to follow her about, she feared the closer the end came, the more she'd lose her nerve. Better to be done with it, she thought. Besides, the sooner she made her announcement to Roger, the sooner her rival would find herself without the attentions of his lordship . . . even if it turned out to be nothing more than a three-month interval.

No more delays, Adriana thought, and plunged headlong into the task she had set for herself. "Roger, I have a matter of grave importance to discuss with you. Perhaps we should go into the hall where we can talk together privately."

The young man raised a brow skeptically. "Grave importance? You mean more important than dancing with you?" He forced a laugh, though it proved a frail attempt at best. He could imagine what kind of statement she intended to make now that the marquess was home. Frankly, he didn't want to hear it. In fact, his father's suggestion was beginning to appeal to him as his only chance for claiming the lady for his own. "I think not, my lady, for to be sure, the idea of holding you in my arms has dwelt on my mind almost constantly these past weeks. 'Twas rare indeed that you allowed me to touch your hand, much less take you in my arms. I don't want to lose the opportunity to do so. I've missed you more in these past weeks than common words can adequately justify. Whenever I'd come to Wakefield Manor and ask to see you, I was informed by your butler that you were either out or indisposed. I was beginning to suspect that you were deliberately avoiding me."

"I'm sorry, Roger, but I've been very busy with other things." It was certainly no lie, merely an exaggeration. But then, after Colton's return, the man should've realized circumstances would change. "Seriously, Roger, I have something important to discuss with you. . . ."

"Later." Claiming her hand, he drew her toward the dance floor. "After we finish dancing."

Adriana pulled back, trying to free herself, but he refused to let her go, and with a mental sigh of resignation, she conceded, not wishing to cause a stir. After tonight, she'd likely never see the man again. She could at least allow him a dance or two. "All right, Roger, but we *do* have to talk. Delaying it won't make it go away."

All around the hall, plumed and beribboned heads came together in a frantic rush as ladies of middling and advancing years craned their flabby, scrawny, or wrinkled necks in an effort to see the miller's son leading Lord Gyles's youngest daughter onto the dance floor. 'Twas a rare occurrence indeed that a man of low estate was granted such a favor from a nobleman's daughter, and the event sparked what could have easily been likened to a feeding frenzy among the busybodies who devoured every comment eagerly whispered behind fluttering fans. Laying bejeweled fingers aside their ears, they leaned forward to catch every juicy morsel, relishing each enticing tidbit as if they hadn't sampled the like of such sweetmeat for months on end. Then they bustled excitedly about to spread the news further, bumping into each other in their haste, weaving in and out, dispersing and converging in their eagerness to carry the news hither and yon. Had any been observing from a high summit, they'd have probably likened the biddies to a mass of plump melons rolling helter-skelter down a steep ravine.

Past and present suitors noticed the ruckus and, in some curiosity, leaned near to hear the reason for the feverish dither. While the rejected sneered and offered rude comments about the lady's choice for a partner, the hopeful were greatly encouraged by the fact that Lady Adriana had finally joined the festivities.

It didn't take that one long to notice the excited pother erupting around the ballroom. Adriana had been expecting the gossipmongers to size her up now that she was the only unattached female left in the Sutton family. After all, when a man had three daughters and no sons, there was always a fair amount of speculation whether he'd be successful in making good matches for all of them or if any would be left without a husband. Adriana just hadn't considered that she'd stir up such a commotion. Having reached the age of twenty and two years and with no apparent betrothal in the offing, she could well imagine they had already considered her destined for spinsterhood.

A fate worse than death, some would lament. In droning tones, others would offer questionable advice as to what could remedy her plight. At the very least, a few would be inclined to suggest that it was a far better fate to wed a miller's son than marry not at all, *as if* she were *that* anxious to wed and had no other choice.

Looking back upon her couturier's last visit prior to Melora's departure, Adriana now wished she hadn't yielded to their suggestion that a spe-

cial gown be made for her so as to leave no doubt that she was being heralded as the last available daughter in the family. The dressmaker had
seemed excited about designing something unique for one whom she had
described as tall, slender, and elegant enough to wear a feed sack and make
it look divine. Though Adriana had never considered herself as one lacking imagination, she hadn't foreseen the couturier's final version, delivered
to her chamber door this very day, as being a garment that would exaggerate her every movement with a glittering array of dancing lights. Beneath
the soft glow of the candles that lit scores of sconces and weighty chan-
deliers, the little crystals made it seem as if fireflies swarmed all around
her. Still, remarks concerning its brilliance would probably seem mild
compared to what some harpies would say about her décolletage.
Although modest in comparison to the apparel of several young ladies,
including the lovely Miss Fairchild, who showed more but had somewhat
less to flaunt, it was definitely not what Adriana was accustomed to wearing even on formal occasions, for it revealed the upper curves of her
rounded bosom rather generously. Truly, had she anticipated the possibility that she'd be at the mercy of malicious biddies, she'd have definitely
chosen a less conspicuous gown to wear, perhaps something that would
have disguised her altogether. Then everyone would've been wondering
who she was rather than her possible fate as a spinster.

Upon facing Roger, Adriana felt as if every eye in the ballroom was
now fastened on them. The apprentice enfolded her slender hand within
his and seemed to hesitate before laying his other behind her shoulder.
Adriana perceived the reason when she noticed the direction of his gaze,
for it seemed momentarily fastened on her breasts, giving her additional
cause to regret that she had *ever* yielded to the advice of others.

Much to her relief, Roger's inspection was cut short by the simple fact
that he was expected to dance. His head lifted, and his brows gathered as
he concentrated on the task of waltzing her around the room. He did so
woodenly, as if it were something he had recently learned and wasn't too
sure about. A moment later, the metal rim lining his sole scraped across
her satin slipper, causing such intense pain that Adriana's mouth flew open
in sharp surprise. With a seriously strained facade of poise, she gritted out
a smile just as Samantha and Perceval swept near.

Behind them came Lord Harcourt whose gallantry readily displayed
itself as he danced past with Berenice. Although tutored by an instructor,
the young lady seemed extremely nervous dancing with the handsome gen-

tleman and repeatedly trod upon his shiny black shoes. His dark eyes met Adriana's briefly, and in his pained smile she was wont to find some humor in spite of the empathy she felt for him. She was convinced she was experiencing a similar torment and could imagine her own gritted smile conveyed as much distress as she strove to force the corners of her lips upward.

Roger's face had taken on a hue reminiscent of scarlet. He definitely felt out of his element amid all the elegantly garbed gentlemen who swept their partners around the ballroom with graceful ease. Even the previously lame Lord Colton had far more grace than he had been able to master since the instructor began the task of teaching him just where to place his seemingly oversized feet in a waltz and other dances. "I'm truly sorry, my lady. I was never trained in any of the social graces. It has only been within the last month that I've had the opportunity to learn." He looked rather sheepish. "I guess I need more practice. Would you prefer to sit?"

"If you wouldn't mind," Adriana replied and tried to ease his chagrin. "But you needn't fret about your dancing, Roger. Not everyone can learn when he's young. In time, you'll become more proficient."

His expression brightened. "I'll try very hard not to make another mistake if you'd grant me another dance now. I do need the practice, and dancing with you is definitely preferable to the instructor."

"Later," she said, wondering if her feet would ever be the same. "Right now, I need to talk with you."

Roger let out a muted, agonized groan. "Not now. Come dance with me instead."

"A rest would likely do you good, Roger," she replied forthrightly. "You were dancing on my toes more in the last few moments than you were when you first began. Perhaps some wine would help relax you."

"Would you care to join me in a glass?"

Wine was the last thing she needed to muddle her brain. She had to remain alert to avoid offending the man if at all possible. "Perhaps later."

"I'm reluctant to leave you," he insisted.

Adriana sighed, frustrated by the clinging tenacity of the man. "Then perhaps we can have our discussion now."

His face darkened, and as his eyes moved about the room, he seemed to sulk as he glowered at no one in particular. "I know what you're going to say, and I don't want to hear it."

"Then perhaps I don't need to waste my breath since you've acquired such keenly intuitive powers."

Of a sudden, Adriana felt a presence behind her. Then she saw Roger's eyes flare, indicating trouble ahead. She was about to turn when a request came over her shoulder.

"May I have this dance, my lady?"

Smiling in relief as she recognized Lord Harcourt's deep voice, Adriana faced the handsome gentleman. "Of course, my lord."

She turned back to excuse herself from the apprentice, but his hotly glowering eyes warned her that he was none too pleased by her eagerness to dance with another after she had just refused him. In a low whisper, she chided, "I never promised to spend the entire evening with you, Roger. I only granted you permission to come. Lord Harcourt is not only a guest of ours, but he happens to be a close friend of mine, and I shan't let your ominous scowls keep me from dancing with him . . . or, for that matter, any other man. Kindly refrain from using such tactics or I shall ask you to leave forthwith."

Roger's lean jowls tensed and flexed as he retreated several steps, then he swept his hand before him and bowed deeply as if doing obeisance before a queen. "My lady."

Fretting that she had been too harsh in chiding him, Adriana watched Roger plow his way through the guests in a most ungentlemanly fashion, causing people to turn and stare after him in astonished wonder after being shouldered roughly aside by the man.

"Never mind the fellow, Lady Adriana," Riordan urged in a low murmur, leaning near her shoulder again. "Obviously he fears his grasp on you is too frail and would hold you prisoner if he could."

Adriana faced the marquess with an uneasy smile. "I didn't realize he'd be so upset. I'm sorry you had to witness that."

" 'Twas the lad's fault for imagining that he could monopolize your time tonight. If he did indeed think you'd devote the entire evening solely to him, then I, for one, resent his audacity. The sad truth is that I'm not alone in desiring as much of your time as you're willing to spare, and though I'd like to dispense with all your smitten admirers so I can have you entirely to myself, I suppose, in lieu of that, I shall have to share your company, at least until a more permanent arrangement comes about."

Smiling at his humor, Adriana yielded her hand to him. "Then lead me out onto the dance floor, gallant lord. Only there will we be safe from intrusions."

"Your wish is my command, my lady," he avowed, drawing her hand to his lips for a kiss.

Riordan Kendrick was as light on his feet as he was easy to look upon, Adriana mentally reaffirmed after several turns about the ballroom. Of all the suitors who had previously been vying for her hand, he had been the only one who had appealed to her. In the past, she had enjoyed dancing with him more than any other. Even now, she found herself relaxing in his arms, but her heart was not the same as it had been even two months ago. If nothing else, she had to be true to herself by admitting that Colton Wyndham had stolen a march on everyone. Yet, Colton really didn't want her; he was merely going through the motions of addressing himself to their courtship for the sake of his mother and the contract his father had proposed.

"You're looking as radiant as the very stars overhead, Adriana," Riordan murmured, his dark eyes warmly devouring her face as he awaited her reaction to his familiar address.

"And you, Riordan, are as kind as always."

The flash of white teeth against his sun-bronzed visage was no less than dazzling as he accepted the lady's response as an invitation to discontinue the formality that had heretofore existed between them. "If I'm always on my best behavior around you, Adriana, 'tis merely that I'm hoping to convince your father that I'm a worthy prospect for a son-in-law. Lord Gyles said he had to consider other proposals before he could answer my petition for your hand. Should he respond in the affirmative, which is truly my heartfelt desire, I must warn you of my wayward side. I'm a disreputable rogue at heart."

Adriana tossed her head in disbelief as she chuckled. "Aye, I saw how disreputable you were when you danced with Lady Berenice. So much so I'm wont to contradict you and call you a gallant gentleman."

"She has a very pretty face."

"She does indeed," Adriana agreed, having long been of the belief that the only reason Berenice indulged herself with food was out of anxiety. Sadly enough, when she was around her widowed father, who was not only handsome but also fairly persnickety about everything being as close to the state of perfection as possible, she was tense most of the time, fretting that she'd never be able to live up to his expectations. The elder seemed blind to all the exceptional qualities his daughter had; he saw her as flawed merely because she was plump and, for that reason, was wont to malign her. "If the right man came along, he could probably do wonders for her."

Riordan slanted a dubious grin down upon Adriana. "Do you have anyone in particular in mind?"

She smiled, realizing the nobleman had read too much into her casual comment. "You would be the right man in any case, my lord. In spite of your wealth and incredible good looks, you're as chivalrous as anyone I've ever known."

Encouraged by her words, he urged with more fervor, "Then persuade your father to favor my request above all others posthaste and let me commence courting you with all sincerity."

"I'm afraid I cannot do that, Riordan," she replied and knew of a sudden that if she confided in him, her secret would be safe. "A contract committing me to another was signed years ago when I was but a child. Should that agreement be dissolved after a three-month courtship, then I shall certainly ask my father to consider your petition."

"We could be happy together," he cajoled.

Her shining eyes swept his handsome face. "That may well be true, Riordan, but I am honor-bound to the agreement my father signed."

A mischievous gleam lit his dark eyes. "Was this agreement put down on parchment that can be easily torched . . . or was it set in stone?"

His humor evoked another smile. "Both, I'm afraid, at least until the gentleman makes up his mind."

Riordan looked astounded. "You mean the man isn't sure he wants you? Is he a raving lunatic?"

"I'm afraid he didn't appreciate his father arranging the matter without consulting him."

"Can he not see the precious gem that has been offered him?"

Greatly heartened by the man's praise, Adriana smoothed his lapel. "You make me feel as if I were a queen, Riordan. No woman could do better than to marry you."

"Then come away with me tonight, Adriana, and pledge me your troth in wedding vows. I swear to treat you like a queen for the whole of your life. Your father would forgive us once he realizes how much I adore you."

Adriana feigned a musical chuckle, reluctant to take him seriously though she sensed he was. "I'm afraid I'm bound by the contract my father signed, my lord. I cannot escape it that easily."

The spark of hope that had momentarily lit his eyes dimmed forthwith as he heaved a sigh. "Three months, you say?"

"Aye, three months."

His eyes caressed her face as if he sought to memorize it. "I shall pray fervently that you will be freed from all your obligations after that length of time, if not before. Until then, Adriana, be confident of my unwavering desire to have you for my wife."

"You honor me, my lord."

They halted as the music ended, and though Riordan asked for another dance, Adriana could see Roger pacing impatiently about beyond several guests.

"I'd better not. I have a matter to discuss with Mr. Elston. I'm afraid he isn't quite as understanding as you have been about my need to honor commitments."

"I'll stay with you."

As much as Adriana wished she could accept Riordan's comforting presence, she laid a gentle hand upon his arm and shook her head. "'Twould only rile Mr. Elston to have you near, Riordan. If you would, go dance with Berenice again. Perhaps her father would treat her more kindly if he thought she had gained the attention of a gentleman like yourself."

She offered him a grateful smile, wondering if Colton would ever be as gallant. Mentally she heaved a dubious sigh and, as Riordan departed, faced the apprentice who rapidly approached with a harsh, angry scowl. She accepted his invitation to dance, and they progressed like wooden sticks around the dance floor until Riordan swept past with the fair-haired Berenice in his arms, evoking a caustic jeer from Roger. "Obviously that dandified jackanapes knows a rich dowry has been laid upon the broad bovine and is merely seeking to pad his purse."

Adriana's temper ignited. "Don't ever speak so disparagingly about my friends again in my presence, Roger. I won't tolerate it! And if you don't mind being the recipient of my criticism, I'd say you have much to surmount before you equal the likes of such an honorable gentleman as Lord Harcourt. As for Lady Berenice's dowry, 'tis as vast as you say, but in all likelihood, his lordship's fortune would make her father's seem mediocre!

If you're not aware of it, Lord Harcourt will become a duke one day, and a very fine one, I might add."

Much humbled by her ire, Roger grudgingly yielded an apology. "I'm sorry, my lady. At times, I fear my jealousy rules my head."

Adriana was not so easily placated. "Then I suggest you keep a tight rein on your envy lest I come to regret the day we ever met."

When the music finally ended, Adriana's toes once again felt as if they'd been caught in some cruel device of torture. Gritting her teeth in a stiff smile, she had cause to wonder if her attempt resembled a grimace as several acquaintances passed, for they looked at her rather oddly. Barely able to walk for the pain, she tottered gingerly to a settee at the far end of the ballroom near the place where her family stood. After lowering herself rather cautiously to the velvet cushions, she released a sigh of relief and began to work off her slippers beneath the hem of her gown. Her toes had taken the brunt of abuse; even wiggling them seemed to increase the pain. She decided right then and there that Roger would have to be told forthwith that their friendship could not continue. Even if she weren't entering into a courtship with Colton Wyndham, she'd never be able to bear dancing with the apprentice again.

"Perhaps I should go fetch refreshments for you since dancing seems beyond my realm of expertise," Roger suggested.

"I believe I could use a glass of wine right now," Adriana conceded, deciding a small amount would likely relax her and get her through the arduous announcement she had to make. If it proved strong enough to dull her agony, then that, too, would be acceptable.

"I shan't be long, my lady."

"Please, take your time," she urged with all sincerity. She definitely needed time to collect her wits for the ordeal ahead.

Mathilda Maxim approached, and with an exaggerated sigh of her own, plopped herself down on the bench beside her niece. "I don't know about you, child, but my feet have been trod upon more times this evening than there were Frenchmen at Waterloo. I'm beginning to think the dance instructor hereabouts needs to be taken out and shot to relieve us all from future misery."

Giggling at the woman's dry wit, Adriana nodded in full agreement. "I know exactly what you mean, Aunt Tilly. Believe me, if I were able to hide a large bowl of medicinal water beneath my skirts, I'd be tempted to soak my feet, stockings and all."

Tilly winced as she doffed her own shoes beneath the covering of her hem. "I think I've been widowed too long."

Adriana's curiosity was sharply tweaked, for it was rare indeed to hear such comments from the feisty woman. "Why is that, Aunt Tilly?"

The older woman responded with a mischievous grin. "I never knew there were so many gorgeous older gentlemen in the world until I came here tonight. Tell me that I'm not dreaming."

Laughing in delight, Adriana nodded. This sounded more like the Aunt Tilly she had always known. Looping an arm through the woman's, she hugged it affectionately. "Oh, I'm in full agreement. I'd be as befuddled as an ol' spinster if I had to make a choice between any of them. Still, I do think Lord Alistair is a cut or two above the rest. He certainly comes from good stock."

"He *is* quite handsome, isn't he?"

"Oh, indeed," Adriana agreed with an amused chuckle, admiring her aunt's effervescent spirit.

As if making up her mind, Aunt Tilly thrust her slender feet into her shoes and then rose. Patting her niece's shoulder, she announced, "I'm going to make myself available for a dance somewhere within close proximity of the area where I last saw Lord Alistair. If I see any nice young gentlemen while I'm looking around, I'll direct them over here. I've seen several who'd put my own sons to shame."

"If it's all the same to you, Aunt Tilly, I think I'll just sit here and rest my feet for a few moments more before I try dancing again."

"Nonsense, child. You're much younger than I and far too beautiful to be sitting here contemplating your squashed toes. I believe I saw Lord Alistair's nephew without a partner not too long ago. I'll see what I can do for you in that area."

"Please, not just yet, Aunt Tilly," Adriana pleaded desperately, afraid Colton would think she had put her aunt up to asking him to dance with her. "My feet really do hurt and are in dire need of a rest."

"All right, child, but only for the time being. If I don't see you dancing fairly soon, I'll find some nice handsome gentleman to send over."

Relieved that her aunt had acquiesced to her pleas, Adriana released her breath in a long, grateful sigh. Some moments later, she had to smile at Tilly's engaging ways as she saw the woman being swept about the ballroom by Alistair, for the man seemed no less than delighted to be with the attractive woman.

Eleven

※

I T seemed for a time that every bachelor in the room sought out Adriana to ask her for a dance. She graciously complied to as many as she could, knowing it would save her toes from further injury. Some moments later, she found Roger pushing through the throng of hopefuls with a glass of wine. He seemed intent on discouraging her admirers as he pressed it into her hand. Adriana promptly realized she either had to accept it from his grasp or have the wine sloshed over her gown. It nettled her that he could be so persistent, but Roger's ploy worked to his advantage, for the hopefuls finally went off to find other partners.

Trying to curb her irritation, Adriana settled upon a nearby bench and sipped from the crystal goblet as she once again worked off her slippers beneath her hem. Roger plied her with a string of inquiries, to which she responded with silence, a noncommittal shrug, a nod or a shake of her head, preferring not to answer any of them for the moment. He seemed mainly curious about the ones who had invited her to dance and if she were interested in any of them. She hardly considered that any of his business since he wasn't really a friend or, for that matter, even someone she enjoyed having around. He had simply proven unrelenting in his quest to be with her, which hardly seemed a viable reason for her to tolerate him any longer. In fact, she didn't even think she really liked the man. Indeed, it seemed an appropriate time to tell him that he could no longer call upon her.

A dozen or so close acquaintances her own age and gender descended upon her before she could do so, crowding around her with vivacious chatter, leaving Roger feeling out of sorts with the lot of them as questions about this gentleman or that were eagerly presented, making it obvious the young ladies' interest centered mainly on titled aristocrats. Finally, unable to bear being the only male in the midst of so many fluttering females, Roger offered a terse excuse and departed.

Nearly a score of hawkish bachelors swooped down on the gathering to pluck this chick or that one from the brood. Adriana smilingly declined several, not wishing to embarrass herself by revealing the fact that she had lost one of her slippers and, for some moments now, hadn't been able to find it.

Sighing forlornly as everyone deserted her, she was fraught by fear that she'd soon be at the mercy of Roger again. This time, for sure, she would tell him that he'd no longer be welcomed at Wakefield Manor after the evening was over. Yet she hardly wanted to face *that* prospect without her slippers on. At least, while wearing them, she'd be able to walk away if the apprentice became too ornery.

There seemed no graceful way of finding her shoe without forsaking all pretense and bending down to search for it, but that option threatened to cause her more humiliation than she really cared to invite. When a scant moment later a more subtle approach came to mind, she rose gracefully from the bench and considered her surroundings in the manner of a queen surveying her court. Edging forward slowly, then to the left and then to the right, she searched about with the toes of her bare foot. Upon finding the errant slipper at last, she was just sliding her foot into it when a large hand swept beneath her elbow, sending her teetering sideways in surprise. A gasp of astonishment had barely escaped her lips when a darkly garbed arm came around her waist, saving her from a fall. In an instant, her head was filled with a pleasing manly cologne, a very strange occurrence indeed, considering she had never noticed Roger's use of toiletries before this moment in time.

Adriana knew she should have been grateful the apprentice had saved her from the humiliation of a fall. Even so, she was incensed that he had tried to take her arm in the first place. Had he not done so, she would never have lost her balance.

Gnashing her teeth in vexation, Adriana shoved her foot securely within her shoe and turned on him. Then she almost stumbled back in sharp surprise as she found herself facing a neatly tied white silk cravat set off by a silk waistcoat and an elegant coat of the same costly black cloth. Her gaze rose by several degrees until she found white teeth gleaming back at her from a handsomely bronzed face.

"Colton!" Her voice gave generous hint to her astonishment, sounding more like a hoarse croak than the sweet tones to which she was certain he had recently been so attentive.

A soft chuckle flowed from his lips. "You needn't sound so shocked, Adriana. You must have known I'd make my claim on you sooner or later."

"No . . . I mean, I really hadn't been expecting you to come over." *Not when he had been plying the lovely Miss Felicity with his charming smile.*

"The way you turned on me, I came close to ducking," he teased with an unrelenting grin. "I seem to remember that even as a child you could give me a pretty good wallop when you had had enough of my tomfoolery. You didn't seem at all bashful about doing so either."

A blush infused Adriana's cheeks, for she had come close to doing that very thing. "You startled me, that's all."

"My apologies, my dear, but after several attempts to find you free, I finally decided I'd have to come and stake my right to dance with you in spite of all the besotted admirers who seem reluctant to turn loose of your skirts. The miller's son seems especially tenacious tonight. Have you told him yet?"

"No," she admitted testily. "I haven't found a convenient moment."

"I'd be willing to perform the deed if you can't bring yourself to do it, my dear," he offered, his eyes gleaming into hers.

"I'm sure you'd be delighted to give him such news," she rejoined coolly, "but I wonder if your intentions would truly be of the benevolent sort, considering the last time you two were together you sent him flying across the room."

"Certainly tender toward you, my dearest Adriana," he avouched. "I'd be saving you from a task you obviously find loathsome to perform. As for him, well, you *could* say the swiftest cut is the most humane way to sever a tainted limb." He lifted his broad shoulders in a casual shrug. "At least, that's what the surgeons told me when they were contemplating the removal of mine."

Elevating a brow, she directed a brief, meaningful glance toward his right limb. "Aren't you thankful you didn't follow their sage advice?"

Colton chuckled. "I am indeed grateful, so if you'd rather not have me enlighten Roger, I shall leave the telling to your more kindly care . . . for a price. . . ."

"For a price?" she repeated, highly skeptical. "And what may that be?"

"I'm here to rescue you from your brief, spinsterish solitude before some other gallant intrudes." He grinned with sudden amusement. "I believe Sir Guy Dalton was searching for you a few moments ago, but Lord Riordan sent him chasing after a phantom. Remind me never to accept directions from your smitten swains. I may end up in Africa again."

"I've been without a partner for at least the last dance or two," she informed him rather coolly and asked outright, knowing full well the answer, "Where have you been?"

"Out taking a breath of fresh air," he answered simply. "I wasn't all that interested in dancing with any of the other ladies and had grown vexed waiting for my turn with you. I now know the outer perimeter of Wakefield Manor better than I do my own home." He glanced down at his well-shod feet. "I even paused to polish the dew off my shoes, anything to get through the interminable wait."

A likely story, with Felicity waiting in the wings, Adriana thought with a fair bit of peevishness. "'Tis very noble of you to try and save me from my fate, my lord, but really, you needn't trouble yourself on my account."

Once again she had cause to wonder if her cheeks would ever regain their normal coloring under his predatorial perusal. Although still miffed by his gall to flaunt Felicity beneath her very nose, Adriana had to admire the way he looked. Never had she seen a more handsome or debonairly garbed man. Indeed, she doubted if even Riordan, whose attire at all times was the very example of discriminating taste, could come close to equaling Colton's finery this evening.

Feigning a nonchalance that she struggled hard to convey, Adriana swept a hand in the approximate direction she had last seen the blonde. "Please, feel free to continue dancing with your partner."

Smiling down at her as he leaned toward her, Colton laid one wrist atop the other behind his back. Unable to resist the delectable scent of her elusive fragrance, he nearly closed his eyes in pleasure as it twined through his senses. It was a simple fact, the lady smelled as intoxicating as she looked, and he knew, were he ever to return to the battlefield, her beautiful face and sweet essence would sustain him through the fiercest of battles. "At the present moment, my dear, I'm without one."

Adriana chuckled, making light of his predicament. "What? Can it be that Miss Fairchild has forsaken you for another? I find that difficult to believe, considering the wealth of praises she has been liberally attaching to your name recently. You must have been visiting her often to inspire such glowing tributes."

Amusement broadened his roguish grin. "You've been listening to those confounded gossips again, Adriana."

"I . . . I certainly have not!" she protested, and was forced to endure the scalding heat of another sweeping blush. Petulantly she lifted her fine nose into the air, doing her best to snub him. "I merely saw you dancing with Miss Fairchild, that's all."

"Once only. It seemed the thing to do until Stuart came back."

"What does Stuart have to do with it?"

"Why, my dear, he brought her. . . ."

Adriana tried her best not to gape in astonishment. "Stuart brought her?"

His darkly translucent eyes danced as he took note of her surprise. "Well, actually, if you really want me to be specific, my sister and brother-in-law brought them both, having been urged by you to bring whomever they would. Samantha didn't think you'd mind since the both of you invited her on your ride the day of my return, and Stuart seemed interested in her." His gray orbs continued to sparkle with mischievous delight as he peered at her closely, making much of his incredulity. "You didn't think *I* had escorted her here, did you, my dear? Why, shame on you."

"I'm not your dear," Adriana declared, lifting her winsome nose higher still. "So stop calling me that."

"Oh, but you are *my* dear . . . according to my father's wishes," Colton needled. Never had a woman made so many attempts to banish him out of her life, and never had he enjoyed a challenge more.

Adriana wished he'd stop grinning at her. He seemed highly amused, no doubt at her expense. Unable to think of an adequate riposte, she shrugged briefly and then remembered much too late that her décolletage had a tendency to gap away from her bosom with such movements. As if bidden, the gray eyes dropped into her neckline, prompting Adriana to clasp the shiny onyx pendant of her necklace as she sought to shield her bosom from his inspection.

"Too late," he murmured, leaning toward her with a devilish grin. "I've seen everything you have hidden there and have been lusting after you ever since."

Ignoring the little thrill that shot through her, Adriana spread her lace fan before her and plied it with zealous fervor as she sought to cool her burning cheeks. "You have some nerve reminding me of your forwardness to spy on me like some naughty little boy peeping through a knothole."

His brows quirked skeptically. "Did I make any pretense about what I was looking at?"

"No, and I doubt I've ever met a more brazen rake."

"The appropriate word is 'candid,' my dear." His lips twitched teasingly. "Besides, I could hardly feign indifference in the state I was in, now could I?"

The fan fluttered vigorously as her face became as hot as smoldering embers. Adriana dared not glance around for fear someone would discern her discomfiture. Instead, she muttered for his ears alone, "Why don't you go back and dance with Felicity. She may enjoy your form of bawdy humor."

"You're jealous, my dear, and without cause," he accused. "I have no interest in the woman."

Adriana peered up at him curiously. "If you have no interest in her, then please explain why you visited her."

"Visited her?" Colton shook his head, totally bemused. "I've never done anything of the sort."

She closed her fan and tapped it against his handsomely garbed chest. "You were seen leaving Mr. Gladstone's house. Now tell me true, who else would you have been calling upon if not Felicity?"

Colton had to think back a moment before he recalled his visit to the old miller. "Well, my dear, if you're so curious, then I shall tell you. Samantha and I went there solely to pay our respects to Mr. Gladstone. We never saw Felicity. In fact, her mother said she wasn't feeling well."

"Oh." Suddenly elated, Adriana shrugged her shoulders, intending to apologize, and remembered too late her revealing bodice.

After catching another glimpse of the lace-encased fullness beneath her gown, Colton cleared his throat rather sharply and glanced around, deciding he'd better refrain from indulging in such titillating sights for the time being. One peek was hardly satisfying; it only whet his appetite to see her beautiful body once again unadorned by anything more than the natural raiment of her loosely flowing black hair.

Searching for something exceedingly less pleasurable to settle his mind upon in his quest to cool his hard-pressing hunger for the lady, he turned this way and that in search of the apprentice. "Where the devil has Roger gone to? Wasn't he supposed to be your guest tonight? Or did you perchance say your companion?"

"Roger is *neither* my guest in the way you infer *nor* my companion," Adriana stated, miffed that he should even mention the man. "I merely told him that we'd allow him to come when he asked me if he could."

"I thought you told me—"

"Never mind what I said. That's the way it is. Roger is merely an acquaintance I met while shopping for a gift for a servant. Thereinafter he took it upon himself to visit me."

Colton's face brightened. "Excellent. Then that means you're free to dance with me."

For a moment, Adriana seemed unable to do anything more than stutter. "I d-don't know that I care to d-dance just yet."

Colton's lips curved into a taunting grin. "Nonsense, Adriana, before I came over here, you were looking like some prim little spinster hiding out in shame in her lonely little corner, all but forsaken by every male in the room, including Lord Harcourt who seems for a change unduly attentive to Lady Berenice tonight. Should I assume you've told *him*?"

Beneath his inquiring stare, she inclined her head stiltedly. "As a matter of fact, I have."

"Well, at least that much is behind you. Obviously the gossips aren't aware of your army of suitors. They were chattering up a veritable storm about your dim future as the youngest offspring in your father's household when I passed several moments ago. If I'm going to save my reputation as a man of taste, you must establish yourself as one who has more hope of marrying young."

The last thing Adriana wanted was this man's sympathy. "You needn't feel constrained to save *my* reputation from gossipmongers, my lord," she said snidely. "Roger will eventually return. If not, I suppose I can tell him about our impending courtship some other time."

Colton snorted derisively. "The lad should do wonders for your notoriety. Left to his care, every poverty stricken yokel in the area will be bleating at your door."

"You don't have to be so disparaging about a man simply because he lacks wealth and a title," she chided, wondering how it was that she could feel all warm toward the handsome nobleman one moment and, in the next, desire to hang a large pot over his head. "There are many honorable gentlemen in that same predicament."

"Aye, I got to know quite a number of them in my years away from home. I called many of them my friends, but I care not for the likes of Roger Elston."

"Can you tell me why *exactly*?" she prodded irritably. "Mayhap I could better understand your aversion if you were to explain it to me."

His broad shoulders moved upward indolently. "'Tis a feeling I have, nothing more."

"And do you often base your contempt for a person merely on a feeling, my lord? Perhaps you've mistaken intuition for an upset stomach."

His eyes danced as they delved into her own. "Was that what Father was suffering when he got the heady notion we should be wed?"

Silenced by his jibe, Adriana turned her gaze away from him in a lofty manner. Only when she felt his hand settle rather possessively upon the small of her back did she face him again with a fair amount of surprise.

Giving no heed to her look of astonishment, Colton urged her toward the dance floor. "I hope you don't mind dancing with a man hindered by a limp."

Although Adriana had seen no slightest evidence of a flaw in his step earlier, she hoped they could forego such exercise for the sake of her own poorly trampled feet. "We could just as well sit. As you know, it wouldn't be the first time for me tonight, and if your abilities are anything like Roger's, I strongly suggest we do."

"Absolutely not!" Colton stated emphatically. "At least not while that malapert-untutored-in-social-graces is still on the premises." With a gentle, yet unrelenting pressure, he pushed her forward.

She peered at him over her shoulder, feeling like an errant child being prodded by a parent. "You're rather persistent, aren't you?"

"I suppose," he allowed, accompanying his reply with a facial shrug. "At least the men in my company thought so."

"I'm not one of your men," she retorted and had cause to wonder what would follow as she heard his soft chuckles.

"Believe me, my dear, I've never mistaken you for one of them, not even for an instant."

"Thank you for small considerations," she responded, exaggerating her gratitude.

His eyes gleamed tauntingly into hers as she chanced another glance. In spite of her snide retort, his smile remained undiminished, his hand on her back unrelenting. "You're welcome, my dear, but it took no mean mental feat on my part to recognize the difference. None of my men ever looked even remotely appealing to me, especially while soaking in a bathtub."

"Shush!" Adriana scolded, flushing scarlet again as she looked about to see who was near. "Someone will hear you!"

"Not while the music and chatter of the busybodies are causing such a din. If you're not aware of it yet, the gossips have now noticed that you're with me instead of Roger."

Adriana cast a surreptitious glance about and realized what he said was true. Another rippling wave of excitement was making its way through the elderly matrons.

When they reached the dance floor, Colton faced her as he swept his gaze over the heads of the majority of guests, searching for the one he had earlier defamed. "Frankly, considering the lad's eagerness to assault me and challenge my right even to come near you, I shall enjoy staking my claim on you."

Adriana had cause to wonder if Colton was genuinely interested in her or merely eager to thwart Roger's aspirations. The idea was enough to cause the back of her neck to prickle. "Just to spite the lad, as you call him?"

Folding his hands behind his back again as if he were standing in a library with a roomful of men rather than on a ballroom floor with her, Colton grinned down at her, undeterred by the fact that dancing couples were forced to halter their steps in order to go around them. "Why, if needs be, my dear, I'd even be tempted to marry you just to frustrate that young whelp's ambitions."

The dark eyes flared, evidencing Adriana's heightening irritation. "You needn't worry that I will accept your proposal, my lord. My father did allow me some choice in the matter."

The corners of his mouth twitched with amusement. "Singed your pretty feathers a mite, did I?"

Her icy glare pierced him. "Your pardon, my lord, but the last time I looked, I wasn't wearing any."

"Crystals, then," he corrected as his sparkling eyes swept her from head to toe in a way that made her blood race. Stepping near, he slid an arm behind her waist and captured her slender hand within his. "Even without such ornamentations, my pet, you'd still be a rare beauty," he murmured softly and waltzed her around the dance floor before offering another conjecture. "I'm sure your friend, Lord Harcourt, thinks so; he seems to be having trouble keeping his eyes off you this evening. But then, he was having difficulty with that very same thing when I first met him, even more so at Melora's wedding. I believe he fancies himself in love with you."

"Have you grown annoyed with Lord Harcourt because he asked me to dance? Is that also why you're upset with the *lad*?"

"I'm not annoyed with Lord Harcourt. He's a very sensible man, and a gentleman of honor. 'Tis also apparent he has incredibly good taste, especially in women. As for the lad, you already know my feelings toward Roger." He shrugged. "As for myself, I'd be satisfied if you were to smile merely for my pleasure."

"What can you expect from me?" Adriana retorted. "Not knowing what these next three months will bring, I find myself in a bit of a quandary. I can only wonder why you're even considering courting me. I know how much you value your freedom."

For a lengthy moment, his translucent gray eyes probed the dark depths of hers. Did he indeed want his freedom more than he wanted her? That had been the question haunting him in recent weeks, yet even now he was wont to dismiss his growing enthrallment with the lady. "I came back to do my duty to my father and my family by assuming the marquessate, Adriana, and if I find that that also entails marrying you, I shall do so."

"You needn't go to such extremes," she stated, wounded by his callous commitment to the existing contract. "I'm quite willing to accept another if you're truly averse to the idea of marrying me."

Colton couldn't explain away the nettling sense of irritation that came swiftly upon him. "By that, I suppose you mean Lord Harcourt."

Adriana raised her dainty chin a notch. "As you said, my lord, he is a gentleman. I could do far worse for myself."

"Would you prefer him over me?" Colton asked, sharply elevating a brow. His growing annoyance gave him cause to wonder if he would be as dedicated to rejecting their betrothal if it meant losing her to another man. Previously he had only considered his determination to get through the courtship without making concessions to commitments that would likely lead people to think he was merely kowtowing to his father's decree, yet he hadn't really considered she wouldn't be there for him to court on his own after the three-month tenure.

"If you have no regard for me, then 'twould be in my best interest to marry a man who wants me. . . ."

"Are you saying that Kendrick asked you to marry him?"

"Yes, I believe he said something to that effect." Adriana tilted her elegantly coiffed head as if trying to recall Riordan's precise words. "In fact, he urged me to abscond with him this very night."

Something strangely vexing roiled within Colton. It was an experience he had only had some inkling of once before, but this time he recognized it for what it was. Bluntly he asked, "Have I reason to be jealous?"

Adriana laughed rather skeptically. "Why should you be? I was under the impression that for a man to experience jealousy he must consider himself in danger of losing a cherished love to a rival. 'Tis apparent you don't care a whit about me, so why would you be envious?"

"You could be mistaken." A meager smile was the best he could manage.

Adriana tossed her head with a scoffing laugh. "What is that very old adage, my lord? Seeing is believing?"

The darkly translucent eyes gleamed back at her. "Father said you had backbone. In fact, he said a lot of things about you that I couldn't believe at the time. When I left home, you seemed like such a wee little mouse, afraid of your shadow, except when you got angry with me for pestering you and Samantha. I think during our courtship I shall enjoy searching for all those assets Father claimed you had."

Adriana wondered if he was deliberately discounting what she had said or if he was merely dense. The latter seemed highly unlikely. "Don't you understand that I'm giving you leave to dispense with this whole thing, not only the betrothal, but the courtship as well."

Colton lifted his chin thoughtfully. Losing her was the last thing he wanted, of that he was confident. "Lord Harcourt seems to be a man of excellent taste and character. He fought valiantly during the wars and was also in line to make general if he had stayed in, but he chose not to. I would be willing to wager you're the main reason he came home. Admiring the man as I do, I think 'twould behoove me to probe the matter of our betrothal in much greater depth. My father thought you were special; obviously Riordan is of the same conviction. Before I can make a fair and prudent judgment for myself, I must come to know everything about you. The only way I'll be able to accomplish that is by courting you as the contract demands."

"You're intentionally dismissing the importance of what I'm trying to tell you," Adriana accused, thoroughly frustrated.

Capturing her gaze, Colton plumbed the dark depths as he stated with conviction, "I mean to accomplish my part of the agreement, Adriana. If you have no intention of honoring your father's word, then please tell me now, and I won't trouble you further."

Adriana bristled. "That has always been my purpose, my lord. I merely offered to withdraw whatever claims I have on you because I thought you wished to be free of the agreement."

"Now you know better."

"I have difficulty discerning your thoughts, my lord. Your actions seemed to suggest the converse."

"Your actions, my dear Adriana, suggest to me that you are the most contrary young lady I've ever met," he countered. "I should hope in all truth that is not the case."

Adriana felt properly put in her place, knowing she *had* been brusque with him almost without exception since his return.

Colton swept his gaze over the top of her head as he considered the sea of dancers moving in time with the music. Perhaps she didn't realize her deepening effect on him and was actually trying to do the honorable thing by releasing him from his commitment, but as much as his pride might have rallied at his freedom to choose his future bride, the idea of losing his firm grasp upon Adriana Sutton went sorely against his grain. He supposed in that respect he was no different from Roger, except that he had an advantage his father had arranged for him. "I can't blame Lord Harcourt for wanting to marry you. You could brighten any man's life."

Not sure how she should take that particular statement, Adriana peered up at him suspiciously. "Do you have a fever, my lord?"

A soft chuckle escaped Colton's lips as he glanced down at her. "How many compliments must a man bestow upon you, Adriana, before you recognize them for what they are?"

"Compliment, you say?" she asked in a doubtful tone as she probed the dark gray orbs for what they would reveal. If she had expected him to offer confirmation under closer scrutiny, then in that she was to be disappointed.

"Find anything?" he teased, his eyes glinting with amusement.

"No, I didn't," she admitted. "Probably because you're very adept at hiding the true import of your words behind that wayward grin of yours."

Laughing softly, he whirled her around the ballroom in ever-widening circles, moving with an easy strength that readily compensated for the slight limp that still lingered. "And you, my dear Adriana, have a very suspicious nature. Have you really no idea how beautiful you have become?"

Even more wary now, she reminded him, "You once called me a scrawny little gamine, remember?"

His darkly shining eyes dipped briefly into her bodice for another glimpse of the womanly fullness scantily adorned by creamy lace. "I can easily attest that that statement is no longer true, Adriana. If you must know, I can barely refrain from ogling you."

His probing inspection proved puissant in its knee-weakening ability to dismantle her composure. It left her nigh breathless, reminding Adriana of his leisured perusal from the vicinity of the tree weeks earlier. If anything, that singular memory was far more heady in retrospect than any of the other encounters she had had with him, and that rather mystified her, considering how he had perused her in the bathing chamber. Yet in that cubicle she had not been cognizant of the almost tangible yearning that she had seen in his eyes outside the church. Nor had he, then, seemed as cocksure of himself or his appeal. If anything, his desire for her had seemed vulnerable, as if he were indeed afraid of losing her. "Is that what you were doing outside the chapel after Melora's wedding?"

Colton accepted her inquiry in stride. "I was simply admiring your assets, my dear. A man would have to be blind not to appreciate everything about you. I might have done so at closer range, but your army of suitors had you well barricaded. When you stormed out of your parents' drawing room, I came to the conclusion that you didn't want me anywhere near you until our courtship began. As much as I yearned to whisk you away from all your admirers that day outside the church, I was certain you'd resent it."

Adriana lowered her gaze to the dark sheen of his silk waistcoat, wondering why she should be even remotely susceptible to his antics. "You were unusually bold about it. The way you looked at me made me feel . . ."

After a lengthy silence during which she failed to finish her statement, Colton peered down at her curiously. "Yes?"

"Never mind, it isn't important," she mumbled, looking elsewhere in an effort to hide her burning cheeks.

"You're blushing again, which means you're embarrassed by what you almost said," he murmured warmly. "When you were a child, you'd turn the brightest red imaginable when I'd catch you and Samantha sneaking animals up to her room. Obviously you're hiding something positively wicked ... in relationship to your virginal innocence, that is."

Adriana's head snapped up, and though she made several attempts to protest, she managed nothing more than, "I never ... !"

Smiling down at her, he raised a querying brow. "Made you feel naked? Is that what you were about to say?"

Fully aware of the flaming heat in her cheeks, she groaned aloud. "*Nooo!* I would never say such a thing!"

"No, but you *were* thinking it," he accused, his eyes dancing with delight. Unable to resist her evocative fragrance, he leaned his face near her temple once again, letting the scent waft through his senses.

"What if I were?" she snapped, brushing a hand upward over the mass of soft ringlets cascading from her crown and in so doing forcing him to straighten. "It seemed your intent to make me feel that way!"

"I was just remembering how beautiful you looked in the bathtub," Colton acknowledged, wrenching a shocked gasp from her.

"A gentleman would never remind a lady of such an encounter!" she scolded, blushing furiously. "Nor would he have remained there one second after realizing the tub was occupied by someone of the opposite gender, especially when he was in such a shockingly shameless state himself!"

"You must forgive my vulnerability as a man, Adriana," he replied smoothly, seeming totally indifferent to her attempt to make him feel ashamed. "Such sights as I saw before me then are far too rarely glimpsed by those restricted to military encampments for weeks or months on end, which accurately described my state just prior to that point in time. To be sure, I was overtaken by a hope that your presence in my bath was actually an invitation.". Another shocked gasp brought his one-sided grin into play again. "But then I realized you were quite distressed to find me there and, in all likelihood, had never in your life seen a naked man before, especially one who had been caught up in his lust for you."

Adriana would have bolted right then and made good her escape, but Colton chuckled softly and swirled her about in widely turning circles until she was nigh giddy. Lowering his head, he indulged himself once again in the tantalizing bouquet of roses as he breathed above her ear, "Would you tear yourself away from me merely because I'm being honest?"

"Stop turning, please," she begged, her head reeling. "I'm feeling faint."

"I will ... *if* you promise not to fly away," he bargained, easing the intensity of his circling rotations.

She gripped his sleeve in an effort to keep herself upright, wondering what discomfited her more, his uncompromising honesty or the fact that he said he desired her. "You leave me little choice."

Ceasing his lazy whirling, Colton led her in a fairly simple dance, allowing her to settle herself. After a moment, he peered down at her. "Feeling better?"

Had she run a long and difficult race, Adriana would have felt no less winded, but that breathlessness had nothing to do with her actual physical state, but rather the emotions that had begun racing through her womanly being. This man, who had once been so adamant in his refusal to consider their future together, had just said he desired her. Had he swept the floor out from under her, he could not have astonished her more. "I would if you'd allow me to sit down."

His soft chuckle seemed to entangle her mind. "Roger is waiting for you, and I don't want to lose you, least of all to him of all people. Besides, we must talk seriously about our courtship."

"I don't intend to demand more than what you're willing to give, my lord, if that's what you're afraid of," she answered, hoping to lay hold of her sanity once more. The fact that she was still in his arms after what he had said to her seemed viable proof of her lunacy.

Colton sighed heavily, as if thoroughly frustrated. "Adriana, if we're going to be together as a couple for at least three solid months, I insist you call me Colton."

"Colton it is, then," she complied, with a single nod affirming her concurrence.

A sigh of exaggerated relief wafted from his lips. "I'm delighted we have finally vaulted over *that* hurdle. *Now* we can get on to more important details."

Adriana readily offered her opinion. "'Tis now my understanding that we're both committed to seeing this agreement through to the end, whatever that may be ... if only for the sake of our parents. Do you concur?"

Again he responded with a lazy shrug. "It could be the end ... or possibly even the beginning. Who knows what will come of it?"

"You needn't try to assuage my feelings. As long as the contract has been signed, I've realized the limited possibility of a wedding actually taking place even if a betrothal follows our courtship. So, please spare me your pretenses. There is no need for them."

He pondered her answer for a moment before offering an undeniable truth. "Our parents hope otherwise."

"Yes, I know they do," Adriana conceded in a small voice. Disappointing her mother and father would be the last thing she wanted to do.

"We should at least make some sort of pretense for them."

"I guess we should, at least a nominal one. If they see more than that, they'll likely be encouraged."

"We can't have that, now can we?"

Did she really see his lips twitch? "They don't expect much now; to give them hope would only cause them greater hurt when we part."

Colton's brows gathered thoughtfully. "I've never courted a woman halfheartedly before. I'm not sure I'm capable of restraining myself in that area. In fact, my dear Adriana, this chicanery you propose will probably prove more difficult than you can imagine."

She lifted her own slender shoulders nonchalantly, only to remember too late that his consuming eyes were ever watchful for invitations of that sort. "Marriage with me or your freedom, sir. That is the choice you'll be facing. 'Tis as simple as that."

"Not quite as simple as that," he countered after peering into her bodice again. Perusing her creamy breasts was a temptation he couldn't seem to resist. He was fascinated by the way the fullness seemed to flow with almost fluid grace into the shallow lace undergarment. From a distance he had casually noted how tightly other women's breasts had been pressed above their fashionably low décolletages, and he had been led to wonder if there had been any small degree of roundness left underneath those mounds. "Nevertheless, we shall see the way of it as our courtship progresses. I do think, however, that we should proceed with all possible haste."

Adriana's suspicions were evoked anew. "Of course, I understand. You wish to have it behind you so you can get on with your life?"

His palm moved upward between her shoulder blades, pressing her closer against him, and in gently swirling her about again, he had cause to catch his breath in sharp reaction as their thighs brushed. The contact left him battling a familiar ache, the intensity of which could've been likened to being hit in the gut, very much like what he had experienced weeks ago when he had watched her laughing and flirting with her courtiers outside the church. The fact that he desired her perhaps more than any woman he had ever known had dawned on him with startling clarity during those moments he had stood underneath the tree. No one could've even come close to guessing the difficulty he had had remaining there merely as an observer and not staking his claim on her. Her escape to her parents' landau had frustrated him to the extent that he had been motivated to move to a place where he could continue to view the proceedings unobstructed, where his eyes could feed on her every gesture, smile, shake or nod of her bonneted head.

Though only just awakening to sensual emotions, Adriana was not to escape unscathed. There was a slow, strength-shattering roll in the lower pit of her stomach that all but took her breath away; it definitely weakened her knees, leaving in its wake a gnawing, hungry craving that seemed to pulse at her very core. Awed by the feelings sweeping through her, she lifted her gaze to find Colton watching her closely, as if searching for something beyond her ken.

Even as she stared up at him, fraught by confusion, he seemed unable to keep his eyes elevated. They swept downward into her bodice again as the cloth loosened over the delicious fullness. From there, his gaze roamed upward slowly over the ivory column of her throat until it reached her mouth. For a wild, mad moment he wondered what it would be like to taste her quickening breath in his mouth and kiss the tempting softness of those lips that parted in . . . Was it surprise? Or . . . passion?

He managed a smile, but it was somewhat strained as he redirected his attention elsewhere, a much needed requirement to regain control over his mind and body. With fierce dedication he lent his thoughts to an area he was loath to recall, the battlefield whereupon he had last fought. While cannonballs hurtled down all around them, stripping life and limb from many of them, he had led a charge into that thick fray with the burgeoning knowledge that if he and his men eased their assault one whit, the day would be lost. They had fought with desperation during the whole bloody conflict, and at long last a sense of victory had finally rallied their lagging strength. In the next moment, a shell exploded nearby, sending shards of debris searing into his leg as the blast hurled him aside. Dazed, he had struggled to his feet and fought valiantly on until they had gained the day. By the next afternoon, his wound had begun to putrefy, and when he had thought of his approaching death, an image of his sire had come to mind.

"You know as well as I that my father was said to have been a man of keen intuitive intellect," Colton mused aloud, breaking the lengthy silence between them. "He was adamant in his belief that we would be good for each other. Call it an experiment, if you would, this courtship of ours, but I'd like to find out for myself all the reasons my father had for thinking that." He laughed rather ruefully. "As you know, my dear, I'm a rather skeptical individual; I didn't like having my life laid out for me in the usual customary rote . . ."—his brows shrugged upward as he made his point— "by my father. Yet I will do all I can to honor his memory as I earnestly probe the whys and wherefores of his reasoning. I can only ask that you bear with me as we go through this pretense together. The task will hardly be offensive to me. You're an incredibly beautiful woman, Adriana, and yet, in spite of having known each other early on in our lives, we have become, as you said, little more than strangers during my absence. Before I can ask more of you, I must come to know you personally." Tilting his head contemplatively, he asked, "Has my honesty offended you?"

"No, Colton," she replied, offering him a hesitant smile. "If truth be told, I prefer your frankness, for you see, in the time that it will take for you to discern my true nature, I hope to discover yours. As with any couple, getting to know each other is part of establishing a firm foundation upon which a marriage can be built. Determining the character of the other is vital in making a prudent choice before the vows are spoken. Although I cannot expect much to come from our courtship because of your past resistance, I shall be willing to give you every chance to judge whatever merits I may have as a wife."

"Thank you, Adriana," he murmured softly.

It took a moment before she could answer him, but when she did, Adriana was amazed to find her voice weak and trembling. "I know we have much to learn about each other, Colton, but I tell you truly, I'm not much changed from that little girl you once rejected. Three months from now, we may decide to take different paths other than the one your father intended for us. Should that occur, I hope we shall each be tolerant of the other's feelings and somehow manage to remain friends for the sake of our families."

The corners of his lips twitched in amusement. "Strange, but I thought you had changed a great deal since I left home. As much as I've searched, I cannot find that light smattering of freckles that once bridged your nose." His eyes followed the straight, delicate lines of the mentioned feature before moving to her softly curving lips. "Truth be told, my lady, I don't recall ever being tempted to kiss that little girl I left behind."

Adriana gave him a challenging look. "I think, Colton, 'twould greatly behoove you to proceed with caution."

"A little kiss here and there is harmless. . . ."

"A little kiss here and there is dangerous," she countered, thoroughly convinced of that premise where he was concerned.

A dark brow arched wonderingly. "Are you so fearful of losing your virtue, Adriana?"

"With you? Aye!" she answered with a finality that brooked no discussion, knowing her mother would be horror-struck if she could hear their conversation. "I've not wandered the world hither and yon as you have done, Colton. I've never been subjected to constant dangers or the uncertainty of war. I've always known where I would sleep, and, thus far, that has always been entirely alone. I don't know about you, what your experiences have been, but even as a young man you seemed to have a way about you that drew young maidens to you like a swarm of bees to honey, and that, frankly, worries me. There are certain things I want from a husband, among them love, honor, fidelity, and a wealth of children we have made together. If, after this courtship, you still want me as your wife, I'll gladly yield you all that I have to give as a wife with as much joy, passion, and devotion as I'm capable of feeling. But until that day wherein we become one, I must guard my heart, because I'm very susceptible. When I was a little girl, I simply adored you, but you broke my heart. If that were to happen again, it would be far more shattering to me the second time around."

"You've made your case, Adriana," Colton murmured, delving into those large, ebon pools that watched him so closely in return.

"Then may I assume that you'll limit the persuasiveness of your manly ardor where I am concerned?"

"I'm not sure I can make that pledge and keep it."

"Why not?" she asked in all innocence.

Colton mentally sighed, wondering if the woman knew how beautiful she really was. Glancing around as he sought to find an appropriate answer, he realized suddenly that the music had stopped. In some amazement he swept a more thorough inspection around the perimeter of the dance floor. From what he was able to discern, they had been the only ones dancing for the last few moments. Everyone else had moved to the sidelines to watch them. Most of the guests simply smiled in amusement, while others were more enthusiastic and emphasized their appreciation with hearty applause and shouts of "Bravo!" and "Encore!"

Percy teasingly heckled from a safe distance off. "You've been involved too long in the wars, my friend. Any pretty face, and you lose your wits over her."

Colton chuckled good-naturedly and waved off the comment with a hand. Then he grinned down at Adriana who laughed and shrugged in spite of the fact that her cheeks were again glowing with a vivid blush. "I do believe, my dear, that we've stolen center stage of the Autumn Ball."

Twelve

❈

GRACEFULLY mimicking the flamboyance of an actress on a stage, Adriana swept a slender hand before her as she sank into a deep curtsey. To the continuing delight of their audience, Colton followed her lead with an ostentatious bow, dissolving onlookers into hearty laughter and vigorous clapping. The din proved too much for Adriana to bear. In spite of her grin, she cringed and covered her ears in an attempt to spare herself the pain of the thunderous applause.

Not every guest was that appreciative of the ovation the couple was receiving. When Roger returned to the ballroom and realized that Adriana had been claimed by Lord Randwulf, he had forged through the guests, shouldering people rudely aside as he sought to gain an unobstructed view of the couple. Once the music had ended, he had felt his vitals twist with acrimony as he became privy to whispered comments that eagerly espoused the belief that Lord Randwulf and Lady Adriana had been made for each other simply because the couple *looked positively sublime together*. Over his shoulder, he had cast angry glowers toward the elderly biddies responsible for offering those galling observations, evoking highly offended gasps and derogatory comments on the crudity of the miller's son before the lot of them had stalked off in haughty irritation with him.

Similar praises were being heaped upon the couple by acquaintances and family members, who had gathered at the opposite end of the spacious ballroom, very near the place where Felicity and Stuart were also observing the gracious responses of the lady and the marquess. It was a comment Jaclyn made to her father that stripped away Felicity's hopes of winning the handsome man.

"You know, Papa, as much as Colton balked when Lord Sedgwick first proposed his betrothal to Adriana, he certainly doesn't appear to be opposed to it now. In fact, he can't seem to take his eyes off my sister. But then, to find another equally as beautiful as she, he'd have to travel the world twice around."

Gyles chortled. "She is a pretty thing, isn't she? But then, I have two other daughters who are just as winsome."

Jaclyn patted her sire's arm affectionately. "As much as Melora may object to the idea, Papa, I've become convinced after my lengthy absence from home that in the area of looks, Adriana has far surpassed the two of us. With her dark hair, large eyes, and height, she's far more elegant. If I may be permitted to boast about my own sister, I'd even be wont to say that she has become a rare beauty."

Felicity mentally sneered at the Suttons' eagerness to laud one of their own, casually disregarding the fact that her own father had frequently been guilty of that offense. Their compliments, however, didn't bother her nearly as much as the news that there was already a betrothal in existence between Lord Colton and Lady Adriana. A dark, impenetrable gloom descended forthwith upon her expectations. As much as she had yearned to win Colton Wyndham for herself, that just didn't seem feasible now with the couple committed to each other. Usually a death of one or the other or a serious indiscretion on the part of the female were the only things that terminated agreements of that sort. She couldn't expect Lady Adriana to be so foolish as to disgrace herself in the latter fashion, and as much as Felicity was led to contemplate what advantages there would be if Ulysses threw his mistress and broke her lovely neck the next time she urged him over one of those steep hurdles she enjoyed taking, it seemed doubtful that such an event would occur so fortuitously in her own favor.

So, how in the world would she ever be able to find another aristocrat to marry? She didn't have the lineage to circulate in the same lofty spheres where they could be found. Although the idea of being a marchioness had temporarily spoiled her to less distinguished titles, she'd now be willing to take what she could get. At the moment, even the title of viscount seemed appealing. Still, she couldn't imagine there'd be that many aristocrats vying for her hand, if any. She was merely an accountant's daughter, and of late, her father had been too involved in trying to straighten out his own difficulties with her mother and grandfather to be of any help directing her. All the predictions he had made in his zeal to see her married to a member of the aristocracy were being unequivocally undermined by a simple betrothal that had obviously been in place well before she had ever come into the area.

"You'd think Lady Adriana had a hook through Lord Colton's nose the way he seems to be doting on her." Indicating the couple with a toss of her blond head, Felicity hoped to draw a comparable comment from her companion, but in the lengthy silence that followed her remark, she looked aside and found Stuart's eyes almost hungrily devouring the dark-haired woman. Unable to suppress her deepening disappointment, she questioned with wounded pride, "You, too?"

Stuart's brows lifted in surprise as he realized she had been addressing him. "Your pardon, Felicity. Did you say something?"

"*I did*," she replied dejectedly, "but 'tis obvious you have *another* woman on your mind. You were staring so hard at Lady Adriana just now that I have to wonder why you're standing here with me when you could just as well have bestowed *all* your attention on her."

Stuart lifted a querying brow, rather amazed at the petulance of the young woman. "I didn't realize I was staring at her so intently."

"Well, you were, and making me feel like an ugly toad in the process," she muttered. "If you're so interested in Lady Adriana, why don't you go over and ask her to dance? You needn't feel constrained to stay here with me just because your brother and sister-in-law brought us here together. I'm sure Lady Adriana would be delighted to know she had captured your attention along with the rest of the other gentlemen here."

"Your pardon, Miss Felicity, but I believe Lord Colton and Lady Adriana are very close to being betrothed, if not that very thing," Stuart murmured.

Felicity shot him a mutinous glance. "Otherwise, you wouldn't have even bothered dancing with me."

Stuart refrained from denying the young woman's brusque assertion. Anything he'd offer in an effort to make amends would likely be refuted, and with good cause. He *had* been looking at Adriana with all the yearning he had recently been feeling.

Had Colton lent even a passing consideration to what the couple were discussing, he wouldn't have been at all surprised, but he had no wish to devote any portion of his consideration to others at the moment, not when he was in the company of the woman who had relentlessly been haunting his dreams since his return home. Considering the fact that *his father* had selected the lady for him ten and six years ago was the most amazing thing about it all. How could his parent have been so insightful to have envisioned Adriana in her prime and to know that she would bestir his son's heart as perhaps no other would? Had it all been coincidence, or had his father really been so insightful?

Settling a hand on the far side of Adriana's slender waist, Colton pulled her close against his side with the hope that his boldness would be enough to keep other suitors at bay until the ball was over. The difficulty would come later when he'd have to forget the way she had felt in his arms and the curiously provocative scent of roses that had filled his head.

Adriana could hardly ignore the familiarity Colton exhibited toward her. Curiously she peered up at him, drawing his smiling regard.

"Yes, my sweet?"

Adriana wasn't sure she liked coming to the rather unnerving realization that her knees were inclined to wobble whenever such smoothly spoken endearments came from the lips of this man. It certainly didn't help her composure to feel his lean, hard fingers tightening upon her waist as he bent his head near her own to hear her response.

"Did we not agree that we should be discreet at all times lest our parents be encouraged?"

"Did we?" he asked, as if the idea had never entered into his consideration.

Taking into account that Colton Wyndham was no addlebrained nitwit, Adriana had no recourse but to believe he had deliberately dismissed her earlier suggestion. In spite of that probability, she pressed him to do what they had tentatively agreed on. "Do you not think we should? 'Twould likely prove beneficial."

His wide shoulders lifted indolently. "I'll have to consider such a notion at greater length, my sweet. It may hinder my ability to accurately access the integral worth of our courtship. If Father was so adamant that you'd be good for me, then surely I should delve without reserve into the matter of our relationship even when we're with our parents."

Adriana almost gulped. The powerful volley of sensual persuasiveness that Colton Wyndham was capable of launching against her womanly being could reap devastating results. She hadn't realized until her sister's wedding how susceptible she really was to falling in love with the man. When his eyes had delved to the depths of hers, he had all but turned her heart inside out and nibbled at its tender core. Were he to continue such delectable assaults on her senses, it might well mean the collapse of her resistance and her ultimate doom. She had not yet forgotten his confident declaration about pleasuring her.

Feeling very vulnerable to his charm, she tried to convince him otherwise. "Surely, Colton, you can see the wisdom of sparing our parents the anguish of having their expectations cruelly dashed after three months of contrived enthusiasm on your part."

"Contrived?" Canting his head at a museful angle, Colton debated her use of that particular word and the charge she laid to him. "I don't think I've *ever* deliberately *contrived* enthusiasm for a lady in all my life, certainly not one who appeals to me. If they happen not to, I simply dismiss myself from their presence. At the moment, Adriana, I'm looking forward to becoming better acquainted with you in the weeks to come. If you feel a need to warn our parents, perhaps you should advise them not to take too much stock in what they see until the day I actually propose. Considering the circumstances that bind us together for the present time, that seems the simplest solution, one that will not hinder me overmuch."

Adriana's heart sank. Already she could foresee the disaster looming ahead of her in the months to come. What defense had an innocent virgin against a man adeptly skilled in the art of seducing women?

The guests smilingly opened a path for the couple, allowing them to move through their midst. As they did so, old acquaintances greeted Colton with enthusiastic pats on the back, hearty handshakes, or humorous quips spoken from afar by those unable to breech the crowd. The resulting laughter caused Adriana to cringe, requiring her to lean closer to her own friends to hear their whispered comments lauding the handsomeness of the swain at her side.

The enthusiasm evoked from acquaintances and friends did much to reinforce the jeer that snidely twisted the apprentice's lips as the couple approached the door where he had stationed himself. Seeing his hopes dissipating before his very eyes, Roger had decided he'd have to try to halt his lordship's possession of the lady by his own physical endeavors. It didn't matter that the marquess was an experienced soldier, or that he was taller, stronger, and skillfully adept with his fists. Roger was desperate. It was either dispense with Colton Wyndham or see his aspirations fade into oblivion.

Here at the central door of the ballroom was where he would begin his efforts to dislodge the retired colonel from the heart of the maid. A strategic placement of a chair and his splayed-leg stance beside it came nigh to forming a barricade for the two. Whether it would prove impenetrable remained to be seen.

Contemplating the hindrance threatening their departure from the room, Colton had to wonder if he'd soon be involved in another altercation with the apprentice. If such a confrontation came about, he promised himself he'd give the lad an even harsher lesson than he had before. Perhaps it would serve the whelp his just due if he beat some truth into that dense brain of his, for Roger did indeed seem slow at grasping the facts. The truth of the matter was that the lady was not his and would never be.

Adriana's steps faltered as she neared the door. She turned slightly to peer up at Colton, but the pressure of the manly hand resting on the small of her back urged her gently forward.

"No need to fear, Adriana," Colton murmured. "If Roger insists on settling this matter with violence, I shall invite him outside. There'll be less chance of our disrupting the festivities out there."

Sneering in contempt as Adriana sought to move around the barrier he had placed to prevent their departure, Roger stepped forward to block her path. "Well, it certainly has become obvious tonight that you don't have the fortitude to declare your independence and have now capitulated to the late Lord Randwulf's plans to marry you off to his son. I thought you were made of sterner stuff, but I realize I was mistaken. I should never have let myself believe there was any hope for me, not when there was a title of marchioness dangling before your fine nose. You make me sorry I ever hoped you'd be different." Turning his lips as if repulsed by what he saw, he swept his gaze down the length of her, yet his heart ached most dreadfully as he feigned disgust, for she was absolutely the most ravishing creature he had ever seen in his life. With her fine, porcelain skin, silkily lashed dark eyes, and softly curving mouth, she put to shame all the painted doxies he had ever sampled in London. "You're just like every female who has ever been born, ambitious for a title and prestige—"

"Excuse me, Mr. Elston," Colton interrupted curtly. "You're making much ado about a matter the lady had no hand in devising. I sought her out for reasons of my own. If you have some claim upon her that restricts her from dancing with anyone but you, I wasn't aware of it. Nor do I know of any constraints that require your permission ere I approach her." Elevating a dark brow, he probed caustically, "Do you have such a claim upon the lady?"

Roger glowered back in sullen resentment, knowing the nobleman was the only one who had any entitlement to the beauty. The contract Lord Sedgwick had laid out for his son had guaranteed him a right no other man could dissolve, yet Roger refused to concede that point, allowing his sulking silence to convey his unyielding objection to what he considered a grave injustice, if to no one but himself.

"I thought not." Bestowing a succinct smile on the younger man, Colton drew Adriana's arm through his with a deliberateness the apprentice could not easily overlook. "I believe the lady has something to say to you, Mr. Elston. If you'll kindly remove yourself to the library, we shall follow."

Adriana lifted her gaze to Colton, prompting him to lower his head near hers. "Perhaps it would be better if I spoke to Roger in private."

Colton shook his head. As desperate as the apprentice was to have her, he wouldn't put it past the man to force her against her will in hopes of bringing about a marriage, though he seriously doubted her father would tolerate such abuse without killing the man. In any case, he had no intention of allowing the apprentice such an opportunity. "That wouldn't be wise, my dear. There's no guarantee that Mr. Elston wouldn't try to harm you."

"Harm her?" Roger repeated incredulously, as if he had never once thought of taking the lady by force. "My lord, let me assure you that you're the only one I'd really like to harm!"

The gray eyes chilled as they lifted to meet the blazing green eyes. "You made that apparent the first day we met, sir, but you obviously haven't taken to heart the lesson I gave you then. Would you like to try again? I'd even allow you to throw the first punch. Who knows? Perhaps you'd be luckier this time."

Roger twisted his thin lips in a derisive sneer. "As much as I'd enjoy beating you to a pulp, I must decline your invitation."

"Too bad." Colton smiled blandly. "Perhaps we could have settled the matter once and for all, because you do seem foolishly bent on making a nuisance of yourself. However, if you should reconsider, you'll find me with the lady."

The green orbs flared at the nobleman's taunt. Having already received a harsh demonstration of the nobleman's capabilities, Roger didn't care to get into another physical confrontation with the man, since he had not fared well during the first one, but he just couldn't hold his resentment in check and lashed out in derision in another area. "Not everybody likes to bow and scrape before aristocrats. As for myself, I find such a task loathsome."

"Not every aristocrat is as forbearing as Lady Adriana. *As for myself*," Colton countered acidly, "I have no intention of letting some blustering, wet-behind-the-ears popinjay mar this occasion. I rather suspect Lord Standish wouldn't be as tolerant of your despicable manners as his daughter has been. If you wish to join us, the lady and I will be in the library. Otherwise, Mr. Elston, you may take your leave forthwith."

This time the pale green eyes flashed with fire as the marquess's insults nettled an area that had become most sensitive in recent years, his boyish looks. Yet Roger dared not make much ado over the man's statements, for fear the lady would also come to think of him more as a youth than a man. "What? Have you now assumed authority here that you can bid guests to come or go?"

A crisp twitch of Colton's lip sufficed as a sneer. "Being a close, intimate friend of the family, I believe I'm well within my right to oust a troublemaker from the premises. And you, sir, have definitely made yourself out to be one."

"You're not lord here," Roger snarled in guttural tones. "You're merely a guest . . . just as I am, and you have no right to order anyone to leave."

Colton laughed chidingly. "If you'd care for me to summon Lord Standish, I shall do so. Considering your penchant for causing trouble, I have no doubt the result will be the same."

Roger opened his mouth to retort, but the nobleman swept past him, realizing they had aroused the curiosity of a considerable number of guests who were now craning their necks in an effort to see what was taking place at the entrance to the ballroom. Roger gaped after the couple for one long, astounded moment and then, glancing quickly about, noticed that several women were eyeing him furtively as they whispered to each other behind their fans. Beyond them stood men of wealth and lofty circumstance, who were not above scowling in haughty disapproval as they peered down their long noses at him.

The buzz of conjectures making their way around the ballroom soon drew Gyles's attention to the apprentice, the only culprit in sight. Although Roger felt the weight of the elder's questioning perusal, he refused to yield him so much as a glance. Ignored or not, Gyles took matters into his own hands and signaled to the musicians. Once again a lilting melody drifted through the room, and as his guests began to dance, Gyles begged leave from those with whom he had been conversing.

Colton drew Adriana to one of a pair of settees that resided near a diamond-paned oriel in the library. He had no doubt that during the day the location and comfort of the furnishings would prove advantageous for reading. At the moment, however, it was a place where one could easily view the myriad stars twinkling in the night sky.

"Roger won't let my challenge go unanswered, Adriana. I have every confidence that he'll be here forthwith," he stated with conviction. "And if I know your father, he should be making an appearance fairly soon himself."

"There won't be any serious trouble, will there?" she asked, blaming herself for the way Roger was acting. If she had allowed her father to turn the apprentice away from their door on his first visit, or anytime thereafter, none of this would have been happening.

"Nothing your father and I can't handle," the marquess reassured her. "No need for you to fret."

Colton hadn't been in the Suttons' library since he had left home, and as he began to stroll about the room, old memories, vividly refreshed by the familiar surroundings, came winging back. Countless shelves with books tucked in every available space lined nearly every wall from floor to ceiling and were interspersed with various portraits, landscapes, and framed sketches from bygone eras. The exception and only change he could discern in the library was a large, fairly recent portrait of the four Sutton ladies hanging in a place of honor on the wall behind Lord Gyles's massive desk. The artist had captured Adriana in all her regal beauty standing beside her mother's chair. On the opposite side of their parent were her older sisters, Melora sitting on a bench in front and Jaclyn standing slightly behind her. Although the two pale-haired, blue-eyed women were beautiful in their own right, in his opinion Adriana, with her tall, sublime form, dark tresses, and beautiful eyes, was far more exotic than her sisters.

Colton smiled as he recalled the days of their youth. While growing up, Adriana had been pitied by a goodly number of acquaintances and relatives who hadn't possessed the same keenly perceptive foresight as his father. Distant kin had considered the girl something of a blemish on an otherwise handsome family. Colton had to admit that he hadn't seen much hope for her himself, but he was now deeply obliged that his parent had refused Jaclyn and Melora as a replacement for one whose looks could have easily put to shame so-called goddesses of ancient lore.

Other reasons made him just as grateful for his sire's intuitiveness. He now towered over the diminutive pair, but that wasn't the only disadvantage to their size. As a newborn, he had been fairly large, and so might his own offspring be. Of the three, he gave Adriana the best chance of bringing a child of his into the world without suffering undue trauma. It was just another practical reason to consider very carefully and from every aspect the choice his father had made for him so long ago.

Roger stalked into the library, prompting Colton to calmly return to the end of the settee where Adriana had taken a seat. Folding one wrist atop the other behind his back, he faced his adversary in the manner of one carefully biding his time before a battle.

Roger curled his lips in derision beneath the unflinching gray eyes and sardonically cocked a brow as he considered the man's protective stance, but it was Adriana's casual acceptance of her intended's sheltering presence that cruelly wrenched his heart. It was as if she already belonged to the man.

Of a sudden, Roger wondered why he had even come to the library. It had been obvious in the ballroom that the lady was committed to the pact her father and Sedgwick Wyndham had signed years ago. Although Lord Gyles had bound her to the contract before she had been old enough to determine her own mind, the culprit had really been Sedgwick. Had he not been the one who had first conceived of the nuptial agreement and then had persuaded the others of its merits? Lord Standish and Adriana had merely been pawns in his little game.

Still, whatever the intensity of loathing Roger had once felt toward Lord Sedgwick, he was now convinced that his hatred for the son had quadrupled in comparison. He could wish the nobleman no less than the same fatal fate as his sire.

Turning back to the door, he laid a hand upon the knob and pushed the barrier toward the jamb. He had no idea what the next moments would bring; he only knew it would not be the end of it, by any means.

"Lord Standish will likely be joining us," Colton announced, halting the man.

Smirking in derision as he faced the retired colonel, Roger allowed his insult to carry forth without the issuance of a single word. If his adversary needed the elder's support, then obviously the one who could confront the two of them without assistance was the better man, was he not?

Undismayed by the venomous disdain visible in the glowering green eyes, Colton offered the man a bland smile. He had faced the dangers of battle too many times to be overly concerned about the abhorrence of one who, by his own words, had never known what it was to confront an enemy on a well-bloodied battlefield. "Let's just say that Lord Gyles will be an impartial witness should I again be forced to correct your manners, sir."

Roger turned his lips in a caustic sneer at the marquess's unwavering inclination to treat him like an errant youth. That fact nettled his hackles as no other insult came close to doing.

Stalking stiff-legged across the room to the settee where Adriana had ensconced herself, he felt his vitals roil in deepening resentment as Lord Randwulf settled a hand upon the lady's shoulder, as if to reassure her that he wouldn't let any harm come to her. To see his adversary's fingers casually resting upon the creamy bare skin fanned the flames of Roger's resentment and jealousy to an agonizing degree. What other man had been allowed to touch her hand, much less some meager part of her body?

In spite of the time and distance that had once separated the lady and her intended, the two now seemed of one accord, as if Colton Wyndham were already her husband. It was just another reason for the rowelling vexation Roger was now experiencing. Feeling totally stymied by Adriana's willingness to accept the marquess as her future betrothed, he heaped a full measure of scorn upon her. "Let me spare you the trouble of making an announcement that has become all too obvious tonight, my lady. You're going to yield yourself to the late Lord Randwulf's dictates and enter into courtship with his son."

Her dainty chin lifted at his scathing tone. "Perhaps you did indeed hope I would ignore the contract my parents signed, Roger, but that has never been my intent."

A loud clearing of the throat announced the entrance of Lord Standish, who peered at his daughter to affirm her safety. "Everything all right here?"

"Not altogether, Papa," Adriana replied in a voice that was noticeably strained. Not since Colton's return had she felt so much tension. "I was just about to explain to Roger that I must ask him not to visit Wakefield Manor again after tonight or to follow me about to other places."

Roger twisted his lips in sardonic revulsion. "You must pardon me for *ever* thinking you had a mind of your own, my lady. Why, you're just as spineless as all the other women I've ever known."

A prickling along her nape and a stirring of her temper reaffirmed within Adriana's mind that she was not as cowardly or weak-willed as Roger suggested. He had definitely been successful in raising her hackles. "Roger, I'm afraid as far back as a year ago you erred in thinking that we could be anything more than casual acquaintances. 'Twas apparent from the very beginning that you wanted something more from me, something I *never* had any intention of offering you. At the very best, you were nothing more than a distant friend, someone who took it upon himself to follow me about and even intruded when he had not been invited. I should've told you months ago that your efforts to see me would avail you nothing. You've known for some time now that I've been pledged to another from my youth, and yet you continued to visit me as if that would never come to fruition. I tell you now that nothing you could've said or done would've ever changed that."

Roger glared back at her through gathering tears. "You couldn't even tell me! You let me go on hoping like some poor, blind fool!"

Adriana was repulsed by his whining complaint. "I never once led you to believe that it could be otherwise, Roger. I had obligations to my family . . . and to others. I tried to tell you earlier tonight that I couldn't see you again because your jealousy and aspirations had made it impossible for us to continue on as friends, but you refused to listen, so it's down to this. . . ."

"Tonight!" he barked. "You'd have been kinder had you told me a year ago, before I ever reasoned in my heart that I would do anything to have you! Why did you let me go on believing there was some hope?"

"How quickly you forget the many times I made that evident. The first time was when you took it upon yourself to come here without invitation. Thereafter you infringed upon my hospitality and that of others every chance you found, following me to the homes of my friends and elsewhere. Had I refused to see you at the very beginning, this wouldn't be happening now. I never wanted you to be hurt, Roger; I never expected you to hope for anything more, but friendship was all I've *ever* been able to offer."

"You knew I wanted more from you, and yet you never warned me that you'd be considering another as your husband."

Adriana's stomach turned. His maudlin distortions of the truth were no doubt intended to make her feel sorry for him; he just didn't realize that what he was arousing within her was a nauseating sense of repugnance. "That's not true, Roger, and you know it. My father is here to affirm that he explained the situation to you quite carefully when you asked for my hand." She paused, glancing down at her tightly clenched fingers, desperately trying to collect her aplomb, and felt a calmness settle over her as Colton gently squeezed her shoulder. Sensitive to the comforting pressure, she lifted her gaze to Roger. "Perhaps you foolishly imagined some miracle would happen to change my mind, but even if Lord Randwulf hadn't returned, I would've married another man from among my peers. The simple fact is, Roger, you've never been anything more than a casual acquaintance, and a rather persistent one at that."

The apprentice straightened his coat with an outraged jerk. "Well, I hope the lot of you will be happy together." The glower he bestowed upon each readily annulled his statement, for it clearly conveyed his loathing for them. "You probably will be, considering you've had everything in the world delivered to you on golden chargers."

"If we have," Colton retorted, rankled by the slur that often came from commoners who were wont to complain about the class distinction but were reluctant to do anything to improve their own circumstance, "it's because our forebears were willing to fight and die for king and country. Because of their allegiance, they were granted titles and land. Before that, our ancestors had little, if anything, but they were ready to sacrifice the very breath from their bodies to achieve honor and greatness, which was far more than you seemed disposed to do for your country in our latest confrontation with the French."

Upon facing the man, Roger lifted his upper lip in a derisive sneer. "Some men enjoy killing; others do not."

Turning crisply on a heel, he stalked toward the door, yielding Gyles a glare as he did so. Upon reaching the wooden barrier, he flung it open with enough force to cause it to rebound against the raised molding of the adjoining wall. Just as quickly it swung shut on his heels.

"I know now that I should have told Roger the first time he came out that I couldn't see him anymore," Adriana murmured. "Had I done so, he wouldn't have been here tonight."

Colton squeezed her shoulder again. "Obviously Roger was hoping for a miracle. He made it abundantly clear the day of my arrival that he was cognizant of the contract between us."

"You're right, of course," Adriana conceded, releasing a troubled sigh. "He was indeed aware that your return would doom his aspirations. His animosity toward you that day readily evidenced that fact."

" 'Twould seem the lad didn't take our altercation seriously," Colton replied.

A troubled sigh slipped from Adriana's lips. It was a long moment before she directed her gaze toward her father. "Do you suppose we should be getting back to the ballroom now, Papa? Mama will be wondering where we are."

"Yes, yes, of course," Gyles agreed, releasing his own breath in much the same manner. "Your mother will be fretting. Why don't you two join the others. I'll follow in a moment. I'd like to indulge in something a bit stronger than wine. It has been a most trying day."

Colton smiled, wondering how he'd cope with suitors quarreling over a daughter. But then, that seemed far better than having to watch a plain-faced spinster pining her heart out for want of a beau. "If I may have your permission, my lord, I'd like to dance with your daughter again."

Chortling, Gyles waved them off. "Be my guest, as long as I can stay here and leisurely sip a brandy." He glanced around as if fearful of someone overhearing. "Don't tell my wife. She condemns the stuff as being less than genteel, but I'd rather have it any day over port."

Colton chuckled. "Aye, my lord, and so would I. 'Twould seem we share my father's tastes."

"A man of excellent taste, I might add," Gyles replied, and then chortled. "He certainly foresaw my Adriana as a jewel in the rough. Now look at her."

"I have been, all evening," Colton averred with a broad grin and was wont to marvel at how comfortable his hand felt riding on the small of Adriana's back as he escorted her to the door. A scant three months ago, he would never have imagined such simple, yet totally gratifying pleasures.

They were just leaving the library when a shocked gasp drew their attention to the woman standing in the hallway. The look of astonishment on Felicity's face seemed to convey that her thoughts were not all that favorable for Adriana's reputation.

Colton wasn't inclined to offer reassurances of their innocence, at least not at this point. "Were you looking for anyone in particular, Miss Felicity?"

"Mr. Elston seemed terribly angry when he stalked past me in the hall just now," she explained, glancing from one to the other. "I was just a bit bemused, that's all, wondering what had upset him. I didn't realize the two of you were in the library."

Colton smiled briefly. "I'm afraid Roger was hoping he could win Lady Adriana for himself, but it was explained to him that that wouldn't be the case. He didn't care for that idea."

"No, I imagine it wouldn't be . . . to his liking, I mean," Felicity replied with a rather frail smile. Hearing footsteps, she glanced toward the library door as the elder Sutton made an appearance.

Having heard the exchange, Gyles had deemed it wise to present himself for his daughter's sake. Smiling as he glanced toward the couple, he rumbled, "I thought you two were going to dance."

Colton gave him a crisp half-bow. "Aye, my lord, that was our plan . . . unless you've changed your mind about giving your permission."

"And why should I?" Gyles inquired quizzically and blustered a bit as he strove to control a grin. "Unless, of course, you're a rogue at heart."

"I may well be, my lord," Colton acknowledged, grinning. "Your daughter could be in danger."

The elder stroked his chin reflectively, wondering if he should read anything into the marquess's statement, and cocked a brow meaningfully. "Perhaps I should warn you, sir, that if warranted, I'm not above changing your status from bachelor to bridegroom."

Colton had the feeling the man would prove a formidable foe to best should anyone offend his daughter. He laughed to ease the elder's fears. "I hear that you're a fair shot, my lord, so be confident of my good intent. I shall take special care to treat your daughter with utmost respect."

"Good!" Gyles chortled and waved them off. "Now you'd better go before the musicians decide to take another break."

Smiling, Gyles stroked his chin as he watched the couple strolling down the hall together. It was rare indeed for a man and a woman to complement each other to such a degree. His old friend had certainly chosen well for his son, but then, Gyles was of a mind to think he could have done far worse for his daughter. As for the future, that was anyone's guess.

With a tenderness rarely exhibited by a man who had spent half his lifetime in the military, the marquess drew the lady's arm within the bend of his elbow as his glowing eyes delved into hers. Beneath that consuming gaze, the dark orbs seemed unusually soft and pliable above a gentle smile. It was not at all surprising that the man paused and, pulling the lady near, pressed his lips to her brow for an unusually long moment, causing Gyles's heart to swell with spiraling hope.

Mentally rubbing his hands together in relish, he could only imagine the future rewards to be had from his daughter's union with the handsome man. *And what beautiful grandchildren they will make for us!*

Clearing his throat as he got down to the business at hand, the Earl of Standish faced the young lady who was staring rather miserably after the two, or perhaps, more precisely, the Lord of Randwulf. "People have been known to get lost in this old Tudor mansion, Miss Fairchild. Its many wings seem to confuse strangers. Would you care to be escorted back to the ballroom?"

In something of a breathless panic, Adriana fairly flew toward the stairs, thankful no one but Colton was in the hall to take note of her rapid flight *or* her flaming cheeks. Over the balustrade, she noticed his face had become a rigid mask as he sought to suppress the manly instincts goading him. Like some sleek, powerful panther prowling the narrow limits of his cage, he paced the shadowed confines of the corridor, grinding the clenched fist of one hand into the palm of the other.

Upon reaching the landing, Adriana couldn't resist a last glance back at the handsome marquess. He had paused to watch her ascent, and beneath the consuming heat of his eyes, she felt thoroughly divested of her garments as those gray orbs ranged slowly upward.

The lady's elevation allowed Colton a view of trim ankles clad in dark silk stockings. From there, his lusting gaze ranged upward with equal admiration. Having stored within his memory every detail of those long, shapely legs bereft of clothing, he could envision the lush, dainty place where they joined and the smooth, creamy hips bejeweled by nothing more than a tiny navel. Her slender waist dipped inward smoothly from her hips, and from there his mental eye roamed upward to well-rounded orbs adorned with nipples as soft and delicate as blushing pink rose petals. His gaze lifted to her gracefully wide shoulders and higher still, until at last his smoldering gray eyes met her worried gaze.

"Hurry," he silently mouthed, finding it hard to drag his mind free of the tantalizing image of her standing in nothing more than her own fine, unfettered, womanly raiment.

Responding with a jerky nod, Adriana lifted her hem and hastened toward her bedchamber. Upon entering its spacious privacy, she swung the portal closed behind her and then leaned back against it, totally shaken and thoroughly amazed by what she was experiencing. Her knees felt too weak and shaky to carry her across her chambers. Yet infinitely more disquieting was the strangely pleasurable throbbing at the core of her womanly being.

It had begun innocently enough shortly after a group of twenty or so matrons of various sizes, shapes, and ages had rushed giggling through the ballroom door, promptly meeting a barrier of musicians and dancing couples who, in a quest to escape outdoors for a bit of fresh air, had converged on the opposite side. At the time, Adriana had wondered what chicanery the older women had been about and could only believe some new, titillating gossip had come to their attention and they were eager to spread it. They had proven redoubtable in their zeal to forge through the nearly impregnable throng that had been halted at the doors. The two opposing bodies pressed forward, the musicians and guests on one side and the matrons on the other, each group eagerly striving to slip past while unwittingly confining in a compact knot everyone who had been caught between.

Having found herself trapped in the crush of people, Adriana had felt her heart racing nearly out of control as she struggled desperately to cope with a fearful dread of severe confinement. Colton's long, muscular torso had proven formidable in its steely hardness, and in rising panic, she had sought to free herself until she had heard him mutter a curse. Trembling uncontrollably and on the verge of bursting into tears, she had tried to placate his anger by apologizing and admitting her own horror of being crushed.

"I'm sorry, Colton, truly I am, but I can't seem to catch my breath, and I fear I'm going to panic!"

At the time, Colton had had cause to recall an incident, which had happened a year or so before his departure from home. Adriana had come to Randwulf Manor to spend the night with his sister, and after dinner the two had set into playing hide-and-seek. As diligently as Samantha had searched, she had failed to discover the younger one's hiding place and ran to look for her in another wing. Hearing screaming sobs moments later,

Colton followed them to the guest room across the hall, where he discovered that Adriana had become trapped in a small chest after the latch had fallen shut behind her. In releasing her, Colton had found himself almost strangled by her fierce embrace as she shivered and wept. Thereinafter, she had been absolutely terrified of being enclosed in tight places or rigidly confined by some constricting force.

Pressed in from all sides in the ballroom, she had been nearly beside herself. Understanding her anxieties, he had settled his lips into her coiffure and, in a hushed, harried whisper, attempted to soothe her fears. "Please, dearest, just calm down. I'm not angry with you but at myself for having my mind too much on other things. Just be confident that we'll be out of this soon enough, and then you'll be free, but for pity's sake, Adriana, please keep still until we do. What you're doing to me is giving *me* cause to panic . . . for fear I'll embarrass us both once we're out of this. If you have no idea what I'm talking about, just remember what you saw in the bathing chamber."

For added emphasis, he had nudged his loins against her, causing her eyes to widen as he made her crushingly aware of his arousal. He had made no excuses for deliberately shocking her, merely peered down into her widening eyes as the dawning took effect.

Once the knot of people loosened enough to allow them to slip free, he had refused to let her fly lest he draw shocked stares from guests. Not having known what else to do, Adriana had stayed close in front of him, allowing her skirts to shield him from prying eyes as she led the way into the hall. She had thought they were safe then until a plump, matronly straggler scurried across their path in her eagerness to join her compatriots, forcing the brunette to an abrupt halt and, in turn, causing Colton to collide into the back of Adriana. The sharp gasp that had been snatched from her had closely emulated his. Had she sat upon a hot brand, she could not have jerked her hips forward any faster from the manly firmness she had felt against her buttocks.

Adriana heaved a sigh over her inability to cool her thoughts *or* her body. After doffing her gown, she draped it over a chaise and made her way into the bathing chamber. There, she wet a cloth, wrung it out, and laid it over the back of her neck. Her whole body was in desperate need of whatever cooling benefits the dampened linen could provide. Never in her life had she felt such burning heat in her cheeks or such quickening fires in the depths of her being as she had in that moment wherein Colton had nudged his hips deliberately against her. Why she hadn't been outraged by his audacity was a mystery beyond her immediate comprehension. But then, even in her adult years, she had never been able to escape the inexplicable feeling of belonging to him.

Adriana heard her bedchamber door open and then close rather gently. Certain that Maud had come to lend her assistance, she felt a surge of relief. The woman could knead her shoulders and relax her as no one else could, at times leaving her feeling as limp as a rag doll, all cozy and calm and ready to face another challenge.... Except Adriana didn't think she wanted her reserve tested by another delicious onslaught similar to that which she had recently experienced. Once was quite enough for one evening ... at least, until a marriage bound her to the man. Otherwise she couldn't predict what would happen.

"Maud, you're such a dear for coming to my rescue the very moment I needed you most," she warbled. "If you'd kindly massage my neck with scented rosewater, I'll be able to return downstairs in fine form. No one is as gifted at soothing frayed nerves as you are."

Footfalls were muffled by the oriental rug cushioning the floor of her bedchamber, yet Adriana had been ensconced in the same rooms for most of her life, and she knew from the odd shadow cast onto the bathroom floor by the lamp burning near her bed that something definitely wasn't the way it should be. There was no evidence of a frilly cap adorning a rather large, frizzy head. Instead the shadow evidenced a fairly small head with locks closely clipped....

A startled gasp escaped Adriana as she recognized the strangely distorted silhouette. Her chemise was a delicate combination of lace and satin, hardly worthy as a suit of armor. Its clinging tenacity caused her to snatch a towel over her bosom before she grabbed a bottle of essence. As the intruder stepped through the bathing chamber door, she whirled to face him.

"Get out of here, Roger, before I scream!"

The apprentice shrugged casually, unconcerned by her dictates. "I can't do that, Adriana. I need you ... I want you ... I *must* have you. No other woman will suffice."

"*You blackguard!*" Incensed, she threw the cut-crystal bottle at him, opening thin gashes along his cheek and earlobe.

Stumbling backward in retreat, Adriana thrust her arm out to indicate the path he should take to remove himself forthwith from her room. "Get out of here, Roger. *Now!* Or you will have to answer to my father. So help me, if you dare touch me, you'll never leave this room alive."

Wiping away the blood trickling down his cheek, he advanced with purposeful strides as his eyes perused the lustrous fullness visible above the towel. "Your threats are useless, Adriana. I'm going to have you, just as I promised myself months ago! I'll be long gone before your father comes up here, but if you think I'm afraid of him, I'm sorry to disappoint you. He's an old man, after all."

Adriana opened her mouth to scream, but immediately Roger leapt forward and clamped a hand across her lower face to stifle her outcry. His efforts enraged Adriana. She was incensed, determined, and strong. If she could control a stallion that most men feared, chief among them the apprentice, she vowed to give the fool a fight he'd long remember. Then he would see what her father would do to him.

Doubling a small fist, Adriana thrust it upward with all her might, hitting Roger's bony chin, rattling his teeth and knocking his head back hard against the wall. In the next instant, her knee came up and hit him hard in the groin, something interesting she had learned about men from her first encounter with Colton after his return home. It caused even more of a reaction from Roger who nearly gagged as he doubled over in pain. In spite of his agony, he reached out a hand and, seizing her arm, hauled her forward against the wall with such brutal force that she was sent reeling from it in a dazed stupor.

A short distance down the hall, Maud paused to listen, somewhat bemused by the dull thuds she was hearing. Just a few minutes ago, cautious footsteps had seemed to draw near her mistress's bedchamber. Now it seemed as if a scuffling noise came from its spacious confines.

Shaking her head, Maud rejected the notion. In such an old house, she couldn't be sure what she was hearing came from human sources. Her mother had often warned her as a child to be wary of strange bumps, groans, and ghostly shapes flitting through old houses.

Still, the sounds had done much to evoke her curiosity. Many guests were in the house, and there was always a possibility that some of them had gotten lost. It was the servants' duty to direct them toward the right area. Cautiously she advanced down the hall, fervently hoping it was a human making the noises instead of something eerie.

"M'liedy? Is 'at yu?" she called, and grew troubled when she received no answer. Settling her mind forthwith on one living and breathing culprit, she heaved an annoyed sigh and bustled down the hall with more vigor, laying the fault for the furtive scampering on a new maid in the household. Thus far, the chit had seemed far more inquisitive than industrious, having already been caught preening before her reflection while holding one of Lady Adriana's best gowns in front of herself. Henrietta Reeves had warned the chit not to go rifling through her ladyship's possessions ever again. Another infraction would likely see the girl packing her bags.

"Where be yu, Clarice? I know yu're up ta no good 'gain. Yu'd best come out now, or I'll be tellin' Miss Reeves on yu."

"Yu callin' me?" a voice from the opposite end of the hall inquired.

Maud whirled in surprise, wondering if her hearing was going bad. "What be yu doin' now, girl? Didn't Miss Reeves warn yu—?"

"Lady Melora said for me ta help Becky pack up the last o' 'er belongin's she left 'ere aftah the weddin' an' ta tidy 'er room afore she an' Sir 'Arold come upstairs tonight."

"An' yu've been 'ere all along? Wit' Becky?" Maud demanded.

"Aye," the girl answered and threw a thumb over her shoulder to indicate the other servant who had stepped to the open doorway behind her. "Becky be 'ere ta says so's 'erself."

Maud frowned in bemusement and, half turning, peered down the corridor toward the area from whence she had first heard the furtive footsteps.

"Is anyone 'ere?" she called, and when no answer came, glanced back at the two servants who were watching her rather oddly. The older woman decided forthwith that she needed fortification from her young mistress, or at the very least Miss Reeves or even Mr. Charles. One thing for sure, she was *not* going to search the long corridor alone.

Approaching the stairs, she announced to the other two servants, "I'll be goin' downstairs ta find Lady Adriana, an' then I'll be 'avin' a good looksee down the 'all. If'n yu 'appens ta sees 'er ladyship up 'ere, kindly tell 'er I'm lookin' for 'er."

Colton turned from the ballroom entrance, somewhat bemused by the weighty footfalls on the stairs. Instead of the beauty he had been waiting for, a middle-aged servant came into view. It seemed like ages since Adriana had gone upstairs, and he had begun to worry about her. "Do you know if the Lady Adriana will be down soon?"

Maud was clearly taken aback. "Why, I thought m'liedy was down 'ere enjoyin' the ball."

"She went upstairs to her bedchamber some moments ago after telling me that she was only going to refresh herself."

"I wonder why she didn't bid me ta come 'elp 'er . . . ," Maud muttered, half to herself as she canted her head in sudden perplexity.

"Do you think she's all right . . . ?" Colton asked anxiously, realizing he hadn't actually seen Roger leave the house. Considering the apprentice's propensity for physical intimidation, Colton wouldn't put it past the man to take Adriana by force, for it was obvious now that he had absolutely no chance of having her any other way.

"I'll be seein' for meself where m'liedy is," Maud declared, turning her bulky self promptly about.

"I'm coming with you," Colton announced, bolting up the stairs. "She may be in danger if Roger is still in the house."

"Roger? Why would—?"

"No time for explanations now," Colton shot back, as he leapt past the servant. His right leg twitched beneath the strain of his rapid movements, but he refused to yield to the discomfort. After reaching the head of the stairs, he glanced up and down the hall as he questioned the woman. "Which way from here?"

Winded from her climb, the portly Maud pointed in the appropriate direction to speed the man on his way. His running footsteps, muted to some degree by the carpet in the hall, drifted back to her before she managed to drag enough air into her lungs to speak. "Turn left an' then two doors down ta the right o' the corridor," she called after him. Realizing he'd likely shock her mistress if he entered her bedchamber unannounced, she added, "Me mistress may not be decent."

"I'll apologize *after* I know she's safe," Colton flung back. All he could think of was Roger and his desire to have the girl for himself.

Colton grabbed the curved handle of Adriana's door, but upon finding it locked, he laid an ear to the wooden plank in an effort to hear what was going on inside the room. The sounds emitting from the chambers were muffled, as if one straining under a great load. Jiggling the handle more insistently, he called through the wood, "Adriana, are you all right?"

Almost on the heels of his question, a stifled scream came from within, prickling his hackles and giving him impetus. Taking a step back, he raised his left leg and applied a well-heeled foot with driving force against the door, very near the handle, and with enough strength to send the portal flying open as the strip of wood around the lock gave way beneath his determined assault.

Emitting an angry snarl, Roger rolled away from Adriana and leapt to his feet. Having failed to subdue her ladyship sufficiently to accomplish what he had set out to do, he could now foresee a frantic bid to escape. His face stung from the deep gouges the beauty had wreaked with her fingernails, having raked them with savage intent from his brow to his chin. His lips were sore and distended from the blow he had received when she had thrust a fairly sharp elbow into his mouth. It certainly hadn't helped when she had turned into a raging virago and, with viciously sharp teeth, had started gnashing vulnerable areas that came within reach, launching him into a bit of a panic as he tried to save his ears, throat, even his nose from those deadly fangs. As fine, bright, and gleaming white as her teeth were, he suffered no doubt now that they had been made primarily for bloodletting.

Unable to foresee the pleasure of mounting an unconscious woman, he had refrained from driving a fist into her lovely jaw as he tried to protect himself. He had wanted her fully awake when he took her, so she'd know forevermore that he had her before any of her lordly aristocrats. He especially yearned for the marquess to be aware of that knowledge, and just maybe the man would decide against marrying her. In spite of her valiant struggles, he had managed to loosen his trousers and actually been in the process of unbuttoning his underwear when the door had burst open and his adversary had come charging in, sending him scrambling off the bed in heightening panic.

Stumbling awkwardly to his feet, Roger raised a leg to flee, but his falling trousers took revenge upon him, binding his ankles firmly together, and sending him flying headlong into the corner of a sturdy armoire. A sudden flash of pain exploded inside his brain, and in the next instant blood began dribbling from his brow. Darkness descended, narrowing his world considerably until nothing but a black void remained as he crumpled into an unconscious heap upon the floor.

"Are you all right?" Colton demanded, rushing to Adriana as she hurriedly scrambled to her knees. So little remained of her undergarments, she might as well have been naked. The lace camisole had been ripped to shreds; only a few remnants hung from her waist. Of her pantaloons, a meager strip fell over her hip. What little was left of her stockings were strewn over the rumpled velvet counterpane where the struggle had ensued.

The lady was shaking so badly, so much in a fog, and so intent on hiding her nakedness with the thin scraps of her clothing that Colton had to grab her arms and shake her to bring her to her senses, at the very least to claim her attention. "Adriana! Are you all right?"

A choked sob escaped her as her face crumpled, and she nodded jerkily as tears began to well forth. Repulsed as she had been by Roger's rough caresses and lusting kisses, she could not subdue her convulsive shivering. The apprentice had managed to frighten her to the depths of her being, yet, for all of that, she was grateful for having come through his assault unscathed except for her trauma, a few bruises, and scrapes. Her hands still ached from the fight she had launched against him. Indeed, it felt as if the skin had been scraped from her thin fingers. If not for his inability to keep her physically restrained and avoid the blows she had laid on him as he sought to unfasten his underwear, she would've likely become his victim well before Colton had knocked on her door. It had been a veritable tug-of-war over possession of her undergarments, with Roger trying to haul down her pantaloons while she had struggled desperately to hold them firmly in place. Her undergarments were now nothing more than a few token scraps, insufficient to hide her nakedness from a lord of the realm.

Colton's ire rose with mounting fury as he viewed the paths Roger's greedy fingers had taken, for reddened streaks marred the creaminess of Adriana's round breasts, stomach, and thighs. Her throat bore a rash, no doubt from a bearding even a boyish face could produce.

Adriana's hands shook uncontrollably as she sought with one purpose in mind to secure her modesty, but as much as she tried, her failure could not be avoided. Tears streamed unchecked down her face, attesting to her shame and distress. In some embarrassment, she laid an arm over her breasts as she settled her free hand over her womanhood, the best she could manage under the circumstances.

"You look like you can use this," Colton murmured sympathetically as he doffed his coat and laid it around her shoulders. It reached almost to her knees and was so large she looked like a little girl in her father's coat.

"Thank you for coming to my rescue," she croaked, lifting her gaze to his. She saw his face through an indistinct blur as unchecked tears impeded her vision. "If not for you, I would've been . . ." After what had just possibly been her most terrifying experience with fear, she could not force the words through her lips. She swallowed against the rawness in her throat as she brushed at the wetness flowing down her cheeks. "But how did you know Roger would be up here?"

" 'Twas merely a simple deduction that left the man no other recourse in his attempt to have you," Colton murmured. "He could either take you by force or not at all. Obviously he decided to take advantage of this evening's ball and the fact that your family is downstairs entertaining friends."

Colton wasn't able to count the number of times since the night he had found the lady asleep in his bath that his memory had conjured up such sights to which he was now privy. His coat was a stranger to her winsomely curved form and refused to conform, yielding him an unhindered view of the lady's unfettered breasts.

Considering the tears that streamed in cascading rivulets down her cheeks, he pointed inside his coat. "My handkerchief . . . will you fetch it?"

Still very much in an emotional fog, Adriana patted her hands over the garment in search of hidden pockets, but to no avail. Her brows gathered in confusion until he took hold of the lapel and, pulling it outward to allow him enough space to move his hand beneath the coat without the threat of touching her, reached down inside to the inner pocket. Traumatized by her near ravishment, she offered him no resistance. It really hadn't been Colton's intent to shock her more than she had been already, but upon drawing the linen from its niche, the back of his hand brushed across a soft, pliant peak, causing Adriana's breath to catch sharply in her throat.

"I'm sorry, Adriana, I didn't mean to . . ." Words failed him as a convulsive shiver shook her, and he had to wonder after her recent trauma if she would faint. Then her dark eyes lifted and delved almost pleadingly into his. If ever he had wondered what it would feel like to be drawn out of himself and absorbed into softly appealing orbs, he found himself experiencing that very thing. Never had he known the consuming warmth that could fill his very being with a feeling of . . . Was it love? Compassion, perhaps? Or simply desire? Whatever name could be laid to it, it seemed to draw him forward like a disembodied spirit.

"Glory sakes alive!" Maud gasped as she stumbled into the room, snatching Colton abruptly to his senses and causing him to quickly reverse his steps. Having been forced to delay her ascent of the stairs because of an attack of wooziness, the maidservant now scurried toward her mistress with a look of distress, taking in the wildly tossed coiffure, the bruises and red marks evident around her soft mouth, and the bare knees barely visible beneath the oversized coat. "What's been goin' on in 'ere?"

She halted abruptly with mouth agape when she espied the apprentice lying sprawled in total oblivion near the armoire. As the realization dawned, she turned eyes widened in horror upon Adriana again. "Merciful 'eavens, m'liedy, what did 'at filthy rat do ta yu?"

Adriana wiped at the cascading rivulets flowing down her cheeks before managing to shake her head. "No real harm has been done to me, Maud," she choked out. Pausing, she cleared her throat in an attempt to dislodge the thickness that still impeded her tone. "But that is only because Lord Randwulf arrived in time to save me from the apprentice. Thanks to him, the worst I suffered from Roger's attack has been a few bruises and scrapes."

Reaching for the handkerchief Colton still clasped, she searched his face through a blur of tears as she drew it from his grasp. He was still staring at her, trying desperately to disentangle his mind from the encroaching vines that had entangled his thoughts a brief moment earlier. What craziness was he experiencing? he wondered. Indeed, even now he felt as if he were being absorbed into those dark, liquid pools.

" 'Is lor'ship thought yu might be in danger, m'liedy, what wit' Roger still in the house," Maud rushed on to explain, remembering that not too long ago her mistress had seemed dismayed by their approaching courtship. " 'E wouldn't wait till I 'ad a looksee. 'E come sprintin' hisself up 'ere ta make sure no 'arm were done ta yu."

"I'm grateful he didn't delay, Maud," Adriana replied shakily, her eyes delving into the gray orbs as she tried to find some reason for Colton's apparent befuddlement. Bestowing a tremulous smile upon her maid, she assured the elder, "If not for Lord Randwulf, Roger would've likely accomplished what he had set out to do."

"Then 'tis thankful I am as well 'at 'is lor'ship come rushin' ta yur aid, m'liedy, for none other could've reached yu in time." The maid crossed to the bed with a tentative inquiry. "Can I fetch a dressin' gown for yu, m'liedy?"

Adriana snuggled the lapels of Colton's coat up close around her neck as she folded her arms beneath her bosom. She didn't dare let the woman see what little remained of her underclothing. "Papa needs be told immediately what has happened here, and you'll have to be the one to carry the news to him."

Knowing the rage that would likely consume her father, Adriana glanced toward the unconscious apprentice, hardly expecting a shiver of revulsion to shake her so thoroughly that she was forced to sit back upon her heels.

"*Please,* get that man out of my sight," she bade in a strained whisper, turning her face aside as if he were something too hideous to look at.

Colton mentally shook himself from his thoughts and, in compliance with the lady's wishes, stepped toward Roger. "Maud, if you can show me a place where this unwelcome baggage can be sufficiently confined until his lordship is ready to deal with him, then I shall take care of that matter posthaste."

"I'm thinkin' 'twould serve 'at wily beggar 'is just due if 'e spent some time in the linen closet," Maud announced, motioning toward the adjoining room. "'Tain't 'ardly big enuff for a body tu breathe, much less twitch a muscle."

"Sounds like just the place for our Mr. Elston," Colton quipped.

Lifting a lip in a disdaining sneer as she considered the apprentice, the maid offered some insight of her own. "For a paltry li'l apprentice, 'e sure 'as some uppity ideas, what wit' 'is forcin' 'isself 'pon me mistress like 'e were expectin' 'er pa ta take it all in stride. The bloke don't know it, but 'twere 'is good fortune yu gots ta 'im befo' 'is lor'ship, else yu'd be carryin' out a corpse."

Squatting down beside the unconscious man, Colton rolled him over and considered the large, swollen gash that now marred the once-smooth brow. An open split from hairline to eyebrow still oozed dark blood. A sticky, red pool of it had collected on the oriental rug, causing Maud to fuss as she fetched a wet cloth to clean the stain and a dry linen to wrap around Roger's head. As the servant busied herself scrubbing the spot on the rug, Colton laid Roger over his shoulder and carried him into the bathing chamber. The linen closet provided even less room than a casket, causing a smile to play on Colton's lips as he squeezed the apprentice into the narrow space. At the moment, he could think of no one more deserving than the apprentice of being initiated into the horrible dread of close confinement.

Maud finished her task and approached the door, announcing that she was going down to inform Lord Gyles of the attack on his daughter. "'E won't take kindly what's been done up 'ere, m'liedy. I can almost 'ear 'im bellowin' now."

"Perhaps it would be wise if you told him beforehand that I haven't actually been harmed," Adriana cautioned. "He'll be less likely to fly into a rage and make a scene in front of the guests if he has been assured that I'm all right. But whatever you do, don't say anything to Mama, or she'll be flying up here in a near faint. For the time being, just say that I'm not feeling at all well and won't be down to bid farewell to the guests. Do you understand?"

"Aye, m'liedy. If'n it's all the same ta yu, I'll be lettin' yur pa do the tellin'. Yur ma 'as a way o' gettin' more outa me 'an I means ta tell."

By the time Colton returned to the bedchamber, Maud had already left on her unenviable mission. Adriana was now perched on the edge of her bed with his handkerchief pressed over her mouth as she tried desperately to muffle her harsh sobs. In gentle compassion Colton rested a hand upon her coat-shrouded shoulder. "Are you going to be all right?"

Embarrassed at being caught weeping, Adriana hurriedly wiped at her tears. "I will be once the shock of Roger's attack ebbs." Her breath fluttered outward in a lengthy sigh as a violent shudder shook her. "I've never been more frightened in my life than when I had to fight off his attack."

"I told Maud that she should have Charles escort your father into the library before she breaks the news. At least, if he lets out a bellow of rage in the library, none of the guests will be able to hear him."

Self-consciously, Adriana rose to her feet. "That was wise, of course. My father does have a temper, in spite of his efforts to deny it."

"I'd better leave so you can get some clothes on before he comes up," Colton murmured thickly, unable to resist flicking a glance beneath his coat again. As much as he had been appalled by Roger's aggression, he knew well enough the goading lusts that could drive a man, especially when such a sublime feast of womanly perfection was nigh at hand. What he saw was exceedingly more than he could bear without suffering the throbbing pains of pent-up desires. "Your father won't take it kindly if he finds me ogling you, especially after you've nearly been ravished."

As she stared up at him, wide-eyed and vulnerable, Colton lifted both hands to the lapels of his coat. For a long moment, it seemed as if he stood on the threshold of the rest of his life as he struggled with an overwhelming desire to kiss her. As much as he yearned to caress a silken breast and press his hand upward between her thighs and make her groan with longing, he knew it would be a foul, dastardly thing to do in light of what

Roger had tried to take from her, virtually an impossible one with her father coming posthaste. Yet she seemed so trusting, so willing . . .

It may have been the hardest thing he had ever done, but with a halting sigh, Colton pulled the lapels of his coat together, denying himself the solace he craved. Looking embarrassed, Adriana murmured an apology, making a belated attempt to secure her modesty, as if she considered herself at fault for not having done so sooner. Her chagrin gave him cause to wonder if she actually thought he didn't desire her. If she only knew the unrelenting passion he had been struggling to subdue since his return home, she'd banish that idea posthaste. Indeed, he could hardly think of anything but his yearning to take her in his arms and to penetrate her sweet, womanly moistness.

"Dearest Adriana, do you have any idea what a temptation you have been to me tonight?" he breathed as he laid an arm about her shoulders and lowered his face into her sweetly smelling hair. "I want to touch you, love you, and have you respond to my ardor with all the passion you're capable of exhibiting, but you've suffered a horrible shock tonight, and 'twill take time for you to forget what Roger tried to do to you. Whatever comes from our courtship, please be confident that I care for you."

She turned her face upward to look into his. Once again, their eyes melded as they had earlier, and he felt as if his heart were being drawn out of the cage he had erected around it. The yearning to hold her close seemed far beyond his ken, and yet, of a sudden, his arms were crushing her against him as his mouth plummeted downward to ensnare her lips with a fierce, consuming ardor, demanding, ravishing as his tongue delved in the sweet moistness of her mouth. His hand found its way beneath his coat and slid over a bare buttock. It was a sweet, rapturous delight, but as enjoyable as it was and as much as he could lose himself in the ecstasy of it, Colton knew it couldn't continue, not when her parent could walk in and find her all but naked in his arms.

"I must go before your father finds us and mistakes me for the culprit," he muttered huskily as he lifted his head, yet he seemed unable to leave her even then. He kissed her again with all the passion he had been holding in check, slanting his face across hers and greedily plying his tongue through the honeyed depths. He felt a convulsive shiver go through her, whether from fear or desire he could not tell, but some sanity returned at the thought that she might be afraid.

"I shouldn't be doing this after what you've just been through," he whispered raggedly, lifting his head. His eyes caressed her face almost hungrily. "I must leave...."

Setting her from him abruptly, he strode toward the door, already feeling the agony of unrequited passion. Somehow he'd have to cool the lust gnawing at his very being and try to forget how soft, sweet, and enticing she had felt in his arms.

Adriana gasped. "Colton, your coat...."

He turned in time to catch the garment in midair, and the last glimpse of Venus arrayed in nothing more than a few shreds of cloth left an impression that would haunt him mercilessly for weeks on end, oftentimes bringing him up from the depths of slumber in the agony of inflamed lust.

Thirteen

✳

A PENSIVE sigh slipped from Colton Wyndham's lips as he approached the wide expanse of mullioned windows that provided a view of the rolling, partially forested countryside typical of the vast acreage included within his holdings and that which surrounded his ancestral home. Normally he would have reveled in the variety of wildlife that could be seen from the windows, but this morning he hardly noticed the pair of deer grazing in a distant field, the rabbits scurrying in the grass beyond the gardens, or the small flock of birds flitting to and fro outside the windows and around the eaves of the manor. As in recent weeks, he found himself once again beset by visions of Adriana elegantly garbed or in all manner of disarray, laughing, crying, sleeping, or awake, but always paramount in his imagination, enslaving his thoughts with her melodious siren's song. Like some puckish sprite with dark, luminous eyes, she flitted in and out through the shadowed fringes of his mind, vexing his concentration no matter how meager or great the task in which he tried to involve himself. Though he had once thought himself immune to the subtle ploys of women, he had begun to suspect that he would never be free of Adriana, no matter the depths or heights he'd traverse or the continent to which he'd flee in a quest to seek his independence. Yet, as much as she ensnared his thoughts, he found his dreams even more daunting to his manly pride, for within them he seemed more her slave than conqueror, as she led him into fantasies no virginal maid could even imagine, much less instigate.

A month earlier, he had traveled to London to deal with matters relating to his marquessate, and he had thought while there he'd seek easement for his goading passions with Pandora and thereby thrust the younger woman out of his mind. More fool he to think he could escape the dark-haired beauty so easily. So preoccupied had he been with Adriana and the quandary in which he had become entrapped that he couldn't even rally enough enthusiasm to visit Pandora, much less imagine his ardor could be stirred to *any* degree by the actress. And yet, that very same night, his musings had drifted back to that moment wherein he had found Adriana lying asleep in his bath, and his desires had risen full mast in a thrice of a moment, and no amount of pacing had been effective in alleviating his goading lusts.

Colton groaned inwardly, recognizing the taut rope upon which he balanced. He had lost count of the months that had passed since he had last made love to a woman, definitely the better part of a year. If he didn't find relief fairly soon for his manly needs, the pain he was experiencing would leave him a damned eunuch! He was sure of it!

What had his father done to him?

He halted suddenly, startled by the blame he readily cast elsewhere. His sire wasn't at fault; it was his own doing. He could have rejected his parent's edict, paid the Suttons remuneration for his affront, and claimed the right to choose whomever he pleased for a wife. And yet, he had been loath to walk away from the opportunity to test the strong attraction that seemed to bind his heart and mind to Adriana. It was she who had set her gentle hooks into him, making him virtually useless to other women.

By providing an escort in the form of Samantha and Percy, he had thought to get through their courtship without pressing his suit beyond acceptable measures. Being chaperoned in such a manner certainly kept him from getting too carried away and compromising the lady's innocence. Unfortunately, the presence of his kin also caused him enormous frustration. More times than he cared to recall, he had found himself trying to subdue a strengthening urge to find a secluded niche private enough to kiss and caress the beauty until she could not withstand his ardent besiegement any longer and would yield to his manly persuasions. Any dark, secretive alcove would have seen him lifting her skirts and having his way with her.

Try though he did, he couldn't thrust from mind her eager response to his kiss or her acquiescence to the possessive claim his hand had made on her buttock after Roger's attack. He knew well enough that if ever he began fondling her again, there'd be no turning back.

So much for standing firm against his father's edict. He was nothing more than a bleating lamb skipping merrily along toward his own slaughter!

Only one month remained of their courtship, and he didn't even know if he'd be able to keep his hands off the lady long enough to allow a big wedding to be planned. The more they were together, the more he could foresee the risk of her standing potbellied with child before a rector.

Thus far, he had exerted every measure of restraint he had been capable of rallying in an effort to quell the procreative instincts that could goad a man and, with equal urgency, to revive that small shred of pride compelling him to stay true to his resolve and remain his own man. Even the thought of that idea had now become rather laughable. To be sure, what Adriana had managed to do with his perseverance in the last several weeks was no less than criminal. To wit: While shaving recently, he had nearly sliced his own throat, albeit accidentally, when it suddenly dawned on him what had been flaring through his brain, *Courtship, be damned! Get on with the wedding and let the bedding be done!*

Had he lost his wits? Did musings of that sort seem even remotely akin to what he was capable of thinking? He had never met a woman he couldn't thrust easily from mind . . . that is, until he had returned home and realized the girl he had rejected years ago had become a dazzling beauty. As adamantly as he had revolted against the idea of accepting his father's choice before his departure, it didn't placate his pride one iota to realize that Adriana was swiftly becoming *his* choice.

Frustrated, he was. Of that, he had no doubt. No one, especially the lady, had any notion how much control he had to maintain over himself to keep from absconding with her.

That event would certainly raise a few eyebrows!

So, what was he to do? Continue on as if his vitals hadn't been knotted up so tightly in his stomach that he wanted to groan in pain? It seemed as if the previously invincible gutstrings of his self-control were playing an entirely different tune lately, and he was sure if he listened closely enough, he'd hear amid the chaotic rhythm presently vexing his manly mood the distant tolling of wedding bells, all because of a beautiful, charming, heroic young woman with whom he was falling deeply in love.

L$_{ORD}$ Randwulf and the Burkes have arrived, my lady," the butler announced after Maud had let him into his young mistress's bedchamber. "They're awaiting your presence in the vestibule. Shall I show them into the drawing room?"

"No need, Charles. Please inform them that I'll be down directly. I won't be but a moment more." Adriana swept a hand toward the chaise where Maud had laid out her red velvet cloak. "Would you be so kind as to take my wrap down with you please, Charles?"

"Yes, my lady." The servant smiled. Of the three Sutton siblings, only the Lady Adriana voiced her requests with such sweetly appealing pleas.

As the steward left and Maud busied herself with setting the chambers in order, Adriana rose from her dressing table and retrieved the Christmas present she had made for the elderly Samuel Gladstone. She had every hope the fleece-lined velvet stocking cap would be effective not only in keeping the old man warm during the cold nights ahead, but in warding off maladies that could very well weaken his valiant spirit and aging body. He was such a treasure to the people of the town and the area encompassing it that she had no doubt that he'd be sorely missed if he were to expire.

It wasn't until Maud glanced around that Adriana realized she had heaved another troubled sigh. It seemed she had been doing that much too frequently of late, but as in the past, it failed to ease her pensive mood.

"Is all well wit' yu, m'liedy?" the older woman inquired worriedly.

"Of course, Maud," she replied, hoping to ease the servant's concerns. Heartening herself, however, would be a different matter entirely. As much as Colton had escorted her to this or that affair during the past two months, it had always been in the company of others. It seemed a convenient way for him to provide evidence that he was doing nothing untoward during this three-month tenure. At its conclusion, she fully expected him to announce that he had paid his full due to his father's edict and had decided he preferred freedom over marriage with her. The Burkes' verification of his gentlemanly comportment would give him an easy, viable escape. That gloomy prospect weighed down her spirits perhaps as nothing else had ever done. What else could she believe except that Colton Wyndham wanted to be free of her forevermore?

Enough of this! Adriana mentally chided herself and gathered together the ragged shreds of her tenacity. If Colton dismissed her from his life, then surely she'd be better off without him, for she'd be loath to marry a man who didn't want her. Getting over the hurt, however, would prove an horrendous ordeal, but given enough time, she'd eventually manage. She had certainly survived his first rebuff; she would endure the second. Still, she had never known how much her heart could be moved by a man until Colton had come back into her life. Their courtship had caused her moments of painful confusion, yet, just as often, pleasure that lightened her heart and made it soar. Merely being with her handsome courtier had done much to enlighten her as to the many delights to be found in a relationship between a man and a woman. Even small deeds seemed much more evocative when he performed them, such as when he pulled her arm through his and escorted her here or there. To see the smile that normally followed such services seemed to lift her whole being on airy wings.

Colton's gallantry had been sweepingly evident even at the commencement of their courtship. The Sunday following the Autumn Ball, he had arrived at Wakefield Manor in the afternoon to formally initiate it. With a grin reminiscent of his boyish years, he had presented her with a lavish bouquet of flowers, admitting somewhat sheepishly that a servant had collected them from the conservatory, albeit with Philana's permission. That unexpected awkwardness in so stalwart a man had touched her in ways she had never known possible.

Faced with the prospect of having every word he uttered in the manor being overheard by her parents, he had invited her to take a stroll with him through the gardens, which in late October had certainly not been at their best. Yet she had readily concurred, knowing there'd be enough of a nip in the chilled breezes to redden her nose and cheeks and disguise the blushes that were wont to sweep into her cheeks whenever she recalled not only her lack of clothing when he had kissed her the night after Roger's attack, but her yearning to have him hold and comfort her.

The lofty hedges surrounding Wakefield gardens had afforded them cozy places of privacy, and her tensions had begun to ease soon after he had engaged her in conversation. Until that moment, Adriana had never realized what a complex individual Colton had become. He had talked candidly about his experiences in the military, and, in subtle ways, confirmed his streak of independence. During his military career, he had had several unexpected confrontations with the enemy wherein he had been forced to improvise and make decisions contrary to orders he had been issued rather than see his men needlessly slain. No one after hearing his stories could doubt his self-sufficiency, and she had felt honored that he had revealed things about himself that he hadn't been inclined to tell his own kin, much of which had had to do with the rift he had caused by his departure from home and the difficulty in coping with the horrendous emptiness of his loss and his separation from his family. After being sent to Africa, however, he had been too busy to think of home and what he had left behind, and much of his remorse had faded from conscious thought.

When he had recounted humorous incidents that had happened during his career as an officer, Adriana had found herself laughing beyond measure at his tales and, in every respect, enjoying their repartee. He had a relaxed, compelling manner about him, and what seemed even more admiring in her estimation was the fact that he was capable of laughing at himself and openly jesting about his idiosyncrasies. Those he mentioned seemed far more charming than vexing. In short, she found him a truly remarkable individual, the sort she'd have chosen to marry had she been given a chance to make the selection herself.

Invited to stay for supper later that evening, Colton had assured her parents that it would not only give him great delight to do so, but would also please his mother who was no doubt hoping and praying that he'd enjoy his visit. He had sat across the table from Adriana, from whence he had seemed liberally disposed to peruse her for the better part of the meal. Much later that evening, as he was preparing to leave, they had stood together outside the front door of Wakefield Manor and held hands as they spoke of family and other things. Then, after snuggling the hood of her cloak close about her face, he had kissed her in a way that had set her heart to fluttering. It had been a sweet little morsel that had united their lips and threatened to engage their tongues as his own whisked tantalizingly across her mouth and slipped briefly inward. Quite abruptly, however, he had set her from him, cleared his throat as he overlapped his redingote in front of himself, and then had briskly taken his departure, leaving her smiling in secret pleasure as she wandered back into the house and up to her bedchamber. Long after snuggling beneath her bedcovers, she had still been reveling in the fact that their kiss had affected him in ways she would never disclose to anyone.

Since that first visit, her parents had been encouraged by Colton's apparent eagerness to get on with the courtship and had remarked numerous times on his suave, impeccable manners. Adriana didn't dare tell them that when it suited his purposes, Colton Wyndham could also be a devil-ish rogue and a bit of a roué at times.

Properly chaperoned by the Burkes, they had spent several days of the following week in Bath where they had shopped, attended plays, musical events, and other social gatherings. By the end of that same expanse of time, nearly everyone in England had become aware that they were *a couple*, or so it had been bandied about by numerous rumors.

As for Roger, her father had come close to killing him the night of his attack on her person. When the young man finally regained consciousness well after the guests had left, the elder had pressed a cocked pistol very close to the tip of Roger's nose as he voiced his indignation. Such a dis-play of paternal rage had left the apprentice quailing in terror and plead-ing for his life amid a profusion of frightened tears. It had only been her mother's wise counsel that had caused Gyles to concede that killing the man would only arouse the curiosity of the gossips. Nevertheless, her father had warned Roger that if he dared approach within close proximity to her ever again while she was unattended that he'd well rue the day. For that offense, he would either be chased down and gelded on the spot or be forced to face far more serious consequences, which would come upon him when he least expected it. For the time being, however, he would allow Roger to go about his affairs without bringing charges against him. It wasn't that Gyles had felt the least bit merciful toward the man; he had just had a sharp aversion to his daughter's name being sullied by an avaricious band of talebearers who'd make much of her near-ravishment.

Concluding his apprenticeship shortly thereafter, Roger had assumed management of the mill and proved his potential by bringing in profits purportedly equal to those once reaped by the original owner, Thomas Winter, a feat Edmund Elston had failed to accomplish in spite of his inclination to laud his own ingenuity. After cruelly maligning his son over his failure to win Lady Adriana, the elder had evidently received his just due, or so some of the mill's employees had whispered, for shortly there-after the elder had suffered a seizure that had left him bedridden and in something of a confused stupor. The fact that the rebuke had taken place in front of the workers had all but severed the tenuous rapport that for the last year had existed between sire and son. Still, there were those who had been cognizant of the fact that Edmund Elston had written out his will well before their rift and, because he had no other next of kin or close friends, had named his son heir of all his possessions and properties.

Some had even predicted upon the man's demise that Roger Elston would become a fairly rich man. Edmund's constitution, however, had soon negated all the morbid predictions he would soon die. His housekeeper even went so far as to say that she saw daily improvement in the man.

Purportedly Roger was now wooing Felicity. For some unknown reason, Stuart had lost interest in the miller's granddaughter shortly after the Autumn Ball, and, to everyone's surprise and Adriana's immense delight, he had begun courting Berenice Carvell, whose proportions in the recent two months had diminished by a noticeable degree. As a result, her comeliness was becoming more and more apparent. As for Riordan Kendrick, he had been rather reclusive since that same event, seeing no lady at all, only intimate friends, or so the rumors had gone. Hearsay had it that he was supervising repairs currently being made to his own private chambers at his estate on the far side of Bradford, and that both London and Bradford woodwrights had been engaged to create paneling beautiful enough to please a discriminating marquess. His housekeeper, Mrs. Rosedale, knew only that he had wanted to make some changes in the manor, for what reasons she wouldn't even speculate. No one had been able to obtain further information, as much as the overtly curious were wont to query many of his household servants whenever they'd venture out to shop. They only repeated what Mrs. Rosedale had volunteered, and nothing else was forthcoming. Their inability to discover his lordship's reasons left gossips all the way from London to Bath in a veritable quandary for fear they were missing some juicy tidbit.

It was upon Riordan Kendrick and his aspirations to have her for his wife that Adriana sought to turn her thoughts as she made her way from her bedchamber. To some degree, Riordan's proposal of marriage served to reassure her that she was honorably desired by someone. Still, upon nearing the central hall where her escort awaited her, she hoped that just once she wouldn't be able to liken Colton to some gorgeous phantom being who had come down to earth for the express purpose of stealing her heart and perhaps even her very soul.

"Good evening," she greeted, forcing a cheery smile as she approached her handsome courtier and their chaperones. If truth be told, she yearned to return to the privacy of her bedchamber where she'd make a desperate attempt to forget that Colton Wyndham had ever returned to disrupt her life. Much to her regret, she had fallen in love with the man, and she despaired of the moment wherein he'd coldly kiss her cheek and terminate their parents' agreement. It certainly didn't help the pace of her heart to discover that her frivolous wish of an earlier moment had been to no avail, for he was the very epitome of a tall, flawlessly handsome, aristocratic gentleman.

Samantha hurried forward and fondly pressed a kiss upon her friend's cheek. "You took your own sweet time getting down here," she teased with a grin. "Why, if I were at all suspicious, I'd be inclined to say you have no wish to attend Mr. Gladstone's Christmas party." As her eyes searched the dark, luminous depths and found no hint of joy, she queried more pointedly, "Or is it that you wish to avoid Roger and Felicity, who'll certainly be there?"

Though her closest friend and confidant had hit close enough to the truth to make her almost flinch, Adriana feigned surprise as Charles brought her velvet cloak. "Why should I wish to avoid them?"

"Because, you goose," Samantha replied with warm, chuckling laughter, "Felicity is wont to claim to every sympathetic ear that you led Roger merrily along until Colton came home. Of course, dear Roger, bless his black heart, magnanimously nods in agreement." She clasped the thin fingers and, finding them trembling and as cold as ice, searched the dark eyes with growing concern. "We don't have to go to Stanover House at all if you'd rather not, Adriana."

"We're going," the younger woman declared resolutely, taking herself firmly in hand. "We'll be visiting Samuel Gladstone, not his granddaughter. After that, whether we stay or go will be entirely up to the three of you."

As much as Colton sought to maintain a gentlemanly serenity in Adriana's presence, he felt his vitals once again being turned inside out. It happened each and every time he laid eyes on her, for she was the very fabric of every lofty vision he had ever formed of the ideal woman. There had been many times while in her presence when he had felt like a simple lackey before a queen. This evening she looked no less than regal in a dove-gray, silk-lace gown that clung sublimely to her slender, curving form.

Having halted Charles with a hand upon his arm, Colton silently claimed the lady's cloak from the butler and stepped behind her. Leaning near as he spread the garment around her shoulders, he murmured above her ear, "Your perfection leaves me besotted, my sweet."

The warm, mellow tones of his voice undermined Adriana's efforts to remain distantly detached from the man. His words seemed to resonate through her being, much like a lover's caress stroking vulnerable areas. She felt doubly defeated when his lean knuckles brushed her bare shoulder. Although nearly dissolving in bliss, she managed a wavering whisper in spite of the tremor he evoked within her. "You're very gallant, my lord."

Her delicate scent was merely one of the many temptations Colton was forced to confront whenever he was near the lady. She always smelled as if she had just emerged from a swirling sea of rose petals. Although he'd have greatly preferred to limit such delicious assaults on his poorly depleted restraint, he was beginning to suspect that in comparison, standing firm against Napoleon's forces had been child's play.

Although clearly capable of recognizing the folly of lingering overlong at such tasks, Colton couldn't resist straightening her collar and smoothing the garment over her shoulders. Touching her even casually seemed far more stimulating to his goading desires than anything he had experienced heretofore with other women. So, too, the sights to which his gaze was privy as he stood behind her. His height gave him the advantage, for he could from that angle peruse her creamy breasts to a greater depth, a view he deliberately sought more than he cared to admit even to himself. He was always eager for a fresh glimpse of the pale orbs or their delicate pink peaks barely visible through the gossamer lace trim of her satin chemise.

From across the room, it had seemed at first glance as if she wore nothing at all beneath the lace scrollwork of her gown. As much as his manly propensities would have been greatly heartened by such sights, he knew Adriana would never have worn anything so risqué. She was a refined lady, after all. Still, whatever hopes he had briefly nurtured were dashed when he realized a flesh-colored silk facing lined her lace gown from shoulder to hem.

"I overheard Samantha teasing you," he murmured for her ears alone, leaning near to catch the fragrance of roses wafting from her temple. It always seemed far more delectable in that area than any spot he had yet discovered, leading him to think that she dabbed a tiny drop or two of perfume there as a finale to her grooming. "You needn't fear Roger while I'm with you. I won't let him hurt you, Adriana."

A smile flitted tentatively across Adriana's soft lips as she turned to look at him over her shoulder. No one but Colton, her parents, and a few trusted servants knew of Roger's attack upon her person. Colton hadn't even told Samantha, which was well, for her friend would never have been able to carry off the pretense of being nice to Roger.

Though Colton made every effort to resist the appeal of those innocent, doe-eyed looks, he could feel the meager store of his resolve waning.
He could only imagine what his heart was doing. At times such as these,
he had cause to wonder why he delayed asking for the lady's hand. If
merely for the sake of his pride, then he could believe the only one he was
punishing was himself, for he couldn't imagine a virgin being tormented
by cravings of the magnitude he had recently been suffering. And if in a
tiny segment of his brain he was still entertaining hopes of seeking his
freedom after being so sweetly cajoled by the lady for the whole of their
courtship, then he had no doubt that the moment of his departure would
be akin to a fool tearing out his own heart and trampling it carelessly
underfoot as he walked out the door.

"We'd better be on our way," he breathed, endeavoring to curb his
unabated longings. He moved around to her side and offered his hand.
"Mr. Gladstone will be expecting us fairly early this evening."

"I heard it said that Felicity arranged everything in accordance with her
grandfather's Christmas feasts from previous times," Adriana replied,
feigning a bright smile as she tried to rally her enthusiasm. "Considering
how crowded Stanover House has been in the past, 'twill be fortunate if
we even get to see Mr. Gladstone, much less chat with him."

"I believe that's exactly why he urged us to come early," Colton replied,
grinning aside at her. "I think the old man is quite fond of you and
Samantha and doesn't wish to miss an opportunity to see you both."

A smile curved her soft lips. "Well, we happen to be just as fond of
Mr. Gladstone."

"I really don't think you're aware of your effect on men, my dear," he
challenged. Though his grin seemed to suggest that he was teasing her, he
was never more serious in his life.

Her brows gathering in bemusement, she peered up at him. "What do
you mean?"

He reached out a hand and brushed a stray curl from her cheek as his
eyes probed hers. "For my own protection, my dear, I think I'd better keep
you ignorant of your winning appeal. It's becoming more and more difficult to withstand your assaults."

Her brows gathered in confusion. "Assaults? What do you——?"

"Perhaps I'll explain in time," he replied, slipping his hand beneath her
elbow. "As for now, Percy and Samantha are waiting for us."

Colton turned, accepted his top hat from Charles, and then presented his arm to Adriana. After whisking her out the front door, he handed her into the landau and then politely waited for Percy to perform the same task for his wife. Only after his brother-in-law had taken his seat did Colton climb in. As usual, the only place left vacant was in the most torturous area, right next to the dark-haired temptress. Though weeks ago he had ascertained that he'd be better off riding atop the coach with Bentley, it still wouldn't have been far enough away to allow him to banish Adriana from his manly awareness. As he settled into the seat beside her, he almost closed his eyes in ecstasy as her delicate fragrance twined through his senses, entangling his mind like a silken rope. As stalwart as he had once been while practicing the art of war, he could almost feel his own manly determination dissipating whenever he was near Adriana, but then, more likely it was his heart dissolving in her hand.

Soon after the landau pulled away from Wakefield Manor, Samantha leaned across and rested a gloved hand upon her brother's knee. "Percy and I have an announcement to make."

The exterior lanterns cast enough light into the carriage to readily illumine Colton's white-toothed grin. "You're selling your town house in London and moving into a larger one."

His sister sat back with an astonished gasp. "How did you know that?"

"Percy told me tonight shortly after your arrival."

Samantha tossed her head saucily as she cut her eyes askance at her chuckling husband. "I don't know what I'm going to do with him," she fussed prettily. "He has never been able to keep a secret."

"Tell them," Percy urged, squeezing her hand, "or I will."

"Tell us what?" Adriana pressed, exchanging a curious glance with Colton.

"I am in a family way," Samantha announced proudly, this time drawing a whoop from her brother who reached across to shake his brother-in-law's hand.

"Oh, how wonderful, Samantha!" Adriana warbled, feeling all warm and content of a sudden.

"Congratulations to you both," Colton chimed in. "How far along?"

"Three months or so."

He calculated the time in his head. "So the baby should be born about—?"

"My best guess is the middle of May or perhaps into June," Samantha hurriedly finished for him before leaning back with a radiant smile.

"Does Mother know?" Colton asked.

"I ran upstairs soon after we arrived at Randwulf and told her while you men were enjoying a libation in the drawing room."

Colton's broad shoulders shook with laughter. "I'm sure she was absolutely thrilled at the idea of becoming a grandmother."

"Of course," Samantha acknowledged, as if the idea of her mother's elation was something totally expected. She grinned contentedly. "Considering how long Percy and I have been married, Mama had almost lost hope that such an event would ever take place, but now, merely the anticipation of having a baby in the family has brought a spark of life back into her eyes. She'll likely want as many as Adriana and I can produce, so you'd better settle this courtship of yours fairly quickly, Colton, so Mama can look forward to another grandchild coming soon after ours is born."

In overwhelming embarrassment, Adriana turned her face to the window as she struggled against the onslaught of a scalding blush. She wished her friend wouldn't be so bold about such things in her brother's presence. Being constantly pressured to marry her would likely force the man to flee to another part of the world, just as he had done when his father had first presented his proposal for their betrothal.

Difficult as it was to remain unruffled at the idea of Adriana getting with child, Colton managed a smile for his sister, but he had to wonder how his mother would react if in the very near future he'd dispense with his restraints and step over the boundaries of protocol in his mounting desire to make love to Adriana. His self-control was so badly frayed now that it wouldn't take much at all to goad him beyond the point of no return. Each passing day saw a further weakening of his will, pushing him toward the narrow bridge suspended over the bottomless gorge. An unwary step and he could well find himself hurtling headlong into matrimony *after* he took her virginity.

Jane Fairchild is as warm and gracious as an angel," Samantha declared in muted tones shortly after the vivacious woman had shown them into the elderly miller's home. "But frankly, I think her daughter has become something of a witch since we first met her. I swear, as piercing as Felicity's glare is, I'm sure it's going to bore a hole right through us, Adriana. She looks like an adder waiting to strike."

"Shhh, someone may hear you," the younger woman cautioned, squeezing her friend's fingers warningly. She glanced around to see if she could detect heightened interest on the faces of those standing within close proximity. Seeing no evidence of such, she felt a surge of relief that her friend's whisper had not been overheard above the low drone of voices in the crowded parlor.

Samantha lightly scoffed. "Considering the way Felicity's eyes have narrowed, I wouldn't put it past her to have read the words right out of my mouth. Witches are like that, you know."

"Perhaps we should join the men upstairs and pay our respects to Mr. Gladstone before he becomes thoroughly spent. Jane said he wasn't feeling very well this evening, so I would imagine he's not up to all this company. If Colton and Percy are acceptable to the idea, we should perhaps consider taking our leave fairly early. Felicity certainly doesn't seem to want us here, and I'd rather not feel beholden to her."

Samantha chanced another glance toward the blonde and shivered, feeling a cold chill go through her. She couldn't remember ever being the recipient of such venomous glares. "What did we ever do to deserve those icy daggers? As much as we thought we were doing her a favor by inviting her on our outing, she seems to begrudge us now."

"I believe her resentment, dear friend, has something to do with the contract your father dreamt up."

Once again sliding her eyes askance toward the one who, by some strange turn of events, had become something of a nemesis to each of them, Samantha could think of no other reason for the change in the woman. "You mean because you have Colton and she doesn't. As *if* she ever stood a chance with my brother."

"I don't *have* Colton," Adriana corrected in an emphatic whisper. "He's very much his own man."

"Well, if I'm able to read anything from Felicity's glares, I'd be inclined to say that everybody else believes you do, and she's hearing their gossip."

"Then *everybody* is wrong. Now let's go upstairs before I become vexed with your constant insistence that Colton and I are as good as betrothed. And while I'm speaking my mind, I wish you wouldn't talk so freely about my having his children in his presence. I'm sure it embarrasses him as much as it does me."

"Doubtful," his sister rejoined, following Adriana into the inner hall. "I don't think anything embarrasses him. More likely than not, seeing the world as part of an army of men has made him impervious to almost everything."

Pausing on the bottom step of the stairs, Adriana turned on her friend in a bit of a huff. "If *he* is, then *I* most certainly am not, and if you insist upon carrying on with such talk, henceforth I shall refuse to go anywhere with you while Colton is present. So I urge you, Samantha, stop trying to prod him into marrying me. If he doesn't lose his temper, then I surely shall."

Casually dismissing the younger woman's threat with a shrug of her slender shoulders, Samantha glanced everywhere but at her companion. "You're just being overly sensitive about it, that's all."

Heaving a frustrated sigh over what she had come to consider a careless disregard for propriety, Adriana managed a subdued retort. "I could say *you're* being *overly insensitive*, my dear, but I doubt *that* would do any good."

Samantha flicked a brief sidelong glance at her friend and then looked back a second time almost as quickly. Upon closer inspection, she began to giggle as she stared intently at the tip of Adriana's nose. "I do believe Felicity's glare has left its mark on you or else, you naughty girl, you've been playing in the soot. Whether you're aware of it or not, you've acquired a dark smudge on your nose. I hope it isn't your *witchy* temper evidencing itself again."

In sudden consternation, Adriana glanced down at her gloved hand and discovered the leather near her fingertips now bore a dark blotch of ink. She remembered the guest book lying open on a table near the front door and could only believe the elderly lady who had entered before them had accidentally smeared ink on the pen. Stripping off her gloves, she whispered urgently, "Hurry, wipe off the smudge before someone else sees it and thinks I've grown a wart or something worse on my nose."

"Warts go right along with being witchy, you know," Samantha teased, her eyes dancing.

Adriana sighed in exasperation. "Are you going to play the simplepated buffoon or will you be cooperative for a change?"

Once again, Samantha's slender shoulders moved upward in placid response. "I don't have anything with which to wipe it off."

Adriana cast her eyes briefly upward as if passionately praying for patience, and then, mutedly issuing a mutter about *some testy individuals*, hurriedly searched through her heavily bejeweled handbag for her own dainty, lace-trimmed handkerchief. "Getting back to what we were discussing a moment ago, *Lady Burke*, this courtship was not your brother's idea. It was forced upon him. You'll only give him more reason to resent it if you persist with your suggestive comments about my having his baby. If you *do not* desist, he just might be tempted to leave Randwulf Manor as he did before."

"Bah! 'Tis time Colton marries whether *he* realizes it or not. He's not getting any younger, you know, and if he intends to sire a dynasty, he'd better get started instead of merely thinking about it. He just may lose the opportunity. Which reminds me, I've heard that Lord Harcourt is having his personal chambers enlarged to include a lavish bathing room. The gossips are nearly beside themselves, thinking he's planning on getting married and not telling anyone." Samantha leveled a suspicious squint upon her friend. "Would you happen to know anything about that?"

"No, of course not," Adriana replied, hurriedly drawing the handkerchief from her purse and wiping at the spot on her nose. "Why should I, of all people, be cognizant of what he's planning?"

"*Because*, my dear friend, you're the only one he has shown any interest in for over a year or more. He has made no bones about desiring you as his marchioness. Did you happen to tell him that you're committed to a contract of courtship?"

"Is the smudge gone now?" Adriana asked, trying to ignore the woman's probing questions.

"No, you goose, you've only made it worse. Let me have the handkerchief. I'll wipe it away."

Submitting herself to the other's care, Adriana waited patiently as her friend scrubbed away the blotch. It was no easy task, considering that it felt like the skin was being scoured off right along with it.

"There, your nose is just fine now . . . except for its bright red hue," Samantha teased and then laughed as her friend groaned in annoyance. "It isn't really *that* bad, but for that bit of service, you must tell me all you know about Lord Harcourt's plans to marry."

"I have no idea what he intends. Ask him, if you're so curious. He'll likely tell you if you're bold enough to ask." Preferring not to be questioned further, Adriana turned abruptly about and continued up the flight of stairs, ignoring Samantha's petulant mutterings.

"You're being awfully secretive about this," the elder complained, following close behind. "Perhaps I should warn Colton. . . ."

Adriana mentally scoffed. *As if that would do any good!* "Go ahead, he may decide to let Riordan take over the courtship."

"*Riordan?*" Samantha's tone peaked in the area of the incredulous. "You're calling him *Riordan* now?"

Adriana managed a noncommittal shrug in spite of the fact that she wanted to kick herself for making such a slip. "Do I not call your brother Colton?"

"You're as good as betrothed to him," Samantha declared. "I certainly hope *that* is *not* the situation between you and *Riordan.*"

They were on the upper flight of stairs when Adriana happened to glance up and then almost gasped in alarm as she saw Roger. He had halted several steps above her, from whence he smiled at her leisurely as his gaze slowly swept her from charmingly coiffed head to dainty slippers.

"Good evening, Mr. Elston," Adriana gritted out stiltedly, hating the way her voice trembled. All the trauma she had experienced during his attack swept over her again in a thick wave, nearly choking off her breath. Beneath his bold perusal, she felt as if she were being stripped naked.

"'Tis indeed a pleasure to see you again, my lady," he said magnanimously, as if he had never once thought of raping her. "I hope you've been well . . . and happy."

She wondered if he detected some strange emotion in her expression, for he canted his head thoughtfully as he considered her. She made every effort to sound gay and lighthearted. "Yes, of course, very happy, very well, thank you. And you?"

"As well as can be expected, under the circumstances."

"I'm sorry, I did hear that your father was ailing, and I know that must be a tremendous source of concern for you. Please allow me to offer my prayers and wishes for his speedy recovery."

He inclined his head, acknowledging her gracious request. "You're as kind as always, my lady, but I wasn't referring to his malady, but mine. . . ."

Her brows gathered in confusion as her eyes briefly swept him, but for the life of her, she could detect no sign of frailty. "Have you perchance fallen victim to some illness?"

His smile was brief enough to be terse. "I'm afraid 'tis a matter of the heart, my lady. It has been seriously wounded, and I fear 'twill never mend."

"Oh."

He cocked a brow as he gave her a dubious smile. "Nothing more to say, my lady?"

"What is there to say, Mr. Elston?"

"And your courtship with Lord Randwulf? Is it going well?"

"Why, yes . . . of course. I mean . . . very well."

Thoughtfully Roger tapped a thin knuckle against his chin as he studied her for a lengthy moment. "Why is it that I sense something amiss, my lady? Your lovely face is not as radiant as I've seen it in the past. Should I think your courtship has gone awry? Are you not happy with the marquess?"

"Yes, of course. Why should you even ask such a ques—?" She halted abruptly, sensing a presence on the landing above the stairs, and lifted her gaze to find Colton watching her with a solemnity she had not noticed in him since the day of his arrival. He had obviously been hovering there as her guardian in case Roger did anything out of hand. It was equally apparent that he had been listening to every word of their exchange. In the moments that followed, his eyes delved deeply into hers until Adriana thought she could not bear his intimate inspection without absconding like a feckless coward. Indeed, he seemed to probe to the very depths of her mind.

Following her gaze upward, Roger managed a bland smile for the nobleman. "You may indeed have some legal claim upon Lady Adriana, my lord, but from all appearances 'twould seem *that* entitlement has not appeased the lady's heart."

Smirking with satisfaction as Colton scowled, the miller continued his descent, taking special pains to make no imprudent movement as he passed Adriana. From the area of the front parlor a moment later, Felicity heralded his approach by drawing another woman's attention to her *"handsome escort."* In the ensuing moments, Adriana was sure even from where she stood rooted to the stairs by Colton's probing stare that she could hear the blonde cooing.

Samantha's hand coming to rest upon her arm reminded Adriana that they had been on their way upstairs to visit the elderly miller. She hastened up the remaining flight and, at the landing, found Colton awaiting her there. Drawing her hand through the bend of his arm, he allowed his sister to precede them as Percy stepped to the landing to await her with a hand extended. Following the couple, Colton escorted Adriana into the miller's bedchamber.

"My ladies," Samuel Gladstone cried in a croaky voice as he saw the beauteous pair. He held out a hand to each. "'Tis a very great pleasure ta see yu both again. Yu're rays o' sunlight shinin' inta me drab room."

As older matrons moved aside to allow the pair access to the miller, Adriana and Samantha left their manly escorts and went to stand on either side of the old man's bed. Accepting his extended hands, they either squeezed or patted them fondly before leaning near to place doting kisses on the elder's pallid cheeks.

"You're looking as handsome as always," Adriana informed the miller, her eyes glowing with as much radiance as her smile.

His blue eyes shone with merriment as he chided, "Ah, m'liedy, don't yu go fillin' me addled head wit' yur pretty lies now. 'Tis swimmin' enough as 'tis, but I thank yu kindly just the same. Yu both always bring a bit o' life back inta me heart wit' yur visits."

"Then we shall have to come more often, won't we?" Samantha suggested, as she squeezed his hand affectionately. "But be warned, you could grow bored with us."

Mr. Gladstone chortled. "Doubtful, doubtful." Turning his head upon the pillow, he indicated the pair with a broad thumb as he winked at a wizen-faced elderly man standing on the far side of the bed, just behind Adriana. "Ah, Creighton, me friend, don't it jes' tear yur heart out 'cause yu're not gettin' any o' this fine attention 'ese liedies be lavishin' 'pon me?"

"Now, don't yu be tryin' ta make me jealous, Sam," the old man fussed jovially, displaying sparse and crooked teeth in a broad grin. "'Ere I be, a bachelor 'ese many years, an' I'm jes' now seein's what I've been missin' all this time."

Amid the laughter evoked by his remark, Adriana found herself stumbling hurriedly backward as Felicity rudely pushed her way to the old man's bedside. It was just another thorn in Felicity's flesh that her own grandfather was among those smitten with the lady. Adriana had been successful in stealing the hearts of gentlemen everywhere. Surely, Samuel Gladstone would evidence a partiality for his own granddaughter. In an endeavor to prove that premise, Felicity took the elder's hand and sought to press a kiss upon his leathery cheek.

Mr. Gladstone promptly turned his face aside and, lifting a hand, tried to ward off her attempts. "None o' 'at now, not aftah yu've been ignorin' me very existence since I bid yur mother ta take o'er management o' the mill," he rumbled. "I won't accept affection when yu only give it in front o' a houseful o' guests. 'Tis no ne'er mind ta me how yu've been slightin' me. I've come this far wi'out yur coddlin'; I can get by wi'out it what li'l time I 'ave left on this earth. See ta yurself, girl."

"Grandpa! What are you saying? I've been busy planning these festivities for you. I just haven't had time to spend with you," Felicity insisted, her face flaming from his harsh rebuke. She leaned forward expectantly. "Here now, let me kiss you so you'll know how much I care for you."

"I want nothin' from ye," the elder muttered, pulling a sheet over his head, in so doing forbidding her access.

Felicity strove hard to maintain her dignity as she retreated from the old man's bedside. Stiltedly, she went to the doorway where her mother, upon entering the room, had paused.

"He's growing more senile by the day," Felicity complained, struggling to keep her composure in spite of her vivid blush. "I don't know what we're going to do with him."

"Senility had nothing to do with it," Jane Fairchild replied and casually shrugged her thin shoulders. "I can't blame him. Had you not been so caustic when he asked you to help me, he wouldn't have snubbed you in return. One usually reaps what one sows."

"Now I know where you learned your little tricks," Felicity hissed and stalked out of the room, her back as rigid as a plank of seasoned oak. Several moments later, the front door slammed, indicating her angry departure from the house.

Colton approached the bed, prompting Samuel to lower the sheet from his head. The miller eyed him quizzically as he drew Adriana's arm through his, and then a slow grin stretched across the elder's lips.

"So, yu've come back from the wars an' taken yurself the fairest maid in all o' Wessex, have ye?" The miller chortled as he snuggled his chin into the rumpled collar of his nightshirt. "Can't says as I blame yu none. 'Twould be me own pick if'n I were kin ta yur sister an' Lady Adriana was agreeable."

"I shall bring both ladies with me the next time I visit," Colton rejoined, bestowing a broad grin upon the man. "Their presence seems to rejuvenate your spirits."

"Come often," Mr. Gladstone urged enthusiastically. "I'm a poor, sickly man in much need o' bolsterin'."

Colton threw his head back and laughed in hearty amusement. "Aye, I shall do that very thing just to make sure you will enliven our lives for many a year to come."

In the concluding hours of their outing together, the dispersal of the occupants of the landau was in sharp variance to what had become the normal rote. Whereas the Burkes' country manor was farther away than Randwulf Manor was from Bath, Bradford on Avon, and all the other places they normally went, the married couple usually had their driver deliver them to the Wyndham mansion, from whence they left in Colton's landau to collect Adriana from Wakefield Manor, which was even closer yet to all the areas to which they ventured. On the return jaunt, Adriana had always been the first to be returned home. Shortly after the foursome had partaken of a meal at an inn outside Bradford on Avon, however, it became apparent that Colton had other plans in mind for the evening, for he instructed Bentley not to stop at Wakefield at all, but to go immediately to Randwulf Manor, where the Burkes' carriage awaited them.

Samantha had been greatly heartened by the events of the evening, and although she would never have admitted as much to Roger, she saw a reason to be thankful for the miller's comments, for he had obviously shaken Colton's steel-bound confidence. She just hoped they'd produce the results she yearned to see, that being her brother's proposal of marriage. Yet she couldn't help but feel a deepening empathy for Adriana, who seemed greatly unnerved by the changes Colton had implemented.

When the conveyance halted outside Randwulf Manor, Colton briefly alighted and cordially offered his adieus to his sister and brother-in-law. He spoke mutedly to Bentley a moment and then climbed back into the landau.

Adriana could hardly ignore Colton's efforts to secure their privacy or the fact that he had chosen to ensconce himself beside her rather than in the opposite seat. His gray eyes glowed with the reflected light of the carriage lanterns as he watched her unrelentingly for a lengthy space, heightening Adriana's tensions until she could hardly bear the suspense.

"Is something amiss?" she asked in a voice that quavered.

Even in the meager light, her unparalleled beauty proved a strong lodestone from which Colton could not drag his gaze. "Nothing untoward, Adriana. I merely wanted to talk with you privately for a few moments. We haven't been able to do much of that lately, and I thought it especially needful tonight."

"Why tonight?"

Colton canted his head, considering how best to approach the subject. Although in the deep recesses of his mind he had sensed that something had been troubling Adriana for some weeks now, it had taken the miller to awaken him to the realization that the radiance had gone out of her smiles. "My concern has much to do with what Roger said this evening."

Adriana managed a nervous little laugh. "You shouldn't let what he said bother you, Colton. You must know he would enjoy having his revenge upon you in any manner available to him. What he said was utter nonsense."

The marquess remained silent for a long moment before asking her outright, "Should I believe you're displeased with me or our courtship?"

"Nooo..." she moaned, and then cringed in chagrin, fearing she had sounded much like Melora when she hadn't been able to cope with some minor adversity. Averting her face in embarrassment, Adriana directed her gaze toward the moonlit, snow-patched hills looming in the distance. The fact that they were going in the opposite direction from her home had not escaped her attention. In a voice fraught by emotion, she asked, "How can any woman be displeased with you, Colton? If I can discern anything from the countless rumors being bandied about, you have become the dream of every woman living in the area."

"Is that the way you feel about me?"

Adriana groaned within herself. If he only knew how her heart ached for fear of losing him, he wouldn't even consider asking such a question. "I have always held you in the highest esteem."

"Even after I left home?"

Rather than leave herself open to his unyielding stare, Adriana lowered her gaze to her lap and began toying with the decorative beadwork on her purse. "I must admit that even at so young an age I was wounded by your harsh refusal to consider me suitable for your future wife, Colton. There are some young girls who cherish a vision of a handsome knight in splendorous armor and dream of that one marrying them and carrying them off to some wondrous place. That fantasy was shattered for me the day you left home. The fact that you had always been my hero made your rejection all the more painful, but you must remember that I was merely a child and didn't fully understand your anger."

"Let me look at you, Adriana," he cajoled gently, but when she complied by lifting her head, his brows gathered in perplexity. The tears glistening in the long, silken lashes were difficult to ignore. Laying a lean hand alongside her cheek, he gently wiped away a droplet with his thumb. "What is troubling you so much that you feel a need to cry?"

Embarrassed because she couldn't contain her emotions, Adriana responded with a frantic shake of her head. "I'm not!"

His hand moved downward to the creamy column of her throat, and he had cause to marvel at the rapid pulse he felt beneath his palm. She was far more upset than she wanted to admit.

Soothingly he stroked a thumb beneath the delicate structure of her jaw. "It hasn't rained in days, Adriana, and yet I can plainly see your lashes are wet. If those aren't tears, then what would you have me believe they are? Particles of snow?"

Adriana recognized the threat of her emotions welling forth in greater volume and sought to turn aside, but his hand, gentle yet unyielding, remained on her throat, refusing to allow her to escape his close inspection. She could do nothing but submit to his probing gaze.

"Please tell me why you're crying," he murmured pleadingly.

She brushed awkwardly at the tiny rivulets streaming down her cheeks, angry at herself for being so vulnerable in his presence. "Please, Colton, just let me go."

"I will when you tell me the reason for your dejection," he bargained gently.

Blindly fumbling at the drawstrings of her handbag, Adriana tugged it open and sought to find her handkerchief, but to no avail, for the dainty, lace-trimmed cloth was no longer there. She realized that Samantha had failed to return it. "I really don't wish to talk about this now," she mumbled miserably, drawing her beaded purse closed again. "My tears have nothing to do with our courtship."

Removing his hand from her throat, Colton drew a clean handkerchief from the inside pocket of his frock coat and pressed it into her palm. "On the contrary, Adriana. I think our courtship is at the very heart of your gloominess, and if you'd care to enlighten me, I'd be most grateful...."

A disconcerted shake of her head was her only response.

A heavy sigh slid from Colton's lips. "I won't pressure you about this matter any further, Adriana. If your parents know why you're so miserable, perhaps they'd be willing to enlighten me."

"Please, Colton, don't trouble them," Adriana pleaded, wiping at the tears that refused to be checked. "'Twould only distress them to know that you're upset with me. Just take me home and leave me to my misery. The matter is of no real importance."

"On the contrary, Adriana, it *is* to me," he countered, "and if I *am* upset, it's only because you are, and yet I'm unable to fathom what has distressed you. Besides, after Roger's attack, I can't leave you in such a state at Wakefield Manor without your parents' suspicions being aroused. They'll likely think I've seduced you. . . ."

An abortive laugh escaped her. "Oh, I'd be able to assure them that you've been a perfect gentleman, so perfect I'm sure you can't wait for our courtship to end. The sad fact is that nothing at all has changed since you left home to escape your father's edict." She cast her teary gaze downward at she entwined her fingers. "You feel no more affection for me today than you did then."

"That's not true, Adriana," Colton argued, wondering how she'd react if he were to tell her just how often he woke from his dreams in a rutting heat, all because of a pressing desire to make love to her.

Adriana blew her nose daintily in the handkerchief he had provided and then, in a voice fraught with tears, offered a solution to her problem. "I dislike this pretense we're going through, Colton, and have decided that it would be best if I released you from your commitments. Henceforth from this night, you may go your way without worrying about our courtship. I want no more of it. *Indeed,* I can bear no more of it! 'Tis bruising my heart, and I cannot continue."

"You're not being rational, Adriana," Colton argued. Reaching out a hand, he rested it gently upon her forearm as he sought to calm her. "Please, love, you'll feel different on the morrow."

"No, I won't! I'll feel exactly the way I do now!" she cried, throwing off his hand. Her voice broke with emotion as she demanded, "Please! Just d-don't call me your love. I'm n-not your love . . . nor have I e-ever been."

"Adriana, for pity's sake . . . be reasonable," Colton pleaded and tried to draw her toward him.

"I'm freeing you from your commitment, Colton," she declared resolutely, shrugging free. "There's no more to be said. The courtship is entirely finished between us!"

Colton launched a strenuous protest. "You cannot absolve me of my obligations to my father. . . ."

"Well, I do-*oo!*" Adriana insisted, her voice catching rather weirdly, this time in a hiccup. "I don't w-want to continue with this travesty a-any longer. I tell you it leaves m-me fretting."

"Seeing Roger again has obviously distressed you," Colton reasoned decisively, leaning back in his seat. "A strong toddy will help soothe you. I shall ask Charles to prepare you one once we reach Wakefield."

"I shan't drink it!"

Ignoring her retort, Colton braced an elbow on the armrest beside him and laid two fingers aside his cheek as he braced his thumb beneath his chin. Peering intently into the darkness beyond the window, he stated doggedly, "I intend to discuss this matter with your father, Adriana. If you're upset because of Roger, then I'm sure your parents will agree that the two of us must avoid any place where there's even a remote possibility that we'll meet up with the miller."

"I d-don't w-want y-you to discuss *anything* w-with them! Don't you understand?"

Elevating a dark brow, he turned his gaze on her once again. "Should I then believe, dearest Adriana, that you're upset solely with me?"

"I'm not your dearest. So d-don't call me that!"

"On the contrary, you *are* my dearest, far more mine than any other's, I'll warrant," he stated with finality and received a mutinous glower for his declaration.

"I'm n-not s-saying anything more to you, Colton Wynd-h-ham."

"You needn't, my dear. I'm quite capable of discussing this matter with your father, and to great length, if need be. To my knowledge, I've treated you with all the deference of a dedicated suitor and have given you no reason to be annoyed with me. Yet it seems you are. I can only hope your father can enlighten me as to what more you may be expecting from me, because at the moment I find myself thoroughly bemused."

Adriana glared back at him in the gloom. "I forbid you to speak to my father!"

Colton slid his now little-used cane from its niche beside the seat and rapped the handle against the carriage roof before offering her a succinct smile. "Nevertheless, my dear, I intend to . . . with or without your permission."

Adriana sought to present her back to her stubborn suitor but found herself bound by her own cloak, which being of like fabric as the velvet seat, refused to yield. When the ties threatened to strangle her, she was forced to tug them loose. Upon throwing off the garment, she scooted close to the door in an attempt to distance herself from her companion, though it proved much more a mental separation than a physical one.

"You may ignore me if you wish, Adriana, but I can promise you 'twill change nothing. I intend to talk with your father until I get this matter settled between us. I have no intention of ending our courtship unless he has reason to believe that your contempt for me is beyond the measure I can bear."

When Bentley finally drew the steeds to a halt before the gray stone facade of Wakefield Manor, Colton alighted forthwith and turned to offer assistance to the lady, but with an eloquent toss of her head Adriana rejected his invitation. Promptly throwing open the door nearest her, she kicked out the step and scrambled down in a most unladylike fashion. Upon hearing Colton's muttered curses as he stalked around the boot of the carriage, she whirled in the opposite direction and scurried toward the well-matched four-in-hand. In her eagerness to escape, however, she failed to note that the hems of both her chemise and lace gown had been snagged on the metal-forged step, resulting in the rending of both garments as she stalked rapidly away in a fair tizzy.

Upon rounding the end of the conveyance, Colton immediately espied the ensnared hems and the swiftly separating garments. Under more intimate circumstances, he'd have admired the lady's scantily attired derriere till his eyes crossed, but he was sharply averse to the idea of allowing Bentley that same privilege.

Mentally cursing the lingering stiffness of his leg, he rushed forward as swiftly as he could in an effort to halt the vixen's flight. "Adriana, stop!" he cried. "You're tearing your garments!"

He caught her arm and promptly received for his trouble her beaded handbag across his face.

"Get away from me!" she shrilled.

"Dammit, Adriana, listen to me!" he barked irately, throwing up a hand to ward off another blow.

Missing him completely, Adriana swung her purse around again in a wide circle, unaware that she had also gained her freedom from the step. "Take your leave, sir, before I *really* lose my temper!"

His hand shot out and seized her wrist. "Stop this nonsense, Adriana! I have to tell you—"

With a snarl of rage she snatched her arm away and immediately became convinced that she had left a goodly portion of her skin in his grasp. She would not be at all surprised if she later found her wrist bruised. "Leave me alone, Colton Wyndham. I have nothing more to say to you."

"Adriana, for pity's sake, listen——"

"Bentley!" Glancing over her shoulder as she stalked toward the lead team, she discovered that she already held claim to the elderly driver's slack-jawed attention.

His query was at best cautious. "Yes, m'liedy?"

"If you have a care for your master, you'd better take him home. And if he should desire to return here upon the morrow or any time thereafter, kindly ignore him. You may save him from getting a hole shot through his left leg."

"Yes, m'liedy," the servant meekly replied, but made no attempt to comply. Ducking his head deeper into his driving coat, he let matters take their course, for he had already learned that, at a time like this, it was far better to pretend daftness and delay the execution of such orders.

"Dammit, Adriana!" Colton barked irately. When she came around once again in full readiness to deliver another wallop with the purse, he was ready for it and flung out a hand to halt its flight. Angrily he indicated her skirts. "You've ripped your garments, and at the present moment, you're showing off your backside to Bentley!"

Adriana gasped in shock, realizing she was definitely feeling a chill against her rear. Frantically she clasped a hand behind her back and groaned aloud at her predicament as it immediately came in contact with her scantily covered buttocks. Twisting about in a tight circle, she sought to catch hold of the far side of her severed skirt. Absurd as it was, her efforts left her more or less chasing her tail.

Bentley made an heroic attempt to ignore what was going on as he laid a broad hand over his eyes and lifted his shoulders to bring up the stiff collar of his dapper coat. It served to muffle his hearing, but the laughter, which intermittently shook his shoulders, was not so easily suppressed.

Adriana noticed the driver's self-imposed restraints and gave up trying to preserve her modesty. Not caring in the least what Colton could see, she stalked toward the manor. He had, after all, viewed her completely naked on a pair of occasions.

Of a sudden, Adriana found herself facing the incensed marquess who, in spite of his past impediments, had outdistanced her in his zeal to halt her flight. Standing firmly rooted in her path with arms akimbo, he dared her to test his patience further by going around him.

Heaving a vexed sigh, Adriana peered toward the livery. "Bentley, are you aware that your master is annoying me?"

The driver parted stubby fingers ever so slightly, enabling him to peer at the lady without compromising her modesty overmuch. He managed a heavy gulp. "Well ... I ... well ... maybe not, m'liedy."

" 'Twould seem your master is proving himself very, very foolish. If you care a whit for his hide, you'd better drag him back into the carriage before I fetch my gun. I'd certainly hate to do him more damage than he suffered in the war. Do you understand me?"

"Yes, m'liedy." Bentley decided he'd better not ignore her threat, considering that even as a small child, she had walloped his present master and even blackened his eye once when she had had enough of his tomfoolery. Scrambling down from the seat, he diligently avoided looking at the severed gown as he scurried toward his employer. "Milord, don't yu think we'd better go now? Her liedyship really seems displeased wit' yu right now. Mayhap aftah she calms down a bit, yu can come—"

"Dammit, Bentley, this is none of your affair, so stay out of it!" Colton barked. "Now get back to the carriage where you belong!"

"Don't curse at him!" Adriana cried and swung her heavily beaded purse around again, this time catching Colton in the eye and causing him to stumble back in pained surprise.

"What's going on out here?" a male voice bellowed from the front portal.

Whirling away from Colton as he clamped a hand over his throbbing eye, Adriana ran into the opening arms of her father. Burying her face against his stalwart chest, she released a floodgate of tears.

Deeply concerned over his offspring's welfare, Gyles settled an ominous glare upon the younger man as that one staggered toward them. "Sir, if you've harmed my daughter in any way, let me assure you, marquess or not, you won't live to regret it. This time I'll take matters into my own hands."

Colton tried to focus his blurred, watery gaze upon the incensed earl. "From what I've been able to ascertain from your daughter's gibberish, Lord Gyles, I believe the problem stems from the fact that the converse is true. I swear to you that, where she is concerned, I've closely adhered to a gentlemanly code of conduct and have returned her to your care in the same unspoiled condition."

Adriana plucked at the lapels of her father's velvet robe. "Papa, please, just send him away."

"Has he hurt you, child?"

"No, Papa, he hasn't touched me at all."

Clasping a trembling hand to his brow, Gyles sighed in relief. After Roger's attack, he had become ever wary. A moment passed before he managed to regain some measure of his equanimity. He was then wont to question her further. "Then, daughter, what has the man done to make you weep so?"

"He has done absolutely nothing, Papa. He has been a perfect gentleman. . . ."

Peering at father and daughter as he held one hand clasped over his injured eye, Colton threw up the other hand in a fine display of derision. "*Now*, my lord, perhaps you begin to see the light of it. . . ."

Adriana snuggled her head upon her father's chest. "He doesn't want me now any more than he did ten and six years ago."

"That's not true!" Colton barked. "I *do* want her, very much in fa—" Startling himself into abrupt silence, he tilted his head, wondering if the lady had socked his senses loose. What he had almost admitted would have led him posthaste to the altar, and in a manner his father had planned for him. Did he not have some last shred of resolve left?

"Please, Papa," Adriana mewled, plucking at the decorative patch on his velvet dressing robe. "Let's go inside. I don't want to talk about Lord Sedgwick's contract ever again. If Lord Riordan still wants me to marry him, I will be amenable to his proposal."

"Now just a damn moment!" Colton roared, causing the elder's brows to fly upward in amazement. "I have some rights here!"

Gyles patted the air in a calming motion, hoping to placate the enraged man. Not since Colton rebelled against his father's edict had Gyles heard the man raise his voice with such intense ire. It gave him reason to hope he really cared for his daughter. " 'Twould behoove us to settle this matter later, my lord, after you and Adriana have had a chance to think this thing through more rationally. 'Tis apparent my daughter is upset, and to lengthen this discussion at this present moment would only heighten her distress. Give her a day or two to settle down, and then we'll talk about it again."

Colton champed at the bit, anxious to settle the matter before Adriana did anything they would both be sorry for later. Samantha had informed him of the rumors concerning Riordan that were making their way around the area. Now, after hearing the girl say she'd accept the man's proposal, his jealousy prodded him unmercifully. Of all Adriana's past suitors, Riordan was the one he feared most. The man had the wits, looks, and charm to steal the lady from him. Only the contract his father had initiated years ago gave him some advantage over the other man, and if that was all the weapon he had to halt the girl from marrying the man, then he'd argue till he was nigh blue in the face before allowing Adriana to terminate their agreement. As much as he personally admired Riordan, he had no doubt that he'd prove the nobleman's worst enemy if they became embroiled in a confrontation over the lady.

"Lord Gyles, you have not heard my side of this fray yet, and I most respectfully petition you to do so ere you lend an ear to Riordan's plea for your daughter's hand. Have I not more of a right to her than he does?"

"I shall give you a fair hearing," Gyles declared. "Of that, be confident. I only ask that you allow me some time to talk with my daughter and to hear her grievances against you. I won't commit her to another man until you have been given every opportunity to voice your petitions and complaints."

Though Colton was disinclined to leave, out of the corner of his undamaged eye he could see Bentley silently pleading for him to relent. Grudgingly he did so.

Squinting at father and daughter as he held a hand clasped over part of his face, he gave them a shallow bow. "Until a later time then."

Pivoting about, Colton stalked to the landau and climbed inside. From the window, he watched Gyles lay a comforting arm around Adriana's shoulders and escort her inside. The door closed behind them, seeming to signal an end to the courtship that Colton had been agonizing over for the last two months and longer. The hollow feeling in his chest removed any doubt from his mind that he could no more live without Adriana than he could his own heart.

Colton drew his cane from its place of residency beside the seat and rapped the handle against the interior ceiling of the landau, giving the signal for Bentley to take them from this place. The conveyance lurched into motion, and in the lantern-lit gloom that surrounded him, Colton stared morosely into the darkness beyond the window as he clasped a handkerchief over his injured eye in an effort to stem its unrelenting watery flow.

Fourteen

❉

HARRISON shifted the candlestick to his left hand and rapped the knuckles of his right upon the door of the marquess's bedchamber. He was fully aware that his lordship had returned home in a fretful mood only a couple hours earlier, and then, much sooner than usual, had secluded himself in his private chambers. Under normal circumstances, he would not have disturbed the man, but the courier had advised him the missive was of grave importance. "My lord," he called through the heavy, wooden portal. "A messenger has just arrived from London, bearing urgent news for you."

A loud crash, the splintering of glass, and a smothered curse preceded a gruff request to delay any entrance at the moment. Within the chambers, Colton dragged the sheet over his naked loins as he swung his long legs over the edge of the bed. He doubted that he had closed his eyes even once since he had turned down the wick and snuffed the remaining flame. His mind had been too busy foraging over possibilities that could preclude the continuance of his courtship with Adriana and the legalities that he'd be willing to put into play to halt the termination of their future together. For the life of him, he just couldn't let her walk away as she now seemed determined to do. His heart would shrivel in sorrow.

With a laborious sigh, Colton threaded his fingers through his tousled hair, looked across the room toward the dancing flames cavorting in the fireplace, and then again at the glass-strewn carpet near his bed. His injured eye was nearly matted shut and undoubtedly would need a bandage if he had to go anywhere.

"Come in, Harrison," he called out, "and make sure you bring enough light to aid you where you step. I've just knocked over a lamp."

"Forgive me for waking you, my lord," Harrison replied as he hurried across the room.

"I wasn't asleep," Colton admitted.

The steward placed the candlestick upon the table and gave the missive over to him. Breaking the waxed closure, Colton unfolded the parchment and, clasping one hand over his eye, began to read the contents of the message as the elder set about cleaning up the broken glass.

Miss Pandora Mayes is near to dying and begs you to come with haste.

"I must travel to London immediately, Harrison," Colton announced. "Tell Bentley to ready the second carriage with the working steeds and bring along another driver. We'll be traveling fast and hard, and I don't want to wear out our best horses. As for the glass, you can clean that up later."

"Shall I pack a satchel or a trunk for you, my lord?"

"A couple of changes of clothes and essentials should I be detained over the weekend. Hopefully, if I am delayed, I'll at least be back by Monday morning."

"That would be nice, my lord. I'm sure your mother would enjoy having you home for Christmas for a change."

"I'll make every effort to return in time."

In less than an hour, Colton was in the coach and being whisked eastward toward London. Shortly after dawn the next morning, they reached the outskirts of the city, and from there, Colton directed the second driver to the actress's town house. When finally the conveyance was drawn to a halt before the place, Colton quickly alighted.

"I may be awhile, Bentley," he informed the man who had been slumbering inside the coach. "There's a stable and an inn down the road apiece. Do what you have to do for the animals and get some food for yourselves. Perhaps you can even find a place to rest for an hour or so. If you're not here when I come out, I'll come looking for you at the inn."

"Aye, milord."

At the entrance of Pandora's town house, Colton rapped his knuckles against the solid plank. Eventually it was opened by an elderly, darkly garbed rector. The man seemed somewhat surprised when he noticed the bandage over the younger man's eye.

"Your lordship?"

"Aye, I'm Lord Randwulf. Are you the one who sent the note?"

"I am, my lord. I'm Reverend Adam Goodfellow, rector of the parish church in Oxford where . . . Miss . . . ah . . . Mayes was once christened. She bade me come to London to attend her in these her last hours and asked me to notify you."

"Have you been here long?" Colton inquired.

"I arrived yesterday, my lord, after being sent her note. The surgeon was with her, but left her in my care, having given up all hope of pulling her through."

"May I see her?"

The wizened man swung the door wider and beckoned Colton in. "I'm afraid there isn't much life left in Miss Mayes, my lord. Indeed, sir, I rather suspect she has been holding on merely to see you."

"Then you'd better lead me to her."

"Of course, my lord," the clergyman replied and shuffled about. His stride was no faster, and in the narrow confines of the corridor, Colton felt hindered by the slow progress of the ancient.

"If you'll excuse me, Reverend, I believe I know where her bedchamber is."

"Yes, of course," the man replied with a meaningful inflection. Flattening himself against the wall of the narrow passageway, he swept a hand before him in an invitation for the younger man to pass.

Colton did so quickly and, upon reaching the far end of the hall, pushed open the door on the right. The bedroom was lit by the meager glow of a single oil lamp sitting atop a bedside table. Residing like a pale wraith in the bed that he had shared with her numerous times was the actress whom he had not seen for at least nine months. In the scant light, her eyes seemed nothing more than dark shadows hollowed out in a death mask. Her cheeks were sunken, her lips ashen. The vivacious bloom that had once brightened them was no longer evident.

Although seemingly entombed in the dark gloom, a plump, frizzy-haired woman of perhaps thirty or more sat in a chair in a corner of the room. Her blouse had been pulled aside an ample breast at which a tiny newborn nursed, but it was her slovenly appearance that made Colton mentally cringe.

Colton approached Pandora's bedside with silent tread, and as he drew near, her lashes fluttered slowly open. A faint trace of a smile curved her lips as her eyelids hovered droopingly over hazel orbs.

"Col . . . I'm glad you've come. I was so afraid you wouldn't," the actress rasped, as if thoroughly spent. She managed a frail smile and then peered at him more closely, noticing his patch. "Did you lose your eye in the war?"

"No, I merely got something in it last night." *A lovely vixen's handbag.*

Pandora reached out a slender hand toward him. "Sit beside me."

Colton lowered himself to the edge of the bed and, gathering her hand close against his chest, leaned forward to search the darkly shadowed eyes. At one time the hazel orbs had sparkled with life and seemed vividly alive, but now their lackluster seemed part of the darkness that encircled them, visually foretelling her approaching doom. "I came as soon as I could, Pandora. What ails you?"

"You . . . have . . . a daughter, my lord," she rasped weakly. "You . . . planted . . . your seed . . . within me . . . the last time . . . you were here."

The shock of her statement filled Colton with cold dread. Almost as suddenly his mind became inundated with visions of Adriana. "But . . . but you said you weren't able to have any children. You swore to me you couldn't!"

"*Ahhh*, that was before you came along," she managed, a frail smile sketching across her pale lips. "Took . . . a bold man to do the deed, . . . but you . . . were he. . . ."

Colton was stricken by remorse. "And you're dying *now* because of *my* seed?"

"Oh, *you.*" Pandora tried to laugh, but quickly forsook the notion, too exhausted to exert herself to that extent. "You needn't blame yourself. 'Twas a difficult birth."

Colton reached out and smoothed the limp, curling hair away from the ashen cheeks. "I know several knowledgeable physicians living here in London. My family has used them enough to verify that their reputations are above reproach. I'll send my driver to fetch one."

She lifted a hand to halt him. "'Tis far too late for me, Colton. I've lost too much blood, but . . . there . . . is one . . . thing . . . I would ask of you."

"What is that?" He held his breath, fearful of her request. Even before they had ever made love, he had warned Pandora that he would never marry her. With far more to lose now than ever before, he couldn't bring himself to even contemplate capitulation to that request.

Her dull eyes pleaded with him for a long moment before she issued an appeal. "Let . . . the Reverend Goodfellow . . . say the . . . words over us . . . ere I die . . . Colton."

Throughout his career as an officer, Colton had gone to great lengths to avoid wedlock, especially with ambitious women. In spite of his tiff with Adriana, she was the *only* one he had *ever* wanted to marry. Jolted by a sharp aversion brought on by the actress's appeal, he gave no heed to the words that spilled from his lips. "But I'm as good as promised to another. . . ."

"I will die . . . tonight, Colton. Would . . . there be . . . any harm . . . in allowing me . . . some peace of mind in my last hours?"

He remained taciturn, unable to commit himself when marrying the woman would likely mean that he'd be losing Adriana.

"Please, Colton . . . I know . . . you explained . . . how you wouldn't marry me . . . but I'm . . . I'm begging you . . . for my sake and for our child. . . ."

Colton felt a prickling along his nape. His instincts urged him to use extreme care in making any decisions. "What is to become of the child?"

The woman's thin lips twisted ruefully. "I would . . . ask that . . . you take her . . . home with you . . . and be a . . . good father to her. You will . . . in time . . . come to . . . see how much . . . she favors you. She . . ." Pandora swallowed with difficulty, and it was a long moment before she gathered enough strength to continue. "Although I haven't . . . been with another man, I know . . . you need proof . . . that she . . . is yours. As you will see . . . our daughter . . . has a . . . purplish birthmark . . . upon her backside . . . just like her father."

She gestured rather lamely to the woman in the corner. "Alice . . . has been . . . cleaning the theatre . . . for some time now. She lost her newborn . . . only yesterday . . . and has consented to watch . . . over mine."

Thus bidden, the scruffy woman rose from the chaise and brought the infant forward. Halting beside Colton, she seemed to smirk as she took the child from her breast, making no attempt to cover the large-nippled, blue-veined, filth-crusted melon as she turned the newborn over. Uncovering the tiny rump, she thrust the girl's buttocks close to the lamp and, with a grimy finger, pointed to the identifying mark.

Colton's heart sank. As often as he had glimpsed reflections of himself in mirrors he had passed while striding naked across a room, he knew for certain the dark splotch had the same shape as the one he had been born with; his father had had one and his grandfather before him. The presence of the birthmark seemed to confirm the child was his, yet he wasn't ready to accept what he saw at face value. After all, its presence endangered whatever future he had with Adriana, and as much as he had first balked at that idea upon his return home, the very thought of losing the girl now aroused within him a desire to escape the trap into which he now found himself plummeting. Although the identifying birthmark looked genuine, he couldn't resist testing its authenticity by rubbing a thumb across the baby's hind part to make sure it hadn't been deftly applied using the grease paint of an actress.

Alas, his efforts to wipe away the stain proved to no avail. If indeed a fake, then it had been crafted by a gifted artist, for the purplish splotch seemed genuine.

Loath to commit himself to what Pandora was asking of him, Colton remained expressionless as the nursemaid returned to her chair. A part of him compelled him to do the right thing by the child. After all, if the birthmark was authentic, she belonged to a long line of Wyndhams, of which he was the last and only hope for the continuance of the name. He certainly didn't want to have any of his offspring, even one begotten in the heat of lust with an actress, reduced to a pitiful state as an outcast of society, but there was also a side of him that urged caution. If he yielded to Pandora's plea and she didn't die, then he'd be forever bound to her, and that had never been his intent.

"Reverend . . . Goodfellow . . ."—Pandora's words were now nothing more than frail gasps as she lifted a hand and feebly indicated the rector— "said any bastard child . . . is forever doomed. . . . He also . . . said . . . I couldn't . . . be absolved . . . of my sins . . . unless I marry the father of my babe."

Colton might've argued the latter point with the man had he been of such a mood, yet that was far from the issue now raging in his mind. At the crux of what was eating at him was the quandary: whether to do the noble thing or leave a daughter of his to suffer the stigma of being born a bastard whelp throughout her lifetime. Could he condemn an innocent to such a fate? He and Pandora had known what they had been about when they had indulged their passion, but the child, as innocent as she was, would be the only one to carry the burden.

"I'm ... dying, Colton ... help me," she gasped pitifully. "I don't want to burn in hell. ..."

Had his father been alive, Colton knew the elder would have had just cause to give him a stern lecture on the follies of a man sowing wild oats and then having to reap the harvest of foolish behavior. Now here he was, facing a decision he had once deemed totally out of the question. As many warnings as he had given to those he had bedded, those admonitions now seemed as dust underneath his feet.

Colton sighed heavily. "Though I've had little experience in getting married, I believe a license is required."

Reverend Goodfellow stepped forward with a hand clasped to his chest. "In my years as a rector, I have counted myself fortunate to have been in various positions wherein I was able to do some notable favors for those in higher positions. As a result, I have been able to obtain for Mistress Mayes a special license from His Grace, the archbishop. Only your signature is required, my lord. ..."

Colton realized there was still a bit of rebellion in him. "The devil you say!"

The elderly man peered at the nobleman curiously, trying to determine what had incensed him. "The documents must be signed and witnessed, my lord. Have you aught against solidifying the nuptials with your signature? Or is it that you do not wish to marry the mother of your child?"

The trap was closing in around him; Colton could feel it choking off his hopes and aspirations like some dark, unseen hand at his throat squeezing off the life-giving air or, more accurately, all the joy from his future. His greatest regret was his beautiful Adriana. When it meant losing the woman he had come to desire with his whole being, he was averse to rectifying his imprudence even for the sake of the child. How could he even hope that Adriana would marry him after this?

No sound came from the bed, and Colton glanced around to find the actress's eyes closed, her breathing shallow.

"'Twould seem you have little time to remedy the matter, my lord," the rector surmised. "Mistress Mayes is near to dying."

Colton felt a pervading coldness spreading through his being. Venting a laborious sigh, he muttered none too happily, "I will marry her."

"And the child? Will you be taking her home with you?"

"She'll be raised as my own," Colton avouched with an equal lack of enthusiasm.

It seemed but a brief moment had passed before the marriage vows were being uttered, feebly by Pandora and rather brusquely by Colton. Needless to say, he felt like a wayward lad who had been caught in a trap of his own making.

"The wet nurse informed me earlier that she'd be willing to take care of the child if you wish her to go home with you, my lord. Does that meet with your approval?"

That idea pleased Colton about as much as getting married, but he could see no way out of that predicament at the present moment. " 'Twould seem I have little choice if the child is to be nourished."

As the rector gestured for the wet nurse to gather up the baby's belongings, Colton found his stomach churning at the overt crudity of the woman. Making no attempt to hide her oversize breast, she laid the tiny nursling aside and rose to her feet. When she noticed Colton eyeing her, she gave him a wide, rotten-toothed grin and, wiping a finger over her dribbling nipple, pushed the digit in and out of her mouth suggestively, making much of her enjoyment as she slowly licked the finger.

Colton felt his stomach roil and turned away in sharp repugnance. He had been propositioned before, many times in fact during his years as an officer, but he seriously doubted such an invitation had ever come from a more repulsive creature. He could only wonder at the men who'd been of a mind to bed such a disgusting crone, but he promptly recalled having seen a fair number of males who'd probably have made the crone look like a saint.

"Her name is Alice Cobble, my lord," the rector announced, drawing his attention back to the woman. "She said her husband was killed in the war, so she has no one now. For her wages, she'll require no more than a tuppence or two besides her keep. I have every confidence that she'll serve the babe well."

Of one thing Colton was sure, he had never seen a filthier creature in all his life, nor was he looking forward to the idea of enduring her presence in his carriage on the long ride home, for the foul odor emitting from her body was so offensive it set his stomach awry. Her frizzy hair was definitely in need of a good washing; it stuck out in oily spikes from underneath the ragged kerchief tied around her head. Even now, she made no effort to cover her naked breast, as if she were actually flaunting it for his benefit. The fact that the babe had nursed at anything so filthy made him wonder just how soon he'd be able to find a replacement for the woman after reaching home. He hoped fervently it wouldn't take very long.

Colton turned back to Pandora and realized her strength was rapidly ebbing. Gesturing to her, he asked the rector, "Can you not help her?"

The man stepped to the bed and pressed his fingers against the actress's wrist. Then, with a pensive sigh, he withdrew and sadly shook his head. "I doubt your wife will last the hour, my lord."

"I will stay with her."

"There's really no need, my lord. She'll be gone soon enough, and if you tarry, your coach will likely be overtaken by soldiers who've come home to find work scarce and vittles beyond their ability to earn. They've been gathering into bands in the city, and are creating havoc in retaliation for being casually dismissed by the governing bodies of this country—in other words, the aristocrats who are enjoying wealth beyond measure while the common soldiers are starving."

"I've fought alongside many of those men and can sympathize with them. I'm willing to take my chances. I wouldn't want Pandora to die alone."

"I'll be here, my lord."

"Just the same, I will sit with her," Colton rejoined resolutely. "I've never been a husband before, but I'm of the opinion that a man shouldn't desert his wife when she's dying."

"You're right, of course," the rector admitted. "I was merely thinking of your safety."

"No need. I've faced greater dangers than rabble-rousers in my lifetime and have learned to take care of myself."

"Yes, the young woman spoke of your bravery under fire."

"Col . . ." a weak voice called from the bed.

"I'm here, Pandora," Colton assured her. "I'm not going to leave you."

"I only ask . . . that you be . . . a . . . good . . . father . . . to our daughter. . . ."

With that request, she closed her eyes and ceased her breathing.

Reverend Goodfellow checked her pulse and then solemnly lifted the sheet up over her head. "She's dead, my lord."

Colton heaved a remorseful sigh over her passing and then rose to face the elderly man. Reaching into an inside pocket of his coat, he withdrew a purse heavily weighted with coins and pressed it into the man's hands. "This should be enough to pay for the special license and to see that Pandora is buried in a respectable place with a proper headstone to mark her grave. Her daughter will in time want to know where her mother has been laid to rest. Where may I find you after I settle my affairs at home?"

"I have a small rectory on the road to Oxford, my lord," the man replied. "Your wife shall be buried there." Shaking out the coins into the palm of his hand, he stared at them in amazement. "You've been most generous, my lord."

"Buy food for the soldiers with what is left over. I'm sure you know a few since so many were required to win the war," Colton urged. Turning on his heels, he motioned rather unenthusiastically for the wet nurse to follow as he took his leave. The woman secured the baby more firmly in one arm and hefted a small, tattered satchel in her free hand before complying.

COLTON had assumed that it would be difficult telling his mother what he had done, but he had never imagined she would collapse upon hearing the news. Only his quick action saved her from hitting her head upon a marble-topped credenza. With Harrison scurrying in front of him, opening doors as he called for Philana's personal maid to run ahead of them, he had carried his mother to her chambers where he had laid her gently upon her bed. As her maid bathed her face with a cool, wet cloth, Philana slowly revived, but upon remembering what had caused her trauma, she groaned and laid a trembling hand over her eyes.

Colton quietly bade Harrison to go downstairs and show Alice Cobble to the nursery. "And have one of the servants instruct that woman on the importance of bathing and washing her hair," he added in a muted tone. "If she refuses, she'll have to answer to me. If not for the child, I wouldn't tolerate that filthy creature's presence in my house under *any* circumstances, so I urge you to lay down the usual ultimatums for women who work in this house."

"Yes, my lord."

When the door closed behind the steward and the maid, Philana rolled her head upon her pillow and looked at her son through a blur of tears. "I was so in hopes you'd marry Adriana," she choked miserably. "All these many years she has been like a second daughter to me. I cannot bear to think of losing her. Neither Sedgwick nor I wanted to consider how we'd ever cope if you married another. Now my greatest desire has been dashed."

Colton squeezed the slender, blue-veined hand consolingly, but could offer his mother no comfort in that area. Although Adriana and he were not even betrothed yet, he couldn't expect her to ignore his indiscretion, especially after their recent confrontation. He could summon little optimism that she'd take this recent news well. To his parent, he could only say, "I will talk to her."

"I fear 'twill do no good," Philana whispered sadly. "In truth, I don't know if she'd be able to bear the shame. 'Twould take a grand lady indeed to subject herself to the sympathetic stares people would be inclined to bestow on her should she marry you. It would've been difficult for me; how can I expect another woman to overlook such humiliating circumstances?"

CHARLES greeted Lord Colton decorously at the front door of Wakefield Manor on Christmas Eve. "I'll tell her ladyship that you're here wishing to see her, my lord."

"Is there someplace where we can talk without being disturbed?"

The butler was aware of the altercation that had occurred between the marquess and the lady and could understand the man's request for privacy. "If you'll go to the library, my lord, I shall inform Lady Adriana that you're awaiting her presence there. 'Tis unlikely you'll be interrupted since Lord Standish and Lady Christina went to the Abernathys' to take presents to the children. I believe they had planned on staying for a time, at least until Lady Adriana went to join them."

"Thank you, Charles."

Colton made his way down the hall to the specified room and entered its confines. His heart was truly heavy, and he could rally little enthusiasm for the task ahead. Then, too, after their last squabble, he wouldn't put it past Adriana to have Charles convey her regrets.

Once again, he found himself standing before the portrait of the Sutton ladies, but there was only one face among the four he cared to consider, the dark-haired goddess whom he now feared he was about to lose. After all his past objections to his father's decree and the stilted reserve he had somehow managed to convey during his courtship with Adriana, he was filled with a cold dread that after his recently coerced marriage, she would banish him from her presence and never let him see her again.

In the past few hours, it had dawned on him that he'd never feel complete as a man without Adriana as his wife. Fearing she'd reject him, he had found himself struggling to overcome an ominous sense of defeat in his personal life, the like of which he had never experienced before, not even when the enemy had managed to gain the upper hand on the battlefields.

"You wished to see me?" a silky voice queried from the entrance.

Colton's heart leapt with relief, and he turned with a hopeful smile, but it became immediately apparent that Adriana was in no mood to return it. He moved toward her. "I was desperate to talk with you about some matters."

"If it's about the other night, I have nothing more to say," she stated coolly, crossing to the fireplace. Turning her back to him, she stretched her slender hands toward the fire in an effort to warm them, for her fingers had turned to ice as soon as Charles had made the announcement that Lord Randwulf had arrived and was wishing to see her. No one knew how difficult it was for her to remain aloof from the man; already he seemed an intrinsic part of her. Dismissing him from her life would be similar to severing a limb or, more truthfully, squeezing the very life from her heart.

"I acted badly," she admitted over her shoulder, "and for that, I must apologize, but I meant every word I said. I cannot go on hoping that you'll eventually change your mind and come to want me as your wife. 'Twill mean less anguish for me if I separate myself from you now and go on about my life as if you had never returned."

"Although you may have difficulty believing this, Adriana, I am most desirous of having you as my wife."

She turned with a brow arched at a skeptical angle and saw for the first time the dark bruise around his eye. She hadn't realized she had hit him so hard, but for that she would apologize later. For now, she was intrigued and wished to delve more thoroughly into his statement. "When did this come about?"

"Actually, I've been aware of it for some time now, but have foolishly been putting off acknowledging that fact. Once upon a time, I was repulsed by the idea of having my life laid out by the contract and betrothal to which my parents had committed me. Yet, as much as I wanted to rebel against our courtship, I found myself wanting ... nay, needing you."

Adriana wanted to smile with joy, but the grim expression on his face made her wary. "Has something happened?"

Colton heaved a laborious sigh and turned aside, scrubbing the palm of one hand against the knuckles of the other. "Sadly enough, an event has occurred that has left me doubtful that you'll accept my proposal of marriage."

Adriana was suspicious of his intent and yet immensely curious. If he meant to cast the blame on her for rejecting their nuptials, she could only wonder how he would go about it. "Go on. I'm listening."

Colton brushed a hand over the elaborately carved wood adorning the tall back of a Tudor chair, feeling terribly out of sorts with what he had to tell her. He was certainly not proud of it. "I was called to London the other night, and there found that a woman I had known for some years had given birth to a child."

Suddenly Adriana's knees went weak. Stumbling to the nearest chair, she sank to its tapestry seat. Her insides had grown cold with dread, and as she clutched the ornate wood on either side of her, she waited for him to continue, to tell her that the child was his and not some stranger's. "Are you in love with her?"

Colton half-turned and peered at her, amazed that she already knew what he was going to tell her. Her head was bowed, the tendons in her hands stood out rigidly as she gripped the arms of the chair. Her slender shoulders had slumped forward, already conveying an attitude of defeat. "No, not really. She was merely an actress I had ... ah ... visited now and then. She once told me she was unable to have children. ..."

"How do you know for certain the child is yours?"

A heavy sigh slipped from his lips. "I have a birthmark on my backside, which I inherited from my father, and he from his father before him, and so on. Actually, I believe it originated many years ago with a Viking. It's shaped rather like a flying seagull."

"Yes, I've seen it."

He turned with a curious brow raised. "You have?"

"The night you interrupted my bath."

His lips compressed in a soundless O.

"'Twould seem the presence of such a birthmark on your offspring is convenient for the actress, but not so convenient for you. Do you intend to marry her?"

"Reverend Goodfellow from Oxford spoke the words over us while I was there."

Adriana could only stare in mute defeat at her lap. So acutely did she feel the heaviness of her heart that she found herself suddenly heaving, threatening to throw up the bitter bile from her empty stomach. She had been unable to eat because of the anguish of separating herself from Colton, and now she was paying for it. She wanted to die in mortification when he rushed forward to lend assistance, but she shook her head and then abruptly clasped a hand over her mouth as her stomach convulsed.

"Step outside a moment," he urged, slipping an arm beneath her shoulders and dragging her up against him. "There's a nip in the air. It will help settle your stomach."

Adriana had no strength to refuse his directive or aid and allowed him to whisk her outside.

"Breathe deeply," he advised, holding her close. "'Twill help."

She complied, not because he had bade her to, but for her own good. What little dignity she had remaining would be better served if she could dispense with her queasiness and send the man on his way. Yet it was some moments before she had enough strength to push herself free from him. As she tottered haphazardly back into the library, he followed close behind and reached out a hand to steady her as she reeled, but she avoided his touch as if he had contacted the plague.

"'Twould be better if you leave now," she said stoically after slipping back into her chair. "Now that you're a married man, we shouldn't be alone together. Please go. I would feel better if you did."

"I'm a *widower*, Adriana," he stated, stressing that declaration. "Pandora died before I left her town house."

"And the child?"

"She is with a wet nurse at Randwulf Manor."

"I see."

"I couldn't very well leave her alone in the world."

"No, of course not. You did the right thing. She'll have all the advantages you can afford."

"Adriana . . ." He laid a hand upon her shoulder.

She lifted her gaze solemnly to his. "Yes?"

When he saw the painful sadness dulling her beautiful eyes, remorse dragged his spirit down into the depths of a dark abyss with chains more weighty than he seemed able to bear. If anyone had ever denied there could be a hell on earth, then in that moment he was sure he could have proven them wrong. "Can you possibly forgive my mistakes and accept me as your husband?"

Once upon a time, Adriana might have heard those same words and been jubilant beyond measure, but now she could hardly manage a frail smile. "I shall have to consider your proposal at some length before I can give you an answer, Colton. Until then, I have no other recourse but to consider myself entirely free of any commitments to you and to the contract our parents signed. Your marriage to another woman has terminated that agreement."

His heart had never felt so heavy. "Will you allow me to come back tomorrow?"

"No, you'd better not. I need to be alone for a time and think about my future. As much as I love your family, I'm not at all sure I want to marry you now."

"Have you come to hate me in so short a time?"

"I don't hate you, Colton, but I must consider that prior to fatherhood, you showed no real interest in me as your wife. It seems a bit late now for a proposal of marriage. If you had wanted me, you should've shown some evidence of that during the past two months, but you didn't."

"I've been interested in you ever since I came back," he protested in desperation. "I can't even think of anyone but you. You haunt my dreams at night, and I wake wanting you beside me, yearning to have you with me every moment of the day."

"Nevertheless, your actions led me to believe that you were unwilling to accept me as your wife. Now I feel a reluctance to consider you as my husband. I must be given time to think through your offer in depth and ponder what my feelings toward you now are. In the meantime, if you'd kindly refrain from visiting me, I would then be able to determine my desires and hopes for the future without being unduly swayed one way or the other." She swept a slender hand toward the door. "You can find your own way out."

Fifteen

❀

Iт had seemed the way of it in ages past and probably would be the way of it in future times. Trouble followed trouble; so, too, sorrow and death. At times, the end of life came singularly, other times in pairs or in much greater numbers. No one could predict the whys and wherefores, or even when or where the dark-cloaked reaper would appear. The only thing that was certain was that he would eventually come to everyone; no one was exempt or excluded. There was, after all, a time to live, *and, inevitably*, a time to die.

The schism between Colton and Adriana grieved Philana so deeply that she nearly shut herself up in her chambers the day following Christmas, but that, of course, was not the English way or the exemplary conduct of a marchioness. She had to carry on stoically though the burden on her heart seemed too weighty to bear. It was doubly hard when word came that her niece, the young woman's husband, and their newborn had been killed when their coach had broken away from their four-in-hand and overturned as it rolled into a ravine. It was another painful death blow that had struck hard at the hearts of Philana and Alistair. Only a thrice of years ago, they had grieved over the passing of their sister and then, three months later, their brother-in-law. The couple had left only one child, a vivacious young woman who, in recent years, had married a viscount, whose own parents of late had also died. What made the deaths of the younger couple and their child more difficult to bear was the fact that they had met their end just outside of London after a band of discontented soldiers, who had been cashiered from the ranks to mete out a shoddy existence in the slums, had taken out their spite on the first available aristocrat, who had himself lost an eye in an earlier campaign against the French.

Relatives and friends of the Kingsleys gathered in London for the funerals, and it was at this sad event that Philana was able to speak with Adriana, who had journeyed with her parents to their London home near Regent Park, where they had met up with her sisters and their husbands before attending the funeral.

"Edythe was barely twenty," Philana explained through the gathering thickness in her throat. "She must have died shortly after giving birth, for the child was very much as he would've been had no one given Edythe aid during his birth . . . except that the cord had been cut and tied. Perhaps one of the soldiers took pity on Edythe and delivered her son. Of course, no one will ever know now what really happened. Even so, it was such a terrible waste of innocent lives. 'Tis difficult to understand why soldiers, once loyal to this country, would have gone after their coach. Courtland Kingsley had proven himself a courageous soldier in prior conflicts with France, but after the loss of his eye, he had to resign his commission because of his limited vision. Still, his own men had honored him as a valiant officer who had been willing to fight right alongside them." Her lips trembled as her sorrow welled forth, and when Adriana reached out to take her hand in gentle empathy, the elder clutched at it, as if in a moment of hopeless despair.

When Adriana later sought out Samantha among those at the cemetery, she found her friend leaning heavily upon the arm of her brother who was escorting her from the gravesite. The women embraced each other desperately for a long moment as Samantha struggled to contain her sobs. When finally Adriana stepped back, she kissed her friend's tear-streaked cheek and then acknowledged Colton's searching gaze with a sad smile and a stilted nod as he tipped his hat politely. His eyes, however, spoke volumes, but she was deaf . . . and blind to the pleas they conveyed.

COLTON lowered his teacup to its saucer and considered the strained smile his mother had pasted on her delicately structured face. As much as she made the pretense, she couldn't hide the anguish that for the last week had been tormenting her. Her niece's tragic death had been difficult for her to bear, but he was painfully aware that her distress had begun well before then, when he had told her about Adriana's stoic dismissal. He had carefully couched his words, desiring to spare his parent the anguish that ofttimes comes with the failure of heartfelt aspirations. Since then, the sadness in her blue eyes and their frequent mistiness had evidenced the morose depths of her despair.

It wasn't that he hadn't expected his mother to react in such a manner. Indeed, he had feared much of what was happening would come to pass after learning of his father's decree. The fact that it had been compounded by the deaths of Edythe and her small family made it even more arduous. Adriana had been his parents' only choice for a daughter-in-law. She had been like a daughter to them, and the very real possibility that those expectations would never come to fruition now was too bleak a prospect for his parent to accept without suffering the pangs of deep regret.

"I must ask you something," Philana announced quietly, studying her teacup intently as she returned it to her saucer.

"Yes?"

"Did you ever visit Edythe when you were in London this past year?"

Colton's brows gathered in bemusement. "No, I'm afraid after my departure from home years ago, I never saw her again. Why do you ask?"

"I ask because of a mark the physician's found on the newborn's backside."

Sitting back in his chair, Colton stared at her mother in growing bewilderment. She didn't have to say anything more. "But how can that be? She was not kin to the Wyndhams. Neither was Courtland."

"How well I know that," Philana murmured, and then struggled to present an intrepid smile, but it was tremulous at best. "Not unless your father . . ."

Colton refused to hear her conjecture. "Father would never have touched Edythe . . . or any other woman. You were the only one he *ever* loved . . . or, for that matter, desired. I never once saw him look at another woman in the manner you suggest. I may've had my failings, Mother, but Father was faithful and true in everything he did. He took me to task too many times in my youth for my own propensity to cavort rather freely with the girls, and he reminded me fairly often that it was not a gentleman's way for me now to believe that he'd have gone against his own moral code."

"Then how would you explain the presence of such a mark on the newborn's backside?"

"Did you see it for yourself?" Colton pressed.

"Of course not. As you know, they wouldn't allow the caskets to be opened because of the length of time. . . ." She clasped a hand over her mouth as she felt her gorge rise.

Colton reached out and, resting a hand upon his mother's, did his best to reassure her. "Then obviously what the physicians described was not the same that I bear now or what my father bore before me. I am the last of the Wyndhams, and even Latham cannot claim the mark, because his forebears before him never did. I cannot tell you how very, very sorry I am that I didn't take more pains to protect my family's honor. Foolishly I believed Pandora couldn't have children and that it was safe to be with her. I have been caught in a trap of my own making, and nothing, absolutely nothing I can say now can erase my error in judgment. My daughter is an innocent victim, and because I couldn't bear to think of one of my own suffering the plight of bastardy, I am where I am. If I were given a chance to do it all over again, I would never have bedded her mother, but as for allowing an innocent to pay the rest of her life for my indiscretions, I cannot . . . and could not bear that thought. The blame is mine; I must suffer the consequences."

"She seems to be a very pretty child," Philana said mutedly, unable to meet his gaze. "The servants have made inquiries about a wet nurse in the area. Hopefully, we'll find one to replace Alice soon. I must say her manners are . . . a bit unusual."

Colton managed a stiff twitch of his lips, the best attempt at a smile he could convey at the moment. " 'Despicable' is the word, Mother."

Harrison entered the drawing room, bearing a small silver tray upon which lay a letter sealed with red wax. He offered it to the marquess. "This missive arrived for you from Bath this past moment, my lord."

"Bath?" Colton repeated in some bewilderment.

"Yes, my lord. I believe it bears Lord Standish's seal."

Philana sat up, a small glimmer of hope brightening her eyes. "Perhaps Gyles has managed to persuade Adriana to give you another chance."

Colton doubted that possibility. The girl had a mind of her own and wasn't easily swayed when it came to choosing a husband, not even by her father. He had seen evidence of that the first time he had visited her at Wakefield Manor, when she had set them all back upon their heels by her angry departure from the drawing room.

Breaking the waxed seal, Colton unfolded the dispatch and began to read. The message it bore presented his options bluntly.

If you have any smallest desire of presenting your petition of marriage to my daughter, I strongly suggest you come to the Lansdown Crescent at Bath ere the closing hour of the Assembly Room Saturday night. The Marquess of Harcourt seems to have taken Adriana's presence here and your lack of such as an indication of a possible estrangement between the two of you. He has sent a request for an audience with me, and I can only believe he means to speak with me again regarding the matter of his marriage to my daughter. I can assure you if that is not Lord Harcourt's intent, there are others here eagerly vying for her hand. Though I trust my daughter to choose wisely, she will not make a decision in your favor unless she is convinced that you desire her to be your wife. If I have mistaken your affection for her, please disregard this summons. Be it known that I deeply honor the memory of your father, and it is only for that reason I send this letter. I cannot fault Adriana if she does not wish to marry you. Our plans are to stay in Bath until after the New Year.

"What is it, dear?" Philana asked. "Do I dare hope that it bears encouraging news?"

"I must go to Bath," Colton declared, coming to his feet in sudden haste. He dropped the letter on the table beside his mother as he stepped around it. "This will explain everything. I'm not sure when I'll be back."

It wasn't long before Bentley was reining the four-in-hand onto the lane that, moments later, led them past Wakefield Manor. Less than an hour had passed since Colton had read Gyles's letter, and in that expanse of time the wind had risen and dark clouds had gathered overhead. Though the onset of evening was still a pair of hours away, the dreariness of the approaching storm seemed to have aged day into night.

Complying with his lordship's request for speed, Bentley cracked the whip over the backs of the secondary steeds again and again, urging them onward to their fastest pace. There were occasions for overt showiness, but the mission his lordship seemed to be on required the maximum effort from the sturdier team. Time was of the essence.

As the conveyance entered the gloominess of a heavy copse of trees, Bentley eased his demands only slightly as the four-in-hand approached a familiar, undulating curve, which took them past thick stands of trees growing close upon the road. The landau swayed from side to side as it sped around another curve and had barely ceased its sideways motion when a warning shout from Bentley and a muttered cursing caused Colton to brace against a sudden, jolting halt.

"What's wrong?" he demanded, swinging open the door and making a partial descent to the step.

"There's a tree across the road, milord," Bentley announced over his shoulder as he tied off the reins. "The wind must've blown it down."

Colton stepped to the lane and snuggled the top hat firmly upon his head as his redingote swirled chaotically about him. Once he strode past the lead pair of horses, he came into view of the barrier and, after assessing the situation, deemed the size of the tree challenging but manageable. Briefly he squinted against the wind before lending his consideration to how best to go about moving the obstacle to the edge of the road where it would be out of their way. Facing the servant, he explained his idea. "Between the two of us, Bentley, we should be able to swing the top of the tree around until the whole of it is lying alongside the road. Considering its size, it shouldn't prove too difficult if we both carry it."

Bentley promptly made his descent to the ground and together, at the count of three, and with all the strength they could exert, they hefted the upper portion of the tree and carried it to the side of the road in spite of its broken limbs and tangle of leaves with which they were forced to contend. The heavier portion of the trunk scraped up soil and grass where it had become ensconced, slowing their progress. It proved an enormous feat, but one they managed to accomplish. Bentley even had enough breath left over to chortle over their success.

Dusting his hands off, Colton grinned. "Now let's get to Bath before we find our way again hampered, this time by a rainstorm."

He was just approaching the stump of the tree when he realized it had not collapsed beneath the force of the wind as they had supposed. Rather, it had been chopped down and, from what he could ascertain, fairly recently from the sap that was still oozing from its firmly rooted base, around which lay a pile of fresh chips.

Continuing on a short distance beyond the stump, Colton paused as if to consider the sky overhead and then turned, lifting his head a slight degree to keep his searching eyes hidden beneath the shadow of his brim. Listening intently, he carefully scanned the woods from right to left. The gravel on the well-worn road crunched slightly beneath Bentley's boots as the hulking man strode past the team, but another sound, the clicking thud of a rifle misfiring, set Colton's nerves on end. It was too close for comfort!

"Get down!" he bellowed toward his driver as he, himself, raced as swiftly as he could toward the landau, the door of which he had left open. Besides a few saplings, it alone offered the closest cover for him. In the next instant, a loud explosion of gunpowder, ignited by a firing pin, produced the forceful trajectory of a leaden ball. The resulting, ear-splitting sound snatched a start from Bentley, who promptly ducked in wide-eyed alarm.

The leaden missile met its intended mark, boring a hole into Colton's back and sending him sprawling forward with a sharp gasp. On the heels of that report, a barrage of exploding gunfire was unleashed upon the pair, most of which pelted the landau with lead shot very near the place where Colton had gone down. As painful as it was for him to move, he was forced to drag himself beneath the conveyance, which at best afforded him little security.

"Milord, are yu hurt?" Bentley cried, having made his way past the front wheels. He squatted down on his haunches on the far side of the landau and craned his neck to look underneath. When he saw the glistening red on the back of the redingote, his heart plunged to morbid depths as fear pierced it. He could only believe the nobleman was either dead or dying. "Milord, are yu alive?"

The piercing agony of his wound delayed Colton's answer a moment as he lay with his brow braced on a forearm. Finally he rolled his head on his arm, enabling him to peer sideways at Bentley, who clasped a hand over his swiftly pounding heart as his breath escaped in a sigh of relief.

"I'm wounded but far from dead, Bentley. Have you a weapon and shot with you?"

"Aye, milord. Brown Besses, both o' 'em. I gots plenty o' shot, too. Yu might says I likes bein' prepared at all times."

"Should we escape alive from these brigands who've attacked us, I'll see that you're supplied with more accurate weapons in the future. As for now, we can only hope our attackers are within range of the shot. Can you reach them without getting your head blown off?"

"Well, considerin' the trouble we'll be in if'n I don't, milord, I'll be doin' 'at very thing right away. I just checked the loadin' this morn'n, just like I've been doin' e'er since yur cousin an' 'er family were killed."

No sooner were the words out of Bentley's mouth than he was again on his feet, scurrying alongside the carriage, this time toward the front. Shots liberally pocked the wood and fine leather sheathing the conveyance as he climbed onto the spokes of the wheel and reached behind the dickey seat. He cursed loudly as the leaden balls sprinkled the landau, sending sharp splinters flying into his face, but upon reaching the weapons and a bag of shot, he clasped them firmly in one arm and hastily began his descent, though not fast enough. An enraged snarl was wrenched from his lips as a ball sliced across his cheek, leaving a groove that readily spilled blood over his dapper livery. The wound gave him impetus. He promptly dropped out of sight and, hunkering down low, scampered back toward the spot where his lordship had taken shelter. There, he delivered two of the weapons into the capable hands of the retired colonel.

Bentley squinted against the stiff breezes that flowed beneath the carriage as he watched the younger man reposition himself. "Do yu ken how best ta take 'em, milord?"

"Go to the front of the carriage, and see if you can drawn them out, but stay out of sight," Colton bade. "It's bad enough that I've been wounded without having you incapable of getting us out of here. I'll see if I can pick off one or two while they're watching you. Hopefully that will send the rest of them fleeing in fear of their lives."

"How many do ye make 'em out ta be, milord?"

"From the shots pelting the landau while you were getting the rifles, more than we can repel without reinforcements. You'd better start praying for a miracle."

While on bended knee, Bentley bent his head, muttered a few words, and then, after a breathless "amen," scurried forward.

A brief curtailment of gunfire had followed his disappearance, spurring Bentley to pop his head into view again. "Yu bloody bastards!" he railed. "Show yur ugly faces."

Quickly he ducked out of sight again, just as several leaden balls pelted the landau. On the heels of this new barrage, Bentley heard the fairly loud roar of a Brown Bess discharging from underneath the wheel base. On its heels came a distant scream. He chanced a peek through the windows of the landau in time to see a man clasp a hand to his profusely bleeding throat and then tumble forward in a senseless heap.

Another gurgling cry was evoked from another of the villains soon after Colton drew bead upon a tattered red coat visible through the brush. The man staggered into an opening, causing Colton to suffer a deep regret as he recognized the coat as one worn by foot soldiers of the English infantry.

"Bentley, stay down!" he bellowed. "I've got to talk with these men!"

The coachman was certain the younger man had taken leave of his senses. "But, milord, they're tryin' ta blow us ta kingdom come!"

"Do as I say! Stay down, and don't draw any more fire!"

A sorely garbled comment, closely resembling an oath, sufficed as a promise of compliance. Petulantly, Bentley folded his arms across his chest, convinced his lordship was courting disaster.

Colton endured the piercing agony centered around the hole in his back as he dragged himself closer to the front wheel. The effort cost him a fair measure of his remaining vigor, and after completing the excruciating task, he was forced to rest a moment. By dint of will, he took firm hold of his resolve as well as his rapidly dwindling strength and called out to the rabble, "Men, why have you attacked my coach? Are you not some of the same fighting men I fought alongside against our enemies? If you have no real ken of the men you've attacked, let me introduce myself. I am Colonel Wyndham, recently retired from His Majesty's armed forces."

"Colonel Lord Wyndham?" Surprise was evident in the voice of the one who answered, but it was one Colton recognized.

"Sergeant Buford, is that you? Good heavens, man! Why have you repaid me for saving your life by attacking my coach?"

"Milord, I ne'er dreamt for an instant it were yu we'd been stirred up ta attack! Please, yur lordship, yu've gots ta believe me! A fella told us 'at a Lord Randwulf was bootin' out families o' dead soldiers who'd been his tenants afore the war an' were forcin' their children ta do his drudgery in his work houses in order for 'em ta eat."

Colton didn't know which galled him more, his wound or the vicious slander. "Who tells those lies against me? I am Lord Randwulf. I assumed my father's marquessate after his death. He owned no work houses, and the tenants residing on our lands have been living there for many a year. As for the widows and families of dead soldiers, they are secure in their cottages, doing what they can for their own betterment."

"Don't knows the bloke's name, milord. Nor 'is face, neither. He wore a mask whilst 'e were wit' us."

"Is he among you now? I would speak with this man who has taken it upon himself to fabricate these lies against me."

"'E were just 'ere, milord. 'E's the one what shot yu. . . . Took 'em two tries ta do it ta ye, too, aftah 'is own weapon fizzled." Cautiously Buford rose to his feet, fearing he'd be shot. After realizing he was fairly safe, he stood upright and glanced around the area. "Why, the gent's taken 'is bloomin' leave, milord. Maybe 'e lit out wit' the idea o' lettin' the rest o' us be 'anged for what 'e started. 'Twould 'peer 'e duped the lot o' us, milord, an' for 'at, I must beg yur pardon."

"Your apology is accepted, Buford. Now I urge you and your co-horts to go back to your homes and families, and stop this chicanery. If you do not desist in this foolishness, I can assure you that eventually you'll pay for what you're doing. If you need work, then by all means, come to my manor. I'll see what can be done for you, but for heaven's sake, cease this idiocy ere you're arrested and strung up for killing innocent people."

"Are yu wounded, milord?" Buford asked worriedly. "I saw yu fall when the bloke shot yu. 'Twould be a bloomin' shame if'n yu died from some-thin' we'd been involved in. Can we 'elp yu, milord?"

"The conniving bastard shot me in the back, all right, but I haven't time to see to my wound. It's crucial that I get to Bath."

Bentley stuttered in sharp surprise before he launched into a vehement protest. "Milord, Bath's an hour away, an' the manor only a few moments. Yu could die if'n we don't turn back. Once a physician looks at ye, then if'n 'e says you're able, we can go on as before."

"Just help me into the carriage, Bentley, and continue on to Bath. We'll find a doctor there in good time."

"Milord . . . please . . . I'd be deeply grieved should yu expire along the way. Yur mother'd ne'er forgive me. Yur sister'd likely 'ave me scalp, jes' like I been 'earin' 'bout from 'em far-off places in the Colonies."

"Dammit, Bentley, do as I say! I won't be swayed by your arguments. My future happiness may well depend on our ability to reach the city in good time."

"Well, what 'bout yur life?"

"I'm not ready to give it up just yet, Bentley, and the longer you stand there arguing, the longer it will take you to get me to a physician. Besides, it's only a scratch."

"Only a scratch," Bentley mumbled morosely, climbing to his seat. "*Humph*, wit' a 'ole like that, 'e'll likely be bleeding ta death afore I e'en gets 'im 'ere."

THE city of Bath was exactly the place where she wanted and needed to be at this precise moment in time, Adriana decided dejectedly as she gazed out on the lantern-lit city from the second-story bedchamber of her aunt's town house, where she had been ensconced shortly after arriving with her parents. That had been several days ago, and, since then, her aunt had taken them on lengthy walks, accompanied them on visitations to old friends and distant relatives, encouraged them to shop frugally, dress tastefully, and follow the very pleasant customs of the city, for it was here that divisions between aristocrats and gentlefolk had ceased to exist, that is, if one minded one's manners, a requirement if one wanted to be accepted. Yet, in spite of her aunt's vivacious and clever wit, which frequently evoked well-deserved chortles from guests, Adriana still struggled to subdue the tears that quickly began to flow whenever she let down her guard and relented to the agonizing pangs she had been suffering since terminating her courtship with Colton Wyndham.

The distance between Bath and Randwulf Manor had allowed her to separate herself, if not emotionally from the handsome man, then surely in actuality. Even so, regrets continued to press down hard upon her, especially when she was alone. She wished now she had had the foresight to release Colton from the contract ere their courtship ever commenced. Had she done so, she'd have saved herself the enormous grief that now weighed down her spirit. Every instinct she had been capable of feeling had screamed a warning of the improbability of their ever getting married, but like a simpleton she had allowed herself to believe there existed a small, finite chance. And so, much to the injury of her heart, she had allowed herself to fall more deeply in love with the man every day they had been together.

A light rap of knuckles sounded on the bedchamber door, drawing Adriana's somber attention away from the thoroughfare below. At her call for admittance, her mother swept in, valiantly feigning a cheery smile. In spite of her deep concern for her daughter, Christina had endeavored to convey an optimistic facade, though in truth her own heart was breaking for her youngest offspring. It was the best she could do under the circumstances, for she found herself totally bereft of the talent for working miracles and absorbing into herself all the anguish the girl was now suffering. "Lord Alistair just arrived, dear. Will you be coming down soon?"

"Yes, Mama," Adriana replied, hardly aware of the dejected sigh that slipped from her lips in accompaniment. "I'm ready to leave whenever you are."

"That will be soon, dear."

A genuine smile of delight touched Christina's soft lips as her eyes swept over her daughter. The dark-blue silk sheath that her youngest wore was sublimely appropriate for one so tall, lithe, and graceful. The minuscule beads lightly embellishing the gown caught the radiance of a nearby lamp, causing the lovely creation to glitter like tiny stars upon a night-blue sky. Teardrop pearls dangled prettily from small, sapphire-encrusted studs, adorning the lobes of dainty ears. Twining delicately about the base of her neck was a gold choker finely tooled to represent diminutive branches of a tree, the twigs of which were studded here and there with minute sapphires. A fairly large, solitary teardrop pearl hung over the hollow of her long, elegant throat.

The jewelry was the only accoutrement her daughter wore with the costly gown, but Christina was convinced she needed nothing more, for it was a fact that some of the simplest garments complemented a rare beauty far more than frilly or elaborate attire. Indeed, there were times when Christina had to admit, but only to herself, that in pulchritude and grace, her youngest daughter far surpassed her sisters.

"You're looking especially lovely tonight, dear. Alistair has just arrived and informed us that Samantha and Percy will also be there tonight at the Assembly Rooms with Stuart and Berenice. From what your aunt has been telling me, many of your past suitors have been making inquiries about you and intend to be at Lansdown tonight as well in hopes of renewing their own courtship. Of course, I doubt you-know-who will be there." Christina dared not mention Colton's name for fear of touching off another lengthy bout of tears. She did, however, think it a shame the man wouldn't be there to see just how eagerly other swains welcomed his very noticeable absence from Adriana's side. It would certainly serve the libertine his just due to realize the zeal other gentlemen freely evidenced in their desire to win Adriana for themselves. Perhaps it was her own entitlement as a parent to feel put out by the man for what she considered a personal affront against her daughter, but then, she couldn't dismiss from mind another who'd grieve almost as desperately if the couple parted forever.

Christina heaved a sigh of lament for her old friend. "Dear Philana was simply mortified by his sudden fatherhood and marriage to that actress.

She was quite put out that special licenses could be bartered by favors to the archbishop in order to legitimize such hasty nuptials. Nevertheless, dear, she hopes you will forgive her son and reconsider his proposal of marriage, but I had to tell her that I didn't see any chance for that occurrence. As handsome a husband as his lordship would make, a woman must be able to trust in the integrity of her spouse. Yet there are those who seem fiercely loyal to him and defend his actions. As much as poor Alistair is trying his best to remain discreetly mum about the matter in Tilly's presence, 'tis obvious he admires his nephew a great deal. He has even spoken in his favor to your father, going so far as to argue that his lordship's actions could be considered noble when compared to other aristocrats who turn their backs upon illegitimate offspring while arrogantly pretending they've done nothing scandalous. At the moment, however, Alistair doesn't want to set Tilly awry by his defense when 'tis evident she's just as loyal to you. If I can believe my eyes, I'd be inclined to say the man is very much smitten with your aunt."

Adriana offered a meager smile, the best she could manage under the circumstances. "He's probably more stunned than anyone by his infatuation, having managed to remain a bachelor all these many years."

"Yes, I can understand why he'd feel that way," Christina agreed. "As long as we've been friends with the Wyndhams, he has never seemed overly enthusiastic about courting women or even getting married. Perhaps you-know-who gets his independence naturally. Still, it will be interesting to see just how it all comes out with Tilly and Alistair. Like you, she is not without her admirers. Even so, I don't know that her three sons will take kindly to having a stepfather. Being full-grown and with children of their own, they can hardly protest, especially since Tilly would ignore their advice anyway." Having said that, Christina smiled as she beckoned to her daughter. "Come along, dear. By now, your father is probably pacing the floor, wondering what's keeping us."

No sooner had their party arrived at Lansdown Crescent than Adriana found herself besieged with requests from handsome gentlemen vying for her attention, or at least hoping for a dance or two fairly soon, or even later on. As far-fetched as it seemed to Adriana, word that she was in Bath without her usual escort had spread even to London just since the previous day, for sons of their Regent Park neighbors had come to Bath to test the waters, but only those rippling around the daughter of Lord Standish.

Sir Guy Dalton had stood at the forefront of the collection of young men who had been watching for her. As soon as Adriana entered, he had swept into a flamboyant bow and immediately engaged her in a vivacious conversation about the city and the approaching New Year, two days hence. Although Adriana smiled and chatted with the young knight for several moments, she graciously demurred his invitation, having no other wish than to join her own parents when he tried to coax her into one of the seats the Reverend William Dalton had reserved in the Assembly Room for his family and their guest, the archbishop.

The music in the ballroom was both soothing and uplifting, and in spite of her recent gloominess, Adriana felt somewhat rejuvenated, at least enough to dance with Sir Guy and several other young men who had been keeping a close eye upon her. Still, after returning to the sidelines, she was unnerved when Roger Elston stepped close in front of her.

"My lady." He smiled into her eyes as if entirely guiltless of any previous wrongdoing.

Her mouth stretched tightly in a crisp smile as she inclined her head in a meager nod of recognition. "Mr. Elston."

She would have brushed past him immediately, but he advanced in the direction in which she sought to flee, guilefully preventing her escape as he looked casually about the hall. Then, as if totally unaware of her wish to leave him, he smiled down at her and found icy shards boring into him. His gaze descended from those dark orbs as if drawn irresistibly to her bosom, the higher, creamy curves of which were set off to perfection by the shallow bodice of her darkly hued gown. Whether the man was merely seeking to refresh his memory or contemplating something more devious, Adriana could not determine, but she was no less incensed.

"Rather surprising to find you out and about without your gallant escort," Roger remarked loftily. "Has his lordship forgotten you perchance, or found another lady with whom to wile away his time?"

Adriana pointedly snubbed the miller by turning aside and vigorously fanning her burning cheeks. As persistent as always, Roger stepped forward until they were once again standing shoulder to shoulder. His eyes scanned the dancing couples nonchalantly as he sniffed a pinch of snuff.

"As for myself, I'm in quite good company, having escorted the very beautiful Miss Felicity and a pair of casual acquaintances of hers, who've been craving to see Bath for themselves for some time."

"Have you become a guide of late, Mr. Elston?" Adriana asked coolly and flicked a glance behind him to smile at Felicity and the two young ladies, each hardly much older than ten and seven, who were nearly chirping with excitement as they glanced about the ballroom.

"Indeed, no, my lady. I'm far too busy with the mill to take on such whimsical tasks. Indeed, so swamped was I with orders to fill today that my livery barely made it to Gladstone's house at the appointed hour."

"That's nice," she replied coolly and was about to walk away when he caught her arm. Turning her head to look at him, she gritted out a smile as she warned, "Take your hand off me, Mr. Elston, or I shall start screaming this very instant."

He complied forthwith. "Goodness, I didn't mean to distress you, dear lady. I only wanted to introduce you to Felicity's friends. Impressionable young girls, they are, truly bedazzled by aristocrats, it seems. They'd be especially honored to meet you. Of course, between Felicity and her friends, I find myself perplexed, wondering which one to lay the honor of a marriage proposal. But then, Felicity is the only one who still resists my manly quests and appetites. She's such an innocent, poor dear. As for the other two I must confess they have left me somewhat jaded by their eagerness to please." He patted a hand to his yawning mouth as if terribly bored. "Why, they lift their skirts for any smallest whim of mine and don't mind that there's three abed. . . ."

Cheeks burning, Adriana turned abruptly from him and started making her way through the crowd toward her parents. Their presence promised her absolute safety. When she drew nearer the place where they stood, she realized her father had been watching her keenly, and though he voiced no question as she joined him, his eyes bespoke his concern.

"Just angry, that's all, Papa," she acknowledged at his silent question. "The man is an utter cad. Too bad you didn't cut him like Maud said you threatened to do. You might have prevented the debauchment of two silly maids."

Gyles harrumphed in some discomfiture. "Maud shouldn't be reddening your innocent ears by repeating my ominous threats, girl."

Smiling up at her father, Adriana laid a hand upon his finely tailored sleeve. "Papa, I've been around horses long enough to know the difference between a gelding and a stallion. Mr. Elston should definitely be a gelding."

Gyles winked at her above a grin, having given up all hopes of trying to suppress it. "One of these days, girl, I may consider performing that service, just to keep you safe from that ogre, though it's too bad about the silly maids. Obviously they never learned that some men are dastardly sorts, but I'm afraid there's nothing we can do to enlighten them. They're old enough to know better. Besides, if they've ignored the admonitions of their parents, 'tis doubtful they'll accept advice from strangers."

"They probably never had a father like you who cared enough to want to protect them." Smoothing a hand fondly over his crisply tailored lapels, she smiled up at him adoringly. "I love you, Papa, more than any man on Earth."

"Now who's being dishonest?" he questioned gently, delving into eyes that in recent days had lost much of their lively sparkle. "There is one you love through and through."

She blinked away a start of tears. "Aye, Papa," she admitted sadly, "but I fear he doesn't love me."

"We shall see the way of it, my dear, perhaps even as early as tonight. Who knows?" He patted her hand reassuringly and then, sweeping a glance about the ballroom, casually motioned across the room toward its entrance. "Now there's a familiar face, and I believe he's searching for you."

Adriana's heart leapt within her bosom, for she could only imagine that Colton had indeed come and was looking for her. Cheeks rosy, she searched in the direction her father had gestured and felt a sharp twinge of disappointment as she caught sight of the very handsome Riordan Kendrick. Apparently he had just arrived, for he was peering about as if he were indeed trying to find someone.

Equal to her father's height, Riordan had the advantage of being able to look over the heads of the women and the vast majority of men. He seemed rather methodical in his quest as he glanced about the room until Adriana finally felt his eyes settle . . . and stay . . . on her. A slow grin traced across his lips. With the same unswerving dedication, he pressed through the chatting couples who had collected behind the chairs and benches of the spectators seated around the ballroom floor.

Adriana couldn't believe that word of her estrangement from Colton was spreading so quickly, but here again seemed viable proof of the alacrity with which it was advancing. Riordan Kendrick was obviously taking the initiative to press his suit.

She had almost forgotten how handsome the man was . . . and just how dedicated he had been to have her for his own. Still, when she returned his smile, it was as if something had gone missing from her spirit. As much as she had once believed she'd be pleased to have Riordan as her husband, she couldn't easily accept that premise now, not while the image of Colton Wyndham still loomed unrelentingly in her mind . . . and her heart. Perhaps in time the agonizing pain would diminish, and she could consider the ones who really wanted her, chief among them, Riordan Kendrick, who as far back as nearly two years past had evidenced his fierce commitment toward that end.

"My lady, mere words cannot fully justify how much I've missed you these past months," he murmured warmly as he halted before her. "I made every effort to keep my mind from dwelling upon the lady whom I had lost and to absorb myself in overseeing renovations to my private chambers at my country estate, desiring not only to assuage the vacancy lingering in my heart, but to find a way to win you for my wife. Should I dare hope that your presence here in Bath and the very noticeable absence of your usual escort is reason for me to rejoice?"

A vigorous flagging of a handkerchief across the room caught Adriana's attention. Curious to know who in the world would be so bold in the Assembly Room, she leaned aside slightly to peer past Riordan's arm, since his height blocked her view. The distressed individual was none other than Samantha, motioning to her rather frantically from across the ballroom. Considering her friend's lack of aplomb, Adriana could only believe something of a serious nature had upset her.

Laying a hand upon the marquess's arm, Adriana looked up at him beseechingly. "Your pardon for being so rude to excuse myself at this very moment, Riordan, but I must find out why Samantha is beckoning to me. She seems terribly distressed, and I can only wonder what has happened. . . ." Adriana could not allow herself to continue, for her heart had turned suddenly cold at the thought of Colton lying dead or wounded somewhere.

Riordan glanced around to see for himself what was going on behind him and readily affirmed that Samantha did indeed seem greatly disturbed. "Here, follow me, and stay close," he bade chivalrously, taking Adriana's slender hand within his. "The crowd is far too dense for you to maneuver through it easily."

Adriana was quite willing to let him pull her along behind him, for his tall, broad-shouldered form easily forged a path through the mass of people. As soon as they neared Samantha, the woman rushed toward her and clutched her arm in desperation. Her face had lost most of its color, and though she was making every effort not to break down, her lips were trembling with the threat of that possibility.

In rising concern, Adriana grabbed her friend's arm. "My goodness, Samantha, what has happened to upset you so? Where's Percy? Is he all right?"

"Bentley sent someone in to fetch him earlier, and he just now rushed back to tell me that Colton is in the carriage outside and is wanting to see you."

A rush of joyful excitement shot through Adriana once again before reason intruded and suppressed her elation. Did he really think she'd fly into his embrace so easily after he had kept her at arm's length all during their courtship? Conveying a casualness she definitely didn't feel, she lifted her shoulders in a blasé shrug. "So, why doesn't your brother come inside?"

"Colton has been shot in the back, Adriana, and he refuses to seek out a physician until he has an opportunity to speak with you. Bentley said they were attacked on the road shortly after leaving home, and my brother has come this far in spite of his wounds, determined to see you."

The dreadful news pierced Adriana's heart with cold shards of mounting fear. For a second time in so many moments, she faced the marquess to plead for his gracious understanding, this time, however, in trembling disquiet. "Riordan, please forgive me, but I must go to Colton."

"Perhaps I can be of some help," he offered, the joy fading from his dark eyes. Clasping her shaking hand within his, he sought to rally her courage. "Having dressed a good many wounds in my experience as an officer, Adriana, mayhap if I were to accompany you both outside, I could be of some assistance."

"Please hurry then," Samantha pleaded, readily accepting his advice and whatever help he'd be able to give. "Colton could be dying for all we know."

The faces of the onlookers registered shock as the three almost ran toward the entrance, but it mattered naught to the women and even less to the man who followed closely behind. Bentley was waiting beside the landau, the sorry condition of which had drawn a crowd of close and casual acquaintances anxious to know what had occurred, and if any of the

Wyndhams had been hurt in what the driver merely explained was an attack by unknown factions. As to his employer's condition, Bentley answered them by repeating the words that had been issued to him earlier. "His lordship, but 'tis only a scratch."

As the ladies hurried from the curving, elegant edifice, Percy made a careful descent from the landau, not wishing to cause his brother-in-law any greater discomfort than he was already suffering.

"Do you ken if his injuries are serious?" Samantha asked her husband as he extended a hand to help her in.

"Your brother claims it isn't," Percy murmured, "but you'd better brace yourself for the worst, my pet. He seems to have lost a lot of blood. His coat is nigh soaked through in the back."

In mounting dread, Adriana bit into a slender knuckle as she waited for the man to assist his wife. When Percy finally turned to her, his face was solemn, his blue eyes in the lantern light bereft of their usual sparkle. The plea in her own tear-filled, dark orbs was readily discernible.

"I can offer no assurances, Adriana," he murmured regretfully, squeezing her thin fingers to communicate his own concern. Gently he handed her into the coach.

Samantha had taken a seat beside her brother, and when she looked around and met her friend's worried gaze, she could only press trembling lips together and offer a noncommittal shrug. Adriana's shaking limbs threatened to collapse beneath her. Somehow she managed to reach the cushions in front of Colton. Yet her heart grew cold with dread as she considered the one she had come to love so desperately.

Colton sat slumped in the far corner of the rear seat with an elbow braced upon the rest, the hand of that same arm pressing hard against his midriff, as if with it he endeavored to brace himself up. In the glow of the lampposts his face appeared pale and drawn. It also became evident that he was having some difficulty in rallying enough strength to speak. "Forgive my shoddy condition, ladies," he rasped through a wry grin. The stiffness of his pale lips vividly attested to the difficulty he was having hiding his agony. "I started out in good form, but between there and here I ran afoul of miscreants who seemed intent on killing me. . . ."

Adriana clasped a hand over her mouth to smother a fearful moan. Her companion and friend, whose own quaking tone clearly conveyed her mounting concern, voiced the question burning within her mind.

"Why didn't you turn back, Colton, and have our surgeon tend your wound?"

"I had to tell Adriana . . . that I do indeed love her . . . and am most desperate to have her for my wife." His eyes flicked toward the door where Lord Riordan stood listening to their exchange. "You see, I was terrified . . . of losing her . . . to another. I did not chance a delay for fear of what the evening would reap . . . if I . . . didn't at least tell her . . . of my love."

Adriana brushed at the tears now streaming down her face. His family would not be able to tolerate his death, nor would she. Not only did she love him with every fiber of her being, but if he were to die, she'd never forgive herself, for she'd be haunted by the fact that the rift between them had prevented him from searching out a physician in a timely fashion. That guilt would hound her to her grave. "We must get you to Aunt Tilly's posthaste and find a surgeon to take care of your wound."

The smile that turned his lips proved feeble indeed. The same shaft of light streaming from the lamppost illumed his smile and the smoky gray eyes that settled unswervingly upon her. "Not until you promise to marry me, Adriana. Tonight would be fine, if not this very moment."

"You may well die if your wound is not soon tended," Adriana choked, trying hard to hold back the threatening sobs.

"Better to die than to live without you," he whispered, extending his free hand toward her.

Amid a flood of cascading tears, Adriana reached out and settled her fingers within his grasp.

"Will you be my wife, Adriana?" he rasped.

She nodded vigorously. "Yes, oh, yes!"

Directing his gaze to Riordan, Colton managed a weak smile in spite of the searing pain piercing his back. "Should I not make it through this, my lord, be it known that you would be my choice for the lady's husband. She could do no better, upon my demise of course."

Even in so serious a moment, Riordan did not miss the other man's unquenchable humor. Inclining his head briefly, he accepted the compliment the other bestowed upon him, but he was wont to answer forthrightly, "Had the two of you not been promised, my lord, I would've moved heaven and earth to take Adriana from you, and though I do most desperately yearn to have her as my own wife, I would not want our marriage to come to fruition through your death. On a matter more pertinent to your present needs, if you'd allow me to accompany you to the town house, perhaps between Percy and I we can be of some assistance getting you to a bed. Although the ladies have proven immensely resourceful in the past, I'm afraid they lack the strength to accomplish that feat."

"Your offer is most kindly accepted," Colton managed weakly. "I fear I don't have enough vigor left to maneuver myself into a house . . . or to doff my clothes even if I were to get that far."

Riordan turned to find Sir Guy standing at his elbow. The younger man had been listening intently to their exchange and seemed genuinely concerned. Considering the knight among his friends, Riordan urged him, "If you'd kindly tell Adriana's parents that she'll be returning to her aunt's town house without delay, 'twould alleviate their anxiety should they realize she's missing."

"I'll see that someone in the family is told of the situation," Sir Guy replied. Before departing on his errand, however, he stepped to the open door of the carriage. Clearing his throat slightly in an effort to claim the wounded man's attention, he soon found himself searching pain-glazed gray eyes. "I sincerely wish you well, my lord," he averred in all truth. " 'Twould be ill-met indeed if an honored hero of our lengthy conflict with France meets his end because of the foul deeds of our own countrymen. I shall hope and pray that you defeat their foul purposes by living a long, happy, and prosperous life. Concerning the matter of your happiness, if you wouldn't mind assistance in that area, I'd be willing to direct my father's attention to your needs. Since you and Lady Adriana are legal residents of Wiltshire, he'd certainly be able to issue you a marriage license. However, His Grace, the archbishop, just happens to be in Bath, inspecting various churches under his auspices, and has come to the Crescent tonight as my father's guest. I believe he'd be willing to dispense a special license to one of our country's finest heroes. With his signature on the document, then no one in the world would be able to challenge your marriage to Lady Adriana."

"Thank you, Sir Guy," Colton murmured gratefully, managing a frail smile. "Whatever the cost, I'd be interested in extending such a sum to have His Grace validate the license."

The knight turned abruptly, intending to set himself upon his errands, but immediately found himself facing Roger Elston, who, after meeting his gaze, cast a sardonic glance into the carriage beyond him. Touching a handkerchief to his left nostril in a lofty manner, he inquired, "Is anything amiss?"

Sir Guy didn't know why his hackles rose; perhaps it was the vague smirk that seemed to turn the miller's lips that goaded a brusque reaction from him, but then, he had never really liked the miller's son, especially his efforts to convey some viable claim on the lady when there were lords aplenty seeking her hand. "Not anything the Lady Adriana hasn't taken care of by agreeing to marry his lordship. In fact, I was just about to go in and arrange for my father to perform the nuptials tonight, by special license signed by His Grace, the archbishop, of course."

Roger's eyes turned icy. "You'd do that for the haughty bastard after desiring the lady yourself?"

"Unlike some men I know," Guy said, raising a brow meaningfully as their eyes dueled like glinting sabers, "I'm not a vindictive loser. Besides, considering his lordship's valiant service to his country, I'm sure *most* people would agree that he's deserving of such an honor. That's more than I can say for those paltry fellows who saw fit to excuse themselves by feigning serious disabilities."

"You poor, misguided fool," Roger sneered caustically, dismissing the other's pointed jibe. "Do you honestly think Wyndham's involvement in a few skirmishes makes him more worthy than any other?"

"A few?" Sir Guy's abortive laugh negated the other's disparagement. "More like a hundred, I'd say, dear chap. In any case, such an argument is redundant since Lady Adriana has already accepted his lordship's proposal of marriage." Lifting a hand, he tapped his forefinger against the miller's chest as he delivered what a knowledgeable swordsman, such as himself, would've defined as a verbal coup de grâce. "Which leaves you, buffoon, no chance in a million."

Roger sought to throw off the other's nettlesome touch, but with the swiftness of a talented foilsman, Guy swept his hand upward, deliberately jarring Roger's chin, evoking a noticeable rattle as the miller's teeth came forcefully together. Roger promptly snarled a profusion of epithets, liberally assailing the briskly departing knight, who now seemed eager to complete his mission.

Percy approached the fretfully pacing Bentley, who, upon espying him, hurried forward to meet him with the hope that he had encouraging news. None was forthcoming. In somber tones, Percy gave the driver instructions to the Lady Mathilda's town house. Dejectedly, the driver turned and climbed to his seat.

Adriana vacated the forward seat of the landau to make room for Percy and Riordan, but in refusing to release her hand, Colton dictated the seating arrangement, forcing her to claim the narrow space between his sister and himself. To spare him further discomfort, Adriana refrained from pressing back into the seat until Samantha slid aside to give her more room. Even then, Colton refused to let her move away, obliging her to remain close beneath his arm. Entwining his long fingers through hers, he rested their clasped hands in her lap as his shoulder overlapped hers and the back of his arm rested against her soft bosom. Lovingly she stroked the muscular firmness of his arm and rubbed her cheek against his shoulder as he slowly lowered his head against the far side of the landau. A moment later, her heart leapt in her bosom as the long fingers fell limp in her grasp.

"Oh, no, please, no!" she cried, bringing the other occupants forward in their seats. Frantic with fear, she searched for a pulse as she pressed trembling fingers against Colton's throat. Her anxiety quickly soared when none could be found. Choking on a sob, she renewed her efforts and, upon detecting a steady throbbing beneath her fingertips a moment later, went limp with relief. In some embarrassment, she glanced around at the others who were staring at her in rowelling concern.

"He's all right. His pulse is strong. He only fainted."

Samantha clasped a trembling hand over her mouth, trying to smother her sobs in spite of the flood of tears streaming down her cheeks.

"Dearest friend, forgive me for frightening you," Adriana pleaded through her own tears as she threaded thin fingers through the other's. Samantha's grip tightened, and together they struggled against their burgeoning fear as they leaned their heads together. As always, their hearts were bound as one in their love and concern for the man.

Sixteen

❄

IMMEDIATELY after Bentley drew the landau to a halt in front of Lady Mathilda's residence, Riordan stepped down and swept Adriana to the ground. Flying to the front portal, she rapped the iron clapper frantically against its metal base as Riordan assisted Samantha. In the silence that followed, Adriana could hear hurrying footfalls approaching the vestibule.

The steward, an energetic man in his early forties, pulled open the door a discreet distance and, upon recognizing the lady, stepped aside as he offered a cordial greeting. Espying the procession of people who followed her, he promptly swept the portal wider to accommodate the broad-shouldered men who were carrying a third who gave every indication of being unconscious.

"Hodges, we need a physician posthaste," Adriana announced anxiously as Percy and Riordan brushed past her with their burden. "Do you know of one who's well esteemed here in Bath? Lord Randwulf has been shot by miscreants and needs urgent attention."

"There's a physician Lady Mathilda holds in highest regard, my lady. I shall send my son for him forthwith."

The steward faced the youth, a boy about twelve, who had followed him into the hall. "You're the best rider we have here, Caleb. Ride over to Franklin Croft's place and bid the man to come with all possible haste."

"Yes, sir!"

Adriana caught up her skirts and flitted past Percy to lead the men upstairs. Her aunt occupied the largest bedroom in the house. Her parents were ensconced in the more spacious of the two guest chambers, which left the one she occupied as the only room that could be easily spared.

Swinging wide the door, Adriana ran ahead of the men and whipped down the covers on the bed. At the end of the short procession came Samantha, who was trying to explain to Hodges what had happened, according to what Bentley had told Percy.

Adriana sought the butler's advice as she indicated the bed. "Should we not spread older sheets over the mattress and bedding to protect Aunt Tilly's fine linens?"

Hodges had already foreseen that likelihood before sprinting up the stairs after them. He faced the door just as a maid, clutching an armful of older linens, rushed in. Adriana quickly helped the woman spread out several protective layers over the mattress and, after the men lowered their burden to the bed, began loosening Colton's waistcoat.

Displaying an uncompromising dignity and discretion as he stepped beside the young woman, Hodges clasped one hand in the palm of the other as he spoke in muted tones. "Lady Adriana, this is no task for a young maiden, such as yourself. I must insist that you and Lady Burke make yourselves comfortable downstairs and leave the matter of undressing his lordship to the three of us." Sweeping a hand about to indicate Percy, Riordan, and himself, the steward gave every indication that he had taken charge of the situation and was well able to handle everything from that perspective. "In the past, your aunt has been good enough to help Dr. Croft when he has treated soldiers returning from the war. On a number of occasions she has offered my services as well. Knowing in advance the items Dr. Croft will need to remove the lead ball and repair his lordship's wound, I've already set servants to boiling the instruments as the physician usually requires and to gather bandages and whatever else is needed. I'm sure you'll agree, my lady, undressing his lordship and cleansing his wound is neither for the delicate in nature nor an unwed maid. Be confident his lordship will be in capable hands, not only now, but especially when Dr. Croft arrives. The man is an outstanding physician and has treated some very difficult wounds with fine results. I can readily attest to that, having personally seen some of the miracles he has performed. There is therefore nothing for you and Lady Burke to do now other than sip a little port while you wait for Dr. Croft to arrive and do his best by his lordship."

Reluctant to leave, Adriana looked back at Colton, but Samantha laid a gentle hand upon her arm. "Come, dear. Hodges is right. The men are far more capable of readying my brother for the surgeon than we are. We haven't the skill to treat serious wounds. If you'll remember, we never had much success in that area when we found animals that were severely injured. The best we could do was let our fathers put them out of their misery."

Worried tears blurred Adriana's vision. "But if he should wake and want me . . ."

Samantha patted her arm in a motherly fashion. "The men will tell him that you're waiting downstairs and will return as soon as Dr. Croft gives his permission."

Hodges's predictions proved trustworthy, for Caleb arrived with the physician on his heels less than a quarter hour later. The older man tipped his hat politely to the ladies as he hastened from the vestibule and then spoke to the youth over his shoulder as that one followed hard on his heels.

"I shall need a strong libation to cleanse the wound and to administer to the patient. Do you know of any in the house, young man?"

"I believe, sir, my father already has what you need upstairs."

"Excellent. Then please be kind enough to direct me to the patient," he bade, sweeping his hand before him in an invitation for Caleb to precede him.

Adriana abruptly came to the awareness that she was tagging along behind them when Samantha halted her with a gentle hand upon her arm. As if coming from a daze, she turned to her friend, her concern for Colton ravaging what little remained of her composure.

Samantha slipped her arms about her and murmured resolutely, "We must pray and trust the surgeon to do his best, Adriana."

It was almost an hour and a half before Dr. Croft finally emerged from the upper room with his coat draped over his forearm. Rolling down his sleeves, he began his descent as Adriana flew to the stairs and clutched the newel with slender, white-knuckled fingers. Though her question remained unspoken as she watched him, her eyes pleaded with him to give her an answer. The middle-aged physician smiled pleasantly. "You must be the young woman his lordship has been demanding to see for the last half hour."

"He's alive?" she cried jubilantly as Samantha ran forward and embraced her from behind.

"Of course," Dr. Croft informed her, as if he had had no doubt of his abilities. "I've made it a habit throughout my profession not to lose patients unnecessarily, and this one definitely has a lot of life left in him. That was made plain enough when he cursed at me a time or two." The surgeon's lips twitched with amusement as he took full note of the lady's glowing delight. "He didn't seem very appreciative of the fact that I forbade anyone to do his bidding when he commanded that you be brought up to the room, but the ornery buck is alive . . . and very well, considering." Lifting his hand, Dr. Croft rolled a lead ball between his thumb and forefinger as he perused it through square-rimmed spectacles. "I thought the man could do without this bit of lead, but you may want to give it to your grandchildren in years to come and tell them how their grandfather never muttered a word during its removal, a feat I've rarely witnessed. That's certainly more than I can say when I told him he'd have to wait to see you."

"He lost consciousness in the carriage and appeared to have been much weakened by his loss of blood," Adriana ventured tentatively. "How will that affect him now?"

"Actually, he didn't lose as much blood as you may have supposed. The shock and pain probably caused him to pass out, but he has abundant resilience, that one. His wound wasn't life-threatening . . . and will not be unless it becomes tainted, which I've taken measures to prevent with a mixture that not only discourages putrefaction but eases his discomfort to a goodly extent. Of course, the brandy also helped considerably in the latter area. In fact, he seems fairly spry now for a man who recently had a hole bored into his back, which thankfully missed vital organs." Dr. Croft flicked his graying brows upward. "He has the idea that the two of you will be getting married tonight. Do you know anything about that?"

Adriana didn't quite know what to say in response. "Well, Sir Guy *did* say he was going to send his father, the rector, over to perform the ceremony, but I'm not sure he was serious."

Dr. Croft threw a thumb over his shoulder to indicate the one in the upper room. "Well, I can tell you right now his lordship is, and if you want to keep him abed, you'd better think of a way to placate the lad if you don't intend to marry him toni—"

A loud rapping of the doorknocker brought Caleb running once again from the servants' quarters. When he opened the front portal, a tall man, dressed in black attire with a white collar, politely withdrew his hat from his graying head.

"I'm the Reverend William Dalton. My son sent me here with a special license from the archbishop with instructions to marry a couple in some haste." Upon recognizing the good doctor, he looked rather sheepish as he harrumphed uncomfortably. "Good evening, Franklin, I sincerely hope I'm not too late. Has the child been born yet?"

Laughing in hearty amusement, Dr. Croft beckoned the man inside. "Come in, William, and rest your mind. I came here to tend the wounds of a man seriously injured, not a woman giving birth to a child. I believe the couple desirous of getting married has been promised to each other for the last ten and six years, at least that's what his lordship said moments ago. 'Twould seem after such a lengthy period, 'tis time they marry, eh what?"

The rector chortled in obvious relief. "Well, *that* does seem fairly reasonable. Shall we commence with the ceremony? My wife would like me to get back to the Assembly Room as soon as possible. She gets a mite flustered when she has to entertain important guests in my absence."

Dr. Croft swept a hand in the general direction of the upper room. "I'm afraid you'll be required to perform the nuptials upstairs, William. I forbade my patient to leave his bed for several days. If he'll stay there a week, I'd be even happier." Lifting a hand to indicate Adriana, he predicted, "I'm sure he'd be willing to comply with my orders if the beautiful lady here would consent to be his nursemaid and hover over him to make sure he stays put. Though we've not actually been formally introduced, I believe this is the young woman his lordship intends to take to wife, the Lady Adriana."

The clergyman stroked his chin thoughtfully. "Well, uh . . . seeing as how the man is seriously incapacitated, perhaps the wedding should be postponed until he's on his feet again. I don't know that I've ever performed a ceremony while the groom has been lying abed."

Dr. Croft laughingly scoffed at his suggestion. "His lordship is quite adamant that the marriage vows be exchanged tonight, and if I were you,

William, I'd humor the fellow. As I've just witnessed, he can exhibit a fairly nasty temper when he's kept from his betrothed. He also has a wide range of epithets that may do much to broaden your vocabulary, though I give you fair warning, 'twill not necessarily enhance it." The doctor's mouth twitched as he relented to his ready wit. "Must've been tutored by the French while he was fighting them hand to hand. 'Tis unimaginable that a proper English gentleman should say such things."

"Oh, yes, I see." The rector's graying brows flicked upward rather worriedly. "Well, no help for it, I suppose. Humor the man, that's what we should do, so let's be about it."

It was evident that Colton's patience had worn thin by the time the group entered, for he was scowling like an ill-humored tyrant. After the bandages had been applied and secured by winding them across his chest, a sheet had been drawn up over his hips, but in turning from his stomach onto his side, he had tested the freshly sutured flesh more than he had intended, making him excruciatingly aware of the searing pain that pierced through him during that repositioning and far less mindful of the fact that the sheet had become ensnared between his thighs and was now snugly adhering to the torpid fullness in that area. His navel had not only been exposed by that movement, but also the thin line of hair tracing down his flat, hard belly.

The good reverend began to bluster a bit in red-faced discomfiture as he became aware of the younger man's inadequate attire, but when the bride-to-be hurried to the bed and clasped hold of the strong, brown hand that had been extended to her, the elder's disquiet increased significantly. His cheeks reddened forthwith at the shocking impropriety he was now witnessing. Clearing his throat in chagrin, he turned to request assistance from Percy. "Do you suppose you can find something to spread over the injured man while the ladies are in the room?"

Percy's brow quirked above an amused smile as he glanced at the two women. From all appearances, they seemed oblivious to Colton's near nudity. "Well, one's his sister, and in the next few moments the other will be his wife. I can't see where it matters much."

"Nevertheless, the sheet seems painfully inadequate for a wedding ceremony," Reverend Dalton pointed out, feeling especially unnerved by the sight. It was bad enough the man's lower belly was exposed without one being made painfully aware of the cloth clinging to his private parts. He was just thankful his lordship kept his wits in the lady's presence and didn't thoroughly shock them all.

Amid his chuckles, Percy relented to the pleading look his wife gave him and took pity on the red-faced rector by spreading a light quilt over the bridegroom's lower half. Colton hardly noticed, for his gaze was focused entirely upon his bride-to-be.

"What of your parents?" he asked in some concern as his eyes searched the beautiful visage hovering close above his own. "Are they here yet?"

"They're with Aunt Tilly and your Uncle Alistair. Considering their delay in joining us, I can only imagine they've been told of my return to the town house but nothing more than that."

Colton's lips curved in a slow grin. "Won't *they* be surprised when they finally arrive?"

Growing suspicious of the glowing warmth in his eyes, Adriana leaned near. The strong odor of the intoxicant that Dr. Croft had given him prompted her to arch an elegant brow suspiciously. "Are you sure you're sober enough to know what you're doing, my love? I don't want you to complain later that you had been duped. Perhaps we should delay the nuptials until your head is clear of the influence of spirits and you're on your feet again."

"Absolutely not! I don't want to chance losing you," Colton declared and cast a quick glance toward Riordan. Although his rival was trying to put on a brave front, his dark eyes had lost their lively sparkle. Having been very close to losing Adriana himself, Colton fully understood the heartache the man was suffering and felt great empathy for him. "I may lose out altogether if I wait, and I don't want to take that chance, considering I have serious competition right here in this room. Let's proceed with the ceremony."

Believing she was doing what was right and beneficial for her heart and future happiness, Adriana stood beside the bed and repeated her vows with teary-eyed conviction. Her hand was clasped securely within the one belonging to the man to whom she had been promised years ago, and though Lord Sedgwick was not alive to realize the culmination of his heartfelt aspiration, it was a fact his foresight had been instrumental in bringing about their union. Had it not been initiated by the elder years ago, Adriana knew she would've likely thrust the memory of Colton Wyndham far behind her and accepted Riordan's first petition. She had no doubt that she would've been happy with the man, but a greater love had reentered her life, and thereinafter she had been held captive by the yearning of her heart. Only by marrying Colton would she be able to utterly appease that longing.

When the good reverend asked for the ring some moments later, there was some confusion, for that small detail had been forgotten. Colton would not let the request go unfulfilled, however. For nigh on to twenty years, he had worn a small family ring on his little finger, and it was this he tugged off and, though it proved too large, slid over the slender digit of his bride as he repeated the reverend's words. "With this ring I thee wed, with my body I thee worship, and with all my worldly goods, I thee endow...."

Tears were streaming down Samantha's face by the time the ceremony ended, and with an exaggerated sigh of relief, she threw her arms about her friend and joyfully wept with her. "At last, we *are* sisters through and through!"

Congratulations were warmly extended, and also a warning . . . from Dr. Croft.

"My lord, I urge you to consider your injury. Although I've liberally dabbed on a paste that has deadened the pain and will reduce the possibility of infection, I plead with you not to stress the wound overmuch. There's time later for you two to . . . ah . . . get acquainted."

Percy couldn't restrain his amusement, which spilled from him in hearty chuckles. "What are you asking him to do, Dr. Croft? Ignore his wife after he's finally permitted to take her into his bed? 'Twould take a blessed saint to do that, especially when the lady is as beautiful as his bride. Frankly, if my brother-in-law doesn't mind hearing a fair sampling of my opinion of him, I think he misses sainthood by a wide margin."

"Percy, behave yourself for a change," Samantha bade, her cheeks glowing though she seemed unable to subdue a smile. "You're embarrassing me. No telling what you're doing to Adriana."

Percy chuckled as he drew his wife's hand through the bend of his arm. "I don't foresee her cheeks cooling for the next month, my love, so she might as well get used to the heat."

Adriana did indeed find it difficult to subdue a blush, but Colton grinned as he accepted Percy's comments as a fairly accurate assessment of his character. He had never claimed to be a saint, but considering how profoundly his bride now held his heart ensnared, he could believe there was more of a chance of that possibility coming into fruition in the future.

Reaching out, he took his bride's fingers within his clasp and, with his free hand, drew her head down to his for a long, gentle kiss. When they finally parted, Riordan was no longer in the room.

Colton bestowed a grin on the physician. The strong brew of which he had liberally partaken had done much to dull his pain, but not the desires that had inflamed his mind and body for the last few months. "I shall try not to stress myself unduly, Dr. Croft, but I won't promise anything more than that."

The physician flicked his brows briefly upward, sensing it would do him little good to reason with his lordship. But then, it was much as Percy had said. The pulchritude of the maid would have made it difficult for any man to ignore her. "Nevertheless, I ask you to be careful. I understand that you were a hero in our confrontation with France. However, consider yourself for the time being as delicate as a newborn. You're not to move around needlessly, so I suggest that you let your bride coddle you for several days. I'll leave a supply of powder and instructions with Hodges on how to mix it and treat the wound after it has been cleansed or should the pain become too intense. I recommend that it be applied four times a day to prevent the flesh from becoming tainted. Tomorrow I shall return to make my own assessment, and if you're worse off, I'll have to send your wife far from here to give you time to heal."

"I shall carefully adhere to your instructions, sir," Colton avouched with a grin. "I'd certainly hate to be separated from her after I've finally taken her to wife."

At last, the couple were alone, but Adriana took the doctor's advice to heart and offered a solution. "I'll sleep downstairs so you won't be tempted to move about."

Colton shook his head resolutely as a slow, meaningful grin curved his lips. "Nay, madam, you'll sleep with me here in this bed, and if I can't find a way to make love to you without opening up my back, then at least I can hold you within my arms. And please don't bother undressing anywhere else or putting on a nightgown. If you do, I'll just have to come searching for you or be forced to remove the gown from you myself. Either way, I could injure myself, and of course you wouldn't want that. So I urge you, Wife, to consider the mayhem you'll cause if you fail to heed my entreaty. I've been waiting too long to find out whether the vision I saw in my old bathing chamber is actually real or merely a figment of my imagination. If the latter, then I should be praised for the degree of perfection I created in my mind. If genuine, then I want to hold that vision within my arms and to savor it thoroughly just as I've been yearning to do since I returned home."

"If that is your desire, my lord," Adriana murmured, her lips curving in a fetching smile. After their troubled separation, she was relieved that she could be with him.

Those warmly glowing eyes seemed to brand her as she lifted her hands behind her neck, but freeing the catch on the gold and sapphire choker caused her difficulty and sent her to her knees beside the bed. "I need your help unfastening my necklace."

When she sought to lower her cheek on the mattress to give him access to the tiny latch, Colton halted her with a finger beneath her chin. Lifting her face, his eyes probed the darkly shining orbs. "Leave the necklace for the moment, my pet, and kiss me instead. For too long now, I've been try-ing to avoid kissing you the way I've been yearning to do for fear of where it would lead us, but I needn't worry anymore about getting you with child. Simply put, madam, I'm nearly starved for the taste of your sweet lips and all the other temptations I found myself facing whenever I was near you."

Adriana recalled his kiss on the night of Roger's attack and grew heady with anticipation. Only the one he had bestowed on her at the onset of their courtship had come close to equaling that singular exchange. Noth-ing since then, certainly not his gentlemanly pecks upon her brow or the swift brush of his lips upon hers, had even hinted of his desires.

Pushing herself to her feet, she leaned over him to deliver his request, but his right arm came around her hips as he silently urged her to lie alongside him. As she kicked off her slippers, he tossed aside the quilt that had been spread over his lower half and then patted the narrow space beside him. Willingly complying with his silent urging, she lifted the silken skirt to climb atop the mattress, but was forced to raise it far above her knees to accomplish that task. Had she issued an invitation for her husband to peruse the sights, he couldn't have been more eager to respond. Ensnaring his gaze, those long, sleek limbs sheathed in dark silk stockings enticingly secured above her knees by beribboned, black lace garters did much to shatter the notion that nothing would ever transcend the spiral-ing heights to which his admiration had soared when he had perused her naked form in the bathtub. Already he had stored within his memory diverse views of her; this one would be lodged in a niche among the most tempting.

"Didn't your mother ever tell you that you're not supposed to stare?" Adriana teased, seeing where his gaze was fastened.

Grinning, Colton swept his hand along her thigh as she pressed alongside him and nestled her head within the crook of his arm. "I can't help it. The sights enslave me." He dragged his gaze away from her shapely legs long enough to give her a grin. "Truly, my love, I've never seen the equal of *your* perfection."

Smiling, Adriana ran her fingers through the fascinating feathering of dark hair covering his chest. "Believe me, sir, you're far from imperfect yourself."

At the insistent urging of his knee, she lifted a slender limb and laid it over his hip, allowing his thigh to encroach between hers. Her heel found a comfortable niche beneath his firmly muscled buttocks as her eyes delved with glowing warmth in his. His face slowly lowered to hers, and soon his lips and tongue took possession of hers, searching, demanding, consuming the delectable sweetness until his delicious assault left her feeling faint, and yet he would not relent. He drew her tongue into the warm cavern of his mouth where a flaming torch stroked over it with a slow, evocative rhythm that suggested something more erotic.

Drawing back with a trembling sigh, Adriana whispered, "The way you kiss leaves my head whirling in an eddy. Soon, I fear, my racing heart will take flight."

His hand slid over her breast, causing Adriana to catch her breath at the scintillating shock of pleasure he elicited as the tips of his lean fingers teasingly scrubbed across a nipple. She arched her back, thrusting the soft mound upward to reap the full measure of his attention. He bestowed it in a way that made her tremble as his thumb strummed with slow deliberation across the sensitive peak.

"You're beautiful, my love," Colton murmured huskily, leaving a trail of kisses down her throat, "but you have too many damned clothes on."

"You don't," she stated with a teasing grin as she drew back to savor the sights. Somewhat in awe of her handsome husband, she swept a hand over the steely bulges of his shoulders and traced slender fingers downward along the bandages crisscrossing his chest. With almost adoring reverence, she stroked the rippling thews, the taut ribs, the manly nipples, and began to brush kisses over the ridges and hollows. Colton watched her, amazed by her gentle passion.

Rising up on an elbow, Adriana stared into his eyes with all the ardent emotions she had kept tightly reined for some weeks. "I love you, Colton Wyndham. I always have . . . and always will. When I was a little girl, you were my idol. Now that you're my husband, I want to be made complete by you, to become part of you, to know you as I've never known you before."

The gray orbs shone with unmistakable ardor as Colton slipped a hand behind her head and pulled her face down to his. Their mouths were soon forged in another rapacious devourment of lips and tongues that blended the honeyed sweetness of her mouth with the brandy flavored taste of his.

Increasingly beset by his desires, Colton swept a hand downward to her thigh, above the place where a frilly garter secured her stocking, and slid it upward beneath her gown. It was not long before he drew back and stared at her in some astonishment. "Madam, you're not wearing any pantaloons."

Adriana blushed, wondering if he'd think her forward. "The skirt of my gown was so narrow, the pantaloons caused unsightly bulges, so I decided not to wear them. I never once imagined anyone would find out. Do you think me lewd, sir?"

Colton chuckled. "Banish the thought, madam. I approve of your decision. It certainly makes it easier for what I have in mind."

Coyly smiling into his shining gray eyes, she inquired, "What is that, my lord?"

"Need you ask?" He grinned into her shining eyes. "Undressing you is the first order of business, madam. After that, copulation, of course. The sooner we get to the latter, the sooner I'll be satisfied."

His fingers plucked at the placket running down her back as their kisses grew wilder and more frenzied. When the garment loosened, allowing him to drag it down in front, she quickly wiggled free of its silky confines and tossed it behind her into a nearby chair. When she faced her husband again, he was leisurely devouring the sights. The white satin chemise clung to the ripe orbs as if reluctant to be parted, while the delicate netting of the lace teased him with minute glimpses of the pale pink it swathed.

"Has anyone ever told you how utterly beautiful you are without your clothes, madam?"

A smile curved Adriana's soft lips as she pressed her brow against a lean cheek. "Only you, my lord."

"Believe me, my dear wife, since my return home, I have become your most ardent admirer."

Eager to view her beautiful body unfettered, Colton dragged the lace straps from her silken shoulders, encouraging her to slip her arms free. Soon he was perusing those luscious mounds as he tugged the garment down nigh her waist. She hastened its removal with a wiggle and slid it past her hips, drawing his eyes downward as she kicked free of it.

Adriana hardly knew the moment it slid to the floor, for her husband promptly lifted her up higher against him. His mouth was there waiting to devour the luscious orbs, quickening fires in the depth of her being. In a moment of pure bliss, Colton pressed his face between the creamy fullness and closed his eyes, savoring the silkiness of her skin and the delicate scent of roses. He was very, very thankful to be alive and to be married at last to this woman who had held his mind ensnared for the last several months.

"I'm glad you never offered me a demonstration of how pleasurable it is to be naked in your arms before now," Adriana whispered tremblingly. "Otherwise, I'd have likely yielded to your invitation to pleasure me long ago."

"The best is yet to come, my beauty, and now that you're my wife, 'twill be even more pleasurable," he breathed as his hand slid down over her smooth, creamy belly. His lean fingers encroached into the moist, womanly softness and, ever so gently, plied their magic, snatching her breath and making her writhe with the ecstasy he evoked. As if with a will of their own, her thighs slowly parted, welcoming his deftly voyaging caresses. Waves of heightening bliss began to wash through her, thoroughly amazing Adriana at the sensations she was experiencing, yet as much as her cheeks flamed at the boldness of his caresses, she could not bring herself to turn aside and halt the fires that had begun flaring upward from her loins. Indeed, his evocative titillation set her whole being aflame.

"What you're doing feels too marvelous to be proper," she whispered shakily. "If you do not desist, I will likely dissolve."

"Perfectly suitable for a husband to search out all the secret places his wife has managed to withhold from him ere they wed, my sweet. Is it not to your liking, too?"

Her voice was faint, breathless. "Very much so."

The fact that she was garbed in nothing more than stockings seemed rather ridiculous considering all the other vulnerable womanly areas were fully in view. Yet when she sat up to loosen her garters, Colton's hand closed around her wrist, gently halting her. "Leave the stockings, my love," he rasped. "I want to feel you against me."

He lifted the sheet aside, inviting her to press close against his naked body, in so doing, causing Adriana to stare at his blatant maleness. Though it was a bold reminder of what she had seen in the bathing chamber, it seemed immensely threatening of a sudden. Lifting her gaze, she stared into those smiling gray orbs.

"I can't be around you without being effected, my love," Colton murmured huskily. "It's what I've been battling ever since the Autumn Ball. If not for the constant presence of our chaperones, I would have had my way with you every time we were alone in my coach . . . or anyplace else that proved private."

Adriana stared at him in astonishment. "But I thought you merely wanted Samantha and Percy along to provide proof of your gentlemanly comportment so you could break away cleanly after our courtship."

Colton softly hooted at such a notion. "It was difficult enough keeping my hands off you when others were around. Getting you entirely alone would have been certain disaster. I had visions of us standing before the rector after your belly had grown heavy with child."

Throwing back her head, Adriana relented to her overwhelming joy and laughter. "I thought you didn't want me!"

Colton took her hand and closed it around the throbbing hardness, drawing a shocked gasp from her. "Is this not proof of my desire for you, madam? It's what has beset me throughout the whole of courtship. Even now, I can hardly endure the pain after my lengthy abstinence. Indeed, I had begun to fear I'd become a damned eunuch, wanting you as I did, and not being able to appease that longing."

"But your wound. Won't you find it hard to . . . ?"

"Banish the thought, my love. I could have one foot in the grave and still desire to make love to you."

"You should follow the doctor's advice," she cautioned as he pulled her full length against him.

"You could do all the work and let me reap the pleasure," he cajoled with a wayward grin as his eyes glowed into hers.

Smiling, she traced a finger over his lips. "You'll have to show me what to do."

His hand swept down to her thigh and dragged a stocking and garter free as she lifted a sleek limb to accommodate him. "I will, my love, but first, I must make you ready for me."

Would you like me to take the other stocking off?"

"Um-hmm," he murmured, slipping his hands behind her nape and unfastening the choker. "And your earrings. I may want to chew on your ears a bit, considering it has been a craving of mine for the last several months."

Giggling, Adriana unfastened the costly jewelry from her earlobes as his hand once again claimed a ripe, creamy breast. "You have the strangest quirks, Colton Wyndham."

"You'll have a lifetime to become familiar with them, Wife, but I would be about more serious pleasures now."

"Such as?" She twisted away slightly to lift her right leg into the air. Stripping off the last silk stocking, she sent it fluttering to the floor beside the other.

"Crossing the last bridge before we become one, my love."

Adriana lay in quiescent stillness, indulging in every blissful thrill, every delectable delight he stirred within her as he worked his magic upon her womanly softness, but when his open mouth claimed her breasts once again and began to suckle her, she felt almost consumed by the pleasure he wrought. Driven by the intensifying pleasure, she reached out and laid claim upon the manly hardness, drawing a sharp gasp from him as the hot blood surged through him.

"Please, Colton . . . I can bear no more. Whatever you're waiting for, wait no longer, I beg you."

"I needn't, my love. You're now ready for me," he whispered. The dewy moistness readily affirmed that she was eager for what was coming.

Lying back upon the pillows, he met her questioning gaze as she rose up to peer down into his face. He smiled with a devilish gleam in his eyes. "I hear you ride Ulysses without a saddle at times, my dear. I have a horn but no saddle. Are you brave enough to try? 'Twill be painful at first."

"You've made it impossible for me to refuse. I've never felt so . . . so . . . wanton before."

"Making love is not wantonness when it's between a couple who has been bound in marriage, love. 'Tis an honest desire, and right now, I want you more than anything in the world."

Rising to her knees, she moved astride him as their gazes melded. Her voice was barely a sigh as she softly whispered, "With my body, I thee worship."

His hungering eyes swept over her alluring form in one long, lingering caress as he pressed himself into the narrow niche, evoking a shiver from her as she felt his heat. With one swift, descending movement, she took him into her, snatching gasps from both of them. Nearly consumed by her womanly warmth, Colton closed his eyes, luxuriating in the joy of being one with her. He sought to bide his time to let the shock of his intrusion ease, but as she had ridden Ulysses, so his young wife rode him until he could not hold back. Waves of rapturous bliss washed over them again and again until they were being swept toward the pinnacle of ecstasy. Myriad bubbles, as finite as the air they breathed, seemed to course over, around, and through their bodies as the heightening swells surged through them, sweeping them aloft with ever-strengthening billows until they were soaring on towering waves that carried them to the outer regions of the universe, seemingly among the very stars.

Much later, Adriana was just dozing off, nestled spoon-fashion within the protective curve of her husband's body, when he whispered near her ear, "Still sore, madam?"

She giggled, wiggling back until she came up in contact with the manly firmness pressing beneath her buttocks. "Do you have a reason for asking?"

He nibbled at a dainty ear as his fingers brushed over a pliant peak. "Aye, I'm a lecher in want of more of the same, and you are the only morsel I crave."

"That's good enough reason for me," Adriana replied with smiling eagerness. Turning to face him, she snuggled alongside her naked husband as her fingers swept over his broad chest and slid lower still, causing him to catch his breath. Finding him ready for her, she rose above him, and their fevered kisses led them on and on and on . . .

ACCORDING to the delicate chimes of the clock in the bedchamber in which the couple had been ensconced, it was well past the hour of midnight when they were both abruptly awakened. A lamp was thrust close in front of their faces, and a loud raging roar rang out, snatching startled gasps from the two who sprang upright in unison from the mattress where they had been nestled closely together. A sharp wince of pain contorted Colton's features as he was suddenly reminded of his painful wound, and though immediately repentant of his hasty movement, he held up a hand to shade his eyes from the intrusive glare. Beyond it, he saw a raging snarl contorting Gyles Sutton's face. In all his life, he couldn't remember ever seeing the man so furious.

"I invited you to Bath to present your case to my daughter, not to fornicate with her!" the elder bellowed in thundering tones. "Now get up out of that bed, you debaucher of babes, and fight like a man!"

As he sought to lay hold upon the younger man, Adriana threw up a hand to ward off her parent. "Papa, no! It's all right!"

Gyles's eyes flared anew as he gaped down at his daughter. Glancing down in the direction he stared, Adriana gasped and hastily snatched for the sheet to cover her naked breasts, but it was far too late. Her father's face took on a ruddy hue that clearly attested to his fury.

Christina groaned from the doorway where she had been halted in shock. Her distressed moan evidenced her own horror after noticing the dark, telltale rosy color imbuing those delicate peaks. Of all her daughters, she had never dreamt she would *ever* find her youngest in bed with a despicable rake. Indeed, there had even been times when she had doubted Adriana would ever choose a husband to wed.

Gyles's roar of rage threatened to bring down the ceiling on their heads. Had the plaster not been firmly attached, it might've made him immediately repentant of his unrestrained wrath. He shook a clenched fist at Colton who, upon seeing the fire flashing in the dark eyes of the elder, had cause to wonder if he'd have to brace himself against the older man's attack. "So, this is how you repay me for trying to help you! You libertine! You sneak thief! You stole my daughter's virtue behind my back. I have a good mind to cut you here and now!"

"Papa, we're married!" Adriana blurted.

"What?!" Gyles staggered back in stunned surprise.

"We were married tonight by Sir Guy's father. We had a special license that His Grace, the archbishop, signed!"

Gyles stared at her with mouth agape. "But . . . but why couldn't you wait . . . to be married . . . in a church?"

"Colton's coach was attacked near Randwulf Manor, and he was shot in the back. We wanted to be with one another, and marriage was the only way we could be together without worrying about what was proper, what was not. Samantha, Percy, Lord Harcourt, and Dr. Croft were here as witnesses. 'Tis all quite proper, I assure you, Papa."

Gyles stumbled back several more steps, wiping a hand down his face, as if still unable to believe the legality of their union. "You should've been married in a church, with your whole family there as witnesses."

"We're no less married now than we would've been in a church, Papa. Reverend Dalton had us sign all the documents. He can attest to the fact that they are valid."

" 'Twas my fault," Colton volunteered, trying to placate the man, knowing he'd probably have been just as enraged under the circumstances. "I was afraid of losing your daughter, and I didn't want to take that chance. I was the one who pressured her into marrying me tonight."

"Actually, Sir Guy arranged it," Adriana explained, trying to spare him some of her father's resentment. She looked at her sire pleadingly. "But if you would be willing to consider my feelings, Papa, I didn't want to wait any more than Colton did. I love him, and I want to be with him for the rest of my life."

Gyles cleared his throat and glanced back at his wife who was smiling in relief. "What do you make of this, my dear?"

"I think they're legally married, dearest, and we'll have no more to say about it . . . except . . ."—she smiled at the couple, her blue eyes radiant as she concluded—"good night."

Gyles blustered a bit, remembering the names he had called his new son-in-law. "Yes, well, that seems the only thing we can say, now that we've awakened the whole house."

Adriana couldn't resist an inquiry. "Where were you, Papa? We sent Sir Guy to tell you that we were returning here to have Colton's wound tended. Why didn't you come then?"

Gyles harrumphed. "All I heard was that you had returned here with Samantha and Percy and, and, well, I just assumed you couldn't bear being at the Assembly Room anymore, what with Roger there and all. Then Alistair sprained his . . . ah . . . ankle . . . probably trying to keep up with your aunt, and we had to find a doctor to make sure it wasn't broken. Tilly's physician wasn't home, and we had to go all over Bath searching for one she considered as worthy as Dr. Croft." He stroked his chin reflectively as one dark brow arched suspiciously. "With what has taken place here tonight, it makes me wonder if Alistair's injury was merely something he just feigned after talking to Sir Guy. The two of them seemed equally intent upon whatever they were discussing . . . or else conniving. 'Twas no good, I trow, at least from Alistair's end of it."

"Come along, dear," Christina urged sweetly. "You'll be imagining all sorts of things about poor Alistair if we stay here much longer. His ankle *did* seem bruised, which leaves me seriously questioning the possibility that he'd injure himself merely to keep us from delaying his nephew's marriage to our daughter. Now let Adriana and Colton get some sleep. Poor dears, you probably frightened them nigh out of their wits."

The giggles that flowed from the couple's bedchamber a moment later made Gyles pause after closing the door behind him. "They must not have been *too* frightened."

Christina smiled as she slipped an arm through his. "Just remember how impetuous you were when we were young, dear. If you'll recall, I had to slap your fingers more than once to make you cool your heels before our wedding."

His hand strayed downward possessively and claimed her backside. "You still have the most fetching derriere I've ever seen, madam."

She cast a glance awry to find a familiar leering grin upon his handsome lips. Tossing her head with a saucy laugh, she warned, *"Humph,* it had better be the *only* one you've ever seen, sir, or I will see *you* cut. There are some things I'm averse to sharing, and one of them is *you.*"

THE morning sun filtered through the Austrian lace curtains, softly illuminating the bedchamber where the newly married couple was nestled together in the bed. It was just intrusive enough to drag Colton up from the depths of a heavy slumber. Except for the pain presently reminding him of the wound in his back, he felt far more rested and relaxed than he had in previous months, at least since he had discovered a dark-haired nymph slumbering in his bath. In spite of his injury, he seemed very much invigorated by their activity during the night. Never had he imagined a bride could be so eager to accommodate her groom, but she had proven quite acceptable to the idea that she was his and he was hers.

Grinning to himself, Colton turned his head slightly on the pillow as he ran his fingers through his hair. The dark, thick strands were wildly tossed, so much so that he could just imagine his untidy appearance. Considering the past hours and what they had entailed, he was immensely thankful to be alive and ... to be finally married.

His bride had been wonderfully enticing and responsive to his lustful bent. Indeed, in all his years as a bachelor he had never dreamt that when he finally wed, his bride would be mounting him. He could only marvel at her willingness to offer her virginity upon the fleshly horn of passion so they could complete their union, and yet, she had done just that in her sacrificial desire to be one with him. Not so long ago, he had thought he couldn't love her any more than he already did, but what he was feeling toward her now seemed to affirm unequivocally that he did indeed cherish her far beyond the measure that he had once considered himself capable of experiencing.

Smoothing a dark, luxurious strand out of his way, he pressed a gentle kiss upon her brow as his hand settled around a lusciously soft breast. Plying a thumb slowly over a pliant nipple, he whispered, "Time to wake up, sleepyhead."

Shaking her head to convey her displeasure with that idea, Adriana bent a knee and rested it upon his thigh as she burrowed closer against him. Sleepily she mumbled, "Can't we stay here forever?"

"I need a bath, and you'll have to give it to me," he persisted with a chuckle. "Unless, of course, you want me disobeying the doctor's orders."

"I've never given a man a bath before," she mumbled beneath the borders of the covers. "I wouldn't know where to begin. . . ."

"Where would you like to begin?" he asked warmly, nibbling at a dainty earlobe.

Adriana's eyes popped open as the answer came readily to mind, but she dared not give him an answer, for fear he'd think her a wanton.

Colton peered down at her. "I could make a suggestion if you're willing to consider it."

Feeling his warm perusal, Adriana struggled not to smile. "And where is that, sir?"

His hand captured hers and pulled it forward before settling it over the hardened shaft. "It needs serious attention."

"Before or after your bath?"

"*Before* would be even better. I'm anxious to taste you again."

"You're insatiable," she accused with a giggle, evidencing her own eagerness to comply as her fingers tightened beneath his.

"Aye, but only for you, madam," he breathed near her ear before his lips moved on to caress her cheek. His hand freed hers, allowing it to play at will while his own slid behind her hip. "Has anyone ever told you what a winsome derriere you have, madam?"

"No, never."

"I've always had a fetish for breasts myself, but, my dear, you certainly have the shapeliest backside a lonely man would dare dream of in a far-off camp. I really do enjoy snuggling up to it. It warms me to the core."

"You do seem to enjoy cuddling, sir."

Arching a brow, he peered down his nose at her. "Are you averse to cuddling, my dear?"

Adriana wiggled closer until her breasts and loins were cleaving to him. "Does that appease your curiosity, my lord?"

"It may answer my question, but it also bestirs my cravings for more of what you have to give. But then, perhaps that was your intent. You do seem to enjoy the delights to be found in a marriage bed." He nuzzled her ear as his hand moved leisurely down the front of her. "Of course, there's nothing quite as sweet as this little haven here to bestir a man's lust."

Her breath caught in ecstasy as he intruded into her softness. She was somewhat amazed at the delicious sensations he could evoke within her when, only a moment ago, all she had wanted to do was sleep.

Sometime later, a perfumed bath was prepared in a small copper tub in the bedchamber. Beneath the admiring gaze of her husband, Adriana set about bathing herself. Never in her life could she remember ever wanting anyone present during her baths. Maud had always prepared everything for her, and then had busied herself doing other things until she had concluded her perfumed ritual. Soon after stripping away the robe she briefly donned to allow servants to prepare her bath, she had realized the pleasure that could be derived by having a man in attendance. Her husband had been keenly observant of everything she did well before she had lowered herself into the warm, fragrant water. His eyes fed upon every detail of her womanly form as she soaped private areas, and in some embarrassment, she had urged him to close his eyes, to which he had responded with a slow shake of his head and a lecherous grin.

"Never in a million years, my beauty. I want to know everything about you, in particular those places you're wont to keep secret. Nothing is hidden or forbidden between a married couple; everything is openly viewed and shared. All I have is yours; whatever is yours is mine. 'Tis a fair pact when two are joined as one."

On those terms, Adriana was more than willing to comply. Beneath his careful scrutiny, she had pushed herself to her feet and, from several pitchers of warm water, had rinsed away the soapy residue from her body. After stepping out onto a large cotton rug that the servants had spread beneath the tub, she had toweled herself dry, rubbed scented lotions over her skin, and then donned pantaloons, stockings, and chemise, the bodice of which she had left unbuttoned between her breasts in compliance with the wishes of her handsome spouse, in so doing allowing him a generous view of the rounded orbs and the deep valley between. Over this, she had tied a light linen wrapper snugly about her waist and then pulled the bodice aside her breasts, willingly fulfilling her husband's behest.

Once the copper tub had been removed, preparations for a basin bath were then made. Along with its initial appearance came fresh towels, linens, a pail of comfortably hot water, and a second basin. Immediately Adriana set about preparing not only her husband for his bath, but also the bed itself. Folding down the bedcovers to the far end of the four-poster, she bade him to roll first to one side, to allow her to place a thrice-folded older sheet underneath him, and then to the other, enabling her to finish spreading it beneath him, precluding the possibility of the feather mattress getting wet. Next she gathered linens with which to wash and dry him, but when she offered to borrow a nightshirt for him from her father, Colton smiled and shook his head.

"I haven't worn one since I was a boy, madam. I don't intend to start now. As for what you may enjoy wearing to bed, I prefer to feel you naked against me, especially when I wake up in the middle of the night. Besides, when you don't have anything on, it's easier to make love to you."

Her eyes glowed into his as she brushed a hand admiringly over his chest. "I'm beginning to think we're going to be spending a lot of time together in bed."

Arching a brow, he gave her a lecherous grin. "You should be forewarned, madam, I'm not going to limit myself to making love to you in a bed. Anywhere that's convenient and private will serve my purposes just as well."

"Then perhaps I should rephrase that with the prediction that we'll be spending a lot of time making love."

"Definitely a more truthful prediction, my sweet."

Adriana soon realized that bathing her handsome husband was an utterly satisfying experience for a new wife, especially since he seemed to take advantage of her proximity by touching her in ways that evoked her gasps. He certainly wasn't timid about what he displayed, either, but she soon found a cure for that by spreading a linen towel over his loins.

"Do you really think that's going to save you, madam? Or are you thinking it will perhaps vanish?"

"I'm not as apt to be distracted this way. You can hardly expect a new bride to see anything else when that's being flaunted in full view. In fact, I'm beginning to suspect you have no modesty, sir."

"Men don't worry about modesty as much as women do, my dear. When a watering hole is discovered in a desert, the only quest men have after quenching their thirst is bathing away the grime."

Through her undergarments she could feel his fingers encroaching between her buttocks and wiggled her hips in an effort to shake them off. "If you don't behave yourself, sir, we could be here until sunset tonight."

"You still have to wash my lower half," he needled with a grin.

"I'll wash your feet and legs first," she announced, directing her attention toward that very thing.

"Otherwise, you're afraid we won't get finished with the bath?" Offering the conjecture, he canted his head in an effort to peruse her flushed cheeks from a better angle.

"Something like that," Adriana replied, busily bathing and drying his feet, ankles, and calves. It occurred to her as she did so that there wasn't any part of her husband's body that was less than admirable. His feet were long and bony, his shins razor sharp beneath a meager covering of hair, his thighs lean and tautly muscled. As she progressed upward, she noticed the previously dark red and purplish area that had once surrounded his old wound had faded to a paler hue. Over time she could imagine the scar itself would be the only thing visible, but even that would eventually be less noticeable. "Your old wound definitely looks better now than it did when you first came home. Does it bother you anymore?"

"Only a twinge or two now and then, but nothing really painful."

There remained no other section to wash but his loins, and she tried her best not to blush as she complied with his instructions, which he definitely seemed to enjoy giving. When she chanced a glance at his face, she found him watching her with eyes glowing above a smile.

"You needn't feel embarrassed," he said. "That part of me is as much yours as anything else I have, perhaps even more so. In a few months, my nudity will seem commonplace to you."

"I doubt anything about you will ever seem commonplace to me," she argued in all truth. "I think you're the most beautiful man I've ever met or, for that matter, ever seen."

"Beautiful, my dear?" His brow jutted upward as he cocked a brow in wonder. "'Tis a very curious word to use for a man."

"Nevertheless, you're beautiful to me. You always have been."

His hand squeezed her backside affectionately. "Come, my sweet, give me another kiss. I'm hungering for you again."

Casting a meaningful glance toward his loins, she laughed. "Aye, I noticed."

As if declaring his bath complete, she dropped the linen towel in a heap over his privates and, with a wide smile, leaned over him. Through her clothing, she could feel his fingers intruding again in the cleft between her buttocks. From very close range, her dancing eyes searched his. "You must have been a very naughty boy when you were growing up," she accused. "There's still evidence of your wayward bent even today. Or is it that you're just trying to feed a fetish for the hind parts of a woman?"

He chuckled. "As your husband, I enjoy searching out all your hidden places, madam. I've never felt so complete in all my life as I do right now. I think I like being married to you."

Grinning into his sparkling eyes, she wiggled her hips in an effort to dislodge his fingers as he sought to resume his teasing search. "That's good, sir, because I'm going to be your wife for a very, very long time."

PHILANA Wyndham had been escorted by a maidservant to the door of the upper chambers wherein her son had been ensconced. According to the young servant, Lord and Lady Standish had departed the house with his mistress an hour earlier with intentions of visiting Lord Alistair at his hotel room to check on how he was faring with his injured ankle. The young miss informed the elder that the only one who had remained behind was Lady Adriana, who was presently with the injured man.

The fact that Adriana was with her son assured Philana that it was safe to enter the designated bedchamber without knocking. After all, the girl had hardly been speaking to her son before his most recent wounding. However, upon swinging wide the door, she promptly decided that she should've been more discreet, for her jaw plummeted forthwith when she saw her son lying on the bed, virtually naked except for a rumpled cloth elevated rather suggestively over his privates, his hand firmly clasping Adriana's backside, and the girl half lying across the bed toward him. It certainly didn't help Philana's composure when she realized that their mouths were locked in a deep, penetrating kiss. The shocking scene nearly caused her to collapse right then and there.

"My goodness, I should've knocked!" she gasped, clasping a trembling hand to her throat as she sought to survive the suffocating heat of a blush. "I just didn't expect . . ."

Having straightened much like a stiffly sprung spring, Adriana spun about to face the intruder. The stunned expression on Philana's face clearly conveyed the fact that Adriana was the last person on earth she'd have thought capable of such overt wantonness. Abruptly the older woman's gaze dropped to the lace-edged chemise and its display of rounded bosom and liberal glimpses of rosy nipples, prompting Adriana to hurriedly pull her dressing gown together in painful embarrassment.

"I've come at a bad time, 'twould seem," Philana struggled to choke out, averting her gaze from the pair as Adriana began to pull up the sheets and quilts to cover Colton's lower half. "When Bentley announced last night that my son had been seriously injured, I hastened to come this morning to see how he was faring. I never expected this . . . I'm sorry, I certainly didn't mean to intrude. I shall leave. . . ."

"Don't, Mother," Colton bade gently. "What you see before you is perfectly acceptable, believe me."

Philana's hackles rose at such a foolish declaration, and she glared back at her son. "Since when did it become perfectly acceptable for a rapscallion like yourself to sully a young woman whom I had previously deemed a lady? Have you no regard for honor, my son?"

Colton's lips curved upward in a cajoling smile. "I guess it became acceptable the moment I married her."

"Married?" Philana clasped a trembling hand to her bosom. Could it be true? Had they really gotten married? Or was this some sort of faraway intention they were merely contemplating? "You don't mean that Adriana actually exchanged wedding vows with you, do you? After all that has happened?"

"I did last night, Mama Philana," Adriana murmured with a gentle, somewhat apologetic smile. "Colton wouldn't have his wound tended unless I agreed to marry him."

"Oh, I see." Philana arched a delicate brow and nodded knowingly. "He always did seem a bit too manipulative with the young ladies. His father didn't know what to do with him, and as for me, I'm totally at a loss." She lifted a smile to Adriana. "Perhaps you'll be better at handling him than I ever was, my dear, but in any case, I'm delighted to have another daughter in the family, especially one I've admired all these many years. Sedgwick would be so very proud of this match. He always believed in it, that it would be good for you both. Now you'll have a chance to find out for yourselves whether his prediction has merit."

She held her arms out in invitation to the young woman, and eagerly Adriana accepted, hurrying forward and encircling the elder with her own as they came together. Tears of joy lit Philana's eyes when she finally stood back and cupped her daughter-in-law's beautiful face lovingly between her hands.

"Thank you, dear child, for forgiving my son and for making me so very happy today. Although Bentley assured me Colton would live, I had to find out for myself that he was being taken care of. Now I can rest assured that he's in good hands, and that this is the beginning of a dynasty that I feared would be dying out. May God bless you both with many, many children."

Seventeen

❋

"Just where have you been?" Jarvis Fairchild railed at his daughter as she tiptoed through the front door of Stanover House at the crack of dawn.

Felicity clasped a trembling hand over her pounding heart and peered intently through the murky shadows in an effort to locate her parent. She finally saw him ensconced upon the settee. She tried to smile, but the best she could manage was a grimace. Her father's face was a mask of pure rage, and even in the gloom she thought she could see dark shadows beneath his eyes. "Papa, what are you doing down here in the parlor? I thought you'd have been upstairs sleeping. You nearly frightened me to death!"

Jarvis leapt from the settee and strode irately across the room until he stood before her. Their noses almost met as he lowered his face to hers. Even in the shadowy room, his flaring eyes vividly evidenced his rage.

"I asked you a question, girl, and I want an answer, *if* you'd be so kind! Do you realize your mother and I haven't slept a wink all night? When you didn't come home, I rode over to the Elstons' to inquire into your whereabouts, but a servant said Roger hadn't returned either. Then I raced over to the homes of the other two young ladies who went with you, but they were both quite bemused as to where you were since Roger had said he'd be bringing you back here. For all your mother and I knew, you could've been abducted, possibly even ravished, whether by Roger or some other foul debaucher was anybody's guess. Now you come skulking into your grandfather's house as if you were no better than a thief about to make off with the silver plates. I want an explanation, girl. *Now, if* you don't mind!"

Felicity made another attempt to smile, but once again, it fell short of her mark. It was noticeably pained, much as she was. She was bruised, sore, and thoroughly repentant for having gone against something she had first deemed foolishness. Yet, after everything had been said and done, it was much too late to do anything about it.

"Papa, I know you had every hope that I'd marry an aristocrat, but after learning that Lord Randwulf and Lady Adriana were pledged, and with the viscount pining for her, there seemed little chance of that happening. Roger is becoming very wealthy, Papa . . . and . . . well, ah, we took the liberty of getting married here in the county. Then we went to an inn. That's where we've been."

"Surely you weren't that foolish!" Jarvis railed, becoming thoroughly incensed. "Where's the bloody beggar? I'll slice his cods out right now." Filled with a sudden desire to reap vengeance, he peered intently beyond her to see if his new son-in-law was hiding like a conniving little weasel beyond the front door.

"He's not here, Papa. He thought 'twould be better if I told you first, and then the two of you could meet after you had calmed down." Felicity twisted her fingers together worriedly. Her smile was no less pained. "As for gelding him, Papa, 'tis too late for that. Our marriage has already been . . . ah . . . consummated."

"You've betrayed me!" Jarvis bellowed, grinding his teeth as he strode irately about the parlor. He shook his tousled head in outrage as he lamented his dashed dreams. "All this time, I believed you'd marry above your station in life. I did everything I could to bring that event into realization. No bookkeeper's daughter ever dressed so well, nor had so many of her wishes granted! Now, 'tis all for naught. You've undone me, girl! You went behind my back and betrayed me by marrying a young whelp of an unlearned man!"

"But, Papa, they're wealthy! Roger promised to array me in riches and costly jewels. . . . The mill will be his shortly. He's sure of it." In spite of her bridegroom's many promises, they did little to assuage her anguish over being ravished on her wedding night. She had made the mistake of drawing away from Roger and asking him to give her a chance to ready herself, but her request had only provoked his temper. He had started yanking at her clothes in his impatience to mount her, and then had held a hand clasped over her mouth as he raped her, thrusting into her so brutally that the sheets had been well-bloodied by his cruel abuse.

"And just who will pay off the moneylenders after Edmund Elston takes off or passes on?"

Clasping a trembling hand to her throat, Felicity stumbled back in stuttering surprise. "Wh-what do you mean, Papa?"

"I mean that Edmund Elston has either been losing large amounts of money from the mill or pilfering it for his own uses. There's no telling how little will be left to go into your new husband's coffers once his father dies."

"How could you possibly know that?"

"One who is in a position to know visited me recently with a proposition that if Edmund . . . or Roger . . . is forced to sell because of the dwindling resources in their accounts, he could almost warrant that the mill would be sold at a particularly economical price that I could afford. If that should happen, then I'll no longer be beholden to your mother *or* your grandfather. I'd have a mill of my own, to do with as I please."

"But where would you get the funds to purchase such a mill even at a bargain?" Felicity quizzed in bemusement. "Mama warned me not too long ago to be careful of every farthing, and to be content with the clothes I have, and here you are declaring with a certainty that you'd have the moneys to buy the Elstons' mill."

Jarvis presented his profile to his daughter as he raised his head aloft. "Never mind where the money will come from; just be assured I have enough to make such a purchase."

"Perhaps this man you know is merely speculating in hopes of winning your confidence in another venture. I only say that because Edmund's mill is becoming very productive under Roger's management."

Throwing up a hand, Jarvis turned aside and strode across the room as he offered a conjecture. "Perhaps Edmund is tucking portions of his wealth safely away and is planning on leaving Roger with the responsibility of paying his workers after he flees to unknown destinations with what he has taken."

"But . . . but Roger's father is bedridden, Papa."

Jarvis jerked sharply about with a condescending brow raised. "How convenient for Edmund. He can pretend to be in a stupor and avoid having to answer his son's questions . . . that is, if Roger *ever discovers* his hopes for the mill is being squandered by his father and that the funds are dwindling in their accounts." Jarvis stalked to a front window and gazed out upon the city for a long moment. The darkness of the past hours had already started receding before the onslaught of the approaching dawn. Thoughtfully peering over his shoulder at his daughter, he asked, "Have you ever wondered how Edmund came to have such wealth?"

Felicity frowned in deepening bemusement as she related what she had been told. "Why, I believe Roger said his father's second wife died and left him everything that she had inherited from old Mr. Winter."

"Died?" Her father laughed caustically. "Murdered, more likely."

Felicity's hackles rose. Angry or not, her parent had no right to defame a man who was at best a stranger. "How can you lay such foul charges upon the man when we weren't even living here when she died? And how can you possibly know enough about Mr. Elston even to insinuate such a thing?"

"Once upon a time, Roger's mother was my aunt's closest friend. It seems that while they were living in London, Edmund abandoned her and their young son and started making the rounds with all sorts of loose women. He seemed able to charm them all; though it has always befuddled me why even a simpleton would believe anything he'd say. Along about the time his wife was killed, he was helping an old friend drive liveries. My Aunt Clara just happened to witness the incident in which Roger's mother was run down by one. At the time, she was convinced that the driver, although masked by a scarf against the cold, was none other than Edmund Elston. Of course, before my aunt got up enough courage to report the incident and her suspicions to the authorities, she was killed in much the same manner. None of the rest of us ever dared follow up on her version of Mrs. Elston's death for fear of being run down in the same manner."

"You mean Edmund Elston is a murderer?" Felicity asked, much agog.

"If you have a care for our lives, girl, you will never repeat what I've just told you, not even to Roger. He may shush you up by similar methods if you jeopardize his chances to wrangle some lucre from his father, though surely he's the one to be pitied, considering there's a strong likelihood that nothing will be left once his father expires or vanishes mysteriously into the dark of night."

"Papa, why didn't you tell me all this before?"

"I didn't know you'd marry the bloody beggar," Jarvis shot back. "The last I heard you had attracted Lord Harcourt's attentions."

Felicity waved a hand to make light of that particular story, which had been much of her own making. "I was mistaken."

Jarvis was curious. "Where are you and Roger going to live now?"

"In his father's house, of course."

"And what if Edmund decides to murder you like he murdered his two wives?"

Felicity shivered at the very idea. "Well, I guess I'll just have to make sure that doesn't happen."

"You'd better start tucking away some funds for yourself, girl. I'd rather not have to support Roger's whelp in my old age."

Felicity lifted her chin and dared to point out a recent fact. "Seems to me after Grandpa and Mama caught you laying off workers and pocketing their wages that Mama's the only one doing the supporting now. The mill is thriving again after they hired back everyone you had laid off."

"How do you know that?"

"I came downstairs late one night to get a book that I had left in the parlor, and I overheard you arguing with Mama. I assumed that's why you've been sleeping down here ever since."

"Your mother thinks she knows better than I. . . ."

Felicity wouldn't let him go very far with that claim. "I believe I overheard her pleading with you to reconsider what you had done, and to return the money to Grandpa's coffers. You refused."

"He's old and rich," Jarvis shot back. "'Twouldn't hurt him none to share some of that wealth with his offspring."

"Papa, you're not his offspring, Mama is, and she's very careful to return every farthing or tuppence to his purse after she pays Lucy and the other servants. From what I understand, you deliberately went out of your way to pilfer funds that were not yours. Mama taught me well enough as a child that that is thievery. So if you know what's good for you, you'd better make amends. I've come to realize that she and Grandpa have a nasty way of paying out retribution. You could just find yourself back in London at the same old counting house you left if you try to outsmart the pair of them. In fact, I've heard stories from Grandpa's friends and foes alike that he has a special way of serving up justice on a large platter to those who deserve it. He calls it, appropriately enough, dispensing a bit of wisdom to those in dire need."

"Bah, he's doddering and senile."

"Not nearly as much as I once thought or even as much as you'd like to imagine, Papa. In fact, I don't know that I've ever met a more perceptive man. You'd do well to heed my advice or you may be forced to suffer the consequences, because you're not nearly as clever as you think. The pair of them have it over you by a wide margin."

"You dare instruct me, girl?"

Felicity managed a bleak smile. "Better a gentle urging, Papa, than a harsh recompense, would you not agree? Or as Grandpa would say, a bit of wisdom dispensed to one in dire need?"

Without waiting for his response, Felicity took her leave through the front door. After all, now that her father knew she was married, there was no further need for pretense. But then, she wasn't so dense that she hadn't known he'd be waiting up for her after Roger kept delaying their departure from the inn. It seemed her groom had a sadistic fetish for forcing what was unnatural upon a woman and, even after his brutalizing rape of her, had refused to leave their room until she had yielded to some of his demands. It had either been that or stay there with him forever. The whole experience had been a horrible nightmare wherein she had found herself the victim of a monster posing in the innocent facade of a handsome lad.

Felicity quietly approached the bed wherein Edmund Elston had been confined since his first seizure some months ago. This was the first chance she had had to visit her father-in-law's room with some measure of privacy since her marriage five weeks earlier. There was always someone around, precluding that possibility, if not Roger, then the servant who had been hired to tend the elder. Staring down at the man, she couldn't imagine how her father had ever arrived at the far-fetched notion that Edmund had somehow been able to deceive Roger. Before his health had collapsed, she had only seen Edmund in passing, but she vividly recalled him as having been a robust, rather handsome, if ill-bred, individual who had seemed impressed by his own importance. His tasteless and flamboyant attire had ofttimes made her thankful her own mother had cautioned her against overt showiness. Still, his attire had seemed to go right in line with the personality of the man.

The difference between her initial impression and what she saw before her now was as sharply dissimilar as midnight from noon. Only a thin layer of wrinkled flesh seemed to cover Edmund's skull. His hair was gone, and his hollowed cheeks bore a strange, whitish hue. Beneath parchment-thin lids, his eyes gave every appearance of having retreated back into his head. Or perhaps the dark shadows encircling them was partly to blame for that perception. His mouth hung agape, and his gauntness made the previously narrow space between his badly stained teeth far more pronounced. Dried saliva had left a whitish trail where it had earlier drooled from a corner of his lips and trickled down the side of a badly emaciated cheek.

"Papa Edmund . . . are you awake?" she inquired diffidently, not knowing what to expect. If her father's warnings were justified, she was probably endangering her life, yet the debility of the man could not be denied. If he weren't already at death's door, then he was close enough to smell the netherworld.

A flicker of movement behind an eyelid assured her that her inquiry had at least been heard, but whether it had actually penetrated the invalid's awareness, she could not determine.

"Do you want anything? Perhaps some cider or even a little tea?"

"Wa . . . ter," he rasped in a whisper so faint she could barely make it out.

Turning to the bedside table, she poured a small amount of liquid into a glass from a carafe a servant had left there. "Here, I'll help you," she offered, slipping an arm beneath the man's frail shoulders as he tried to lift his head. His breath was foul, and in sharp repugnance she averted her face. Still, she had recently discovered there was within her a sizable measure of her mother's fortitude. She was a married woman now, and she had come to realize in that brief, month-long marital hell she had been forced to endure that she would have to look to the security of her future . . . and to that of her offspring. Although Roger was the father, she considered the growing entity within her womb entirely hers. She wanted the child; her husband did not. In fact, there were times when he was so rough in his lovemaking that she could believe he was trying to make her miscarry. If that ever happened, she had already promised herself that she would leave him and plead with her family to shelter her until she could find a haven far from his vindictive revenge.

Edmund's condition was far more serious *and* repulsive than her grandfather's. That was clearly evident. Yet there were things she had to find out for herself, and to get to the truth of the matter while there was still time, she had to go to the only likely source who had that knowledge. If the man expired, her chances of obtaining the truth would be sharply reduced, if not altogether negated.

Edmund revived ever so slightly after taking a deep sip and, upon collapsing back into his pillows, stared up at her in bemusement. "'Oo are yu? From what I can recollect, I've ne'er seen yu 'ere afore."

"I'm your new daughter-in-law, Felicity. I'm here to help you get well, Papa Edmund."

His ashen lips quirked upward in a frail smile. "'Tis a cer . . . tain . . . ity yu're not Mar . . . tha Grim . . . bald."

"No, Papa Edmund, I don't even know who she is."

"Just . . . as . . . well. Ye . . . would . . . na . . . be . . . impressed."

"Was she someone Roger was supposed to marry?"

"I'll leave . . . 'at . . . for 'im . . . ta be . . . sayin', girl. Just . . . know . . . yu're . . . a . . . damned . . . sight . . . prettier."

"How are you feeling? Is there anything I can get for you? Some food perhaps? A little port?"

"Don't . . . agree . . . wit' . . . me. I've 'ad too many spirits in me life, an' they're eatin' away at me innards."

"What about some food? Perhaps some medicinal herbs from the apothecary."

A thin finger fluttered upward weakly, drawing Felicity's attention to the fact that the nail was strangely streaked. The hand itself seemed scaly, as if the skin were actually in the process of drying . . . or dying.

"Mayhap . . . a . . . bit . . . o' porridge . . . or puddin' . . . just ta . . . soothe the . . . misery in me . . . gut. 'Tis . . . so . . . unbearable . . . at times . . . I . . . yearn . . . ta die."

Carefully avoiding contact with the man's skin, Felicity laid a hand gently upon his arm where the nightshirt covered it. "I shall ask Cook to prepare you some porridge and pudding immediately. Is there anything else I can get for you in the meantime?"

"Where's . . . Roger?"

She watched the man closely, wondering if she'd see anything in his reaction that would be indicative of his concern over the mill's accounts as she led him on. "I believe he's looking over the books. There seems to be a discrepancy somewhere. Just where, I can't imagine. I can only repeat what I've heard, that there are apparently more coins going out than coming in."

Edmund struggled to push himself up on his elbows, but quickly collapsed upon the mattress, too weak to leave it. Rolling his head on the pillow, he gulped as he sought to take a breath. "Roger'd ... do better ta manage ... the mill ... an' leave ... the books ta me, girlie."

"But, Papa Edmund, you've been too ill even to know what day it is, much less tally the mill's accounts."

"Tell 'im ... ta leave off ... till I'm ... on me feet ... again."

Leaning over the man, Felicity offered him a smile as she patted his arm in a motherly fashion. "I will tell him what you said, Papa Edmund. Now rest yourself. There's certainly no need for you to get in such a dither about the accounts. 'Twould seem like such a small matter for Roger to worry you about ... unless, of course, you happen to know why they can't be balanced. If so, you should consider letting him know ... to save him endless searching."

"Just tell 'im ta leave off, girlie. 'E has ... no head ... for tallyin'."

Eighteen

❀

COLTON Wyndham swept his bride into his residence overlooking Hyde Park in London, and promptly became mindful of the fact that Seward, the small, wiry, elderly butler, who had been elevated to the status of head steward of the house long before Sedgwick Wyndham had ever started having a family, was grinning like a wizened monkey. The thin man snapped his fingers and, amazingly, a flood of people, mostly garbed in black, others from the kitchen wearing only white, seemed to scurry from every nook and cranny to form a lengthy line for the new mistress's inspection. Even Cook was there, having been hired a score of years earlier to round out the staff for the mansion. Now she reigned supreme over the kitchen and the preparations of the food. It seemed every one of the servants wore a smile as broad as the butler's and was eager to greet the newly wedded Wyndhams immediately upon their return from their two-month honeymoon spent in warmer climes, which had indeed proven advantageous to the master's recuperation. By the time the last smiling maid was introduced, Adriana's head was nearly reeling with a blur of names. Imagining the difficulty she'd likely encounter remembering which name went with what face, she laughed and clasped her hands to her pinkened cheeks.

"In all my past visits here, I never realized there were so many servants on the premises. I shan't be able to recall everyone's name at first, so, please, please have pity on me."

Laying an arm about her waist, Colton squeezed it affectionately as he drew her against his side. "Aye, they'll do that for you, my dear. After all, they've no other choice since you're the new mistress of the house. Yet, as much as they'll be learning your preferences, I doubt they'll be expecting to lose their hearts to you. Having experienced that very thing myself, I should warn them to be on their guard, or they'll be scampering around here, ignoring my demands while they're eagerly doing all they can to please you."

The amiable chortles evoked from the servants readily evinced the possibility of that occurrence. Of all the past visitors to the Wyndhams' London manor, it had been Lady Adriana who had always evidenced a vivacious charm and caring thoughtfulness that had evoked their fondness. They couldn't have been more delighted now that she was mistress of the manor.

"Dinner will be served at the usual hour, my lord," Seward informed the marquess, unable to contain his own grin. "Considering your lengthy jaunt in the carriage today, I thought perhaps you and madam would enjoy having your meal served in the warmth and privacy of your chambers. No doubt, after your extensive travels these past two months, you'll welcome an opportunity merely to relax."

"An excellent idea, Seward," Colton replied with enormous enthusiasm. "Lady Adriana and I are indeed weary after such a tedious ride today and would like nothing better than to soothe our spirits in such a manner as you suggest." He paused as if a thought had just occurred to him and held up a forefinger. "One more thing, after our dessert, I would very much enjoy a hot bath. It seems to soothe my wound."

"Aye, my lord, I shall see that one is prepared for you and that your wishes are carried out as you have stated. I shall also caution the servants not to disturb you after the dishes have been collected." The elder's lips twitched ever so slightly. "Travel does seem to weary a body, and of course, wounds do need leisured time to heal properly."

"Very good, Seward."

Smiling warmly at his bride, Colton offered his arm. "Shall we go up now, my dear? I would enjoy getting comfortable. What about you?"

Adriana curbed her own smile as she tucked a slender hand within the crook of her husband's elbow, knowing well what they'd be doing soon after the servants had been dismissed for the night. She had come to believe her stalwart husband could be nigh dead and still be desirous of copulating. Their honeymoon had been proof enough of that. "That does indeed sound inviting after a lengthy trip."

Colton's grin widened as he gently patted her hand. "I was certain you'd agree, madam."

COLTON stripped away the last of his garments beneath the warmly admiring gaze of his wife and motioned for her to make room for him as he stepped near the oversized tub.

"I thought I'd like to take a bath alone for a change," she teased, her teeth tugging at a bottom lip as she sought to curb a grin. Deliberately reclining against the rounded end of the copper tub, she leisurely soaped her breasts, taking puckish delight in teasing him with her nakedness. She flicked a glance upward toward his boldly displayed passion, secretly pleased that he was already desiring her. "You haven't let me do that since we've been married."

His devious chuckle was well contrived. "Make room for me, wench, or I'll have your hind-part in my hand. I'm coming in whether you want me or not."

Heaving an exaggerated sigh, Adriana lifted herself upright and scooted forward. "I'll never get clean if you keep insisting that we take our baths together. You always seem to have other purposes in mind rather than merely bathing."

"That may well be, madam. After all, you have such luscious places upon which I enjoy feasting, yet I can't see what difference it makes who actually bathes you as long as you get clean."

Settling into the water behind her, he laid an arm around in front of her, capturing a rounded, soapy breast in one hand as he thrust his free hand underneath her, just forward of her buttock. Lifting her back within the spread of his thighs, he snuggled her closely against him.

She tossed an impish glance over her shoulder. "Comfortable?"

"Not entirely," he breathed as he nuzzled her ear.

Wiggling her hips, Adriana resettled herself, but hardly expected the jolt of scintillating excitement that spiraled upward through her as her womanly softness came in contact with his manly flesh. Her husband's breath caught, assuring her that he had also been affected. She shivered in rapturous bliss, and her dark eyes were soft and warm with desire as she turned her face in profile to him. "Better?"

He nibbled a dainty earlobe between his teeth as he made her keenly aware of his excitement. "Do you have any doubts, madam?"

Adriana smiled as his fingers brushed across a soft nipple. "Perhaps we wouldn't have so much difficulty fitting together if you didn't get so carried away *before* you got into a tub."

Leaving a trail of kisses across her shoulder as he progressed inward toward her nape, he cajoled softly, "You could consider facing me, in which case we'd fit together perfectly."

The luminous eyes closed dreamily as he taunted her once again with his maleness. She rolled her head slowly upon his shoulder, luxuriating in the languid caress of his mouth. "Knowing you, I fully expect that event will follow shortly."

"You've come to know me through and through, madam."

Considering he was always surprising her with new and exciting experiences in the world of sensual pleasure, Adriana rejected his conjecture as anything holding merit. "Not in a thousand years."

Leaning forward over her shoulder for a fresh view of her creamy breasts, Colton lifted a saturated sponge and stroked away the whitish foam adhering to the womanly fullness, causing his wife's breath to halt and then ease outward in a blissful sigh as he gave first one delicately hued peak his undivided attention before moving on to the other.

"I like that," she sighed tremblingly, deliberately thrusting the sensitive peaks forward to reap as much pleasure to be found from his touch. The sponge was forgotten as his brown hands came forward to gently clasp the pale orbs. He felt a shiver of desire go through her as his fingers plied the delicate nipples.

"From the moment I wake in the morning till I fall asleep at night," he rasped against her ear, "I'm besieged with freshly brewing desires amid a profusion of memories we've made together in the various beds in which we've been ensconced these last months, my love. I even crave you in my sleep."

"Yes, I know." She sighed and then giggled when he canted his head to peer down at her in some curiosity. "Well, I'm not necessarily oblivious to the changes in your body when we're snuggled up in bed. I enjoy waking up and feeling you hard and eager against me. One day, I may even take advantage of the fact that you're asleep."

Chuckling softly, he pressed his lips into her sweetly scented hair. "I give you leave to wake me anytime, madam. Giving you pleasure always reaps more of the same for me."

"I can't remember a time since we've been married, my dear husband, when you haven't teased, titillated, poked, evoked, intoxicated, ignited"— she paused to catch her breath and then sighed contentedly—"and completely appeased my desires. You definitely have a way about you that bestirs my yearnings and makes me eager to be one with you."

Colton grinned at her exaggeration. "For a moment there, I was sure you were going to compliment my rutting talents."

Giggling, she wiggled her bottom against him teasingly. "Finish your bath, husband. I want to go to bed with you."

"What can we do there that we can't do here?" he whispered against her ear. Slipping a hand down between her thighs, he plied the silky softness that readily opened to him.

Soon Adriana found herself writhing with the ecstasy he created within her until she could bear it no longer. Rising to her knees, she turned to face him, her eyes aflame with hungering desire as she searched the smoldering gray orbs. Laying her hands atop his broad shoulders, she moved her body in slow, sinuous, seductive invitation, feeling as if bubbles of delight were bursting within every fiber of her being beneath the delicious caresses he plied to more sensitive areas. When at last he guided the hotly pulsing blade into her warm, moist sheath and pulled her down upon him, a convulsive shiver went through her. Her head fell back, spilling darkly curling tendrils from her loosely confined tresses as her loins began to caress his. The throbbing passion intensified as their bodies cleaved together and their gasping breaths became moans of blissful pleasure until they soared together from the limitations of the universe and began to ascend to galaxies far, far beyond. It was much later when they finally drifted to earth, once again wrapped in each other's arms.

"I love you, madam, more than mere words can convey," Colton whispered against her brow, seriously doubting he had any more strength left in his limbs.

Adriana finally braced up on his chest and smiled in eager delight as she scrubbed her slender fingers through the feathering of hair covering that broad expanse. "Tell me when you first realized you loved me."

Colton lifted his head musefully, as if he were having some difficulty remembering back. "Why, if you're really curious when that emotion began to thwart my bachelor status, I believe it was when you crushed my manly parts."

Laughing in amusement, she delivered a playful blow to his chin and then proceeded to recline alongside him. "Well, if it's any consolation, my husband, I was sure I had destroyed my maidenhead during that same encounter. I couldn't sit comfortably for a whole week."

He canted his head to peer down at her, seeming a bit confused. "I would never have known. It still looked intact when I perused you in the bathtub."

His comment wrenched a feigned gasp from her, prompting her to push herself up from his chest. "You didn't!"

Chuckling, he lifted his naked shoulders in a casual shrug. "A man always looks when he has the opportunity to peruse at close range a worthy subject, and you are indeed *most* worthy, madam."

Adriana sat back and tossed her head, pretending to be miffed. "You were absolutely despicable, that's what you were. Ogling me while I slept, you should've been ashamed of yourself."

"I was too intrigued by the sights to feel anything but overwhelmed by my lust for you, my dear. To that, you can attest."

The corners of her lips turned upward enticingly. "Aye, 'twas a bit shocking at the time, but I've grown rather fond of the view."

"Oh-oh!" He peered down at himself, drawing her curious attention to the same area.

"Lecher!" she accused with a grin.

"Lecher, am I? I'll show you what a lecher I am."

With a laughing squeal, she scrambled up and swung a leg over the side of the tub in her haste to flee, allowing him another delectable view. Her breasts were set wondrously abounce as she danced backward, away from the tub. His devious chuckle sounded menacing as he swung a leg over the side and began to stalk her. Though she watched him carefully to determine which way he would go, he feinted to the left and then caught her as she lunged toward the right. Sweeping her up in his arms, he growled as he made a pretense of devouring her throat.

"Colton, behave yourself," she scolded, her voice a strange mixture of giggles, feigned reproaches, and playful shrieks thrown in for good measure. "The servants will hear us."

"They shouldn't be listening at the master's door, madam. I'll have to talk to them about that."

Changing her tactics to pliant submissiveness, Adriana slipped her arms around his neck and didn't mind at all that he lifted her upward to languidly devour a soft nipple. Trembling at the pleasure he created with her, she asked huskily, "Have I told you recently, my darling, how much I adore you?"

"I seem to recall you saying something like that when you were slipping off to sleep last night, and then the night before, and the night before that," he whispered softly, raising his head to find her parting lips approaching his. "I don't care how many times you say it, I never grow tired of hearing it."

"I never thought it possible, but our union has brought me joy beyond measure. I can only hope and pray that nothing happens to disturb the blissful haven we have found together."

THE Wyndhams' homecoming to Randwulf Manor was first heralded by the gardener, who espied his lordship's new landau coming smartly down the lane from some distance off. The aging man scrambled up from his knees near a flowerbed in which he had been directing several of his newest helpers in the planting of flowers. Scampering hurriedly up the stone steps, he whisked open the front door of the manse and gave his old friend happy tidings of the couple's imminent return. With a buoyant grin Harrison conveyed the news promptly to his mistress, who by then was having her tea in the drawing room, where, after reveling the past three or so months in the fact that Colton was now married and deeply in love with the very one his father had chosen for him, she had been content merely to relax and gaze lovingly at the portrait above the mantel and recall the former days of her own marriage.

No one thought of informing Alice Cobble of the couple's return. Nevertheless, her ears were well attuned to the excited dither and chatter of servants. Thus, with the young child draped facedown over her forearm, she made a point of sauntering into the main hall just as the master laughingly swept his bride past the vestibule.

Adriana's jubilation promptly ceased in the wide corridor beyond the archways as she caught sight of the slovenly garbed woman. The frazzled hag held the tiny girl as carelessly as she would a bag of grain. Although the baby's gown was finely made and edged with costly lace, it was badly wrinkled and soiled. For barely a moment, Alice jostled her burden upright, allowing Adriana to see the girl's huge, haunted blue eyes, chapped cheeks, and runny nose. The realization of the baby's less-than-sublime condition went through the younger woman like a cold shiver. Feeling suddenly sick to her stomach, she clasped a trembling hand over her mouth. A fretful moan escaped her lips as she squeezed her eyes tightly shut and made a desperate attempt to stem her queasiness.

Unable to ignore his wife's distress, Colton bent near solicitously, but when she shuddered convulsively after casting another distressed glance beyond him, he looked around in curiosity to see what had provoked this reaction from her and mentally cursed when he espied Alice Cobble, not only present against his wishes, but in the same slovenly condition she had been in when he had first brought her from London. Furthermore, his daughter looked very much like a tiny, pitiful waif.

Sharply incensed, he faced Harrison forthwith with a blunt question. "Why is that woman still here in that condition? And the child...why does she look like that?"

The steward spoke in a low murmur, securing their confidentiality. "My lord, we cannot find a wet nurse anywhere in the area. We've looked high and low, and with each passing day, the woman becomes more impossible, as if she knows we want her gone and yet are unable to send her on her way because of the child. Your mother doesn't dare complain about the baby's appearance or state of health, for she is immediately beset with threats of Alice's departure. If not for the child, her ladyship would have seen the woman dismissed months ago, especially since that had been your behest, my lord."

"Get her out of my sight," Colton growled through gritted teeth. "Among her many offenses, she happens to be upsetting my wife."

Alice Cobble strode forward boldly, displaying black, rotting teeth in a taunting grin, as if it weren't already apparent that she had been reveling in the power she held over the household. "Aftahnoon, yur lor'ship," she crowed and then cackled gleefully, causing the baby to whimper at the ear-piercing sound. "We thought yu'd ne'er return from cavortin' 'bout the countryside wit' yur new missus. Been more'n three months since yu left 'ere fer parts unknown." Her eyes shifted to Adriana, and her seemingly unruly lips twisted sneeringly as she inclined her head ever so slightly. "Yur liedyship."

"Go back to the nursery, woman," Harrison bade sharply, gesturing in the general direction of the stairs as he stalked toward her. "Your presence is not required down here. Now leave us."

"Why, I thought 'is lor'ship 'ould be wantin' ta see 'is li'l chit 'pon his return. Seems ta me a man what cares fo' 'is offspring 'ould be anxious ta visit wit' 'is brood first off aftah bein' 'way so long. Gor', yu've been gone so long the chit's nigh grown."

The steward caught her plump elbow and, in spite of the fact that she outweighed him by a goodly margin, turned the termagant skillfully toward the stairs. "Away with you, I said!"

Alice leaned back to peer over her shoulder at the marquess. "Will yu be comin' up later ta sees yur chit, milord? She's a mite scrawny, 'at she be, but jes' the same, real pretty ta me way o' thinkin'. Mayhap 'er liedyship'll be wantin' ta come up wit' ye."

"Cease your prattling, woman!" Harrison insisted angrily as he sought to give her a sharp shake. "Or so help me, I shall stuff a rag in your mouth!"

Alice squawked. "Yu an' 'oo else, yu li'l bitty crow? I've wrestled be'er men 'an yu ta a stan'still' in ale 'ouses, I 'ave, an' if'n yu don't gits yur bloomin' 'ands off'n me right away, I'll be gnawin' on 'em wit' me teeth." As if to strengthen her threat, she bared her blackened fangs, causing Harrison to stumble back in sharp aversion for fear of being wounded by those foul shards.

Philana fought a moment of queasiness herself before the wet nurse finally took her leave. The elder's distress was readily apparent in her blue eyes as she looked toward her daughter-in-law in helpless appeal. "Forgive us, dear child. We've not been able to control that woman since she came here. I'm sure she knows we're unable to find a replacement for her and delights in playing havoc with everyone in this house. I shan't expect that you'll be able to tolerate her any better than we have done. 'Twould definitely require someone with more stamina than any of us have thus far been able to gather."

In spite of the lingering nausea that still assailed her, Adriana crossed the hall with opening arms and managed a courageous smile as she embraced the elegant woman. "We can't allow Alice to disrupt our lives, Mama Philana, as much as she may delight in doing so. We shall carry out our search for a wet nurse posthaste, even if we must go to London."

"Maud is here, dear," Philana informed her, hoping to banish Alice from their thoughts, if only for a few, peaceful moments. "She arrived in the hired livery perhaps an hour ago and said you were on your way. 'Twould seem her driver made better time than yours did."

"Colton and I stopped at an inn to have a bite to eat. I was enormously hungry, so much so your son cautioned me against getting fat." She made an attempt to laugh in spite of the fact that, after seeing Alice, she wasn't at all certain she'd be able to keep what she had eaten in her stomach.

Philana laughed softly, making every attempt to present a cheeriness she didn't necessarily feel in her spirit after their confrontation with Alice. "Bentley was rather put out that Colton had left him behind to tend to my traveling needs, few as they were, and chose to take Jason from our London house for your lengthy excursion. Maud, however, seemed quite pleased that she had been allowed to attend you throughout your absence from home. She's upstairs now in the master's chambers, unpacking your satchels and trunks."

Adriana laid a gentle hand upon the elder's forearm, deciding it was far better to be truthful. "Right now, I'm not feeling at all well, Mama Philana, and I'd like to rest for a while."

"That is completely understandable, child. Alice would cause anyone to suffer more than they should. I've found that out for myself on more occasions than I care to count, and have often retired to my bed thoroughly spent and with a terrible headache throbbing in my temples."

Adriana sought to give the elder hope. "I shall look in on the child when I'm feeling better. In the meantime, I suggest you send a rider with a note explaining our needs to my aunt in Bath. I have no doubt Aunt Tilly will be able to find us a wet nurse. She seems to know everybody from Bath to London and has many faithful friends who'll help scour the countryside in an effort to help us."

"In that case, I shall send Alistair on that mission posthaste." The corners of Philana's lips twitched in amusement. "He's eager to find *any* excuse to visit Tilly."

Managing a smile for the woman, Adriana squeezed her thin hand. "Let's hope Alice will be gone from here ere the week is out, if not sooner."

Philana didn't dare pray for such a miracle. Turning the other cheek was something she could likely do, but tolerating that shrew was another thing entirely. "As much as I desire to see the vulgar woman gone, dear, I can't imagine she'll leave here without causing some dreadful disturbance. She's such a rude woman and does everything she possibly can to test our tempers and our patience. Indeed, she seems to revel in the fact that she distresses the lot of us."

"We'll put an end to that posthaste," Adriana declared and was about to turn away when she realized she hadn't heard anyone call the baby by name. Facing her mother-in-law again in some curiosity, she inquired, "What do you call the child?"

"I fear, dear, she has no name as yet," Philana admitted rather sadly. "I've been waiting for Colton to name her, but of course, he has had other things on his mind and probably hasn't thought about doing so. 'Twould be presumptuous of a grandmother to take on that responsibility. Thus far, we've just been calling her Baby Girl."

"I'll ask Colton about naming her tonight. She should be christened fairly soon, and will need a name for that event."

"I've always liked the name Genevieve myself. Had I been fortunate to have another daughter, she would've been christened Genevieve Ariella."

Adriana leaned near to kiss the elder's cheek. "'Tis a beautiful name, Mama Philana. I shall mention it to Colton later."

Happy tears brightened the blue eyes as the older woman searched the beautiful visage. "Thank you, dear child, for marrying my son. He would never have been happy without you. Nor would the rest of us."

Adriana managed a heartfelt grin. "If you're taking count, Mama Philana, you should include me in that number, for I love your son more than words can fully define. I think I've always loved him."

"No doubt, dear. You always seemed to enjoy tagging at his heels when you were younger. Now he seems to enjoy tagging at yours."

ONE look at the pale, beautiful visage of her young mistress sent Maud scurrying to find a basin of cool water and a cloth to wash her face, which she then proceeded to press upon her brow. "Lie down an' rest yurself, m'liedy. Yu look as ill as death warmed over."

"Funny thing, that's exactly how I feel." Adriana gulped, holding the cool cloth clasped to her brow as she collapsed back upon the bed.

"Come now," the servant urged, "lift yurself an' let me help yu off wit' yur clothes. Yu've been in 'em all day, an' 'tis sure yu'll be more comfortable wit'out 'em."

Adriana groaned much like a petulant child as she yielded to the woman's command and held her arms aloft. "Leave me my shift," she bade listlessly. "I may have to heave up my stomach, and I don't want to have to scurry through these chambers stark naked while I search for a basin."

Straightening at her statement, Maud peered at her curiously. "What ails yu, mum? Did the long ride from London wear on yu?"

A negative shake of the dark head gave mute answer, but when slender fingers suddenly came up and pressed to the whitened lips in an effort to halt an outward flow, the maid's brow quirked in wonder.

"I don't want ta alarm yu none, mum, but could it be that yu're wit' child?"

Adriana promptly sat down again, fearing her legs would give way underneath her as the shock of that possibility settled down on her. She stared across the room as if stunned. "'Tis true I didn't come at my normal times, but I thought it was merely due to the excitement of being with Colton on our honeymoon."

"How long have yu been feelin' this way?"

"Actually, the nausea only came upon me today, when I saw that creature . . . Alice . . . holding that pitiful little girl. Poor little thing, my heart went out to her. She seemed . . . so . . . so . . . desperately miserable. . . ."

"Well, yu know how yu've always been 'bout 'elpless critters an' li'l orphans, mum. 'Twouldn't be at all surprisin' if that's all what made yu sick." She nodded, as if settling her mind resolutely upon that possibility. "That's all it probably was, nothin' more."

"Yes, I suppose you're right," Adriana replied. "Otherwise, missing my flux right off as I did, I must consider that I got with child the first week of our marriage."

"Was 'at the only one yu missed, m'liedy?"

Adriana stared at her as the dawning came. "I haven't had one since his lordship and I have been married.

"'E's a bold one, m'liedy, that he is."

"Say nothing of this to anyone, especially to the older servants. They're enormously loyal to Philana and will hasten to tell her, and I'd rather not have that happen before I have a chance to talk with Colton. If it's just the excitement of being with him that has caused me to miss my regular times, I don't want Philana getting her hopes up only to see them dashed. Neither do I want everybody sizing me up until I find a convenient time to tell his lordship. That opportunity might not come for several days yet, considering how upset we all are over Alice's presence in the house. 'Twill be better to make such an announcement after she's gone."

Maud chortled. "Yu can expect the servants 'ere ta be lookin' yu o'er anyway, mum, seein's as how yu'll be the only one what'll be bearin' offspring wit' the Wyndham name. 'Ey cannot 'elp but 'ope ta see signs o' yu carryin' the master's babe."

Adriana smiled as she laid a hand upon her stomach. "I think we're *all* hoping that will come to pass fairly soon, Maud."

THE tinkling chimes of the mantel clock dragged Adriana up from the depths of sleep. Lying on her side within the curve of Colton's long body, she listened to the delicate notes until finally the twelfth heralded in the hour of midnight. When silence once more came back to reign, she cuddled more closely against her husband, kissing the sheltering arm under which she lay. A smile curved her soft lips as her hand moved below her waist. As was Colton's preference, she was naked, as was he, and though her fingers slowly plied the silky smoothness of her stomach, she could detect no slightest evidence of a life growing within her womb. In spite of cautioning Maud against indicating such a possibility to anyone, she had nevertheless been tempted to tell Colton, but had decided to wait after all, considering his lingering irritation over Alice. Her monthly cycles had always come at regular intervals, and except for her brief nausea when Colton had told her that he had married another, she hadn't been sick to her stomach in some years, at least not since she was ten and four and had run a high fever and been confined to bed. That illness had passed ere the week had gone, and she had been in good health ever since.

Adriana had no doubt that Philana would be thrilled at the prospect of another grandchild on its way, but would Colton? He enjoyed their intimacy to such an extent that she had cause to wonder. Would he be repulsed by her rounding belly or perhaps the awkwardness that would eventually hinder their lovemaking? Or would he be just as thrilled as she to imagine the marvel their love had created?

Closing her eyes, Adriana heaved a contented sigh and was just drifting off to sleep again when an indistinct sound prompted her to fling them wide again. Wondering what she had heard, she turned her head on the pillow to listen more intently. Was it the wailing of the wind? Or, more disturbingly, the bawling of a baby from some distant area of the manse?

Adriana strained to catch the sound more distinctly and, as the seconds flew past, became more convinced that that was indeed what she was now hearing, a baby's harsh crying. There was only one child in the house, and from that little one's haunted expression, Adriana could only believe the little cherub was in desperate need of loving attention.

Taking care not to awaken her husband, she slipped from his side, donned her nightgown and dressing robe, and then pushed her slender feet into satin slippers. In the hall outside the master's chambers, she paused to listen in an effort to determine from whence the wailing came. It was definitely some distance away, but where exactly?

Adriana hurried in one direction, but decided forthwith that she was not on the right bearing. Whirling, she ran past the door of her husband's chambers and went up a flight of stairs that took her to the third level. It was a part of the mansion that she hadn't been in since her childhood. It was an older section and had always seemed rather dark and forbidding, even ghostly at times, tempting Samantha and her to test each other's courage by hiding out in its many nooks and crannies, forcing the seeker to follow, cautiously at best.

The wailing grew louder, leading Adriana on nearly at a sprint. When finally she reached the room from which the harsh sobbing drifted, she found the door standing ajar and a shaft of light streaming from the narrow opening into the wide hall. Laying a hand upon the barrier, she pushed it carefully inward just enough to allow her to peer inward without being seen.

The first thing that came into view was Alice Cobble, sitting in the middle of the bed with her back braced against the heavily carved Jacobean headboard. In one hand, she held a crystal decanter, from which she literally sipped. A lamp burned on the table beside her, and in its radiance the griminess of her nightgown was clearly apparent. The garment hung open over one large-nippled, blue-veined mound, and was so old and rotten it had become all but transparent, no doubt due to its filthy state, Adriana surmised. That was hardly the most pronounced cause for her lack of modesty, however, for her nightgown had been hiked up to her thighs and she lay with one leg bent and the other widespread.

Adriana didn't dare let herself imagine what the woman had been doing or just whose attention she had been trying to attract. Even so, it was not hard to imagine the hag's predilections were of the vilest sort.

Alice cackled suddenly, wrenching a start from Adriana. "'Ere 'ey was, 'is lor'ship an' 'is missus, lookin' likes 'ey couldn't be parted for all the wool in Bradford . . . 'at is, 'til I comes 'pon 'em wit' the chit." The crone smirked gleefully. "Aye, I planned it real good, I did. 'Eir 'eads is likely still aspin-nin'. *Humph*, serves 'em right for wantin' ta gets rid o' me. O' course, 'twouldn't be too long aftah 'ey did 'at 'is lor'ship would figger out jes' what I'd been doin' 'hind 'is back. Then 'ere'd be 'ell ta pay, sure as I'm adrinkin' 'is port. An' then 'e'll be askin' questions, wantin' ta knows what's goin' on. 'Tis only a matter o' time afore 'e figgers out 'e's been tricked. Missus 'Igh an' 'Aughty ain't gonna waits forever. No, sir, she ain't! 'Bout 'at time, 'is lor'ship an' 'is missus is gonna knows 'ell's done come up from the depths."

"What's the meaning of this outrage?" Adriana demanded, pushing the door wide as she stalked inward. The baby's wails had grown harsher, and although she had listened to the hag's inane gibberish in an effort to dis-cern what she was talking to herself about, Adriana couldn't ignore the child's needs any longer. She went directly to the crone's bedside and was repulsed by the fact that Alice made no attempt to cover her own naked-ness. "You were hired to nurse and take care of the child. Instead, she's howling from neglect and there you are, sipping my husband's port. Pack up your belongings and get out . . . immediately!"

"An' jes' 'oo's gonna nurse the brat?" the woman challenged with a con-fident, black, snaggletoothed grin. She swung her legs off the mattress, but, in making an attempt to rise, stumbled over her own filth-crusted feet and listed heavily to the side, much like an old tar upon a storm-tossed ship. When finally she came up hard against an armoire, she grinned back at Adriana with a confident leer. "Yu wouldn't dare let me go, missy. Why, the chit'd starve."

"She's starving now, and yet you're so deep into your cups you haven't even noticed. If need be, I'll soothe her with a sugar-tit until we can find a woman who'll at least nurse her until another can be employed full time. In the interim, I want you gone from here."

"Mayhap yu'd better ask 'is lor'ship afores yu sends me packin', missy. 'E jes' might resent yu layin' the law down ta me."

"My wife has told you to leave," Colton barked as he strode inward, garbed in a long, velvet robe and leather slippers. "And that's exactly what I want you to do. In fact, you can get out of my sight ere the hour is past. The stableboy can hitch up a cart and take you as far as Bradford. From there, you'll have to make your own way to London or wherever it is you'll be going, just as long as it's far from here."

"Yu owes me wages, yu do!" Alice railed back and then elevated a brow as she peered askance, curiously eyeing the younger woman as she hurried across the room to the baby's crib. When Adriana lifted the tiny girl and cuddled her closely against her, a derisive sneer drew up the hag's upper lip. She didn't hold with spoiling a chit. They were better off learning at an early age that their wailing wouldn't get them what they wanted in life, but that would hardly be her affair anymore if his lordship did indeed intend to let her go. What *was* her concern was getting her just due, and for that, Alice was willing to do more than a little ranting and railing. Turning upon his lordship again, she lifted a clenched fist and shook it at him threateningly. "I ain'ts leavin' 'ere 'til I gets what's comin' ta me."

"And that may be more than you bargained for, hag," Colton retorted acidly. "A boot in the rear would likely serve you a fit recompense."

The shrew squawked and, turning about-face, flipped up the tail of her nightgown as she bent over and waggled her bare backside at him, cackling in glee as she snatched a shocked gasp from Adriana. For good measure, she made a foul gesture between her legs. "Come on, lovey. Puts yur poker in 'ere so's yur missus can sees hows it's really done."

"On second thought, you'll get no wages," Colton barked sharply, thoroughly incensed. His comment brought the woman around with a raging snarl that displayed her foul, decaying teeth. Undeterred, he jeered into her murderous glare. "You just used up what was left of them. The liberty you took with my port could've been waived, but your latest infraction cost you the full sum."

Alice shrieked and shook a grimy fist at him. " 'Ere yu are, rich as all get out, an' yu begrudge me a li'l prank."

"Serves you right for being so despicably vulgar and letting the child go without proper care and nourishment while you've been in here poking yourself and guzzling down my port," Colton shot back in heightening ire.

He recognized the extent of his own indignation when he realized he was literally shaking with rage. His hands were clenched into hard-knuckled fists, and his stomach, which had knotted in revulsion over what he had just seen, began to twist and churn. In an effort to calm himself, he slowly exhaled, and glanced aside at Adriana who was clasping his daughter closely against her bosom as she strolled toward him. Her soft cooing and gentle cajoling was closely reminiscent of that which he had heard from past times when she had been inclined to nurture orphaned or wounded animals. For a brief moment, the squalling ceased as the child rooted eagerly at a softly rounded breast. Alas, no nourishing nipple could be found through the dressing gown, and once again the baby started thrashing her tiny fists in outrage.

"Poor little darling," Adriana murmured in caring, sympathetic tones. "We'll see you fed ere long. That much I promise you, Genevieve Ariella."

"Genevieve Ariella?" Colton repeated with a bemused smile, drawing a hesitant glance from his wife.

"Your mother said she liked the name, but if you'd prefer another, I'm sure she wouldn't be offended."

Smiling, he reached up a hand and lovingly smoothed his wife's tousled tresses as she leaned into him. Her soft, gentle ways did much to banish the fury raging within him, and he couldn't resist lifting her small chin and placing a soft kiss upon her winsome lips. "'Tis a good name, my love, one that will likely suit her. As for you, madam, you look quite motherly holding the babe. We should think about having a houseful."

Once again, Alice lifted her lip in a ridiculing sneer. "Yu bloody bastard, 'twould serve yu proper if'n yu ain'ts gots any seeds in yur coffer."

Colton laughed harshly as he bestowed a disdaining sneer upon the woman. "'Twould seem I've already put that question to rest. . . ."

Scathingly Alice swept her eyes over him. "'Twouldn't surprise me none in the least if'n Miss Pandora filled yur ears wit' rot."

Canting his head quizzically, Colton peered at the woman. "Are you telling me that Pandora tricked me into thinking the girl is mine?"

Avoiding his probing stare, Alice cut her eyes aslant and shrugged noncommittally. "Much as I'd cackle in glee ta knows yur cods be all dried up, I guess 'ey ain't, seein's as how yu put yur family mark on the babe's arse. Jes' sayin' 'twould serve a bloke like yu 'is proper due if'n yu can'ts make no mo' brats wit' yur fine an' proper liedy so's yur family name can be carried on. I been hearin' some o' yur servants talkin' amongst themselves 'bout 'ow's yu're the last male in yur family."

As much as Adriana had considered waiting to announce her childbearing state to her husband, she couldn't resist frustrating the hag's mean-spirited aspirations. "No need for you to leave here foolishly hoping that is the case, Alice," she chided, causing both Colton and the ogress to look at her in mounting confusion. "I am already with child."

A joyous cry erupted from Colton, drowning out the woman's foul curse. For good measure, he laid an arm about Adriana's shoulders again and brought her close for another kiss, this time with open mouth and probing tongue.

"Colton, for shame," Adriana chided, blushing at his display of fervor. Still, she had trouble curbing a pleased smile as her fingertips stroked dry the sweet dew of passion lingering on her lips. "What will Alice think?"

"Alice bedamned, madam. This is my ancestral home, and you're my wife. You're carrying my child in your womb and holding another close against your heart. At this moment, I can't possibly imagine how I could love you more than I do right now or, for that matter, have loved you since the dawning of time."

As much as another kiss from her husband pleased Adriana, it failed to satisfy the baby. Withdrawing from Colton with a radiant smile, she murmured, "I must go down now and wake Cook. I do so hope she knows how to prepare a sugar-tit for Genevieve."

"Couldn't regular cow's milk be warmed and given in the same fashion as a sugar-tit?" Colton asked.

" 'Twill give the chit runs," Alice volunteered caustically, stripping her plump, blue-veined body bare, once again thoroughly scandalizing Adriana who stared at her agog. The hag scratched her private parts shamelessly, making the younger woman spin about with a mortified groan, a reaction that drew cackles of glee from the crone. "What's the matter, lovey, yu wants ta do it fo' me?"

"Get some clothes on, you old scold!" Colton roared, once again feeling his temper rising. "You're disgusting enough with your clothes on, but you're damned revolting without them—"

"Likes I was sayin'," Alice interrupted caustically, lifting an upper lip to sneer at his lordship again. "The li'l tike'll likely starve afore yu finds 'nother wet nurse." Just the same, she complied with his command by waggling her hips into a skirt, not caring how much she set her flabby stomach rippling and her mountainous bosom swaying with her movements. After yanking a dowdy top over the heavy melons, she chortled as she heckled Adriana. "Yu can turns yurself 'round now, yur liedyship, but yu'd best keep it in mind, yu ain't gonna be lookin' no better'n me several months from now."

Colton arched a brow incredulously. "You really can't be serious, ol' hag. Or are you so blind to your own hideousness that you have the gall to compare yourself to one who, in my estimation, is nigh perfect?"

Snarling epithets to herself, Alice bundled her few clothes together and tied them in a large shawl. Facing the couple, she offered a jeering conjecture. "So's, yu've made up yur minds, eh? You're gonna let the chit starve. Don't says I didn't warn yu."

Colton met his wife's gaze worriedly and realized they were both suffering the same qualms. Yet he dared not suggest delaying the woman, for there was no guarantee she wouldn't take out her spite on his daughter. "We'll find another, my love," he said, trying to comfort his wife. "I'm sure the servants know of a woman in the village who'll at least suckle Genevieve until a more permanent wet nurse can be engaged."

"So's her own babes can starve?" Alice inquired caustically and then curled her lip in derision. "'Taint likely."

"Nevertheless, we'll find someone who'll be willing," Colton stated resolutely.

"I'm sure you'll want to see Alice sent on her way posthaste," Adriana responded, briefly bestowing a cold, withering stare upon the hag. Alice was the coarsest creature she had ever come across in her entire life, and she just couldn't bear the idea of the woman staying another moment in a home that had never known such depravity. Her eyes immediately softened with love as she looked back at her handsome husband. "I'm going to ask your mother's advice. She'll be able to tell us what we should do."

Moments later, Adriana and Philana were hurrying down the main stairs when the sounds of a carriage halting before the manor aroused their curiosity. Philana ran at once to a front window and, peering out through the moonlit darkness, espied the glowing lanterns of the landau that had come to a halt in the drive below the stone steps. The manly figure standing at the open door of the conveyance was unmistakable, and in elated surprise she spun about to face her daughter-in-law. "Alistair is here, dear, and he's helping a young woman out of his carriage. That can only mean one thing!"

Both women hastened to the front portal and in their eagerness suffered a bit of confusion over which one would actually draw open the door. With a joyous laugh, Philana finally took care of the matter herself since Adriana was trying her best to placate the furiously squalling baby. Nearly ecstatic with relief, the elder yanked open the heavy portal so quickly that she caught her brother standing before the door with a fist suspended in midair.

For Alistair, the hardest part seemed to be recovering his aplomb with his jaw hanging aslack with surprise. In the following moment he reclaimed enough of his wits to close his mouth. Straightening his coat, he managed to assume a more lofty air as he strolled inward. Very proud of himself, he bragged, "Efficient as always I am. Mathilda found a wet nurse for you in Bath, and I took the liberty of transporting the young woman directly here in case you were desperate." He cringed slightly at the volume reached by the screaming youngster, and then cleared his throat. "Yes, well, 'twould seem the young lady and I have arrived in the nick of time, eh what?"

"Uncle Alistair, you're such a dear, dear man," Adriana exclaimed happily and gave him an enthusiastic, one-armed hug. "Please do bring the woman in. The baby is starving!"

"This is Mrs. Blythe Fulton," the man announced a moment later as he ushered the woman into the vestibule. "Her husband was killed at Waterloo. Only a pair of days ago, she gave birth to a   Although I understand little of these matters, Mathilda has assur   that Mrs. Fulton is most anxious to find work as a wet nurse and to obtain relief, not only from her serious lack of funds, but from her . . . ah . . . ah . . . painful condition."

Philana offered a conjecture as she faced her daughter-in-law. "Mrs. Fulton will no doubt want some privacy, dear. As much time as it's taking for my son to rout Alice from her room, I wonder if she's proving difficult. Do you think we should ensconce Mrs. Fulton in a room downstairs for the moment or dare we show her to her bedchamber upstairs? I had servants freshen the sheets and linens in the room across the hall from Alice's, just in case we were fortunate enough to find someone. I even had Samantha's old crib moved in there."

"Colton's chore in ousting Alice is definitely not one I envy, Mama Philana, but we shouldn't let that woman's presence dictate what we do for her replacement. Mrs. Fulton would likely be more comfortable if she were settled immediately into rooms of her own. Why don't I take her upstairs to the chamber you readied? The sooner she can nurse the baby, the better we will all feel."

The two younger women were just approaching the stairs leading to the upper floor when Alice's harping tones all but drowned out the baby's wailing.

"As much as I've looked 'igh an' low for it, I still can't finds me gold ring," she complained as she stalked out of her room. Half-turning to direct her comments to Colton, who followed upon her heels, she insisted, "Yu're gonna haf ta makes good me loss, do yu 'ear? Me po' dead husband give me the ring aftah 'is ma passed on."

"If *ever* you had one," Colton retorted, highly skeptical of the idea that the unruly hag had ever had a gold ring *or* a husband.

"I ain't leavin' 'ere wit'out h'it, no I ain't!" Alice declared, setting her jaw with stubborn tenacity. When she heard hurrying footsteps on the stairs and the infant's squalling coming nearer, she tossed a triumphant smirk back at Colton. "Maybes I ain'ts leavin' 'ere, aftah all."

"You're wrong there, Alice," Adriana interjected from the stairs as she came into view of her husband and the shrew. "You *will* be leaving, posthaste in fact. We've been fortunate enough to find *and* hire a wet nurse for Genevieve this very hour."

Colton felt his own jaw sagging in astonishment and was so curious he had no time to rejoice at Alice's look of stunned disbelief. "How in the world did you manage that, madam?"

Adriana smiled smugly. "Uncle Alistair came to our rescue again, my love. Even as late as it was, your uncle made the trip from Bath to bring us Mrs. Fulton . . . just when we needed her most."

Adriana gently rocked the baby in her arms, trying to soothe her some small whit as she settled a bland stare upon Alice. " 'Tis doubtful that you and Mrs. Fulton will ever meet again, so I shan't bother introducing you. I shall, however, wish you a speedy journey from Bradford since I'm rather fond of the vast majority of its inhabitants."

Colton pressed a knuckle against his lips to subdue his amusement as Alice brushed past the two women in bristling fury, having forgotten her earlier quest. If she could dismiss the gold ring from her mind so soon, it seemed to confirm his suspicions that she had never possessed one in the first place.

"I shall introduce you to my husband later," Adriana informed Mrs. Fulton, giving the child over into her arms. She inclined her head to indicate the room that would belong to the woman henceforth. "For the time being, however, you and the baby can become better acquainted in your chambers. 'Tis certain the little darling needs your immediate attention, do you not agree?"

"Oh, yes, my lady, and I am most anxious to give it," Blythe Fulton assured her, trying not to wince from the discomfort she was presently experiencing.

"I shall awaken some of the servants and have your baggage brought up to your room," Adriana informed her. "I assume your cases are still in his lordship's carriage."

"No need to bother the servants, my love," Colton stated. "I can bring up her baggage myself." Cocking a brow sharply, he leveled a forefinger at his beautiful wife. "I'll see you in our chambers shortly. We need to talk about babies and such."

Smiling, Adriana stroked her hand along the length of his arm as they passed. "My pleasure, my lord."

"No, mine," he murmured, tossing back a sly wink above a grin just as their fingertips slipped free of the other's.

Nineteen

✻

Felicity donned her bonnet and a light shawl before slipping out of Edmund Elston's house and hurrying up the dirt lane toward Bradford. She was confident that Roger would be gone on his errand to Bath long enough to allow her to accomplish what she had been yearning to do for some time. Her first destination was the apothecary shop, where she hoped to purchase the same herbs Adriana and Samantha had once given her grandfather. She had no way of knowing whether the elder had just been lauding the benefits of their gift merely because of his admiration for the two women, who purportedly had done many good deeds for the people in the area, or if the medicinal herbs had actually improved his condition. By bestowing upon him such a gift, she hoped to get back into his good graces. Yet, after her haughty conduct, she could rally little optimism that she'd be able to make amends though she now regretted her actions with all her heart.

For years, she had been inclined to discount her mother's instructions on the merits of integrity, moral behavior, and self-esteem. Instead, she had considered her father an example to follow. She had allowed his derogatory opinion of Samuel Gladstone to become her own. Yet, at some point in her life, her mother's lessons on honor, virtue, and kindliness must've taken root in her own character, for her respect for Jarvis Fairchild had plummeted the very day she had learned he had been pilfering funds from his father-in-law's woolen mill by laying off workers without removing their names from the roster of employees requiring wages. His thievery had made the sterling attributes of her grandfather shine bright in comparison.

When she had married and moved away from Stanover House, she hadn't realized just how much she'd come to miss the old man, his wit, and his wisdom. Perhaps such admiration came from one gaining maturity. Since her union to Roger more than five months ago, she had become the recipient of some fairly harsh lessons about life and its hazards, which had made her far more appreciative of the values she had previously considered.

For instance, marriage could definitely be a nightmarish pit of demented debauchery when a woman had a husband like Roger. Not only did he have the manners of a boar in bed, but at times he became irrational, even furious when she didn't readily perform his strange requests, many of which seemed vile and sordid. In spite of her reluctance and tearful pleading, he'd force her against her will as if she were merely a plaything to be used for his pleasure alone. She was forever in fear of what he'd do to her child when he slammed into her tender parts with such vehement force, as if he were some crazed demon, unable to obtain pleasure without dispensing a heavy dose of pain. If he had hated her and used such tactics as punishment, she could not have been more anxious about her welfare.

The bell hanging above the door of the apothecary shop tinkled charmingly as Felicity pushed it open and slipped within. A chubby-cheeked man with a short frizz of white hair running around the lower portion of his balding head leaned outward from a narrow aisle lined on both sides with countless shelves, upon which resided neatly organized, labeled glass bottles filled with various herbs.

"Yes, miss? May I be of some assistance?" he asked solicitously, adjusting his wire-rimmed spectacles in a quest to see her better.

"Why, yes, if you would," Felicity murmured, offering the apothecary a tentative smile. If of late she had become diffident around men, it was only that she was now inclined to wonder how many were hiding an evil side. "More than eight months ago, my grandfather, Samuel Gladstone, received some medicinal herbs from two ladies of the peerage. He praised their benefits so highly that I thought I'd purchase more of the same for him. One of the ladies is Lord Randwulf's sister and the other has since become his wife. Do you happen to recall what those herbs were and, if so, would you be able to supply me with a fair sampling that I can take to my grandfather?"

"Why, I recall them very well, miss. In fact, I was the one who suggested those particular herbs to the two ladies. I thought they'd give your grandfather some vigor and possibly help his condition, but I fear they're fairly rare and, for that reason, quite costly, miss."

Felicity placed a pair of earrings on the counter between them. "Would you take these in trade? I believe they were worth a goodly sum when my father purchased them months ago."

The apothecary tilted his head thoughtfully as he peered at her above his eyeglasses. "Are you sure you want to part with them, miss? They are quite lovely, and you'd surely look fetching wearing them."

"Missus, actually. Mrs. Elston, to be exact." Felicity nodded in response to his inquiry. "Yes, I'm willing to trade them. I have nothing else with which to barter."

The apothecary could imagine the sacrifice the young woman was making in trading the earrings and sought to suggest a less arduous alternative. "Business seems to be going well at the mill, Mrs. Elston. If you don't have the funds at this very moment, I can give you the herbs if you'd care to ask your husband to stop by later and pay me. I'm sure he could afford—"

"No, I'd rather not ask him. Nor do I wish you to reveal to anyone that I was even here, making such a purchase. Do you understand?"

"Yes, Mrs. Elston. I can be quite tightlipped when I need to be."

"I'd truly be grateful if you were, Mr. . . . ?"

"Carlisle, Missus. Phineas Carlisle. And don't you worry none, Mrs. Elston, I won't tell a blooming soul." Personally, he had never liked the Elstons, having become highly suspicious of the way the late Mrs. Elston had gone from a healthy, effervescent individual to a listless, depressed, and totally forgetful creature soon after her marriage. He had seen opium work much the same way, and at the time he couldn't help but wonder if Edmund had started giving his wife large doses without her knowledge to create the impression in people's minds that she had been afflicted by some horrible malady. He would've enjoyed proving his theory after her death and bringing evidence of her murder against the man, but he hadn't been able to. If Edmund had killed his second wife by such a method, then he probably purchased the opium in London, the sources for which would've been difficult, perhaps even impossible to discover. As for the son, this was Phineas's first real hint that his initial perception of Roger Elston had some merit.

Felicity offered the man a gracious smile. "I was wondering while I'm here, Mr. Carlisle, if you could possibly help me with another matter."

"If I can, madam."

"Prior to my marriage to his son, my father-in-law was stricken with a mysterious illness. His fingernails are strangely streaked, and his skin is scaly and dry. Would you happen to know a malady that could cause that sort of reaction?"

Mr. Carlisle folded his right arm across his portly middle and braced the elbow of his left upon its wrist as he stroked a finger musefully across his upper lip. *Interesting how one's foul deeds were wont to come home to roost.*

"Well, right off, Mrs. Elston, I don't know of any disease that would cause that particular reaction. However, I once warned a young lady against the dangers of taking small doses of arsenic to make her skin fairer. She was very vain and exceptionally pretty, but I'm afraid the saying is true: Pride goeth before the fall. . . ." He flicked his bushy brows upward. "Or, in her case, death. At her funeral several months later, I noticed that her skin, which had once been so soft and creamy, had a scaly look to it and her fingernails were strangely streaked."

Felicity felt a terrible coldness spreading through her, and she had to gather her courage before she could bring herself to make another inquiry. Even to her, her voice sounded unusually frail. "Is arsenic fairly common, Mr. Carlisle? And if so, have you sold any within the last year?"

"Arsenic has been around for some time, madam. It was identified perhaps as much as two hundred years ago, but from what I understand, it existed well before that event. As for selling it myself, the answer is no, dear lady. I've been avoiding doing so since the young lady died. I have no wish to see another foolish woman kill herself by such a method merely because her conceit prevails over common sense."

"Is there another apothecary in the area?"

"No, madam. However, I've seen an old acquaintance of mine from London who has been visiting fairly frequently of late. He has become quite prosperous in that trade and now owns several apothecary shops. He has a fine carriage, far better than anything I could ever afford. He also seems to have become quite fond of your husband's fabrics in recent months. He left the mill with a large bundle of woolens tucked beneath his arm not too long ago." Phineas didn't dare tell the lovely young woman that the man was also a conniving scoundrel who was eager to be rich by any means he could employ.

"And his name?"

"Thaddeus Manville."

Felicity had no knowledge of such a name or the man to whom it belonged. As much as she'd have enjoyed exhibiting what both her father and mother had taught her about accounting, her offer to help Roger in that area had been curtly rejected. In fact, she hadn't been allowed anywhere near the ledgers. Roger had forbidden her even to enter the mill, giving the excuse that he didn't want her interrupting his work.

Felicity accepted the medicinal herbs that Mr. Carlisle bundled up for her and, with a gracious farewell, made her departure. Still, she couldn't help but draw comparisons between Edmund's symptoms and those that Mr. Carlisle had taken note of at the young lady's funeral. Could Edmund have been poisoned some months back? And, if so, by whom?

W<small>HO</small> is it?" Jane called, hurriedly descending the stairs after hearing first a knock and then the telltale creaking of the front door as it was being opened.

"It's Felicity, Mama. I've come for a visit."

Jane couldn't contain her elation nor the happy tears brightening her eyes as she beat a hasty path toward the parlor in her eagerness to greet her daughter. She entered with arms widespread and ran to meet her offspring. With a muted cry, Felicity evidenced her own joy and relief at being welcomed back with such fervor as she flew into her mother's warm embrace. In view of her past behavior, she had almost feared she'd be shunned.

"Oh, my precious, precious girl, I've missed you so very much," Jane avouched in a voice that had grown thick with emotion. "Why haven't you visited sooner? I went to the mill a time or two to see how you were getting along, but Roger said you didn't wish to be disturbed, especially by me. Have you been well? Happy?"

"Yes, I've been well, Mama." Preferring not to answer the second inquiry, Felicity hurriedly pulled away and held out the small bundle of herbs. "I brought Grandpa a gift. I thought I'd come and read to him from the Bible if you think he'd enjoy that."

"Of course, dear. He'd be delighted. He has missed you."

"Missed me?" Felicity was bemused . . . and dubious. "But I thought he didn't like me."

Laughing, Jane laid an arm about her daughter's slender shoulders and gently shook her. "You little goose, he may have been put out with you for a time, but kin is kin, and that's the way it shall always be with your grandfather. You're his granddaughter. Both of you have the same blood flowing in your veins. How could he not care for you?"

Unable to contain the moisture welling forth in her eyes, Felicity searched her mother's face and found love brimming over in the other's teary smile. "Mama, I'm so sorry for the way I acted. Can you ever forgive me for being so utterly selfish and despicable?"

Jane clasped her daughter close against her, joyful tears streaming down her cheeks. "Say no more, dear. All is forgiven . . . and forgotten. You are my dearest love, my pride and joy."

Felicity's composure broke, and as much as she sought to quell her emotions, harsh sobs shook her. Both mother and daughter remained locked in a fierce embrace, their past regrets washing away as their love for one another flowed upward from the depths of their hearts.

When at last they parted, Felicity searched her handbag for a handkerchief and blew her nose as she tried to reclaim her composure. Jane watched her, trying to discern what remained hidden. Instinct told her that something was not quite right in the life of her daughter, but she had no idea what that could be. Gently, she laid a hand upon the other's arm. "What has happened, Felicity? Is everything all right with you?"

"Of course, Mama." Felicity didn't want to fret her mother and bravely tried to smile. It seemed a task beyond her capability. She finally shrugged as she gave an excuse. "I guess now that I'm with child, I realize how much of a burden I was to you, I mean, the way I acted and all."

"You're with child?" Jane pulled away with a buoyant laugh, but it died in her throat as she caught a brief glimpse of the sadness dulling the beautiful blue eyes of her offspring. Immediately the look of hopelessness was forced behind an artificial smile, and once again Felicity was pretending to be happy. Worriedly Jane cupped the delicately boned chin within the palm of her hand as she carefully perused the girl's face. "Something *is* wrong. What is it?"

"Nothing, Mama," Felicity tried her best to laugh in an effort to put to naught her mother's insightfulness. "Nothing at all."

"Is something the matter with Roger?"

"Roger is fine, well, never been better."

"Roger may be fine, but I know my daughter well enough to perceive that something is not quite right. Although I do not wish to pry, I plead with you to trust me to help in any way I can."

"Mama, I just don't know what you're talking about. I'd better go upstairs now and read the Bible to Grandpa. I can't stay long. After my visit with him, I'll have to leave."

F ELICITY couldn't believe she had actually found an opportunity to slip into the mill's office without fear of Roger finding her mulling over the books. He had left for London before workers had departed the previous day and, for that sojourn, had made plans to stay over until Sunday. She certainly didn't mind that he hadn't invited her to go along with him. If anything, she was relieved she wouldn't have to endure his deviant abuse in bed for that space of time.

Her handsome but utterly depraved husband had seemed especially aggressive with her right after she had gone to Stanover House, causing her to wonder if he had found out about her visit through a casual comment from townswomen or some other harmless soul and had sought to dissuade her from ever calling upon her mother again. The pain he had elicited had definitely heightened her dread of him and made her wary of visiting her relatives, at least in the light of day, when townspeople might see and later comment on it to him.

So great had been her ordeal during those several days that it had seemed as if Roger had released her from a torture chamber when he finally turned the bulk of his attention to a new undertaking of his, directing carpenters in the task of converting a little-used storeroom just off the gift shop and his adjoining office into a private haven for himself. It was obvious he was expending a greater sum to bring workmen all the way from London, but he had casually given the excuse that locals were not skilled enough to satisfy him. Felicity had to wonder if that were truly the case, why Lord Harcourt, who was clearly a man who appreciated quality, had employed a good many woodwrights from Bradford while refurbishing his own chambers.

Naturally, for this proposed room, Felicity hadn't been allowed to view any plans or projected expenses. It seemed her husband only wanted her for one purpose, to pleasure him in bed, and casually dismissed any other talent or knowledge she had out of hand.

Upon the room's completion, shortly after the mill workers had left for the day, furniture arrived from London in two large tarp-covered wagons hitched to teams of stout drays. Curious to see what Roger had purchased, Felicity crept into her father-in-law's upper-story bedchamber while the elder slept. For some reason, it was a room her husband didn't think she'd ever enter, much less frequent. He was mistaken, however, for she did so fairly often, having discovered that its windows afforded her a broad vista of everything that transpired in front of the mill.

In spite of the large tarps and padded quilts wrapped around the pieces, she glimpsed enough gilded arms and heavily carved legs to have no doubt that Roger's private cubicle would be grand enough for royalty. Such ostentatious tastes definitely seemed out of place in Bradford on Avon, even more so in a woolen mill.

Now that Roger was in London and she had an opportunity to search through his accounts without fear of discovery, Felicity intended to acquaint herself with both. Unfortunately, soon after entering the mill, she discovered that her husband had taken measures to safeguard his secret room by locking its door. As for his ledgers, he had not been so careful. He had left the key for the cabinet where they were stored in full view upon his desk, no doubt believing she wouldn't dare enter his office without his consent. Little did he guess her growing concern for herself and her offspring and her reluctance to go to the poor house should he lose the mill.

Felicity had to give as much credit to her mother as her father for her own astuteness in mathematical matters. Although to her knowledge, none of the counting houses in London had ever hired a woman, her father had asked for her assistance in completing his work there on different occasions. As for her mother, Samuel Gladstone had once taught his daughter, Jane, and she, in turn, taught her daughter.

It didn't take Felicity long after initially perusing Roger's books to discover that large sums had indeed gone out in various amounts to two individuals. Their identity couldn't rightly be determined, however, since only the initials *M.T.* and *E.R.* were marked beside the extraction of funds. She lost track of the hours she spent just trying to find names to correspond with them, and her burgeoning frustration did much to heighten her fatigue.

It was nearly midnight when Felicity finally turned down the wick in the small lamp she had lit over the desk. Hoping to continue her search in bed, she tucked one of the ledgers beneath her arm and locked the door of the office behind her before returning to the house. She had entered and was just crossing the hallway to the bedchamber she shared with Roger when she was brought up short by the realization that the room was occupied . . . by her husband.

"Roger, I wasn't expecting you until Sunday night!" she exclaimed, her heart hammering within her chest as she halted within the doorway. Clandestinely shifting the book to a table residing in the hallway next to the door, she forced a smile and then hurried forward to bestow a wifely kiss upon her boyishly handsome spouse.

Roger averted his face, rejecting her offering, and then peered down at her coldly. "Where have you been?"

Knowing she hadn't been able to hide the ledger very well, Felicity shrugged and swept a hand to indicate the place where she had left it before entering the bedchamber. "I overheard some gossip about your father trying to cheat you, and . . . well, I just wanted to find out for myself if that were true. I brought one of the books back to look through when I have more time."

"No need to worry yourself about such things, my pet," he said, moving past her to fetch the book. "I'll do that for you. In any case, if Father *has* managed to cheat me, he's in no condition to do so now. With each passing day, he seems that much closer to death." Tucking the ledger beneath the frock coat that he had slung over the back of a chair near the door, he turned to her again, unbuttoning his waistcoat as he smiled meaningfully. "I decided to return tonight, because I was overtaken with a peculiar desire to instruct you in something entirely different."

Felicity went cold with dread at that ominous portent, yet in light of the fact that he had caught her with the book, she didn't dare hint of her aversion. There had been times when she had striven valiantly to preserve some meager scrap of dignity in spite of what he forced her to do, but she had learned that such efforts only made her husband more malicious. Tonight she saw the necessity of complying with Roger's every wish. Then hopefully he'd turn his mind to other matters rather than stew over the fact that she had entered the mill without his permission.

Plucking open her bodice, Felicity did her best to convey enthusiasm in a seductive smile. She just hoped Roger wouldn't notice how violently she trembled with the fear-instilling uncertainty of what he'd require of her this time. "You must have read my mind."

Twenty

❋

MY lady, there is a young woman here who insists upon seeing Lord Randwulf and claims the matter is of some urgency, but she refuses to give her name or any indication what her visit is about."

"His lordship is outside walking the dogs, Harrison," Adriana replied. "Perhaps I can be of some assistance to the lady."

The steward seemed to hesitate before venturing further. "Your pardon, my lady, but the woman is not a lady in the same sense that you and the Lady Philana are."

The lovely brows gathered in confusion. "You mean the visitor is not an aristocrat?"

"No, madam, she is not. Neither is she a lady."

"Oh." A moment of pensive silence followed as Adriana considered his statement. "My goodness, Harrison, I truly hope she's no kin to Alice Cobble. I don't know that this household can bear another sampling of her sort."

"Much more comely and cleaner, to be sure, my lady, but her manner of attire leaves one to imagine that she has had more worldly experience than one who has been carefully protected from unsavory influences."

"I think I shall have a look at this . . . ah . . . comely creature who wants to see my husband," Adriana declared softly. Considering Colton's earlier forced marriage, she could only wonder what other light-of-love had emerged from his past.

"As you wish, my lady." Harrison inclined his head in a shallow bow. "I shall show her into the drawing room."

As the man withdrew, Adriana approached the long, standing mirror in the dressing room and thoughtfully inspected her reflection as she turned from side to side. Her childbearing state was too far advanced for anyone to mistake her condition though she had trouble herself believing she had been married for five wondrously perfect months. Her union with Colton had been the sweetest bliss she had ever known. Indeed, each new day, especially now that June was nigh upon them, seemed filled with its own special euphoria, each night rapture beyond her wildest imagination, not only in the merging of their bodies, but in the deepening awareness that their unborn child was a unique entity forged by their union and yet an altogether separate individual. The hard knotting of her belly evoked their laughter as they lay side by side watching the small gyrations going on beneath the small, creamy, protective mound, which once upon a time had been flat stomach, and then feeling beneath their hands the wonder of their baby moving. Colton didn't seem to mind at all that she had lost her winsome shape; indeed, he gave every indication that he was now just as eager to view her naked as he had been before. Ofttimes, he'd take the rose-scented oils and lotions she was wont to rub over her body and perform the task for her. Yet he seemed far more methodical about it, obviously enjoying the intimacy marriage and expectant fatherhood afforded him. Never once had she dreamt that he'd be such a wonderfully attentive, tender, and adoring husband, or that her love for him, which before their marriage had seemed far beyond the measure of reasonable logic, could deepen with each passing day.

Although the weather was fairly warm, Adriana laid a lace shawl about her shoulders to hide to some degree her rounded shape. As she did, she realized how anxious she had become in the last few moments. In spite of her assurance that Colton loved her, the thought of facing another woman from his past unsettled her as nothing had done in some months.

The visitor, upon hearing the lighter, feminine footfalls progressing rapidly across the marble floor of the central hall, turned from the mullioned windows of the drawing room with a brow raised in curious wonder, fully expecting to see the marquess's mother. She was somewhat taken aback by the appearance of a younger woman and was immediately put to confusion. Her gaze swept the beauty full length, from sedately coiffed dark hair to the slender leather slippers barely visible beneath the hem of her gown, but it was the roundness beneath the intricately woven shawl that made her eyes harden.

The stranger's chin raised loftily. "I came here to see Colton, no other."

"I'm Lord Randwulf's wife," Adriana replied, rather piqued at the liberty the other took using her husband's name. She concluded her own inspection of the caller in much the same manner as she had been perused and had to agree with Harrison. Although quite beautiful, their guest did indeed lack the elegance and refinement of a lady well tutored in social graces. Applications of rouge had been made to the woman's cheeks, dark kohl lined her eyelids, and her softly curving mouth was vividly painted. Her garments also conveyed a boldness in both color and design that led one to mentally question her profession. Wrapped about her head was a paisley turban, from which a tightly curling mass of dark hair streamed over her shoulders and down her back. Large, gold filigree earrings dangled from pierced earlobes. A necklace of brightly minted gold coinage of questionable value, along with various other chains, hung about her neck. In height, the stranger was shorter than she, Adriana determined, but overtly rounder in places most men would have appreciated. Such attributes were deliberately flaunted. In spite of the hip-length, loosely flowing magenta robe she wore, her bosom seriously tested the shallow bodice of her empire gown, which readily revealed the deep valley between her breasts. If she wore any undergarments at all, then that possibility remained questionable, for the silken cloth clung to her suggestively.

In a guise of serenity, Adriana offered their guest a smile. "Since you're now acquainted with who I am, may I be allowed the pleasure of knowing the name of the one to whom I am speaking?"

The red lips angled upward patronizingly. "Well, I guess you may address me as Lady Randwulf . . . or Wyndham, if you'd prefer."

Adriana frowned, thoroughly confused. "I assume, then, that you're not related to my husband since he's the last of his family to carry on the Wyndham name."

"Colton Wyndham *is* my husband," the visitor announced with a challenging brow raised, "which, of course, makes you no wife at all."

Had she been struck a debilitating blow, Adriana would have reacted no differently. Staggering on trembling limbs to a nearby chair, she eased herself carefully within its confines. As if sensing her distress, the baby moved suddenly within her womb, causing her to gasp in sharp surprise and clasp a hand to her tensed belly.

"Now don't lose the little bastard," her guest cautioned with a smirk. "Of course, the way things stand now, 'twould probably go better for you if you did. The slander will be bad enough without people cruelly ostracizing your chit for the sins of his parents."

"Who are you?" Adriana cried in anguish. "Did you come here for the sole purpose of tormenting me? Or do you have some ambiguous motive in mind?"

"I don't know what you mean." The visitor had definitely never heard the word *ambiguous* before. "I simply came here to stake my claim upon my husband, and I find you living here under his roof. As for my name, I am Pandora Wyndham, and if I'm not mistaken, my daughter is living here with my husband."

Adriana now understood only too well. "Obviously you're not quite as dead as my husband was led to believe. Yet I cannot help but wonder where you've been for the last five or six months. Had you sent some missive informing him of your good health soon after you and he were married, the two of us would never have wed." Considering the length of time it had taken the woman finally to come forward and make them aware of her existence, Adriana couldn't resist a bit of sarcasm. "Was that a minor detail you failed to consider months ago, or merely a lack of etiquette? Whatever the case, you're a bit late informing us that you're not dead."

"I did *die*, at least for a moment or two, as the good rector will attest, but I revived. Yet I was so weakened by the birth of my daughter that friends immediately whisked me off to warmer climes in hopes of bringing about a full recovery. As you can see, their nurturing attention rejuvenated me, and I have returned to England to claim my husband and my child."

A sharp whistle in the main hall alerted Pandora to the approach of the one she had come to see. Colton's voice verified that fact as he instructed, "Go find Adriana."

The joyful barking of the wolfhounds changed forthwith into a vicious growling that evoked a frightened screech from Pandora as the two animals came bounding into the room, sending her stumbling hurriedly back in rising panic. She halted only when the back of her head hit the mantel, where she was forced to a terrified halt. Hysterically, she tried to shoo the hounds away, flicking her hands outward cautiously, as if afraid one of them would snap off her fingers or take a large chunk out of her arm.

"Get away! Get! Get!" she shrilled. "Get away, you beasts!"

"Aris! Leo! Behave yourselves!" Colton commanded from the main hall.

Obediently the pair sat down on their haunches in front of their captive and looked back over their shoulders as their master approached the room. The dogs' proximity made Pandora wary of even moving, much less crossing the room to greet the marquess.

"Adriana, who in the world was doing all that frantic screeching? Do we perchance have a visitor—?" Colton's words halted abruptly as he entered the drawing room and finally saw the woman the dogs had cornered. "Pandora!"

"Get these animals away from me!" she railed in outrage, indicating the pair with a wary flick of her hand. "You shouldn't have beasts like that running loose in the house! They could kill somebody!"

"Leo, Aris, come," Adriana urged, snapping her fingers. Wagging their tails, the wolfhounds readily answered her summons and received from her several fond strokes along their backs before they plopped themselves down on the rug near her feet.

Pandora glared at the brunette, realizing she could have called off the animals just as easily as the man. In nettling ire, she lifted her upper lip in a caustic jeer at that one, allowing her unspoken insult to convey her thought.

In spite of the venom bestowed upon her by the actress, Adriana returned her gaze unwaveringly before lending her attention to her husband, whom she eyed quizzically. For one so mentally astute, it was taking him an unusually long time to recover his aplomb. Obviously, he was trying to understand all the whys and wherefores of how this situation had come about, much as she had been.

Pandora sought to salvage as much of her pride as she could manage after the dogs had sent her fleeing like a squealing pig. Difficult as it was, she lifted her head in an elegant manner, as if posing for a stately portrait. "Well, Colton, aren't you happy to see me?"

"Not especially," he retorted brusquely. "I thought you were dead."

"I was, at least for a moment or two, but I revived. And now I'm here to claim my rightful place as your wife."

"*The devil you say!*" he barked, his gray eyes flaring. "I have only one wife, and she is the one you have most recently met!"

For a moment, Pandora's jaw sagged in shock at his thunderous declaration as he swept a hand about to claim Adriana as his only true spouse, as if he'd fight heaven and hell before relenting to any other state of wedlock. The tenacity he displayed while making that statement left Pandora feeling as if he had just slapped her across the face. Making every attempt to keep her chin elevated in a guise of dignity, she insisted, "Legally, Colton, *I* am your wife. Nothing you can say or do can change that."

"Well, I intend to! Although I agreed to let Reverend Goodfellow speak the words over us, 'twas done merely to give Genevieve my name and protection."

"Genevieve?"

"The child to whom you gave birth, but now I'm wondering if she really is mine. Perhaps you tricked me into marrying you . . . for what purpose I cannot as yet say exactly, although I have the distinct feeling that I'm about to learn what that is." His lips turned sardonically. "Lucre, no doubt."

The woman blinked her eyes, a bit perplexed. "I'm not sure I understand the meaning of that word . . . *lucre.*"

"Profit, money." His wide shoulders lifted in a casual shrug. "It's all the same."

"Oh, Colton, how could you even suggest that I'd stoop to such a despicable level? Genevieve is our daughter, and, as her mother, I only want to be with her . . . and you."

He seemed to grow increasingly museful as he lifted his head to the decorative molding edging the lofty ceiling. "How long has it been now since you supposedly passed on? Six months? Or has it been seven? At least long enough for my wife to be nearly six months along with child. Considering the length of time it has taken you to get around to telling me that you didn't die as I was led to believe, I seriously doubt that you've had *any* desire to be with Genevieve. I'm sure whatever you were doing, you were enjoying yourself immensely. Otherwise, I would've heard from you sooner. What made you finally come? Did your funds run out? Or did your lover decide to toss you aside for some new diversion?" He caught the sudden flare in her eyes and decided the latter conjecture was closer to the truth, if not the very reason for her appearance. "Is that it? Were you rudely spurned by your rich admirer? I can more easily entertain that notion than I can believe you had any desire to see Genevieve."

"Of course, I've wanted to see her, Colton. She *is* my daughter, after all . . . as surely as she is yours."

"Is she really mine?" His tone suggested that he now had serious doubts about that possibility.

"Of course she is. How could you have forgotten that she bears your family's mark? Tell Alice to bring the girl down here, and I'll have her refresh your memory. That mark is incontestable proof that she is your offspring."

Adriana opened her mouth to explain that Alice was no longer living under their roof, but Colton surreptitiously motioned to her behind his back, silently bidding her to remain silent. She readily complied, perceiving he had some viable motive in mind.

Facing the actress, he inclined his head briefly. "I shall ask one of the servants to convey the news that the child is to be brought down."

"Genevieve?" Pandora arched a brow after Colton had excused himself and, with a condescending smirk, turned to peer at Adriana. "Who thought of that? Please don't tell me *you* did. Otherwise, I'll have to change her name once I root out the little baggage trying to usurp my marriage."

Adriana folded her hands in her lap to keep from responding with sarcasm to the woman's slur. Considering the length of time the actress had been gone, she could only imagine that if Pandora's union to Colton had been valid, then its continuance went against every precept intended by God and man, especially if she had indeed been involved with a lover. "The child was named by her ladyship, the marchioness."

"Colton's mother, you mean." Pandora tossed her head and laughed, seeming to revel in a moment of anticipation. "As much as I've resisted the lure of the title, I shall be pleased to hear my so-called friends addressing me as the Marchioness of Randwulf. They'll soon be licking spittle from my shoes and offering me parts they've recently been giving to mere chits."

"I believe my husband has something entirely different in mind than what you're presently coveting," Adriana replied succinctly. "So if I were you, I wouldn't count on your acquaintances doing obeisance just yet."

Pandora chortled derisively. "As much as Colton may resent our marriage, my dear, I'm afraid there's no escape for him. After all, I have proof. The document he signed will confirm our marriage."

Adriana held her peace, not knowing what would follow. She felt equally weak and sick inside, as if her greatest joy had been snatched from her life. She couldn't even take comfort in the movements of their baby who seemed especially active in her womb, perhaps sensing her distress.

Colton returned to the drawing room with the announcement, "Genie is being changed at the moment. She will be brought down directly."

"We must talk at length about our child and our marriage, Colton," Pandora responded, moving toward him with a hand outstretched, as if to make another appeal for the judiciousness of her reasoning.

If a lightning bolt had struck the floor right beside Colton at that instant, he could not have reacted any faster. Clearly conveying a reluctance to be anywhere within close proximity of the actress, he eluded her attempts to approach him and, in the rapidly dwindling space she left him, stepped over the dogs lying at Adriana's feet. Settling on the settee beside his young wife, he reached out a hand to her lap. Entwining his long fingers through hers, he settled their clasped hands in the hollow of her gown defining the place where her thighs joined as he rested the back of his hand against her softly rounded belly. His bold familiarity would've definitely been out of place in the company of others, but in the presence of *this* visitor, Adriana eagerly welcomed his intimacy and was not in the least bit embarrassed by his forwardness.

Pandora could hardly mistake the unspoken message Colton had just delivered. He had made his choice; he would have no other.

Feeling a burgeoning annoyance at the increasing frequency with which she was being uprooted by younger women, Pandora glared back at the couple. Knowing her most recent lover had done that very thing didn't assuage her pride one meager speck.

"Does Genevieve favor me?" she asked in an effort to redirect the man's attention away from where it obviously was.

Colton's answer was curt, evidencing his brewing vexation. "Not particularly."

"Then you, perhaps."

"Absolutely not."

"But surely she favors one of us."

"I see no resemblance whatsoever. Genevieve is dainty, blue-eyed, and dark-haired. 'Tis only the last trait either of us can lay claim to."

Pandora took exception to his blunt remark and lifted her chin. "Just what do you call dainty if I'm not that very thing?"

Colton laughed caustically. "Do you even know what the word means, Pandora?"

"Of course I do!" She flung her hand toward Adriana. "Am I not more dainty than she? Why, she stands nearly half a head taller than I!"

"And I'd venture to guess that even now, when my wife is far along with child, you must outweigh her by as much as two or three stone." Sweeping a hand toward Adriana, he declared with pride, "She is what one would call delicately beautiful, not only in appearance, but her character as well. I've never been able to say the same about you, Pandora."

The actress's eyes ignited at his audacious insult. She had always considered herself beautiful beyond the measure of most women, and it infuriated her to be compared unfavorably with one of her own gender, especially when that one was younger by six years or more. "You're only saying that because you're angry with me, Colton."

He managed a lame smile, as if only tolerably amused by her supposition. "Believe what you will, Pandora. I'll say no more."

Some moments later, Blythe carried in Genevieve and, after giving the child to Adriana, bobbed a pert curtsey and promptly took her leave. The baby squealed in glee as she recognized the man sitting beside her. Smiling at her obvious show of elation, Colton swept the tiny girl up in his arms and rose to his feet. Gently jouncing her in his arms, he approached the actress.

"This is Genevieve Ariella Wyndham," he announced to their visitor. "As you can see, Genie favors no one here." Now able to closely compare the child to the actress, Colton was led to speculate. "In fact, Genie is so completely different from you that I have to wonder if she's really yours at all. Her skin is fair, yours is not; her mouth is winsome and small; yours is—"

"Of course, she's my daughter!" Pandora insisted. "I even died giving her birth, though I'm very thankful to be alive today. I'm also intent on claiming my due, that being my daughter and my husband. You can't deny we're married, Colton. I have papers to prove it. As for the child, I remember quite clearly that she bore your ancestors' mark upon her buttock. If you've forgotten that small detail, let me remind you now by showing it to you."

She snatched the child from him, wrenching frightened screams from the tiny girl and in so doing bringing Adriana flying across the room in motherly concern. Pandora turned aside, preventing the younger woman access. When Adriana persisted, Pandora raised a shoulder to prevent her from reaching Genevieve.

"Genie doesn't like strangers," Adriana declared, moving around in another attempt to take the girl from the actress.

Once again, Pandora gave her an ignoring shoulder. "She's *my* daughter!"

"Please let me have her," Adriana pleaded in rising concern, and then reasoned, "If you must see her backside, I shall uncover it for you myself."

Another piercing scream of terror from Genevieve caused Pandora to cringe in pain. That seemed to convince the actress of the expediency of handing the girl over. She did so, almost shoving the baby into Adriana's arms in her haste to be rid of her. "Here! Take the nosy little whelp if you must! But I would have you show Colton the birthmark of his forebears."

Holding the bawling child close against her as she returned to the settee, Adriana rubbed a hand soothingly over Genie's back as she softly sang a lullaby against the girl's dark curls. Slowly the sobs were hushed and, in their stead, came the happy gurgling of a baby who felt secure in the arms of a loving, caring, familiar person.

Several moments passed and still Pandora saw no evidence that her demands would be adhered to anytime soon. Settling a glare upon the younger woman, Pandora asked sharply, "Well, are you going to show us the birthmark or not?"

Deliberately ignoring the woman, Adriana continued to play with Genie, patting her tiny hands together and gently chucking her chin as she sang a children's rhyme. Soon the girl was patting her hands together herself and squealing in delight as she wrinkled her nose and lifted a sparse-toothed grin to the woman who nurtured her with as much devotion as a mother.

Pandora lost patience and, in strident tones, railed at Adriana, "If you're not going to do as I asked, then I most definitely will!"

She stalked toward the pair menacingly, causing the hounds to leap to their feet. The animals' fangs were promptly bared in savage snarls as low growls issued forth. Just as quickly, the actress stumbled back, a trembling hand clasped to her throat.

Colton chuckled softly as he moved around behind the animals and settled once again on the settee beside his wife. "'Twould seem you are mistaken, Pandora."

Upon espying him beside them again, Genevieve squealed in glee and pumped her tiny arms up and down as if coaxing him to take her. Colton did so, much to her babbling delight.

The actress assumed the role of a poorly beleaguered mother, hoping to win sympathy from the man. "Are you so cruel, Colton, that you'd actually keep me from my own daughter?"

Slowly shaking his head at her antics, Colton chuckled in amusement. "Too bad you never learned the art of genuinely weeping on cue, Pandora. Perhaps I'd be more convinced of your sincerity. The simple truth is, even if you are in truth Genie's mother, she doesn't know you as such, and I'll not allow you to frighten her again. If it pleases my wife, she will show us the birthmark . . . when it suits *her*, not *you*."

Pandora could see no advantage in protesting his decision. If she had learned one thing about the retired colonel, he was not moved by feigned tears or plaintive whining. Her last ploy had achieved nothing. Deeming a more gracious manner favorable to her mission, she retreated with a muted, "Very well."

Not in the mood to accommodate their unwelcome guest, Adriana did indeed take her time baring Genie's backside, but when she finally acquiesced, to the astonishment of both Pandora and Colton there was only the faintest evidence left of what had purportedly been a Wyndham birthmark. Even that had become so faded in areas on the girl's buttock that it was no longer recognizable as anything closely resembling a bird in flight.

"Call Alice down here this instant," Pandora demanded in roiling rage. "I want to know what you've used to get rid of that mark. It must be some kind of deviant trick of yours, something you've rubbed on to hide it, because it was there clear as day when the girl was born. Alice will probably know what you've used and will take it off."

Colton was pleased to announce, "Alice was let go some time back, Pandora, along about the time we hired a new nursemaid, a woman to whom Genie has since become attached."

"The little brat would grow attached to anyone with a full teat!" Pandora snapped.

"She didn't seem that fond of Alice, and I can honestly say from my limited experience, I've never seen bigger breasts nor ones bared as freely as Alice seemed inclined to do. If truth be told, Genevieve seemed quite discomforted by the hag's neglect."

"Alice probably spoilt the chit and made her contrary."

"Genie was not contrary, but somber and listless. As you can see for yourself, that is no longer the case. What I'm wondering is where you ever managed to find someone as despicable and callous as Alice."

"I told you. She cleaned the theatre where I worked."

"Then I shall make a point of visiting her there to find out what concoction she applied to Genie's buttock, no doubt at your behest, so I'd think the babe was my daughter. Obviously since Alice hasn't been here to reapply it for the last two or three months, the mark has faded to what we now see."

As if stricken by an inner fear, Pandora stared at him, her eyes conveying something akin to panic before she managed a laugh. "I doubt if Alice would've gone back to the theatre. In fact, you probably won't ever be able to find her."

"Then I shall have to go to Oxford to search out the Reverend Goodfellow," Colton mused aloud. "I have friends there. They'll know where his church is."

Pandora waved a hand in a vague direction. "The good rector has moved beyond our shores. I'm not sure where. Ireland, perhaps. Somewhere far beyond my ken."

Colton managed an abortive laugh. "How convenient for me that he has."

The actress seemed taken aback by his statement, yet, at the same time, bemused by it. "What do you mean?"

"He can't serve as a witness to our marriage."

"Oh, but there's a license with your signature on it."

"Can you produce such a document? You'll have to, you know, if you intend to verify its authenticity before a magistrate. 'Twill be a requirement in your claim against me."

"No, I don't have it now, but I know where it is."

"Where?"

"Well . . ." Pandora chewed on a bottom lip, "I'm not sure just where I put it exactly since I've been gone for a while. It may take a little searching. It must be in one of my trunks I left with a friend."

"Reverend Goodfellow said he'd take it to his church in Oxford. Once I locate his church, I'll ask the rectors there to search for it, and then have the archbishop determine its legality, just in case it's a forgery of some kind. He'd certainly be willing to do that for me, considering he signed the license permitting my nuptials to Adriana."

"Your high and lofty friends won't be able to undo our marriage,

Colton," Pandora flung caustically. "You'll have to face the fact that our marriage is legal and binding. The document will prove that beyond your attempts to deny its validity."

"Well, if it's all the same to you, Pandora," Colton said almost pleasantly, "I'll proceed as I see fit." Canting his head, he gathered his brows in museful reflection. "Which leaves me wondering where I should actually begin my search. I seem to recall a story you told me a few years ago about your brother being so skilled at duplicating certificates that he was able to pass himself off as an Oxford scholar. Forging a marriage certificate would be fairly simple in comparison. Is your brother also an actor? Perhaps he did you a favor by performing the part of the good Reverend Goodfellow . . . for my benefit, of course. I shall have to look into that theory, especially if no one can tell me who this Reverend Goodfellow is or where his church is located."

Pandora's eyes flared with venom. "If you dare mention this matter to anyone outside your family, Colton, you'll only see yourself disgraced. 'Twill soon be bandied about that the woman you're living with is with child. I'm sure you can imagine the shame she'll suffer after word gets out that she's going to bear a child out of wedlock. For her sake, you'd better go no further with this matter. Besides, if you intend to seek out all the rectors at Oxford, you'll find them busy nowadays, what with the returning soldiers having so much difficulty finding work and food."

"Too busy to accept a worthy donation for lending their attention to such a matter, an amount that would allow them to help soldiers who can't find work or food for their starving families? I'm sure they'll take into consideration what I've already done in an effort to ease the hardships of our soldiers and to hire those who can work. Surely, in light of that, a rector of a church would not refuse me. But then, I can understand why you wouldn't want me to seek their help. If Reverend Goodfellow doesn't exist, then my investigation will likely lead to your brother's arrest and, quite possibly, your own."

Pandora wrung her hands as she paced about the room, feeling unduly pressed by the man's insistence. Over the years she had come to know him well enough to realize that he could be damnably persistent when he was inquisitive about a matter or when it came to getting at the truth. Hadn't her brother warned her about the colonel years ago? He hadn't ceased his investigation into the disappearance of munitions and gunpowder until those responsible had been hanged for treason for selling large stores of

English arms and supplies to the French. The fact that her brother had narrowly escaped with his life and the ragged clothes on his back had thereafter made him wary of trying to dupe the man. Nevertheless, the thought of being able to glean not only revenge but great wealth from the present Marquess of Randwulf had proven a strong incentive.

Laughing softly, Pandora commended herself on her skill as an actress as she deftly turned the subject away from the marriage certificate. "You needn't go to all that trouble looking for the document, Colton. If you really want me to remain silent about our marriage, you have only to show some generosity toward me instead of the soldiers. . . ."

Colton cocked a brow above a bland stare. Her offer was no less than what he had been expecting since finding her in his drawing room. "In what form?"

"Well, in a sizable payment that would keep me comfortable for the rest of my life."

"Extortion, in other words."

"Hardly that, Colton. I only ask for a little compassion, seeing as how I'm giving up my rightful place as marchioness and entitlement to . . ."— she swept a hand about to indicate everything within sight and much of what was not—"all this."

He grew pensive. "At the moment, I'm not in favor of accepting your offer, Pandora. It has always been my wont never to relent to the demands of those who try to wrest some gain from tragic or difficult situations, but I must consider others who'll likely be hurt by scandal. I shall give the matter further consideration. Should I agree to your terms, I'll need to know where you'll be staying in case I have to reach you. Or are you on your way back to the theatre?"

"I'm afraid I'm no longer employed there." Having recently suffered the pangs of bruised pride in her career, Pandora lifted her chin a notch, her feelings smitten by the brutal severing of what had once been a lucrative and, in the world of the theatre, a very prestigious position. "It seems another actress has been found to take my place, someone who's younger and supposedly more talented—but I'm sure in time they'll realize their mistake and come crawling after me, begging my forgiveness. But I digress from the pertinent issue. If you must know, I had planned on staying in the area for a time . . . this house, in fact, seeing that I *am* legally your wife." She elevated her chin in the guise of a suffering martyr, as if sorely wounded by his rejection. "But I can see you don't desire that now, since you've found someone younger to service your needs. Of course, you know your present love is, at best, only your mistress since I am still legally your wife. You won't be able to change that unless you obtain a divorce, but to do so would involve a lot of difficulty and notoriety."

As if he hadn't heard the woman, Colton jounced Genevieve up and down on his lap, educing gleeful shrills, which soon made the actress cringe and clasp her hands over her ears, as if in dire pain.

"Do you have to do that?" Pandora railed. "I fear my hearing will never be the same after today."

Upon espying Adriana's smiling face close by, Genie decided she wanted to bestow some loving attention on her and promptly gave her a slobbery wet kiss upon her mouth. Fairly often she had seen the man give the beautiful lady something similar while they were together. If that was not enough, the child sat down rather abruptly on what was left of Adriana's lap, and then, as if deciding that sitting wasn't actually what she really wanted, immediately sought to pull herself up by grabbing what was handy. Adriana almost yelped as the baby's tiny fist closed over the place where her gown protruded . . . and the vulnerable nipple beneath. A woman's breast was familiar territory to the youngster, who, upon leaning forward, searched about with an open mouth for the hidden peak.

Laughing at the innocent antics of the tiny girl, Colton took pity on his wife and lifted Genie onto his lap. As much as Adriana sought to ignore her discomfort, she felt like dissolving in pain. Leaning against her husband, she folded the shawl across the front of her bosom to hide the telltale wetness over her breast and tried to await the ebbing of her discomfort.

"Ah, the joys of parenthood," Pandora derided and then smirked pointedly toward the woman's softly rounded belly. " 'Twould seem you're doing your best to supply the Wyndhams with a new heir. Too bad 'twill be born a bastard."

Colton felt his wife shudder beneath the actress's taunt and promptly settled the back of his arm at a slant across her torso, as if to physically shield her from the other woman's ridicule. Laying a hand alongside her thigh, he snuggled her close against his side. "It's all right, my love," he murmured, seeking to ease her fears. "We'll come through this in good order. That much I promise you."

His assurances ignited the fires of jealousy in the one who observed his tender nurturing. "Well, you can tell her that if you think it will help,

Colton," Pandora sneered caustically, "but I really don't know how you're going to make good on your pledge, seeing as how the two of you aren't really married."

The woman had cause to stumble back as she saw the feral gleam in the gray eyes that turned upon her. Never had she seen Colton Wyndham in such a rage.

"You leave me no other choice, Pandora," he retorted coldly. "Be it known that I will now search heaven and hell for proof that the vows you and I exchanged were nothing more than a farce, and if they weren't, then I shall go before the highest magistrate in this land and plead my innocence of any wrongdoing and my ignorance that you were still alive when I married my wife. I can assure you, I will use every advantage at my disposal, even the fact that I'm a war hero, to gain the right to cast you out of my life forever and to seal my marriage with the only woman I've ever loved. Do you understand me?"

"I'll make you pay if you try to brush me off without a farthing!" the actress railed in ear-shattering tones, wrenching a frightened whimper from the tiny girl. "You won't be able to keep Genie. I'll demand my rights as a mother, and I won't stop until she's given back to me!"

"Then I'll just have to prove that she isn't yours, won't I?" Colton rejoined snidely. "It may take me a while, but I think I can do that."

A baleful gleam came into the actress's eyes. "You hopeless, besotted fool! You don't know what scandals you'll be facing if you dare refuse me. Believe me, I'll get my revenge on you and your child-bride, even if I have to bed down with every magistrate in this country in order to see it done. I can be immensely persuasive when I want to be. I'll play the victim to the hilt while I scheme and lie and tell all sorts of outlandish tales about you both. Once I'm finished, neither of you will be able to hold your heads up in London, much less around this paltry place you call your country estate."

Collecting her poise, Pandora assumed a more dignified posture and inclined her head briefly to Adriana and then to Colton. "Thank you for your hospitality, such as it was. . . ."

"One more thing before you leave, Pandora, if you don't mind," Colton interjected, his tone pleasant in spite of the threats the woman had just leveled against them.

Having already advanced toward the drawing room door, Pandora halted promptly, certain he had decided to relent. Stepping back to face him, she arched a brow expectantly. "Yes, what is it?"

"Perhaps you can save me the trouble of asking the performers of the theatre where you worked if Alice Cobble did indeed work there and was with child during the latter part of that period. If need be, I'll explain that you're trying to claim her child as your own. I'm sure there'll be those who'll be eager to negate the idea of your childbearing state as well as your dying performance in your town house the night you supposedly died.

"I'll also ask them if they know of the substance Alice Cobble used to create the birthmark on Genevieve's backside and to touch it up thereafter. It must've been some enduring stain to resist my attempts to rub it off that night, and of course, since Alice never saw my birthmark, I must assume that you made a pattern from my own. Did you trace it while I slept?" He laughed shortly. "I must have been pretty exhausted during that event, but then, there were many times when I was so physically and mentally drained from fighting that all I wanted to do was sleep. Perhaps with his forgery skills your talented brother reduced its likeness to an appropriate size for a baby and made different patterns for Alice to use as the child grew. Too bad for you that the crone was so despicable that no one here could abide having her around. Without Alice on hand to reapply it, the mark soon faded."

His theories stunned Pandora into momentary silence, for she had to wonder how in the world he had thought of everything they had done so precisely. The man was far more clever than even she had suspected.

Clasping a shaking hand to her throat, she stared at him as if unable to fathom what he was talking about. "I'm not sure I know what you mean."

"Before you knew who I was, you told me you were incapable of having children, and in the ensuing years, you never got with child. I'm sure you had other lovers, but I never saw any evidence that you had given birth. It was only after I was proclaimed a hero by the *London Gazette* that you actually learned that I was in line for the marquessate. Once I gained the title, you supposedly bore a child. Convenient for you, yet your barren state throughout our lengthy affair leaves me wondering how you came to have Genie. If Alice got with child while working as a cleaning woman at the theatre, then I'm sure you'd have seen some advantage in bartering a healthy stipend for her babe. Perhaps you might have even given her a purse at the time of your agreement and then promised her a larger one once she delivered into your hands a live newborn. After all, if your scheme worked, you'd become wealthy, and Alice certainly seemed callous enough to comply with that kind of bargain. Of course, that leaves me seriously bemused, how an ugly woman like Alice could bear a child as dainty and pretty as Genie. Yet if her own baby died, she'd have likely gone to great lengths to steal another woman's newborn in order to obtain the purse you promised her.

"So, again, what if . . ."—Colton lifted his wide shoulders in a casual shrug as he expounded further—"she stole the babe outright or practiced a bit of midwifery to get her hands on one. Whether boy or girl, it wouldn't have mattered, just as long as it was alive. Alice could've easily told Genie's real mother that her baby had died and left her own dead infant in her stead."

Canting his head thoughtfully, he continued to muse aloud for Pandora's benefit. "If I were to let it be known throughout the highways and byways of England that I'd give Alice a very handsome reward if she could provide undeniable evidence of the girl's parentage, I think she'd be willing to give me what I seek, even if it meant putting to naught your little gambit. Alice seems the kind of woman who'd want to hold some leverage over you to make sure she got her full due . . . or perhaps even more than she had actually been promised. Have you considered what the odds are of Alice having secured irrefutable proof that you're not Genie's mother?"

"I've heard enough of your inane gibberish," Pandora declared irately, seeing her hopes for great wealth being sundered by the man's speculations. "I'll be staying at the inn outside of Bradford until I hear from you, and if I don't, I'll let the authorities know you are twice wed and both your wives are living."

With that, she stalked out the drawing room and, upon seeing Harrison hastening toward the door, angrily waved him out of her way.

"Thank you kindly, but I can let myself out! And may you all be damned to hell!"

Twenty-one

❋

R OGER Elston glanced up from his bookkeeping as the bell on the front door heralded the entrance of a customer. His eyes lit up instantly when he saw the lady, for she seemed to have the same bold manner of the actresses he had once been wont to visit in London. In fact, he thought he recalled seeing this one perform while he had still been employed at the orphanage. Once upon a time, he had had to save up enough coin to indulge what had then been his favorite pastime, viewing the performers in their provocative costumes. Now he was able to afford and *demand* much more from the funds he pilfered from the mill.

Though the overflowing bosom of this one was partially covered by a robe, the pale, luscious mounds seemed to test the restraint of her silk bodice, as if eager to be free. The woman didn't seem to mind that he stared at her overt display. Indeed, she smiled at him rather coyly before bending forward to search the merchandise laid out on the table between them, making it obvious that whatever undergarment she wore beneath, it was meant more for the purpose of enticing rather than concealing. His hand itched to explore the deep valley between those orbs and tweak the nipples that thrust impudently outward through the cloth of her gown.

Pandora smiled at the handsome young man, allowing her eyes to briefly scan his narrow trousers. He didn't seem the least bit abashed by his display, but awaited her reaction as he offered her a half-grin. He wasn't as old or perhaps as experienced as the men she had been enjoying as lovers in recent years, but she could imagine he'd be willing to do *anything* to please her. After Colton Wyndham's adamant refusal even to consider her as his wife, she needed to reaffirm her appeal for her own peace of mind. At one time, she had been convinced the colonel really cared for her. Now she had to wonder if that had only been part of his persuasive charm, making every woman feel special while she was in his arms. His wife had certainly seemed to idolize him, but then, Pandora mused resentfully, it had appeared her love had been returned tenfold.

Smiling coyly at the young man, she offered an explanation for her presence. "I left my shawl in London and have need of something to keep me warm tonight while I'm here in this quaint little town. I wasn't expecting it to turn cool this evening, but as you've probably discovered for yourself, it has. Would you happen to have a shawl or something that would suffice to keep me warm?"

Hastily Roger stepped to a cabinet in the corner and produced one of the mill's finest woolen wraps. The beauty's eyes widened in delight as he shook it out and displayed its exquisiteness.

"How lovely!" Pandora crooned excitedly, admiring the piece. Just as quickly, her brows gathered. Pursing her lips, she feigned a look of dismay. "But as much as I desire the piece, sir, I fear it's beyond my means."

"For such a rare individual as yourself, madam, the piece would require nothing more than a few moments of your time," Roger breathed, luxuriating in her sweet fragrance as he removed the robe. In its stead, he draped the ornately worked woolen shawl around her shoulders, managing to brush his hand over a ripe breast before tucking the ends of the wrap around her arms. Standing close behind her, he ogled the half-concealed melons with growing eagerness and leaned down to nuzzle her ear. "I can make it worth your while, my beauty."

"Really?" Pandora cut her eyes askance, awaiting his proposition, and didn't mind hugging herself to tempt him beyond his means to resist. In ready compliance her bodice gapped away from the pale orbs, bringing into view their rosy peaks. "The shawl is so wondrously warm. I'd *love* to have it."

Roger stared at the luscious melons, seriously tempted to slip a hand down inside her bodice, but he couldn't chance an employee finding them, for it would then be all over town that he had been dallying with a customer. "I have a private room near," he murmured, extending a hand to indicate its direction. "It has a comfortable chaise where we can sit . . . and talk together."

"Do you have some port?" Pandora inhaled deeply until she was nearly out of her bodice and then released her breath, once again leaving her bosom in full view for barely an instant. At an early age, she had learned the art of enticing men and had gained much from their eagerness to savor what she had or could do to pleasure them. "I'm so in the mood for a glass of port."

Roger smiled. "As a matter of fact, I do."

Stepping away, he indicated the dark hallway leading to the private room he had made secure. Never had he imagined he'd be using it so soon after outfitting it with necessities. Much to his delight, such an opportunity was now at hand, and he just couldn't resist. He had even padded the walls to some extent to prevent workers from becoming curious about what he was doing within. Taking a nap was one thing, fulfilling his every fantasy with a wanton was another.

"Come into my private parlor, dear lady, and I shall pour you a libation and we can drink a toast to your new shawl."

Pandora slipped an arm through his and hugged it close against her breast. "I shall never forget how generous you've been, giving me such a costly gift. How can I ever repay you?"

"Your company for a time is payment enough."

Pandora's eyes lit up as he pushed open the door of the inner room. It was furnished extravagantly with an ornate credenza upon which sat a silver tray with several crystal decanters containing different brews. A half dozen silver candelabrum stood between a like number of standing mirrors and these in turned encircled a wide, luxurious, red velvet chaise, upon which lay a filmy red peignoir. It was fairly simple to surmise that the occupants of the chaise would be able to observe from every angle everything that transpired there.

Strolling across the room, Pandora sank upon the cushioned piece and found herself duplicated many times over in her audience of mirrors. She sighed in pleasure as she stroked a hand over her thigh, managing to hike up the hem of her gown to show a trim calf. Then she cooed in admiration as she lifted the negligee before her face and considered the room through its thin veil. "You must be rich to afford such luxuries."

"I'm rich enough to afford this and a few other things besides," Roger boasted, locking the door behind him.

"Such as?"

He strolled forward, doffing his coat. "A mistress who'd be willing to comply with my every desire and whim, and one with a vivid imagination of her own." His fingers plucked open his shirt. "I'm not an ordinary man and would be very generous with a woman who could overlook a few minor inconveniences in order to please me. Is not variety your pleasure, too?"

"How generous?" Pandora asked, licking her lips in anticipation. She flicked her eyes over his chest and shoulders as he tossed his shirt aside; she had seen more manly brawn in her years as an actress, but the lad had a certain boyish appeal. It had been some time since she had felt inclined to yield her favors to a mere boy, but then, she had a need to feel young again.

Roger reached inside the credenza and produced a pair of gold earrings. Dangling them before her eyes, he murmured warmly, "This is only a small sampling. There is much more to be had should you please me."

"Well, these will do for starters," Pandora assured him, smiling warmly as she plucked them from his grasp. Doffing her own, she attached the heavy rings to her ears and reclined upon the chaise as she drew up her skirts to show a shapely thigh entirely bereft of pantaloons. Taking his hand, she stroked it along the shapely limb. "In return, I'm willing to give you more than a fair sampling of what I can do to pleasure a gent."

"We'll get to that part in good time, my beauty, but first, I have other things in mind."

W HAT are we going to do?" Adriana asked later that night after Colton had stretched out in bed beside her.

He sighed heavily. "As much as it distresses me to search for Alice, that may be our only option if we intend to prove that we're legally married, my love."

"Do you think we are?" his wife asked worriedly.

"I can almost promise you we are, my sweet," Colton murmured, wrapping an arm about her shoulders and pulling her close against him. "Pandora became very nervous even at the first when I started asking about Reverend Goodfellow, which leads me to think that he was no rector at all.

Perhaps he *was* her brother or some actor she had promised to pay once she received monies from me. I'm not sure exactly what I'm missing here, but from the moment you bared Genie's bottom and found nothing more than a faded blotch, something has been nagging at me, some detail or fact I fear I may be overlooking. Perhaps 'tis nothing more than a memory or an event from the past, but as much as I try, I can't seem to bring it clearly to mind."

"It seems rather wicked to make love when we're not sure if we're married," Adriana ventured beneath his warming kisses a moment later.

Colton pulled back to view her worried face and gave her a teasing grin as he tugged the sheet down past the lustrous orbs. Gently he plied a forefinger around a soft nipple, evoking a shiver of pleasure from the one who watched him with adoring eyes. "Haven't you ever wanted to feel positively wicked once in your life, my love?"

His tongue replaced his finger and moved with intoxicating slowness over a pliant peak, causing Adriana to catch her breath at the sensations he created within her. At the gentle urging of his hand, she readily opened herself to him, making no pretense as to her own desires and cravings. Threading her slender fingers through his thick crop of hair, she whispered with bated breath near his ear, "If this is wickedness, my love, then surely I am doomed, for I have become your most ardent slave."

BENTLEY had taken Philana to the Wyndham residence in London two days previous. The following morning a small army of servants accompanied her to the Kingsley residence in Mayfair a short distance away. She wasn't looking forward to sorting through the possessions of her late niece, but she had determined to put the ordeal behind her. Even as loyal as their servants were, she couldn't leave them with such a perplexing task, for they wouldn't have any idea what to do with the furnishings and everything else that had belonged to the young couple other than pack it all up and load it into endless carts. If there was anything that could be donated, sold, or thrown away prior to storing it in the attic or upper rooms of their house on Park Lane, then it would indeed save on the labor of getting it up there and the available space.

What Philana came across as she directed the servants in the careful wrapping of family portraits made her cease her work and return to the

Wyndhams' Park Lane mansion posthaste. The next morning, Bentley lent her a helping hand into the landau, and just before dinner that evening, she arrived at Randwulf Manor. After hurrying up the stone steps to the front portal, she swept into the house and then went in search of Colton, having been told by Harrison that her son was working in the library on documents he intended to present before Parliament.

Having missed the earlier sessions because of his most recent wound and his three-month recuperation during his honeymoon, Philana knew that Colton felt pressed to make up for lost time. In that quest, he had also been making preparations to move his family to their London mansion where they would remain, at least for the most part, until August when Parliament would again adjourn well in time for the hunting season.

Adriana had spread a quilt out on the oriental rug in the library and had settled on it to play with Genie. The two of them were well in view of Colton whose laughter was often evoked by the playful antics of the child, who seemed to delight in wrinkling her tiny nose and flirting with either him or the lady.

When Philana entered, Adriana rose immediately to her feet and lifted the happily squealing Genie in her arms. "Mama Philana, we weren't expecting you back for several days."

The baby was especially delighted to see her grandmother whose eyes seemed riveted upon her. Placing a trembling hand beneath her tiny chin, Philana lifted the small face to catch the dwindling light from the glass-paned doors. As she studied the girl's face intently, sudden tears brightened her blue eyes, and then a joyful grin swept over her whole face.

"What is that you're carrying there?" Adriana inquired, inclining her head toward the small, cloth-covered painting her mother-in-law held close to her breast.

"A portrait, my dear, one you and Colton must study very carefully before I ask you whether or not I'm mad."

"You, mad?" Adriana chortled at the woman's humor. "Well, if you are, Mama Philana, then the rest of us must be raving lunatics. Tell us, what madness are you imagining?"

With a graceful sweep of her hand, Philana motioned them toward the settee. "Please, take a seat there together," she urged, and as they complied in some bemusement, she propped the cloth-covered painting up in a wing chair located across from them, and turned up the wick in a lamp residing on a table next to it. When the couple had settled themselves, she presented her request. "I would like both of you to tell me if you recognize the child in this portrait."

Again the two exchanged bemused glances before Colton gathered his brows and acknowledged, "After being gone so many years from home, Mother, I don't have much of a recollection of family members. I seriously doubt that I'll be of much help identifying the person in the portrait."

"Do your best, dear," she urged with a confident smile. "'Twill not be as difficult a task as you might imagine."

Slowly Philana lifted the cloth from the portrait and stood back in nervous anticipation to allow her son and daughter-in-law to study the painting as long as necessary. Yet as soon as Adriana and Colton saw it, they frowned in confusion and then peered up at Philana.

"Where did you find that?" Colton asked. "And how can it be? We never had an artist in here to paint Genie's portrait."

Philana lifted her trembling chin as tears began to stream down her cheeks. "It isn't Genie, my son."

"But who . . . ?"

"'Tis Edythe, when she was just a little older than Genie is now."

The jaws of the couple fairly sagged in astonishment for barely an instant, then Colton leapt from the settee and, in two long strides, reached the chair. His wife wasn't far behind him. Snatching up the portrait, Colton tilted it in order to catch more of the light as Adriana looked over his arm.

"I could almost swear that's Genie," he declared.

"'Tis quite a shock when you first see it, isn't it? And then you find yourself wondering how anyone could have painted our darling little girl's portrait without our knowledge." Philana was having difficulty controlling what could only have been joyful tears and hurriedly dragged a handkerchief from her purse. "After the servants discovered it, I had to find better light myself to make sure I wasn't dreaming."

Colton's brows gathered in confusion. "But how do you know for a certainty that it *is* Edythe's portrait?"

"Her name and the date are on the back, dear. It was painted when she was only one year old."

"What are you thinking, Mother?" Colton queried, not wishing to voice any conjectures that might upset her.

Philana didn't hesitate to express her opinion. "I believe without a doubt that Edythe gave birth to Genie before she died. God only knows what miracle brought the child into our home, but that is what I believe with all my heart."

"And the child who was found with Edythe?" Adriana probed, and then turned to peer up at her husband. "Do you suppose your conjectures were right after all about Alice Cobble losing her child and then stealing another to give to Pandora? If her babe did indeed die as you suggested, then she might've carried it with her with the intent of stealing another wherever she could and leaving her dead infant in its stead. A live newborn would've been the only sure way she'd have received what Pandora promised her. If she came upon the soldiers while they were chasing the Kingsleys' coach or rummaging through it, she'd have likely hidden herself for fear of being killed and then searched the conveyance after the soldiers took their leave just to see what she could find. The physicians did say there was evidence that someone had helped Edythe deliver her babe after the coach overturned, because the cord had been cut and tied. If Edythe was indeed in the process of giving birth when Alice searched the conveyance, then Alice would've probably been overjoyed at the prospect of getting her hands on a live newborn to take to Pandora."

"That sounds logical to me," Colton acknowledged, "especially since the boy who was found with Edythe bore the Wyndham mark on his rump. That's what I've been trying to remember since Pandora's visit. There was no other way the babe could've had that mark. Father would never have bedded Edythe, and I certainly didn't."

A smile traced across Philana's lips. "Edythe was too much of a lady and too much in love with Courtland for me to consider that she'd have gone behind his back to do such a thing. Sedgwick never gave me any reason to believe he had ever been untrue to me. We were always together, mainly at his insistence. Ofttimes, he avouched that I was as much a part of him as his own heart."

"Of course you were, Mama Philana," Adriana reassured her gently, slipping an arm around the older woman's waist. "Throughout all the years I can remember, that seemed the way of it. He loved you very, very much."

Philana nodded, growing firm in that belief. "Alice likely put the Wyndham birthmark on her son's backside while he was still alive, but couldn't take it off once he died. If you suffer any doubt, consider how long Genie's mark has lingered just since Alice's departure. All Alice would've cared about anyway were the coins she'd been promised. I just hope she didn't kill my niece in her greed."

"'Tis unlikely she did, Mother, considering that Courtland and the driver were both dead," Colton replied. "Still, if she *did* kill Edythe, then she should pay for that crime. I will notify the authorities to be on the watch for the woman."

"Even if Alice did kill Edythe, she'll lie and say she didn't," Philana stated with conviction. "And who of Edythe's family is in a position to say she did? No one."

"Now that we have the portrait, we'll be able to offer some evidence that Genie was Edythe's daughter, and that Alice gave the babe to Pandora." Colton nodded thoughtfully. "Of course, even if we do manage to find Alice, we'll have to wade through her lies to get to the truth, but a threat of a hanging might just shorten her lying tongue."

Philana heaved a lengthy, wavering sigh. "I feel as if a terrible weight has been lifted from my shoulders. All this time, I'm been grieving over Edythe and her family when her daughter has been here all along offering me solace. It truly seems a miracle, and tonight I shall begin, and continue henceforth, to express my heartfelt gratitude in my prayers, first because we have Genie with us, and second, because there's reason to believe she truly is Edythe's daughter."

FELICITY watched the entrance of the mill as the last of the workers filed out and then, in heightening impatience, perched upon the window seat in her father-in-law's bedchamber as she awaited Roger's departure. He had told her earlier that he would have to take the cart on an errand after the mill closed, and that he wouldn't be home for supper. His absence would give her another chance to look through the ledgers on the remote possibility that she had overlooked some pertinent information that would help identify the people whose initials matched the ones she had found.

As anxious as she had been to return to the mill and peruse Roger's ledgers after her first search, he had seemed reluctant to break away from his office, as if compelled to stay and finish his work, whatever that was. He had ordered her to bring his food to him at noon, more than the usual he had said since he would have someone helping him, but, once again, she had been warned not to go much beyond the front door.

While delivering his food, Felicity had espied quite by accident a small vial of a liquid substance wedged between books in the glass cabinet behind his desk. Roger had been talking to workers down the hall at the time and had had his back to her. Deeming it fairly safe to creep to the bookcase, she had opened the door very quietly and slipped the bottle into her apron pocket before gently closing the cabinet. At his sudden approach, her heart had nearly leapt into her throat, but she had raced out, telling him over her shoulder that she had forgotten his bread and had to run back to the house to fetch it, which had actually been the truth and a fortuitous oversight she had decided after espying the vial. In the house, she had dribbled a tiny portion of the contents into a clean vial and then had slipped the original back into her pocket before racing back to the mill. Roger had been nowhere in sight when she returned the vial to the bookcase in his office. Leaving the basket of bread on his desk, she had scampered out.

Anxious to know exactly what the substance in the vial was, Felicity had immediately taken what she had collected to Mr. Carlisle and asked him to identify it if at all possible. He had first sniffed it and then tasted a tiny bit on his tongue. Then he had smiled with a kindly twinkle in his eye and announced that it was merely laudanum, nothing more. Greatly relieved by his answer, she had dared hope that Roger really hadn't poisoned his father in spite of her recent suspicions.

Felicity straightened on the window seat as she realized that Roger was finally emerging from the mill. He seemed in some haste as he donned his frock coat and began to arrange his cravat. He raised a knee to climb into the cart, but halted abruptly, lowered his foot to the ground, and then, after glancing around, began fastening his breeches.

Felicity raised a brow curiously, wondering what he had been doing this time, if it had merely been an oversight after visiting the privy or if he had been involved in something a bit more sordid; but then, she wasn't really interested in his prurient diversions. In fact, if he found a mistress who'd demand *all* his attention, she'd be greatly relieved. At least then she wouldn't have to worry about her baby.

Felicity waited a quarter hour after the cart disappeared from sight before she finally deemed it safe to leave the house. Where Roger was concerned, it was wise to be cautious, she had learned. He was not always predictable, especially when it came to remembering things. As much as he thought himself mentally astute, in her opinion he fell far short of that mark. If he had forgotten anything and been forced to turn back for either that or some other reason, she didn't want him to catch her with her nose in his ledgers.

Felicity flitted across the moonlit yard, and then pressed back into the deeper shadows of the overhanging roof for another moment or two to make certain that no one was roaming about. Reassured that she was all alone, she thrust a hand into the pocket of her apron and withdrew the weighty ring of keys she had found in Edmund Elston's tall secretary in his bedchamber. She had absolutely no idea what the individual keys opened, but she was curious to find out. After her last intrusion into the mill, Roger had never left the spare key in the house again, and she had not been able to find another until she had thought of searching through Edmund's room. The Elstons, she had come to believe, were mean and conniving men, and because of that reason, she felt a need to protect her-self, or they'd likely dispense with her in one fashion or another.

Finally finding a key that would unlock the front door of the shop, she slipped inside, closed the portal behind her, and then secured her privacy by latching it. To further provide for her safety, she closed the shutters over the windows. She had no wish to be unduly surprised if Roger returned sooner than expected. In providing an alternative way of escape in case she'd have to race out the rear of the building, she searched through the keys again until she found one for the back door. She just hoped she'd have time to lock it behind her before her husband entered the premises.

Keenly aware that she'd have to snuff the flame posthaste if she heard the cart returning, she lit the lantern hanging over the desk. Moments later she became totally immersed in the ledger, noticing that more expen-ditures had been entered, this time exorbitant amounts. Beside them were the initials E.R. She also saw where a smaller sum had been deducted, in itself quite hefty. M.T. had been marked on the line near the latter. Yet, as many times as she searched through the entries, even going back repeatedly from front to back through the ledger, she just couldn't seem to find names to match.

Restlessly she paced the confines of the office, thoughtfully flicking the end of a pen against her cheek. E.R.! M.T.! Who were these people to whom her husband was giving large sums? If he paid for either the furni-ture or the new room with any of the mill's funds, surely he'd have been given a receipt with a name on it or some such thing.

Returning to the desk, she braced her hands on its edge and stared at the book upside-down, racking her brain as she ran through a mental list of Roger's acquaintances. Basically, he had no friends to speak of, especially among the male populace. Women, it seemed, were merely a tool he used for his lascivious purposes. Bereft of close companions as he was, he had to be paying business acquaintances for services rendered and undisclosed. But here again, she wasn't cognizant of any who had initials to match those noted in the ledger.

"E.R. and M.T.," she hissed, angry with herself for not being able to find any clue to the identity of the two. "E.R. . . . E.R. . . . E.R. . . . Elston? Elston?" Her eyes brightened as the thought came, "Elston, Roger?"

Though she knew it was only a twinkling of a possibility that the initials were actually his, only reversed, she searched her memory for someone with the remaining initials, T.M., when turned about. The only name she could recall was the one Mr. Carlisle had given her, Thaddeus Manville, the apothecary from London. And it just so happened that Roger was fond of going to London, and Mr. Manville was especially partial to Elston's woolens. Or was he?

A dull thud from somewhere nearby caused Felicity's heart to lurch in sudden trepidation. Hurriedly she turned down the wick in the lamp and crept to the front windows, where she peered out through a niche in the shutters. As frantically as she searched the darkness beyond the mill for Roger's cart, she couldn't see any sign of it. Another thump snatched a gasp from her and made her whirl abruptly about as she realized she had mistaken the direction from whence the first sound had come.

Cautiously she tiptoed into the hall, half afraid that Roger had gone around behind the mill and entered from the back. "Roger? Is that you?"

Once again, her heart nearly jumped from her chest as another bump intruded into the answering silence. It seemed to come from Roger's newly furnished private chamber, a room she had never been permitted to see, much less enter. She crept to the door and jiggled the handle. Promptly, three loud thumps came against the door from the interior of the room.

"Is anyone there?" she called through the portal, but immediately felt like a dunce for asking such a ludicrous question. Of course, someone was there, and whoever it was obviously wanted out!

Not more than two days ago, Felicity had been ordered by Roger to go to the alehouse and fetch him a brimming pitcher of the dark brew. Upon her return, she had found him standing at the door of his new room with an arm raised and his hand on the molding above the portal. At her entrance, he had made a show of yawning and stretching, which had seemed rather far-fetched considering she had seen enough to know he had shoved something onto that narrow strip of wood. In spite of his silly pretense, it had been all-too-apparent what he had been doing ... what else but hiding a key? Perhaps it was just as well that she hadn't remembered that incident right off. Otherwise, she'd have already been confronting the person imprisoned in the room.

Curiosity had a way of leading a person into an area that could well prove life-threatening. Felicity was well aware of that fact and yet she considered her choices, whether to ignore the thumps and continue perusing the ledgers or to discover the identity of the person Roger had secluded in his private room. The decision was hardly debatable, at least not for someone who had already discovered the evil lurking behind a handsomely boyish face. She was fearful enough of Roger without allowing his unrelenting intimidations to control every facet of her life. She had to see what he was up to this time.

Dragging a chair near the door, Felicity climbed atop the seat, slid slender fingers along the uppermost part of the doorjamb, and promptly found what she had sought. "Sly you are not, Roger!"

Clasping the key to her breast, she stepped to the floor and, once again, paused to consider the consequences of her actions. Although determined to release Roger's prisoner, she was also more than a little wary, not knowing what would likely happen if she erred in thinking her husband was the only culprit. *But he had already proven he was one of the foulest sort!* reason argued. Resolved to find out the identity of the one he had locked behind the door, she fetched a lantern and placed it upon the seat of the chair to lend her much needed light as she tried to fit the key into the lock. Shaking fingers definitely hindered her progress. Yet she had to know what and who was in the forbidden room.

Thrusting the key into the tiny niche, Felicity turned it once, heard a "click" as the lock was freed, and was about to reach for the knob when the door was snatched inward. Almost immediately, out stumbled a woman, totally naked except for wildly snarled hair flowing almost to her waist. Her face and body were terribly bruised. On the inside of her thighs, matted blood had dried, sending cold shivers of dread through Felicity. She entertained no smallest doubt that Roger was responsible for the woman's sorry condition.

"Help me," the wild-looking female pleaded in desperation. "Please, oh, please, help me escape that vile madman. He'll likely kill me if I remain."

"Who are you?" Felicity asked, completely stunned by what she was seeing. She had never dreamt that Roger would go so far as to actually hold a woman captive for his prurient purposes. "Why are you here?"

"I'm Pandora Mayes, an actress from London," the woman explained, on the verge of tears. "I came to the mill to buy a shawl yesterday. Or was it a year ago? It certainly seems as if an eternity has passed since then." She shivered in revulsion. "The miller said he'd give me the shawl if I'd be nice to him, but I never imagined what he'd demand of me in return or that he'd keep me a prisoner to serve his demented pleasure night and day. He forced me to drink some laudanum before he left me last night, but I don't think I could've escaped anyway, not after what he did to me. I've never been so violated in so many different ways in all my life. I thought I'd die before he finished with me. I've been so frightened, and I'm too ashamed to say what he did." She shuddered convulsively. "I must leave here before he returns, or he'll kill me. I know he will! He promised he'd come back tonight, to continue with what he had started before he left. He said he had to run an errand, and then he'd be back. Knowing he'd be gone for a while, I took a chance that someone would hear me. Now I'm free, and I must get away. There's no telling what more he'll do if I can't find a way to escape."

The actress's sorely used condition and the terror she conveyed at the idea of falling into Roger's hands again brought Felicity face to face with the realization that her husband had treated her fairly well in comparison. Knowing how difficult it had been to tolerate his abuse herself, she was moved by compassion and mentally searched for a way to help the woman escape. Her grandfather came to mind.

Laying a hand upon the woman's arm, she stated what was obvious. "You can't leave here without any clothes. Do you have any?"

"The miller refused to return them. He told me to wash and perfume myself before he returned, but I've done neither."

"I'll run back to the house and fetch some clothes. If you can, you'd better get washed. You . . . ah . . . smell . . . used."

"I *have* been *used*, numerous times in fact . . . by that *filthy bastard!*"

Although Roger had vented worse language in her presence, Felicity had never heard a woman spew forth the like. "Ready yourself as much as you can while I'm gone," she urged. "I'll return shortly with something for you to wear. My grandfather has friends who'll see you safely to London, but we'll have to walk up the hill from here. Do you have any shoes?"

"That's the only thing that sorry lecher left me," Pandora sneered in venomous hatred of the man.

Briefly considering the voluptuousness of the woman, Felicity decided forthwith that it would be futile to bring back anything more than a nightgown and a cloak. Although they were nearly the same height, the woman was far more buxom and generally fleshier. With her long, frizzy hair, painted nails, smeared rouge, and eyes smudged with black kohl, she definitely looked the sort to be found in houses of ill repute.

Felicity sprinted back to the house, but in her haste to return with the clothing she had collected, she failed to notice the cart parked in the lane on the far side of the mill. Snatching open the door of the office, she rushed in, busily separating the garments until she realized Roger was standing in the middle of the room with arms akimbo and his scar-separated brow arched to a lofty height above a menacing glare. Letting out a frightened screech, she whirled about-face and made a frantic attempt to flee. Immediately he was behind her, catching a hand in her hair.

"So, my little dove, you were curious, eh?" he snarled in her ear. "Well, we all might as well have a glass of port while I figure out what to do with the two of you. Of course, I could take you both to London and sell you to the brothels there. . . ." He snickered snidely as Felicity clutched a trembling hand protectively over her protruding stomach. "As dainty and fetching as you are, my sweet, you'd probably lose our chit ere the first week is out. The men will certainly be delighted to taste such a tempting little morsel, even if you are with child."

He sent her spinning across the room and chortled in amusement as her haphazard dervish ended in a rather ungraceful plop into a chair beside Pandora, who was literally quaking with terror. The tears the woman had wept just since Roger's reappearance had dissolved the rest of the kohl lining her eyelids, leaving black streaks coursing down her cheeks.

Roger sauntered about, taking his own precious time making his den of iniquity secure as he locked his private haven, bolted the front door, and latched the shutters. As he passed through the room, he smiled insipidly at the pair. "We can discuss where I'll be taking you over some port, so please don't stray while I'm fetching it, ladies. Should you dare, I can promise you that I'll make you both extremely sorry you disobeyed me. I have this cruel little device called a barbed rod. The metal spikes on the end will likely take the flesh off your backs in short order."

He disappeared down the hallway and, after a lengthy moment, finally reemerged bearing three goblets. Betwixt the fingers of one hand he clasped the stems of two as he lifted a third to his lips and leisurely sipped from its rim. Holding the portion in his mouth to savor it more fully, he rolled his eyes as if transported to paradise and then smiled as he swallowed the liquid.

"Divine, if I may so myself," he boasted, as if entertaining two ladies from the upper classes.

He extended the hand bearing the two goblets to Pandora. Fearful of refusing, she peered up at him warily and, with badly shaking fingers, plucked one free of his grasp.

"You needn't be so terrified, my pet. Drink the port. 'Twill give you courage. Who knows? I may even take pity on you and finish what we started earlier. My wife could use a few lessons in the art of making a customer happy before she is forced to yield to their various requests."

A convulsive shudder went through Pandora, evidencing her own growing horror of what he suggested.

Stepping before Felicity, Roger presented the last glass to her and perused her face admiringly as she accepted it with a cautious glance upward. "You are a real beauty, my pet," he mused aloud, caressing her cheek in a display of affection. "I shall be greatly saddened to take you to London. After all, I did love you . . . in my fashion . . . but, of course, not as much as I loved Lady Adriana."

A sharp gasp was wrenched from Pandora, who looked up at him in surprise, drawing a curious smile from the miller. Immediately she dropped her gaze to her naked thighs, fearful of claiming any portion of his attention.

"Ah, 'twould seem you are acquainted with Lady Adriana. How so?" When she failed to answer him, he leaned toward her and railed at the top of his lungs, making both women start and tremble violently in their chairs. *"How do you know her, slut? You're not of the peerage!"*

"L-Lord Col-Colton," Pandora stuttered fearfully. "I've known him . . . for some time."

"I shall assume *that* was before he returned and married the beauteous Adriana. . . ." Although he waited, he had to resort to a vicious backhand blow across the actress's face before he gained an answer.

"Y-yes, I-I only m-met her yesterday or m-maybe it was the other day. I c-can't remember. I've l-lost track of time," Pandora stuttered. Reaching up with the back of her hand, she wiped away the thin trail of blood that trickled from a corner of her mouth. "I n-never saw or even h-heard of h-her until I went to Randwulf Manor the other day."

"A regal beauty, isn't she?" Roger mused, sipping his port with a lofty air. "I almost had my pleasure of her, but his lordship intruded ere I could force myself upon her. Of course, I shall never forget how she thrashed me before he appeared. I owe her for that. Sometime very, very soon, I'm going to have her bleeding and begging me for mercy, and then I'll make her do everything I want. She'll be sorry she didn't let me make love to her then."

Felicity peered askance at Pandora as the trembling woman lifted the wineglass to her lips. Briefly they exchanged glances, and Felicity frowned, shaking her head warningly, but Roger bent toward her with a smile, halting her attempt.

"What's the matter, dear? Are you jealous?" He smirked. "You needn't be. The wench means nothing to me, merely a plaything with whom to wile away my evenings, a knowledgeable diversion, to be sure, but nothing meaningful. I would've returned to you once I became bored with her. That was not far off, believe me. Her continuous sobbing and pleading wore on my temper until I was nigh ready to thrash her."

"Are you really going to take me to a brothel in London, Roger?" Felicity asked, amazed that she had been able to get the words out through her fear-constricted throat. She had never been so frightened in all her life. "It would likely mean the loss of your child."

He waved a hand with a casual air, dismissing that issue as none of his concern. "I care not for children, nor your rounding shape, my dear. However, I will miss you to some extent. I'm immensely fond of beautiful women, and you're among the finest, I must admit."

"But not to be compared to Lady Adriana," she managed in a snide tone, as if she truly resented that fact.

"Oh, I see you *are* jealous, Mrs. Elston," he crooned and then chortled as if amused by the idea. "You were certainly envious when Lord Colton turned his attention upon her, weren't you? Oh, I know how you adored the man, my dear, but one of these days he's going to be sorry he ever came back from the wars. I intend to have his cods on a roasting stake, and then I'm going to mount Adriana as many times as I please while he's forced to watch. I owe him that before I kill him."

Felicity couldn't resist asking, "Do you hate everyone, Roger?"

"Why, no, my dear. I don't hate you. Or Adriana. Haven't I treated you well and loved you in my fashion?"

"In your fashion?" Felicity demanded incredulously. "Hurting me whenever you touched me? Is that what you call love? Or would it be better described as brutality?"

He waved a hand arrogantly to dismiss her argument. "There are definitely those I hate. Some I've shrewdly removed, and no one's been the wiser. Others have yet to feel my revenge. I had Lord Colton in my sights once after rallying men to aid me, but he lived in spite of the hole I put in his back, and he married Adriana that very same night. I hated him for that! I hated his father before him, and I took my revenge upon him, subtle though it was, but that is neither here nor there. What I must decide at this present moment is what to do with you fair damsels."

Roger strode to the far end of the shop, allowing Felicity to dump the contents of her goblet into a tall copper kettle that sat beside her. Pandora craned her neck to see what she had done and then briefly sneered at the waste of good port. Before Felicity had a chance to stop her, the actress raised her own glass and finished the wine off with one flip of her wrist. Felicity stared at her in paralyzed horror, knowing with a certainty that she had just gulped down a lethal dose of arsenic.

The miller turned and, seeing their drained glasses, set aside his own. "Time to be about the business of taking you two to wherever I'm going to take you," he announced and then gestured toward the nightgown and cloak that had fallen from Felicity's arm when she had entered and which now lay in a heap upon the floor. "You might as well let dear Pandora wear those things you brought over, my dear. 'Twould be difficult to explain to anyone we pass why I have a naked woman riding in the back of my cart."

Beneath Roger's smirking gaze, Pandora dragged on the nightgown and then wrapped the cloak about herself. As he silently gestured for her to move toward the door, she complied, afraid to do otherwise. Bidden in like manner, Felicity followed the woman, and a few short moments later, the two of them were climbing into the back of the cart as Roger freed the reins.

It didn't take Felicity long to realize they were not heading toward London after all, but in more of a westerly direction, toward the rolling countryside interspersed with lofty manors and sizable estates through which the River Avon twined. It was also an area where Roger could dispense with them fairly easily and they wouldn't soon be found, if at all. If she didn't manage to get away from him alive, it would probably take weeks, perhaps even months, before anyone found their bodies.

Beside her, Pandora began to groan and writhe in agony. Fearing to do otherwise, Felicity emulated her as best as she could. When she heard her husband's sadistic laughter, her neck crawled at his callousness. For all his talk of being fond of her, he seemed highly amused by the idea that he had been successful in poisoning her. It was actually what she hoped he'd believe. Indeed, her ploy would likely be the only way she'd be able to escape alive from this ordeal. It all depended on what her husband intended to do with them *after* he decided they were dead. She was not particularly fond of being buried alive, but then, Roger was not all that ambitious either, especially when it involved hard work, which digging a grave definitely was. Considering his aversion to any laborious task, there was a strong chance that he'd just dump them somewhere alongside the road and be done with it. She prayed desperately that that would be the way of it, and that it wouldn't be long after he had left them that she'd be able to find help.

Pandora finally stopped her anguished moaning, and again Felicity followed her example. Even so, she reached across very carefully and pressed her fingers to the woman's wrist. Alas, she could detect no pulse and could only conclude the actress had indeed died from port that Roger had poisoned.

In an area that was totally unfamiliar to Felicity, Roger finally halted the cart, dragged Pandora to the end of it, and, from there, let her body plummet to the ground. Taking hold of her wrists, he hauled her away from the road and then along a ridge that Felicity suspected ran parallel to a stream or perhaps even the River Avon. In the distance, she thought she could hear the burbling of a swiftly moving stream.

While her husband was engaged in the task of disposing of Pandora, Felicity tore off a tiny portion of her chemise and stuffed the piece into her mouth, hoping fervently it would be sufficient to stifle whatever sound would be evoked from her if Roger let her fall to the ground as he had Pandora. Even with her precautions, she was fearful that some grunt, gasp, or similar sound would issue forth from her mouth, which would indeed prove immensely hazardous for her. If Roger wasn't thoroughly convinced she was dead, she wouldn't live out the hour.

Roger straightened as he reached a place favorable for his purposes. Bracing a booted foot upon the voluptuous actress's hip, he sent Pandora rolling down the slope, and a short space of time later, a distant splash evidenced the fact that her body had rolled into the stream at the bottom of the ravine. Panting from his exertion, he made his way back to the cart.

Felicity's heart lurched in her breast as Roger clasped a hand around her ankle and hauled her toward him. Her skirts were nigh to her waist by the time she reached the end of the bed, but he tugged her around until she was lying parallel with the edge. She held her breath in agonizing fear, dreading her descent, praying she and her baby would somehow survive the fall.

Roger leaned forward over her and, slipping his arms beneath her, lifted her up in his arms, causing Felicity to grow weak with overwhelming relief. She was much smaller and therefore lighter than the actress had been. Perhaps for that reason, Roger had decided she would be more manageable if he just carried her. In view of the rocks that jutted up here and there over the area he was traversing, he'd have certainly exerted himself far more had he dragged her to the same place from whence he had rolled Pandora's body down the hill.

Felicity had to keep reminding herself over and over to stay as limp as a drowned puppy while Roger carried her toward the spot from which he would launch her toward the stream. Although it became more of a mental feat than a physical one, it left her head lulling loosely over his arm. Although it strained her neck muscles, the position allowed her to see the general area toward which he was taking her, albeit from an upside-down angle. They finally halted along a rise bordering a burbling stream, which Felicity could barely see at the bottom of the rock-strewn hill. Although the moon was out, she had no way of knowing actually how steep the incline was or the distance to the water. She could only hope that she'd still be alive when she finally came to rest.

For a long moment, Roger stood laughing to himself, as if he were actually anticipating whatever was coming or perhaps cheering himself for his ability to dispense with two more victims. Silently, fervently, Felicity prayed that whatever he was planning, she wouldn't end up drowning. If she couldn't stop him from killing her, she'd much rather have her head cracked open and lose consciousness than suffer the mind-reeling horror of not being able to breathe.

As much as she tried to prepare herself, Felicity almost panicked when he swung her this way and that in a quest to gain momentum. Then, quite abruptly, he let her go, and she found herself hurtling through space. Seized by fright, she came close to thrashing her limbs wildly about in a frantic attempt to somehow right herself, but she knew any movement would be visible in the moonlight, and it would mean her ultimate doom. If Roger saw anything that seemed even remotely suspicious, he would come after her. Thus, she remained frozen as much as she was able . . . Mentally, it was much like moving at a snail's pace while everything else around her was speeding past her with lightning quickness. Whether she'd be alive or dead when she came to rest, she had no way of predicting.

She did indeed fall to earth on soft turf, but upon rolling helter-skelter down the hill, she slammed belly-first into a boulder. If not for the rag she had stuffed into her mouth, the impact would have left her gagging in sudden agony. Pain seared through her, and immediately she felt a wetness gushing forth from her loins, and she knew at that very instant that Roger had finally managed to kill her baby!

It was a very long moment before Felicity could bring herself to move. She feared every bone in her body had been broken, but when she heard the distant rattle of hooves on the road, she realized that Roger was leaving and that it was safe for her to drag the gag from her mouth. She did so, and promptly heaved up her stomach. With each spasm, the gushing fluid flowed more profusely from her loins, but now it was warm and sticky. Although the first had likely been that which surrounded a baby in the womb, she knew this could only be blood, and that if she didn't somehow find help very, very soon, she'd probably bleed to death. *Somehow* she'd have to crawl, climb, or claw her way back up the hill to the road and trust that some passerby would come along and take pity on her before it was too late.

RIORDAN Kendrick sat glumly in the corner of his landau as he stared out the window into the night. Since Adriana's marriage to Colton, he had had no heart for the gathering of friends and acquaintances, yet this evening he had finally relented to Percy's plea to join the couple for dinner. Seeing Samantha in the latter stages of her pregnancy only reminded him of what he had missed not being able to claim Adriana as his wife. At times, he found himself inundated with impressions, her silken arms twining about him in the darkness, her soft lips responding to his, her thighs opening to welcome his throbbing maleness into her sweet, womanly softness.

Gnashing his teeth, Riordan rubbed his chest, wishing he could relieve that damnable, nagging emptiness where once a heart had throbbed with life . . . and hope. He was wise enough to know he *would have* to get over the pain of losing Adriana and turn his mind toward the task of finding another woman whom he could love, but as yet, he hadn't felt the least bit ambitious about motivating himself in that area. None of the available maidens in the area appealed to him. The ones he had once thought might have had a chance of satisfying him if he had been forced to choose another were now married. But even then, he had considered them only briefly, not wanting to face the loss of his ideal. He had loved Adriana deeply, would probably always love her, but as painfully brutal as the truth seemed to be of late, she now belonged to another who had proven his love for her just as strongly. Colton had certainly seemed willing to die to ensure their union, which left him, Riordan, sadly coveting the wife of another man, a man whom he admired and respected . . . and totally envied.

Riordan frowned in sudden perplexity as he realized his driver was drawing the landau to a halt on the open road. "What is it, Matthew?" he asked when the older man opened the small window above the forward seat. "Why have you stopped the carriage?"

"There's someone lyin' aside the road, milord, an' if'n I can believe me poor eyes, I'd make it out ta be a fair-haired lady, sir. She may be dead . . . or perhaps bad hurt. Shall I climb down and have a look, milord?"

"No, keep your seat, Matthew. I shall see to the matter myself."

Riordan pushed open the carriage door and stepped lightly to the ground. Making his way forward alongside the landau, he paused beside the dickey seat to receive a coach lamp and directions from the driver, who then pointed toward the inert form. Lifting the lantern high to light his way as he progressed toward the dark shape, Riordan watched for any meager sign of life. The fine leather soles of his boots crunched against the roadbed, but he could detect no smallest evidence of reaction from the woman, who was curled in a small knot on her side near the edge of the road. From what he could determine, she was already dead, or at the very least unconscious.

Squatting down on a well-shod heel beside the woman, he lifted a slender wrist in his hand and searched for a pulse. It was faint but still detectable. He set the lantern on the road near her shoulder and then proceeded to turn her over.

"Mrs. Elston!" he cried, promptly recognizing Samuel Gladstone's granddaughter. He vividly recalled having met the beauty a number of months ago when he had visited the miller. Although at the time he had hardly been cognizant of any woman other than his lovely Adriana, he had been pleasantly taken aback by the girl's exceptional pulchritude in spite of the fact that he had considered her pale blond hair and blue eyes the exact opposite of his ideal, which Adriana had unknowingly done much to solidify in his mind. Later, he had heard some talk about Samuel's granddaughter having married the young miller, the same cad who had been so rude and possessive of Adriana during the Autumn Ball. However briefly he had considered her, Riordan had mentally marked the lady off his list of alternatives.

A trickle of blood had dried after flowing from the corner of the lady's mouth, and there was a dark bruise upon her cheek and brow. Though he gently shook her, he received no response, not even a flicker of an eyelid.

Bending over her, he slipped an arm beneath her back and then slid another under her knees until he realized her skirts were saturated. Withdrawing his hand, he held it near to the lantern. His concern for the lady spiraled to greater heights as he realized it was blood. He folded back her gown and petticoat as he searched for some indication of an oozing wound that perhaps needed to be tightly confined to stem the flow. The inside leggings of her pantaloons were soaked with a thicker, darker hue, and when he spread a hand over the gentle mound that formed her abdomen and applied pressure, the resulting surge of blood made him realize his talent for binding up wounds did not extend to the area of miscarriages.

Bundling her skirts around her lower torso, he lifted her up in his arms and hurried back to the carriage. "Forget the lantern, Matthew. Take us home as quickly as you can. Dr. Carroll must be fetched immediately. Mrs. Elston is in the process of losing her baby, and if she doesn't receive help soon, she will likely bleed to death."

When they arrived at Harcourt Hall, Riordan whisked the young woman from the conveyance, bade his driver to make haste collecting the doctor, and then rushed into the Gothic manor. Calling for his housekeeper, Mrs. Rosedale, to come running, he leapt up the stairs, taking them two at a time and, with a broad shoulder, pushed open the door of a bedchamber just down the hall from his own suite of rooms. Maidservants came scurrying into the chamber on the heels of the housekeeper who, with her usual pragmatism, promptly sent her master elsewhere as the younger women began undressing the girl.

Soon after bathing Felicity and tending the minor abrasions that still oozed blood, the servants laid out more towels and sheets as they awaited the physician. Other than servants, there were no women residing in the house. Thus, they sought out the master and readily received permission to use one of his nightshirts for the lady. They knew by the lack of times the garments had appeared in the wash that the master normally didn't wear them. The only time anyone had ever noticed he had done so was when guests were in the house and various circumstances necessitated his appearance after he had retired to his chambers. Though the maidservants searched through his armoire, they could find none any smaller than the rest. Firstly, they hoped the lady would survive to wear what they finally selected, and then, secondly, would be able to keep the garment together thereafter, for it had no ties and, even on a man, the opening for the neck would have plunged to at least mid-chest. They didn't dare imagine the depth it would go on a small woman.

Dr. Carroll arrived in the coach and promptly became breathless and flustered by the alacrity with which his lordship escorted him upstairs. The master of the house seemed unaware of his long strides, which forced a shorter man to redouble his efforts just to keep up. Nevertheless, upon entering the chamber wherein the young lady had been ensconced, the physician rolled up his sleeves, washed his hands and, with the aid of the more knowledgeable matrons, set about his labors.

Remorseful tears were still flowing down Felicity's cheeks a pair of hours later when Riordan was finally allowed into the chamber to see his bedridden guest. In some embarrassment, Felicity burrowed deeper under the damask coverlet and hurriedly brushed at the streaming wetness, trying her best to put on a brave front.

"I understand I owe you a debt of gratitude for finding me and saving my life, my lord," she volunteered in a small voice.

Riordan drew up a wing chair close beside the bed and smiled as he took her slender hand within his grasp. Covering it with his free hand, he made a point of correcting her. "I'm afraid I did nothing of which you claim, Mrs. Elston. My driver was the one who first noticed you lying alongside the road, and as for saving your life, well, the good physician did that, I'm sure. I did, however, send a man to Bradford to inform your husband that you're here."

"Oh, no!" Felicity sprang up from the pillows in alarm as her heart leapt into her throat. "Roger will kill me, just like he tried to do earlier."

Riordan set back in his chair, completely astounded by her claim. He watched the lady in some confusion as she tried in painful embarrassment to pull his nightshirt over a pale shoulder, from which it had fallen after her sudden movement. He'd have more fully appreciated the soft, creamy, pink-nippled breast that had come briefly into view had he not been so astonished by her declaration. "But, Mrs. Elston, why in the world would you think that? What could you possibly have done to enrage a man so much that he'd seek to murder you?"

"Roger didn't seem the least bit enraged when he set about to kill me, my lord," Felicity informed him as she hauled the coverlet up beneath her chin again. "In fact, he did his foul deeds as if he enjoyed the challenge. He was very cold and methodical about everything he did. If not for the fact that I had begun to suspect that he was poisoning his father, I would likely be dead now, too."

"Too? Did someone die?"

"Roger murdered an actress tonight in the same manner in which he tried to dispense with me."

The dark, magnificent brows of the handsome man flicked upward as he debated whether to believe the charges this woman laid upon her spouse. "Would you care to explain more fully, madam?"

Tears blurred Felicity's vision as she related the events of the evening. Solemnly Riordan drew a clean handkerchief from his coat and pressed it into her trembling hands as he listened. Finally, in a voice fraught by sorrow Felicity concluded her tale.

"Near the place where you found me is either a stream or a river. If you return there, you will find the body of the woman Roger poisoned. It's hard to imagine I've been living with a sadistic madman all this time, but that became painfully evident tonight. There's no telling how many others Roger has managed to murder since he came into the area."

Riordan was completely taken aback by the foul acts of the miller. "I must send a servant immediately to inform the authorities of your husband's deeds, Mrs. Elston. Hopefully, they can find the woman's body before Roger receives word of your welfare and returns to the ravine to hide the woman's corpse. If he accomplishes that feat, he could easily swear you lied for your own purposes. We can't let that happen." Leaving his chair, Riordan strode purposefully toward the door as he spoke over his shoulder,

"Please be assured of your safety while you're here at Harcourt Hall, Mrs. Elston. No one will be able to harm you while you're under my protection."

It was some moments before his lordship came back to Felicity's bedside. Once again, he settled into the chair beside her. "You said that you had begun to suspect that Roger was poisoning his father. How did you arrive at that conclusion?"

"I noticed Mr. Elston's fingernails were oddly streaked and that his skin had an unnatural, scaly look about it. I asked Phineas Carlisle, the apothecary in Bradford, if he had ever seen symptoms like those before, and he informed me that he had once warned a young woman about the dangers of taking small doses of arsenic to lighten her skin. Later, at her funeral, he noticed her nails were streaked and her skin scaly."

"Strange, but when I visited the late Lord Randwulf's sickbed, I recall wondering what sort of illness would've caused his fingernails to become streaked. He had always been quite a fastidious gentleman and enjoyed having his manservant file and buff his nails until they bore a soft sheen. I had been there previously on some impromptu business while the elder was having that done. At that earlier time, his nails bore no streaks. It was only later, when he lay abed from some strange malady, that I noted the difference. Actually his lordship died mysteriously. Physicians couldn't determine the cause, though he was sick for several months. Do you think Roger could've poisoned him?"

Her mouth and throat were parched, no doubt due to more than her lengthy explanation of the night's events, making it difficult to answer the man. Begging his pardon for her delay, Felicity reached for a glass of water residing on the bedside table and, much to her chagrin, was forced to snatch the silken coverlet as it and the oversized nightshirt slid away again from her bosom. Clasping the comforter beneath her chin, she blushed profusely, hoping he wouldn't think ill of her. "Your pardon, my lord, the nightgown seems so large and unmanageable, I can't seem to keep it in place...."

Riordan chuckled, having thoroughly enjoyed the brief glimpse he had had of the lady's breast. The sight reassured him that he was very much alive and still desirous of having a wife to appease his manly needs. "It should be, Mrs. Elston. It happens to be mine."

"Oh, yes, I see."

"Please, continue with what you were saying," he urged soothingly, noticing how disconcerted she had become. Still, he couldn't help noting how much more enchanting the vivid bloom on her cheeks was than her previous pallor. "I asked you if you thought Roger could've poisoned the elder Lord Randwulf."

Clasping the damask quilt firmly beneath her chin, Felicity tried to put her thoughts into perspective. "Roger said he had taken revenge upon Lord Colton's father. If Roger had actually thought the elder stood in his way of getting Adriana, then it's my belief that he would've gone to some measure to dispense with the man. He does seem fond of using poison, and I found in his ledgers where he has been paying a London apothecary, Thaddeus Manville, immense sums of money, no doubt guaranteeing the man's silence while ensuring his supply of poison."

"I'll need to tell Lord Colton about this matter," Riordan mused aloud. "Roger definitely wanted Lady Adriana for himself, and if he has been willing to kill others, then I can believe he would have tried to remove his greatest obstacle before Lord Colton actually came home from the war . . . and that would have been Lord Sedgwick."

"'Tis amazing to me how many men wanted Lady Adriana," Felicity stated softly. "I'm afraid I was jealous and not very nice when I had the chance to be. Now, it seems as if my life is over."

"Nonsense, my dear," Riordan replied, chuckling softly as he gathered the slender fingers within his grasp. "You have your whole life ahead of you, and if there is one thing upon which I'm willing to wager, that would be the resilience of Samuel Gladstone's descendants. I'm amazed by your mother's tenacity to manage the mill, run Stanover House with easy efficiency, and still have time to nurture that father of hers as if he were one of her own offspring."

"My mother is quite an amazing woman," Felicity admitted, deeply ashamed she had ever been so rude to her parent. "I wish I were more like her."

"No doubt you will be in time, my dear. You just need to get your feet under you. Although I know this is not something a bachelor should be discussing with a young woman, Dr. Carroll assured me there is no reason for you to fear that you'll be unable to have other offspring in the future."

Although relieved to hear that bit of news, Felicity felt a warm surge rushing into her cheeks at the uninhibited frankness he conveyed announcing her childbearing potential. "I think Roger was disappointed when I got with child, but I truly wanted a baby."

Riordan squeezed her fingers reassuringly. "You'll have others in time, by a different husband, of course. Roger must pay for what he has done, and that usually requires a hanging."

"Roger made it clear that he didn't mind killing me. I heard him chortling sadistically after I began to mimic Pandora's death groans, and then later, just before he threw me out over the ravine, I heard him laughing as if in triumph. My life will certainly be over if he catches me alone."

"He wouldn't dare enter these premises, especially while I'm here, and I promise you, Mrs. Elston, I won't leave you until your husband has been caught. You're under my protection here, and I have a full staff of loyal servants who'll keep us alerted. I rather suspect that Roger is a bit of a coward when he has to face another man, and though he seems to enjoy taking his spite out on women, in this case he'll have to face me before he can get to you."

"I have no idea why Roger is so resentful of women, whether it stems from the fact that Lady Adriana rejected him for Lord Colton, or if his malice runs far deeper than that. It wasn't long after I married him that I realized what a horrible mistake I had made. He seems to have a lot of hatred bound up within him. My father told me once there was a witness to his mother's death. The woman swore that she had seen Edmund Elston at the reins of the livery that ran over the first Mrs. Elston. That event occurred shortly after Edmund abandoned Roger and his mother, and although I doubt that Roger actually suspects his father of killing her, the bystander who saw it was later killed in the very same manner. My father warned me to keep quiet about it, or else I'd likely be killed, too. Truly, 'twould seem Roger and Edmund are far more alike than either of them would ever suspect."

"Lovely people," Riordan jeered disdainfully. "Remind me not to turn my back on either of them."

"Edmund is near death and, because of that reason, has become fairly harmless. I wish that were also true of Roger."

"I think it's expedient that I warn Lord Randwulf to keep a watch out for Roger," Riordan replied. "I shall send a missive over to Randwulf Manor this very hour."

"Roger boasted that he had shot his lordship the very same night Lord Randwulf married Lady Adriana. You could be saving them from certain disaster by sending such a message posthaste."

"So, the little weasel did try to kill Colton, eh?" Riordan muttered half to himself. "I knew he had it in him to kill Adriana's suitors." Rising to his feet, he excused himself forthwith. "I shall return to speak more about this matter, Mrs. Elston, but I must do as you have advised and warn my friends."

"That would be wise, considering Roger's predilection for murdering people," Felicity murmured, winning a smile from the marquess.

Clicking his heels together, Riordan swept her a bow. "Your every command sets wings to my feet, my dear."

Felicity couldn't help but chuckle as she raised a skeptical brow. "I do believe, my lord, that your tongue is gilded with sentiments to win the hearts of many a maid. I think it would behoove me to keep my own heart secure behind lock and key."

"Too bad," he rejoined with a teasing grin, "unless, of course, I barter lessons from a thief and become proficient at picking locks." Striding to the door with a chuckle, he laid a hand upon the knob and, turning briefly to look at her over his shoulder, gave her a flirtatious wink and a wayward grin before making his departure.

The door closed behind him, and Felicity lifted the coverlet to assess to what degree she had revealed herself to the handsome man. She groaned aloud, finding one breast fully exposed, and hurriedly tried to remedy that problem by tucking the huge nightshirt up close beneath her chin. Alas, it wouldn't stay. It fell over her shoulder almost as soon as she let it go.

Riordan was back sooner than expected, catching her just after she had taken a dose of laudanum the doctor had prescribed. Although she had followed it with a copious measure of water, the horrible taste threatened to play havoc with her composure. His alacrity in returning could only have been attributed to his long legs, for her eyes were still a-blur from her efforts to defeat the convulsive heaving.

Riordan seated himself again at her bedside and began expounding on new theories. "This evening, Lady Samantha told me about a servant who had died rather suddenly at Randwulf Manor after quaffing the late master's brandy. My understanding is that when Mrs. Jennings collapsed, the decanter containing the brew was broken to pieces. Had it not, others would've likely partaken of the brew. Lord Colton found her dead in her hut the next morning and thought she had merely imbibed too much. I suspect differently. Perhaps Lord Sedgwick died in much the same manner, and the poison simply didn't react as swiftly in his case because he limited his intake to what he normally had, which wasn't very much at all. If Roger did indeed poison the contents of the decanter before Lord

Sedgwick died, then that leaves me wondering if he left the tainted brew in the decanter. Considering no more reports came of people dying in like fashion at the manor, I must assume he got rid of the lethal brandy and just put a new dose into the decanter after Lord Colton's return, but was thwarted in his attempt to poison his rival by the unfortunate Mrs. Jennings. Roger then tried shooting him, in the back no less. I shall have to tell Lord Colton how truly blessed he has thus far been not to have expired from Roger's murderous attempts."

"I noticed you dancing with Lady Adriana at the Autumn Ball," Felicity acknowledged hesitantly. "You, too, might have become a target of Roger's envy yourself had you persisted."

"Oh, I wanted to, believe me," Riordan admitted, rubbing a thumb across the surface of the lady's delicately boned hand. "But Adriana was bound to Lord Colton by a contract their parents had drawn up years ago. As much as I was tempted, I couldn't very well snatch the lady away in the dead of night and carry her off to faraway places."

"I rather gathered that Lady Adriana has had a veritable host of suitors smitten with her over the years. Although I readily acknowledge her beauty is beyond what most women can claim, I'm left wondering if that is the only reason men find her so appealing. Her father was especially generous with the dowries he set aside for his daughters, but I haven't heard nearly as many rumors about her sisters. Would you mind explaining to a woman who was once envious of Lady Adriana why men have been so taken with her?"

"No longer envious?" Riordan questioned, a grin softening his pointed inquiry.

"I'm afraid after what I've been through with Roger, I may never trust another man again." Felicity looked at him curiously. "Do *you* even know why you were attracted to her ladyship?"

Growing thoughtful, Riordan leaned back in his chair. "Lady Adriana is like a breath of fresh spring air among women who seem to chatter on incessantly, giggle, gossip, snip or snipe as they prissily mince along wherever they walk. She conveys no false pretensions about who she is; she's as honest to herself as she is with those who seek her company. She'll beat a man at a horse race and then tease him unmercifully through his blustering, and yet she can be totally sympathetic to him in other ways or to people in desperate need. Many needy folk have been wont to praise her benevolence to them as well as to orphans who've been left bereft of home and parents. As she once nurtured stray animals when she was young, so she has turned that compassion in her adult years toward people. . . ."

"Say no more, please," Felicity begged with a teasingly dubious smile. "You've hardly begun and already I know I'll never come close to measuring up to your ideal woman."

Riordan chuckled. "I suppose I get a little carried away talking about the lady. No one knows how much I envy Lord Colton, and yet I greatly admire him and believe he's deserving of such a woman. It's obvious he loves her as much as she loves him."

"Thank you, my lord, for sharing your thoughts, but I fear at this moment the laudanum the doctor prescribed is beginning to have some effect on me. I'm feeling very, very tired of a sudden." She blinked eyelids that had suddenly grown heavy. "Perhaps we can continue this discussion tomorrow."

"Of course, Mrs. Elston. . . ."

"Please, don't call me that," she begged drowsily. "Felicity will do. I have no desire to be associated with Roger anymore."

"I understand completely, my dear," Riordan murmured, but had cause to wonder if she actually heard his reply before closing her eyes. Her breathing readily deepened in slumber, and as he watched her sleeping, he was reminded of his earlier admiration of her when he had visited Stanover House some months ago.

Curiously, he thrust a finger through a golden curl and became intrigued by the way it seemed to twine of its own free will about his digit. His eyes passed over her bruised face, and he was rather amazed to find the shape and delicate structure appealed to his senses. Her slender nose had the sassiest tilt, her eyelids the longest, darkest lashes for a woman with such fair hair, her brown brows wide-sweeping above eyes that had seemed the bluest blue he had ever seen. As he had viewed earlier and now mentally envisioned, her round breasts were ivory hued, crowned with delicate pink, definitely exquisite enough to bestir his rutting instincts.

It was much, much later when Riordan Kendrick rose from the chair beside the bed and made his way to the door. He was rather amazed at the lightness of his heart. Where hours ago it had seemed dark and vacant, now it was airy and full of hope. Would wonders never cease?

Twenty-two

✻

LORD Harcourt's housekeeper bustled into the guest bedchamber where the miller's wife had been ensconced and, with a wave of her thin hand, shooed away the pair of maids who, after her morning meal, had bathed and freshly gowned the young woman.

"You have visitors, Mrs. Elston," Mrs. Rosedale announced with a pleasant smile. "Lord and Lady Randwulf have come to see how you are, and of course, my employer, Lord Harcourt, is inquiring into your health this morning as well. Are you up to seeing anyone after your ordeal?"

"I must look terrible," Felicity replied, clasping a hand to her bruised face.

Mrs. Rosedale smiled. "My dear, if most young ladies looked half as fine when they're at their prettiest as you do after being so sorrowfully used, then this would be a very fine world indeed."

Felicity smiled, but immediately winced as she was harshly reminded of the cut on her lip. For the moment she could bear no more display of enthusiasm and carefully responded to the housekeeper's inquiry. "I'd be honored by such a visit."

The young woman whom Felicity had once imagined that she detested swept into the room with a smile and a large bouquet of flowers. Following close on her heels was her handsome husband. Lord Riordan sauntered in behind them at a more leisurely pace and came to stand at the end of the huge Gothic bed as the couple approached the invalid's bedside.

"You're looking quite remarkable in spite of the recent trauma you've been through, Miss Felicity," Adriana bade cheerily. "I should hope to fare so well under similar circumstances."

"Thank you, my lady. You're very kind to visit me after my hateful behavior toward you. Please forgive my foolishness."

"All is forgiven, Miss Felicity," Adriana said kindly and, reaching out, gently squeezed her hand. Then she laughed as she indicated the bouquet she carried. "We stole these from Mama Philana's garden. Aren't they lovely?"

"Oh, yes, they're beautiful," Felicity agreed, thankful she was alive to see such a wondrous array of flowers.

Adriana handed them to the smiling housekeeper. "I'm sure you're better at arranging these than I am, Mrs. Rosedale. Would you be so kind? My sisters always demeaned my lack of ladylike talents." She chuckled deviously as she lifted her elegant chin. "Aye, but I often enjoyed my revenge when they tried to remain seated in a sidesaddle while racing over the hills and vales we traversed."

Felicity's eyes dropped to the gentle protrusion underneath Adriana's shawl and grew suddenly misty-eyed before she averted her face.

"It's all right," Adriana soothed gently, catching the young woman's glance. Reaching out, she rubbed Felicity's arm sympathetically. Riordan had told them everything, sparing the blonde the difficult task. "You'll have another baby by a husband who'll treat you like a rare treasure, mark my words."

"Where is Roger now?" Felicity asked, searching the faces of her three visitors. "Have the authorities been able to find him?"

"Not yet, Miss Felicity," Colton said, settling an arm behind his wife's back as he stepped to her side. "I imagine Roger lit out for places unknown when he received news that you had been found alive. He'll likely be afraid to show his face in the area."

"Nevertheless, I won't feel safe until he's caught."

Riordan pulled up two more chairs for Colton and himself as Adriana settled into the wing chair in which he had ensconced himself the night before. Smiling at Felicity, he stated, "I've told the Wyndhams everything we discussed last night and our theories about the elder Lord Randwulf's death. Have you been able to recall anything more that may be of further value to them?"

"I'm afraid not," Felicity murmured sadly. "Had I known sooner what Roger was doing, I may have been able to save Miss Mayes, but I wasn't aware of his murderous attempts on the Wyndhams until he admitted taking his revenge. As far as I'm aware, he had only met Miss Mayes for the first time when she came into the shop at the mill." Felicity turned to meet Colton's gaze. "Was she a friend of yours? She said she knew you."

"I became acquainted with Miss Mayes a number of years ago," he acknowledged. "We were friends until some months ago, at which time she led me to believe she had died giving birth to my daughter." He reached across to gently squeeze his wife's hand. "Since then, there has been evidence to indicate that the girl I was led to think was mine is actually the offspring of my cousin who was killed when their coach overturned. The child was taken shortly after her birth and later presented to me as my own progeny. We're still searching for the woman who actually stole the babe away and later delivered her to Pandora. Frankly, I doubt that either woman was cognizant of our relationship to the child. However, I do consider it something of a miracle that Genevieve is where she belongs, for she has no blood kin other than my mother, my sister, Uncle Alistair, and myself."

Felicity was amazed that Lord Colton could be so frank about his liaison with Pandora. "I shall not breathe a word of this to anyone, my lord. I may have been foolish once, but I was forced to grow up under difficult circumstances while living with Roger. I now regret being cosseted by my father. I should've more closely adhered to my mother's instructions rather than to his. I'd truly be honored if you and Lady Adriana were to forgive my past offenses and consider me as a dedicated ally."

Under Adriana's smiling regard, Colton reached across and squeezed the young woman's hand. "We would be pleased to have you as a friend, Miss Felicity. Although fairly soon we must be going to our home in London since Parliament is in session, your visits there would be greatly welcomed. As my wife nears her time, we'll be going out less, and would enjoy your company if you're of such a mind to travel that distance. We'll be returning here to the area about the middle of August, at which time we'll be neighbors again."

"Have you a preference as to the gender of your child?" Felicity asked tentatively. "I was hoping for a daughter myself. . . ." She could not bring herself to continue and, in the following moment, found Adriana's hand replacing Colton's and gently squeezing hers.

"It would be nice if we had a boy to continue the Wyndham dynasty," Adriana explained. "After that, whether girl or boy, we'll be grateful for whatever will be born to us. I think we both would enjoy having a large family. 'Tis sure, with the scarcity of Wyndham kin, we need to have a houseful."

Colton grinned as he boasted, "After all the animals my sister and wife rescued when they were young, I'm sure they'll both prove wonderful mothers. I've already seen evidence of that with Genie. She loves my wife as dearly as she would a mother."

A subtle rap of knuckles on the chamber door and a prompt response from Riordan preceded Mrs. Rosedale's entrance into the room. All eyes turned to mark her advance as she came toward the bed, smiling brightly as she bore the enormous bouquet of flowers beautifully arranged in an elegant vase.

"Have you ever seen such lovely blossoms?" the older woman warbled. "Makes me wish I were a gardener."

"I'm glad you're not, Mrs. Rosedale, or else I'd be out the best house-keeper in these parts," Riordan quipped with a grin.

"Oh, don't waste yer time sweet-talkin' me, ye handsome rogue," the woman teased with an infectious chortle. "I'm too old for ye ta flatter. Ye'd be better off devoting your attention ta either Miss Felicity or her lady-ship instead o' tryin' ta wheedle a smile from me."

Riordan grinned at the beautiful invalid with the loosely curling blond hair flowing across the pillows. "Well, since her ladyship is already mar-ried, I guess I shall have to bestow my consideration upon Miss Felicity, seeing as how she'll be coming available in the not-too-distant future." ·

Colton smiled wryly. "Just make sure your decanters are all tightly sealed to keep the contents pure, at least until Roger is imprisoned. One never knows where culprits might be lurking."

ALICE Cobble was not nearly so difficult to bear when she was facing a charge of murder. She seemed almost humble and contrite as she sat in the presence of her former employer while guards stood near enough to ensure their prisoner didn't misbehave or attempt an escape, though there was little chance of that. She confessed all, but denied she had killed the lady who had given birth to the girl child.

"I was makin' me way past the bridge when I caught sight o' the carriage comin' down the road an' men on 'orseback chasin' aftah it. I nearly broke me bloomin' neck, jumpin' off'n the bridge in time ta save meself from 'ose miscreants. Just 'bout 'at time the team come free an' the coach went careenin' o'er the edge. I hid 'hind some trees near the bridge an' watched as the soldiers climbed down ta search the coach. Well, pretty soon 'ey lit out, an 'at's when I decided ta 'ave a look-see at wha' maybe 'ey left behind. 'Ere I was, wit' a dead chit in me satchel an' no idea 'ows I was gonna find 'nother ta give Miss Pandora so's I'd gets me money. Well, me luck proved good for a bloomin' change. I sneaked a look inta the coach an' seen the liedy astrainin' down like she was gonna bear the li'l bugger right 'way, so's I thought ta meself I'd 'elp 'er deliver the babe an' then switch it wit' me own dead chit. Well, 'ere weren't no real need for me ta worry what the liedy'd think aftahward, considerin' she was near dead. She died aftah the babe slipped free, so's I took the li'l tike as me own, an' left me li'l boy aside the liedy. By then, I'd already painted the mark on 'is hind end jes' like Miss Pandora's brother said for me ta do. They tol' me ta put the mark on regular like in months ta come, usin' the patterns what 'er brother made, an' lettin' 'em sorta grow wit' the chit, so's Miss Pandora could come back ta fleece yu regular like once she returned wit' her rich fella. I heared some rumors 'bout 'er bein' cast off by the bloke what found a younger liedy more ta 'is likin', an' 'ere yu're tellin' me today Miss Pandora's been murdered by an ornery miller."

Colton peered at the hag. "Did you happen to know the rector who was there the night Pandora supposedly died?"

"Aye, we 'ad it all worked out, jes' like a play, yu might say. Miss Pandora's brother played the part o' Rev'ren Goodfella. Jocks were a real wily li'l critter, 'at 'e were, more'n 'alf as young as 'e made 'imself out ta be 'at night. O' course, the way Miss Pandora painted 'im up, not e'en 'is own ma could've guessed 'is age."

"And the marriage certificate? Was it a forgery?"

"Aye, Jocks were real clever 'bout doin' 'at kind o' stuff. I seen 'em fixin' it up meself. Whilst 'e was doin' 'at, Miss Pandora boasted a lot 'bout what Jocks 'ad done in the past. 'E seemed ta think 'e were a real smart fella, 'e did, but 'ey also said ye nearly carped 'im when ye caught men sellin' English arms ta the French."

Colton sat back in his chair, remembering that incident very well. Only one of the thieves had been able to escape, and that had only been because a strumpet had enticed English soldiers to watch her lewd dance instead of the prisoner. Though the men had only described her at the time, Colton now considered the possibility that they had been entertained by none other than Pandora Mayes.

"Why didn't Pandora just ask a real rector to come and marry us?" Colton had also been wondering about that possibility long before he had heard evidence to prove his theories correct. "That would've been the simplest thing to do, and then Pandora would've had real proof of our marriage."

Alice Cobble cackled in glee. "Yu don' thinks yu were the only bloke what she pretended ta marry, do ye? She tricked some real 'igh an' 'aughty lords so's she could threaten ta bring 'em down ta the gutter wit' what she knew 'bout 'em if'n they didn't give 'er what she asked for, only some o' 'em first fellas she *really* did get hitched ta, wit' proper licenses an' all. Accordin' ta rumors I heared 'bout her, she were a real looker back maybe eight or ten years ago, an' she 'ad 'em 'ristocrats feedin' out o' 'er hand, so ta speak. Then she wed this 'ere real wise 'awk, a magistrate, 'e were, jealous ta 'is very bone. 'E started lookin' inta 'er past, an' learned 'e weren't the only one what she'd married. She'd been wed 'most as many times as 'e 'ad toes. Well, 'e threatened ta cut 'er up an' feed 'er ta the fishes, so's she skedaddled fo' 'er life. Aftah 'at, Pandora was kinda skeered ta be callin' on rectors what'd turn 'round an' file papers in places where this 'ere magistrate could look 'em o'er."

"Didn't this magistrate know she worked at the theatre?"

"Aye, 'e did, at least whilst theys were sparkin' together." Alice cackled in glee. "Aftah 'is 'awk got real mean, Pandora 'ad Jocks an' a friend watchin' for the bloke, an' whene'er they'd see 'im comin', Pandora'd pay 'er understudy ta perform an' say she'd been 'ere all along, pretendin' ta be Pandora."

"How do you know all this?"

Chortling, Alice laid a grimy finger to her temple. "'Cause I'm clever, I am, an' gots ears ta 'ear. 'At's what I do best, listenin' in on folks, jes' like I knowed yur ma an' yu wanted ta gits 'nother wet nurse ta replace me. Whilst I weren't cleanin' the theatre, it tickled me fancy ta listen in on Miss Pandora an' 'er lovers. Don't remember yu, though, maybe 'cause yu were off fightin' the war so much. Pandora an' Jocks talked many a night when 'ey thought no one was 'round. 'Ey were real cozy, yu might say."

Colton cocked a brow at the hag in silent question.

Alice cackled at his shocked expression. "Like two lovebirds, 'ey were."

Colton shook his head, wondering how in the world he had ever let himself get mixed up with such a woman. For too long he had considered himself safe because of Pandora's claims of being barren, but like all the rest of the fools she had led along on her silken string, he hadn't realized just how great an actress she had really been. It was probably a miracle that he hadn't come down with something that would've ruined him for the rest of his life. "And Jocks? What happened to him?"

"Latest word is 'e gots 'isself killed in a knife fight shortly aftah Pandora went ta Bradford."

Having been burdened by a pressing desire to hurry home to his wife almost from the time he had departed, Colton excused himself momentarily from Alice and went to discuss the accusations against the scruffy woman with one of the officers in charge. "In this instance, I'm convinced that the crone is telling the truth. In view of the fact that my cousin's husband and driver were both killed when their carriage came free of the four-in-hand and overturned, there is no reason for me to believe that my cousin would've survived the crash without also suffering fatal injuries. If Alice hadn't come along and helped the lady deliver her child, likely her daughter also would've died. Therefore, if you have no other charges against the woman other than what I've laid against her, then in my opinion she can be released. Should you feel a need to question her further, I'm sure she'll be at the theatre where you found her working."

Returning to the room where he had left the hag, Colton dropped a small purse upon the table before her. "This is a reward for saving Genie, but if I ever see you anywhere around Randwulf Manor, Bradford on Avon, or my home in London, I'll have you arrested for sheer spite. Do you understand me?"

"'At I do, gov'nor," Alice assured him, totally convinced that he was serious. "I thank yu kindly for the coins, an' yu can bet I'll be keepin' me distance from yu. Ain't no reason for me ta leave the theatre an' trot on o'er ta where yu live or ta 'at li'l hole in the wall yu call Bradford."

"Good. Then we understand each other."

STARTLED upward from an afternoon nap, Adriana sat with a hand clasped over her palpitating heart as her eyes carefully searched the familiar nooks and crannies of the spacious bedchamber that she shared with her husband. Nothing seemed different, everything appeared to be in its place. Yet something had snatched her awake. Whether it had only been a bad dream or some distant sound, she could not say, but the lingering impression now hovering in her mind was of a sound similar to the mourning moan of an animal that had just lost its lifelong mate.

"Leo? Aris? Are you there?"

No answering bark or similar reassuring response from the animals was heard. In fact, the house seemed strangely, almost deathly quiet. Colton had left for London very early the previous day to talk with Alice. Having had no desire to sit in on that conversation, or endure the lengthy ride in a jouncing carriage when their baby seemed especially restless and wont to roll and twist in her womb, Adriana had begged to be excused from the trip in spite of the fact that her husband had been totally against the idea of leaving her. While Roger was still free to commit mayhem, Colton had argued, it wasn't safe for her to be alone. Even when she had smilingly reminded him there were many, many servants in and about the house, his concern for her welfare remained of paramount importance to him. She was tired, she had admitted when he had kept insisting, and might just sleep the day through, which had definitely been her intentions while he was gone. If he wanted to stay home and watch her sleep, she had said with a coy smile, then that was entirely up to him. But, of course, there was the matter of Alice to deal with, and he could do that more efficiently without her tagging along or delaying his progress with her frequent trips to the privy. Reluctantly he had acquiesced but had given Harrison implicit instructions that everyone in the house should watch over their young mistress and, if necessary, guard her with their lives. Maud had fervently assured him that she would stay near.

Samantha's time was near at hand, and shortly after Colton had left for London, Philana had departed in the opposite direction for the Burkes' country residence where she planned to stay until her grandchild was born. Samantha had been pleading for her to come and spend some time with them anyway, Philana had explained, and this seemed her best opportunity yet.

Leaving the enormous Jacobean bed, Adriana slipped a silken wrapper over her chemise and brushed out her long hair, allowing the softly curling tresses to flow freely down her back. Departing the master's chambers, she progressed toward the staircase. She was anxious to alleviate the sudden trepidation that had swept over her and to affirm that everything was just as it should be in the manor. She had no idea when Colton would actually return. He had only told her that he would rush back as soon as he concluded his business with Alice. Having had a fair sampling of how ornery and difficult the woman could be, Adriana didn't hold out any hope that he'd be home soon enough to please her, or in any kind of good humor after questioning the vexatious hag.

Adriana's slippered feet beat a rapid staccato on the stairs as she made her descent. When she came to light upon the marble floor in the massive great hall, she glanced around apprehensively, hearing nothing, seeing no one. By rights, she should've heard some sound from the servants as they went about their duties or even the patter of rushing feet as they hurried through the manse. Instead, the house was as quiet as a tomb.

"Harrison? Where are you?"

No answer came, giving rise to a goading fear. Harrison was entirely dedicated to the family. Had he been able to, he would've responded to her call.

Throwing caution to the wind, Adriana raced through the archway leading into the vestibule and snatched open the front door. Stepping beyond the portico, she glanced about the immediate grounds. No one was in sight, not even the gardeners.

In deepening confusion, she returned to the interior and glanced briefly toward one end of the drawing room before wandering back to the massive great hall. There she turned slowly about in a circle as her eyes swept the corridors and probed the nooks and crannies beyond the stone archways surrounding the central room on both levels. There was absolutely no sign of *any* servant, much less Harrison.

In renewed determination, Adriana decided that she had to be more methodical in her search and began in that endeavor by returning to the drawing room, this time entering it rather than merely glancing into it. She had barely moved past the tall wing chair residing near the entrance when she halted with a sudden gasp, espying Harrison's crumpled form in front of the massive fireplace. A thin trickle of blood trailed from his temple into his gray hair, causing her heart to lurch with sudden fear.

Flying across the room with her dressing gown spreading outward like giant wings, Adriana knelt beside the steward and frantically searched for some sign of life. Greatly relieved by the steady pulse she found beneath his stiffly starched shirt-cuff, she sought to reassure herself that he had not been assaulted but had merely stumbled and hit his head. Considering his advancing years, there was always that possibility. Yet, after straightening his thin legs and placing a pillow beneath the elder's head, she espied a diminutive, blood-smeared marble bust lying on the floor near the corner of the marble hearth. Its present location and somewhat gory condition was enough to send her apprehension soaring, for that particular bust usually sat on a table near the entrance to the room.

Leaving the man, Adriana hurried downstairs to the kitchen to fetch a bowl of water and a cloth with which to cleanse his wound, but when she entered, she promptly halted, seeing it completely devoid of those who usually worked there. Even so, water was boiling in several pots, and in a large bowl whipped egg whites had begun to lose their consistency.

"Cook? Where are you?"

Silence continued to reign unbroken, congealing her fear into a cold, hard lump in her throat.

Of a sudden, Adriana realized her heart was thudding against the wall of her chest. An abandoned kitchen at Randwulf Manor was definitely not normal. Indeed, as tightly as Cook ran her domain as well as the help allotted her, preparations should've been in progress for the evening meal.

Catching sight of a pitcher of water, Adriana snatched it up, grabbed a cloth and a small shallow basin, and then ran out. In spite of its length, she was sure her hair was standing on end as she hastened upstairs again.

At the entrance to the drawing room, she momentarily set aside the items she had collected and dragged the wing chair away from the doorway, providing herself with an unobstructed view of the passageway and the great hall beyond it. She had no wish to be caught unawares by an intruder in the same manner as Harrison had.

Collecting the items she had brought from the kitchen, Adriana knelt beside the elderly butler and began bathing the blood from his temple and cheek, all the while keeping a wary eye out for the culprit whom she now feared was lurking somewhere within the house. All she could think about was Roger, and the people he had poisoned. Somehow he had managed to get past the dogs and slip into the house. As much as that idea terrified her, it seemed the only logical explanation for Harrison being unconscious and the servants missing.

As many times as she glanced toward the drawing room entrance, absolutely no one came within range of her vision. Realizing that her fears were mounting with each passing moment, Adriana resolved to search the house from end to end in a quest to find some help. Someone of a friendly nature had to be in the house! He just had to be!

"Aris? Leo? Where are you? Come here, boys!" she called, desperately hoping she'd hear their toenails clicking against the marble floor as they responded to her summons. "Oh, please, please come. . . ."

Then the thought dawned. *Perhaps Roger had poisoned the animals!* He had always been afraid of them. How better to dispense with the pair than to poison them! But how? He'd be too afraid to approach them. Even if he did, they'd never take anything from his hand.

The terrifying thought sent her flying down the corridor toward the gallery where the pair enjoyed sunning themselves. Reaching the archways that served to divide the room from the corridor, she peered within. Although less brilliant than in the winter, the strange configurations of colored lights steamed into the room, making it difficult to accurately discern what was real and was not. Holding up a hand to shade her face from the subdued radiance, she moved past the entrance, not at all certain what she'd find.

"Aris? Leo? Are you here?"

"As a matter of fact, my dear, they are," a familiar voice replied, snatching a startled gasp from her. Frantically she glanced about, searching out the devil who had entered her home.

"Roger! What are you doing here?" she demanded, her spine prickling with fright as she espied him sitting much like a king in a large wing chair. He looked very lofty, smug, and amused. Obviously he was enormously pleased with himself.

Searching back through her memory, Adriana wondered how she could have overlooked his presence in her anxious quest to find servants. Yet even this late into spring, the sun still created strangely deceptive shafts of light that confused the eye. Less than a month from now, that problem would cease, at least until the coming of late autumn. She was now convinced that Roger had been sitting exactly where he was for some time, no doubt smirking in demented amusement as he watched her dashing hither and yon.

"I've come to pay my respects, my beauty," he stated, seeming very self-possessed. His eyebrow arched to a lofty height at the scar that fractured it as his eyes lowered to her rounded stomach. Then his upper lip lifted in a disdainful sneer. "I see your husband has been taking his pleasure of you, my dear, but I can almost promise you by the time I'm finished with you, that little part of him will be dead."

Clasping a trembling hand over her belly, Adriana stumbled back, her heart chilling with fear. Once again, she searched about with her eyes, wondering why she had heard nothing from the dogs, and then gasped in sudden agonizing horror as she found them both lying on the floor beyond Roger. Their tongues hung unnaturally out of their mouths as they lay sprawled upon their sides. She had no other recourse but to believe they were dead.

"You've killed them!" she railed, tears filling her eyes. "You foul, stinking son-of-a bastard!" At the moment, it was the worst name she could think of, but almost as soon as it came out of her mouth, Adriana realized it didn't sound quite the same way that Shakespeare had phrased his defamation in *King Lear* and had to conclude that she had probably besmirched the man's talents by seriously misquoting the insult. Nevertheless, her slander suited this particular popinjay perfectly, considering the insinuated affront made its descent from the sire rather than from the mother.

"I certainly hope so, and as you can see"—Roger casually swept a hand about to indicate the pair—"'twould seem so in spite of the fact that I was in somewhat of a rush to leave the mill after receiving word that my wife was still alive. I had cause to momentarily reflect on whether I had grabbed the right bottle from the chest of little treasures that Thaddeus Manville has been keeping well stocked for me. In my haste, some of the contents sloshed over the outside of the vial, smearing the ink so badly I could no longer read the writing, but in any case, whether I inadvertently picked up the laudanum instead of the poison, the animals cannot help you now."

"Aris and Leo would never have taken anything from your hand!" she declared. "How did you manage it?"

The miller chortled in amusement, as if truly reveling in his clever feat. "I searched about the area outside the manse for the dogs' most recent kill, knowing they'd go back to it. I dribbled poison over it and then waited. They returned to the house soon after feeding upon their spoils and were let in by Harrison, as is his usual wont. If the dogs are not already dead, I'm sure they will be in time. I don't make too many mistakes."

"How did *you* get in?"

"I slipped in behind the scullery maid after she went to collect vegetables from the cold bin. Once we gained the kitchen, I held her hostage with a pistol pressed to her temple and threatened to shoot her or the first one who moved. Now they're all snugly locked up in the cold bin outside, along with the gardeners and the vegetables."

"And the rest of the servants?"

"Oh, I had the scullery maid summon them downstairs, too. She didn't want to, poor little thing, but the pistol barrel boring into her cheek convinced her that she'd better cooperate or else. Except for poor Harrison, all the other servants are in the cold bin, including your maid who received a large bump on her noggin for trying to attack me. She fell like a plummeting stone."

"And Harrison? What did you do to him?"

"Well, I thought I could sneak up behind him, but for an old man he has amazingly keen hearing. After he caught sight of me, he ran to get the iron poker from the fireplace, but I threw a small statue at him and took him down with a blow to the head. Is he alive?"

"Barely."

"Too bad. I thought I had killed him."

"You're evil, Roger. Very, very evil. When I think that you murdered Lord Randwulf because of me . . ." She searched her mind for a way to make him fully aware of the remorse and agony she had recently suffered after learning he had poisoned the elder. Her eyes hardening, she looked at him coldly. "I can only plead to God that I'm forgiven for ever allowing you to follow me here. I should've declared you a nuisance long before you ever thought of murdering Lord Randwulf. How could you have done such a horrible thing to that fine gentleman? He never did you any harm."

"Didn't he?" Roger shot back, growing incensed. "He tried to separate us! He couldn't stand the idea that you would marry someone other than his precious son! Well, that was enough motive for me!"

"As you have since discovered, Roger, his death availed you nothing," she pointed out acidly. "I would never have married you. You were merely an acquaintance, and certainly not a very commendable one. You were disagreeable and petulant, short of temper with anyone who seemed even remotely interested in me, yet most of them were friends I had known all my life or nearly so. In fact, you were envious of people I never would've considered marrying."

"I hated them all, especially Lord Sedgwick and that other one you married. Lord Colton!" Roger's upper lip lifted in a contemptuous sneer. "I loathe him more than anyone. I tried to poison him, too, but from what I hear, the Jennings slut helped herself to the brandy I spiked with poison the afternoon he returned home."

Adriana swept her gaze scathingly over the miller. "'Twould seem you used any petty excuse to kill those you consider your enemies, Roger, even Pandora Mayes, whom you sought to hold captive for your own sordid little pleasures. As much as I pitied you for what you once suffered as a boy, that is no longer the case. You're not worthy of anybody's compassion. In fact, you're nothing but a spineless coward. Your very presence here in the home of that grand gentleman you murdered sickens me to the core." Her own lips turned, clearly conveying the revulsion she felt toward him. "'Twould have been a merciful act for the world had you been killed right along with your mother when your father ran her down with a livery. You and your father are truly alike, both vile, depraved, wicked *murderers!*"

"What are talking about?" he barked irately, bolting from his chair and striding forward.

Adriana stood her ground and lifted her chin, defying him to strike her as she met his gaze. "Obviously, you've been ignorant all this time of the extent of your father's sins."

"Whoever told you that my father ran over my mother?" he railed in her face.

"*Please*, Roger, lower your voice. There's absolutely nothing wrong with my hearing."

"*Tell me!*"

With a casual shrug, Adriana complied. "There was a witness to that event, Roger. Unfortunately, that witness was dispensed with in the same manner in which your mother was killed. 'Twould seem the driver of the livery who ran over both women was none other than your father. In fact, he probably married and killed his second wife for the sole purpose of acquiring the mill and her wealth."

Roger staggered back in shock and laid a hand across his brow as he struggled to recall the incident that had taken his mother's life. He could remember jumping aside just as the livery came upon them. Had he not done so, he would've also been killed. "Are you entirely certain about this?"

"How can I be? I wasn't there, but you must have been. Weren't you? What did you see?"

Clenching his hands into white-knuckled fists, Roger twisted this way and that, as if wrestling with a demon . . . or his own memory. A low snarl escaped his lips and quickly gained in volume and raging intensity as he raised his fists skyward and shook them violently as if berating the very heavens for his troubled past.

" 'Twill do you no good to shake your fists at God, Roger," she quipped with a full measure of sarcasm. "Perhaps you'd better aim your fury in the opposite direction, for I'd be willing to guess that in the not-too-distant future you'll be in the netherworld, screaming in agony as the devil's welcoming heat singes your hide."

"What devil?" Roger scoffed in rampant derision as he turned a sneer upon her. "You don't believe in those old wives' tales, do you?"

She smiled complacently. "When I look into your eyes, Roger, I see vivid proof that the devil exists, because right this very moment I can see how successful he has been at bedeviling you."

The miller stalked toward her threateningly, but again, she stood her ground. He lifted an arm to backhand her, but she raised her chin with all the pride she could muster, hoping he couldn't discern how violently she trembled.

"You seem to enjoy abusing women, Roger," she dared to taunt, despite the intense glower flaming in those green eyes. "Why is that? Didn't you love your mother? From the little you've told me about your past, I can only believe you did, so why this hatred of women?"

"You don't know what I've had to suffer beneath their cruel devices," he sneered, lowering his arm as if the idea of beating her senseless right then and there was inconvenient for him. "Had you that knowledge, you'd be pitying me instead of heaping your sympathy on those whom you claim I've abused."

"Then tell me, and perhaps I'd be able to feel more compassion for you."

"Who wants your compassion?" he jeered. "I wanted your love, and you refused to give it. I have no need of your pity."

"Everyone needs a little pity now and then, Roger," she reasoned. "If we were all infallible, we wouldn't need anything or anybody. We'd be towers of perfection and piety unto ourselves, and we all know that isn't possible."

"I could've used more of someone's benevolence in the orphanage, but there was none to be had. I was starved, beaten, hung by my wrists until I was sure my arms were being torn from their sockets, but did I get mercy when I pleaded and sobbed for it? Ha! Miss Tittle beat me with a rod until blood oozed from my lacerated back. That day I swore to wreak vengeance upon that bitch and her minions, and I had it, too. If there *is* a hell, then I'm sure they're writhing in it now."

Shivering at his cold-bloodedness, Adriana had serious cause to wonder after listening to his ranting if there was any end to the wickedness he had committed. "You killed the women at the orphanage?"

Flicking his brows upward above a lazy smile, he slowly waggled his head. "Not all at once, you understand, but that's where I learned the benefits of poison . . . rat poison, to be exact . . . arsenic, if you will. I made everyone there think there was an epidemic going around, except, oddly enough, it was only happening in the home where I had been imprisoned. There were five altogether I killed there, and no one *ever* became mindful of what had been done to them. No one ever thought to look at the supplies of rat poison. We had lots of those foul critters running around, and many's a time the orphans had to eat their droppings right along with whatever was cooked for them from the stores of vittles those vermin had been chewing on."

Adriana clasped a hand over her mouth as her gorge came threateningly close to erupting. Her whitish pallor drew a smirk from the apprentice.

"If you think I exaggerate, my dear, then you should visit some of the orphanages in London sometime. I'm sure you'll see much the same thing."

The sound of a carriage arriving in the drive in front of the entrance steps down below brought Roger spinning around in sudden alarm. Adriana seized her chance, fearing what would happen if she didn't warn the arriving party of the dangers that awaited them.

The miller may have been fast, but, even as a child, Adriana had played enough games of tag with Samantha and other children to know how to skirt around an extended hand, which was precisely how Roger sought to catch hold of her. He missed on his first attempt, and when he lunged toward her again, she whirled quickly about, causing him to lurch off balance as he found nothing in his arms but thin air. He teetered on one leg, trying to regain his equilibrium as she scurried toward the front entrance, all the while screaming at the top of her lungs in an effort to warn the ones who were about to enter.

Colton hadn't been able to wait until the landau came to rest. He had flung open the carriage door and lit at a run toward the stone steps, bolted up them three at a time, and arrived at the front door in a frantic attempt to abate the nagging dread that had haunted him all the way from London. Throwing open the door, he charged inward to find Adriana racing toward the entrance with the miller stumbling and sliding on the marble floor behind her. Colton raced toward his wife and, wrapping his arms about her, swung her around out of harm's way, just as Roger launched himself off the floor in an effort to tackle her and take her down. The best the miller caught was her slipper, which readily slid off her foot as he fell to earth.

Colton pushed Adriana toward the entrance, bidding her to leave, and turned to lunge at the man. Alas, Roger snatched forth a loaded pistol from his coat, the sights of which he quickly directed toward the face of the retired colonel.

"Twitch your lip and I'll put another hole in your head right above the one you call a mouth," the younger man warned with a snide smile.

Colton had no choice but to spread his arms. Even so, he stepped this way and that to keep his wife safely behind him though she sought in desperation to move around in front of him. "Stay where you are, Adriana," he bade sharply. "If you don't, I'll have to attack him!"

Rising cautiously from the floor, Roger smirked at them. "So quaint the way you two are trying to save each other, but 'twill do neither of you any good. Before I leave here, you'll both be dead, and this time I'll be the one who'll be laughing in triumph."

"Why must you kill Adriana?" Colton demanded. "She has never done you any harm."

Roger shrugged, as if somewhat amused by the man's question. "I'm afraid your wife must pay for making the wrong choice. You see, she chose you over me, and I won't take any of your leavings, especially since she has your brat growing inside her. You'll both die, and the babe right along with you. Actually, you could say that I've had my revenge upon this household in many different ways. First Lord Sedgwick"—he chortled as Colton's eyes narrowed ominously—"then the dogs . . ."—he watched the man glance in surprise at his wife, who nodded sadly—"and, of course, 'twill give me the greatest pleasure to do away with you, milord. That will truly be an achievement I can revel in for many a year to come. A decorated hero who fought under Wellington. Forsooth, dealt a death blow by a simple miller. How sad, they'll lament. Then, finally, my beautiful Adriana, whom I will truly regret losing, but there's no help for it, you see. If left to live, she'll manage to tell someone of my deeds eventually, and I can't allow that to happen. I must protect myself."

A sound thoroughly familiar to both Colton and Adriana made them peer curiously beyond the miller. A smile tracing across the manly lips caused Roger's hackles to rise, and then he heard it, too, the sound of toenails clicking against the marble floor.

Startled, he twisted half around to look behind him, and immediately his breath was snatched sharply inward as he saw the lone figure standing at the arched entrance separating the great hall from the vestibule. There stood Leo, the largest of the wolfhounds, with his hackles erect, his head lowered at a menacing depth, and his fangs bared in a sinister grin. The low growl that issued forth from the canine's throat caused Roger to scramble freneti-cally about as he sought to find a place of safety. He saw the door of the drawing room ahead of him, but in his haste, his metal-clad soles seemed inclined to slip on the marble floor. He just couldn't seem to get enough traction to move, much less advance. Even so, when Colton sought to charge him, Roger swung his pistol around as he shakily aimed it somewhere in the area of his lordship's chest. When his feet finally ceased their frenzied shuf-fling, he was able to sidle around toward the entrance of the drawing room.

Leo moved forward, slowly stalking his prey, placing one paw on the floor in front of him before bringing forth the other, causing Roger to whimper in terror as he saw a very real possibility of his impending doom. This time, to be sure, no commands to "sit" or "stay" were forthcoming from either Colton or Adriana.

"Call off that animal!" Roger shrieked in panic. He swung his pistol about, turning it on Adriana. "Or, by heavens, I'll blow her beautiful head off her shoulders!"

The sudden flash of pain that in that instant seemed to fill Roger's head was enough to drive him to his knees. His jaw descended ever so slowly as the outer corners of his eyelids drooped heavily over a dazed stare. Another blow was delivered against the side of his head, and a third slammed into it from the opposite side. Tongue lolling loosely from his mouth, Roger collapsed facedown on the marble floor.

With quiet dignity, Harrison withdrew a handkerchief from the inner pocket of his coat and proceeded to wipe away the blood and hair that encrusted the end of the poker as Adriana raced toward him with arms held wide and tears filling her eyes.

"Oh, Harrison! Dear, dear Harrison, you saved our lives!" she cried jubilantly, hugging and kissing the servant, who tried not to smile. Still, he was inclined to turn his cheek to get the most from her kisses.

"My pleasure to be of service, madam. I couldn't let that brute get the better of us, now could I?"

Colton chuckled as he joined his wife in conveying his heartfelt grati-tude. The three of them soon turned to extend their enthusiastic gratitude upon Leo, who yawned as if extremely tired.

"Roger said he poisoned the dogs," Adriana informed the two men, "but he also admitted he may have picked up the wrong vial by mistake. 'Twould now seem he did and gave the dogs a sleeping potion rather than the arsenic."

"Then where is Aris?" Colton asked, glancing around.

"He's in the gallery," she replied, leaning against her husband's long frame as he slipped an arm about her. "I'm sure since Leo is alive, Aris must be, too."

"And the servants, where are they?"

"In the vegetable cold bin, outside."

"I shall let them out immediately," Harrison informed the couple and gingerly felt the large lump on his head before drawing away his hand and rubbing his fingers, which were now stained red. "Mayhap I can get Cook to wrap a bandage around my head. I fear it's still bleeding."

"I'll be pleased to do that for you right now, Harrison," Adriana offered. "His lordship can let the servants out and send someone to fetch the sheriff, and then we'll have a look at Aris."

Not too many moments later, the household was pretty much back to normal. Roger had been tied up and dragged behind the tea table where no one would stumble over him and where he'd be easily accessible to the sheriff. He still hadn't regained consciousness, and it seemed doubtful that he would before the authorities arrived.

It was soon officially determined that the two wolfhounds had merely been given a dose of laudanum rather than poison, for Aris awoke yawning as if from a long nap. The dogs enjoyed the attention Adriana bestowed upon them in the drawing room as she knelt beside them and taught Genie how to stroke their long coats. Colton opened a fresh bottle of brandy just in case Roger had been tampering again with any of the brews in the decanters, and he proceeded to pour Harrison a glass and one for himself. Watching as the pair of dogs eagerly bestowed their affection upon Adriana and Genie, the two men chortled in hearty amusement as the pair made faces evidencing their disgust after being licked across their mouths and cheeks by the hounds. Nevertheless, Adriana sputtered in happy protest, not only thankful that the animals were alive, but that they themselves were, too.

Moments later, Philana swept in, waving her arms excitedly as she fairly scurried to the door of the drawing room. "Finally, at long last, I'm a grandmother! I rushed here to be the one to deliver the news to everyone. I now have a grandson."

"'Tis wonderful news, Mama Philana!" Adriana cried with a joyous laugh and accepted Colton's smiling assistance as she scrambled to her feet. Running to her mother-in-law, she embraced her affectionately before leaning back to ask, "Is Samantha all right?"

"Of course, dear child. She's happy as a lark," Philana declared light-heartedly. "But I must confess, I'm feeling a little spent after all the pacing Percy and I were doing outside their bedchamber while Dr. Carroll was with Samantha. I can definitely assure you that no one in this house has had such a traumatic day as I. Very happy I am that it's over, and I can finally relax."

The hearty laughter made the woman stop and stare at family members and servants in some bemusement.

"Well, I am!"

Epilogue

❄

ADRIANA gently jiggled her wailing son in her arms, trying desperately to shush him long enough for the rector to conclude the christening ceremony, for which they had returned from London to see accomplished in the same church in which Colton had been dedicated. The baby had slept through his earlier feeding, refusing to be awakened, and was now thoroughly incensed that he couldn't have what he demanded. Try as he did to latch on to something familiar as he nuzzled his mother's bodice, he just couldn't seem to find what he wanted.

The pained expression on Reverend Craig's face clearly evidenced the fact that the infant's lungs were in good working order. Even Gyles Suttons' eyes seemed to water when his grandson's shrieks pierced the level beyond that which he could easily tolerate. Philana and Christina stood together with proud smiles, as if luxuriating in the moment. As for Colton, he gave every indication that he was highly amused by his son's display of temper. Smiling broadly with fatherly pride, he stood beside his wife as the good rector arduously went through the motions of christening Gordon Sedgwick Wyndham.

When Adriana was finally able to retire to a private room to nurse her son, she was pleased to be joined by Samantha who was on the same maternal quest, that being to find a quiet spot to nurse her own son. The two babies looked very much alike and seemed to eye each other rather speculatively after being laid side by side. It was fairly safe to predict that these two, like their mothers, would grow up to be inseparable friends.

Later, the two women found their husbands standing with Riordan and his bride, the most radiantly happy Felicity Kendrick, who seemed to relish her husband's gentle consideration. It was a stark, but thoroughly welcomed contrast to the abuse she had received from Roger. With the assistance of a manservant, Jane Fairchild had brought her father, Samuel Gladstone, in a chair on wheels. Jarvis Fairchild was noticeably absent, but that didn't seem to bother the industrious woman, for she conveyed a vivacious wit as she chatted with her new son-in-law, daughter, and other aristocrats who had become close friends with the Gladstone family throughout the years.

In bed that evening, Adriana lay nestled against her husband's side as Leo and Aris slept not too far away, indulging in the warmth radiating from the fireplace. Gordon had just received nourishment from his mother's breast and was sound asleep in his tiny crib. As for Genevieve Ariella Kingsley, she was ensconced in her own room a short piece down the hall, with Blythe in the bedchamber next door and, as always, ever eager to see to the needs and care of the beautiful little girl, who would grow up with full knowledge of the wonderful couple who had been her real parents.

"It's hard to believe that Riordan and Felicity are already expecting a child," Adriana mused with a smile. "She must have been caught on the very first night, too. Two months already, and as radiant a bride as I've ever seen."

Colton stroked a hand over his wife's thigh, admiring its sleekness. "Felicity seems quite happy and content now that she's married to Riordan, and I can certainly imagine why she should be after what she went through as Roger's wife. Jane's ecstatic over the idea that she'll soon be a grandmother. She's very fond of Riordan, and of course, he's very fond of his mother-in-law, as I am of mine."

Adriana giggled. "You'd better be. You have no other choice."

Her husband grinned down at her. "Now, I wouldn't say that. I left home once when I didn't like the arrangement that had been laid out for me."

"Oh, I know!" Adriana feigned a heavy sigh. "You've always been stubborn about having your own way."

"Madam, be honest. Would you have been confident of my love had I agreed to my father's edict at the very beginning and gone to the altar out of duty?"

"Well, Samantha and Percy are very much in love, and they did that very thing," she reasoned.

"I'm not Percy, and you're not Samantha, and I'd say that we're every bit as happy as they are, if not more so. At least, you needn't worry about my ever straying. I've indulged in that kind of life enough to know I prefer the one I now have with you. If you're not aware of it, madam, I'm very much in love with you."

She snuggled her head contentedly upon his shoulder and brushed her fingers admiringly over the neat feathering of hair covering his chest. "And I you, milord."

It was some moments before Adriana rose up on that formidable expanse and peered down into her husband's smiling eyes. "I believe Gordon is going to look exactly like your father."

"Me, madam! He's going to look like me," Colton corrected with a gritted grin.

Smiling, she seemed to mull over his answer for a long moment as she glanced about the room. Finally, she lifted her shoulders in an impish shrug. "Well, if it bothers you so much not to get *all* the credit, then I suppose I can allow that he does look very much like you. But . . ."

Colton held up a hand to halt any further argument. "I know, madam! I've heard it all my life. I look just like my father before me."

Smiling, she pressed her slender nose against his cheek. "I'm glad you do. If you're not aware of it, sir, you're an admirable specimen of a man, and I'm so very, very glad you're mine."

Another long moment passed before she lowered her chin upon the arm she had braced on his chest. "Did Riordan say anything to you about witnessing Roger's hanging?"

"He did."

"And? What did he say?"

"He said he felt it necessary to assure himself—and Felicity—that she would be safe from that monster forevermore. In spite of all the people he killed, Roger proved to be a full-fledged coward when he faced death himself. He wept and pleaded for mercy all the way to the gallows, but of course he never extended any compassion to any of his victims, so he received none in return."

"Mr. Fairchild is certainly pleased by the fact that Felicity is now married to Riordan," Adriana said. "According to Jane, he predicted a gentleman of the peerage would ask her to become his wife. Since Edmund passed on, and Jarvis bought the Elston mill, his attitude toward Samuel Gladstone has changed for the better. He seems to admire the elder much more now and, from what I've heard, he has repaid all the funds he directed into his coffers after laying off Creighton and others, who've now all been hired back. Felicity said her father is even courting her mother now, as if she weren't his wife at all. Of course, the fact that they've been living apart for some months may have had much to do with his repentance. Perhaps he finally realized what a jewel of a wife he had and that he was going to lose her if he didn't make amends."

Chuckling, Colton rolled to his side to face his young wife and slid a hand down her naked back, settling it fondly over a tempting buttock. "As Shakespeare wrote, madam, all's well that ends well."

Adriana's eyes gleamed with merriment as they warmly melded with his. "Lecher."